COMPLETE
SERIES

The
SUMMER
twins

DEBRA ST JAMES

THE SUMMER TWINS

Complete Series

_____

DEBRA ST JAMES

The Summer Twins – Complete Series

Website: *www.debrastjamesbooks.com*

Email: *debrastjamesbooks@gmail.com*

Published by: Debra St James Author

Edited by: Double AA Author Services

Formatted by: Debra St James Author

ISBN: 978-0-6454536-8-3 [Paperback]

ISBN: 978-0-6457395-5-8 [Discreet Edition Paperback]

ISBN: 978-0-6454536-2-1 [Ebook]

THE
SUMMER
TWINS
book one

loving
SUMMER

DEBRA ST JAMES

inspiration

This story was inspired by the lyrics ...
—> _Only Heart by John Mayer_ <—

a note from debra

Thank you so much for picking up my debut,
Loving Summer.
I started writing this book in January 2020—*before* COVID struck and
changed the landscape of our world—and published it in February
2021.
I had read plenty of romance books, but had never put pen to paper
(so to speak) myself. I knew the type of story (more like book boyfriend)
I wanted to write, but I didn't know *how* to write it, so I just started.
Never in my wildest dreams did I think I'd finish *this* story, let alone go
on to write more books, creating an interconnected world readers
would fall in love with.
In 2025, I decided to re-read my catalog to create a 'spicy' chapters
graphic I could use on social media. I honestly cringed when I read
this book (I'm my own worst critic). I've learned and grown a lot as an
author since I wrote and published this book and felt embarrassed that
what I thought was pretty amazing wasn't written very well.
I waffled back and forth over the idea of leaving it as is, but eventually
decided to revise it. So, I spent January 2026 re-editing it. I haven't
changed the storyline at all, and I haven't gone deeper with emotions,
like I do in my more recent work, because I didn't want to lose the
naivety of this story. Instead, I focused on correcting and improving
the sentence structure, grammar, and readability of the story.
I hope you enjoy it, fall in love with the characters, and go on to read the rest of my
stories!

playlist

Only Heart ... *John Mayer*
Man Alive ... *Diesel*
Only to Be with You ... *Roachford*
Praise You ... *Fatboy Slim*
Best of You ... *Foo Fighters*
Are You Gonna be my Girl ... *Jet*
You are my Sunshine ... *Jasmine Thompson*
A Thousand Years ... *Christina Perri*
Here Comes the Sun ... *The Beatles*

You can check it out here:

https://tinyurl.com/lovingsummer-spotify

ONE

-oliver-

[fifteen months prior]

"Fuck, this humidity might kill me! Explain again why I couldn't send my usual donation this quarter, rather than spend five days in this shitty hellhole?"

The people here are fantastic and are very appreciative of our work, but I don't like to be away from my business for this length of time. Plus, the humidity and bugs have been driving me to despair. I can barely see a smooth area of skin on my arms and legs from all the fucking bites.

"I want people to think you're a compassionate human being, as opposed to the dick they currently think you are! You really had no choice since I organized this little jaunt behind your back," Jase snickers, clapping me on the back.

It's true. Most people think I'm an asshole because I'm solely focused on making my company the best it can be. I don't dedicate *any* effort to building relationships with people outside of my business —*why bother with people?* All they do is hurt me and let me down. My business has never disappointed me, cheated on me, or broken my trust. It makes sense to invest all of my time there. I don't care if people think I'm an asshole because of my choices. Being perceived as a dick helps to keep people from trying to get close to me, so I consider it a win. My singular focus has made me successful beyond my expectations, and that's why, at thirty-two, I could retire and play golf for the rest of my days.

Fuck that, though.

Besides the fact I hate golf, I thrive on the excitement of closing multi-million dollar deals for my clients—it makes waking up in the morning worth my while.

"C'mon, you only have another twenty-four hours to play nice with others, then you can go back to living your lonely life far above the rest of us mere peasants." He points high in the sky, shielding his eyes from the sun, as if indicating my floor in my building—Stone Tower. "You can do it, man!"

"My life isn't lonely. I have plenty of willing women lining up to keep me company," I scoff. "I doubt you can say the same."

"Nope. Can't say that I do." He shakes his head. "I spend my time with family and friends because I don't want *plenty of women*; I want that one special lady." He actually holds his hand over his heart and looks off into space when he says, *that one special lady*. What a sap. He's naïve if he believes in that happily ever after bullshit. "You should try it some time."

"Ah yes, that elusive *special lady*. Don't go down that road man, you'll only end up broken-hearted and destroyed." I dismiss him. "I'm good."

Been there, done that. I thought I'd found that *special lady*—turned out she only wanted my money and the social status that came with dating me. When someone higher up the corporate ladder came along, she ditched me real fast. I won't be making that fucking mistake ever again. The women I see agree to my terms, which satisfies my needs and keeps them at the distance all women should be kept. They know it's only a physical arrangement most of the time. Occasionally, I'll invite a woman to attend a business function with me, which also benefits her by increasing her public profile—we both get what we want.

"Whatever. Not all women are heartless bitches."

Yeah, I've heard that before, too. This is a regular discussion for us. He's still single and I'm still safe.

———

After ordering room service, I climb into the shower, enjoying the spray on my tired muscles after working another ten-hour day. The extreme heat and humidity are sucking the life out of me.

Even though I didn't want to come here, the sense of satisfaction I feel at seeing our hard work coming to fruition is more than I would have anticipated outside of a successful business deal. It feels fucking fantastic to know I've used my bare hands to help build a school for this struggling community; that I've contributed to making a better future for kids in this community. My lips actually tip up with pride. With an education, who knows where life will take them? That's a fucking unbelievable thought. I'll never admit it to Jase, though. I don't want to give him the satisfaction of thinking he made the right call—it would go to his head and give him the permission he needs to go behind my back again to organize another philanthropic vacation.

I know how important school can be because it saved my life. It was my one constant as a kid and into my teen years. It was the one thing I could focus on and pour my energy into. My singular focus on doing my best in school earned me the scholarship I desperately needed to get into the college of my choice so I could follow my dream, which led to my eventual success. Without school to focus my energy, I don't know where I'd be today.

According to Bob and Ella, the couple who birthed the idea of this project, a couple of volunteer teachers from the States will arrive tomorrow. Apparently, one of them has won a ton of awards in her field and will work with the local teachers to help them establish a suitable curriculum for elementary-aged students; while the second teacher will help establish the curriculum for the middle and senior students. Which is why we need to complete the construction tomorrow. There isn't much left to do, so we should finish the work by tomorrow afternoon; then we'll head back to our *real* lives tomorrow night.

It's been fucking exhausting working on this project *and* keeping on top of everything back home.

After dinner, I grab a cold beer out of the mini fridge and crack open my laptop to catch up on work emails. Once I've done as much as I can, I climb into bed to get a decent night's sleep, ready to start all over again at the ass crack of dawn tomorrow.

"Pass me those nails, man."

"How about a *please*? Pass me those nails, *please*?" Jase calls out over his shoulder with a grin.

I'm not sure how I've worked with him for the past five years, since he's such a sarcastic bastard. Luckily for him, he's the best assistant I've ever had, and I don't have to worry about offending him. He's easy-going, efficient, organized, wicked smart, *and* manages to keep up with me, if not occasionally knowing what I need *before* I do.

"Pass the fucking nails! I'm nearly done with this window."

"Sure thing, boss. Here ya go. It would be nice if you said please occasionally."

"Hey, less of the *boss* thing. You know I don't want anyone else here knowing who I really am. It's bad enough that Bob and Ella know. I only agreed to do this if we kept it on the down-low. Unlike you, I don't care if everyone thinks I'm an asshole. The only thing that matters is taking people's investments and making them a shit ton of money."

"I get where you're coming from, even though I think you're wrong. You pay me the big bucks to watch out for you. Remember? This is me watching out for you."

Turning to take the nails from Jase, I spot a striking woman walking toward us with a duffel on wheels. She's genuinely struggling with it on the uneven terrain and if I weren't struck dumb, I'd offer to help. Tiny denim shorts show off a stunning set of shapely legs that end in a pair of battered red Converse. Raising my eyes to skim the rest of her exquisite body, my eyes catch and pause on the perfect amount of cleavage visible above her tank.

Woah! If I can see the tops of those sensational tits, that means every other asshole can, too.

I scan the area, noticing she's garnered quite a bit of attention from the other men working on site, which I'm not happy about.

Her fiery red hair, tied in some sort of intricate braid, has fallen over her shoulder. I don't recall ever seeing hair that color before; it reminds me of a sunset at the end of a scorching hot day.

Even though she's finding it tough to maneuver her duffel, she's wearing the biggest smile and her big blue eyes are sparkling like she's some kind of fairytale princess.

She's like sunshine streaming through gloomy gray clouds.

No wonder every guy within a five-mile radius is checking her out. She's the quintessential girl next door, except she's stunning.

"Put your tongue back in your mouth, boss man! You're making a scene." Jase points out with a laugh.

Shit, I didn't realize I'd been staring at the woman—something I never do. "Fuck off," I grumble.

Jase moves toward her, helping with her duffel and situating it on the veranda.

She stops in front of us while I glare at Jase and gives us an award-winning smile. "Hey there! I'm pretty sure I'm in the right place. I'm supposed to meet Bob and Ella at one, but I think I'm a bit early. Are they around?" She looks around expectantly as if they're going to walk out of the building at any second. "Oh, sorry, I'm excited and forgot my manners. My name's Kate."

She's obviously nervous because her words come out in a rush. Her nose, dotted with freckles, scrunches up as she thrusts out her delicate hand for me to shake, but Jase steps in before me, greeting her with a friendly smile—*asshole*. I scowl at him, but he ignores me, moving closer to her.

"Hey. Nice to meet you, Kate." He raises his chin, offering a friendly smile. "Bob and Ella stepped away for a bit, but they'll be back shortly. I'm Jase and this is Oliver."

He's so damn polite, making me appear more of an asshole because I haven't said a word.

"Hi, nice to meet you guys. How long have you been working on the construction?" She studies the building. "I'm excited to start and can't wait to see what I'll be working with. This is such an incredible opportunity."

She's almost bouncing on her toes. Far too sweet for the likes of my cynical ass, but I'll be damned if I can stop thinking about getting my hands and mouth on her sweet curves.

"Are you one of the teachers?" I finally ask as I step in front of Jase, forcing him back a step.

"I sure am! I'm a kindergarten teacher back home. I'm spending part of my summer vacation here to help Bob and Ella get the elementary part of the school established. It's going to be vastly different from anything I've ever done before, but I love a challenge and you know, kids are kids, no matter where they live," she says with a shrug.

Yep, sweet as honey, this one. *I wonder if she tastes as sweet?*

"How long have you guys been here?"

"Jase and I have been here for five days. We're on our way home later tonight. We need to return to the real world and our actual jobs." But damn, I wish I were staying longer, so I could see this woman naked. To pull that long, fiery-colored braid of hers back, so I can lick my way up her slender throat and trail my hands along all that smooth ivory skin encasing those shapely legs, which I could wrap around—

"Oh yeah. What do you guys do for work? Are you in construction back home?"

Her question jolts me from my thoughts of having her for a night, dragging me back into the conversation.

"I work for this—" Jase starts, pointing toward me.

"Nope. We work in corporate investments," I cut Jase off before he opens his big mouth and outs me as his boss.

He gapes at me as if I've lost my mind.

He knew the deal.

"Oh wow. I bet this was quite an experience for the two of you."

Her eyes keep wandering down my body. I took off my shirt because it's fucking hot. I work hard for my body, so I certainly don't mind that she can't keep her eyes to herself.

Jase smirks at me. "Yeah, we're used to suits and ties and temperature-controlled offices. It's been a wake-up call. I'm going to appreciate the luxuries of using my own shower, sleeping in a comfortable bed, and not sweating bullets all day." *I hear ya, brother.*

He winks at Kate.

Fucking winks!

The bastard thinks he's so fucking smooth with the ladies.

She laughs.

Fucking laughs at him, but she's still looking at my chest.

I run my hand down my torso to adjust my shorts and sure enough, her eyes follow the path. I haven't taken my eyes off her, and when she finally looks up and notices I've caught her ogling me, she swallows hard and blushes.

Now that's what I'm talking about! That's the reaction I want from her.

To have a woman look at me like I'm a piece of meat as opposed to a walking credit card is something else. Most women back home know who I am, which means they only look at me for what I can give them, not for the man I am.

It's rather refreshing.

TWO

-kate-

OH MY!

How embarrassing. He caught me ogling his impressive body.

Wait, is that an eight-pack? Is that even a thing?

He's beautifully defined. He even has that awesome V thing, pointing to the promised land that hot guys have. I thought only guys on the covers of my favorite reading material had that—oh, and Chris Hemsworth. *So hot!* And that sexy trail of dark hair leading down into his shorts, like a trail of graham cracker crumbs, guiding me to a house of candy. He's a lot to take in. I don't know where to look first.

I've been here five minutes and I've already embarrassed myself. *Keep up the good work, Kate!* But there's something about him besides a hot body. He seems very intense, and he gives me the impression that he's laser-focused when he finds something or someone that he wants.

When I was walking toward the building, I saw them working, their skin glistening with sweat. It was like discovering my very own hot guy club as their muscles pulled and stretched as they hammered and lifted the timber. Both men are the same height and build; one with darker hair, the other lighter. The one with lighter hair is, dare I say, almost pretty. But for some unknown reason, my eyes keep moving back to the dark-haired one named Oliver.

A tall, slim, middle-aged man with weathered skin and a graying ponytail, and a stout but attractive blonde woman with an enormous smile approach from the side of the building, saving me from myself. I'm guessing they might be the couple I'm looking for. I've been communicating with them via email for the past several months but have never met them in person.

Bob and Ella founded the non-profit organization called *Schools for Everyone* after they retired from teaching. In the past eight years, they've helped two other communities like this one. They help to secure funding and volunteers to build schools in remote communities all over the world. They'll stay with the project until it's self-sufficient before moving to their next one.

I didn't want to miss the opportunity to work with such an inspirational couple. Helping them work with this small island community in the middle of the Java Sea is a dream come true for me.

"Hey, you must be Kate. I'm Bob and this is Ella." He gestures to his wife. "It's lovely to finally meet you in person."

He steps in for a hug, closely followed by Ella. Oh, I love that. I'm also a hugger.

A growl rumbles behind me, and I turn toward the sound. I catch Jase grinning from ear to ear as he pats Oliver on the back in a reassuring manner. Oliver's eyebrows are slashed low over his mesmerizing green eyes, while his mouth forms a firm, straight line. He's scowling at me as if I've broken his favorite toy.

"I see you've already met Oliver and Jase," Ella acknowledges.

"It's great to meet you both, and yes, we were just introducing ourselves. It looks like they've done remarkable work here," I say as I gesture to the building behind us. "I'm a little early. I was too excited to stop at the hotel first. I hope you don't mind that I asked the driver to bring me straight here from the airport."

Ella smiles, taking hold of my hand. "Not at all. We're grateful you could give up your valuable time to help us with this project. You sounded perfect in your application for this volunteer position. We feel incredibly fortunate to have you onboard."

A blush rises from my chest in response to her words—I hope I don't disappoint them.

"How about we show you around and then we'll deliver you to the hotel to settle in? We can chat about the plan for the coming weeks over drinks," Bob suggests as he picks up my duffel like it weighs nothing.

Ugh, it felt like it weighed a ton to me.

"That sounds great. I have a rough plan ready for you guys and the local teachers to look at. I can't wait to get started." Rubbing my hands together, I turn toward Jase and Oliver. "Bye, guys. Perhaps I'll see you later?"

Oliver observes me as though he's studying an exhibit, making me feel self-conscious. "Doubtful. Once we've finished here, we'll be heading out late tonight."

His stare and body language are freaking full-on; I've never experienced anything as intense before. My body burns as though I'm about to combust from the potency alone and he hasn't laid a single finger on me.

"Ohh-kay then. I guess a big thank you is in order for all of your hard work."

Leaning in, I hug Jase goodbye as Oliver watches me like a hawk. *Maybe Jase is his boyfriend, and he doesn't like other people touching him?* When I step across to hug Oliver, I'm unsure if it's such a good idea, but I don't want to appear rude. I don't know what it is about him that says *stay away from me*, but draws me to him in equal measure. As I wrap my arms around Oliver's large body, there's a tectonic shift beneath my feet and I realize my mistake instantly. His torso is naked, meaning I'm touching his glorious, bronzed skin.

He's so hard and *so ... male* and smells so good and *so ... male*.

Ugh. Get it together.

It takes him a few beats to reciprocate my embrace, but when he does, his large hands engulf my back. He's much bigger than I am, but I like it. I love feeling tiny and feminine in his arms. His body relaxes slightly, and I hear him suck in a breath.

Did he smell me?

As I reluctantly step away, I'm a little dizzy, a little off-balance, and it takes a second for me to get my bearings—wow, he certainly has a potent effect on me.

Luckily, he's leaving today because I don't need any distractions. It's important to me to do the best job I can for Bob and Ella, as well as for the teachers and children who need this school.

———

I stand from the table I shared with Bob and Ella and drag my satchel onto my shoulder. As I look up toward the hotel bar doors, Oliver steps through them and my breath catches. He looks as though he's had a shower—something I desperately need.

He looks around the bar as though he's searching for someone, so I scan the bar. Maybe he's looking for his friend, but I didn't see him here unless he snuck in when I was in the ladies'. His eyes eventually land on me and, if I'm not mistaken, his posture relaxes somewhat, as if he's found who he was looking for. He steps forward, making it to me within five strides. *Geez, how long are his legs?*

"Kate."

"Oliver. I didn't expect to see you here. I thought you were leaving."

"We are, but not for a few more hours. I thought I'd have a quiet drink before heading to the airport."

"Oh, that sounds like a great idea. I'm a nervous flyer, so a drink usually calms me down and stops me from stressing out as the plane takes off from solid ground. I would prefer to travel overseas without leaving the ground." There I go again, rambling like a complete fool. *When will I learn to temper what I say?*

He huffs out a laugh as he places his hands in the pockets of his shorts; perhaps he doesn't mind my rambling all that much.

"That sounds like a fair approach. Would you like to join me for a drink?" He gestures toward the table I was about to leave.

"Uhm, oh." Well, his invitation is unexpected. I figured he was here to have a drink with his friend. "Uhm. I can keep you company while you wait for Jase."

"I'm not waiting for Jase. I *was* hoping to catch you."

Huh! I'm not sure what to make of that. I guess it's only one drink and he'll be gone in a few hours. I'll never have to see him again, which means he won't become a distraction.

"Uh, sure. That sounds … *nice?*" My acceptance of his invitation doesn't sound convincing.

He gestures for me to sit. His tanned forearms and the display of sexy veins draw my eyes as he rests his hands on the back of the opposite chair.

"What would you like to drink?"

My eyes snap back up to his. *Damn.* He caught me staring again, and heat rises to my face from my chest.

Normally I'd stick to soda because I have an early morning tomorrow, but I think I'll need something stronger while I'm with Oliver. "Um, a sweet white wine would be great. Thanks." I grab my purse to give him some money, but he waves it away, then heads to the bar.

He returns with a glass of wine for me and a beer for himself. We each sip our drink; the cool liquid soothing my nerves and my dry throat. He takes the opportunity to observe me, making me self-conscious of my messy braid, bare face, and travel-creased clothes. After twenty-four hours of travel, I went straight from the airport to meet Bob and Ella. Plus, I've been sitting here for the last three hours, so I'm certain I don't look or smell very fresh.

"What made you volunteer to travel halfway around the world to help Bob and Ella build this school?"

I guess we're skipping the usual small talk about the weather. "I'm a teacher back home. My greatest joy comes from helping people, kids in particular. When I saw this opportunity advertised in an education newsletter, I knew I had to apply. Working to build a school from the ground up was a challenge I couldn't pass up. I knew I had to get involved. There was no other option for me." I gulp my wine to shut myself up. "How about you? What made you volunteer?"

He shakes his head. "Not what, but *who.* Jase signed us onto the project without telling me. He arrived at my place last week, packed my bag, and drove me to the airport—explaining the plan on the way. I was pissed at him at first." He pushes his hand through his thick hair. "I don't like taking time away from my work, let alone a full week. It took me a few days to calm down enough to realize the project is worthwhile." He sips his beer and I watch his Adam's apple move up and down. "I'm glad he did it now. It's been satisfying to watch the structure grow from a pile of materials into usable buildings." He chuckles. "Don't tell him I said that, though. It'll go to his head." I chuckle with him.

"Wow. How did he manage to get you off work for a week without you knowing?"

"I don't actually know. Sometimes I think that man can work miracles."

He seems to have a great deal of respect for Jase.

We chat for over an hour and another round of drinks. The day of travel has finally caught up with me, and I can't hold back the yawn that's been trying to escape for the last twenty minutes.

"You must be tired. I'll walk you up to your room. You need to rest, and I need to pack."

"Thanks. It was nice to chat with you." I realize I genuinely mean it. As intimidating as I initially found Oliver, I've felt at ease in his company.

"It's been my pleasure." He pulls out my chair, guiding me from the bar with his hand resting on the small of my back. The heat and electricity from his barely there contact are completely new to me.

Stopping at my door, I lean forward to hug Oliver in thanks. He's quicker to reciprocate my embrace this time. It seems as if he squeezes me a little tighter and holds on a little longer, and I definitely hear him inhale deeply close to my hair. Stepping back from his large body, I put some much-needed space between us.

"Thanks again. And thanks for everything you and Jase have done for the school." I tuck my hands in my back pockets, searching for the key to my room, and his eyes drop to my boobs. *Ugh!* "Have a safe trip home."

"Thanks, and it was no problem. Good luck with the setup."

"Thanks." I turn to unlock my door and as I step inside, Oliver stops me with his hand on my forearm. My skin practically sizzles where his calloused hand touches me.

"Be careful, Kate. Make sure you always keep your door locked. Okay? A striking woman like yourself needs to be careful." The furrow in his brow tells me he's deadly serious about my safety.

"Uh, sure. Thanks again. Bye." *Did he just call me striking?* That's laughable; especially with my messy state at the moment.

"Bye." I watch him turn away, tucking his hands in his shorts as he walks down the passage toward the other end of the hotel.

Well, that was crazy!

THREE

-oliver-

[present]

I SPOT JASE WALKING PAST MY DOORWAY, CARRYING A STACK OF FILES. "Jase, do you have those updates I requested this morning?"

He stops and leans on my doorframe. "Sure thing, boss, I'll bring them by in a sec. Did you hear if your private investigator found Kate yet? Not that it's weird or stalker-ish that you've hired an investigator to find her." He smirks at me—*asshole!*

"I saw something I want and I'm working toward getting it. If you have a problem with that, you're working for the wrong fucking guy."

"I don't have a problem with it—you talk about her as though she's some kind of commodity. She didn't come across as the type of woman you usually spend time with and probably won't go for your usual arrangement."

I shrug. "Probably not, but she's worth pursuing. I know she's not like the usual women I spend time with, but there was something about her that intrigued me. I don't need you to be my fucking conscience." The woman hasn't left my thoughts, and it got to the point where I had to do something about it.

"Well, that's something, I guess." Jase rolls his eyes at me. "I'll get those updates for you."

"I need them ASAP." I turn back to my computer, effectively dismissing him.

I'm unsure what it was about Kate that woke something inside me —she sparked my interest beyond wanting to meet my physical needs.

After spending less than two hours in her company, I could tell there was an innate goodness about her I honestly shouldn't taint, but fuck me, I can't stop thinking about her. I'm compelled to find out exactly what it was about her that caused such a profound reaction in me. Not only is she sexy as fuck, but she's obviously intelligent, compassionate, and brave. I need my fucking PI to hurry and find her. *How hard can it be?*

"Here ya go, the updates you requested. They look pretty good to my untrained eye." He drops the papers on the corner of my desk and pushes them toward me.

His untrained eye is bullshit. He doesn't give himself enough credit for his knowledge in this field. If he says they look pretty good, I'm certain they do, in fact, look pretty good.

"Thanks. This quarter is looking pretty spectacular at this point. Can you get Mike on the phone for me? I want an update on his search."

"Sure thing."

As Jase leaves my office, I scan the updates for this past quarter and I can't help being impressed with what my team and I have achieved for our clients. We're making them a shit ton of money, which is exactly the way I like it.

My phone buzzes with the internal line from Jase's desk. "Mike's on line one for you."

I press the button to connect to Mike and get straight to the point. "Hey, Mike. Have you found Kate?"

"I'm getting close to finding her. I managed to get in touch with Bob and Ella to find out her surname, but they wouldn't budge. They were protective of her privacy."

I had already called Bob and Ella asking the same thing; hoping my substantial funding toward their project would get me the information I wanted, but they wouldn't share any details. Instead, they even reminded me how protective I am of my identity.

"I have a contact inside the airline that flew to the area that day. He ran a search for a Kate on all flights heading to that community, and what do you know? He found Kate and her surname. Her name is Kate Summer. I traced the origin of her flight back to our very own international airport. Which means she's possibly a local girl."

Well, fuck me, she's probably been under my nose all this time.

"There are actually two women named Kate Summer living in this city. It's too complicated to figure out which school she might work at because there are over seventy kindergartens within the city. It'll be easier to locate them via their driver's license."

"How long will it take for you to get their identification for me?"

"I need to get in touch with my contact. I hope to have something for you within the next few hours. As soon as I do, I'll bring it directly to you."

"Good. See you soon."

"No problem."

The conversation with Mike leaves me frustrated. Even a few more hours of waiting to find out who she is feels interminably long. She's been a regular guest in my thoughts since I met her on that school veranda. Sharing a couple of drinks and a brief conversation with her in the hotel bar fifteen months ago left me wanting more. I never spend this much time dedicated to thinking about one woman. I have to find her and spend a night with her. That way I can see she's not everything I've built her up to be in my mind. I haven't been able to spend time with another woman since meeting her because she's fucking invaded my every thought.

I rub the scruff on my chin.

Kate Summer—even her fucking name is like sunshine.

Watch out, Kate. I'm coming for you.

Jase interrupts my musing. With his shoulder leaning against my doorframe, he's the epitome of a laid-back guy—everything I'm not. I'm unsure how we work so well together, but we do. He stares at me as though he's trying to work out where my head's at with a smile on his pretty-boy face. Good luck, buddy, because I don't even fucking know at this point.

"Are you ready to work on *The Parkerville Project* this weekend?"

"Yep. That's why I've been working later than usual every night this week. I needed to free up my weekend so I could do my civic duty for your latest attempt at making me appear less of a dick."

Even though I've been giving him a hard time about working on this project, I *am* looking forward to helping with the makeover of the latest acquisition for *The Parkerville Project*. They do sensational work with kids who need to be removed from abusive or neglectful homes.

In the past, I only threw money at these projects, but Jase is determined to improve my image, meaning my money alone isn't good enough—I have to give them my time as well. At least it's only a weekend this time, as opposed to the seven days I spent working and traveling the year before last—taking me away from my business for far too long.

"You know they're doing great work for the kids—kids whose upbringing isn't that dissimilar to yours." He raises a blond eyebrow as a form of punctuation.

I made the mistake of sharing my history with Jase a couple of years ago and now he loves to use it to guilt me into working with organizations like *Parkerville*. Generally, I don't mind offering financial assistance, however, my time is another matter. I need all of my focus on my business. I don't need any distractions or anything else eating up my time, except maybe Kate—for a night, or maybe two.

"Anyway, I'm heading out. Do you need anything before I go?" He pushes away from the doorframe.

"Nope, I'm good. I'll finish reviewing this data and then I'm heading upstairs myself."

I drop my head back to the document I'm looking at, dismissing him.

"I'm catching up with some college buddies for drinks at *Brady's Pub*. See you at the house on Winchester Street at eight a.m. sharp."

"Sure. Don't drink too much. I don't want to be holding up your hungover ass all day."

He laughs at me, waving over his shoulder as he retreats. Sometimes I envy the lightness he has with his easy smiles and ready laughs. That he has time to spend socializing for the fun of it, not just for business purposes. Then I remember that I'm safer keeping everyone at arm's length. Though I may have a problem with that if I ever find Kate. I have a feeling I won't want any space between us—at all.

———

The buzz of my alarm wakes me at five. Even though it's Saturday, I want to get my workout in before heading to the project site. I tug on my workout shorts and hit my home gym—having a dedicated room with the equipment I need saves me time. Plus, I can avoid dealing with people.

It's leg day and as I lift and pull, stretch, and strain to the sound of *Praise You* and *Best of You* pumping over the Bluetooth system, a layer of sweat coats my skin. While I'm working my body, I run through what needs to be done before I leave for the Winchester Street property. I need to go downstairs to my office to double-check some figures from the data I was reviewing last night.

By the time I've finished my workout, it's almost six so I head to the kitchen, collecting the ingredients to make myself a high-protein breakfast. After showering, I dress in shorts and an old college T-shirt for comfort and ease of movement. I'm not sure what I'll be doing today; a bit of this and a bit of that, I expect.

I still haven't heard from Mike. I've been calling since last night and all I get is his fucking voicemail. Snatching up my wallet, phone, and keys, I slam the door as I step out of my penthouse. Making my way to the subway, aiming to get to the property for the eight a.m. start, I try Mike again. *Still no fucking answer!*

Being early on a Saturday, the subway isn't too crowded and will probably be even less so when I make this ride again tomorrow. I could have driven, but my car is conspicuous and I don't want people to recognize me. Once I clear the subway, I try calling Mike again with the same result. I run my hand through my hair and study the people around me going about their normal business.

I wonder if she uses this subway?

Have our paths crossed over the last fifteen months and I didn't notice? Nah. I would have definitely noticed *her*.

Arriving at my destination, I take in the property we're working on this weekend. The goal is to make it as warm and inviting for the kids as possible. This is where they'll stay after being removed from an unsatisfactory family situation, while the Department of Children's Services locates more suitable family members or approved foster families to take the kids in and care for them permanently.

I'm impressed with the space out front of the property, which would be great for a game of basketball. There's something therapeutic about bouncing a ball and taking shots to center the mind and settle any confusion. The house isn't very appealing, but by the end of the weekend, I'm sure it will be more suitable for its intended purpose.

I freeze mid-step as I spot Jase hugging a woman with the same striking fiery hair as Kate. Now I'm fucking imagining her wherever I go. I think I'm in trouble.

Good ol' Jase is at it again; already chatting up the ladies and making friends. He notices me over her shoulder and says something to her while motioning me over. She turns, and I see her face for the first time. All the breath leaves my lungs in a rush as if I've taken a punch to the gut.

It's her!

My Kate!

Fuck, when did I start thinking of her as mine?

For some reason, it feels right to think of her that way. As she takes me in, her eyes widen and she swallows hard while she takes a step away from Jase—*good girl.* I increase my pace and make it to them in a few long strides.

Jase nods to me with the biggest shit-eating grin I think I've ever seen. "Morning. Remember Kate from our stint building the school a while back?"

As if he needs to remind me.

"Morning, Jase. Kate." I step closer and look her square in the eyes. I want her to know she has my sole attention. "Of course, I remember Kate. I always remember a beautiful woman."

She's wearing something similar to what she wore the first time I saw her. I'm gratified to find she truly is as stunning as I remembered. If she looks this good with no makeup, that gorgeous hair back in a simple ponytail, shorts, tank, and those battered red Converse; imagine how she looks when she's trying.

"I bet you say that to all the women you meet. I'm far from beautiful," she says as she rolls her eyes.

That attitude of hers is going to have to change.

"I was telling Jase how much I enjoyed working with the teachers to create a curriculum for the kids in the community where we met. They were open to some new hands-on ideas for the kids and using the latest open-ended learning techniques designed to encourage self-learning and allow the child to learn and develop at their own rate." She gesticulates like it's an Olympic sport and her stunning blue eyes are sparkling with joy—it's fucking spectacular to watch. "Oh my gosh, sorry. There I go, getting carried away. I can't seem to help myself."

I can't believe she's apologizing for being passionate about her work. I wait until I have her eyes on me. "It's all good, Kate. It's something special to listen to someone dedicated to and passionate about the work they do."

Her shoulders drop, and the worry disappears from her eyes, making me feel ten feet tall that I could do that for her so easily.

Suddenly, a tall, blond-haired, man-bun-wearing guy comes up behind her, wrapping his arms around her waist and lifting her off her feet. She startles, letting out a surprised squeal, while the dick behind her laughs. Without intentional thought, my fists clench and my body prepares to fight. My adrenaline pumps hard, increasing my heart rate and my breaths. All I can see is this guy holding *MY* Kate and a red haze takes over my vision. I'm ready to kill this motherfucker! The linebacker next to him steps toward me with a *don't fuck with me* expression.

Yeah, well, don't fuck with me either, man.

He lets her down. Landing on her feet, Kate spins around, punching him on the arm, laughing the entire time. "Oh my gosh, Toby, don't do that! You scared the crap outta me." Kate presses onto her toes to hug him, all the while smiling her award-winning smile.

He returns her smile and hug readily—a clear familiarity between them. I quickly scan her hands and notice she doesn't wear any rings, nor is there any sign that she's worn a ring for a long period. He doesn't show any signs of a ring either, only wearing leather bands around his wrist. But this guy must be a boyfriend to be so familiar, which pisses me the fuck off.

She turns to us while holding onto his arm with a gigantic smile. "This is my brother, Toby. I wasn't sure if he was going to make it because he's been busy lately." She gestures to the other guy. "This is his, uh … *friend*, Shane." Then she turns back to her brother. "I'm thrilled you could make it. I've missed you so much." She leans in to hug Shane. "Hey, Shane. This is Jase, and this is Oliver."

My hands release and my muscles relax, coming out of fight mode. Jase glares at me, letting me know I'm acting like an asshole, but I don't fucking care.

Toby kisses her forehead. "You know I'll always try to support your causes if I can. I'm happy to get dirty for a couple of days renovating if it makes you happy, Squirt." He acknowledges Jase and me with a nod over her head.

"Hey, don't call me Squirt. I'm the big sister, remember?" She seems affronted by the nickname, but Toby obviously thinks it's hilarious.

"You may be older than me." He glances at us. "By four and a half minutes, but I'm much bigger than you. *Squirt*."

Ahhh, twins! They have different colored hair, but their eyes are the same shade of blue. Shane chuckles as Toby quickly dodges the next swing from his spunky sister. He must be used to their antics. Clearly, the fiery-colored hair reflects her feisty personality. She *is*— hands down—a lethal combination. The siblings obviously have a lot of love for each other, which makes me think about my own lack of siblings. My relationship with Jase is probably the closest to having a brother. Jase is probably the closest person I have to a brotherly relationship.

Sarah, the head coordinator of this renovation for *The Parkerville Project*, interrupts my musing. She gains everyone's attention, thanks us all for donating our time, and *The CornerStone Foundation* for funding the project. Jase winks at me, nudging his shoulder against mine—*obvious much?* I know I don't need to worry because I'm pretty much anonymous. The only person associated with *The Parkerville Project* who knows who I am is Marcus Trainor, the CEO.

Sarah then allocates tasks to people working in pairs. To prepare the floors for sanding and polishing—which are in great condition—she allocates Jase and me the job of removing all the old, dirty carpets and cracked linoleum.

While I work, I'm constantly on alert for any glimpse of Kate as we remove the disgusting flooring, which must have been here since the house was first constructed.

FOUR

-kate-

TOBY, SHANE, AND I HAVE THE DELIGHTFUL JOB OF STRIPPING THE bathroom and separate toilet ready for new tiling, a basin, a combined bath and shower, and a toilet to be installed tomorrow. Toby, Shane, and I—well, mostly Toby and I—chat and laugh our way through the morning as we demolish the small spaces, but the company and the work aren't enough to distract me from Oliver.

I was disappointed when I saw Jase on his own this morning, and I can't deny how relieved I was when he mentioned Oliver was joining us.

I can't believe I actually get to see him again.

He's been a regular starring feature in my thoughts over the past year and a bit, even though I spent less than two hours with the man. I thought my mind had made him into someone more spectacular than he was in real life, but he literally is a twelve on the Richter scale of hotness! Which is great for my eye candy this weekend, but there's no chance someone that handsome would be interested in me.

I mean, I know I'm not ugly, but I'm certainly nothing to write home about. When he said he *always remembers a beautiful woman*, I knew he was being kind because it was so far from the truth, it wasn't funny. I'm going to need to work hard to hide my natural reaction because my attraction to him is strong.

As we work to clear out the bathroom and toilet, I'm on alert for any glimpse I can get of Oliver while chatting with Toby and Shane. He was intense again this morning, and his muscles looked fantastic in his college T-shirt, which looked soft and comfortable. *I wonder what it would be like to spend a night with him, then get up and throw that shirt on?* I bet I'd feel fantastic after a night in his bed.

Too focused on my daydream, I almost tip the wheelbarrow over in the front yard, losing the load. When I look up to determine what stopped the fall, intense green eyes study me as if they can see what I was thinking. Oops, that would *not* be a good thing. The warmth of my blush rises from my chest until it heats my cheeks—I wish I wasn't so fair. Every time I feel the slightest bit embarrassed, everyone immediately knows. I may as well hold a banner over my head with an announcement.

"Oh, sorry. I nearly lost my load all over you!" I blurt without thinking as I work to rebalance the wheelbarrow.

His eyes widen, and crinkles form around the edges as his lips press together. "You can lose your load over me anytime you like, Sunshine."

My blush gets hotter. I must look ridiculous by this point, as I realize my faux pas and the way he threw it right back at me. *Surely he's not flirting with someone like me?* I'm at a loss about how to respond, totally thrown by his candor and how easy it was for him to banter with me.

"Go to dinner with me tonight," he says in a rush, contradicting his normal confidence and catching me off guard with his demand. *It* was *a demand, right?* It certainly didn't sound like a question.

Who does that?

"Uh," I stammer like a fool, quickly trying to gather my wits. "You didn't really ask me. It seemed like you were demanding I join you for dinner tonight." I narrow my eyes. "Besides, I have a date, which means I can't go to dinner with you. Even if you asked nicely." Digging into confidence I don't feel, I raise a single brow at the man.

If you could call my plans tonight a date—I'm not sure why I referred to my evening in that way, only that I wanted to put him off. I spend my Saturday afternoons, which often turn into evenings, at another house associated with *The Parkerville Project.*

I hang out with kids waiting for new, safer living arrangements. We usually bake, learn some new recipes, watch movies, make popcorn, play games, and generally do stuff to distract them from the unfairness of their lives. Some of the kids have had horrendous experiences, and they're still very young. *Too young!* It breaks my heart. I love that I'm able to spend time with them, providing them with some positive, happy experiences. I'm privileged to be able to show them not all adults are bad, and there are people who care.

His eyes narrow and his dark eyebrows form slashes over those tantalizing green orbs. "I rarely *ask* anyone to join me for dinner. Women usually ask me." He seems positively dumbfounded—*cocky much!*

Well, his arrogance just lowered his rating on the Richter scale of hotness.

"Sorry to disappoint you, but I'm too busy most nights to be asking random guys out to dinner." Not that he's totally random, but I'm gonna go with that. "Between work, family, and other obligations, I have little free time."

I collect my wheelbarrow and begin moving away when his hand on my arm stops me, reminding me of the last time we met and sending tingles through me.

"What about tomorrow night?"

I can't believe he's asking *me* out to dinner. It sounds as though he has plenty of offers from other women. Why waste his time and energy on me? I'm a mess. I'm pretty sure I still have glitter in my hair from yesterday's craft activity. "Sorry, but I'm expected at my parent's home for dinner tomorrow night. I'm looking forward to it because Toby's finally back in town after being away for months."

He runs his hand through his hair. I guess he's used to women asking *him* out and he's not used to someone saying *no* to him. He finally releases me so I can empty my wheelbarrow and get back to the guys for the next load.

I miss the pressure of his hand on my arm and kick myself for feeling disappointed at having to turn him down. I don't need some hot guy playing games with me. He'll probably ask me out and then stand me up, or cancel at the last minute, for the fun of it. I know guys like him aren't genuinely interested in girls like me. I already learned that lesson when Michael made a big deal about asking me to senior prom in front of everyone and then never showed. When I turned up on my own, he was dancing with Samantha Riley. I was proud of myself for holding my head up high and semi-enjoying the dance with my friends.

He steps in, taking over the wheelbarrow handles. "Here, I'll do this. Since your brother and his friend are such wimps, they let the woman do the heavy lifting."

I'm pretty sure my eyebrows hit my hairline. I can't believe he implied I can't do manual labor because I'm a woman. Oh, now it's on! I cross my arms, narrow my eyes, and shore up my feet, ready for battle.

"Uh, what did you say?" I tilt my head to the side. "It sounded like you said I'm incapable of handling manual labor because of my gender?" I pause for a moment. "I hope I've misunderstood you." His eyes have dropped to my boobs—*ugh!* "My eyes are up here, Mr. Macho."

I wait until he makes eye contact, but his demeanor is not one of contrition for being called out for sexism; it's more … *animalistic.*

He smirks at me and I'm ashamed to say the action causes tingles in my nether regions.

"Oh, I'm certain you are more than capable of handling manual labor, but you shouldn't have to. It's my job to watch out for you and make your life as easy as possible."

I drop my hands to my sides. *Whaat?* What does he mean, *his job?* This guy is intense. He doesn't have any type of relationship with me —doesn't even know me. He walks away with the wheelbarrow, dumps the load, then returns it to me and walks inside without another word. I glance up, noticing Toby leaning against the porch, and I recognize the concern on his face. He must have witnessed what happened.

As I get closer to him, he takes the wheelbarrow from me and nudges my shoulder with his elbow. "What was that all about?"

"Nothing. Oliver was asking me to dinner, but I'm not interested in being made a fool. I turned him down. Then he started being all macho, implying I'm too weak to push the wheelbarrow!" Shrugging my shoulders, I walk toward the bathroom we're working on.

"How do you know he'd make a fool out of you? He looked pretty interested from where I was standing, *and* he looked frustrated when he walked away from you. He was probably trying to help you. You weren't overreacting, were you?"

"I may have overreacted a little," I say sheepishly. I do have a tendency to overcompensate for my stature when I'm surrounded by giants. "But look at me." I wait for him to look at me, not just look, but study me closely. "Now look at him. Guys that look like him don't go out with girls that look like me. We both know that."

"You're gorgeous, Sis! Any guy would be proud and consider himself lucky to be with you. It's not only the way you look on the outside; you're gorgeous on the inside, too. You have the biggest, most generous heart of anyone I've ever known, bar Mom."

"Aww, Toby, *you* have to say that. You're my brother."

I give him the biggest hug, pressing onto my toes to kiss his cheek. Geez, I always forget how tall he's become. I still remember him before he went through puberty. He had to stand on the step Mom kept in the kitchen to reach the *sometimes* snacks on the top shelf in the pantry.

Holding my shoulders, he pushes me away. "No, I don't. You are one of the special angels put on this earth to make it a better place for the rest of us. People can't help but see the goodness shining out of you."

"Oh, stop!" I playfully hit his arm. "You're gonna make me cry and we'll never get this work finished."

Toby's eyes widen as he retreats from me, holding his hands up in surrender—he can't handle it when Mom or I get upset. We all get back to work, clearing out the bathroom and toilet within the allocated time. I'm impressed with our achievement. I wasn't convinced we'd get everything done.

Things seem to be going smoothly with the renovation up to this point; everyone is on target and ready for the next phase tomorrow. It's exciting to see these people willing to give up their precious weekend to help the kids who will call this place home for however short or long they stay.

By four I'm exhausted and sore, but I need to haul ass home, shower, and then head over to Lloyd Avenue to spend my evening with a bunch of nine-, ten-, and eleven-year-olds. We'll make dinner and watch the latest Avengers movie tonight. I don't mind, I'll get my fill of all my Chris's; you know Hemsworth, Evans, and Pratt—a girl certainly can't complain.

I hear my name as I cross the front yard. When I turn around, I find Oliver jogging over to me. He still looks more than handsome, while I probably look like I've been spat out of a tornado—*as usual*.

"Are you sure you can't cancel your date tonight and go out to dinner with me?" He tucks his hands in his pockets, looking hopeful.

What? For all he knows, I have a boyfriend taking me out for a romantic dinner, and he's *still* asking me out. *Who does he think he is?*

"Yeah, I'm sure. Thanks for checking! Enjoy your evening, and I'll see you tomorrow."

No matter how rude I think he's being, I don't have it in me to be rude back to him or call him out for being inappropriate. Waving goodbye, I spin around to continue on my way.

He steps in front of me again, preventing my retreat. "Can I give you my number? In case you change your mind."

Geez, he's persistent. "I can take your number, but I won't change my mind. My date tonight is important to me, and canceling at the last minute is not who I am. Enjoy your evening, and I'll see you tomorrow." I can't be any clearer.

He holds out his hand, gesturing for my phone. I roll my eyes and place my ancient phone in his large hand. He fiddles around, inputting his number, and then I hear an alert from his pocket. He must have sent himself a message from my phone—sneaky. He hands it back with a sheepish smile and a nod.

"My loss. Your boyfriend is one lucky son of a bitch. I hope he appreciates what he has." He begins to walk backward, away from me. "See you in the morning, Kate."

The way he says my name, the disappointment in his voice, along with something that sounded a lot like respect, almost makes me correct his assumption. Almost. But I don't.

It's better this way.

———

I arrive at the Lloyd Avenue house on time, and Roman greets me at the door. His arms are open wide, ready for a hug. He's the legal guardian for this house and I love working with him because he's such a warm person and understands my penchant for hugs! As I walk inside, the kids rush forward with cheers, high-fives, hugs, and the biggest smiles on the planet. These kids don't trust easily, and that they've given it to me is the greatest honor.

The kids love our big nights in as much as I do. I would never think of canceling our plans—this time with them is especially important in building their safety net and confidence. They need to know they can rely on someone; that someone cares enough to want to spend time with them on the regular. Often, they've never had those types of important connections with the adults in their life. Normally, I would get here much earlier, and we would have baked a cake, cookies, or something equally bad for my hips. The kids understood I had to come later today because of the work we needed to do at the new house.

We cook a simple fried rice dish and heat some ready-made spring rolls for dinner. The kids demolish it in record time while they fill me in on their week. We make popcorn with a generous amount of M&M's ready for our movie and take our regular positions in the living room. Sammy, the youngest of the bunch, snuggles into my side, while Evelyn and Ivy take up the rest of the couch. The boys grab their pillows and make themselves comfortable on the floor. I battle to keep my eyes open after working hard today.

Once the movie's over, I say goodbye to and hug each of the kids and Roman tight, with the promise of returning next Saturday. When I arrive home, I head straight to bed, but sleep doesn't come easy because my mind won't stop replaying all of my interactions with Oliver today.

I sort of feel bad that he thinks I have a boyfriend. Maybe I'll set him straight tomorrow? Maybe I won't? Him thinking I have a boyfriend might be the one thing I need to keep him away.

Ugh, go to sleep!

FIVE

-oliver-

OKAY, I'M OFFICIALLY A STALKER NOW.

I'm not proud of my actions, but I couldn't fucking stop myself from following her yesterday afternoon—my feet seemed to move of their own volition. Positives from the situation, though: I have her number; I know where she lives; and I've seen her boyfriend. He seems a little old for her ... not sure what the fuck's going on there.

Perhaps she has daddy issues or some shit?

Once I get my hands on her, I can sort that out. She won't even remember her own name, let alone his.

From what I saw yesterday, she seems careful with her money—from her worn-out shoes, ancient phone, and the older model car parked out front of her small detached home. Everything suggests she isn't caught up on material things, which adds to her attractiveness in my eyes.

I follow my regular morning routine before heading over to Winchester Street. I paid attention to how she asked for her coffee yesterday, so I stop at the local coffee shop to order Kate and myself a coffee. Hopefully, the gesture will earn me at least a smile. I felt like a dick yesterday when she thought I was implying she's weak. As if anyone could possibly think of her as weak or incapable. She traveled halfway around the world to a remote island community to work with strangers on her own. Yesterday, she bashed the shit out of the bathroom and toilet as she demolished everything in preparation for the new installation. Anyone can see she's strong beneath all those smiles, sparkling eyes, and bouncy steps.

Jase spots me with two cups of coffee and steps forward to grab one. I scowl at him, turning my body to block his access. "It's not for you, asshole."

He laughs at me and nudges my arm. "Good morning to you, too. I guess that second cup is for Kate." He gestures toward one of the cups.

I nod.

"I'm hurt! I've worked with you for over six years. You've known Kate for five minutes and you buy her coffee? Not once have you ever brought me coffee." He puts on a puppy-dog face as he holds his hand over his heart, which I'm sure has some effect on other people, but does nothing for me.

"Fuck off! I need to make amends. I think I was a dick to her yesterday."

He chuckles. "Oh, I'm sure you were. What did you do?"

"I'm pretty sure I implied she wasn't capable of doing any manual labor. That she's weak."

His eyebrows shoot up as his eyes widen. "Oh shit! Yeah, you were definitely a dick to her. I think you'll possibly need more than a cup of coffee to get in her good graces, man." He pats me on my back, then crouches down to retie his shoelaces. He looks back up at me. "You could offer to take her out to dinner or something."

"I tried yesterday. She blew me off for a date with her boyfriend last night, and apparently, she has dinner with her family tonight." I'm still recovering from the sting of her rejection. *She's lucky I like a challenge.*

Jase looks dumbfounded as he responds with a smirk. "Ah, the great Oliver Stone has had his first taste of rejection from a beautiful woman. Ouch! That must have hurt, man."

"There's always a first time for everything. I'd guess you're pretty used to being rejected, huh?" I smirk at my longtime friend and colleague, enjoying our no-holds-barred banter. There aren't many people in my life I can be relaxed with and have a bit of easy back and forth.

He laughs at me. "Touché, man. I'm going to get a cup of coffee since you didn't get one for me."

As he walks away, I spot Kate, Toby, and Shane walking my way. When Toby sees me, he lifts his chin at me and bends toward his sister to say something. She looks up and our eyes connect. My body relaxes, even though I didn't realize I was carrying tension across my shoulders.

I walk toward them, passing Kate the coffee I bought for her, and she takes it even though she's clearly confused.

"Morning. I wanted to apologize for being a dick yesterday when I implied you weren't capable of doing manual labor. I figured coffee would be a good start. I hope I remembered how you like it." I show her my best smile. The one that usually helps me get what I want.

Toby and Shane snicker, while that adorable blush I love rises to pinken her cheeks.

"Good morning to you, too." She raises her cup toward me. "Thank you, but you needn't go to any trouble for me. Although great coffee definitely makes it easier to start my day."

She blinds me with that dazzling smile I've quickly grown addicted to. It was the reward I was hoping for—not bad for a three-dollar investment. Without warning, she steps into me and embraces me. Her warm body presses against mine, and I inhale her subtle jasmine scent and savor having her body this close to mine—she's everything I never expected or even knew existed in this world. After a beat, I return her embrace, careful not to spill my coffee on her, and bring her in closer to me. We fit perfectly, and if I have my way, she's going to be spending a lot of time with my arms around her, protecting her from everything that might take that smile off her exquisite face. She releases me and I'm pretty sure I growl as she steps back.

I don't remember making the conscious decision, but she's quickly moved from someone I want to fuck for a night or two to someone I want to get to know. When I glance up, I find Toby and Jase looking at me with two distinctly different expressions. Jase's lips are tipped up, barely holding back a laugh, while Toby looks as though he wants to go all big brother on me. Then there's Shane ... who appears indifferent.

Kate sips her coffee and her eyes cut across to me. "Mmm. This is perfect. Thanks again."

"You're welcome. Maybe you can allow me to apologize properly by having dinner with me tonight?" I try again because I don't give up when I want something. It works in business, so I don't see why it shouldn't work here.

"Uh, I told you yesterday I have dinner with my family tonight. I don't want to miss it. It's been months since we've had Toby home." She looks at her brother with such love and adoration, and wraps her arm through his, pressing the side of her body against him in affection. "Mom's excited to have the four of us together again."

Toby clears his throat. "Mom probably wouldn't mind a couple of extras. She always makes too much food for the four of us. I could call her and check if you like?"

"No, I don't—"

I cut her off, so she can't deny me again. "I'd appreciate that, man. Thanks." This will be a step in the right direction in my quest to get to know her better.

"Sure, I'll call Mom now. Jase, you want to come, too?"

I look at Jase, telegraphing he better fucking decline the offer. He shakes his head, laughing under his breath at me.

"Thanks, but I'm busy tonight. Plus, I need a break from Olly before I have to see his ugly mug at work tomorrow." Patting me on the back, he walks away to speak with some of the other volunteers. As Toby steps away to call his mom, I step closer to a stunned-looking Kate.

"I'm not sure what just happened." She glances around as if searching for an answer. "Why would you want to come to dinner with my family? You don't know me, and I don't expect any more of an apology for yesterday than the coffee you've already given me today. Not that I even expected that." Her eyes widen as that phenomenal blush rises from her chest. *I wonder how far down that blush goes?* I bet her tits are spectacular when they're flushed that soft pink color.

I ensure I'm in her personal space; partly because I enjoy being close to her, and partly because I don't want her to misunderstand what I'm about to say. Looking down into her denim-blue eyes, I tell her what I want in no uncertain terms. "I *want* to get to know you, Kate. I want to know who you are, what you like, and how you behave around your family. I want to know everything about you. How you taste. How far that blush travels beneath your clothes. How your skin feels beneath my touch. *Ev-er-y-thing.*"

She swallows hard and looks down at those red shoes she always seems to wear. The blush on her chest, neck, and cheeks heightens as her breaths quicken. The pulse point at the base of her delicate neck pounds out a fast rhythm—she's not as unaffected by me as she portrays.

Toby returns, interrupting the moment with a slap on my back. He looks at his sister. "Mom said she'd love to have your friend over for dinner." He turns back to me. "She said Kate's friends are always welcome and they never need an invitation." He smirks.

Good to know.

Sarah gains everyone's attention and shares the progress made yesterday. There are only a few of us who were here yesterday, alongside some fresh faces today. The new men and women have the skills we were lacking yesterday. The prep work had to be completed, ready for them to lay the tile, install the plumbing, and sand the timber floors.

Today, Kate, Toby, Shane, Jase, and I will paint while the skilled workers do their work. We're lucky the fall weather is in our favor because a small group will work outside to make the yard presentable, as well as paint the exterior of the house. Bright, sunny colors were chosen to make the house as appealing as possible for the kids who will call this place home, however temporary that might be.

The installation of new blinds on all the windows, a security system complete with cameras, and all new appliances for the kitchen and laundry will happen tomorrow.

On Tuesday, new furniture will be delivered to outfit the house, making it suitable for up to six kids to stay with a paid live-in counselor, who acts as their guardian while the kids are under their care. Volunteers are also welcome to spend time with the kids, but I'm not sure how often that happens or even if anyone gives their time regularly.

We all start work, and I catch Kate's eyes on me more than once over the course of the day. We all talk and the others mess around to make the tedious work more fun. Shane's quiet, but Kate, Toby, and Jase find it easier to relax and joke around. I have a tendency to become singularly focused on a task and want to keep working until it's complete. The messing around does my head in a bit, but hearing Kate laugh and seeing her smile overrides my annoyance. With her easy smiles and laughs, she is without a doubt like summer and sunshine.

I'm counting down the hours until we've finished here; I'm ready to learn more about her. As we near the end of the day, Toby gives me his parent's address and tells me what time I should arrive for dinner. It's not all that far from here, but I'll have to cross town to shower and change, then drive back in time for dinner.

SIX

-kate-

WE ALL SAY GOODBYE AND I HUG JASE BECAUSE I PROBABLY WON'T SEE him anytime soon. He and Toby have hit it off, so perhaps they'll stay in touch—I guess I may see him here and there. Toby usually finds it difficult to make genuine friends because of his fame. Actually, come to think of it, everyone's been respectful this weekend. I noticed a few glances and a couple of the younger people discreetly asked for a selfie, but they more or less left him alone.

I can't believe my brother, the jerk, invited Oliver for dinner tonight. He's going to be so dead when I get him alone. I *could* text Oliver and tell him not to come. After all, he gave me his phone number and encouraged me to contact him. My fingers hover over a new text message, but it feels rude to ask him not to come. I'm many things, but I'm not a rude person. I never set out to intentionally hurt or offend anybody. I'll stand up for myself or someone else I think isn't being treated properly, but I certainly won't do anything to upset another person on purpose. I guess I can manage to sit through one meal with the guy.

———

When I arrive home, I glance at the time to see if I have enough time to check my neighbor, Margie. I like to check on her every couple of days because she's elderly and lives alone. Her husband passed away five years ago before I moved in, and her older sister passed away last year. Unfortunately, Margie couldn't have children, which means she doesn't have anyone to make sure she's okay. She's a lot of fun and the best neighbor a girl could have. I think she lost her filter over the years because she says whatever she's thinking. I don't think I've ever met anyone as straightforward as her. Plus, it doesn't hurt that she bakes delicious pies. I cook dinner for her a couple of nights each week to make sure she eats properly. Otherwise, I think she would eat canned soup or toast every night because she can't be bothered to cook for herself anymore.

I knock on her door and hear her shuffling toward it, then I hear the locks release. She opens the door with a smile and a hug, ready for me—our usual greeting.

"Hey, Katie-girl. You look like shit." She holds me at arm's length and checks me out from head to toe.

A laugh bursts from me. "Of course, I look like shit. I've been renovating that house I was telling you about."

"Oh, that's right. How'd it go?"

"We got everything done. It's ready for the finishing touches, then the kids can move in." As tired as I am, I feel accomplished. "Anyway, I've gotta go. I'm having dinner with my family tonight." We say our goodbyes, and I head to my place to shower and get ready.

While I'm in the shower, Oliver's words run through my mind—him wanting to get to know me, that he wanted to know how I tasted, and how I felt. Oh my gosh; I think I almost combusted from his words in his rich baritone.

The heat from my blush works its way up from my chest, thinking about how his proximity and words affected me. I don't know how I'll make it through dinner if he comes at me like that again.

I shave and scrub myself, using my favorite jasmine-scented shampoo and conditioner to clean all the paint from my long hair. Heading into my bedroom, I plan in my head what I might wear to dinner. I've felt grimy all weekend, so I think I'll wear my cute yellow midi skater dress with the square neckline. I dry my hair, leaving it loose down my back, and apply a light amount of makeup. After all, it is *only* dinner with my family … and Oliver. I tie on my red micro-suede wedges that I saved for ages to buy, and I'm on my way.

SEVEN

-kate-

WHEN I ARRIVE AT MOM AND DAD'S, THERE'S AN UNFAMILIAR CAR parked in the driveway that I assume must belong to Oliver. It looks very expensive to me, not that I know much about cars, only that they get you from one place to another and they need regular servicing. I walk up the wooden steps to the front porch, where I can hear voices coming from inside. Opening the screen door, I call out as I enter, "Hey, Mom. Hey, Dad."

Mom comes out from the kitchen with her arms open wide, a huge smile on her face, and a sparkle in her blue eyes which match mine. She embraces me tightly, as though she hasn't seen me for months; when, in reality, I was here last Sunday for dinner.

"Hey, Katie-girl. I missed you." She kisses my cheek.

I giggle. "Aww, Mom, I saw you last Sunday for dinner and we've talked on the phone almost every day."

I glance over her shoulder while we're hugging to find Oliver standing in the doorway, looking edible in worn jeans, a fresh T-shirt, and black Converse that are in much better condition than mine. What I wouldn't give to be able to afford a new pair of Chucks. I'm trying to pay my mortgage down as quickly as I can, so I have to be careful with my money. He's watching us as though he's studying a science experiment with the earnestness I've come to expect from him.

"Hey, Oliver. I see you beat me here and you've already met my mom."

I step forward to hug him, steeling myself for the impact of touching him. I try to step back quickly, but he squeezes me closer, engulfing me in his warmth and masculine scent.

"Hey, Kate. Yeah, I've already met your beautiful mom,"—he smiles at her—"and your dad, before he left with Toby and Shane to buy more beer." Mom flicks her eyes between us as if she has a secret. He leans around the doorway, bringing out a large floral arrangement. "These are for you."

I've never received flowers this lovely before. The bouquet is full of different flowers in yellow, red, and orange; reminding me of a warm summer's day.

"He also gave me a bunch. Isn't he thoughtful?" Mom gushes like a giddy schoolgirl. "Your mom brought you up right, Oliver."

Oliver's face blanches, then smooths quickly as Mom walks back into the kitchen to continue preparing dinner, patting his arm gently as she passes.

"Thank you. They're beautiful." I tuck my hair behind my ear. "You don't need to keep buying me stuff to apologize. I've already accepted your apology for yesterday. It's all good." I touch his arm to ensure I get my point across. "I promise."

"The flowers have nothing to do with my behavior yesterday. I bought them because you remind me of summer and sunshine and the flowers made me think of you." He places his hands in his pockets, shrugging carelessly. "I wanted you to have them." He looks me up and down in an appraising manner. "You look absolutely edible in that dress. I won't be able to take my eyes off you over dinner. Your dad's going to want my head on a spike."

I roll my eyes and huff out a laugh. "There you go again, being polite. You can stop. It's unnecessary."

Dad, Toby, and Shane stride inside, saving me from Oliver's intensity. Dad greets me with a giant bear hug, followed by a kiss on my forehead, then offers Oliver a beer.

Oliver's phone rings, so he checks the display, then looks at me with apology in his eyes. "I'm sorry. I need to take this. I won't be long."

He steps onto the back porch to take the call, while we all move into the kitchen to catch up on the adventures my *famous* brother has had over these past months on tour. He's a singer-songwriter, and he's extremely talented—we're all very proud of him. We've always had music in the house thanks to Mom's love of music. I can't hold a tune, but singing came naturally to Toby under Mom's tutelage. Now he's famous and spends half of the year touring and performing to packed stadiums. Shane sees more of him than we do because he's with him twenty-four-seven. He's been Toby's best friend since school, before he became his bodyguard a few years ago, and he's like another brother to me.

Oliver steps inside, obviously finished with his call, which took almost thirty minutes.

"C'mon, you lot, dinner's ready. Let's move this to the table," Mom calls out to us.

Mom's delicious pot roast with all the trimmings fill the kitchen counters, so we work together to help carry the plethora of dishes to the table. Mom and Dad sit at either end of the table, with Toby and Shane on Dad's left, and me and Oliver on his right. I fight for a full, steady breath as he pulls out my chair for me to sit. After we've all settled with plates full of food, Dad sits up straight, his focus directed at Oliver.

"So, Oliver, what do you do for a living?"

Oh gawd, here we go!

"Dad, I'm sure Oliver didn't come to dinner to be put through the third degree." I look at him with my *please stop* face.

Oliver presses his thigh against mine beneath the table, and my skin buzzes at the contact. "No, it's alright," he says to me, then focuses back on Dad. "I work in corporate investments. I've been doing it since I left college."

"I hope you're not after Kate's money to invest because she puts all of her hard-earned money into paying down her mortgage."

Earth, open up and swallow me whole, please. Could this be any more embarrassing?

"Dad, I'm sure Oliver doesn't want *my* money or anything else of mine. He works in *corporate investments*. I would guess that involves working with businesses rather than individuals. Am I right?"

"I beg to differ." Toby smirks. "He wanted a dinner date with you. He certainly *wants* something from you." He winks at me, as though he's in on some big secret, while Shane snickers. *I think I've just turned as red as a beetroot!*

Oliver coughs and looks at Toby and Shane as though he's trying to contain a smile. Then he looks at me with pride, as if it's miraculous I figured out what he does for a living. "One hundred percent." Looking back at Dad, he says, "Sir, I would never take your daughter's money, even if I worked in small investments. She's completely safe with me. I'm not here to take advantage of her in *any* way."

Oh, well, that's a shame. I can think of some ways I wouldn't mind being taken advantage of. Oh my gosh, stop it already!

"That's good to hear, Son." Dad seems pleased with Oliver's answer.

Toby pipes up with a smirk. "The work must pay pretty well because that's a sweet ride you have parked out front. I only took a quick peek. What is it?"

Oliver clears his throat, looking a little uncomfortable as he answers Toby, "It's an Aston Martin Vanquish. It's been a dream of mine to own an Aston Martin since I was young. It's magnificent to drive. I could take you for a ride after dinner."

"That'd be awesome; so long as I get to drive." Toby winks at me as he cracks his knuckles, and Shane shakes his head at Toby's antics. He's always been quiet, but more so since he returned from service.

Oliver presses his thigh against mine under the table again, and I swear my leg catches fire. I gulp down some water in an attempt to calm myself, but it goes down my windpipe and I choke—in a very unladylike fashion. *Ugh.* Oliver immediately rubs my back to ease my discomfort, making me more flustered and worsening my situation.

Will this dinner ever end?

It's Mom's turn to carry on with the inquisition. "Where do you live, Oliver?"

With his arm still resting on the back of my chair, he twists a lock of my hair between his fingers as he answers her. "Uh, I live in the city close to work. It makes more sense with the long hours required for my job. I don't get many opportunities to drive my car because the office is close to home."

"Oh, that's convenient for you. You can roll out of bed and go to work without worrying about getting stuck in traffic." She chuckles.

"Something like that, I guess." He seems happy enough to answer their questions and looks at me as though he's waiting for me to ask him something.

Instead of asking him a question, I tell my family, "Oliver and I met briefly when I went overseas to help set up the new school. Do you remember?"

Everyone around the table nods, encouraging me to go on. "Oliver and his friend, Jase, were finishing the construction of the school so I could work with the local elementary teachers. They did an incredible job."

"Oh, you sound just like our Katie-girl. She's always helping someone, trying to make the world a better place." She looks at me with such pride. "We wish she would slow down a little and give herself some time to meet a nice man and settle down."

Just kill me now!

My mother did not just say that in front of Oliver. I appreciate how he's trying his best to keep his laughter contained. He has quite the sparkle in his eyes, so I can't even complain about Mom when she's produced such a spectacular reaction from him. He looks different when he relaxes and smiles—I'm not sure my defenses can withstand a relaxed and happy Oliver.

I think it's time to give Oliver a break from the inquisition. "How's Nan doing on her Alaskan cruise?"

Dad places his knife and fork down. "She's having loads of fun, so we haven't had regular contact with her." He turns, speaking to Oliver. "My mom is currently living it up on a Royal Caribbean Cruise as she explores Alaska. She's very excited because the ship has an observation pod that rises out of the top of the upper deck. Apparently, it rotates three hundred and sixty degrees to give a spectacular view of the area."

"We named our Katie-girl after David's mom. It turns out she has the same sense of adventure as her nan." Mom looks at me full of love. This, categorically, is my safe place; here with my family, in the home where I grew up.

Dinner settles down. The questions slow and the discussion turns to lighter, more general topics, suitable for the dinner table. We clear away from dinner and Mom serves homemade apple turnovers with ice cream for dessert. She makes the creamiest ice cream you'll ever have, and I can't help but moan in appreciation. Oliver's head snaps my way, and the potency and heat in his eyes steal my breath.

Oh, my! Could it be possible that he *does* honestly think I'm beautiful, and they're not only words? He's had some part of his body touching mine all throughout dinner, and the way he looks at me ... I don't think anyone's ever looked at me that way before.

Once we finish dessert, Toby, Shane, Oliver, and I clear the table and wash the dishes. We've told Oliver repeatedly that he doesn't need to help, but he insists on doing his share. After we've finished, he invites the guys for a ride, leaving Mom and me alone for a while. Mom makes us hot chocolate, and we move into the family room, getting comfortable on the couch.

She wastes no time going straight for the kill. "Oliver's a handsome young man. He seems very taken with you."

I roll my eyes. "Don't start, Mom. Toby invited him here for dinner —not me. He's being polite." I sip my hot chocolate for something to do. "And yes, he's a very good-looking man. That's why I know for certain he would *never* be interested in someone like me. He could have any woman he wants. He told me yesterday he has women asking him to dinner *all* the time."

Repeating the words he said yesterday makes me sick to my stomach. I don't understand why he's wasting his Sunday evening here with my family when he could have dinner with any gorgeous woman he wanted.

Mom looks positively livid. "What do you mean, *someone like you?* You are such a kind soul and beautiful and intelligent to boot. You are quite a catch for *any* man. I'm not sure where you got the idea that you're not a beautiful woman?"

Shrugging, I study my drink, avoiding her gaze; hiding further behind the curtain of my hair. "If I were as great as you say, Brandon wouldn't have cheated on me. He wouldn't have gone behind my back with Crystal, now, would he? Not to mention every single boyfriend I've ever had. They've always left me for someone prettier. Someone more *interesting*." Brandon broke me when he cheated with my best friend. It was out of the blue and completely unexpected. We never had the sparks I experience when I stand next to Oliver, but I thought we were happy.

"He was an idiot! Your father and I never warmed to him. Plus, it's his loss and your gain that he let you go. Not all men are as stupid as Brandon and those other boys, Katie-girl." She glides her hand down my hair, then slides my loose hair behind my shoulder. "Don't let those boys from your past keep hurting you. Promise me you'll open your heart to the possibility of love." She moves closer to me, wrapping me in a hug I didn't realize I needed.

The guys walk inside, and Oliver's gaze immediately snaps to me in Mom's arms. His eyebrows slash down over his arresting eyes as he moves straight toward me. "Everything okay?"

I nod, not wanting him to press me further. Mom gets up to make them each a hot chocolate, carrying the sweet drinks into the family room.

Toby turns toward me. "You spent last night with the kids over at the Lloyd Avenue house, right? How are they?"

Oops, busted!

Oliver's head swings toward me. His narrowed eyes causing guilt to rise for my half-truth yesterday.

"They were great. They're always excited to see me, even though I visit them every week. We cooked fried rice and spring rolls, which they demolished. Then we enjoyed popcorn with M&M's, while we watched the latest Avengers movie. I struggled to keep my eyes open, though. I was pretty tired after the work we did yesterday."

"Did Kate tell you she spends time every weekend with a group of kids in one of *The Parkerville Project's* share homes? She adores those kids." Dad doesn't realize the trouble he's dropped me in. In fact, he doesn't seem to notice the icy vibe coming off Oliver in waves.

"No, she didn't tell me. She told me she had a date last night. But I bet those kids think they're the luckiest kids on the planet when she visits." His expression turns to disappointment. It curls around in my stomach, making me feel terrible for my subterfuge.

We finish our drinks. "Thank you very much for inviting me to dinner. I'd better head home and allow you guys some time to catch up." He stands. "Dinner was delicious. Thank you, Mrs. Summer."

Mom hugs him tight, rubbing her hands up and down his back like she does when she's hugging us goodbye, then Dad shakes his hand and pats him on the back. "You're welcome anytime. You don't need an invitation."

Whaaat? Really? Where's the family loyalty?

Oliver turns toward me. "Would you mind walking me out?"

I know this will be all kinds of tense—it's like I'm walking to the gallows! His big, warm hand settles at the small of my back as we walk, guiding me along. That small amount of contact sends my body into alert mode, and tingles race up my spine.

As we stand beside his car, he rubs the back of his neck. *When did that action become sexy?* Slowly, he raises his head, looking at me in his usual way. "Want to explain to me why you lied about having a date last night?"

Here we go. "Uh, nope! To me, it's a date. I don't cancel on those kids unless I have a prior engagement I've planned ahead of time. I would *never* cancel on them at the last minute unless I was sick. They've had enough disappointment and flaky people in their life. I refuse to be another adult who lets them down."

How dare he be upset I didn't change my plans to suit him—the nerve!

He moves into my space; he seems to like being close. "Fair enough. But you could have said what you were doing. I feel you purposely let me think you were going on a date with a boyfriend. Is there a reason you wanted to shut me down, beautiful girl?"

Uh, geez, he's direct. "Um, see, that would be why. You keep saying things that are definitely out of the realm of what could possibly be true. I *know* you're playing with me—"

He moves even closer—if that's possible—interrupting me. "You can stop right there, Sunshine. Each time I've called you beautiful, you act like I'm lying. Beautiful isn't a strong enough word for how I see you, so that attitude of yours is going to have to change. I won't tolerate you disrespecting yourself like that."

Aaand there go my knees. Is that even physically possible for words to make your knees collapse out from under you?

This guy is freaking smooth. Fortunately, I won't see him again after tonight.

"Now, when can I see you again? Tonight made me want to get to know you even more."

Gently gripping my chin, he directs me to look into his eyes, which I was desperately trying to avoid. His track around my face, checking my eyes and pausing on my mouth—I swear, I stop breathing. I'm going to pass out at his feet at this rate, which would not be sexy—*at all.*

I want him to kiss me, but I don't want him to kiss me at the same time. I can't keep my head straight around him, which is dangerous. He leans in, sliding his bristly cheek against my smooth one, and brushes his full lips across mine. He pulls back ever-so-slightly to check my eyes again and I'm unsure what he's looking for.

Swallowing, I attempt to get my words out straight. "As I said yesterday, I'm pretty busy with work, my family, and other obligations. I rarely have time to catch up with friends or simply eat lunch at work; I'm *that* busy. I honestly don't have time for anything else," I whisper as confidently as I can.

He studies me like I'm an expensive artwork, but he must see what he needs because he nods and gently brushes my lips with his again.

Then he steps away from me. "I'll text you. Eventually, I'll wear you down, and you'll agree to go on a date with me."

I'm not sure why he wants to *wear* me down when he, apparently, *has women asking* him *to dinner*. He steps away from me, and I miss his body heat immediately; god, I'm a mess. Walking around his car, he climbs in smoothly and drives away, leaving me to stand in the driveway wondering what on earth just happened, and why on earth it happened to me.

EIGHT

-oliver-

THE FIRST THING I DO MONDAY MORNING IS CONTACT MIKE. I FILL him in on the events of the weekend and inform him I no longer require his services to find Kate. He thanked me for my business and told me to expect his invoice.

As I end the call with Mike, Jase stops in my doorway. "You've met the parents already, huh? Must be serious." He raises his eyebrows and chuckles. Sometimes he can be worse than an old lady.

"I'm not about to let an opportunity pass me by. I don't do it with my business and I won't do it with something that I want as badly as I want that woman."

"Yeah, but meeting the folks is a bit much, don't you think?" He stuffs his hands in his trouser pockets, his brows furrowed.

"Nothing's too much for her. Now, if you've finished sharing your thoughts, which I didn't ask for, get back to work. I have shit to do." *Like message my girl.*

He holds his hands up in surrender. "No problem, boss."

As soon as he's gone, I pull out my phone to message Kate.

ME

Good morning Sunshine

SUNSHINE

Good morning to you too

ME

Thanks for letting me crash dinner with your family

SUNSHINE

It wasn't left up to me now, was it?

ME

I guess not

Can I see you again?

SUNSHINE

I'm pretty busy atm

ME

I'll let it go

For now

SUNSHINE

Gee, thanks

ME

Enjoy your day

SUNSHINE

You too

I glance at the time and realize I need to check in with the rehab center looking after my father, so I make the call.

"Good morning. Welcome to *Square One*. My name is Doris. How may I help you?"

"Hi, Doris. It's Oliver Stone. I'm calling for my check-in with Dr. Wyatt."

"Oh, hello, Mr. Stone. I'll check if he's available. Please wait one moment."

On-hold music fills the line while I wait to connect with the doctor working with my father.

Dr. Wyatt's deep baritone reaches across the line to me. "Hello, Oliver. Nice to hear from you."

"Hello, Dr. Wyatt. It's that time of the week again. How has my father's week been?"

"He's had a tough week. He's been rather difficult, threatening the staff and demanding to be released. You realize we can't keep him here against his will?"

He vacillates through highs and lows; refusing to attend the therapy sessions and giving the staff a hard time, then being the model inpatient and impressing the hell out of everyone on staff.

"Yeah, I understand. But he's not mentally stable to be out on his own. Are you able to assess his mental health and ensure his long-term habit hasn't created some type of mental health issue?"

"We're already in the process of assessing your father's mental health. There's no point in him kicking his addictions, leaving the center, and then being left undiagnosed and untreated for something else. We need to be sure he can stay clean and function successfully in society, or else all the hard work will be for naught."

I'm happier knowing they're on top of things. It was a tough road getting him into the rehab center in the first place.

"Your father still carries a great deal of guilt about the accident which claimed your mom's life. His behavior has been his coping mechanism *and* his punishment."

Dad lost the desire to live after Mom was killed in a car accident. They had been out celebrating their wedding anniversary—I was seven years old and home with the babysitter. He must have had a few drinks and figured he was okay to drive. Nobody knows what caused the accident, but he drove off the road and skidded sideways into an enormous tree. Mom's side of the car was annihilated, killing her instantly. Dad woke up in the hospital five days later and was charged with her death because he was twice over the blood-alcohol limit at the time of the accident. He was sent to prison for six years. When he was finally released, he spent all his time drinking and escaping into drugs.

"I know he feels that way. I also know I lost *both* parents that night. First, because he was sentenced to time in prison for his actions, then later because he couldn't keep his shit together." I struggle to keep the anger out of my voice, but I'm certain Dr. Wyatt can hear it.

I was sent to live with a family of strangers while my father was in the hospital because there were no other family members to take care of me. Eventually, I ended up in a foster home with a decent family, but I always felt like an outsider. I didn't make life easy for them, getting into trouble on the regular and shutting them out. I was only with them for a couple of years, because they thought I was too much trouble and sent me back to the shelter. Over the years, I was placed with five different families until I aged out of the system. None of the families were terrible. They just didn't know how to deal with a closed-off, troubled kid. I rejected any type of bond or affection and only communicated when absolutely necessary—I'm more or less still like that. I hide it better now.

"I could have easily blamed him for everything, but I didn't and I still don't. A relationship with my father is very important to me. He's all I have left. I purposely sought him out to build a relationship, but he makes it difficult with his addictions. He chooses that path instead of a path with me, his only son."

A couple of months ago, he hit rock bottom. He had passed out in an alley and was badly beaten within an inch of his life. The hospital contacted me when they found my business card in his pocket. From there, I finally got him into rehab. It's the best center in the city with a high success rate. I only hope he can rebuild some semblance of a normal life because I truly miss him.

"I understand and I hear what you're saying. He's been in the cycle a long time, fighting the guilt over losing your mother *and* failing you. He's trying his hardest to become the man he needs to be. But you have to remember, this has been his life for the past twenty-five years. It's a difficult cycle to break."

"I get it. Truly I do. I'm just frustrated."

"That's understandable. You must feel you're doing all the work. Making all the effort. But let me assure you. Your father is working his ass off in here." He pauses, and silence fills the phone. "Why don't you come in for a visit soon? We can all sit and chat. Maybe clear the air a little."

"That sounds good, Dr. Wyatt. I'll get my assistant to set it up in my calendar."

"Good. Good. I'll look forward to it."

Disconnecting the call, I slump back into my chair, running my hands through my hair. Looking out of my windows, not seeing the view, I wonder if I'll ever have a positive, healthy relationship with my father.

———

As I move through my workday, responding to emails, making phone calls, and speaking with clients, my thoughts keep returning to Kate and the way she looked after everyone on the worksite over the weekend. Not only did she manage her own work, but she was also always checking in on everyone else, getting them bottled water, and offering an extra pair of hands to anyone who needed help.

I wonder who looks after her?

I can't stop thinking about the sweet taste of her soft lips—the hot chocolate and my sweet, sweet Kate. I kept the kiss light, even though everything in me wanted to devour her, taste her tongue, and experience her desire.

Her dad and brother questioned my intentions toward Kate during our drive. I explained as clearly as I possibly could that I want her in my life, and I will do everything in my power to make it happen. I think they were as surprised by my declaration as I was.

I'm at a loss to work out at what point my intentions moved from one or two nights to wanting Kate as a permanent fixture in my life. It's so far removed from every relationship, or lack thereof, I've had with women throughout my adult life to date.

I only hope I can be worthy of her goodness.

NINE

-kate-

THE WEEKEND GAVE ME A *LOT* TO THINK ABOUT. I DON'T THINK I'VE ever met anyone like Oliver—in fact, I *know* I've never met anyone like him. He's way out of my league and wholly overwhelming. There's no way I could keep the interest of a guy like him. I can't even keep the interest of a normal man for more than a few months before they look for someone prettier and more interesting.

His message this morning was a surprise. I don't know what type of game he thinks he's playing with me, but I've learned my lesson in the past. I'm nobody's fool. The best thing I can do is steer clear of him—he'll get bored and move on sooner rather than later.

The school day goes by and I drive home. It's my turn to cook dinner for Margie and me tonight. Washing up, I collect the ingredients I need to get started. I make our dinner from memory because I've made this dish several times before, then plate it up to take next door. I knock on Margie's door and when she answers with a big grin; I hand her the dish.

"Hi. How was your day? Anything exciting happen down our street?" She often sits on her small porch, watching the comings and goings on our quiet street.

"Hey. Oh, you know, Pete down the street was chasing Joe's dog out of his garden, and cursing up a storm while he was doing it. Nothing new!" She laughs. She loves watching the antics of the old guys who live down the street, who entertain her regularly.

"Anyway, enjoy your dinner before it gets cold. Have a great night, and I'll see you tomorrow." I hug her carefully so I don't disturb the plate of food, then go back to my place to eat my dinner before it gets cold. Afterward, I plan on having a hot bath and getting lost in my new book by one of my favorite authors.

Soaking in the tub with my new book, I can't help but compare Oliver to the hero in the story. The hero is rather bossy and seamlessly takes charge of the heroine's life before she realizes what's happening. I think Oliver would definitely be like that if the person he was with didn't put some clear boundaries in place.

I lay my head back, recalling last night when he held my chin and touched his lips to mine. He was gentle and respectful—sweet even. I take it further in my mind, and I can almost feel his hands gliding over my curves, down my hips, and across my soft stomach. My body heats, my breasts grow heavy, my breaths quicken, and the blooming of my arousal makes itself known. How easy would it be to touch myself and release the pressure, but I don't want to condition my body to respond to him, so I climb out of the tub and dry off, then head to bed.

After another restless night's sleep, I drive to work to start a new day.

———

It's a usual Saturday morning for me, and I'm busy catching up on laundry and other chores around my house, dancing to my favorite playlist, when I receive a text. When I see it's from Oliver, butterflies erupt in my stomach. We've texted every day for two weeks, and I've come to look forward to seeing his name on my screen.

OLIVER

How's my beautiful Kate this morning?

Oh my! He's pulled out the big guns straight up. Let's have some fun.

ME

Who's this? I think you have the wrong number

OLIVER

Don't who's this me! You know exactly who this is and I definitely have the correct number

Answer me

How is MY BEAUTIFUL Kate this morning?

Oh-kay! No fun to be had here. He sounds pissed.

ME

I'm great. How are you today?

OLIVER

I'm feeling pretty good myself. What are you doing?

ME

I'm catching up on laundry and other exciting chores around the house before I spend the afternoon and evening with the kids at Lloyd Ave

OLIVER

What about tomorrow?

ME

I have prep work to do for school next week and then dinner with my family

OLIVER

Can you spare an hour to catch up for lunch?

Oh, geez, what can I say? I've blown him off a heap already, and he's been incredibly sweet with his texts every day. That he hasn't given up already makes me more inclined to say yes, and I guess he *is* only asking for an hour.

ME

I guess I can spare an hour for lunch. Where would you like to meet?

OLIVER

I'll pick you up at 1

No, no, no. That's not okay. I'm worried that if I give him an inch, he'll take a mile, and if he drives, then I won't be able to leave when I'm ready.

ME

I insist that I'll meet you there or we won't meet at all

OLIVER

Damn Sunshine, you make my life difficult

ME

Sorry (not really) 😊

OLIVER

No need to apologize. I wanted to do the right thing and pick you up, like a gentleman. Maybe someday you'll let me do that?

ME

Maybe

OLIVER

How about we meet at Pier 7 at 1?

Does that suit you?

ME

Sounds great. See you tomorrow

OLIVER

See you tomorrow

Why do I feel as if I've agreed to something that's going to change my life irrevocably? I realize I'm smiling even though I swore I wouldn't give him a chance.

TEN

-oliver-

I PACE AT THE ENTRANCE OF PIER 7, WHERE THERE ARE SEVERAL restaurants, casual cafés, and bars, waiting for Kate to arrive. It's been two weeks since I've laid eyes on her, and waiting for her to arrive has me balancing on a knife's edge.

It's 1:25.

She's late—*what if she's changed her mind and doesn't show?* I run my fingers through my hair, unable to believe she has me this worked up. She has me acting like an inexperienced teenage boy.

I check my phone for any messages, only to find work-related emails which can wait. The realization that I'm happy to put work on hold for an afternoon hits me hard and fast, but I want to give Kate my full attention. Hopefully, she enjoys her time with me and doesn't notice the time, giving me the opportunity to spend longer than the designated hour with her.

When I look up, I spot her walking quickly toward me. She's breathtaking in a pair of light skinny jeans worn at the knees and a navy boat-necked T-shirt, with her favored battered red Converse on her feet. Her hair is tied up but blowing in the wind, and as she spots me, her eyes light up while an enchanting smile settles on her lips.

I hope I get to keep her.

She's everything good in this world.

Taking long strides, I walk toward her, eating up the distance as quickly as possible.

She stops abruptly as I reach her. "Hi," she says, looking up at me with a small smile. Pushing up on her toes, she gives me what I've been needing for the past two weeks—a hug.

It's so simple, but I feel as if I can breathe again.

Having her in my arms is like a balm to soothe my soul.

"Hey," I return with a smile of my own, looking into her sparkling blue eyes. We seem to stand like that; caught up in each other for several moments as everything around us falls away, then she steps back, breaking the spell. She tucks her hands in her back pockets, thrusting her tits out for my perusal. I'm doing my best to be a gentleman and keep my eyes locked on hers, though. *Go me!*

"I'm sorry I'm late. My car stalled in the middle of an intersection, and it took a lot of persuasion on my part to convince the old girl to start again," she tells me as she huffs out a nervous laugh. "I wasn't sure if you'd still be here."

"I'm not going anywhere, Sunshine. I thought you'd changed *your* mind." I shove my hand through my hair. "I don't like the sound of what happened, though. That could have been a dangerous situation. Does your car break down often?"

I'm already working on a plan as to what to do about the old sedan she drives. She needs something safer, more reliable. I'm certain it will cause an argument with her, though—she's an independent firecracker.

Looking up at me, she responds, "Occasionally. It's happening more often as she gets older, but she was my first car, so I'll nurse her through. The car's special to me because she belonged to my nan." She shrugs.

Hmm, I won't be able to get rid of the car, but I would be happier if it had a complete overhaul. "Fair enough. C'mon, let's get something to eat. What are you in the mood for?"

I take her hand in my larger one and we walk along the pier, which juts out over the water, toward the eateries. I like how *natural* her hand feels in mine, as though we were made to fit together. Glancing down at our joined hands, I notice she doesn't have those long, fake nails some women seem to covet. Kate's are a practical length, with a pale pink polish.

She looks around thoughtfully, tapping her first finger against her luscious bottom lip I'm dying to bite. "I love the food at *Declan's Diner*. Mind if we eat there?" She turns, a hopeful expression painting her face.

The place is an institution on the pier, serving diners for the last eighty years. "Sure, let's go."

Still holding her hand, I lead her across the pier, quite pleased she hasn't pulled away—that's a win in my book. We step onto the worn black-and-white checkered linoleum tiled floor, our eyes needing to adjust to coming inside so we can see properly. The first thing that hits me as we enter are the delicious aromas of fish and chips, burgers, kebabs, and whatever else the guys are cooking. The second thing is the heat from all the fryers and grills. I don't get down here very often, but it's always busy because the food is fantastic and comes out fast.

We each study the menu boards for a few minutes, deciding on our preferences. Kate orders a Greek lamb salad wrap with an iced tea, while I order the burger, fries, and a root beer. We sit at a chrome and red 1950s-style table, making general small talk about the pier and tourists while we wait for our number to be called. Opting for a table outside on the pier allows us to people-watch as we enjoy our food.

As Kate unwraps her lunch, she looks at me as though she wants to say something, so I nod, motioning for her to tell me what she's thinking.

"Thanks for lunch."

I place my hand on hers to pause her. "I sense a *but* coming in here, and I know I won't like it, but go on."

"You're right, there is a *but*. I was happy to pay for my lunch. I can't keep accepting your generosity—it makes me feel uncomfortable. It's not like you're my boyfriend or anything." I growl under my breath, and her eyes widen. "I didn't mean you *should* be my boyfriend or anything like that. Oh my gosh, can the earth open up and swallow me now? I can't believe I said that! How embarrassing!"

She's adorable in her embarrassment—her natural blush rising while her hands cover her face. I gently remove them from her face. "Don't hide from me. I told you last time I want to get to know you. *Everything* about you. Remember? Even the things that embarrass you."

She looks properly chastised. "Yeah, I remember," she responds quietly while looking down at her food, avoiding my eyes.

I don't like that our date has taken this negative turn. "Tell me about what you did with the kids this weekend."

I know I chose the right topic to change the mood when her face lights up with the smile I adore and she straightens her body.

"It might be easier to tell you what we didn't do over the course of the afternoon and evening." She giggles. "I'm pretty sure the kids spend all week thinking up stuff for us to do: recipes to try, movies to watch, and games to play. We spent ages taking turns competing against each other, playing racing games with Luigi and Mario on their console. The kids are crazy good. I'm pretty sure I spent most of my races falling off the side of the track." She shakes her head and laughs at herself. "But I'm sure you don't want to hear me wax poetic about hanging out with a bunch of pre-teens."

"I absolutely do. I enjoy watching you light up when you talk about things you're passionate about. I actually find it pretty sexy—who knew?" I finish with a smile to put her at ease.

And the blush is back! I mentally congratulate myself because I love that fucking blush.

We finish eating and decide to walk along the pier, taking in the scenery and other people as we go. We stop here and there, looking closely at items for sale at the cottage craft stalls, which were set up for the Sunday market. Kate seems to be more comfortable with me, chatting freely about different crafts her mom has started and given up over the years.

The fall weather is perfect, with a soft, warm breeze, making the entire experience enjoyable. I even notice she hasn't bothered to check the time, and I've snagged more than an hour with her. "Would you like—"

"Hey, Kate! I thought that was you."

She freezes, and I know from the stiffness in her body and her pinched expression this won't be good. The guy is shorter than me and a little pudgy around the middle. He stands with his arm around a bony blonde woman, who's looking at Kate like she's covered in mud, and me as though I'm a juicy steak she's dying to devour.

He looks at me, pointing his finger. "Hey, I know you. You're Oliver Stone." I stiffen and prepare for Kate to pull away from me. He'd better not blow my chance with her. "What are you doing here with someone like Kate? Surely you can do better than her, man?"

What the fuck did he just say?

My blood boils, and my free hand tightens into a fist, ready to knock this motherfucker out.

Kate attempts to tug her hand from mine, dropping her face toward the decking. "Uh ... hi, Brandon. Hi, Crystal." She looks up at me with wide eyes, then glances around us quickly. "I have to go." She breaks free from my hold and turns, walking away briskly.

I'm torn whether to follow her or to put this dick in his place. The second option wins out, and I turn back to dickface. I straighten to my full height, taking the few steps needed to get into his space. My clenched fists, the pissed-off look on my face, and the tic in my jaw *should* make me appear menacing. "What. The. Fuck. Did you just say about Kate? Tell me I misheard you."

This guy must be as dense as a brick when he smirks at me. "Nah, man, you can do better than her. You're *the* Oliver Stone!"

It's not even a conscious decision when I raise my arm back to swing. My fist connects with his jaw and he falls flat on his ass in the middle of the pier. I leave him there, taking long, quick strides in an attempt to catch up with Kate. It's not easy because a crowd has gathered around us, and I have to weave in and out of groups of people. I can't see her anywhere; she's fucking disappeared. I head toward the parking lot to search for her car, but it's not there.

She's gone! *Fuck!*

ELEVEN

-oliver-

I QUICKLY CLIMB IN MY CAR AND DRIVE TOWARD KATE'S HOUSE, WHICH is going to be fucking awkward since she never told me where she lives. I'm not sure how I'll explain how I found her, but I don't care at this point. I need to see her and find out what that was all about; but above all, I need to make sure she's alright.

When I pull in behind her car, she's at her front door, about to step inside. She turns around when she hears my car. Turning off the engine, I climb out, and even from this distance, I can see she's been crying. She stays locked in position, fidgeting with the hem of her T-shirt as I walk toward her.

"I'm sorry I left like that. I was having a great time with you, but Brandon was right. You can do much better than a girl like me—"

I'm not having this; I step up to her, getting as close to her body as I can. I lift her chin gently to ensure she can see my face clearly, cutting her off mid-sentence. Then I kiss those luscious lips I haven't been able to stop thinking about. It takes her a beat to respond, and I worry I've taken things too far.

Slowly, I pull back to study her eyes, checking I haven't over-stepped, but it doesn't seem as if she wants me to stop. I cup her face in my hands, using my thumbs to wipe her tears away as I move in to kiss her lips again. I start gently, enjoying the warmth of her lips, then I use my tongue to taste her—the iced tea she drank at lunch, and the saltiness of her tears are at the forefront.

Her dainty hands hold my hips as I press in to deepen the kiss, encouraging her to open up and let me in. She does, and it's the best feeling. I sense the importance of her allowing me to taste her like this. Fire licks up my spine as our tongues tangle in a sensual kiss, breathing each other's air and learning each other's taste. We kiss for long minutes, and she finally gives in. I capture her sigh. The chemistry between us is beautifully explosive

I slow down and soften the kiss, finishing with a light peck on her swollen lips, then press my forehead to hers. If I don't stop now, we'll be at risk of being charged with indecent exposure. Her eyes open slowly as she takes a deep breath, smiling timidly.

"I've been wanting to kiss you since I first met you on that stinking hot veranda fifteen months ago, and I was *not* disappointed." She giggles as her cheeks pinken. I notice the curtain drop into place at the neighbor's window and chuckle to myself. Nudging her nose with mine, I whisper, "I'm going to want to do that a lot. Probably a lot more than that, too."

She smiles broadly and I feel ten feet tall that I could do that for her. "I can't believe you kissed me on my porch after what just happened. This isn't my life. I'm not the girl hot guys chase after and kiss!" She looks up at me. "I guess you want an explanation, huh?"

I didn't miss the fact that she referred to me as a *hot guy*. Perhaps I *do* have a chance with her. "Whenever you're ready to talk about it, I'll be ready to listen. Now, are you going to invite me inside?"

Her eyes widen as if she can't believe I would want to be invited inside her home. "Uh, I don't think that's a good idea after what happened." She attempts to put space between us, but I don't allow her. "Truthfully, you *can* do better than a girl like me. I'm not much of anything and you're … well,"—she waves her hand up and down, gesturing to me—"you're *you*."

"I'm not following you. You're going to have to be clearer." I *know* I'm not going to like what she's about to say. She's going to demean herself in my presence yet again, and that's going to piss me the fuck off.

"Oh, come on!" She huffs, slapping the sides of her thighs. "Don't pretend you don't see the disparities between us. Judging by your car, you're clearly a successful guy. You're confident and exceptionally good-looking. You told me that women ask *you* to dinner. You seem to be intelligent, and you're kind and thoughtful—if not a little over-whelming."

I'm not sure what I've done for her to assume I'm kind and thoughtful. I wouldn't use either term to describe myself.

She takes a step back, straightening, and looks me directly in the eye—she's ready for battle. "I can't keep a boyfriend from straying. I'm average-looking at best. I'm a simple kindergarten teacher and spend my free time with my eighty-five-year-old neighbor and a group of prepubescent kids. Is that clear enough for you?" She finishes with wide eyes and a sassy head shake.

Yep, she fucking pissed me off!

I cup her face in my hands, my thumbs resting on her delicate cheekbones, while my fingers slide to the back of her head, cradling it more gently than the anger boiling inside me should allow. Backing her up against her front screen door, I tilt her face up to mine and slam my mouth down onto hers. I give her everything I have, pressing as close as I possibly can.

She has to feel my growing cock, hard as stone, behind my zipper. It would be impossible to miss what she does to me. She can't go anywhere while I have her like this and eventually relaxes, giving in to me and our off-the-charts chemistry. She melts against me, wrapping her arms around my neck, pulling me down—as if she wants us to join as much as I do.

After a long while, I pull back gently to place light, delicate kisses against her swollen lips and the tip of her nose, then I wait until she opens her eyes.

"You've pissed me off. I've told you before, I won't tolerate you disrespecting yourself. Let me tell you the disparities I see between you and me." Using my fingers, I hold her chin so I don't lose her focus. "I see a woman who has the biggest heart of anyone I've ever met. Who gives her time freely to make the world a better place for others without asking for anything for herself. My heart is closed off, and I guard my time as though it's buried fucking treasure—I wasn't sure I had a heart until I met you. I see an intelligent woman with a truck-load of patience to work with kindergarten children day in and day out. I see a caring and thoughtful neighbor, who freely gives her time to make sure her neighbor is okay. I, on the other hand, only focus on myself and my work. I see an absolutely stunning woman with the most ravishing set of legs I've ever seen, a miracle of a smile, because it allows me to breathe, and a great set of tits that I can't wait to get my hands and mouth on." She laughs at my last comment, which is exactly what I wanted. "Surely you can feel what you do to me." I press my hard length against her belly. "I've never, in my life, had such a visceral reaction to a woman. The chemistry between us is palpable, and I would like the opportunity to explore it with you. But you need to trust that what I'm saying is real and stop doubting me or denying this connection we have." She seems stuck for words, so I lay one more gentle kiss on her and reluctantly step back. "I won't insist on an invitation inside this afternoon." I tuck a lock of hair behind her ear. "Be warned. I'm not giving up on you and the idea of us. Enjoy your family dinner tonight. Say hi to your mom and dad, as well as Toby from me."

I do one of the most difficult things in my life—I walk away. She needs time to come to terms with everything I've said. I only hope she makes the right decision—to cooperate because I'm not giving up.

TWELVE

-kate-

STANDING, IF YOU CAN CALL IT THAT, AGAINST MY FRONT SCREEN DOOR in a daze, I realize I've *never* been kissed like that. Full of passion and desire. The need between us was like an independent living organism. My heart is still beating a million miles a minute, and I'm dizzy from the lack of air entering my lungs. I am absolutely floored by what happened; the things he said.

Brandon completely embarrassed me when he told Oliver he could do better than me. The afternoon had been perfect, and I was beginning to think my issues were stupid before Brandon flayed me open, reminding me Oliver *is* totally out of my league. I wanted to make myself as small as possible and escape as quickly as I could before Oliver realized it was true—that he was wasting his time with me.

The sound of the locks disengaging next door captures my attention, and Margie steps out of her front door fanning herself. "My god, girl. Who was that and tell me where I can get one?"

Aaand that does it. I burst into laughter and she joins in. Our laughter eventually slows, turning into girly giggles when she nudges me with her elbow. "That kiss was movie-worthy. I could feel the heat and steam from inside. You need to hold on to a man who knows how to kiss like that. Believe me, men like that are few and far between these days. They're all pansy asses who don't want to mess up their hair or manicure."

Ha! She's spot on there. I experience more chemistry standing next to Oliver than I've ever felt, even in the most passionate of moments, with any of my exes.

"Can you imagine what he's like between the sheets ... or against the wall ... or in the shower?" Margie sighs.

My blush rises when I think about her witnessing the hot kisses we shared on my front porch, and that she's imagining Oliver having sex.

I put my hands on my hips and deadpan. "Were you spying on me, Margie?"

"Absolutely, I gotta get my thrills from somewhere, Love!" She has not one ounce of shame in her game. It's exactly why I love her. We smile at each other as she winks at me. "So, tell me all about that hot hunk of man."

"Well, you probably won't see him around again. He's way out of my league—"

Margie holds up her hand in the universal sign of stop, interrupting me. "Stop right there! There was no *out of my league* from where I was watching. You two are stunning together, and the chemistry was off the charts. He would be lucky to catch and keep a young woman like you. Mark my words, I'll be seeing him around here quite often."

"But—" I try to explain, but she cuts me off again with a slash of her arm.

"No *buts* about it. Now go inside and get ready to visit with your family for dinner. Make sure you say hello to everyone for me."

Margie glares at me while hugging me tightly, then heads inside, engaging the locks. I guess that's that then.

THIRTEEN

-oliver-

I'M DOING MY BEST TO FOCUS ON MY WORK WHEN JASE STROLLS INTO my office and makes himself comfortable in the chair opposite my desk. He looks as if he wants to sit and chat for a while, but I'm too discombobulated to carry on any kind of meaningful discussion this morning. He slouches back in the chair, rests his right ankle on his left knee, looks at me, and waits me out.

I raise my brows. "Okay, I'll bite. What's up?"

"That's what I want to know. You don't seem your usual self. You look a little, shall I say, disheveled." He waves his hand around in my general direction. "You've missed your nine-thirty check-in with *Square One* for your father, and I've had a call from a guy named Brandon. He's threatening to sue your ass for his fractured jaw." He finishes with raised eyebrows.

I glance at the time, realizing he's right—*fuck!* Kate has my head in such a spin. I barely slept last night, and I can't seem to focus—on anything. I've never experienced these kinds of feelings for a woman before. Jase drops his leg, places both feet on the floor and leans forward, resting his elbows on his knees.

"Talk to me. What's going on?"

I huff out a breath. "It's Kate."

His posture straightens, and that relaxed air about him vanishes. "Is she alright? Nothing's happened to her?"

I wave him off. "No, nothing like that. Unless you count her dick of, I assume, an ex-boyfriend humiliating her." Thinking about it has a red haze entering my periphery, my fists clenching, ready to fight.

"What do you mean?"

"I finally got her to agree to go on a date with me yesterday afternoon." Nodding, he smirks while gesturing for me to continue. "We were having a brilliant afternoon. It felt surprisingly natural, as though we're in sync. Then this guy approaches Kate—Brandon." I raise my eyebrows. "When he sees she's with me, he says, 'What are you doing here with someone like Kate? Surely you can do better than her, man?'. She shut down, then took off before I could stop her."

"What the fuck?" Jase looks as though he wants a piece of the bastard as well. "I hope you set him straight as well as punched him in the jaw. Any guy would be lucky to have a woman like her." Glaring at him, I tense. I don't want him to consider he should be with Kate, but I'm also relieved he thinks highly of her. He raises his hands in surrender. "Hey. Calm down, I don't mean I'm interested. I *know* she's all yours."

Relaxing back in my chair, I swipe my hand down my face. "Damn right I set him straight. He deserved what I gave him and more. The lawyers can deal with his slimy ass." I almost smile—it felt good to knock that asshole on his ass in front of his current girlfriend.

"Good, glad to hear it. I would have done the same. I guess things are moving forward with you two, then?"

Shaking my head, I stare at my desk, gathering my thoughts. Looking back at Jase, I suck in a deep breath. "I don't know. By the time I decked Brandon and chased after Kate, she was gone. I turned up at her house, catching her before she went inside. She thinks she's not good enough for me." I poke my chest with my thumb, shaking my head. "She thinks *I* can do much better than her. That she's not beautiful enough to be with someone who looks like me." My blood boils all over again.

"Her ex must have done a number on her. She's going to need you to show her how wrong she is; help her rebuild that self-confidence." He studies me as if to check if I'm up for the job. "What are you going to do?"

"First of all, I kissed the shit out of her and told her she wasn't to disrespect herself like that ever again."

Jase snickers.

"Then I laid my cards on the table." I scrape my hand down my face. "I've never been this invested in spending time outside of sex with a woman. I want to get to know her and soak in all her goodness. I told her I wanted to be with her, and I would consider myself very lucky if she would give me a chance. Then I left her to think about it." I pause, looking out of the floor-to-ceiling windows. Jase generously allows me the time. "I'm hopeful she makes the choice to let me in and gives this thing between us a chance to grow."

"It sounds like you did the right thing. She'll come around."

"I hope so."

But I'm not convinced.

"Can you find the closest coffee shop to Northwood Elementary? Place a recurring order for every Monday to Friday to be delivered to Kate Summer in the Kindergarten. Make sure she gets a large skinny latte with a vanilla shot in a reusable cup with some type of pastry each day. Make sure the pastry isn't the same two days in a row unless she shows a preference for a particular type. Then make sure they let me know which pastries she prefers."

He makes a note on his tablet. "Sure, boss. You don't think that's a little excessive? You might scare her off."

"She told me she's too busy to eat lunch most days. I don't think it's excessive at all. I plan to look after her so she realizes she needs me in her life. This week we'll start with coffee. Next week we'll include lunch. I need to find out if she has any allergies. Actually, make sure they deliver the coffee before school starts. She probably can't have hot drinks once the students enter the room."

"I'll get right on that, but don't say I didn't warn you when this bites you in the ass, and she tells you to leave her alone." He shrugs. "I'll also contact your lawyer about Brandon."

"Thanks, Jase. Appreciate it. Now get out and let me get back to work. Next thing I know, you'll want to paint my nails and braid my hair." My lips lift in a half-smile.

He huffs out a laugh. "You wish."

He offers me the bird over his shoulder as he leaves my office, and I can't help but laugh.

———

I haven't heard from Kate for almost forty-eight hours when my phone buzzes around twelve-thirty. As I reach for it, I see it's from Kate. A true smile breaks, and I can't open my phone quickly enough. This is exactly what I was hoping for.

SUNSHINE

Thanks for my coffee and pastry this morning. This is the first chance I've had to respond. But please stop buying me things. I don't need it

ME

You're more than welcome and I'm not going to stop looking after you. You need someone to take care of you and I'm going to show you I'm that man

A few minutes pass and I figure the conversation is over.

SUNSHINE

Woah! Slow your roll, big guy. I'm not some little woman who needs a big strapping man to take care of me. I've been doing fine this long, and I'm certain I'll continue to do fine all on my little ol' lonesome

Fuuuck! I went too far, and I didn't mean it like that. But hey, I raise my brow at the phone. She said I'm a *big strapping man.* I'm happy with that.

ME

I didn't mean it like that. I know you are a highly capable woman. Please let me make it up to you. Can I take you out to dinner tonight?

SUNSHINE

It's all good. You don't need to make anything up to me

She totally ignored my dinner invitation. What's it going to take to get this woman on a proper date? I hope I haven't fucked my chances before I even get started.

SUNSHINE

I also, uh, wanted to apologize for my breakdown on Sunday. I'm sorry you had to witness my self-loathing and I'm rather embarrassed 😔

Oh, Sunshine.

ME

You have nothing to be embarrassed about. I hope I made it abundantly clear I want to get to know you, Kate. Spend time with you. See where this chemistry might lead

I've never felt this way about a woman, and as much as it shocks me, I like it. A few minutes pass before her next message comes through.

SUNSHINE

I think I would like that very much

Yes! It's like I've won the lottery. I abruptly stand from my chair, knocking it back as I throw my fist in the air to celebrate.

Feeling more settled, I finally get my head back in the game and back to work. We have a big quarter coming up, and I need to prep for a meeting with my senior staff tomorrow to ensure we're all on the same page.

FOURTEEN

-kate-

OH, THAT MAN.

He's certainly different from any man I've ever encountered before. The girl took me by surprise when she arrived from *Coffee and Cookies* with *my* coffee order. When she told me someone had phoned in an order yesterday to be delivered to me—I didn't understand what she was talking about. I rarely buy takeaway coffee or pastries, because I'm watching every penny. When I asked her who placed the order, she smiled at me and said his name was Oliver. She asked me to tell her if I liked the pastry she had selected for me, presented my coffee in a reusable coffee cup, and left. As I took a sip, I couldn't resist closing my eyes while I absorbed the rich flavor and aroma—no wonder they're considered the best coffee place around.

I spent the morning walking on clouds because I felt special. It's not everyday someone pays attention to how I like my coffee, and then organize a delivery. Even Emma, my friend, and the first-grade teacher in the class next door noticed. She said I looked even more energized than I usually do. When Jack pulled Sue-Anne's hair, I was still floating in the clouds. But then I messaged to thank him for the coffee, and it things got a little out of hand! He comes across as a bit of a caveman —a sweet and thoughtful caveman, but a caveman all the same.

I wonder if he would be that bossy in the bedroom? Aaand there goes my blush again!

After a restless night's sleep, I mentally prepare for a new day as I drive to work. When I arrive, the girl from *Coffee and Cookies* is waiting by my classroom door with another cup of coffee and an interesting-looking pastry. I'm going to put on ten pounds at this rate. I never eat this type of food regularly. Sure, once in a while, but certainly not two days in a row.

"Morning, I guess this is from Oliver?"

"Good morning to you too!" She has such a cheerful demeanor for this time of the day. "Bingo! Oliver strikes again. Let me know if you like the pastry. It's a new creation of mine. Have an awesome day!"

She collects the cup from yesterday, waving as she leaves. I can't help but sigh at his kind gesture, but I don't want to encourage him to keep spending money on me. These types of expenses can add up without realizing it. Before you know it, you've spent twenty dollars here and thirty dollars there, and then you can't make your mortgage payment. I grab my phone and shoot Oliver a quick message before the kids arrive.

ME

Good morning! Thank you once again for my coffee and pastry. I appreciate your kind and thoughtful gesture, but I must insist you stop. It truly is unnecessary. I hope you have a great day

OLIVER

Good morning, Sunshine. You are more than welcome for the coffee and pastry. Enjoy them and think of me. Have a productive day

Oh, I will certainly think of him. *How can I stop?* I hope I'm not seeming ungrateful for my delicious treats, but I'm not used to having a man spoil me without expecting something in return. I drink my coffee, made exactly how I like it, and eat the delicious chocolate-filled pastry, finishing in time to greet my energetic students. As I greet each child, I can't clear my head of thoughts of a hot, bossy green-eyed man named Oliver.

———

Each morning, I'm greeted with coffee and a pastry. I won't fit into any of my clothes at this rate. I started to share the pastries with Emma—I figure I'll be eating fewer calories that way. Each day, I send him a thank you text which also asks him kindly to cease and desist. On Friday afternoon, my phone vibrates on my desk.

OLIVER

Good afternoon Sunshine. Do you have anything that you're allergic to?

ME

Why?

OLIVER

I wanted to check to ensure I'm keeping you safe

ME

You don't need to worry about that. I can keep myself safe. Thank you for checking in though

OLIVER

Do you have any allergies? Answer, or I'll keep texting you until you tell me anyway. Your choice!

ME

Geez, you're one persistent dude! No, I don't have any allergies. Happy?

OLIVER

Unbelievably so

Well, that was weird. He's too much! I don't know what to make of him. Honestly, I don't. I've never experienced anyone like him before.

FIFTEEN

-oliver-

IT'S BEEN TEN DAYS SINCE I'VE LAID EYES ON KATE. TEN DAYS TOO long for my liking. If I want to make any headway with her, I'm going to have to push forward because I *know* she won't come to me.

> ME
>
> Can I see you tonight?

Perhaps I'm being pushy, but I need to have her in my arms again —and soon.

> SUNSHINE
>
> I can't tonight. I'm cooking dinner for Margie. I try to cook for her a couple of nights each week to make sure she eats properly

Why am I not surprised? From what I can work out, she always looks out for everybody else.

> ME
>
> I can bring Chinese food, or whatever you like
>
> Enough for the three of us

I sit, staring at my phone like a teen, impatiently waiting for her response, which doesn't come. Maybe I pushed too hard, too fast. I need to slow down and tread gently with this woman, or I may scare her off. My phone vibrates as I turn back to my computer. I pick it up as if I'm an addict, receiving the message I was hoping for.

SUNSHINE

Sorry I took a while to respond. I had to check with Margie. That would be great. Margie and I love Chinese food. We'll see you at 7

Aaand, touchdown!

ME

See you soon Sunshine. Get home safely

Well, this is interesting. I don't think I've ever left the office before seven, and I need to order dinner, pick it up, and get to her place *by* seven.

"Trinity Fox has dealt with Brandon," Jase announces as he steps through my office door.

Turning his way, I raise an eyebrow. "Good. I like how she works. Swift and sharp."

He nods. "Yeah. She threatened to sue him for public embarrassment and humiliation. He backed down straight away."

I huff out a breath. "Of course he did. Goes to show how weak and insipid the fucker obviously is."

"Yeah." He thumbs over his shoulder. "I'm off to grab lunch. Do you want me to bring anything back for you?"

"I could eat a sandwich. Use the card."

SIXTEEN

-kate-

IT'S FOUR BY THE TIME I WALK OUT TO MY CAR TO DRIVE HOME. I can't believe Oliver's having dinner with Margie and me tonight. I'm not sure whether I'm more excited or nervous about having him in my home.

I stayed to display the giant shapes the children put together from our shape hunt today. We wandered around the school, identifying the different shapes the children could see in the built and natural environment. They took photos of the different shapes with their tablets, then I printed them on the school printer. The students then sorted them into categories of images of the same shape. We took it one step further, making a giant shape using the shapes in each category. It was great fun, and now the kids are determined to identify shapes everywhere they go. I live for that stuff. The best part of teaching kindergarten is watching the students develop confidence in their skills and knowledge over the year. I love forming a bond with them and watching them grow as learners.

I frown as I look at my yellow blouse covered in green paint and glue from our craft activity this afternoon. I don't want Oliver to see me so messy. I desperately need to have a shower and change before he arrives.

I pile all of my gear in the back seat of my car and climb in. Nothing happens when I turn the key. I pump the gas a few times, then turn the key again. Instead of nothing, I get a loud bang and a plume of gray smoke pours out of the engine bay.

Crap! Now, what do I do?

I scramble out of my car, working quickly to collect all the files I loaded in. Then I step as far away as I can—just in case it explodes. Okay, I'm probably being dramatic, but as smoke keeps pouring out of the engine, I feel justified in my position to stay clear. I guess I need to call a tow truck . This is annoying. I was hoping to pay a little extra off my mortgage this month. I didn't budget for car repairs, but it has to be fixed or I won't be able to get to and from work.

Reaching into my bag, I pull out my phone. As I navigate my way to the phone app, it rings. Oliver's name lights up the screen, so I quickly press to accept the call. "Hey. How was your day? Are you still planning on coming for dinner tonight?" My questions come out in a rush, and I probably sound like a madwoman who might miss out on her fix—which I might, thanks to my car.

His rich laugh fills my ear. "Hey, Sunshine. Of course, I'm still coming for dinner. I was calling to find out if you needed me to pick up anything else on my way?"

He's so thoughtful.

"No thanks, just bring yourself and dinner, of course. I'm having some car trouble. I hope I'll make it home on time. I was about to call a tow truck to pick up my car. Then I'll need to work out how to get home."

"Where are you? I'll organize for my mechanic to come and pick up your car. I can come and take you home."

Oh geez, I'm pretty sure the mechanic he uses for that fancy car of his would be way out of my budget.

"No, that's okay. I'll sort it out. I have a mechanic I use, so I'll get in touch with him. He's my friend's brother. I trust him. But I wouldn't say no to a ride home if it's not too much trouble. I'm still at school."

I hold my breath, hoping he'll be happy to swing out of his way to take me home.

"Of course. I'll get there as quickly as I can. Text me the contact details of the mechanic you use, and I'll organize the tow for you. You go back into the building and wait for me."

Gosh, he's bossy, but I'm not going to complain … I need his help.

"Okay, I'll text it to you now. Hopefully, the tow truck can get here soon. That way, you won't have to wait around. Thanks, I appreciate your help. See you soon."

"No problem. Happy to help any time you need. I'll see you soon."

He disconnects the call, and I carry all my files back inside the building. Lucky for me, the cleaners are still working and the school's still open.

SEVENTEEN

-oliver-

THIS IS THE SECOND TIME SHE'S HAD CAR TROUBLE SINCE I'VE KNOWN her. Once she texts the number, I call her mechanic. It rings several times, and I'm about to call my mechanic when someone finally answers.

"Stanfield Auto Repairs. This is Max. How can I help you?"

"Hi, Max. My name is Oliver Stone. My girlfriend's car has broken down and needs to be towed. Can you pick it up now?"

"Sure. Where is it?"

"Northwood Elementary. Do you know it?"

"Yeah. My sister's a teacher there."

"I need you to do me a favor. She keeps having trouble with the car. I want the entire vehicle stripped and everything mechanical replaced."

He whistles. "That'll mean the only original parts of the car will be the body and the interior."

"Yep. That way, I can rest assured the car is safe and reliable. The car is special to her. It belonged to her nan."

"I have to be honest with you. It's probably going to be more expensive to complete this work than it would be to buy her a new one."

I huff out a sigh. I guessed as much. "She's attached to the damn thing, so this is how it has to be. You need to keep it between us and invoice her for something inexpensive to explain the smoke."

"Okay. I can keep it between us. But it's going to take a considerable amount of time to do the work you want."

"I'm sure you can come up with some excuse for the extra time. It's important she feels she's dealing with her own problems."

"No problem. I'll work something out. I'll see you at the school."

I arrive at Kate's school at the same time as the tow truck. She steps out of the building, loaded down with her bags of files for work. Striding forward quickly, I press a kiss to her forehead as I take some of the load. I've never seen her in her work clothes. She's adorable wearing red ballet flats, a black-and-white striped skirt, and a yellow blouse with green splotches ... of ... is that paint? I have the distinct feeling she loves red shoes. Each and every pair of shoes I've seen her wear are red. I brush a kiss across her lips, and her shoulders drop. I guarantee she's worried about the expense associated with getting her car repaired.

I brush a lock of hair that's come free from her braid behind her ear, but it's stiff. I rub the strands between my fingers ... is that ... glue? She's adorably messy after her day at work, and I'm trying hard to hold back a smile.

"Hey."

She looks up at me, eyebrows drawn tight. "Hey. Thanks for coming, and for organizing the tow truck."

"No problem. I'm always happy to help."

We walk toward the tow truck parked next to her car, and I reach my hand forward. "Hi, I'm Oliver. I spoke with you on the phone."

He nods in greeting, shaking my hand. "Max."

Kate steps forward. "Hi, Max. Thanks for coming out quickly. Do you have time in your schedule to work on my car? I'm going to need it fixed pretty quickly because I need it for work."

"Yeah, of course. It'll probably take a few days, though. You may need to rent a car or borrow one from a friend. I used to offer courtesy cars, but the insurance on them was too much for my business."

"Oh, thanks. Yeah, I'll work out something. Can you please call me when you know what's wrong, as well as an estimate of the cost and time it's going to take?"

Max looks across at me, then back to Kate. "Sure, sure. No problem. I can do that. I'll most likely call you tomorrow afternoon once I investigate the issue."

She tucks a lock of hair behind her ear. "Thanks, I really appreciate your help."

He nods and moves toward her car. "Do you have everything you need out of here?"

"Uh, yeah. It's good to go," she responds, taking the few steps to Max and handing him her car key.

I tuck her in close as Max loads her car onto the tow truck. When he's done, we watch him drive away. Kate slumps against me, releasing a long sigh. I kiss the top of her head, and she looks up at me. "Thanks for coming to my rescue. I hope it's not going to cost an arm and a leg to fix my car."

I squeeze her shoulder. "You didn't need to be rescued." I pull away to study her, noting the tightness around her mouth and eyes. "Come on, we'll load your stuff into my car and get going."

We load her work gear into my car and make our way to her place. I drop her off, then drive back to my office to tie up some loose ends for an overseas client that I need to finish before I can leave for the day.

———

I pull up to Kate's place at ten minutes past with several bags of Chinese food from my favorite restaurant. Considering the way my afternoon went, I did well to get here on time. I chose several dishes because I wasn't sure what they'd like. I figure they can survive on what's left over for the rest of the week.

Her front door is wide open, the only barrier her screen door allowing me to hear her talking with another woman.

"I told you I would see that young man again. You need to listen to me. I know my stuff!"

I assume that's Margie's voice.

"I know what you said. I guess I need to let go of my apprehension and trust what he's showing me. He's genuinely sweet and thoughtful, if not a little overwhelming and intense."

Silverware and crockery clank; they must be setting the table for dinner. I use the break in their conversation to knock on the screen door. Kate comes to the door wearing yoga pants and a loose T-shirt draped off one shoulder, showing smooth, creamy skin interrupted by a red bra strap. Her feet are bare, with red polish on her toes. I could get used to coming home to her greeting me at the door in such a comfortable state. Her hair's wet—she must have washed the glue out of it.

"Hey, you're right on time. I wasn't sure if you could even get here after I messed up your afternoon. Traffic can be hectic at this time of day."

I think she's nervous because she's barely taken a breath. She unlocks and opens the screen door, then stands to the side to allow me into her home. I want to greet her with a kiss, but I don't want to push my luck as I spy her neighbor standing off to the side, observing us with a cheeky smile.

As I pass Kate, her delicate jasmine scent fills my senses, and I want to pause and soak it all in.

"It's unusual for me to be out of the office while it's still daylight." I turn toward Margie. "You must be Margie. I'm Oliver. It's nice to meet you."

I step closer to shake her hand, but she knocks it out of the way and hugs me. My body's stiff, unused to being hugged in a platonic way. Tonight should be interesting. I'm desperate to spend any time I can with Kate, so I wasn't going to miss this opportunity, but having a friendly dinner with strangers is out of my comfort zone. This is the second dinner I'll sit through with people I don't know to spend time with this woman.

"Kate and I are huggers! None of this shaking hands business."

As she releases me, she squeezes my biceps and not-so-covertly nods and winks at Kate.

She blushes in response—I love that fucking blush.

We get situated at Kate's small dining table, dishing up our plates of food. At first, we're all quiet, taking in the delicious aromas and flavors.

Margie swallows a bite of food, then places her fork on the side of her plate. She studies me intently for a moment, then with a serious expression, she asks, "Tell me, Oliver. What are your intentions with my girl, Kate?"

Kate spits out the water she just drank in utter shock. "Margie! I can't believe you asked that. Do you have no filter at all?"

She's mortified, which I find charming. The blush I love is creeping up her throat, burning her cheeks as she attempts to wipe up her mess.

Margie laughs, hitting the table with an open palm. "Oh god, girl, settle down. I was joking with Oliver. He doesn't mind."

Kate turns to me and mouths, "I'm so sorry." Then she shoots Margie a death glare, filled with obvious underlying affection for the woman.

Placing my palm on Kate's forearm, I gain her attention while speaking to Margie. "My intentions are simple. I want to spend time with Kate. I want to get to know her. I want to know *everything* about her. I want to care for her, and have her in my life for as long as possible."

I've repeatedly had to make my intentions clear in regard to Kate. I don't mind. It makes me happy to know she's surrounded by people who care for and love her fiercely. Margie seems satisfied with my answer as she nods and smiles, looking lovingly at Kate who still looks unsure of my intentions, and well, I'm a bit surprised myself by the overwhelming desire I have to get to know her. Not only on a physical level but on an emotional one as well.

We move on, making small talk about each of our days and the happenings in their street.

Kate relays the afternoon's ordeal to Margie. Without hesitation, Margie offers her car, which she barely drives anymore because of failing eyesight, and the tightness in Kate's body releases with a solution to her transportation problems.

I offered to rent a car for her, but she's a stubborn, independent woman—so very different from any other woman I've encountered. She obviously knows I have more money than she does, yet she refuses to allow me to help her.

We finish the meal, and Margie excuses herself, so I offer to walk her to her door, and she accepts; hugging Kate goodbye.

At her door, Margie turns to me. "Please don't hurt my girl. She has such a kind heart and a generous soul."

"You needn't worry, Margie. I have absolutely zero interest in hurting her. I can see exactly how much she has to offer, and I selfishly want it. I want it all, and I want it all from Kate. Now that I've met her, nobody else will do."

She hugs me, pats my cheek, then steps inside, locking up for the evening.

I let myself back into Kate's home, which is as sunny as she is. Comfortable furniture with colorful cushions, rugs, and prints fills the space, giving it a joyful feel that's warm and welcoming. The exact opposite of my cold, clinical penthouse.

She's already cleared the table and is currently standing at the sink, washing the dishes. Her ass looks fantastic in her yoga pants and I can't stop myself from needing to touch her any longer. I step close behind her; my entire front pressing against her back. She pauses what she's doing, turning her face to the side, allowing her to see me. I place my hands on either side of her body, boxing her in. Leaning in, I place gentle kisses and nips along her exposed shoulder, up her slender neck, finally reaching her soft lips—something I've been desperate to do all evening. The plate drops into the water with a splash, and I swallow her sigh. It's as though she's been waiting for me to touch her, to kiss her.

EIGHTEEN

-kate-

MY GOD. *FINALLY!*

From the minute he walked into my home and I smelled his woodsy masculine scent, I've wanted him to kiss me. To touch me. To show me he meant everything he said to me after the pier.

When I saw him in his suit, I'm pretty sure I stopped breathing—holy hotness! I've always been a sucker for a guy in a suit, but Oliver takes it to the next level. I figured it couldn't get any better, but he took off his jacket, undid his tie, and rolled up his sleeves.

I think I had heart palpitations.

The hotness level skyrocketed one thousand percent—it was as though all my arm porn fantasies came to life, right before my eyes. Now, as his warm, muscular body presses against mine, I want to turn around and feel every inch of him.

As he kisses me, the rasp of his short beard is delicious against the sensitive skin on my shoulder. His delicate kisses make me feel as if I'm precious. Losing my grip on the plate I'm washing, it drops into the sink, and I tilt my head, giving him better access to my neck. His kisses heat my blood and goosebumps cover my flesh.

I can't go another minute without touching him.

Turning around, I lift my arms around his neck to pull him closer. I'm so lost in him I forget for a moment that my hands are wet, and run them through his thick hair, but he doesn't seem to mind. Wrapping his arms tighter around me, he squeezes me as close as he can to his body, deepening our kiss. Our tongues mingle, mixing our tastes and our breaths.

It feels incredibly right—I want to keep doing this forever.

He moves his hands to my waist, picks me up as though I weigh nothing, and places me on the counter next to the sink. Nudging my legs apart, he positions his hips in the space he's created. Without breaking the kiss, I wrap my legs around him, pulling him in as close to me as possible. He grumbles, thrusting his hips forward, connecting with my most sensitive area and making me aware of the pulsing need I have to feel him in the most primal way. I can't miss the hardness in his pants, separated from me by layers of thin fabric. The kiss is spectacular and continues for what seems like hours.

Hands groping, mouths joined, sighs and moans filling the air. This is the most erotic experience I've had to date. I'm experiencing more than a physical connection with this man because he somehow reaches into my soul.

The muscles of his back and arms are so hard, so strong beneath my hands. My heart beats out of control and with my chest touching Oliver's, I can feel his is the same.

We gradually pull away from each other to catch our breath, and I bury my face in his neck, suddenly feeling shy. He gently cradles either side of my face, his thumbs resting on my cheekbones, his fingers in my hair. Tilting my head back carefully, he kisses my forehead. It seems he likes cradling my face. I like it, too; I feel cherished every time he does it.

"I've been wanting to do that since I left here ten days ago. The thought of never being able to see you, or kiss you, or touch you again was too much for me. I couldn't concentrate at work; even Jase was worried about me. Please trust what I say and what I show you. Don't let the assholes of your past ruin something that could be incredible between us."

Oh my heart, he's not scared to be vulnerable.

Not like I am.

"I've *never* felt this way about a woman before. It's new and scary for me." He drops his forehead back to mine.

His words bolster me to share my truth. "Believe me when I say I've wanted your kisses as well. I've been thinking about what you said and I'm going to try my best to move forward and let the hurt from my past relationships go." *I hope I can do what I say.* "I might mess up sometimes, or feel inadequate, but I want you to know I am working on it. I'm ready to trust in what you say, and the things you do that show me you care."

Using his hold, he angles my lips for another heartfelt kiss. This kiss is hungrier, more demanding. If he keeps kissing me like this, I may never gain full control of my brain again.

He pulls away, kissing the tip of my nose. "If I don't stop now, I may not stop at all, and I don't want to push you. I want to do this the right way. You're worth more than just a couple of nights."

We eventually finish cleaning up from dinner, and Oliver reluctantly leaves me to the rest of my evening.

NINETEEN

-oliver-

KATE'S MECHANIC CALLS AS I'M ANALYZING STOCK OPTIONS FOR A client. "Hey, Max, what do you have for me?" I ask, my pen ready to record any information I need.

"Hey, Mr. Stone. I can get everything I need over the next two days. It will probably take about a week to put the car back together. That's working as quickly as possible. I'm a sole operator."

"No problem, whatever it takes. Sounds good. Now, what are you going to tell Kate?" It may be deceitful to organize this behind her back and not tell her what's happening, but her car has been unreliable and I'm not comfortable with her driving a vehicle that could potentially leave her in a dangerous situation.

"I'll tell her coolant was entering the combustion chamber. It needed to be drained so I could change the hose. It's a low-cost fix totaling $150, including the tow. I'll tell her I have to order in the hose, which will be about a week, to allow for the additional time."

"Sounds good, Max. Thanks for the call. Let me know if you have any issues and I'll sort them out. Talk soon."

"Yeah, bye."

Over the next several hours, I meet with a new client and speak with existing clients over the phone. I like to keep them up-to-date with changes to their investment portfolio before following up with a formal email. I find that the personal touch keeps our business relationships strong.

My phone buzzes with several messages from Kate.

SUNSHINE

Hey

Max called

My car's only going to cost $150 for the repair and the tow 😊

ME

Hey

That's not too bad, you must feel relieved

SUNSHINE

Yeah, but I'll be without my car for a little over a week

ME

Margie won't mind how long you use her car

SUNSHINE

I guess, I just don't like being a bother

ME

I doubt Margie thinks you're a bother

SUNSHINE

I hope not

ME

Have a great afternoon with your students

SUNSHINE

Thanks. I hope you have a productive afternoon too

———

I want to spend Sunday hiking in the woods with Kate before the weather makes getting outdoors difficult, but I'm not sure if she's an outdoorsy person. I enjoy getting out and about in nature to center myself after being cooped up in an office all day, every day. It helps to reduce my stress levels as well as improve my mood and productivity. I have some important meetings coming up and I want to be functioning at my best. I think spending my day hiking in the woods with Kate would be the best possible way to get me there.

She usually spends her Saturday morning catching up on chores around the house, making it the perfect time to call her to organize a date for tomorrow.

"Hey." Hearing her voice soothes something deep inside of me.

"Hi. How are things?"

"Great. I'm catching up on my usual Saturday chores. How about you?"

"Pretty good. I was hoping I could take you out hiking tomorrow." I hold my breath, waiting for her rejection.

"Oh, I'd love that. I haven't been out for a hike in ages." I release the breath I was holding with a whoosh. I'm surprised since she's been resistant to spending time with me. We organize the details, and I disconnect the call with a wide smile.

———

When I wake on Sunday morning, I'm still smiling in anticipation of spending my day with Kate in one of my favorite places. I shorten my workout because I'll be hiking today and I want to get to her ASAP. After my shower, I eat a protein-rich breakfast, then I'm on my way; stopping only to pick up some healthy snacks and bottled water for our hike.

When I arrive at Kate's tidy home, she's waiting on her small porch wearing the yoga pants that drive me wild. Her hair's in a braid over one shoulder, reminding me of the first time I met her. She grabs her backpack and walks quickly toward my car, her lips spread wide. I climb out, reminding myself to behave like a gentleman and open the door for her; however, I trap her between the side of my car and my body without cognition. I know I've caught her by surprise when her mouth opens with a gasp. I take advantage, capturing her lips in a desperate kiss, and my cock grows, preparing to be inside her. It hasn't got the memo that I'm taking my time with this beguiling woman.

Gentling the kiss, I pull away, finally greeting the woman who has stolen my every thought since I met her and is rapidly stealing my heart. "Hey."

Her eyes open slowly, a shy smile touching her lips. Dilated pupils greet me, and it's satisfying to know she's as turned on as I am.

"Hey." Her swollen lips spread into a proper smile—she looks ravishing.

I release her and help her into my car so we can drive toward the outer limits of the city, where we'll spend our day hiking in the woods among the towering redwood and sequoia trees. She tells me about her latest adventures with the kids from the shelter, and I find I have nothing of value to share. I'm happy to listen. I fear if I talk about my work, I'll slip up and I don't want her to know I own my company—not yet, anyway.

Climbing out of the car, I draw in a deep breath of fresh, clean air. We collect our gear and, holding hands, trek toward the park entrance. From here, we can choose from a variety of walks, ranging from thirty to ninety minutes. We opt for the longer trail and head off, stopping now and then to admire the trees or an amazing view. I take every opportunity to touch her with my hands and mouth, planting kisses on various parts of her exposed skin. The day is perfect.

TWENTY

-kate-

TODAY HAS BEEN PERFECT. OLIVER'S BEEN INCREDIBLY ATTENTIVE, AND it's been wonderful to see him relaxed. He clearly enjoys spending time in nature, which is something I also enjoy. The weather will change soon, making today a great opportunity to experience an outdoor adventure before we're no longer able.

Mom and Dad have a church event tonight, so they've canceled our family dinner, and I'm not ready for our day to end, so I turn to Oliver. "Would you like to stay for din—?"

"I'd love to," he cuts in before I can finish the invitation.

I chuckle at his eagerness. "I didn't tell you what we'd be having."

"Don't care what we eat, as long as I'm spending time with you." Aaand cue the melting heart.

"I have the ingredients to make homemade burgers. We could sit on my small back deck to enjoy them as the sun goes down."

He reaches across, takes my hand and places it on his firm thigh. "You don't need to sell it to me, Kate. If you're there. I'm there. End of story."

Once we arrive home, we work together to prepare our burgers and then sit on my small back deck to enjoy them as the sun sets. We seem to always find something to talk about, but don't necessarily need to fill all the silences. I'm just as comfortable sitting quietly next to him as I am when we're chatting. It's as if we've known each other for much longer than we actually have.

After the sun's gone down, it's too cool to stay outside, so we work together to clean up and move to my couch. Oliver looks huge on my tiny two-seater, but it works in my favor. While he sits on one cushion, I sit to the side of him, with my back against the arm, tucking my legs up. He takes hold of one of my feet and begins to rub it absentmindedly, which feels fantastic after spending the day walking. He switches to my other foot and I sink further into the couch, my body thoroughly relaxed—which seems weird to me when I don't know him all that well. We talk softly about this and that; the music we each like; whether we prefer the beach or the river—we both love the riverside. We talk about how we developed our passion for the work each of us does and, as I get sleepier and sleepier, my eyes droop.

———

The buzz of my alarm causes me to stir, and the sun streaming through my window wakes me completely, and I bolt upright, disoriented—I don't remember getting into bed. As I wake fully, I realize I'm still wearing my clothes from yesterday. Getting up quickly, I walk through my small house to find Oliver missing, and my heart sinks with an instant pang of disappointment. I can't fathom what he must have thought of me falling asleep on him and having to put me to bed last night. Between that and him seeing me covered in paint, with glue dried in my hair during the week, he must surely be second-guessing his choice to pursue me.

I set my embarrassment aside and start preparing for my day. He even thought to put my phone on charge last night, before locking my house to keep me safe—I warm at his thoughtfulness. Unplugging it, I spot messages from him.

OLIVER

I didn't want to wake you. You looked peaceful, absolutely captivating. Have a great day Sunshine. I'll talk with you soon

Thanks for spending the day with me

Oh, my heart! He seems too good to be true.

ME

Good morning. Thanks for putting me to bed. I'm sorry I fell asleep on you last night

Maybe I can make it up to you tonight?

I hope I'm not being too pushy.

I drive to work, starting my day while hoping I'll see him later. As I greet my students at the door and check in with them, I know my smile is a little brighter and my mood a little lighter. We work through our morning routine of puzzles, counting, and songs to get our bodies moving. The joy and happiness on their little faces fill my heart to overflowing. During the first break of the day, I check my phone and am disappointed with the messages I've received.

OLIVER

I'm honored you fell asleep in my presence. Please don't ever apologize

I'm sorry, I have a business dinner tonight which will probably run very late

I try to put the disappointment to the back of my mind, moving on with story time and our fine motor group activities. At lunch, the school office clerk knocks on my classroom door with an impressive floral arrangement from *Blooms and Balloons.*

"These were just delivered for you. You are one lucky girl because these are gorgeous."

"Thanks for bringing them to me." I take them and draw in a deep breath, filling my lungs with their beautiful scent.

"No problem. Enjoy!"

Emma must have seen the delivery pass her classroom because she comes in to investigate as the school officer leaves. "That is one of the most stunning floral arrangements I think I've ever seen. Do you know who they might be from? Is there a note?"

I look through the arrangement to find a card tucked inside a baby pink envelope.

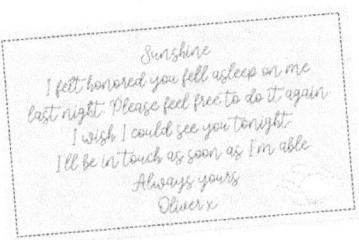

Sunshine
I felt honored you fell asleep on me last night. Please feel free to do it again
I wish I could see you tonight
I'll be in touch as soon as I'm able
Always yours
Oliver x

Emma's giddy as she reads over my shoulder. "Swoon. Who is this Oliver? You've been holding out on me."

It takes me a moment to catch my breath and rein in my disappointment over not seeing him tonight. The gesture of flowers is unexpected, and so … Oliver.

I quickly explain how I met him, that it's all very new, and how determined he's been to establish a relationship with me. I tell her about my fears that he's way out of my league and that one day, I'll have my heart broken by him when he eventually wakes up and realizes this. She swoons at the appropriate times and chastises me for my self-doubt, then hugs me and tells me to *go for it*.

I shoot him a quick text.

ME

Thank you for the beautiful flowers

I attach an image of the arrangement.

ME

I'm disappointed I can't see you tonight, but I understand about prior engagements. Good luck with your business dinner

I'll be thinking of you x

TWENTY-ONE

-oliver-

As I READ KATE'S MESSAGES, I REALIZE I'VE EVER HAD ANYONE WISH me luck for a meeting. It's assumed I have it in the bag—that I don't need luck. Her working-class background and down-to-earth nature are refreshing for someone like me who's constantly surrounded by people who are focused on money, status, and what I can do for them.

Jase pokes his head inside my office, interrupting my musing.

"I almost forgot. I've organized the lunch deliveries you requested for Kate. They'll rotate through various wraps, salads, soups, and subs during the week."

"Thanks, Jase. Appreciate it."

Apart from my sweet messages from Kate, this morning has been an absolute shit show. The meeting with my senior staff went well over the allocated time. If we don't nail these contracts next quarter, we could lose out on more than $375 million. I'm not prepared to lose that sort of money because my staff can't get their heads out of their asses. I made it clear I won't tolerate any sloppy work or anyone dropping the ball. Jase was giving me the look—the one that tells me to *calm down*—but I was too worked up to care.

After putting Kate to bed last night and leaving her to sleep—*alone* —I drove home and spent the night tossing and turning with thoughts of her. How her body felt in my arms as I carried her to bed, and her gentle sigh as I placed her on the soft mattress and covered her with blankets.

I need her in my bed. I don't want to leave her—ever.

I organized a flower delivery from *Blooms and Balloons* because I

109

wanted to make her smile, even though I won't have the opportunity to see it.

Returning to work, I prep for the meeting I have tonight with a new overseas client. I'm completely engrossed in my work, so I startle when my phone buzzes. Hope bounces around in my chest that it's a message from my girl when I notice the time … three-thirty. I grab my phone, and a smile stretches across my face.

SUNSHINE

Hey. I wanted to thank you for my coffee and pastry this morning, followed by a delicious chicken and salad wrap for lunch. Even though I appreciate your very thoughtful and generous gesture, you don't have to go to so much trouble for me

ME

Hey Sunshine. You are more than welcome for the food. I enjoy taking care of you

Fuck! There I go again, making it sound like she can't look after herself.

ME

I KNOW you can take care of yourself, but I want to take care of you too

SUNSHINE

You're lucky you qualified your statement. I was about to send you a not very nice message big guy

I chuckle at her sass.

———

The rest of the day passes in a mash-up of emails, meetings, and phone calls before I need to leave for my business meeting. After work, I make my way upstairs to shower and change, all the while thinking I'd rather get ready to spend the evening with Kate. Last night, sitting on her couch was the most relaxed I've been for … well … I can't remember the last time I felt that relaxed and comfortable.

The kisses we shared and the intimacy of sitting and talking with her are things I've never experienced with a woman before, even though I have been in a long-term relationship. Since that relationship ended, I've never taken the time to get to know a woman, but with her, I want to know *everything*. I crave considerably more than just a physical release when I'm with her, and I'm inexplicably drawn to the woman and the goodness inside of her.

———

When I arrive at the hotel, I allow the valet to park my car and make my way inside to meet my overseas guest. The hostess greets and guides me through the exclusive restaurant to my table. With only a dozen tables complete with rich golden chairs that match the gold inlay on the walls, and the delicate chandeliers hanging overhead, the compact restaurant gleams with decadence. I wish, once again, I was sitting on Kate's couch, rubbing her feet and learning more about her, rather than meeting Lena Rhinecourt.

Lena became the CEO of her father's mining conglomerate when he passed away five years ago. She's a force to be reckoned with, and if I can impress her tonight, I'll close a $500 million investment deal over the next four years.

I'm getting comfortable when the hostess approaches with Lena, so I stand to greet her. "Good evening, Ms. Rhinecourt. It's good to meet you in person finally." I hold out my hand to greet her. She's about my age if I could guess, and most would say she's classically beautiful, but Kate is significantly more attractive, in my opinion.

"Oh, don't Ms. Rhinecourt me. Lena, please. It makes me sound old." She takes my hand, shaking it while reaching up to kiss my cheek, taking me by surprise. I don't give or receive affection from people with whom I have a business relationship—*ever*.

We sit, and the sommelier efficiently takes our drink orders. We begin making generalized small talk about her trip, how long she's staying, and what she hopes to see and do while Stateside. Her Australian accent and terminology make our conversation interesting.

Once we place our order, our conversation turns toward business. The award-winning, Michelin-star chef brings out our meals, outlining the flavors and textures we can expect to experience.

As the meal progresses, Lena constantly touches my arm and leans into me. I'm not ignorant. I know she's flirting, but I *never* mix business with pleasure, and I'm certainly not interested now I have Kate in my life. I would never do anything to jeopardize my chances with her.

Lena excuses herself to visit the bathroom, and I spot a familiar man looking pissed as he walks toward me. It takes a second or two to place him, but when I do, I stand to greet him.

"Hey, Toby, good to see you." I hold out my hand, but he ignores it as he looks at me like I'm shit under his shoe.

"I'd like to say the same, but I can't. This is exactly what my sister is worried about. She's had her share of assholes who thought it was okay to step out on her. She doesn't deserve another one." I'm taken aback by his assumption. "I knew who you were from the get-go, but I figured I'd give you the benefit of the doubt. You seemed like you were genuine when we spoke." His jaw ticks beneath his beard. "That's why I didn't tell you to fuck off and leave her alone. But I'm going to say it now—fuck off and leave Kate alone. If you can't keep it in your pants and be faithful to her, you don't deserve her." His words are cutting, but he couldn't be more wrong.

I'm appalled that he thinks I'm fucking around behind his sister's back. *As if that would ever happen.* "I'm not stepping out on your sister." I hiss. "This is a business dinner. I would prefer to be sitting on your sister's couch rather than sitting in this stuffy restaurant with a woman I have zero interest in, apart from the multi-million dollar deal I'm hoping to close tonight."

"It looked pretty damn cozy from where I was sitting." He gestures to a table close by, where a group of men dressed in casual business suits sit talking and drinking. His friend, Shane, is among them.

"Well, you have the wrong idea. I would never cheat on your sister. I know how special she is, and I would never do anything to jeopardize my chance with her. I'm not letting her go any time soon. You need to get used to seeing me around, Toby."

He must recognize the sincerity and determination on my face.

"Make sure you keep it that way." He steps away, walking back to his companions.

Fuck! I wonder if Kate knows who I am; I don't get the impression she does. Agitation swamps me and I find it difficult to still my muscles, but it's imperative that I do. I suck in a deep breath and take a moment to check my phone to calm myself, noticing it's after ten. When Lena returns to the table, I'm ready to conclude this initial meeting and follow up in the office tomorrow.

Lena leans in close. "Is everything okay? You seem deep in thought."

"Yeah, everything's great. I think we've covered everything we need to this evening. We can tease out the minor details tomorrow in the office at our nine a.m. meeting. Did you want to order anything else, or shall we call it a night?"

Her eyes light up. "Oh, we can have a nightcap in my room." She rests her hand on my arm once again, her voice huskier. "If you know what I mean?"

"Sorry, Lena, but I need to leave. I'm hoping to catch my girlfriend before she turns in for the night." It's best I cut Lena off, letting her know my interest clearly lies elsewhere.

"We could make it quick. She would never have to know."

She's too close to me; her breast now pressing against my arm. Her heavy perfume and glossy red lips are too much, and I crave the natural scent and perfectly soft pink lips of Kate. "Ah, you see, *I* would know. She's everything to me, and I'm not prepared to do anything to jeopardize my relationship. It would be best if we say goodnight now. I'll see you tomorrow morning in my office to continue our business discussion," I tell her in plain terms.

Lena pouts at me like a child—most unattractive. "Oh, that's too bad. I hope she appreciates how faithful you are to her. I'll see you in the morning."

"Would you like me to walk you up to your room?"

She waves me off. "No, that's fine. Go visit your girl."

"I'll send a car to collect you in the morning. Enjoy what's left of your evening."

We both stand, and as I make the move to shake hands, she steps into me, kissing my cheek and whispering in my ear, "Your girl is one very lucky lady."

Lena steps back, hurrying away. When I glance up, Toby's watching me with distrust. I lift my chin toward him as I leave the restaurant. He's going to have to learn to trust me with his sister.

I drive toward Kate's house without conscious thought. When I thought about *catching* her before she turned in for the night, I was only going to send her a text. I had no intention of actually going to her. I know it will be almost eleven when I get there and probably too late, but I'll feel better knowing I'm close to her.

At this point, I get the impression I'm more invested in this relationship than she is, but I think it's because she doesn't trust my intentions. I have to *show* her she can trust me and that I'm in it for the long term. I pull into her driveway where her car would normally be. A car I would prefer to replace, but know the gesture wouldn't be welcomed. I shake my head at my predicament.

I don't think she realizes who I am, and I don't want to tell her because I know it will give her another reason not to believe my interest in her. She already thinks I'm out of her league. If she knows I'm a billionaire, she won't come near me with a ten-foot pole—and isn't that fucking ironic. For once, I meet a woman who garners my full interest, and she won't want anything to do with me *because* of my money and who I am. I need her completely invested in our relationship before I tell her. I only hope her brother doesn't out me before I get the chance.

I'm unsure how long I sit in my car in her driveway—it's probably a bit stalkerish, to be honest, but I can't bring myself to leave. Maybe she's still awake.

> ME
>
> Hey, how was your evening?
>
> Are you awake?

SUNSHINE

Hey

I am now, my messages woke me up

> ME
>
> Sorry, I had to see you

SUNSHINE

What do you mean?

> ME
>
> I'm parked in your driveway
>
> If it's too late, I can leave

The dots bounce as if she's responding, then they disappear. The lights come on inside, and she appears at the open door, waving me inside, and I exhale a relieved breath. She's such a good person. She *should* have told me to *fuck off*. I climb out of my car and make my way to her front door before I know I'm moving.

Stepping inside, I kick the door closed with my foot as I grab Kate's delectable ass, lifting her to press her against the wall. Her shapely legs wrap around my hips as I crash my lips against hers.

We're lost in a passionate kiss and everything around us falls away. Her fingers dig into my scalp as her hot pussy grinds against my engorged cock. Being within five feet of her makes my cock hard, so I have no hope of keeping it under control when she's actually touching me. Miraculously, I slow the kiss and press my lips gently to the tip of her nose. "I missed you."

She pulls back further, looking into my eyes, truly puzzled. "But you saw me last night."

"It's been too long for me. Thinking I wouldn't see you tonight felt … interminable. Throughout the entire day, in meetings and on phone calls, you were always on my mind."

Her eyes soften, her body melding further into mine as she leans forward to kiss me again. This is the first time she's initiated a kiss between us, and it feels like a monumental step forward. We kiss for minutes, maybe hours—time makes little sense when I'm like this with her.

Slowly, she pulls back, gifting me a shy smile and I take in her sleepy state—messy hair, sleepy eyes, a white tank that hides nothing, and her sexy red boy shorts.

"I should say I'm sorry I woke you, but truthfully, I'm not. Pretty sure that makes me an asshole." I shrug, taking her mouth in another scorching kiss.

She pulls away, biting her bottom lip. "You want to come to bed with me?"

My wide eyes must convey my shock because she quickly corrects herself.

"To sleep," she blurts. "I'm not ready for anything else—yet." She looks away briefly, then turns back to me. "Is that okay?"

"It's more than okay. I'm happy to go at your pace."

I sound like a lovesick pussy.

"I'm grateful for the trust you're giving me. I didn't come here expecting anything from you. This has been more than I expected. I would love to sleep with you, but I need to leave early because I have a conference call with an overseas market early tomorrow."

Her radiant smile lights up her entire face. "Then take me to bed. Down the hall, first door on the right."

She holds on like a koala, with her arms around my neck and her legs around my hips, my hands where they belong—on her ass. I carry her to her bedroom; turning off the lights as we go. Carefully, I lay her on the bed, and she scoots back, covering herself, which is disappointing.

Without taking my eyes off her, I remove my tie and jacket, placing them neatly over a chair in the corner of her room. Her eyes follow every movement, encouraging me to take my time to undress for her enjoyment. Next to go are my shoes and socks. I stand, slowly unbuttoning my shirt, when she climbs out of bed and moves into my space to take over. I feel as though I've hit a home run when she willingly puts her hands on me to undo my shirt buttons and drags my shirttails out of my pants. She removes it slowly, sliding it off my shoulders and carefully drapes it over my jacket. Then she turns her focus to my belt, sucking in a sharp breath when she notices what she's done to me and her sexy blush starts moving up from her chest. My cock is fucking hard, and it's more than obvious in my pants. She removes my belt with shaking hands, undoing my slacks and letting them drop to the floor. As she bends to pick them up, I get an unexpected view down her tank at her stunning tits. I can't wait to get my hands and mouth on those beauties. She folds my pants along the creases, drapes them on the chair, then guides me to her bed. Facing each other—her hand on my neck, fingers playing with the hair at my nape—we quietly study each other while my hand rests on her hip as my thumb draws circles over her soft skin.

I tuck a lock of hair behind her ear, looking into her eyes. "You are incredibly striking. You take my breath away, and yet when I'm with you, I feel like I can finally breathe."

I kiss the tip of her nose, guiding her to turn over, allowing me to hold her while we sleep. I wrap myself around her and make the decision to never let her go. The calm and peace she brings me is something money can't buy. All the other shit and noise in my head disappears when I'm with her. I'm not sure I'll ever be able to explain to her what she gives to me. "Goodnight, Sunshine," I whisper into her hair.

TWENTY-TWO

-kate-

I TRY TO SLEEP, BUT MY BODY WON'T SHUT DOWN. HIS BREATHS DEEPEN as his body relaxes, so I take the opportunity to turn over and study him in the darkness. I can barely make out his relaxed features in the limited light creeping through the gaps in my bedroom curtains. It's surreal to study him like this. He looks very different in sleep; relaxed —more boyish. He must feel as though he has a great deal of pressure on him when he's awake because he always looks formidable, yet he manages to find time to be thoughtful and genuine toward me.

When he was undressing, I couldn't help myself. I had to get my hands on his body, which is to die for. I can't believe I invited him to spend the night in my bed, which he readily accepted, knowing I wasn't ready for sex. He suddenly rolls onto his back, scaring the crap outta me and causing me to almost fall off the bed. *Ha!* I can't imagine what he would think if he were to wake up to me falling to the floor on my ass.

The sheet has slipped down, allowing me to appreciate all those sexy abs, as well as the tantalizing trail of dark hair which leads to the promised land, if the substantial bulge in his pants is anything to go by. I almost don't want to sleep and waste this uninterrupted time to study him, but it's probably a little creepy to perv on him while he's sleeping. As hard as I try to stay awake, my eyes droop, and sleep takes me, knowing that I'll be waking up to an empty bed in the morning.

I wake to my alarm and a furnace of hard muscle at my back. My body's on fire from the heat of Oliver's body, and I'm instantly aware of his impressive erection pressing into my backside. My heart races with surprise that he's still here, and I'm worried he's overslept. Attempting to roll over, I struggle to move with the way he has me pinned to his body. His large hand cradles my breast, while his leg drapes over my thigh, tangling between my calves—no wonder I'm roasting.

He kisses the back of my head. "Good morning." His voice is all sexy rasp and has my lady bits waking up in the best possible way.

I turn my head to look at him. "Good morning, hot stuff!"

He smiles and laughs, kissing the tip of my nose. "*Hot stuff*, huh? I'll take that."

"Hot stuff, because you feel like a furnace. I've never known anyone to be as hot as you while they slept."

His body stiffens behind me, and a grumble emanates from his throat.

"Please don't remind me first thing in the morning that some other asshole has shared your bed. The reminder will put me in a bad mood."

Uh oh. When I said that, my previous boyfriends didn't enter my mind. *I mean, is Oliver even my boyfriend?* I don't know what this is with him. He says he wants to get to know me and spend time with me, but what does that mean for a guy like him?

"I can hear you thinking," he murmurs.

He relaxes a little, placing kisses on the back of my head and shoulder, then loosens his hold, releasing me slightly, allowing me to maneuver so I can face him. He immediately leans in for a morning kiss.

I squirm away. "I haven't brushed my teeth."

"Like I care. Kiss me."

I don't need a lot of coaxing and relax into the best good morning kiss I've ever received. Slowly, I pull away and connect with his eyes, noticing the various shades of green within the flecks, ranging from the color of fern leaves to a deep emerald. Colors I've never noticed, because I'm always trying to avoid his gaze. "I figured you would be gone by now since you had a conference call this morning."

"I've already dealt with my conference call. I wasn't ready to leave you, so I climbed back into bed. I must have dozed back to sleep, which never happens. Usually, once I'm awake, I'm up and ready to go for the day. You make me want to stay in bed."

He nuzzles my neck, sliding his hand along my hip toward the small of my back. I notice he's being respectful now he's awake.

"I do need to go, though. I have a nine a.m. follow-up meeting with my client from last night."

I feel terrible that I didn't ask him how his business dinner went last night. *What sort of person am I?*

"How was your dinner meeting? Do you think it was successful?"

He looks surprised I've asked about his meeting. *Doesn't he have anyone interested in him and his life?*

"It went pretty well. We'll sign the contract today, and I'll work to make the initial investment multiply over the next four years."

He looks away from me, takes a breath, and then turns back to me. "I saw Toby at the restaurant. He got the wrong idea and told me to leave you alone if I couldn't be faithful to you."

Why would Toby think Oliver was being unfaithful?

My mouth drops open as the light bulb goes off in my mind. I assumed his business dinner was with a man; I never gave it a second thought. My muscles tense and tighten as I consider the possibility he may have crossed a line. Toby must have seen something he didn't like to approach him like that. *How intimate was this dinner?* Trying to pull away so I can get out of bed and away from him is pointless as he tightens his hold.

"It was a *business* dinner. She flirted a little, but I set her straight and let her know I have a girlfriend."

I suck in a sharp breath, my eyes widening. I'm surprised he referred to me as his girlfriend.

He keeps talking, oblivious to my inner thoughts. "I didn't lead her on in any way because I'm not interested in anyone but you."

He leans forward, kissing me gently, teasing my mouth open to allow him entry. His kisses are drugging, exquisite, and delicious.

I *never* want to stop kissing him.

My body responds to him readily—my nipples pebble and my sex is hot and wet. My body's hot and my breaths labored. His arousal is obvious through the thin fabric of his boxer briefs, and it would be oh so easy to surrender to our chemistry, but I actually need to get ready for work, and so does he.

We gently separate as though it's the most painful experience for both of us.

"I wish it was the weekend and we could stay in bed all day," he grumbles. "I never feel like skipping out on work." He glares at me playfully, as if it's my fault.

The ironic thing is, I would skip out on work today if it meant spending the day with him.

Pressing his lips to the tip of my nose, he rolls out of bed, pulling me up with him. Dragging me in close, he kisses my forehead, then releases me so he can get dressed. I immediately mourn the loss of his body against mine, along with losing the visual perfection of his form. His muscles dance under his bronzed skin as he dresses quickly.

We say goodbye with lingering kisses that I never want to end. He leaves to drive to the city to get ready for work, and I drift through my morning routine in a daze. And before I know it, I'm at work, ready to greet my delightful students for another day.

TWENTY-THREE

-oliver-

THE PAST FEW DAYS HAVE GONE BY IN A BLUR OF MEETINGS, LATE-NIGHT kisses with Kate, and early mornings to get back to my penthouse to start the day all over again.

I'm more than hooked on this girl and am happy to burn the midnight oil to see her for brief moments before we both crash for the night. I want to spend every waking minute with her and if I could bring her into the office with me, I would most definitely do so.

I need to come clean with her soon, but I'm still not convinced she's as invested in our relationship as I am. I'm unsure what it'll take to make her fall as deep as I already am, but I need her tied to me to ensure she won't walk away when I make my confession.

————

Kate finally gets a call from Max that her car is ready to be collected, and I receive the invoice for services rendered. I was right, it would have been cheaper to buy her a brand-new car. The dollars simply don't matter when I see the excitement on her face when we collect her nan's car.

TWENTY-FOUR

-kate-

OVER THE LAST TWO WEEKS, OLIVER AND I HAVE SETTLED INTO A routine of sorts. He sleeps at my place more often than he sleeps at his own, and it almost feels ... *domestic*. I love having him in my space, seeing him relaxed in sports shorts and a tank, dressed casually in jeans, or impeccably dressed in his superbly fitted suits.

Some nights he doesn't get to my place until after ten, and I realize how much time his work takes away from his personal life. I thought I was busy, but he dedicates an excessive amount of time to his job—*I hope his boss appreciates his dedication*. It doesn't matter how late he arrives, or how exhausted he seems, he always checks in with me about my day, my students, the kids at the shelter, my family, and even Margie. I've shared my concerns about his long hours, but he brushes it off as a busy time of the year, with the quarter coming to a close and preparations underway for the new one.

One thing that makes me pause: he's never invited me to his place, and he never talks about friends or family. He seems very isolated in his work. Jase is the only person he speaks about.

This morning, he said he's going to try to get home in time to eat a meal with me, so I've made a chicken and mushroom risotto—his favorite.

I've showered, washed my hair, blown it out, shaved, and scrubbed my entire body because tonight I'm ready to take our relationship to the next level. I'm wearing my sexiest red underwear beneath my lacy black dress. It has the cutest cap sleeves with a fitted bodice and flared skirt, landing slightly above my knees. On my feet, I'm wearing my favorite red wedges. I hope it has the desired effect because I'm pretty sure I trust him with my heart and my soul, and now I'm ready to trust him with my body.

I even bought a box of condoms so I'm prepared.

My nerves are out of control because I get the impression he's a lot more sexually experienced than I am. I mean, it's not like I'm a virgin or anything like that. If the expertise of and confidence in his kisses and touches set my body on fire to the point I could explode, the real thing is going to be something I know I've never experienced before. I hope I'm able to keep him satisfied enough that he doesn't stray or get bored and move on, like my previous boyfriends.

As I add the final touches to my small dining table, making sure everything is perfect for tonight, a flash of light through my curtains signals his arrival.

It's showtime. I can do this. I can be sexy. I can seduce my man.

The knock on my door interrupts my pep talk, making my heart thump as if it's trying to escape my chest. When I open the door, I'm locked in place by Oliver's arresting green eyes and a smile that seems to come more easily these days. I blatantly roam his body with my eyes, noting that he's wearing his most comfortable pair of jeans, which shows off the definition of his strong thighs and firm ass, matched with a college T-shirt, fitting his torso like a glove. He's holding a gift box, which I assume is for me, because he often brings me little treats and treasures he thinks I might like. I've given up trying to stop him because he likes to spoil me.

When my eyes finally make it back up to his, he's checking me out from head to toe, and the heat in his eyes tells me he also likes what he sees.

"Hey. You look edible. It must be my lucky day." He steps into me, grasping one hip firmly. "I feel a little underdressed." Leaning forward, he kisses me deeply, making my heart race and my mind dizzy. "Am I unaware of a special occasion?"

"N-n-nope." I stutter. I wanted to dress nicely since you only ever see me in my lounging-around-the-house clothes or messy from work. But you're right, today might be your lucky day if you play your cards right." I wink, closing the door behind him.

I'm digging deep, attempting to appear more confident than I really am. When he reaches the main living room, his eyebrows rise as he notices I've set the table, complete with flowers and candles. He gifts me a sexy grin and then must remember the gift he has for me.

"Here, this is for you," he says as he passes me the box.

"I've told you, you don't have to keep bringing me gifts. I'm just happy to spend time with you."

I can't quite decipher his expression—maybe disbelief. *Has he never had anyone want to spend time with him?* If that's the case, my heart breaks for him because everybody deserves to have people around them who care.

Opening the box, I'm surprised to see a brand new pair of red Converse shoes. I can't believe he bought these for me. I've wanted, no, needed, a new pair for such a long time, but I always seem to have something else I need to buy or repair.

I launch myself into his arms. "Thank you. My shoes were close to dying on me."

I hold on to each side of his face to pepper him with kisses while he bands his arms around my waist and holds me off the floor as he laughs at my antics. His whole face changes dramatically when he smiles and laughs—it's really something to see.

Watching me while I admire my new shoes, he simply says, "I know. I noticed the rubber sole is almost worn all the way through."

This is the thing: as busy as he is, he's super observant and notices every little thing about me. Last week, he bought me new pillows because he could see that I was struggling to fluff up my old pillows to my liking. The other day, he bought Margie a pair of binoculars because she was complaining she couldn't spy on Pete and Joe down the street. Needless to say, Margie thinks Oliver's definitely a keeper and I agree, but there's a small voice in the back of my mind still holding me back a little.

"Well, thank you, kind sir. I appreciate your thoughtfulness. I'm going to take such good care of these. That way they'll last ages." I stroke them as I would a kitten.

After placing them in the box carefully, I invite him to sit at the table and I serve our dinner.

His mouth drops open, and he looks up at me as I place his plate in front of him. "Is this what I think it is?"

"Depends. What do you think it is?" I smirk.

In a playful way, completely unlike the man I've gotten to know, he smacks his lips and rubs his hands together. "Chicken and mushroom risotto? My favorite meal."

"Ding, ding, ding! Ladies and gentlemen, we have a winner. He guessed correctly," I announce, applauding like a crazy loon, while he laughs at my game show host impersonation. I'm relieved he recognized the dish, and I didn't mess it up.

"It really *is* my lucky day. What have I done to deserve such special treatment?"

"I figured ... well, you always spoil me; it was time to spoil you for a change. You've been very generous and extremely patient with me—I thought you deserved some special attention."

Leaning forward, I gesture for him to meet me halfway. Our lips meet in a sweet, delicate kiss while his hand moves to the back of my head. He quickly takes control—deepening the kiss until I'm lost and breathless. Our kisses get better every time, and I can imagine the combustion that will erupt between us later tonight. The thought has me pressing my thighs together to control the tingles spreading through my nether regions.

Eventually, we eat our meal, chatting about our day. He praises my cooking thoroughly, making it clear how much he enjoyed the risotto I prepared for him. Wait until he gets a taste of the chocolate brownie I've made for dessert.

After we clean up from dinner, we move across to my couch, each with a glass of wine. Whenever we end up here, I inevitably end up straddling his lap—his preferred position—but I'm uncomfortable initiating the sitting arrangement. Usually, I sit on my own cushion, then he situates me where he wants me—but tonight, I *want* to take the lead.

I want to show him I'm ready for more.

I'm nervous I'm going to make a fool of myself and he's finally going to realize he's wasting his time. I wait for him to sit and get comfortable. Then I make my move, hoping I look somewhat sexy.

TWENTY-FIVE

-oliver-

MY BEAUTIFUL KATE SEEMS A LITTLE NERVOUS TONIGHT; SHE HASN'T stopped fidgeting, and I get the sense tonight's important to her for some reason. The last couple of weeks have been out of this world for me. I feel as though I'm coming *home* at the end of each day, not just going to a cold, empty apartment. She always tells me I give her too many things—that I spoil her—but she's the one who's given me more than I've ever had.

She can't seem to decide where to sit—my preference is always on my lap; that way I can study her eyes while we talk and steal all the kisses I want. She finally seems to choose, surprising me by sitting on my lap.

This is a big deal for her ... for both of us. She's showing me a level of trust she hasn't shown me before. I'm honored and humbled by her actions. She rests her forearms on my shoulders; her slender fingers caressing the back of my neck, fidgeting with the hair at my nape. Wrapping my arms around her lower back, I draw her closer, resting her pussy against my hard cock. I'm dying to be inside her, but I promised to go at her pace, and I'm bound and determined to keep my word—even if it kills me. Using my forefinger, I gently direct her chin up to ensure eye contact as my other hand moves down to cup her delectable ass.

"Tell me what's bothering you."

She sighs, turning her head in an attempt to look away from me, but I gently guide her eyes back to mine.

"Um, I'm a bit nervous and might be out of my depth and, well, I'm not very confident and I'll probably be terrible at it—"

I interrupt before she can go any further. "Whoa, slow down. Take a breath with me."

Taking a deep breath, I nod for her to mimic my actions, which she does. She closes those beguiling denim eyes for a few seconds, and when she opens them, her resolve has returned.

"Thanks for that. I needed to calm down a bit. Geez, anyone would think I'm a virgin, with the way I'm acting."

She giggles, and a grumble emanates from deep within me. I don't like to be reminded some other asshole has been inside her, especially since I haven't—*yet*. I have to physically stop my hand from tightening on her lush ass.

"Anyway." She takes another deep breath. "I have a surprise for you. Uh, it's probably easier if I show you."

Gracefully, she climbs off my lap, steps into her bedroom, and returns with her hands tucked behind her back, wearing a coy smile.

"You didn't have to get me anything. You've already spoiled me a lot with your sexy outfit and my favorite dinner."

She steps closer, bringing an empty hand out from behind her back, closely followed by her other hand, balancing a small box ... *of condoms!*

My eyes widen and my cock jumps in anticipation.

Is this what I think it means—is it hopefully my lucky day?

Words escape me at this moment.

"Uhm ... we don't have to do—"

I'm on my feet, crowding her space before she can get the next word out of her delectable mouth that I've pictured around my cock more times than I care to admit. She drops her gaze to the floor, and I *know* she's misinterpreted my surprise and silence.

I lift her chin, holding her eyes with mine. "Is this what I think it means? Are you ready to let me worship your luscious body the way it should be worshipped? Are you going to let me taste you, caress you, feel your body beneath mine? Take me inside you?"

She opens her mouth and closes it again as her eyes widen and her cheeks flush. She nods her head, but that's not good enough for me.

"I need your words, Sunshine. Tell me what you want."

"Uhm, yeah ... all of that. I want all of that with you. Please," she breathes.

"Once I've been inside you, you *will* be mine forever. There's no going back. You'd better be certain this is what you want."

Without wasting a second, I bend forward, lift her onto my shoulder in a fireman's hold, and carry her to her bedroom, while she giggles and squirms. Once inside, I slide her slowly down my body, ensuring she can feel how hard I am, then I take her mouth in a heartfelt kiss. Cupping her face in both of my hands, I direct and deepen the kiss exactly how I want it. She melts against me and her heart beats a rapid tattoo against my chest to match my own. I slowly drag my kisses down her neck and across her collarbone, but her dress only allows me to go so far.

"I'm going to worship your exquisite body. You're going to feel everything I do to you for days. I hope you're ready for me."

"I'm pretty sure I was ready the first time I laid eyes on your naked chest in front of the school." She bites her bottom lip and her eyes widen as though she's said too much.

I'm stunned she felt the same way I did; it seems we've been on the same page all along. I pull back to study her guileless eyes, then cup her face in my large hands, and confess with a whisper, "Me too, Sunshine, me too." Releasing her, I step back slightly, encouraging her to turn around. I collect her silky hair in one hand and gently place it over her shoulder, draping it over her breast. Caressing down her exposed neck and shoulder, I place my fingers on her zipper. "Is this okay?" I don't want to move too fast in case she changes her mind.

"Of course," she replies breathily. Slowly, I slide the zipper down, exposing ivory skin and the lacy red band of her bra.

Could this get any better?

I breathe deeply to compose myself, so I don't ruin my pants like a sixteen-year-old virgin.

"As much as I love you in this sexy dress, it's gotta go."

While peppering kisses along her neck, I smooth my hands up the silky skin of her spine, sliding them across to her shoulders and slipping the lace dress from her arms. She tilts her head, allowing me to press soft kisses from behind her ear to her shoulder. Slowly, I turn her around. She's holding her dress in place, preventing it from falling. Her body language suggests she's on board with what's happening, but maybe her mind isn't quite there yet.

I search her heavy-lidded eyes and ask, "Is this still okay with you?"

She blows out a long breath. Locking her eyes on mine, she releases her dress, dropping it to the floor and creating an inky puddle of fabric around her red shoes. It takes every ounce of self-control to keep my eyes on her face. Every part of me wants to drop my gaze and study her curvy body for the first time.

Holding out my hand, I guide her to step out of her dress, taking the opportunity to run my eyes slowly from her face, down her slender neck to her irresistible tits, encased in red lace. The limited amount of blood left in my brain makes its way to my cock, and I remind myself to slow down. My eyes scan her soft stomach to her matching lace panties, and further still, down her shapely legs, to the sexy red laces wrapped around her ankles. The groan I've been holding back escapes, and I adjust my pants, attempting to release the pressure of the zipper against my painfully engorged cock.

She is my every wet dream come to life.

"I knew you were beautiful. But *beautiful* isn't strong enough to describe you. You're exquisite. I'm one lucky man and I'm going to show you exactly how lucky I feel to have you trust me with your body."

"I'm the lucky one here. I hope I don't disappoint you." She blushes, and it begins from her tits, rising quickly and painting every inch of her alluring creamy skin up to her cheeks.

"There is no way to disappoint me. This experience is already one hundred times better than anything I've experienced before. We're going to be combustible because when we kiss, it's like nothing I've ever felt."

I lean in. Using my teeth, I gently bite and pull her bottom lip, pressing closer to take her mouth fully, tasting every crevice and sharing every breath. Her hands move up to the hem of my T-shirt, attempting to slide it up my body. I take over, grab the back of my collar, and drag it over my head. Tossing it to the floor, we pick up where we left off.

With one hand, I flick the clasp of her bra to release it and gently slide the straps from her shoulders, letting it join the rest of our clothes on the floor. Sliding my hands around her ribs, I glide my thumbs along the underside of her heaving breasts. Her body trembles—not from the cold, but from desire.

I feel the same, Sunshine.

I'm torn between continuing to kiss her lips and pulling away to admire her breasts. The need to see her tits wins out, and I pull back to soak in my fill. They're firm and full, with peachy-colored nipples drawn tight into peaks.

"I've been dying to see these beauties, and they were definitely worth the wait."

Cupping them in my large hands, I drop my head, taking one globe into my mouth. We both groan. If she only ever let me do this to her, I would be a happy man. She tastes like sunshine and I know I'm going to become addicted to her flavor. With a shuddering sigh, her hands move to the back of my head, holding me in place—as if I was going to move anytime soon. Moving across, I pay equal attention to her other breast—*because I'm fair like that.*

She moves her hands to my belt buckle and manages to get it undone, then works to undo my button and zipper. The pressure releases from my cock and the relief is instant, until her hand grips my rock-hard shaft through my boxer briefs, sending whatever blood was left in my body to my engorged cock.

She gasps as I grow impossibly larger under her touch. I watch her eyes widen and can't hold back my groan. My jeans slip down my legs, getting caught on my shoes, so she pulls away, her tits swaying as she drops to her knees to untie my laces and remove my shoes and socks. The sight of her on her knees in front of me causes my cock to jump, leaking precum from the eager slit. I know once I get inside her, I'm going to fucking embarrass myself, shooting my load before we even get started. Stepping out of my jeans, I hold out my hands to pull her back up, then grab hold of her perfect ass to lift her; encouraging her to wrap her legs around my hips.

I whisper into her ear, "I'm going to fuck you so good that you become addicted to my cock. No other cock will ever satisfy you like mine will."

Her entire body shivers in response to my promise.

All we have between us are her lace panties and my cotton boxer briefs. She grinds down on me and the heat of her pussy makes my cock weep. I take the few steps needed to her bed and slowly lower her as she holds onto me, then I taste her silky curves and valleys until I reach her panties. Dipping my thumbs inside the waistband, I begin removing them. Once she catches on to what I'm doing, she releases her legs from around my hips and lifts her ass, making it easier to slide the garment off. She's finally naked, except for her sexy as fuck shoes I've decided to leave on for now. Her hands find the waistband of my boxer briefs as she attempts to remove them, but my cock makes it difficult, so I free myself from the constricting material.

Resting on my forearms on either side of her head, caging her in, I lean down to take her mouth with the need to own her, mark her. I could kiss her mouth for eternity, but I have other areas on my mind tonight.

"I need to taste your hot pussy."

Her muscles lock and her entire body freezes. Not the response I was looking for.

"Oh, you don't have to do that. That's okay, I'm pretty sure I'm wet enough for you to slide right in," she whispers as she blushes and I lose her eyes as she turns her head away from me. Well, that won't fucking do. *At all.*

Using my fingers, I direct her eyes back to mine. "I know I don't have to, but I've been dying to taste your pussy for weeks, if not months. It's what I intend to do. You'll learn soon enough when I make my mind up about something, I'm solely focused on it until I get it."

Her body tenses further at my words, and she attempts to wiggle out from under me.

"Uh, uh, uh, what's wrong?"

I gently hold her in place. If she wants to stop, I'll fucking stop. It'll kill me, but I'll stop.

"Um, nothing."

"It's not nothing. Something I said put the brakes on, and I want to know what's going on."

I watch her pull herself together before she finally speaks.

"I guess I'm worried. Once you get what you want from me, I mean like physically, you'll probably move on to someone new. Someone better. Someone more suited to you. I'm not sure I'm cut out for that, to be honest. Maybe I didn't think this through properly."

Pulling back, I look at her fully, and with the way she's attempting to put space between us, I guess my expression shows how pissed I feel. Shaking my head, I breathe deeply to calm myself because a pissed-off dude in her bed is not what she needs right now. Obviously, I haven't been clear enough with her.

"Let me make this crystal clear. You won't be able to get rid of me, even if *you want* to end this relationship. I've decided that …

You.

Are.

Mine.

I'm not going anywhere. If I could knock you up and marry you tomorrow to lock you down, that's exactly what I'd do. I can't explain what being with you gives me. It's not a material thing; it's nothing money can buy. When I'm with you, I experience peace for the first time—the noise in my mind quiets. When I come here at the end of each day, I'm coming *home*. You give that to me, Kate. I'm not a stupid man. I know a good thing when I see it—you're that good thing for me. You give me a whole lot more than the shitty pillows and shoes I've given you. Believe in what I say, what I show you."

Her body relaxes beneath mine. Her eyes soften and grow glassy as if she's holding back tears. She smiles tentatively, then leans forward to take my mouth in a kiss that blows my mind and almost has me blowing my load.

I slowly pull back to check on her. "Are we all good?"

She nods at me. "Yeah, we're all good. Now, where were we before my stupid insecurities got in the way?"

"I was about to taste your hot pussy. No more interruptions. I need to focus."

She giggles and then spreads her legs wider for me. "Go ahead, be my guest." She winks playfully.

Smirking at her, I slowly make my way down her neck, kissing and sucking lightly, biting gently, soothing with my tongue. I blaze a path down her body with my hands, caressing her tits and stomach, following diligently with my mouth. I'm singularly focused on getting to the promised land between her thighs. I don't know how many nights I've imagined having my head between her legs, but this is more than even I could conjure up in my wildest fantasies.

Shuffling down, I settle my shoulders between her silky thighs, situating my head in the ideal position. My hands cradle her perfect ass once I place her thighs over my shoulders, and I take in her impeccably groomed pussy; swollen, wet pink lips are the perfect sight, waiting for my kisses. I move in, rubbing my nose along her pussy lips, inhaling her womanly scent, then flick my tongue out for my first taste of perfection.

Yes. I knew she would be my favorite flavor.

Her sighs and soft moans are music to my ears. She's enjoying my kisses, but I want to drive her wild. I want to push her to let go. I up my game, biting gently and licking her pussy as though it's the last time I'll ever have her like this. Her hands hold my head with a vice-like grip, and her body pumps with my rhythm. She's getting close to her first release.

Adding pressure to her clit with my thumb, I insert my middle finger into her tight opening until I find her G-spot. Her channel is fucking tight and hot and my cock is dripping against my stomach in anticipation. Massaging both areas rhythmically, I add another finger, making her muscles tighten. Her body convulses as she reverently whispers my name like a prayer, and I smile against her pussy, feeling like a king.

Her body comes down from the high as I slow my fingers and mouth. I gently remove them and wipe my face, then climb back up her body with teasing kisses and gentle caresses.

"That was better than any fantasy I could have possibly dreamed up. Watching you come undone was breathtaking."

"I didn't know it could be like that. That was out of this world," she whispers through her harsh pants, her tits shuddering with each labored breath.

"I haven't even begun. We have all night, and I know I'm going to want to do that again and again. You're addictive."

She grasps my face in both hands and kisses me enthusiastically, attempting to roll me onto my back. I roll, taking her with me, so she straddles my lower stomach. My need to get inside her is growing more insistent by the second, but I work hard to control my instincts to take over and hammer my way inside what I now know is a sensational pussy. Allowing her to take some of the lead, to help her gain her confidence, helps to calm me a little.

She licks her lips as her eyes slowly peruse my body. Leaning in, she starts kissing, biting, and licking down my torso; paying extra attention to my nipples and abs. "Your body is a work of art. I can't believe I'm the lucky woman who gets to be up close and personal with it."

She sighs, her warm breath on my flesh driving me crazy. I have to stop her though because if she gets near my cock, it'll be game over and I desperately want to be inside her when that happens.

"It's all yours, but I need to be inside you when I come. I want that tight pussy of yours strangling my cock."

She sits up, straddling my thighs, then reaches over for the box of condoms. I reach up to massage her tits while she opens the box to remove one, rips it open with her teeth, and rolls it down my length. I don't even try to contain the groan fighting for release at the sensation of her hands working the condom slowly over my shaft, ensuring it's firmly in place. My skin is on fire and my heart thuds out an uneven rhythm.

She leans forward, rising as she holds my cock, swiping it back and forth along her pussy lips. She finally notches the head at her opening and slides down painfully slowly. We both groan at the sensation of my length making contact with her pussy walls for the first time. I watch my cock disappear inside her body, looking up at her in wonder.

Her head has fallen back, her slender neck elongated beautifully. Sitting up, I suck on her pulse point, then move upwards to take her lips, thrusting my tongue inside to dance with hers.

"I was wrong before. Now. Now I've come home. Your pussy is heaven. So tight. So ... hot," I whisper against her lips.

Her walls tighten—*she likes that.*

Sliding my hands up her back, I grip the top of her shoulders to keep her still for a beat, while I revel in the sensation of finally being inside her and giving her time to adjust to my size. She begins to rock her hips, letting me know she's ready.

Thrusting up gently, I fully seat my cock inside, and Kate takes that as a sign to start moving in earnest. She rocks back and forth, adding a swivel of her hips, which is going to work me over too quickly. I want this to last as long as possible. She needs to come before I can let go. I roll her onto her back and, rising on my forearms, I take her mouth as I cage her in, building a rhythm to drive her to the brink.

"That's right, let me fuck this tight pussy," I pant in her ear.

She moans as her walls tighten around my cock—her body loves my dirty mouth.

"So good. Please don't stop."

"I'm never stopping."

Her walls tremble—she's close now.

Sitting back on my haunches, I lift her ass with one hand, while my other works over her clit. I take her in; tits bouncing with my thrusts, skin red and blotchy from exertion, her head thrown back, eyes closed —she's a stunning sight. It doesn't take long to push her over the edge; calling out my name with a long moan, her body tightens around my cock as her release overtakes her.

Now I can let loose, pumping my hips harder through her orgasm feels sensational as her walls convulse around my length. My balls tighten, and my release explodes out of me as I see stars. It seems to go on forever, triggering a second, smaller release for her. My hips gradually slow, and I lower my lips to hers in a languid kiss. With our hearts racing and our skin slick from exertion, we both take a minute to catch our breath.

I *know* I'll never be the same.

She's the first to break the silence. "Wow."

"Wow's right."

Kissing her nose, the apples of her cheeks, and her forehead, I touch my forehead to hers; our eyes connect and hold. The soul-deep connection I feel with her in this moment is extraordinary. The connection I've had with her from the first moment I laid eyes on her only grows deeper and more powerful.

"I'm lost for words. Give me a minute to gather my thoughts."

She giggles, causing her pussy to tighten, reminding me I'm still inside her and that I don't ever want to leave the warm cocoon of her body.

Reluctantly, I pull out to deal with the condom. We're going to need to discuss birth control because I don't want latex between us. Walking into her bathroom, I ditch the condom and wet a hand towel to tend to Kate's pussy. I meant to be more gentle our first time together. Once we connected, I lost my mind and my body took over. A shy smile forms as I wipe gently between her legs.

"I'm sorry. I meant to be more gentle with you. I lost my head and got carried away," I murmur, looking at her swollen lips and the beard rash on her tits while I wipe. Call me an animal, but my chest swells with a sense of pride when I see the marks I've left on her perfect skin.

She smirks at me. "You can lose your head with me any time you like if that's the result."

Oh, she's getting sassy now; I like this side of her. I take the wet cloth back to the bathroom, then I make my way through her home, lock up, and turn off the lights. Snuggling under the covers with my girl, I think about how tonight took an unexpected turn.

"I can honestly say I'm going to want to do that again and again. As many times as you'll allow me the privilege."

"I think we might be on the same page with that idea." She snuggles down, resting her cheek on my chest. Her breaths deepen, her body sinks into the mattress, and I know she's close to sleep, if not already there, and I follow her into a peaceful sleep.

———

I wake Kate in the middle of the night with my mouth on her pussy for round two, and she wakes me in the morning with her luscious lips wrapped around my cock. A perfect start to my Saturday morning. I only wish I didn't have to get out of bed and go to work.

The sound of the elevator doors startle me. I'm the only person in the office, so I get up from my desk to investigate who's about. Stepping out of my office, I'm surprised to see Sonia, my ex, strutting toward me like she owns the fucking place. I haven't seen or heard from her in over four years after she left me via text message. Apparently, she'd *fallen in love with someone else.* I later discovered who she was madly in love with—Robert Sinclair, hotelier and worth more than I was. I've since overtaken his financial worth twice over.

She's wearing the tallest spiked heels I've ever seen with the shortest skirt, which looks more like a belt, paired with a low-cut blouse, showing more breast than it covers. Her lips are painted scarlet, to match the long talons on the tips of her fingers, and I'm surprised she can open her eyes with her heavy-looking eyelashes and thick makeup. She's dressed more like a hooker than a high-society lady.

As she looks forward, she notices me standing in my office doorway. Her botox-filled lips spread in a wide, fake smile, and she adds more sway to her non-existent hips. She's had a lot of work done since I last saw her.

Tucking my hands into my trouser pockets, I straighten to my full height. "What the fuck are you doing here, Sonia?"

The scowl on my face should be enough of a deterrent, yet she moves into my space to hug me; forcing me to step back to prevent her from touching me. Her arms drop to her sides and she fakes a disappointed pout, which looks fucking ridiculous on a grown-ass woman.

"That's no way to greet the love of your life." She steps forward, and I stay rooted to the spot. *Is she fucking delusional?* "I'm sick of you ignoring my calls and texts, so I thought we should talk in person."

I scoff. "Love of your life? Have you hit your fucking head?" I snarl. "It was a long time ago that I felt anything other than malevolence for you." I study her closely and can't see what it was I thought I loved about her. What I thought was love back then was nothing compared to how I feel about Kate now. What we have is authentic and unconditional. What I had with Sonia was convenient and shallow. "I've come to realize what we had was a shitty excuse for a relationship. I'm not interested in anything you think you have to offer."

She manages a look of surprise, which is miraculous with the amount of work she's had done. "Oh, Oliver." She rests her hand on her chest. "I didn't realize how much I hurt you back then to cause you to still be angry with me now. I was stupid. What can I say?" She flicks her platinum hair over her shoulder, attempting to appear contrite. "I made a dreadful mistake. I've missed you terribly over the years, and I'll do anything you ask to win back your love and trust."

I cross my arms, narrowing my eyes in suspicion. "Don't waste your time. As I said, I'm not fucking interested." She reaches forward, attempting to place her hand on my arm, but I step back again. "Don't fucking touch me. Now leave my building before I call security to drag your scrawny ass out of here."

She sighs as if she's negotiating with a five-year-old child. "Okay, I'll leave for now. But I'll show you how much I love you and what I'm willing to do to win you back. I'll remind you how good we were together." She turns and walks back to the elevator, looking over her shoulder to see if I'm watching her walk away—which I am, to make sure she fucking leaves. She smirks and adds more sway to her hips, attempting to look sexy. Rolling my eyes, I wait for her to enter the elevator. When the doors close, I step back into my office to call security, ensuring they escort her out of the building and ban her entry in the future.

I attempt to get my head focused on the account I'm working on, but I can't shake the foreboding feeling that Sonia's going to become a problem. I need to see Kate; she'll settle me.

TWENTY-SIX

-kate-

I COULD BARELY WALK THE MORNING AFTER OUR FIRST NIGHT together last week. It was as though the dam had burst, and now that we had broken the barrier, we couldn't stop ourselves. I think we've christened every surface in my little house over this past week with the amount of sex we've had. Oliver's certainly not one for predictable sex, and you'll never hear me complaining about that.

I can't help but reminisce about last Saturday …

He arrived right after I got home from spending the evening with the kids.
Prowling toward me with determination written all over his face, he thrust
out paperwork I hadn't noticed he was holding in front of me.
I took the papers gingerly from his hand and looked them over, surprised
that he was showing me test results for any STDs.
Then he looked me straight in the eye. "I need to be bare inside you. Please
tell me you're clean and on some form of birth control," he said in a low
tone.
To say it shocked me was an understatement—it took me several seconds to
recover enough to respond. I think he was expecting me to reject his request
by the way his face fell. Even though I was totally embarrassed, I made
sure to make clear eye contact.
In a handful of minutes, I explained I was already on the pill to regulate
my periods. I told him I was strict about taking them every day at the same
time. And while I didn't have paperwork on hand to assure him I was
clean, I embarrassingly confessed how I had to get checked for STDs after I

*discovered Brandon's infidelity. I also quietly confessed that I hadn't been
with anyone since then.*

*His expression at the news that it had been a while for me was rather
comical.*

*He blew out the biggest breath, picked me up, and carried me to my
bedroom. Then he spent hours ravishing me. I wasn't sure how I was going
to walk the next morning, which was an unnecessary concern because we
spent most of the day in bed.*

Breaking out of my recollection, I take a moment to calm myself,
then change into my gardening clothes. The weather is holding out
nicely today, and I want to tidy up Margie's front yard as well as mine
before winter settles in.

Margie has a handful of various-sized pumpkins on her front porch
along with a couple of lanterns ready for Thanksgiving. Ever since I've
lived next door, she's always done a simple display on her front porch,
and I think it's adorable she still decorates for the holidays at her age.
She's going to spend Thanksgiving with my family again this year. My
nan and Margie are heaps of fun when they're together.

I wonder if Oliver has any plans this year, or if he would like to
spend the day with my family?

As I work through the two yards, Margie keeps me hydrated with
cool refreshments and my energy levels up with fresh fruit snacks. The
weeds are everywhere, and several of the bushes need to be pruned, so
I need to keep moving if I'm going to get finished and cleaned up
before it's time to visit my favorite kids.

Oliver parks his car behind mine when I'm about three-quarters
through the task—I wasn't expecting him back this soon. He never
comes over until after I'm home from seeing the kids.

I stand from my crouched position and walk toward him, greeting
him with a hug, careful not to touch his suit with my grubby gardening
gloves. "This is a pleasant surprise."

"Sorry if I'm intruding. I needed to see you."

I pull back to study him. The tightness around his eyes and in his
posture suggests something's wrong. "Are you okay?"

"I feel better now I have you in my arms." He leans forward, laying
a gentle kiss on the tip of my nose, then on my lips. "Can we talk?
There's something I need to tell you."

Biting my lip, I guide him to sit on the front step of my porch as I
remove my gloves. "Sure."

"I need to share something from my past. Something I was trying to ignore, but it seems it won't go away so easily." He grasps my hands in both of his. Looking at where we're joined, he tells me about his ex, Sonia.

He purges everything about their relationship and how it ended. Then he tells me about her visit to his office today, as well as the text messages and phone calls which started about a month ago. He'd been ignoring her, hoping she would lose interest and leave him alone. What he fails to see is that he's such a great guy, it's not possible for any woman to lose interest in him easily.

"She needs help. Her behavior seems desperate."

"She's not my problem. I don't want to have anything to do with her. She's toxic, and I don't want her anywhere near me, or you, for that matter."

"Just because *you* don't want her around doesn't mean she'll stop. I think you need to be careful. Perhaps you need to sit down with her and discuss where you're at now. That you've moved on." I glance across the road. The thought that he may have a secret wish to rekindle what they once had strikes me out of nowhere. "I mean, you have moved on, right?"

He looks at me as if he doesn't understand what I'm asking.

"There's no part of you … deep down, that doesn't want to try again?" He stands abruptly, shoving his hand through his hair. He paces away from me and back again, then pulls me up to stand in front of him. "Maybe it would wor—"

Taking my hands in his again, he frowns down at me. "Unequivocally no. There is not one ounce of anything I feel toward that woman, but distrust and loathing," he says firmly.

"If it's been so long since you've seen her, why do you think she's coming back for you now? What's changed for her?"

"I don't know." He breaks eye contact with me, as though he can't bear to tell me the next words. "I know my bank balance is healthier than it was back then."

He must be reasonably high up in the company he works for, which means he probably earns a pretty good income. I guess that's appealing to some women, and it seems like Sonia is a woman who is attracted to someone's bank balance rather than the actual person.

"What are you going to do?"

"I'm going to keep ignoring her. She'll get bored and move on to some other schmuck."

Typical man. Thinking he can bury his head in the sand and the problem will go away.

We stand quietly, secure in each other's presence, allowing time for our conversation to settle between us. I don't like to think about her coming after him. *What if he changes his mind and decides she's more suited?*

Pulling away, I explain I need to finish the gardening so I can get to the kids on time this afternoon. He offers to help, and we work together to finish the pruning and clean up the mess.

We shower together, which remains platonic because I started my period this morning. I told him, so he didn't waste his time coming over tonight, since I don't feel comfortable having sex during my period. He insisted he'd still be sleeping in my bed with me tonight and every night. He made it clear that, although the sex is magnificent, our relationship is more than that to him.

As we dress, I have second thoughts about leaving him on his own while I visit with the kids, but I don't want to flake out on them.

"Will you be okay if I spend a few hours with the kids?"

"Of course. I'm going back into the office to finish some more stock analysis for a couple of my clients. I'll meet you back here later." He gently tucks a lock of my hair behind my ear.

"You work too much. You should speak with your boss about his expectations and your workload."

He waves off my suggestion. "Nah. It's okay. It's not always like this."

I reach up on my tiptoes to kiss his bristly cheek. "I worry about you."

His face softens, and he slouches a little. "Do you have any idea how long it's been since someone worried about me?"

"No."

"A very long time. Not since I was a boy."

Tears sting the backs of my eyes, and I'm unable to swallow past the lump in my throat. My heart breaks into a million tiny pieces for this man. "You have me now. I care about you and I'll worry about you." I'm not one hundred percent clear about his childhood because he doesn't talk about it, but I get the sense he was very lonely and isolated growing up.

His large hands cup each side of my face as he moves in to devour my lips. This kiss is different from any other we've shared thus far. It's full of passion … and something else I can't quite place. It's deeper, reaching down into my soul, and it's so very Oliver.

We part ways, and I spend the afternoon shooting hoops with the kids. We make pumpkin pie cupcakes ready for dessert, and turkey subs for dinner, in recognition of Thanksgiving later in the week. After dinner cleanup, we play various card games, where Jack and Blake lead the kids in a competitive showdown. I bought each of the kids a new journal from the discount shop, and we spend time thinking about and writing what we are each grateful for while enjoying our delicious cupcakes. I'm astounded when each of them easily lists things they are grateful for—even in their current situation. It's a testament to Roman's dedication to these kids.

When I arrive home, Oliver's waiting for me with a tub of my favorite ice cream, a block of chocolate, and a heating pad, in case of discomfort. I fall asleep with him snuggled behind me, massaging the cramps that started late this afternoon.

———

As we get ready to leave for our Thanksgiving dinner with my family, hummingbirds take over my stomach, and I think I'd better give Oliver a heads-up about Mom. Every time I speak with her, she gives me the third degree about him, and each Sunday, she gets annoyed with me because I haven't brought him over for dinner again. She has her heart set on him sticking around.

"Uh, just a heads-up. Mom's been trying to get the inside information on our relationship. Be prepared for the third degree. It'll probably be worse than last time."

He laughs. "It wasn't that bad. I had a great time with your family. I loved how your dad was watching out for you." He raises a brow. "You know your dad and brother asked me what my intentions were when we went for a drive after dinner."

Oh my gosh, my family is too much sometimes!

I gape at him in shock. I'm certain I'm as red as a tomato as my blush rises with my embarrassment. "Seriously? I'm really sorry." My family has the best of intentions, but geez, they can be embarrassing.

He chuckles, shaking his head. "No need to apologize." He steps into my space, his body heat warming my front. "I set them straight. They know exactly what my intentions are. They were satisfied with my response."

I study him, dying to ask what he said, but I also don't want to know, because I think it'll make me even more anxious about our relationship. I like how it's growing organically at this point.

After I collect Margie, we pile into Oliver's fancy car. I sit in the cramped back seat because it's too difficult for Margie to climb through the front door opening. I'm not sure how Dad, Toby, and Shane fit in here. We arrive after stopping to buy flowers for Mom and Nan, as well as beer for the guys at Oliver's insistence.

He quickly exits the car while I take a calming breath. It'll be different this time; they're going to be able to see I've fallen for him all over my face. Oliver helps Margie out of the car while I wait in the backseat, then he helps me. The three of us walk to the front door, where I knock and enter without waiting for an invitation—which is customary here—calling out "hello" to let them know we've arrived. Mom rushes out of the kitchen with her arms open wide, ready to hug me as though she hasn't seen me in months.

"Oh, my Katie-girl, it's fantastic to see you. I missed you this week." She gushes as she envelopes me in her arms and kisses my cheek.

I roll my eyes. "You saw me last Sunday, and we've spoken and texted every day." This is a regular conversation for us.

Oliver smiles at us, and I don't know if he has people around him to greet him like this. Not that I know for sure, because he doesn't talk about his family. I take mine for granted, and I'm realizing I should appreciate them more. Not everyone is as lucky as I am.

Mom moves on to greet Oliver and Margie, and Dad and Nan step in from the back deck to greet us with the same exuberance.

Mom decorated the house in her usual Thanksgiving style. A range of small, but different-sized pumpkins and candles decorate the center of the table, and the silverware is set in cute hessian bags with fall leaf decorations. On the fireplace is a wreath with the word **FAMILY** made of wooden blocks, surrounded by photographs of our family, including the little boy who lived with us for two weeks when Toby and I were one.

-oliver-

I STEP CLOSER TO HAND THE FLOWERS TO KATE'S MOM AND NAN AND the beer to her dad. "These are a thank you for letting me crash your Thanksgiving dinner."

Mrs. Summer hugs me. "The flowers are beautiful but unnecessary. We're thrilled you could join us."

Mr. Summer pats me on the shoulder heartily in thanks for the beer as his wife releases me.

Kate's nan looks me up and down, testing my bicep muscles. "Who's this hunk joining us for Thanksgiving?"

Oh yeah, she's as spunky as Kate and reminds me of Margie. I bet the two of them are trouble when they get together. I struggle to keep my smile at bay.

"Nan, this is Oliver. He's uh … um …" Kate looks unsure how to introduce me, which won't fucking do—*at all!*

I reach out my hand to introduce myself properly. "I'm Kate's boyfriend. It's a pleasure to meet you finally."

I feel better now that I've clearly stated our relationship. I glance around to find smug smiles on Mr. and Mrs. Summers' faces. Kate's nan slaps my hand away, coming in for a tight hug. A very tight, lingering hug. She's smaller than her granddaughter, but she's deceptively strong for a woman her age.

"Really, Katie-girl? You didn't think to mention you were seeing someone. Especially someone this handsome." She winks at me. I see how it is. She's teasing her granddaughter.

Kate's clearly mortified that I've let the cat out of the bag, but her

145

family needed to know I'm in her life, and I plan to be around for a long time.

"Oh, well … its early days yet, Nan. I didn't want to jinx it." She smiles tentatively, tucking her hair behind her ear.

Toby and Shane arrive, interrupting the discussion with warm hugs and pats on the back. He narrows his eyes at me as he shakes my hand … hard.

"Dinner's ready." Mrs. Summer calls and we walk into the dining room to sit in the same seats as last time, with Kate's nan between her son and Margie. Kate's mom has gone all out with a traditional Thanksgiving meal and decorations.

We take turns around the table to give our thanks.

"I would like to give thanks for my family and our good fortune to have a roof over our heads, food on our table, and an abundance of people to love. I also give thanks for Oliver coming into our lives, and I pray he's happy, healthy, safe, and loved," Kate's mom shares, sounding choked up.

My breath catches, and my heartbeat quickens with a feeling I can't describe. "Thank you for including me, Mrs. Summer."

She raises her hand to her throat, her eyes widen slightly, and she releases an embarrassed chuckle. "Oh, I'm sorry. I didn't think." She looks across at her husband for help. "Of course you're included in our family."

Kate's dad clears his throat, looking back at his wife. Kate's hand settles on my thigh, and I get the impression I've misinterpreted Mrs. Summer's prayer.

"We, uh, actually had a little boy live with us for two weeks when the twins were only a year old. His name was, uh … probably still is, Oliver. Every prayer I've said since then has always included my hope that he's okay. I didn't consider the confusion it would cause. I'm very sorry." She's unnecessarily embarrassed.

"Oh, that's okay. I made an assumption."

"You know, you actually look like a grown-up version of him, to be honest. He was seven at the time and was such a sad, quiet little boy; which was understandable. He'd just lost his mom, and his dad was in a coma in the hospital. He only ever smiled when he was with Kate." She looks at her daughter with a half-smile. "He used to dote on her. We were heartbroken when he left us to go back to his father. We have his photo on our mantel."

My heart's beating a million miles a minute, and I'm worried it's going to beat its way out of my chest. Surely she's not talking about me. I remember being picked up by a man and staying with him, his wife, and their two babies.

That would have to be some coincidence.

Kate squeezes my thigh, breaking me from my confused memories, and I release the breath trapped in my lungs. Her face is pinched tight with concern. While my mind is stumbling around in confusion, I miss Kate's mom and dad serving the turkey and passing the various dishes around the table.

After the initial silence, as everyone tucks into the tasty Thanksgiving meal, discussion begins around the table—everyone catching up on each other's lives. It was like this the first time I joined them for dinner; these people genuinely love each other and are interested in what's going on in each other's lives. I find it difficult to stay focused; my thoughts are stuck on the possibility that I lived with this family.

After Mom died and Dad ended up in jail, I never had this—these deep family connections. I'm unpracticed in this type of situation, but I want to soak up all the genuine love surrounding me.

Kate's nan pipes up, "So, Kate." She looks pointedly at her namesake. "A boyfriend, huh? When did this happen? Am I the last to know?" She looks accusingly around the table.

Margie chuckles under her breath. "It's always the quiet ones you've gotta watch, Kate. You know that."

Kate blushes, while I smirk and slide my hand over to rest on her thigh.

Mrs. Summer speaks up, "Uh, no, Mom, we all found out at the same time tonight. But I'm not surprised by this fresh development. I could tell we would see more of him after the last time he was here for dinner." She smiles at me in a motherly way as she taps me gently on the arm. Mr. Summer and Toby nod simultaneously in agreement with Kate's mom. "I *knew* he was taken with our Katie-girl." She shares a look with Kate that tells her, *see, I told you he was interested.*

I'm happy they're on board with our relationship. I clear my throat. "You're right, Mrs. Summer, I'm very taken with your daughter. I hope to join your family dinners for many years to come, if you'll have me."

Kate's jaw drops open, her eyes widen, and that adorable blush I love is tingeing her cheeks. She probably can't believe I made such a bold statement in front of her family, but it's essential they know how important she is to me. I squeeze her knee in reassurance, while Kate's nan and Margie snicker, nudging each other as they wink at me across the table.

Mr. Summer clears his throat. "You're welcome here, as long as you treat our daughter with the respect she deserves."

Kate's nan mumbles something which sounds suspiciously like, *not too much respect, I hope.* Causing her and Margie to burst into giggles again. Kate must catch it too because her blush intensifies, while I wink at the octogenarians across from me, which they return with interest.

"Yes, sir, that's my plan."

He smiles at me with approval, and I'm satisfied with the result of this conversation. I take pity on Kate, changing the subject to ask Kate's nan about her Alaskan cruise. She spends the rest of our meal telling us all about her adventures.

We clean up, and Mrs. Summer brings out three different pies to choose from for dessert, which go down a treat. Apparently, Toby's favorite is pumpkin, Kate's is pecan, while Mrs. Summer always likes to have apple pie on hand. I get the sense Mrs. Summer enjoys feeding her family and any extras that may show up.

"The meal was delicious, Mrs. Summer. Thank you for allowing me to gate crash."

"You're always welcome."

While eating dessert, Kate's mom asks Toby, "So, how was your dinner meeting with the music executives? You said nothing had been finalized yet, but have you heard any more?"

"Oh yeah, I did. They've offered me a contract to record a new album and take it on tour throughout the country. I'm pretty stoked about it because I have a bunch of new songs rumbling around in my head."

Hugs, congratulations, and cheers go up all around the table, and I feel as though I've missed something important. I turn to Kate with questions clearly written all over my face.

She looks at me with a raised eyebrow. "Toby Summer. *The* Toby Summer." She looks at me as if the name should mean something to me, but I shake my head in the negative. At this stage, everyone's gaping at me.

"I'm offended you don't know who I am," Toby says with a smirk and a twinkle in his eye, hinting he's truly not upset.

"He's been number one on the charts six times in the past three years. How can you not know of him?" she says, totally dumbfounded.

I shrug. "I'm sorry. I don't follow music all that much. I listen to whatever's on in the car when I'm driving. Which isn't very often." Although, since staying with Kate most nights, I'm in my car a lot more often.

She digs out her phone, pulls up a popular music app, selects a playlist, then presses the play icon. Music plays, and I'm relieved that I recognize it. This song was played to death about six months ago. "Oh, I know this one."

Everyone seems to release a collective breath, as if relieved I'm not a complete moron.

I point to the phone. "This is you?"

Toby nods.

"Sorry. I didn't make the connection. I've heard this song a heap, but didn't know the artist's name."

"It's cool, man. Don't stress. Kate thinks everyone on the planet should automatically know who I am." He winks at her and pats me on the shoulder as he walks behind me, taking his dishes to the kitchen sink.

While cleaning up, Shane walks into the kitchen as Toby sidles up closer to his sister. "Hey, can I have your opinion about something?"

"Sure, Tobes. What's up?"

We stop what we're doing to give him our full attention.

"Uh, well, an old classmate from high school reached out to me on social media. He wanted to let me know our high school graduating class is having its ten-year reunion. I guess they couldn't find you because you don't have any social media accounts. They also asked me to let you know about it. But I'm not sure I should go. What do you think?"

He runs his hand through his almost shoulder-length hair—appearing nervous and unsure. Not sure why, if he's as famous as I've gathered from the previous conversation.

"I know you didn't have a great time in high school, and that you felt as though you didn't belong, but look at you now. You should definitely go. Show all the jocks who gave you a hard time how successful and confident you are now." She wiggles her eyebrows. "You never know, Cassia Phillips might be there." She nudges his arm with her shoulder because she's too short to reach his shoulder to nudge. "We'll go together. I would love to see what the bitchy girls are like now and if those too-big-for-their-boots-jocks still think they're all that."

He huffs out a laugh, and Shane smirks. "Oh yeah, Cassia. She was gorgeous ... and smart ... and sweet ... and kind." He has this wistful, faraway expression as he talks about this girl. I'm confused because I thought Shane was his boyfriend. "She tried her best to include me, but I was too damn awkward around her for my own good because I was crushing on her hard. Then she started going out with *Jake the Jock* and broke my heart." He shakes his head. "What if they're still together? I'm not sure I'm up for it."

She wraps her arms around his waist in comfort, looking up at him. "You play to audiences of tens of thousands of people. Millions of people listen to your songs. You *can* walk into a high school reunion with a bunch of nobodies from high school." She squeezes him extra hard. "You've gotta go. You need to show them they didn't win. They didn't crush your spirit, and you succeeded despite them. You *will* walk into the reunion with the same confidence you have when you walk on stage in front of all your fans. Shane and I will be with you for moral support." Shane nods in agreement; the guy never seems to say much.

"I'll think about it. Thanks, Squirt." He shrugs, and she pinches the side of his stomach in retaliation for calling her Squirt. I'm man enough to admit I'm envious of their relationship. I've never had that sibling bond.

I wonder if my parents would have had more children?

We move into the family room, and I purposely wander over to the mantel to study the photographs on display. I've been itching to look throughout the meal but didn't think it appropriate to leave the table. I find the photo I'm looking for.

My heart speeds up. I feel dizzy and struggle to draw a breath.

I can't believe what I'm seeing.

This can't be real.

It has to be some cosmic joke.

Kate's arms wrap around my torso from behind, and she notices the photo I'm staring at.

"That's the boy Mom was telling you about." She leans forward, studying the photograph closely. "Huh. She's right, you could be a grown-up version of him. What a weird coincidence." She squeezes me tight. "Are you ready to leave?"

I feel utterly discombobulated and can only manage a nod in response.

We call it a night, say goodnight to Kate's family and drive back to her house. We see Margie safely inside, then we spend the night tangled in her sheets, making love until late, when we both eventually collapse, exhausted.

As Kate sleeps, I study her closely. I can't believe she's the little girl I used to hold in my arms. I remember the powerful draw I had to her then, and maybe it explains why this is my favorite place in the world to be now.

———

Deciding to call it a day, I drive to Kate's place for the evening. She's still with the kids, but I might check on Margie to see if she wants to share dinner with me. I enjoy spending time with her; she's such a quirky old duck. Once I arrive, I dump my briefcase and step next door to check if Margie's eaten yet. The light shining through the side window lets me know she's home, so I knock on her door and wait for her to answer. After several knocks without an answer, I peer through the side window and see Margie's foot poking out from behind the couch.

My heart pounds in my chest as my adrenaline rushes through my system. I try her front door, but it's locked. I know Kate has a key, so I race back inside, finding it on the hook in the kitchen. I grab it and my phone, rushing back to Margie's.

I hope she's okay.

Unlocking Margie's door is difficult because my hand is shaking like crazy, but I eventually get it open. Moving swiftly to where she's lying, being careful not to jostle her, I check for a pulse; I find it present, but it feels weak. She's unresponsive to my touch.

"Margie. Margie, it's me, Oliver." Still no response, so I immediately call for an ambulance, sharing the address and the limited information I have about Margie. She has a lot of blood on her face and her glasses are askew, so I carefully remove them.

Glancing around, I notice the tipped-over dining chair and broken bulb on the floor nearby—she must have been trying to change the light bulb. Using the blanket draped over the back of the couch, I cover her body to keep her warm. I sweep up the broken glass and grab a clean cloth from her bathroom to put pressure on the wound, which is still oozing blood.

Sitting beside her, I hold her hand and speak to her softly. It's in this moment I realize how much Margie has come to mean to me. She's been kind and welcoming, and she means the world to Kate. I'm going to do everything I can to ensure she's looked after and fully recovers. As I'm about to stroke her hair away from her face, her eyelids flutter open slowly as she lets out a low, pained moan of discomfort.

"Margie. Stay still, help's on the way. It looks like you've fallen and banged your head."

She's clearly disoriented and confused. Her eyelids flutter closed again.

"Margie, if you can hear me, stay awake. Help is on the way. Stay with me, Margie."

She battles to open her eyes again and shakes her head slowly back and forth, obviously causing herself pain if the tight expression on her aged face is any indication. I do my best to stay calm, but my heart's pounding like it's going to burst out of my chest.

"Stay still, Margie. Okay. I'm here. Everything's going to be okay."

She moans again, attempting to lift her hand to her head, which is covered in blood. I gently clasp her hand and lay it back by her side, holding it still as I hear sirens blaring down the street.

Doors open and slam closed, then footsteps sound on the front porch. A voice calls out to announce their arrival, checking they're in the right place.

"Come in," I call, and two paramedics enter. I move out of the way, allowing them to help Margie without my impeding their work. They rattle off a steady stream of questions, of which I can only answer a few, explaining who I am and how I found her. I have no idea how long she had been on the floor, or what happened. I've made an assumption based on what I found.

They carefully lift her onto a gurney, situating her in the back of the ambulance. I collect my wallet, lock both houses, and jump in with them. When we get to the hospital, I'll let Kate know what happened. I don't want to upset her while she's with the kids.

The ambulance arrives at the hospital, and Margie's surrounded by a flurry of activity. She's wheeled down a corridor, and I'm bombarded with what seems like endless questions I can't answer. Questions about what happened, her medical history, health insurance information, and payment information. I don't know if Margie has insurance.

"Look, I'll pay for anything and everything she requires to ensure a full recovery. Just look after her and make sure she gets the very best treatment. Do everything you can for her. Money's no object. I want the best doctors and the top medical treatments and support for her recovery."

The administrator is surprised, especially since I only just finished explaining my relationship to Margie. "Okay, Sir. I'll need you to complete this paperwork."

I'm frustrated that the hospital's focus seems to be on the money, rather than Margie's care, but I snatch the forms from the woman. "No problem."

I'm determined to help Margie in any way I can. *What's the point of having money, especially the obscene amount I have, if I don't use it to help make the lives of the people around me better?* It's been a long time since I've had people around me I truly care about. In the short amount of time I've known Margie, I've grown to care for her very much.

I complete the horrendous amount of paperwork involved in paying for any additional care and hand it back to the woman behind the counter. "Can this remain between us? I don't want Margie or anyone else to know I'm paying any additional costs for her care. I'm happy to offer a large donation to the hospital to keep it between us."

"Sure. I'll put a note on the file."

"Thank you, I would appreciate that. Now, where do I go to be with Margie?"

"Head through those doors. You'll need to wait to be called back." She gestures toward a set of doors on the opposite side of the room.

I walk through to the emergency waiting room and directly approach the clerk at admissions. He dismisses me immediately because I have no familial relationship with Margie. I sit and wait, impatiently. Kate is due home shortly and will probably worry because I was supposed to be waiting for her.

My phone buzzes in my pocket, and I quickly collect my thoughts to answer.

"Hey, I'm home. Your car's in the driveway, but you're not here. Where are you? Are you okay?" Her words tumble out, rushed and panicked.

I run my hand through my hair; I don't want to tell her what's happened. "I'm okay, but Margie's been brought to Mercy Vale General Hospital by ambulance. I'm at the hospital, but they won't let me through to her because I'm not family."

Silence greets me on the other end. "Kate. Kate. You there?"

"What happened? Is she going to be okay? Oh my gosh, I need to get to the hospital!"

"I'll call you an Uber. I don't want you driving while you're upset. Stay put."

I quickly put her on speakerphone, pulling up the app on my

phone, and book her a ride, then let her know her Uber is fifteen minutes away.

"What happened?"

I explain how I found Margie, and that I called 9-1-1 to get her help. We end the call as her ride arrives, and all I can do is sit and wait.

Forty-five minutes later, she bursts through the emergency entrance doors, frantic. I quickly stalk toward her, engulfing her in my arms; drawing her into me, and kissing the top of her head. She sinks into me, releasing the tears she must have been holding at bay. We find comfort in each other's embrace for several moments, then she pulls herself together and peers up at me. Searching each other's face, she nods a little, letting me know she's okay. Together, we head toward the administration desk.

The clerk seems distracted by whatever he's looking at on his computer screen. "Welcome to Mercy Vale. How may I help you?"

Kate steps closer to the counter. "Hi, my neighbor, Margie Watson, was recently brought in. She suffered a fall at home. My boyfriend, Oliver, called 9-1-1, and an ambulance came and brought her here."

"Are you family?" he asks.

"Uh, um, no, I'm not. I'm pretty sure I'm listed as her emergency contact person because her husband has passed and she has no children or other family. Can you please tell me what's happening? If she's okay, at least?"

He turns back to his computer, typing some information, and then he reads quietly for a few minutes. His eyes rise to us, then drop back to his screen. "Ah, here we go. Margaret Watson." He looks up at Kate. "And what's your name?"

"My name is Kate Summer. I'm Margie's neighbor. I watch out for her, checking on her regularly." She grips my hand tighter.

He looks back at the screen and nods. "Yes, I have you listed here. Walk through those double doors, down the corridor, and follow the signs to the emergency ward."

"Thank you."

We don't waste another minute. We rush down the corridor, following the signs to emergency, where we're greeted by another desk. Kate goes through the process of identifying herself *again*, and we're sent through, finally, to see Margie.

She looks every one of her eighty-five years. Her skin is gray, and she looks frail in the hospital bed; very different from the Margie I've come to know and adore.

Kate heads straight to her bedside, taking her hand carefully, avoiding the IV attached to the back. I pull a chair closer to the side of the bed, encouraging her to sit while still holding Margie's frail hand.

"Oh, Margie. What did you do to yourself?" Kate sniffles, and I realize she has tears running down her cheeks.

I stroke her back, offering comfort in the only way I can right now. We sit quietly, side by side, for some time. The only sounds are the beeping of monitors and other various noises throughout the ward. I'm unsure how much time passes, but after what seems like hours, a nurse opens the curtain to enter our cubicle.

"Oh, good evening. I didn't realize anyone was in here. My name is Adele. I'm looking after Margaret this evening." She moves efficiently around Margie, checking tubes, recording information, and assessing the drip of the IV line.

"How's Margie? Do you know what's wrong? Will she be okay?" Kate's questions tumble out rapid fire and the nurse smiles gently at her.

"The doctor in charge of Margaret should be in shortly. She'll be able to answer any questions you have." She finishes her checks, tells us there are snack machines at the end of the corridor, and leaves after returning the curtain to its closed position.

We sit and wait. And wait. And wait some more.

I get up to pace because I can't sit in the chair and do nothing. Even though the pacing is a waste of energy, I need to move. Kate's head has dropped to Margie's bed and her breathing has evened out; she's utterly exhausted.

The curtain opens without warning, and a tired-looking woman in a white coat enters the cubicle. She looks up from her tablet, noticing us with Margie. Kate stirs, sitting up carefully to avoid disturbing Margie.

"Hello, my name is Dr. Fieldman. I'm Margaret's doctor while she's here with us in the ED."

"Margie. She likes to be called Margie. She says Margaret sounds too formal for her liking," Kate firmly states. "What's wrong with her, Dr. Fieldman?" I move next to her as she stands, holding her close to my side.

The doctor studies us carefully. "Are you family?"

"No. We're not. I'm her neighbor. I'm also her emergency contact because she has no living relatives. My name is Kate, and this is my boyfriend, Oliver."

The doctor checks something on her tablet, then looks at Margie and turns back to us. "It seems Margie's fall was quite nasty. She's broken her hip and has a contusion to her forehead, as well as bruising to her face caused by her glasses." A gasp escapes Kate, so I tug her in tighter to me. "We're going to take her in for a CT scan to check she doesn't have a bleed on her brain. Assuming it's clear, we have organized an orthopedic surgeon to replace Margie's hip in a few hours."

The doctor leaves, and we're left waiting again. The time feels interminable in this small room with the monotonous beeping of machines. An hour later, an orderly arrives to take Margie for a CT scan. Kate looks absolutely shattered, so I wrap her in my arms, kissing the top of her head.

"C'mon, Sunshine. Let's get something to eat. Then we'll wait for word." I guide her out of the ward and the hospital. We cross the road to a late-night deli, which seems to be the only place open at this time of night.

While we've been in the hospital, night has fallen and everyone has gone home. It's quiet in the deli, so they quickly take our order and serve it efficiently. The staff here are probably used to having to work quickly for the medical staff who must frequent this place.

We choose a seat at a table next to the window. Kate's shoulders slump forward, her eyes glassy. "I don't know what I'll do if Margie's not okay."

I reach across to grasp her hand. "She'll be okay. They're doing everything they can for her, and we'll be her support as she recovers."

She nods, drawing a shuddering breath.

We eat quickly, then purchase coffee to take back with us. We settle in the waiting room on the ward and wait to hear from Margie's doctor.

TWENTY-EIGHT

-kate-

THE SOUND OF A THROAT CLEARING WAKES OLIVER AND ME WITH A start. We stand quickly, with hearts full of hope that we receive good news.

"How is she, Doctor?"

"The CT showed no internal cerebral bleed, so we've stitched up the wound. The surgery went well. The orthopedic surgeon success-fully replaced her hip, and she's currently being settled into her room. A nurse will collect you once she's stabilized." She refers to her tablet. "She'll be in room three eighteen. Margaret won't be conscious for some time." She glances between us. "I recommend you go home. Get a good night's sleep and come back late tomorrow to check on her progress."

I turn to Oliver. "I'm not leaving her. She has nobody else, and I won't leave her to face this alone." He nods as his eyebrows draw tight. He looks exhausted. I know Margie has grown to mean the world to him in the short time he's known her and he's as worried about her as I am.

"Maybe we should wait to see Margie, then go home to shower and get some sleep before coming back tomorrow." He looks at his watch. "Uh, later today, since she'll be unconscious."

I nod, absently. Even though I don't want to leave Margie, I know it doesn't make logical sense to stay. "Okay." He leans forward, kissing my forehead, then he wraps his arm around my shoulder and tugs me close to his warm body.

The doctor acknowledges our decision, leaving us to wait for the nurse to collect us. After what seems like hours, we're finally led to Margie's room. When I lay my eyes on her, I swear I feel my heart shredding in my chest and I'm unsure my knees can hold me up. The new bandage covering her head doesn't hide the bruising to her face, which looks worse than it did before surgery. She looks unnaturally still among the loudly beeping machines and the multitude of wires and tubes going in and out of her body. I cover my mouth to hold back a sob only to find myself pressed into Oliver's hard chest. One hand cups the back of my head, while the other gently caresses my back.

"Shhh, shhh. She's going to be okay. I promise." His confidence comforts me and I nod into his chest. "C'mon, let's say goodnight and we'll come back later. Okay?"

I say goodnight to Margie, gently placing a kiss on her paper-thin cheek, and then he guides me out of the hospital to a waiting car to take us home.

Once we're back at my place, he silently walks me to the bathroom and starts the shower. As the steam builds in the bathroom, he strips us both naked and guides me carefully under the water, where he washes my hair and body with gentle care and affection in silence. Even though he's exhausted, he takes quiet control, knowing I'm incapable of looking after myself tonight. He dries us both, tucking us into bed after ensuring the house is secure, then he pulls me close to his body, kisses the top of my head, and encourages me to get some sleep. I'm absolutely wiped out; it doesn't take long for me to fall asleep.

———

Slowly, I wake to the sun streaming into my bedroom and the smell of bacon wafting in from my kitchen. I stretch out, roll onto my side, and tuck my hands under my cheek as I gaze out of my bedroom window. I spend a few minutes remembering the events of yesterday and last night, mentally preparing myself to face what's to come. Rolling out of bed, I step into my bathroom, brush my teeth, and take care of business; then I head to the kitchen, ready to see my guy.

Oliver's standing in my kitchen in his boxer briefs and one of my aprons; the sight is comical and sexy at the same time. His back muscles shift and roll as he turns the bacon and stirs the scrambled eggs, while his butt cheeks squeeze and shift in the most delicious way.

Stepping into the kitchen, I press my front to his back, wrap my hands around his middle and place a kiss between his shoulder blades

—he's so warm and strong and has quickly become my home. I turn my head, pressing my cheek against his back, feeling beyond grateful for his presence. "Morning."

He turns his head to gaze over his shoulder at me. "Good morning. How did you sleep?"

I release him, giving him the space to turn around. He shuts off the burners on the cooktop and turns to engulf me in the biggest hug, then he lowers his face to take my mouth in a searing kiss—thank goodness I brushed my teeth.

"What's all this?" I ask, smiling appreciatively.

"I thought I would surprise you with a cooked breakfast. I figured we'd spend most of the day at the hospital, and it would be a good idea to start with a solid meal." He kisses the tip of my nose as if his thoughtfulness is of no consequence. "I called the hospital to check on Margie, but they won't tell me anything, because I'm not family."

His face is drawn tight with worry for Margie. "Thank you for everything you did for Margie yesterday. I'm not sure what would have happened if you hadn't been there."

"I'm not happy about finding her the way I did, but I'm glad it was me and not you." I nod, and try to push down my worry.

We eat the delicious breakfast he cooked and get ready to drive back to the hospital. Mom and Dad are stepping out of Margie's room as we walk down the hall. I messaged them last night, but didn't think they'd get here so early. We all hug in greeting, and if they're surprised to see Oliver, they don't show it.

"Oh Katie-girl, it's such a shock to see Margie that quiet and still. Just the other day, she was giggling up a storm at our dining table." She holds me tight in comfort, knowing how close I am to Margie. "If there's anything we can do to help, please call us anytime."

"Thanks, Mom. I have to work tomorrow. Would you mind checking in on her? Then I'll come by straight from school."

"Of course. I was going to come back tomorrow anyway because I don't have any classes on Monday. Dad can come on Tuesday because he doesn't have any face-to-face appointments. Wednesday, we'll have to work something out. Maybe Toby could stop by?" She brushes my hair away from my face and cups my chin. "We'll work it out together. She won't be alone for long. Okay?"

I nod, smiling at Mom with appreciation. "Thanks, Mom. You're the best." We hug once more before they leave.

Oliver and I step into Margie's room to the regular beeps of the heart monitor, and my heart skips in my chest. I feel helpless to do anything. She still hasn't woken. As we sit in the sterile room, we take comfort from each other, holding hands in quiet support. Having him here beside me offers me a sense of strength, and that everything will be okay.

A nurse breezes into the room, completely focused on Margie and unaware of us. "Good morning, Margaret. How are you feeling today, lovely lady?" When he notices us watching him, his step stutters as his eyes land on Oliver. He looks at him appraisingly, then turns toward me with a wink, mouthing, "lucky lady", causing laughter to burst out of me. "Hi, I'm Stephen. Margaret's day nurse."

I smile. "Hi, Stephen. I'm Kate, and this is my boyfriend, Oliver." It still feels surreal when I think of him as my boyfriend. "It's nice to meet you. How's Margie?"

Oliver simply raises his chin in greeting.

"Oh, the pleasure's all mine." He fusses around Margie, checking her vitals and recording information. "Margaret's been a dream to look after. We had a lovely chat earlier this morning."

I'm surprised; I didn't think she had woken up yet. "Did she wake up?"

"Oh no. But I always chat with my patients as if they're fully lucid. I believe it helps them to stay connected with us." He glances at us as he quickly swaps out Margie's IV. "You should fill her in on what you guys have been up to. Just as you normally would when you see her."

"I never even thought of that. Thanks, Stephen. By the way, she prefers to be called Margie." I smile at Oliver, then proceed to tell her about the delicious breakfast he surprised me with this morning.

Stephen interrupts, "Oh my! A man that handsome and cooks as well. You've done mighty well for yourself." He turns to Oliver. "I don't suppose you happen to have a brother?"

Where I would have expected Oliver to be offended, he huffs out a laugh and shakes his head. "I'm sorry. No, I don't."

"Ah, such a shame." He finishes his work, and as he heads to the door, he tells us Dr. Jackson will stop by shortly.

We chat with Margie about the plans we made for her care, and I tell her about my afternoon and evening with the kids. I can't believe it was less than twenty-four hours ago. I make sure to include every detail.

Oliver listens intently, and I notice his smile comes easily when it comes to the kids. I must remember to ask if he's allowed to visit.

Oliver heads across the road to buy coffee, and I find a cloth to wipe over Margie's face, neck, and arms. As I'm gently massaging her feet, Oliver returns with coffee and pastries. He kisses my forehead, then places the items on the table.

"Margie's lucky to have you in her life." He kisses the tip of my nose. "So am I, for that matter." This man melts my heart.

A man enters the room, interrupting our moment. "Good afternoon, I'm Dr. Jackson. I'll be looking after"—he glances at his tablet—"Margaret during her stay."

Oliver acknowledges the doctor with a nod when I introduce us. I love how he's stepping back, allowing me to take the lead. "How is Margie's recovery progressing?"

"Things are progressing as we would expect." He observes Margie and then focuses back on us. "Margie will probably experience some discomfort from her head wound, facial bruising, and hip. As soon as she's able, we'll get her on her feet, walking short distances."

"That seems fast to get her back on her feet after such major surgery." I'm shocked. I figured she would have to stay off her feet for quite some time.

"Patients have more positive results after a hip replacement if we get them up and moving as quickly as possible. She'll need to follow a detailed recovery program with our physiotherapists over the next several weeks, tapering off until Margie is looking after her body on her own. She'll need to keep up with regular, gentle exercise to ensure she looks after herself and her new hip."

"Thank you, Doctor. Do you have any idea when Margie will wake? I would like to be here when that happens."

Oliver rubs his warm hand up and down my back in support.

"I can't provide an exact time, but we'll aim to start reducing her medication around this time tomorrow. It usually takes time before the patient starts to come around, but this varies from person to person." Dr. Jackson taps his tablet, then moves around to check the machines and drip.

"Thanks, Doctor. I'll come straight from school tomorrow. My mom is going to come during the day to keep Margie company."

"No problem. I'll see you tomorrow." He dips his chin, then leaves.

"Well, everything sounds positive so far. I think Margie's in expert hands with Dr. Jackson." Oliver gestures to the seat and I sit so he can pass my coffee and pastry to me. He grabs his, then sits in the uncomfortable hospital chair beside me.

We sit for another couple of hours, then he suggests we go home for the night; I love the sound of that ... *home*. I can't imagine he would want to live in my tiny place when he probably has a fancy apartment in the city—not that I've ever been there. I can't believe I'm thinking about living with Oliver. It's not that far-fetched; even though we haven't spoken about it, he pretty much lives with me already. He spends every night at my place, and I can't remember what it was like *not* having him in my space. We stop to grab food for dinner and then drive home.

———

When I arrive at the hospital after work, Oliver's already sitting in the chair beside Margie's bed, his laptop balanced on his firm thighs, and my step falters. I assumed he'd be too busy at work to be here during a workday. I lean against the door frame, observing him quietly for a minute or two while he's working.

"Are you going to come in, or are you going to perv on me all afternoon?" He looks up, one side of his mouth tipped up, then he stands and places his laptop on his chair. We both move forward at the same time, crashing our bodies and mouths together as if we haven't seen each other for weeks, not hours.

I peer up into his emerald eyes. "How is she? Has Dr. Jackson been by yet?"

"He came by about half an hour ago to reduce the medicine. It has to be reduced gradually over the next couple of hours." He tucks a lock of hair behind my ear. "So, we sit and wait." He pulls a chair across next to his, gesturing for me to sit.

"Sorry. I didn't even say hello," I say sheepishly, too focused on Margie for manners. "Hey." I smile softly.

He looks at me in the blistering way he always does and returns my smile. "Hey."

"How was your day?" I sit in the chair beside him.

"It's better now. How was yours?"

"Okay, I guess. I found it difficult to focus on the kids. How long have you been here?"

"I came after my meeting finished at one. I figure I can work as easily from here as I can in the office. But I need to step out to make a phone call. Will you be okay for a few minutes?"

"Sure. Go do what you need to do. I'll catch Margie up on my day." He bends down to kiss the tip of my nose, then leaves the room.

Not long after, Stephen comes into the room to adjust Margie's medicine again. "Hi, Kate. How's your day been?"

"Hey, Stephen. Good to see you again. My day will be better when my friend wakes up. Have you had a good day?"

"It's certainly been busy. We need one more reduction in Margie's meds. Then we should begin to see some changes. Where's that hunk of man of yours?"

I smile because Stephen has certainly made his thoughts on Oliver plain. "He had to step out to make a call for work. He'll be back shortly."

We make general chitchat about his day and mine, then he moves on to check his next patient. I'm in the middle of telling Margie all about Emma's latest attempt at dating when Oliver steps back into the room with a sandwich and a cup of hot chocolate for me.

Kissing me on the forehead, he passes the items over. "I figured we'd be here until late, and you probably haven't eaten since lunch."

My heart goes all soft and gooey. "You're always looking after me. Thank you." We unwrap our sandwiches, peeling the paper away carefully so they don't fall apart all over our laps. "How was your phone call?"

For several seconds, he studies me like I'm some sort of puzzle he needs to solve. "You know, I've never had anyone in my life, outside of work, check in on me and how I'm going with my work the way you do." He glances out of the small window and then back to me with a smile. "I find I like it. The normality of it feels ... domestic." His lips widen. "I've never had that before. Thank you, Sunshine." Leaning closer, he skims his lips lightly across mine, then leans back to take a bite of his sandwich. I'm sad that he hasn't experienced something I thought was commonplace in a relationship.

"What about when you were engaged to Sonia? Surely you talked about your days with each other?" I don't enjoy thinking about her with my boyfriend. Apart from what she could get from him, I don't think she was genuine in her affection. It breaks my heart because he was going to settle for that type of relationship, and he's worth a lot more.

"She was only interested in spending my hard-earned money on her various treatments, outfits, and luncheons. She was never interested in me as a person, only what I could give her, closely followed by the size of my cock." He looks contrite when mentioning their intimate relationship. "I was hurt and angry when she left me eight weeks before our wedding to be with someone with a larger bank account. Now, though, I could kiss the ground on which she walks in gratitude for her leaving me. I believe I dodged a bullet there." He looks at me, studying my face closely. "If I was in a miserable, superficial relationship with her, I would have missed out on meeting you. The best thing that's ever happened to me in my life." He reaches across and grasps my hand, kissing the back of it gently, reverently.

"Maybe we should send her a thank you gift." I chuckle. "I consider myself lucky to have you in my life. I can't believe I made it so difficult for you in the beginning, and I'll be forever grateful you never gave up on me."

"Perhaps I should send her on a vacation. That way, she'd stop bothering me," he says evenly, but I'm on automatic alert.

"What do you mean?"

His eyes widen when he realizes his faux pas. "Oh, nothing. Don't worry about it."

I turn toward him, hoping he hears my concern. "I *do* worry about it. I care about you. I don't want you dealing with her on your own. Can I help?"

He sighs and explains she's still harassing him. He's quick to tell me he's done nothing to encourage her or lead her to believe there's any chance of reconciliation, and I believe him.

I'm about to respond when Stephen comes waltzing into the room to complete the final adjustment on Margie's medicine. He says we should start noticing some activity soon.

Once he leaves the room, I return to our conversation. "I think you should inform the police. She's pretty much stalking you."

He huffs out a laugh. "Yeah, I can imagine how that would go. 'Officer, my ex keeps contacting me and showed up at my office.' They would laugh it off and tell me to grow a new set of balls. I don't think the police would take it as seriously as they would if I were a woman, being stalked by a man."

Margie groans softly, and attempts to lift her hand, but can't because of the IV attached there. I quickly move closer, holding her hand still. "Margie. You're okay. Stop moving, we'll get the doctor for you." I keep soothing her, while Oliver goes to find Stephen or Dr. Jackson.

He bursts back through the door with Stephen hot on his heels. He walks straight to me, placing his warm hand on my lower back in unity.

Stephen checks the machines attached to Margie, and she moans again. This time Stephen reassures her that she's okay. He records some information on her file, tells us it will be a little while until she wakes fully, and walks toward the door, letting us know that Dr. Jackson will be by shortly.

We pull our chairs closer to the bed, putting our conversation on hold, while we both observe Margie closely. She squeezes my hand and I quickly look across at Oliver. His eyes meet mine and a small smile touches his lips, letting me know he noticed the tiny movement. I'm not surprised; he doesn't miss much.

His grin grows as he tips his head toward Margie. "She'll be back with us in no time."

I breathe a sigh of relief, nodding. We sit quietly by Margie's side … waiting. It's growing dark outside when I feel another squeeze, and Margie releases another groan. Watching her face closely, she opens her eyes slowly, as she shakes her head side to side on the starchy pillow.

"Margie. We're here. Whenever you're ready, you can wake up," I whisper reassuringly, coaxing her to come back to us. We dim the lights, ensuring they're not uncomfortable for her when she opens her eyes fully.

She moans in response, opening and closing her eyes several times. It takes a little while for her to keep them open to look at us.

"Wh— What happened? Where am I?" She attempts to sit up, but Oliver quickly scoots around to the other side of the bed, gently pressing her shoulders back to the bed.

"Stay still Margie. The doctor will be in soon," he whispers to her.

"Margie. You're in the hospital. You fell off the chair when you were trying to change your light bulb." I'm furious with her. I've told her I'll change her bulbs, but she's stubbornly independent.

I grab the cup of water we've had waiting for when she woke up, and hold the straw to her lips. "Sip slowly, Margie. Not too much."

Dr. Jackson enters the room. "How's my patient?"

"If you're talking to me, young man," Margie grumbles. "I have the headache from hell, and I feel like death warmed up." I smile to myself because it's good to know she still has her attitude.

"To be expected after the nasty fall you experienced. We can offer you something to relieve your pain. Can you tell me, one to ten, one being very little pain, to ten being unbearable pain, what would you rate your pain level at?"

"Probably close to a nine."

"Okay, I'll get the nurse to administer some pain medicine. Do you remember how you fell?"

"I climbed up on a dining chair, so I could change the darn light bulb in my living room. I guess I must have lost my balance. Then I don't remember anything else."

"Okay, Margie. You bumped your head pretty badly. When you came in, your forehead was bleeding profusely, probably because of your blood thinners. You also broke your hip, which we've replaced. You'll have several weeks of physical therapy to get back to your level of mobility before the fall." The doctor looks across at us and smiles. "You have some pretty great people here who I'm sure will be more than happy to help you. I'll tell the nurse about your pain meds, so we can help you feel more comfortable."

Soon after the doctor leaves, Stephen comes in with a bright smile. He chats to Margie the whole time as if they're best friends while administering pain medicine. After a few minutes, Margie's face and shoulders relax. I guess the medicine is working—thank goodness.

We sit with Margie for a while. "You kids should go home. I need my beauty sleep and you're keeping me up."

———

I head straight to the hospital after school to visit Margie, finding Oliver already there, the same as yesterday. He's been worried about her. I stand in the doorway to watch them for a moment with Dr. Jackson. Margie looks much brighter today; her cheeks have more color, and the sparkle is returning to her eyes.

"Thanks, Doctor. I'm not sure how I'm going to pay for all the extra help I'll need. I don't have health insurance."

"The hospital registrar told me the hospital can cover everything you need. Apparently, you fit a particular criterion, Margie. Don't worry about the cost; it's all covered," Oliver tells her.

"Oh, that's wonderful. Thank you so much, Doctor. Such a worry has been taken off my mind."

"You concentrate on getting well." Dr. Jackson leaves the room, and I step inside to join them.

We visit with Margie, updating her on what's been happening since

Saturday. I also take the opportunity to chastise her for changing her light bulb, which she brushes off as only Margie can.

———

We've spent this past week going back and forth to the hospital to visit Margie. The constant back and forth and worry is taking its toll, and we're both exhausted. It will be a relief when she comes home.

The hospital has arranged for a nurse to visit Margie at home twice each day to help her shower and ensure she's able to complete everyday tasks safely. Oliver organized the installation of a temporary ramp to make it easier for Margie to get to her front door.

I've had to let the kids know I won't be able to visit them this weekend because I need to be available for Margie. They were downright sweet, making her get-well cards for her mantle and funny videos for her to watch.

It's finally Friday, and as I leave the school building, I inhale a deep breath. I need to visit Margie before I quickly clean her place, ready for her return home tomorrow.

TWENTY-NINE

-kate-

MARGIE'S EXCITED TO BE GOING HOME TOMORROW. WE'VE WARNED HER repeatedly that she's to follow the doctor's orders to the letter. After a couple of hours, Oliver and I make our way home.

While I clean Margie's place to make sure it's ready for her return, Oliver cooks me breakfast for dinner as a treat. He's been my rock throughout this past week, and I'm not sure how well I would have kept myself together without him by my side.

"I'll clean up. You have a hot shower to wash away the week." He stands, collecting our dishes.

I press up on my toes to land a kiss on his cheek. "Thank you."

He smacks my ass playfully, making me giggle as I head for the shower. When I return to the living room, he has two glasses of wine waiting.

He truly makes my heart sing.

Never in a million years would I have expected the man I met across the other side of the world all those months ago, to have such a soft and gooey center.

I situate myself on his lap, playing with the hair at the nape of his neck. His hands tighten on my hips and I lean in to lay a delicate kiss on his full lips. I pull back enough, allowing me to see his luminous emerald irises, and whisper, "Thank you for taking care of Margie, and especially for taking such good care of me." I lean forward, pressing my forehead to his. "I'm incredibly lucky to have you."

His hand comes up to cup the back of my head as he directs my mouth to his in a deep, sensual kiss that reaches the deepest parts of my soul. "I'm the lucky one."

I feel as if, maybe, I'm falling in love with this man. No, not maybe. *Definitely*.

He passes my wine, collecting his own, and we talk over what the next week will look like in terms of Margie's care.

After another glass of wine, we fall into bed, loving each other's bodies into exhaustion. I fall asleep, listening to Oliver's rhythmic heartbeat beneath my cheek, his powerful arms wound around me, keeping me bound to him—*as if I would ever want to leave*.

———

The weekend passes by in a blur. Between bringing Margie home and helping her out with her steady stream of visitors—including Pete and Joe from down the street—I feel like I've been in a time warp. It's Monday morning already; time to start the school week again. I don't feel prepared or rested, and I can't help but worry about leaving Margie home alone.

As soon as I see the smiling faces of my students, my spirits lift exponentially. We have a great day together reading stories, singing songs, creating towers, and practicing our balancing skills. I high-five each child as they leave for the day, and then collapse in a heap on my chair.

Collecting my things together quickly, I leave earlier than usual. I'll do my work while sitting with Margie; I need to get home and check she's okay. I walk out of the building amid shocked faces that I'm leaving on time, for once.

Over the week, we spend our days working, and our evenings with Margie, before falling into bed, wrapped around each other's bodies, exhausted.

THIRTY

-oliver-

I ARRIVE LATE AT KATE'S ON FRIDAY EVENING BECAUSE MY MEETING with a new investor ran long. I also needed to collect some fresh clothes from my penthouse for the next couple of days. I don't like to be away from her any longer than I absolutely need to. The meeting seemed to take longer than necessary, and for some reason, I felt compelled to search for the photograph I had carried with me throughout my childhood.

I hadn't thought about the picture in years, but I made sure to always keep it safe as I moved from home to home. I brush my finger over the image of me sitting on a couch, holding a baby girl while a baby boy sits beside me. My expression as I look down at the baby girl is one of pure adoration.

That baby is Kate, and the other baby is Toby.

It's like a punch to the gut; all the air in my lungs whooshes out, leaving me dizzy and off-balance. Sitting on the edge of my bed, I attempt to regain my composure.

I'm unsure what to do with this revelation.

Telling Kate means revealing my shitty background, and I'm not certain I'm ready for her to look at me differently. At this point, I'm keeping more secrets from the woman I'm definitely falling in love with than I'm sharing.

She greets me at the door with a gorgeous smile, and I settle now I'm back in her orbit. Knowing what I know now explains the feelings she evoked in me from the moment I laid eyes on her. The familiarity and the instant connection I felt with her. The calmness I find with her —only ever with *her*.

She throws her body at mine as though she hasn't seen me for weeks, kissing me as if it's the last time we'll ever be together. "I'm so happy you're home."

Home.

Now that's something I haven't had since I was a boy. I would love to make a permanent home with Kate. At the moment, all of my belongings are in my penthouse, and I only bring over what I need to get through a day or so. I want to change that, but now's not the time.

"I have some great news for you." She tugs me inside, leading me to sit on her tiny couch, and straddles my lap—just the way I like.

I grab her ass, pulling her closer. "Yeah? What is it?"

Her smile grows wider, if that's even possible. "Well, I asked Roman to check if it would be okay for you to come with me sometimes when I visit the kids. He had to get permission from the higher-ups, but I think it was just a formality." She's bursting at the seams with her excitement. "He messaged me tonight. They've cleared you to volunteer at the shelter with me." I'm truly shocked; rendered incapable of responding straight away. "If you want to, of course. No pressure!" She must think my lack of response means I don't want to.

I cup her face, ensuring she can't turn away. "Of course I want to come with you. I'm surprised you're willing to open up that part of your life to share with me," I whisper, kissing her nose and her forehead. I press my forehead to hers, locking gazes—meadows to sky. "That you want me to be with you means the world to me. Thank you."

This is a giant step forward in our relationship. She's finally showing me a level of trust and openness that terrified her in the beginning, and I know I'm a fucking fortunate man.

Maybe I'll be able to tell her who I am sooner than I thought.

She strokes the hair at the nape of my neck, which feels fucking fantastic. "Let's go to bed," she murmurs huskily as she pulls me to standing. I check that the house is locked, turn off the lights, and join my ravishing girlfriend in bed. Wrapping myself around her, our bodies come together naturally. Loving, joining, combining, fucking until we fall asleep together, just as I hope we do for the rest of our days.

"Morning," I whisper, in between peppering open-mouthed kisses along her exposed neck.

"Morning," she sighs, while tilting her head to give me better access to her smooth neck. "I was going to bring you breakfast in bed."

"I would rather have you in bed. I don't like waking up without you." I nuzzle her neck and spin her around to face me.

She smiles shyly, her natural blush rising from her tits. "Yeah?"

"Yeah." I lean in, taking her mouth in a good morning kiss to begin my day the way I like; though I'd prefer more bodily contact. Our bodies respond instantly, and it takes Kate's control to separate us so we can eat the breakfast she's prepared while it's still hot.

I want to speak with her about our living arrangements and forging forward with a life together, but I'm not convinced she's ready. There's still a lot about me she doesn't know, and it wouldn't be fair to move forward without her knowing all of my secrets.

I'll have to maintain my patience for a while longer.

While she collects another load of laundry, I step next door to check on Margie. She looks fantastic after her ordeal as she shuffles toward the front door using a walking frame. She's only been home for one week, and she's getting around remarkably well for an eighty-five-year-old who recently had a hip replacement.

"Well, hello, young man." She opens the screen door, welcoming me inside with her usual warmth.

I hug her. Since meeting Kate, I've quickly become accustomed to giving and receiving hugs. "How are you feeling, Margie? You look fit as a fiddle."

She brushes off the compliment with a wave of her hand, offering me a cup of tea, which I gratefully accept. Margie's like the grand-mother I never had, and I'm surprised to discover I enjoy her company.

"How are you and Kate going? You've been busy looking after me since my fall and subsequent stay in the hospital." She leans forward, patting my arm. "I hope you both know I appreciate all you've done for me."

"You're more than welcome, Margie. We'll always keep an eye on you." I pause, ensuring I have her undivided attention when I say, "But no more climbing up on chairs. I'll change any bulbs in the future." She tries to interrupt, but I stop her. "Don't be stubborn. Kate was beside herself with worry … and so was I. I don't want to go through that again. Understood?" My expression must deliver my message clearly because Margie looks properly chastised.

She nods sharply. "Understood."

"Good. Now, how's your physical therapy going? You seem to be getting around well."

Margie tells me all about her therapy and the lovely nurse who stops by to make sure she's showered. The agency installed a couple of grab rails in her shower and toilet to make them safer, and I'm pleased with the attention the health workers are giving to Margie's care. I'll need to pay them a personal bonus.

Of course, Margie and Kate think the hospital organized the home visits, and I'm hoping to keep it that way. We finish our tea and I head back to Kate's place to find her sitting at her small dining room table, working on her dated laptop.

She says I work too hard, but she puts in a lot of additional time outside of school hours to provide the students in her class with every possible opportunity. Stepping behind her, I lean down and tug her braid to the side so I can kiss her neck. Then I gently pull her hair back further to raise her face toward mine. Leaning forward, I kiss her lips. "Come on. It's time to get ready to visit your kids."

THIRTY-ONE

-kate-

I'M NERVOUS *AND* EXCITED TO INTRODUCE OLIVER TO ROMAN AND THE kids. I didn't give them any warning that he was visiting today. I wasn't certain if he would be interested in coming along, and I didn't want to disappoint them. They don't need any more disappointment in their lives. When he readily accepted my invitation, happiness burst like lightning, which was hard to contain.

Roman opens the door with his usual smile, his arms open wide in readiness for a hug, and I step in as I normally do to receive one of his enormous bear hugs. Roman's a big guy, making his hugs all-encompassing. Oliver grumbles behind me, and when I turn around, I'm surprised to see the possessive way he's watching our exchange. The kids come out from wherever they've been to greet me, stopping dead in their tracks when they see I have company.

I pull away from Roman, stepping back to grasp Oliver's hand. "Everyone, this is Oliver. My boyfriend." It feels unreal to introduce him as *my boyfriend*. "Oliver, this is Roman, Pete, Evelyn, Ivy, Blake, Jack, and Sammy." I gesture to each person as I introduce them.

Oliver steps forward, shaking Roman's hand, and waving to the kids. "Hey everyone. Thanks for letting me crash your big night in."

He receives a series of "no worries, man" and "no problem" as we step further into the home. It's been two weeks since I've seen the kids, so our catch-up is energetic, to put it mildly. We traipse into the back-yard to shoot hoops while the kids update me on school and friends. Oliver's great with them, joining the game, making it four on four—girls versus boys. A whole heap of smack talk is going down at the moment, and Blake constantly postures into Oliver's space. The girls grow bored shooting hoops, so we move inside to paint our nails and do fancy braids in our hair.

The girls giggle like crazy as we settle down for mini-makeovers, but Ivy's the first one brave enough to ask about Oliver. "So … what does Oliver do for a living?"

I'm not surprised Ivy asks about his job because she's all about job security and earning buckets of money once she's able. Her dream is to become the CEO of a Fortune 500 company. With the way she reads everything she can get her hands on, and her negotiation skills with the other kids in the house, I'm positive she'll fulfill her dream.

"He works in corporate investments. Probably an industry that would interest you. He drives a pretty nice car and lives in an apartment in the city. I would guess the job pays reasonably well." I wink at her.

"Do you think he would let me follow him around for work experience?" she asks excitedly.

I don't know too many eleven-year-old girls already planning out their work experience. "I'm pretty sure he would. You might have to wait until you're a little older, though."

She claps her hands together excitedly, racing to her room to get her journal, which is full of tips and secrets for business success.

"Are you going to marry him?" Evelyn questions. She always shows all her feelings clearly, and her expression is one of concern.

"I don't know. We haven't been dating all that long. Why do you look worried?" I rub my hand up and down her back in soothing strokes.

She glances at the other girls. "If you marry him, you'll probably stop coming here, and you'll have babies, and you won't want to spend time with us anymore."

The other girls nod their agreement, and I'm shocked they're thinking that far ahead. Pulling them all in for a group hug, I comfort them. "My life may change, but I will always make sure I am in each of your lives forever. You can't get rid of me that easily, no matter where my life takes me, or your life takes you. You can always count on me. I promise."

The girls seem satisfied with my answer for now and relax. We finish our mini-makeovers, making general chit-chat about favorite nail colors and hairstyles. We hear the boys stomping in through the back door and know our girl time is about to come to an abrupt end.

Oliver herds the boys through to the bathroom to wash up before touching anything food-related. He winks at me as he passes, making my heart melt. He's come a long way from the guy complaining about interruptions to his work life. Roman, Oliver, and I settle the kids with an afternoon snack, a brownie slice they made after dinner last night, and glasses of milk. Blake situates himself between me and Oliver at the table, and I look over his head to find him attempting to hold back a laugh.

We decide to take the kids to the local park before getting ready for dinner, so we head down the street. Blake hangs back, being very obvious in his attempt to keep Oliver and me separated as we bring up the rear. All afternoon and evening, through afternoon tea, the park, dinner, and games, Blake is like our very own personal wedge.

As we're leaving, everyone cheerfully says their goodbyes to both of us, with wishes for a great week. Everyone except Blake, who's worn a constant frown today. Midway down the path at the front of the house, Oliver pulls me to a stop.

"You know, Blake has the biggest crush on you. He was posturing up to me the entire time we were playing basketball, and I felt as though I was being interrogated by him all afternoon." He laughs, tugging me forward, and plants a gentle kiss against my forehead. I feel his smile as his warm lips press against my skin. He seems carefree. I think spending time with the kids was good for him. I know I always feel great after being in their company.

"I don't think so. He's only watching out for me—he often takes on that role with the other kids. He's making sure you're good enough to date me." I poke my tongue out at him. "Evelyn was worried we'd get married and have babies. The girls were worried I wouldn't want to spend time with them anymore." I shrug.

I probably shouldn't have told him that. He'll think I've been thinking about marriage and babies with him.

Which I have.

Sort of.

But he doesn't need to know that, *yet*.

"Well, she's right about the marriage and babies part."

Whaaat?

My world screeches to a stop, but he keeps right on talking nonchalantly as if what he said wasn't a big deal. "But I know for certain you would never abandon those kids. I'm sure you'll always be a part of their lives in some capacity."

"You're right. I won't ever abandon them. What they fail to consider is that they'll move on with a new family and leave me behind." I'm emotional thinking about losing one of my kids. I need to shake it off, and quickly. "Did Ivy talk to you? She was fangirling over you something fierce when we were doing our nails and hair."

"Yeah, she did. She has a lot of passion tucked away in that little body of hers." He huffs out a laugh. "She asked if she could shadow me for a day. I said I'd tee it up over school vacation, so it didn't interfere with her classwork."

I hug him close in gratitude. "Do you think your boss would mind?"

Oliver stalls for a second, as though he's searching for the right answer. "He won't mind. I know for sure he'd be happy to support and encourage the next generation of entrepreneurs."

"You know, she's only eleven. She can wait to see what you do at work. It doesn't need to happen anytime soon. Thank you though. Her dream is to become the CEO of a Fortune 500 company."

"Yeah, she mentioned that. I think with her tenacity she should be able to make her dream come true. Never know, she may come to work with me one day."

THIRTY-TWO

-kate-

WE'RE BARELY IN THE DOOR WHEN OLIVER TUGS ME AROUND TO FACE him. Sliding his hand under the hair at my nape, he tilts my face up toward his, then whispers against my lips, "Need you."

He takes my mouth in a ferocious kiss, and I readily part my lips to accept his tongue, which strokes and dances with mine. Sharing the same air, in and out, his kiss makes the world around us fall away. He wraps my legs around his slim hips, his hands cupping my ass, as he strides with purpose toward my bedroom.

"I need to be inside you. It was murder spending all that time with you, yet being unable to touch you." He tosses me onto my bed, following to land on top of me. I can't help but giggle at the savage need on his face, and how much he seems to have struggled throughout the afternoon and evening. "What's funny?"

"Nothing. You're acting like a caveman."

"I'll show you how I can act like a caveman the next time you let some other man put his hands on you."

He must recognize the confusion painted on my face.

"Roman." He huffs, his eyebrows nearly reaching his hairline. I still don't get what the problem is. Roman's a forty-five-year-old man who acts more like a favorite uncle than anything else. "He hugged you a little enthusiastically when we arrived this afternoon. I don't like seeing you in another man's arms."

Whaaat? "You can't be serious."

"Deadly."

I need to be on a more even level with him lording over me, so I push to sit up but he keeps me pinned to the bed.

"He's like my favorite uncle. You can't possibly think anything more than that is happening. He's nearly twenty years older than me." I shake my head. "That's just ... ewww!" A shiver runs through me at the thought of anything even remotely romantic happening with Roman.

I mean, he's a sweet man and I've often wondered why he's still single because, I guess, for forty-five, he's good-looking. But no, just no! Actually, now I think about it, I wonder if Emma would like Roman. Now, that's something to think about.

"I can see your brain ticking over. What are you planning, Sunshine?"

"I was just thinking I should introduce Roman to Emma. She's thirty-seven. Do you think Roman's too old for her?"

He leans forward, kissing me with a smile on his lips, shaking his head slightly. "How about you let them work out their own love life, and we'll concentrate on ours? Hmmm?" He rubs his nose across mine, then takes my mouth in a full-on assault, leaving my mind blank of everything except him.

Slowly, both sets of clothes are removed, leaving us gloriously naked. Feeling his warm skin against mine is heaven. His fine dusting of chest hair tickles against my rigid nipples, while his hard dick rubs teasingly against my pubic bone. He turns me on like nothing I've ever experienced. I'm already wet, my sex soft, ready to take him.

He leisurely lowers his hips to line his dick up with my entrance, and at an excruciatingly slow pace, enters me with short, shallow thrusts, gradually increasing in depth and power.

He knows how to bring me the maximum amount of pleasure.

I roam the expanse of his back with my hands, reveling in the feel of his strength and power, and press the heels of my feet into his tight ass, urging him impossibly deeper. He takes the hint, picking up the pace, and our groans and panting breaths fill the space around us.

"I love your pussy," he breathes into my ear. Nipping my lobe, he moves lower to press open-mouthed kisses to my throat.

"I love your dick." My walls tighten, ready to explode, letting him know I'm close. We both groan as I erupt, detonating his own orgasm, and we fly into bliss together.

Groaning.

Grinding.

Grasping.

Kissing.

"Do you think sex between us will always get better? Each time we come together, it's better than the time before." I sigh as he keeps his lower half joined to me, sliding in and out lazily.

Rising on his forearms, his hands cocoon the top of my head, while his thumbs soothingly brush my hair away from my face. He looks deep into my eyes, as though he's attempting to see all the way to my soul.

"I don't know, but I'm willing to test the theory." He wiggles his eyebrows up and down. "Give me a minute, and I'll be ready to go again. Purely for research purposes, of course."

"Of course." I can't help but giggle at this fun side of him. He groans, thrusting gently to remind me he's still inside; as if I'd ever need to be reminded. He carefully slides out and grabs a warm cloth to clean up the evidence of our coupling.

Snuggling into his arms after another round of breathtaking love-making, I'm sated and know I'm safe and loved. Even though we haven't said the words, our bodies make it abundantly clear what's happening between us. I've never felt this cherished or important in a man's life before.

I want so much more with him.

I want *everything*, and I'm starting to believe he wants the same with me.

THIRTY-THREE

-kate-

TOMORROW IS THE LAST DAY OF SCHOOL BEFORE CHRISTMAS BREAK, SO I plan to spend my evening wrapping Christmas gifts. That way, I can give Emma and her boys their gifts tomorrow, and Oliver isn't here to see what I bought for him. My body naturally moves to the upbeat Christmas music I'm playing through my Bluetooth speaker as I cut paper to size, fold, and tape. Applying bows and name tags, I get lost in my head, thinking about my sexy times with my hot boyfriend.

He certainly knows how to please a woman in all ways.

My favorite has to be the wall sex, though. Just thinking about it makes my lady parts clench.

I had given him a key because some nights he's late coming home from work, and I'd just stepped out of my bathroom with a towel wrapped around my hair and another around my body when he walked in.

He took one look at me and I could see his eyes darken—his intent written all over his impressive face and body. He stalked over to me, undid my towel, dropped to his knees, situated one of my legs over his shoulder, and kissed, sucked, licked, and nipped at me as though he hadn't seen me for days.

I've never experienced anything like his mouth on me before. I never knew oral could feel as sensational as it does with him. My previous boyfriends seemed to do it out of some form of obligation or something equally stupid. They certainly never enjoyed it the way Oliver does. He makes it seem as if he could do it all day.

His talented mouth worked over my sensitive lips and clit while his fingers leisurely pumped in and out of my channel. I held onto his head for dear life because it was difficult to remain standing with such an onslaught of attention.

As I came down from my orgasm, he dropped his pants, picked me up, pressed my back against the wall, and thrust his engorged dick inside me. I've noticed he has this habit once he's inside me; he pauses for a bit, studying my face closely before moving. Almost as though he wants to make sure I'm genuinely on board for what's about to happen. He pounded me so wildly, I was worried I was going to break through the drywall, but at the time I didn't care. He felt beyond amazing.

When he's inside me, he's one hundred percent focused on me and my pleasure. He says his pleasure and enjoyment come from seeing me satisfied and falling into an orgasm-induced coma. Ha! Pretty sure I've had several of those over the past few weeks.

I don't think we spoke until we'd both calmed somewhat and caught our breath. With a genuine smile, he said, "Hey."

I could only respond in like, snuggling my face into his neck as he carried me into the bathroom so we could both wash off.

I finish my task, then check my email, finding a new message from Ella and Bob asking me if I'd like to meet. They're going to start a new project and would like to discuss the possibility of working with me.

Oh my gosh!

That's a no-brainer for me; I adored working with them. I learned an enormous amount, and it was a fantastic feeling knowing I was helping the local teachers develop their elementary education program. It was truly an honor, as well as a humbling experience.

We take a lot for granted here. Resources and support for our schools are plentiful when compared to the schools Ella and Bob are establishing in remote communities. I might check in with Oliver to ask if he would be interested in helping on the new project since he was involved previously.

I respond to their email, telling them I'm definitely interested, and when I'm available to catch up for a coffee and chat. Christmas break starts tomorrow, so I have some time on my hands. I'll spend some of the time planning my program, as well as spending extra time with my favorite kids.

Today was crazy hectic. As expected, the kids were extremely excited about Christmas, so they were a bit wild. I didn't mind their excitement; in fact, I found their excitement fed mine.

This is my last opportunity to see the kids before Christmas, so I'm heading over tonight instead of tomorrow because Roman's organized a special Christmas outing with kids from other homes. I dress in my black skinny jeans, a pink sweater, and my brand spanking new red Converse. Gathering my gifts for them, I leave a light on for later and make my way over to Lloyd Avenue.

When I arrive at the house, I bounce up the steps, wondering what they'll want to do tonight. Even though I could walk straight in, I treat this as their home, making sure I show the same respect I would when visiting anyone I know, so I always knock on the door.

Knock. Knock. Knock.

Then I wait.

I'm a little surprised nobody has answered the door, so I knock again, then try the door handle.

It's locked.

I guess it's not unusual, but it *is* unusual for nobody to be home when Roman was expecting me, even though the kids have no idea I'm visiting tonight instead of tomorrow.

Walking around the outside of the house, I attempt to look in the windows, but all the blinds and curtains are closed. Now that *is* unusual in a house full of kids with only one adult. I walk back around to the front and sit on the step, wondering where they may have gone.

Maybe they went to the park a couple of blocks away.

I stride toward it, hoping to find my crew. When I get to the entrance, I look around, but can't see anyone familiar to me.

I guess they're not at the park.

I'm confused because Roman *knew* I was coming this afternoon—after all, it *was* his idea. Pulling out my phone, I shoot Roman a text.

ME

Hey, I'm out front

Where are you guys?

I sit, waiting for a response, but nothing is forthcoming. I wonder how long I should wait around? It won't be long before it's dark, and I'm not sure what to do. As I climb to my feet to head home, my phone chimes with an alert.

ROMAN

Hey, busy atm

Can I call you in 20?

ME

Sure

Hope everything's okay

Maybe I should wait here until I speak with him. I don't want to drive all the way home, only to have to turn around and come back again. Decision made, I wander around the back and make myself comfortable. While I wait for his call, I'll read the book I have on my phone.

I'm getting to a raunchy part of the book when my phone rings, and I quickly accept the call. "Hey, Roman. Did you forget I was coming over today?"

"Hey. Sorry. No, I didn't forget, but something's happened which was out of my control." He sounds frantic; unlike the Roman I know and love. "I don't know how to break the news to you."

"Are the kids alright? Nobody's hurt?"

Panic hits, and my heart beats hard against my ribs. *Why didn't I think that something could be wrong?* Climbing to my feet, I pace across the back porch, wrapping my free arm across my stomach, as if I can protect myself against anything awful he might say.

"Ah, no. The kids are okay. Nobody's hurt. It's nothing like that," he rushes to reassure me.

"Then what's happened? Why aren't you guys here?" I question because I still get the sense something's seriously wrong.

"We were shut down. Early this afternoon, I received a call telling me to pack the kids up and bring them to the main center in the city."

I can't believe what I'm hearing. "Whaaat? What do you mean ... shut down? I don't understand. How can they shut down like that? How could they kick the kids out of their home this close to Christmas with no warning?"

The shock of the news is making it difficult to breathe. I don't understand what's happened and why. *Who would do such a drastic and invasive thing to these kids?* They've already had enough turmoil.

"I don't know all the details yet. I'm probably not supposed to tell you anything because you're a volunteer. They've shut down the fifteen homes spread throughout the city and brought everyone into the central facility. I don't know any more than that. I'm sorry I forgot to let you know we wouldn't be home when you arrived. I got caught up packing, moving, and settling the kids."

He's unnecessarily apologetic when my feelings are the least of anyone's concern.

I pause my pacing and peer into the backyard, full of many wonderful memories with the kids. "Please don't apologize to me, Roman. Your focus should always be on the kids, exactly where it's been today. How are they?"

He sighs tiredly. "Oh, you know what they're like. Their walls went straight back up, and they closed themselves off from the disappointment. Pete's using humor to get through, which is driving Sammy up the wall because she wants everyone to take things seriously. Evelyn's tearful, and Ivy's stuck close by to support her. Jack and Blake have been super quiet, keeping to themselves."

I can picture him shoving his hands through his messy hair as he talks. None of this will sit well with him.

"Do you think this is permanent? Will I be able to see them?" My gifts seem petty now, but I still want to give them to the kids.

"I don't know anything more at this point. I'll try to keep you in the loop if I can. I'm sorry." He sounds knocked down and defeated. Tired.

"No, that's okay. I understand. You focus on the kids. Tell them I love them and I'm still around. Okay? Maybe if you find out more, you can let me know?"

"I will. Take care of yourself."

"You, too. Bye."

He disconnects the call, leaving me feeling unsteady and lost. I sit on the steps in a daze. I don't know what to think, or what to do with myself.

I'm unsure how long I sat, but a chill has reached into my bones and it's completely dark, so I make my way home.

———

Once home, I make a warm drink and sit on my couch, contemplating what I can do to help.

I check my emails for something to do, finding a reply from Bob and Ella. Our schedules don't align for another six weeks, so it will be a while before we can discuss their plans. I pick up my book, but my mind won't switch off and I'm unable to concentrate on the sexy times I'm attempting to read. Turning on the television, I watch my favorite comedy talk show. The host is a bundle of fun. Hopefully, she'll break me out of my gray mood.

I must doze off at some point because I wake to my phone ringing. Before I answer, I notice it's Oliver, so I quickly accept the call. "Hey."

Even before I hear his voice, the tension in my muscles dissipates, knowing he's on the other end of the phone. He was the first person I wanted to talk to about the kids this afternoon. It's scary how much I've come to depend on him—especially since I swore I wouldn't depend on another man.

"Hey, Kate."

I lift the phone away from my ear in confusion, because it's definitely not Oliver on the phone, even though it says it's him.

My heart races and my hands grow sweaty. "Who is this, please? Where's Oliver? Is he okay? Please tell me he's okay!" I stand and pace my living room. I don't think I can handle any more bad news today.

"Hey, calm down. It's me, Jase. Oliver's okay. He asked me to let you know he won't be able to make it to your place tonight."

"Oh." My disappointment is palpable, and I'm suddenly exhausted. "Is everything okay?"

"Sort of. Everything with Oliver is okay. He's been called in to help sort out a work-related issue and it'll probably be an all-nighter."

"Really? The boss expects an awful lot from him. He gives up an enormous amount of his personal life for his job." A long silence draws out on the other end of the phone, so I check if the call has been disconnected. "Jase, are you still there?"

He clears his throat. "Yeah, I'm still here. You're right, the boss does expect a lot from his employees, but he *is* fair. This is a temporary crisis and once it's sorted out, things will return to normal. How about I send you my number? That way, if you ever need anything and can't get ahold of Oliver, you can call me."

"Oh, thanks, Jase. That would be great. Maybe text it through to me and I'll add you to my contacts list." I guess that's it then. It's a little disconcerting that Oliver couldn't call me himself, but I guess he's busy. "Bye, Jase. Thanks for calling me. Maybe I'll see you soon?"

"Sure thing. Take care. See you soon."

He disconnects the call, and within a few seconds I receive a text with his contact details. As I save it to my contacts, I think this information may be handy if I ever want to surprise Oliver since they work together.

I've had a lousy evening. I've missed out on seeing the kids, and now I've missed out on seeing Oliver.

I stop, taking a minute to remind myself that it wasn't my home taken away from me today, and it's not me who has to work all night to sort out some type of crisis at work. Perhaps I'll have a glass of wine and read my book while soaking in the tub before going to bed. Maybe tomorrow will bring some positive news.

THIRTY-FOUR

-oliver-

"WHAT DO YOU MEAN, THE MONEY'S FUCKING GONE?" I SHOUT INTO the phone at Marcus, the CEO of *The Parkerville Project*. I can't believe what I'm fucking hearing.

"We received a call from the bank early this morning, informing us they were foreclosing on our properties. The only one we can use is our central facility in the city because we own that building outright. That was the initial purchase for the organization, courtesy of you. It's the only building we have left." Marcus patiently explains to me, clearly as exasperated as I am. He's the only person within *The Parkerville Project* I have contact with. I like it kept on the down-low that I'm a major contributor. That's why Roman didn't know who I was when we met.

"Where did the money go? It can't have fucking disappeared. I gave you a check for two million dollars last quarter."

I stand to pace along my floor-to-ceiling windowed wall that over-looks downtown.

"We're going to have to engage a financial investigator to find out what happened. I'm sorry I don't have more information. I don't understand what happened." He sounds as exasperated as I feel.

"Send all the financials to my office. I'll see if I can track the money. I'll need access to everything associated with *The Parkerville Project* financials. I'll expect to receive them within the next thirty minutes. If I can't find the trail, then we'll get a financial investigator in to do what needs to be done."

I disconnect the call, expecting my request to be followed since I'm the major financial contributor to the organization, and buzz Jase into my office.

Jase strolls in as if I have all fucking day. "'Sup, boss?"

"Cancel everything on my calendar for the next two days, starting from now."

He looks gobsmacked. I *never* cancel anything. *Ever.* "But you have that follow-up meeting with the Vegas investor—"

I cut him off with a slash of my arm and a stern look. "That's going to have to wait. I just got off the phone with Marcus from *The Parkerville Project.* He informed me the bank has foreclosed on most of their properties because all the money has fucking disappeared."

"What the fuck?!"

"Exactly my sentiments. I've asked him to send me all of their financials. I'll work on following the trail to figure out what's happened to the money." I shove my hand through my hair. I'm overwhelmed by the task ahead of me, but I won't ever show that to anyone—not even Jase.

"Sure thing. I'll get right on rescheduling everything for you. I'll order lunch in and clear the schedules of our team leaders—they can help you work through everything." He turns around as he reaches the door. "I'll help in any way I can. Those kids need those homes to feel safe and secure."

I fucking *know* that. That's exactly why I'm prepared to put my business on hold.

———

Forty minutes later, I sit at my desk looking at piles upon piles of files and folders, attempting to work out the best approach for tackling the problem at hand. I think the best approach is to start at the most recent documents and work my way backward.

I've probably been going strong for about an hour when Jase walks in with our lunch, making himself comfortable on the other side of my desk.

He surveys the mess on my desk, sideboard, and floor. "You're going to need more than two days to go through all of this, even with the help of our team leaders and me."

He passes my lunch over, unwrapping his sub while I do the same. "I'll pull an all-nighter tonight and work across the entire weekend if I need to. Can you contact Kate on my phone? Let her know something important has come up, and I won't be able to make it tonight. If I talk with her, I'll cave and go home. I need to invest the time to sort out this issue as quickly as possible for the kids."

Don't think I didn't notice I referred to Kate's place as *home*. I've felt that way for a while now. The feeling only became stronger when she gave me a key, enabling me to come and go as I please.

Lunch passes quickly, and I'm back sifting through the piles of documentation on my desk and scattered throughout my office. My team leaders arrive to help sort through, and hopefully find a trail that will explain what's happened. We work solidly, unaware of time passing. When I glance at the clock, I'm shocked to see it's after nine.

I call over, "Hey, Jase, did you contact Kate?"

"Oh shit, sorry. I'll do it right now."

I feel like shit for blowing her off, but she has a powerful hold over me. If I make contact, I'll get distracted, and I can't afford to lose focus at this point.

I listen to Jase on the phone with Kate. He looks at me, giving me the evil eye, then responds to whatever she said and offers his phone number to her.

What the fuck?

That's completely unnecessary. I'll only be out of contact tonight and maybe the rest of the weekend. No need to fill my shoes yet! He texts his information to her and hands my phone back.

"What the fuck, man?" His expression is livid. "You still haven't told her who you really are? That poor woman thinks that *your boss expects a lot from you*. When are you going to tell her that you *are* the fucking boss?"

He's pissed, and with good reason. He's been on my case for the last several weeks to be honest with her.

I'm not fucking ready.

I *know* she won't respond well, and I'm terrified I'm going to lose the best thing that's ever happened to me.

I *need* her to be fully invested in our relationship.

I *need* her to be as attached to me as I am to her—so she won't leave me when she finds out who I am.

I've never lied to her. She knows my real name; she knows I work in corporate investments; she knows I live in the city, near work; she knows I earn more money than she does; she knows the *real* me, behind the corporate persona.

I remind myself she could search for me online or her brother could tell her who I am *before* I get the chance—which would be disastrous.

"I haven't found the right time to tell her. When she finds out who I am and how much money I'm actually worth; she'll run for the hills. I can't afford to lose her, Jase. It would ruin me. More than any financial loss ever would."

I know I've shown Jase my vulnerable underbelly, and he could easily use the information against me, but all I see in his eyes is compassion and understanding. He knows she's as down to earth as they come and has the biggest heart and kindest nature. He knows the impact she's had on me since she came into my life.

"Look, man, I know you're worried. But the longer you take to tell her, the worse her response will be."

He pats me on the shoulder, leaving my office to organize dinner for us, while I slump down in my chair, feeling like shit.

———

It's been more than three fucking days since I've seen or spoken with Kate, and I'm like a junkie having withdrawals. I've made no direct contact with her. I can't bring myself to speak with her because I miss her so fucking much that I ache. I was worried that if I heard her voice, I'd break and go to her.

I've barely slept, only an hour or two here and there on the couch in my office, before showering and returning to my desk. It'll all be worth it because I found the trail of missing money. My missing money, since I fund ninety percent of the organization.

For me, it's been fucking personal!

Someone's gradually siphoned the money off into offshore accounts over the past few years. The trail shows money going into several different accounts held in different names, each to a value of less than $10,000; meaning an FBAR report didn't need to be supplied to the IRS. It would have taken a great deal of know-how and time to set the system up and to fly under the radar for as long as they have. Now we need to work out the *who*—though I have my suspicions.

I've spoken with Marcus about bringing in a financial investigator to solidify our case, and he's on board. Mike, the PI I used to find Kate, gave me his recommendation, so I've set up a meeting with him and Marcus for tomorrow morning—Christmas Eve. Marcus also wants to hold a meeting for all interested parties, allowing us to report what we've discovered thus far and our next steps moving forward to stabilize the company. I've readily agreed that people need to be kept informed, but I don't want to spook the perpetrator just yet. To allow us some additional time, the meeting will be held at the end of next week in my offices here at Stone Tower.

I'm beyond shattered, but wild horses couldn't keep me away from Kate any longer. I need to see her, smell her, touch her, and feel her body wrapped in my arms.

Shutting down everything in my office, I lock the door to keep any sensitive information safe, driving straight to Kate's place without stopping.

THIRTY-FIVE

-kate-

MARGIE AND I ARE BUNDLED UP IN OUR WARMEST COATS AS WE SIT ON her front porch. I sit on the step and Margie sits on a chair, enjoying a cup of tea while she updates me on the shenanigans in our street. It's Christmas Eve and I haven't seen or heard a peep from Oliver since Friday morning when he woke me with delicate kisses along my neck and shoulder before he left for the office.

"Did you see Pete and Joe going at it yesterday afternoon?" Margie asks with a giggle. "I swear, I don't need a TV with those two living down the street."

I giggle as well. "Yeah, I can't believe Joe cut the branch off Pete's tree like that. Just because the leaves fell onto his driveway this last fall." I look over at the poor, butchered tree. "As if the leaves on the rest of the tree won't fall and blow over the fence."

"Right! The leaves that fell on his driveway didn't only come from the branch growing over his side of the fence." She laughs extra hard, causing tears to escape her eyes from the force.

"I'm not sure if they would survive if one of them moved from the street. I think they keep each other going with their antics."

"True, very true." Margie's expression turns thoughtful. "So, I haven't seen young Oliver's car in your driveway for the past couple of days. Everything going okay?"

My mood sinks, and I shrug. "I guess so. There's been a big drama at work he's needed to sort out, so he's been radio silent. I've only heard through Jase, a guy who works with him, that he couldn't leave work to come to see me." I smile weakly. "I've missed him beyond what

I thought was possible, Margie. If I'm honest, the depth and strength of my feelings toward him scares the living daylights outta me."

She pats my arm. "Ah, that's the sign of a strong bond, Katie-girl. Only the best stuff is experienced at an intense level, which is scary. That's the stuff worth holding on to." She nods down the street. "Speak of the devil. I believe this is him roaring down our street now."

I turn my head in the same direction as Margie, and sure enough, Oliver's car is slowing down to enter my driveway. As soon as he has his car in park, the engine cuts, and he opens the door. His long strides bring him directly in front of me within seconds.

He picks me up bridal-style, then turns to Margie. "Hi, Margie. Sorry, but I need to steal my girl away. Hope you don't mind."

Even though he's speaking to Margie, he looks at me with that fierceness I've come to expect from him. Dark smudges stain the skin beneath his eyes, and his usual short, tidy scruff is unruly.

Margie waves us off with a slash of her arm. "Oh, pish posh. Don't let me stop you from having your sexy times. Have fun."

She winks at us as she rises to move inside. Oliver carries me inside, kicks the door closed, and orders me to lock it.

"Hey," he whispers as he runs his nose up my neck to my ear, then pulls back to peer into my eyes.

"Hey." I'm at a loss for words. I've missed him terribly, but I don't want to sound like a needy child who can't let her boyfriend get on with his job.

He blows out a long breath, and his shoulders drop into a more relaxed position. "I've missed you."

Oh wow. Tingles buzz across my skin, and my stomach fills with butterflies.

Blowing out a long breath, I study his eyes full of sincerity and release the tension from my muscles. "I've missed you so much. I didn't realize how accustomed I'd become to seeing you every day."

We both lean forward at the same time to meet in a gentle kiss filled with heavy sighs and palpable relief. The kiss quickly amps up in a way I never dreamed possible before him.

I've fallen in love with him.

The realization hits me with the force of a ten-ton truck, and I pull him in tighter to me as he carries me to my bedroom. Sitting on the edge of my bed, he gently pulls away from our kiss. I miss him immediately, and lean forward to follow his lips, which garners a smile from him.

"As much as I want to be inside you right now, I owe you an apology first." I try to interrupt, but he presses his finger over my lips, shaking his head. "No, I do. I wanted to call you many times, but I knew if I heard your voice or even read a message from you I would get too distracted from the urgent work that needed to be done. People, good people, were relying on me to solve the problem as quickly as possible, and I couldn't let them down."

"Your work ethic knows no bounds. I won't say it didn't matter, but your radio silence hurt me. I understand your work is important. It sounds like whatever happened was pretty major, but I didn't like feeling that I wasn't important enough for you to take five minutes to check in with me. It made me feel small. Perhaps I'm more invested in this relationship than you are? But then you're here, explaining why you couldn't communicate, and I feel like such a selfish ass." I hadn't realized I felt that way, but the words purged out of me in a rush. I tug him close, pressing my forehead against his. "Maybe we could find some middle ground?"

"I'm sorry. I truly am. My intention was never to make you feel small, or that I'm not invested in this relationship. I'm an ass. I'm not making excuses, but I'm used to focusing on my work and *only* on my work. Our relationship is relatively new and I forget I need to consider my partner. I was too busy focusing on how *I* felt and didn't consider how *you* would feel. For a long time, I haven't had to answer to anyone. I hope you can forgive me. I promise to do better next time."

He kisses the tip of my nose and presses his forehead to mine.

"I can understand when something important needs to be accomplished. I would appreciate better communication next time, though. It would have only taken you a couple of minutes to make contact. I would have understood that you needed to work. I would never try to take you away from your job because I know how important it is to you." I kiss the tip of his nose. "I missed you more than I thought was possible, and I was worried about you."

His expression is incredulous. He's clearly not used to having someone worry about or show concern for him. Every time I've shown my care and concern for him, it's as if he's never experienced it before.

"I truly am sorry. Having someone who worries about me is unfamiliar territory. It won't happen again."

I nod my acknowledgment. "I'm prepared to let it go this time, but if it happens again, I won't be so forgiving."

He leans forward, capturing my lips roughly, while his hands reacquaint themselves with me. "I could do with a shower. Come with me."

He picks me up as though I weigh nothing, carrying me toward the bathroom. Sitting me on the vanity, he turns toward the shower to start the water, winking at me over his shoulder while adjusting the temperature.

Oh yeah, shower sex. That's my second favorite, after wall sex with him.

We both undress, stepping under the warm water together. He grabs my jasmine soap to wash me. He always looks after me, but I take it out of his hands, soaping up his big body with care—it's my turn to look after him for a change. I want to wash him and show him some TLC because he looks exhausted.

Being in the shower together is a tight squeeze because of his size, but we've made it work before. It means our bodies *accidentally* rub against each other—*what a shame!* Touching his chiseled body is such a decadent experience, and I cherish the privilege every time I get to put my hands on him.

It should be a criminal offense for any one man to be this utterly perfect. From his classically handsome face to his strong, broad shoulders, down his chiseled torso, to that notable V which leads to an impressive dick, by any standards, resting between two strong and powerful thighs.

A sudden feeling of gratitude overwhelms me as I recognize the intimacy of experiencing this with Oliver; that I'm the woman who gets to *see* and *feel* him like this. As I glance up, the green I love so much is disappearing as his pupils dilate. His breathing is choppy, his nipples pebbled, and his engorged dick is rising to prepare for action.

He takes the cloth out of my hand, drops it to the floor, and twists his body under the water to rinse off, then he comes for me with delicious intent written all over his face and in his taut body. His vibe is aggressive, yet his touches are gentle and delicate on my breasts until my nipples peak to his liking. Bending down, he sucks one into his warm mouth, drawing a sigh from me. Even though I'm wet from the shower, the warm wetness of his mouth is sublime, as he moves between both breasts to give them equal attention. My satisfaction is impossible to suppress and a moan escapes. He presses his fully erect dick against my lower abdomen, showing me what my response does to him.

"I love your tits. One day, I'm going to fuck them and paint them with my cum," he growls, then presses my back against the cold tile.

The difference between the front and back of my body is significant, adding to the sensations he's endowing on me as he presses my boobs together, kissing them gently and rubbing his beard across both globes. All I can do is moan at the thought of him sliding his big dick between them. The guy is incredibly sexy, and his dirty mouth adds a level of heat to our sex I never anticipated I would enjoy as much as I do.

He grabs my ass in both hands, lifting me easily. As I wrap my legs around his slim hips, he lines up his dick, drawing me down in one powerful thrust. He groans while all thought escapes me. My breath pushes out of my lungs, and my eyes close in bliss. He fits me perfectly, touching all the parts inside I wasn't aware of before.

As is his usual MO, he pauses, fully seated inside me. He intently studies my face; tracing my eyes, my lips, and a general all-round check-in that I'm with him. I take his bottom lip in a small bite, followed by a gentle kiss, but as usual he takes over, devouring my mouth.

We kiss tenderly, tasting, breathing each other's breaths, then he begins to move inside me. He pulls his body away slightly, allowing us the space to watch his dick moving in and out of me in smooth, precise glides—so hot! I'm on fire; the sensations inside me seem to be growing and expanding exponentially. For a spell, I worry the feelings are too big and the resulting explosion may tear me apart.

"Harder. Harder, please," I moan out. I'm almost there. "Keep hitting that spot. Yeah, that one right there!"

His warm breaths coat the side of my face, and the feel of his muscles shifting and flexing under my hold increases my lust. My breasts press against his slick chest, and I swear our hearts beat a matching tattoo.

"Come for me. Give it to me," he whispers in my ear, nipping the lobe.

It's then that I break.

My vision goes black for a second, and my breaths stall in my chest. For resplendent moments, I'm suspended in that extraordinary place outside of reality. My body spasms around his dick, holding him tight, as my arms hold him tight to me.

"Oh yeah. That's it, give it all to me!" he breathes between grunts, as his thrusts grow erratic. "Your pussy's strangling my cock … just the way I need it."

He falls apart; his dick pulsing and jetting out his cum into me. I don't know how he holds me up and remains standing at this point. Squeezing my pussy as tight as I can around his dick, I run my hands soothingly up and down his back in a gentle glide, calming his body through his orgasm.

He buries his face in the crook of my neck, blowing out a hot breath. "Fucking you is my favorite thing to do, behind being with you in any way that you allow me in your life."

Oh, my heart, he's too much with his sweet words. "Same for me, big guy. Same for me." I press delicate kisses across his shoulder.

We stay in each other's embrace until the water cools. He carefully slides out of me and we both groan at the immediate loss of intimate contact. Gradually, he slides me down his hard planes until my feet make contact with the floor, but he doesn't let go until he's sure I have steady legs. We quickly rinse off, then turn the water off and step out to dry off.

———

Sitting on the couch with a glass of wine, I listen to Oliver order Thai delivery for dinner. I feel deliciously stretched and worked over in the best possible way. Thinking about what he does to me makes me blush.

He breaks me out of my thoughts when he sits on the couch beside me. "It'll be about forty-five minutes. I ordered enough for Margie too, if you want to let her know."

I smile at his thoughtfulness. "Sure, I'll text her now."

After messaging Margie to invite her over for dinner, I put down my phone and turn toward my boyfriend. He rests his hand on my thigh, and I don't think he realizes the sensations he provokes with one simple touch.

"So, tell me what I've missed in your life over the last few days."

Where do I begin?

"To be honest, I've been feeling a bit numb. I had planned to surprise the kids on Friday afternoon, but when I arrived, nobody was home. When I finally got in touch with Roman, he told me the fifteen homes belonging to *The Parkerville Project* had been shut down. All the kids had to move into their central location in the city."

I don't even register I'm crying until he pulls me onto his lap and gently wipes my tears with his thumbs. "Kate," he murmurs harshly. "What did Roman say happened?"

THIRTY-SIX

-oliver-

IN MY SINGULAR DETERMINATION TO SORT OUT THE ISSUE FROM MY END, I didn't even consider how the news of the closures would affect Kate. It just goes to show, I'm not used to having to consider another person in my daily life. Maybe she would be better off if I stepped out of her life. She doesn't need someone as selfish as me messing her around.

I don't think I can give her up, though—proving exactly how fucking selfish I am.

She has the biggest, most generous heart, and she would have taken the closure and displacement of the kids quite hard. I'm not surprised she's emotional about it. I wish I could tell her of my involvement in the project, but that would expose who I am, along with my financial status.

I'm not ready.

See, fucking selfish!

She sucks in a shuddering breath. "Roman couldn't tell me much. Only that the homes were closed down and the kids had to move to their central location. That means they no longer have room to take in street kids or provide them a meal and a safe place to sleep. The repercussions are enormous and far-reaching for all the kids involved. My heart breaks for them." She blinks up at me. "Right at Christmas. What a crappy thing to happen at such a special time of the year."

Mmm, Roman shouldn't tell her anything because she isn't an employee. I can understand his loyalty to her, though. From my understanding, she's only one of a few people who regularly volunteer their time to the program. It's *almost* like she is an employee.

She looks up at me with teary eyes, breaking my heart. "Roman said he's not supposed to tell me anything because I'm not an employee, but he said he would try to keep me in the loop as much as possible. I don't know how I can help."

"I'm sure you could visit the kids," I say, brushing a loose lock of damp hair behind her ear.

"Roman suggested I wait a few days until the kids settle in. He'll let me know when he thinks they're ready. Luckily, I'm on vacation until the Monday after next."

There's a knock at the front door. I open it to find Margie holding onto her cane with a cheesy grin. She winks at me and steps inside.

"I have to say, I'm a little disappointed you two have finished already. I would have thought you'd have more stamina for a man your age." She giggles, patting me on the arm as she walks past me.

This woman is hilarious, and while I don't mind her cheeky comment, I know Kate will be mortified, so this should be fun.

Kate stands to embrace Margie with their usual affection. Margie pulls back, looking her dead in the face. "Well, that's a shame."

Kate narrows her eyes, tilting her head to the side.

"You can still walk. I anticipated you'd be limping, at the very least."

Understanding dawns on Kate, and that adorable blush of hers rises to take over her neck and face. I know exactly where that blush starts, and it has me thinking all kinds of inappropriate thoughts in mixed company.

"Oh, Margie, you have no filter at all." She covers her face with her hands to stem the giggle that's trying to escape but gives up the fight, and they both fall over each other in laughter.

I can't help but join them. We're interrupted by another knock at the door, which is hopefully dinner. Collecting my wallet, I answer the door—exchanging a wad of cash for our delicious-smelling meal. We all move into action, preparing the table, dishing out food, and getting drinks before sitting down to eat.

We chat while we eat. The ladies update me on the latest adventures of Pete and Joe—eliciting more giggles from them and a shake of my head from me.

"Did you tell him Bob and Ella invited you to help them set up another school?"

Kate looks at me. "Uh, no, I hadn't got that far yet."

The pride I have for her fills my whole body. She's brilliant in her chosen profession. Bob and Ella are very selective about who they invite to work with them on projects—only wanting the best of the best. Kate definitely fits the bill, especially after the exceptional work she did at the last school.

"Tell me all about it. Where's the next project?" I already know because my foundation is the largest financial contributor to the project, but I can't tell her that.

"Oh, well, it's going to be a while before we can meet to talk about it. I don't know any details yet. I'm sure they'll fill me in on everything when we meet in six weeks. At this stage, they wanted to know if I was interested in working with them on their next project." She sips her drink, then turns back to me. "Do you think you'll work on building the next school for Bob and Ella?"

I wasn't planning on it, but maybe I should. "I hadn't given the idea any thought, but I don't think I'd be opposed to it if it means not being separated from you."

She smiles at me as though I've shared the best news ever. Her entire face lights up, and it's an arresting sight.

"Oh, that sounds wonderful. You two working together to build and set up a new school."

I nod slowly, turning my attention to Margie.

"Did she tell you that's how we met?"

Margie holds her hand over her heart, shaking her head in the negative. "No, Katie-girl never got around to telling me how the two of you met."

I tell Margie about meeting Kate for the first time. How she was constantly in my thoughts for over a year before I hired a private investigator to track her down. I don't think I've ever shared that information with her, and she looks surprised, to say the least.

"Oh, I never knew that! You were constantly in my thoughts as well. I thought I'd built you up to be way better than you were."

I smile. Knowing she felt the same as I did fills me with hope that a future with Kate is within my reach. "The relief I felt when I saw you at the renovation project for the kids knocked me on my ass," I tell her honestly.

We're both lost in each other until Margie clears her throat. "That sounds like a fated meeting to me. Now I'm going to go home for the evening. Thank you both for dinner, and I'll see you two later."

We all stand—Kate hugs Margie goodbye, and I walk her next door. Before Margie steps inside, she presses up on her toes to peck my cheek. "You are very good for her. She looks happy and content now she's with you. Thank you."

She walks inside, locking her door before I can respond. I head back to Kate's, finding her cleaning up from dinner. We work together and finish up quickly so we can go to bed. I haven't finished showing her how much I missed her over the past few days.

———

Waking up with Kate on Christmas morning is the best gift I've ever received. Her warm, naked body pressed against mine in slumber, touching at every available point, fills me with gratitude that I found her. That she's now part of my life. Looking down at the top of her head resting on my chest, I gently smooth her wild curls away from her face—so I can admire her perfection. The dusting of freckles across her nose, which she tries to cover with makeup; her delicate auburn lashes, lying flush against her pale cheeks; and those tempting pink lips, slightly open in rest.

Her hand resting on my abdomen slowly comes to life, indicating my quiet appreciation time is coming to a close. She nuzzles in closer, then stretches out and slowly opens her eyes, exposing those guileless cobalt irises to me.

She tilts her face up to mine as a slow smile spreads across her lips. "Merry Christmas."

"Merry Christmas, Sunshine." I lean down to kiss the tip of her nose.

She rolls out of bed and sprints for the bathroom, spoiling my fun and dragging a chuckle out of me. She has a thing about brushing her teeth before she lets me kiss her in the morning. Sometimes I'm able to catch her off-guard, but most of the time she's too quick.

When she returns to my arms, she has mischief written all over her face. "Do you realize it's only been three months since we met for the second time?" she asks as she glances between my eyes and mouth. I lick my lips temptingly, striving to distract her from the conversation. I'd rather use my mouth for something other than talking. "It feels like I've known you forever. I want our first Christmas together to be super special." If only she knew that we *have* known each other forever—*sort of.*

She leans forward, initiating a kiss and boosting my Christmas gratitude into the stratosphere. Any time she makes the first move toward intimate contact, it's like I've won a prize. As often as I've taken her body, I always want more. Every time, I promise myself to let her take the lead next time, but I can't help myself. I inevitably end up taking control and this time is no different. Even though she started this time, I'll be the one to finish it.

———

After a shower and a light breakfast of waffles, we sit on the couch to exchange gifts. I made sure not to go overboard with gifts because I didn't want to make Kate uncomfortable. She always chastises me for spending money on her, so I held back. But one day, I'll be able to spoil her the way she deserves.

I bought her a pair of Jimmy Choo Gin flats, made to order in red —her favored shoe color. I figure they'll be comfortable for her to wear to work because she doesn't seem to wear heels very often.

"Oh my gosh, these are so pretty. Thank you." She quickly takes her woolly socks off to try on her new shoes. They fit her perfectly. She throws herself at me as if I've gifted her a new yacht, instead of a measly pair of shoes. Her genuine gratitude for the simple things is extraordinarily rare in my world.

Her second gift is probably more for me than for her. A sexy La Perla cranberry balconette bra—which is going to display her tits magnificently—and matching panties. I can't wait for her to put them on, so I can peel them off … with my teeth.

As she opens the box, the stunning blush I adore rises from her chest, covering her neck to her cheeks. *Oh yeah!* I love that fucking blush; especially now I have first-hand knowledge of where it originates.

She picks up the delicate items and looks at me. "These are stunning. I feel rather spoiled." She leans forward to kiss me, gently at first, and then more forcefully. "I can't wait to wear them. There's something so … so tantalizing about wearing something this sexy underneath your clothes. It makes me feel fiercely feminine and powerful."

And there goes my cock. It's already a constant battle to keep it under control around my exquisite woman, but when she talks like that, I have no chance. I shift uncomfortably on the couch, discreetly adjusting my wayward cock.

She moves off the couch to retrieve the gifts she bought for me, and I can't help but admire her lush, round ass as she bends down. She has three gifts in her hands, and her face is pinched with uncertainty.

"Are those for me?"

She bites the side of her thumbnail. Something she does when she's unsure or nervous. "Uh yeah. I hope you like the things I chose for you. They're certainly not as decadent as the gifts you've given me."

It's been years since I've been given a gift at Christmas time. "I know I'll love anything you've chosen for me because it came from your tender heart."

She blushes again and hands the first gift to me.

I unwrap the box, opening the lid to find a pair of red socks. I look up at her with a smile because I get the reason behind the red socks. She tucks a lock of hair behind her ear. "I love having red shoes on my feet. I'm unsure when it started, but it's the only color I'll wear. I didn't think you'd wear red shoes, and you especially can't wear them to work, but I thought maybe you could have red socks as the next best thing. In my opinion. Of course." The explanation gushes out of her. Whenever she's nervous or anxious about something, her words come pouring out of her mouth, but she has nothing to feel anxious about here.

"I love them. Actually, I've been thinking about getting a pair of red Converse so I can match you."

Her face lights up the entire space, and she breaks into a giggle. "Oh, I'm relieved you didn't think I was stupid."

"Never. I would never think you're stupid."

She hands me the second gift to open. Inside are two pairs of red boxer briefs, and I get the idea there's a bit of a theme happening here. She picks them up, turning them around to show me the back. Printed on one pair is, *This is mine*, and on the other pair is, *Property of Kate*. I burst into boisterous laughter, and she quickly joins me.

"I'll wear these with pride. I love them."

"I'm so pleased. They had a no-returns policy and they're too big for me to wear." She giggles again as she hands me her last gift.

Opening the box, I find a booklet of a dozen handmade love vouchers. Each one offers a variety of experiences Kate's willing to share with me—massages, a picnic in the woods following a hike, specially made favorite meals, breakfast in bed, movie night of my choice, and more. She's put a great deal of thought and care into this gift. My nose tingles, and I have to work hard to keep my emotions at bay.

I whisper a simple "thank you." Then pull her into my arms to bury my face in her neck. This gift shows me she's planning to keep me around in the future. I'm overwhelmed by how full my heart is when I'm with her.

"I know it's not much. I don't have a lot of money to spend, so I tried to make it as special as I could. I hope you like your gifts."

I look into her eyes, full of compassion. "You have no idea what your gifts have given me. Having you wake up in my arms this morning was a gift, but this ... this is next level. Thank you doesn't seem enough."

I press my lips against hers, brushing back and forth, then slide my tongue inside to participate in the kiss. It doesn't take much coaxing these days for her to open up to me. Our kiss is passionate, deep, and all-consuming.

Margie, Kate, and I are expected at Kate's parents' for lunch. I don't want us to be late, which means we need to stop.

———

I'm more nervous than I've previously felt as we arrive at Kate's family home. This time *I know* they're the family who took me in after Mom died and while Dad was in the hospital. I'm not sure how they became involved, and I don't remember them clearly. I *do* remember feeling I was welcome here, and I adored their baby girl—Kate.

I want to confess who I am. Then I can tell Mrs. Summer she can stop praying for me because I am safe, I am happy, I am successful. But I haven't told Kate about my childhood yet, and she deserves to know before I share that information with the rest of her family.

With Christmas greetings out of the way, we sit down to yet another delicious meal prepared by Kate's mom and nan. The food is delicious and serves to remind me it's been a long time since I last celebrated Christmas to this extent. Everyone is genuinely happy to be together, and the chatter around the table is only paused to chew another mouthful of delicious food.

Mr. Summer asks Kate, "Did you find out any more information about what happened with *The Parkerville Project?* Any idea when the kids will go back to their regular homes?"

"Nope, nothing yet. Roman wasn't supposed to tell me anything. I doubt he's going to be able to keep me updated, even though I asked him to." She sighs, her shoulders slumping in defeat. "I feel terrible for the kids. They've had enough upheaval in their lives. They didn't need this."

Mrs. Summer finishes chewing the food in her mouth. "Yes, those poor darlings. I wish we had enough room for them to come here. I would happily take those precious souls in."

I know she would in a heartbeat—she's deeply maternal. She's already made me feel incredibly welcome here with minimal effort.

After our bellies are full of delicious food, we retire into the family room to exchange gifts. I'm shocked to discover they've included me in the gift exchange. I bought for Kate's family and Margie, but in no way expected to be receiving anything in return. I was very wrong. They've included me at every turn, and I hope to be part of this family until my dying day.

———

Leaving Kate's place, I drive toward my sterile penthouse to get ready for my meeting with Samuel, the financial investigator Mike recommended. As I drive, I ruminate over the last months with Kate. She's completely changed the way I feel and the way I think. I can't believe I ever thought *a couple of nights* with her would be enough. I want to be a better man for her, to be everything she needs me to be. Disappearing on her for days at a time is definitely unacceptable behavior, and won't ever happen again.

The realization dawns on me that we've only ever been out on a couple of dates—one of which ended in me punching her ex and her in tears. I need to rectify the situation because she deserves the world.

———

My meeting with Samuel takes longer than expected. I walk him through my discoveries and my suspicions of Errol, the finance officer at *The Parkerville Project*. He looks through the files and notes I've made, then explains his process for tracking the culprit. He's concerned Errol may have already attempted to cover his tracks as soon as we made the discovery.

He's reasonably confident he can trace the money to the source, find the proof we need to have Errol arrested, and gain a conviction. We only have a slim chance of recovering the money. The theft needs to be proven, and the money also needs to still be in the accounts. Jase works diligently to make copies of the files and notes Samuel will need to work through the investigation. As he leaves, he promises to be in touch early next week.

I spend the next hour organizing a surprise weekend away on the coast for us. I assume she won't see the kids anytime soon, as her usual volunteering is on hold. This time away may help take her mind off missing them. Once I have everything squared away, I send her a text.

ME

I have a surprise for you

It takes a few minutes to receive a text and I'm impatient for her response. I can't contain my excitement for her reaction.

SUNSHINE

Oh yeah

Will I like it?

ME

Of course you will

Pack a weekend bag

SUNSHINE

What? Why?

ME

We're going down the coast for the weekend

Don't worry, I'll have you back in time for your family dinner on Sunday night

Those annoying dots bounce on my screen, then stop, then start again. This doesn't seem like a good sign. My phone rings and her stunning smile lights up the screen.

"Hey, Sunshine."

"Are you serious? A weekend on the coast?"

She must be excited because she didn't even bother to say *hi*.

"Yeah, I am. I figured you were probably free, and I missed you terribly on the days I had to work. I also realized on the way to my place this morning, we've only ever been on a couple of dates, and that's not good enough."

I hold my breath, hoping for a positive response.

She sighs. "Yeah, I'm definitely free this weekend because of what's happened." She still sounds heartbroken. "I would love to spend the weekend on the coast with you. Even though it's way too cold to go into the water, we can still have a wonderful time."

The breath I was holding in anticipation of her response releases. "Yeah?"

"Yeah," she whispers. "I think it's just what I need to take my mind off the kids, and it will also give *you* a break from working excessive hours. An extra bonus will be having you all to myself, totally uninterrupted. When do we leave?"

"It's only a one-hour drive from your place. I'll pick you up around four. Be ready."

"Oh, I will be."

She squeals as she disconnects the call. I guess she's happy about our little getaway—which is exactly what I was hoping to achieve.

I buzz Jase, explaining to him I'll be unreachable this weekend and my reason. I can hear his smirk through the phone when he responds with his typical, "yes, boss"—*smart ass.*

I'm *never* unreachable. This is an extremely rare occasion. Kate's changing me in a great many ways and I can't say I'm mad about it.

I spend the rest of the day ensuring I have everything ready for a hectic workload next week; I still need to catch up on what I've ignored these past few days while dealing with the shit show that was *The Parkerville Project*, as well as the Christmas break. Heading upstairs to my penthouse to pack myself a weekend bag, I mentally plan what I'll need to take with me—not that we'll be needing too many clothes for what I have planned. I do, however, want to take her on at least one or two outings. I pack the photo I found of Kate, Toby, and me sitting on her parents' couch. It's time I opened up to her, and this weekend will be the perfect opportunity to do so.

The drive to Kate's is frustrating—traffic is a fucking nightmare to get out of the city center at this time of day. The city always seems to have road closures happening at all hours of the day and night, exacerbating the problem. I arrive at ten past four, aggravated at being late.

She must have been watching for me because she comes out her front door, beaming while dragging her duffel down the steps. The moment is reminiscent of the first time I laid eyes on her.

I quickly exit my car to help with her bag, taking it from her as I steal a gentle taste of her lips. Once her bag is situated, she locks up and says goodbye to Margie. Finally, we're on our way out of the city, toward our weekend getaway destination. My shoulders relax as I place my hand on Kate's shapely, jean-clad thigh.

I glance at her. She's worrying her bottom lip and doesn't look quite as relaxed as I feel. I get the sense something's bothering her. "Everything okay over there?" I ask, keeping my eyes on the road.

From my periphery, I see her look at me. "Uhm. I'm not sure how to say this, so I'll just say it." She sighs and takes a deep breath. "I was so excited when I spoke to you earlier that I agreed to this getaway without thinking about how I'm going to pay my half of all the expenses. You're always spending your money on me, and I don't want to take advantage of your generosity. I feel as though I'm unable to reciprocate fairly."

I squeeze her thigh. "Don't even give it a second thought. I invited you away, which means I expect to cover all expenses for this weekend. Please don't worry about money, I have it covered. It won't break the bank. Truly." I smile at her, squeezing her thigh again, hoping to ease her concerns. I need to lighten the mood. "So, did you pack anything sexy?"

She laughs and her shoulders relax; I've achieved my goal.

"I'm not sure I even own anything sexy, to be honest. Trust you to be thinking about that stuff." She rolls her eyes.

"I'm a man and you're a beautiful woman. I'll always think about that *stuff* where you're concerned. Are you saying you don't think about that *stuff*?" I scoff. I'm offended if that's the case.

"Of course I do. I'm just not as direct about it as you are."

Well, that makes me feel marginally better. The drive down the coast continues with general small talk about the scenery and what she would like to achieve next week before she returns to work.

We finally pull up to the property I've rented for the weekend, and it's as impressive in real life as it was in the photographs I saw online. I'm surprised it was available at such short notice, but I guess not everyone wants to spend time on the coast during winter.

With wide, excited eyes, she turns to me. "This is where we're staying?"

I nod. "Yep. This okay? I didn't want to stay in a hotel. This felt more ... *private*." There were other, more spectacular properties, but I didn't want to overwhelm her.

"Oh my gosh, I can't believe you even have to ask. I've seen places like this on TV or online, but never in real life."

She leans over, wrapping her arms around my neck, awkwardly

pulling me down toward her for a kiss full of joy and gratitude. We eventually separate to exit my car, collect our bags, and make our way to the front door. The butler, who will look after us this weekend, already has the door open in welcome.

"Good afternoon, Mr. Stone. Ms. Summer." He dips his head to both of us in deference. "I'm Gerald. I'll be looking after you this weekend. Please allow me to take your bags and show you around the property."

THIRTY-SEVEN

-kate-

I CAN ONLY GAPE. *A FREAKING BUTLER!*

This is unreal, and so far removed from my life experiences to date. I glance at Oliver, checking this is real, but he's taking it all in stride as if he does this sort of thing every day. We enter the spectacular steel-blue and white weatherboard home to a massive open-plan living area with high-vaulted ceilings. The flooring is light bamboo, making the space feel even larger. The few walls are painted pale gray, with enormous windows across the entire back of the space. I'm drawn to them to admire the spectacular view of the breathtaking white sandy beach below.

I turn around to find my boyfriend watching me, almost as if he's waiting for my approval. I walk back to him, wrap my arms around his torso, and kiss his bristly chin. "This is out-of-this-world phenomenal. I have to be the luckiest woman around. Thank you for organizing this awesome place for us to stay this weekend."

I press up on my toes to kiss his full lips with a gentle touch, but he takes over, deepening the kiss, making it almost obscene. I sense Gerald in the room and reluctantly pull away. Oliver winks at me, wrapping his arm around my shoulder, turning us toward our butler—*our own freaking butler!*

As Gerald shows us around the property, we learn that the glass doors across the back of the house can be opened fully and hidden inside the outside walls—which would make it seem as if we're outside. If the weather was warmer, I'd have those doors tucked away the whole time we were here. As we step out of the master bedroom, a hot tub is situated on an enormous covered outdoor wooden deck, which is bigger than my entire house. Oliver tells me he has plans for me and that hot tub later, and my lady parts cheer in excitement—I can't wait!

The master bathroom boasts the most glorious shower with shower heads coming from all directions. But it's the bath that captures and holds my attention. I'd say five people could fit in that tub, and I'm dying to drop into the warm water with my man. The property has a tennis court, as well as a limestone pathway, which takes us down to our very own private beach, complete with a stone fire pit. Gerald leaves us alone after telling us dinner will be served on the outside deck at seven.

We leave our bags and put on our coats, deciding to navigate the pathway to investigate our very own private beach—*even if it is only for the weekend*. Holding hands, we make our way down the winding lime-stone path until we hit the white sandy beach.

The sun sits low on the horizon, bright orange and red hues fighting to be the last vestiges of light. It won't be long before they lose their battle, and it becomes dark. The wind carries the smell of salt off the water, and the air is cold, so I snuggle closer to Oliver, taking advantage of his size and warmth to protect me against the chilly wind coming off the bluest water.

With his front to my back, he wraps both arms around me, kissing the top of my head. "I love the beach. I never got to spend time here growing up. When I have any spare weekends, I occasionally choose to escape to the coast."

I suck in a breath because it's the first piece of information he's shared with me about his childhood. I want to bombard him with questions, but I don't want to push him on a topic I sense is difficult for him. "I can see the appeal. It's truly special here; relaxing and peace-ful. We're never going to want to leave this place," I whisper.

He tightens his hold, and we both spend quiet moments looking out at the water, our toes buried in the cold, soft sand, as the sun drops below the horizon. The sunset is almost as magnificent as the man holding me, as though he's never going to let me go.

I hope he never wants to let me go.

We meander up to the house, guided by the solar lights along the pathway, and wash up ready for dinner on the enclosed portion of the back deck. A toasty fire, situated to warm inside as well as the area out here, makes the space cozy.

Gerald—*did I mention we have a freaking butler*—brings out wine, crusty bread, and large bowls of seafood arrabiata—*yum*. Perfect for our current location. Over dinner and a couple of glasses of wine, we talk about what it would be like to live on the coast as a local, as opposed to being a tourist. It sounds to me as if he would love to live on the coast and simplify his life.

THIRTY-EIGHT

-oliver-

I WANT TO OPEN UP TO KATE TONIGHT AND SHARE ABOUT MY childhood, but I'm unsure where to begin, or even if it's appropriate at this point in our relationship. I sit in the hot tub, waiting for her to join me, lost in my head, when I hear the door open and close.

She steps out in an olive-green bikini, and I almost swallow my tongue. Those tiny triangles on her tits barely cover her nipples, and the triangle at the apex of her thighs is not much bigger. Her silky, fiery-colored hair is twisted up in some type of knot on top of her head, leaving her smooth neck and creamy shoulders exposed.

She walks toward me slowly. "I wasn't going to pack my bikini because I figured it's too cold for swimming, but I'm glad I did."

Fuck!

She must wear those scraps of fabric to the beach—*in public!*

Every asshole would be able to see her gorgeous body. "Turn around," I growl like a fucking Neanderthal. I'm going to have to find every asshole who's ever seen her in this bikini and cut their goddamn eyes out.

She freezes. "Huh. Why?"

"Because I need to see everything every other asshole at the beach can see when you wear those tiny scraps of fabric that barely cover the essentials."

She laughs at me—*fucking laughs!*

I don't see the fucking humor—*at all.*

"I said, turn around." I grit my teeth, my tone brooking no argument. "Now turn around. I need to see your lush ass."

She rolls her eyes at me but turns around. And yeah, it's as bad as I figured it would be. Those delectable ass cheeks of hers are almost on full display. I take deep, purposeful breaths to get myself under control.

"Get in here before I spank that luscious ass for being on display."

She turns around, stepping into the tub while smiling and rolling her eyes at me. "You're a bit of a caveman sometimes. You know that —right?" She chuckles softly. "I'm only getting in the tub because I *want* to, and *not* because you told me."

"Only for you. You bring it out in me. From the very first moment I laid eyes on you, as you dragged that duffel behind you toward the school." I pull her in close, kissing her nose. "I've never felt this protective of anyone before. This is all new to me."

I feel the fight leave her, and her body softens into mine. I position her on my lap, her legs straddling mine. Grabbing her almost naked ass, I drag her into me, taking her bottom lip in a gentle bite which quickly evolves into an unrestrained, ravenous fucking of our mouths. She grinds her hot pussy against my thick cock, and I squeeze her ass, drawing her impossibly closer. If I could drag her inside of me, I fucking would.

Guiding her hips back and forth, she rocks her soft pussy against my engorged cock, building the rhythm and intensifying the sensations. I pull my mouth away from hers to nudge her bikini top aside with my nose, freeing the globes and allowing me to suck on her luscious tits. Her sighs and moans spur me on. I guide her hips faster and suck her glorious tits harder until she shudders in my arms with a long moan. She collapses forward, slumping into me, tucking her face into my neck. She kisses and licks my pulse point gently, and I release a deep sigh of pure male satisfaction. I slowly glide my hands up and down her back until she collects herself.

Raising her head, she looks between both my eyes and mouth. "That was ..." she sighs. "I don't know. I'm lost for words. Sex keeps getting better and better between us."

I know *exactly* what she means. I nuzzle into her neck, licking up toward her ear so I can nip the lobe, then move back to her jaw and kiss my way up to her mouth. I take her lips in a slow, luxurious exploration. We kiss for what feels like hours, if not days. I could kiss her for eternity, and it still wouldn't be enough.

I reluctantly release her as she slowly pulls away. She shows me her fingers, which look like prunes. "I think it's time to get out."

I nod, assisting her out of the hot tub, and follow close behind. Grabbing towels from the cupboard near the hot tub, we dry the excess water off and step inside to shower off the chemicals. We spend most of the night loving each other's bodies in between brief bouts of sleep.

THIRTY-NINE

-kate-

I WAKE TO OLIVER'S FINGERS SLIPPING INSIDE ME AS I LAY ON MY stomach—my body already reacting, my hips rocking with his rhythm. He slides my leg upward to open me to him, then covers me with his muscular body and slowly glides his dick through my folds and into my pussy. We both groan at the sensation and meet in a slow, languid kiss. My body heats and tingles begin to spread through my limbs. He's obviously been at it a while already.

"Morning." His kisses linger on my neck. "Hope you don't mind that I started without you."

"Why would I mind when I have this to wake up to?" I push my hips back, meeting his leisurely thrusts. "Be my guest to wake me up like this any time."

He slowly rocks into me, maintaining solid eye contact. "I love being inside you. It's my favorite place to be. You feel so fucking good squeezing around my cock. We were made to fit together like this."

His thrusts increase in speed and power as his hand slides under my hips to tease my aching clit.

All I can do is moan and beg him to keep going; I'm incapable of anything else when he's inside me. It doesn't take long before I explode, coming on a loud moan, which I couldn't hold inside if I tried. His dick pulses and he follows me with his own orgasm. Sharing this level of intimacy with him is unbelievably intoxicating.

What a way to start the day.

"Yeah, I agree. What a way to start the day."

Oops, I must have said that out loud. Without pulling out, he rolls us to the side, wrapping himself around me and holding me to him as we catch our breath.

"How did you sleep?" he whispers, carefully sliding out of my pussy.

"Well, there wasn't much sleep to be had because someone kept waking me up throughout the night." Not that I'm complaining, but I'm not sure my legs are going to function today.

"Oh yeah? I don't remember hearing any complaints. A lot of moaning, and 'harder', and 'don't stop' though." His smile is huge, while his mossy-colored eyes twinkle with mischief.

Oh my gosh, there goes my blush. I hate having such a fair complexion.

"And there's that stunning blush I adore." He chuckles and nuzzles his nose into the crook of my neck.

"Oh, stop it! You're not being fair."

"Pretty sure I was being fair last night. I'm reasonably certain you had two orgasms to my one every time." He laughs as if he's told the greatest joke ever, as he jumps out of bed to avoid my playful swing.

―――――

We spend most of the day relaxing around the house, playing tennis, walking along the beach, and lazing on the back deck while being spoiled with a delicious breakfast, lunch, and snacks in between. Oliver's organized a sunset cruise with dinner on a yacht tonight, which sounds divine. I can't believe I'm sharing this experience with him. I keep pinching myself to confirm this is all real.

―――――

Walking toward the pier, I spot a magnificent yacht with an enormous mast docked at the end. With my hand securely in Oliver's as we stroll along the pier past other boats and yachts, I realize we're heading for the yacht I saw from the parking lot.

Wow, this can't be my life right now—it feels like a dream.

I glance up to find Oliver watching me, perhaps waiting for my reaction. My eyes must be as wide as saucers. "Is this the yacht for our sunset cruise?" He nods. "It's amazing. You're spoiling me beyond my wildest dreams. Actually, I've never even dreamed of something like this."

I throw my arms around his neck and press up on my toes to kiss him. It was meant to be a quick peck, but he takes over. He grabs my butt and pulls me tight against his body, making the kiss indecent for public consumption. Eventually, he pulls away from me, leaving me breathless and dizzy.

He looks into my eyes. "You deserve the best of everything, Sunshine, and I'm going to give it all to you," he whispers.

"Oh, Oliver, all I need is you. Nothing else. Just you." I press my hand against his chest, trying to brand my words onto his heart.

His steps stutter a moment as he nods slowly, then he drags me to the end of the pier, and we board the yacht on steroids. After a tour of the decadent water vessel, which leaves me speechless, the crew set about departing the pier and cruising out to sea.

We wander up on deck to appreciate the magnificent view, wrapped in our warmest clothes. Even though the sun is shining, the wind is cold on my face. The crew meets our every need, barely allowing our glasses to empty.

As afternoon turns into evening, we move inside to get out of the cold and partake in a delicious seafood feast. With full bellies and glasses of wine, he begins to share stories about his childhood.

My relief is palpable.

He hasn't shared much about himself, and I was worried he never would. However, my relief is short-lived as he recounts the night that changed his life forever. I rise out of my chair to settle beside him in his, wrapping my arms around him, offering the only comfort I can.

He's lost to his memories. The vacant look in his eyes tells me he's reliving the night the lost little boy learned his mom was never coming home to him—would never hug him or kiss away his bumps and bruises. The little boy who just wanted his mom to hold him and tell him everything would be okay. Even though his dad survived the crash, he also lost him that night.

Tears track down my cheeks, but I don't want to wipe them away and possibly cue Oliver into my heartache for him, because I sense that's the last thing he wants from me.

I feel closer to him at this moment than any other moment we've shared over the past few months.

He's finally let me in.

Allowed me to see who he *really* is and what shaped him to be the man he is today. He tells me about how *The Parkerville Project* gave him a place to stay before being placed with his first foster family, and in between subsequent families. And now I understand why he was volunteering at the renovation project where we reconnected. He wants to give back to the organization that helped him when there was nobody else.

My heart breaks for this man, who missed out on so much love during his formative childhood and teenage years. No wonder he closed himself off, concentrating on his work to the exclusion of people.

He glances at me and then back at his hands. "There's one more thing." He pulls out an old photograph, studying it silently for a few moments. "I'm the boy who stayed with you when you and Toby were babies. I'm Oliver from the photo on your parents' mantel."

He passes the photograph to me, and I draw in a sharp breath as my eyes land on the familiar couch with a young Oliver holding me while Toby sits next to us. The photo must have been one of several shots that day because everything's the same. His expression as he looks down at me as a baby reminds me of how he looks at me now.

I glance up at him. *He* was the boy who stayed with us for two weeks. *He* was the boy who apparently doted on me and only smiled when he was with *me*. It somewhat explains our immediate connection. It's as though we were always destined to be together.

"I can't believe it. Mom and Dad are going to be so surprised."

"Do you think so?"

I nod. "Absolutely." My mind races with the possibilities of *what if*.

What if he'd always lived with us?

What if my parents had adopted him?

What if he'd never come to live with us?

What if we'd never met again?

My thoughts whirl as we sit quietly in our cocoon, watching the dark waves behind the yacht as we sail toward the pier to disembark.

In bed, our bodies come together. Our mouths, hands, and limbs entwined in a way that somehow feels deeper and more connected than we've been before. A level of trust has settled between us, providing me with a sense of comfort and a feeling of home. Lord help me, but I love this man—this complicated, overwhelming, intense, magnificent man. It's in this moment I realize that I've become comfortable with him. No longer fearing that he'll leave me for someone prettier or more interesting.

Oliver surprises me by organizing a visit to the artisan markets which are set up along the pier we visited yesterday. It has a completely different vibe today, with an eclectic array of items being made for sale in front of us.

A young woman, in her late teens, is making a pair of stunning rose gold earrings with delicate rose quartz heart inlays. I notice she has a matching necklace, which she must have finished before beginning work on the earrings. I'm tempted to purchase the set, but it's not in my budget. I'm careful not to show too much interest because I don't want Oliver to spend any more money than he already has on me this weekend. It's ridiculous the amount of money he must have paid for the accommodation and the yacht yesterday, not to mention having a butler at our beck and call.

We keep moving, observing an older lady making the most intricate lace dress overlay I've ever seen, and a man blowing glass to create a unique set of wine goblets. So many people gifted with enormous talent.

I drag Oliver toward a woman about my age, making homemade ice cream. We end up in an argument because I want to pay, but I eventually win, and we enjoy the tasty treat as we continue exploring the various stalls. We spend hours wandering through the maze of stalls and displays, stopping to chat with the crafters about their products and praising their talents.

I excuse myself to the restroom, and when I return I find Oliver speaking with the jeweler who was making the earrings I admired earlier. I see him slip her something with a nod and a smile, then he says something to her and makes his way toward me. She waves to me with a grin and then strolls off toward her stall.

"Are you ready to leave? We need to get on the road if we're going to get you home in time for dinner with your family."

"Yeah, sure. I didn't realize how late it was." I pause and capture his gaze. "I had the best weekend with you. Thank you for spoiling me." I grip his hands. "And thank you for sharing your story with me. I know it wouldn't have been easy, but I appreciate you trusting me." He seems lighter today, not as bogged down.

I press up on my tiptoes, kissing his lips gently with gratitude. He kisses my forehead and nods stiffly. The tic in his jaw reminds me it's a difficult topic for him. Placing his hand on the small of my back, he guides me to the entrance of the market.

We make our way back to the house to pack our belongings. It doesn't take long and we're on the road, heading back to the city. As we get closer to home, I can't bear to let him go. Without thinking of the repercussions, I blurt, "Do you want to come to dinner with my family tonight? We could tell Mom and Dad who you are. I *know* Mom will be relieved to learn you're okay after all these years."

Even though I surprised myself with the invitation, I don't want to rescind it. I want him there with me. It's not like he hasn't joined our family for dinner before, but now I *want* him to come to *every* family dinner.

He glances across at me, eyes crinkled at the corners, lips spread wide. "I'd love to. How do you think your parents will take the news?"

"I think they'll be over the moon. You know you're always welcome. Mom always makes enough food for an army—it won't be any trouble."

Mom's always made it a point to have more than enough food, just in case we want to invite any friends over. It's a sort of open-house policy where our friends are concerned. "I'll message her to let her know you're coming to dinner."

> ME
>
> Hi Mom
>
> Is it okay if Oliver comes over for dinner?

> MOM
>
> Of course it's okay
>
> He's always welcome here
>
> Especially now he's your b-o-y-f-r-i-e-n-d

> ME
>
> Mom!! 🙄

I sigh, rolling my eyes, and Oliver notices, looking at me quizzically.

"I think Mom's excited you're my boyfriend."

He chuckles light-heartedly and lays his hand on my thigh.

———

Dinner is a quiet affair: Mom, Dad, Oliver, and I. Which works perfectly for the news he has to share. I can tell he's nervous, so I'm doing everything I can think of to calm his nerves. I stay close, offering him small smiles and gentle touches. Hopefully, he knows I'm here for him.

As we eat dinner, I take the first step for him. "Mom. Dad. Oliver has something he would like to tell you both."

He looks across at me, full of anxiety. I nod, letting him know it's okay while smoothing my hand up and down his back, attempting to soothe and support him.

Clearing his throat, he begins his story.

By the time he's shown his photograph to my parents and told them his story, we're all in tears. Mom hops up from her chair, pulling him into the tightest hug I think I've ever seen. Even Dad joins in.

"I'm not sure how I came to live with you or why I left. I'm hoping you can fill in the blanks for me."

Dad clears his throat, clearly emotional. "Uh, well, my friend was working as a counselor for the Department of Children's Services when your case came across his desk. They only needed something short-term for you until your father was released from the hospital. He asked me if Emily and I would be willing to look after you until your father was well enough to be released."

Mom takes over. "We fell in love with you immediately. You were such a sad, lost little boy. You had lost more than anyone ever should. Kate seemed to have a special place in your heart—the way you constantly doted on her. It was truly special to watch your sadness vanish when you were with her."

"After I left here, I was taken to a house that was part of *The Park-erville Project*. My father was arrested and eventually sent to prison for drunk driving causing death. I never lived with him again," he shares.

Mom gasps, holding her hands to her throat. "Oh no! Why didn't they bring you back here? I don't understand." She looks across at Dad with disappointment. "We would have kept you as part of our family. We would have loved you and provided you with a solid family."

I think he needed to hear that. His posture relaxes significantly as his face smooths out. Somehow finding peace knowing that he *was* wanted.

FORTY

-oliver-

THIS WEEK IS GOING TO BE A FUCKING NIGHTMARE. I NEED TO CATCH up on what I missed last week, in addition to staying on top of the situation for *The Parkerville Project*.

My *CornerStone Foundation* can't even step in to help financially for the next two quarters, as we've already designated those funds for the *Schools for Everyone* Project. I wish I had enough money available to help both organizations simultaneously, but I still have a company to run with employees to pay, and while I'm a billionaire on paper, a lot of my money is tied up in stocks and real estate portfolios. I call Jase into my office to go over my schedule and plan for *The Parkerville Project* meeting on Friday for any interested parties.

After we've finished preparing for the week ahead, Jase lingers with a smirk. "So, how was the weekend away?"

I lean back in my chair. "It was the best weekend I've had in living memory."

Jase's eyes widen as his smirk becomes a full-blown smile. "That's great news. I'm genuinely happy for you, man. I don't suppose she has a sister?"

I laugh, typical Jase. "Uh, that would be no. Only Toby. Hey, did you recognize him—Toby Summer?"

"Yeah. He's been popular on the music charts for several years. I did my best not to fangirl over him because I'm sure he gets tired of it."

"Huh. It was just me then. I didn't make the connection until I was explicitly told at Thanksgiving dinner. I feel like a dick now."

233

"Nothing new there, you *are* a dick most of the time." He laughs as he rises from the chair to leave.

"Fuck off, asshole. Get to work or I'll dock your pay!" I laugh, turning back to my computer, but not before I notice him giving me the bird over his shoulder. I'm lighter today. My weekend with Kate was exactly what I needed. Sharing my story with her and her parents lifted a burden off my shoulders I hadn't realized I was carrying. Knowing they didn't give me up, that they would have kept me settled a part of my soul that's always felt fractured. Yes. The weekend was the best I've had in living memory.

I get stuck into catching up on emails, phone calls, and reports needing to be finalized for our current clients. Even though I have a lot on my plate at the moment, thoughts of Kate constantly invade my mind. Of wrapping her in my arms, and the way our bodies fit perfectly together.

———

Over the next few days, I work with dogged determination to catch up and get on top of everything that needs to be done. By midweek, I need to know how Samuel's progressing with the investigation. It would be better if we had more information ready for the meeting we have planned for Friday.

I buzz Jase. "Can you get hold of Samuel for me? I need an update. I want as much information as possible for Friday's meeting."

As I'm on the line, I hear Jase's other line buzz, so he disconnects our call. When he buzzes me, he announces Samuel's on line one for me—that's good timing.

I press the line and answer. "Hello Samuel, what do you have for me?"

"I traced the money and offshore accounts. Your suspicions were correct. It was Errol. I've contacted the FBI, the SEC, the CFTC, and other necessary authorities. They'll be moving in to arrest him with an appropriate search warrant this afternoon. They want to ensure the case is as watertight as possible to reduce any chance of him escaping prison time. They're also working to increase the chances of *The Park-erville Project* getting as much of their money back as they possibly can."

That's a relief. "Thanks. That's good news for us."

"No problem. It was a straightforward process for me. You had already done most of the work to find the money. I'll continue working with the authorities until they no longer need my input."

"Sure. Let me know if there's anything further I can do to help the process along."

"I'm sure the FBI and other agencies will need to speak with you and Marcus at some stage."

"Of course. I wouldn't expect anything different. Thank you for everything, Samuel. I'll speak to you soon."

"No problem. Bye for now."

Disconnecting the call, I wipe my hands down my face. When I look up, Jase is standing in the doorway, waiting to hear the latest update.

"They found him. It *was* Errol. The FBI is arresting him this afternoon."

The relief is overwhelming, and suddenly I sag with exhaustion. I didn't realize the toll this issue was taking on me. My shoulders release, and some of the built-up tension evaporates from my muscles.

"That's great news. Do you want me to get Marcus on the line for you? You can update him ahead of the meeting."

"Yeah, thanks, Jase." He nods, stepping out to organize the call.

I spend the next fifteen minutes on the phone with Marcus relaying the information I received and finalizing plans for the Friday meeting. I'm pleased we have more information to share with anyone who attends.

I speak to the bank, which holds the mortgages to the properties, informing them of the situation. Unfortunately, the situation from their end remains unchanged. We have ninety days to come up with the remainder of the mortgage, or we lose all the properties under *The Parkerville Project* umbrella.

FORTY-ONE

-kate-

OVER THIS PAST WEEK, I'VE CAUGHT UP ON MY CHORES AROUND MY little house, worked in the garden, prepared my program for the next term, and prepped my activities for the first two weeks back. Today, I'm going to treat myself to brunch with my colleague and friend, Emma.

She's ten years older than me and has two sons who are at school, one of whom is in my class. She left the corporate world when she was pregnant with her oldest boy, Lachlan, to be a stay-at-home mom. Before her youngest son, Austin, was born, she decided to become a teacher. She wanted to be available for her kids before and after school and during school vacations. Her husband left her because he felt she wasn't the same person he'd married and thought the two boys— particularly Lachlan—were too much trouble. He wanted a corporate wife and the life that goes along with that—*asshole!* The boys are with Emma's parents today, giving Emma time for some self-care.

Sitting in a booth near the window inside our favorite catch-up spot, I spot her as soon as she enters. She's wearing the biggest grin and looks pleasantly relaxed. We hug in greeting and then get to the important business of ordering our coffee and cake, then catch up on our Christmas vacation shenanigans. When I tell her about what happened to the kids I volunteer with, she's visibly upset, offering to help in any way she can. I go on to tell her about my weekend away with Oliver, and she's genuinely thrilled things are going smoothly for me.

"So, have you done the obligatory social media search on him yet?"

237

She's big into social media. Me, not so much. I've always been a pretty private person—the appeal isn't there for me. I've learned from Toby that social media isn't all it's cracked up to be.

"Uh, no. You know I'm not into all that stuff." I wave away her suggestion.

"Geez, girl, I think you're the only twenty-something I know that isn't all over social media. I can look him up if you like?" She grabs her phone, ready to search like the skilled social media stalker she is.

I laugh and wave her off. "No, it's okay. I'd prefer to learn all about him from him rather than from a third party. Thanks for the offer, though."

She shrugs carelessly, tapping her phone. "That's okay. If you change your mind, you know where to come." She finishes her sentence with a playful wink.

We say goodbye because Emma needs to run a few errands before picking up her boys, and I meander to the park across the street for a stroll on this cold, but sunny afternoon. I visit the market to grab the ingredients for Nan's famous chili because Oliver said he'll attempt to make it to my place in time for dinner tonight. He's been working late every day, catching up on the work he missed because of Christmas and the big drama that happened. After the market, I drive home to prepare dinner. I also need to work out if I have anything sexy enough to wear as a special treat to seduce my sexy boyfriend.

———

After spending twenty minutes rifling through my cupboard and drawers, I find my cute herringbone skater skirt and a gray crossover top, leaving my midriff bare. I wear my red Converse that Oliver bought for me, and dry my hair in loose waves down my back.

The chili is almost ready when I hear Oliver come through the front door, dropping his keys on the table where I usually leave mine. He spends most of his time here. It's almost like we're living together. His footsteps come closer, and I prepare myself for seeing him in his suit—*so hot!*

He stops in my bedroom doorway, rolling up his shirt sleeves; he must have already relieved himself of his jacket and tie in the living room.

Mmhm, those forearms.

His eyes trace up and down slowly, from the tips of my toes to the top of my head. I check him out too, my gaze catching on the bulge behind the zipper of his pants, which appears to be growing before my very eyes—*oh my*.

Yes, please.

Licking my lips, I continue trailing my way up his torso until I get to his face. His expression is one I imagine a starving man wears. It's a look that makes my panties wet and thighs clench.

He leaves the room, confusing me with his sudden departure. After about thirty seconds, he returns, making a beeline straight for me. Crowding my space, he presses his body tight against mine. One hand lands on my hip while the other goes to the back of my head, underneath my hair, holding me in place.

"Hey," he whispers against my mouth.

"Hey."

His mouth crashes against mine, his tongue parting my lips to make its way inside. His kisses make me dizzy and incoherent. All I can do is grip his biceps and hold on for his delicious assault. Warmth spreads throughout me, and my sex softens in preparation. Wrapping my arms around his neck, I pull him in as close as possible. He slides the hand at my hip down to the back of my thigh, which he smoothly lifts, wrapping my leg around his hip. This close, I can't miss the unmistakable erection filling his trousers. His other hand smooths down my back to my butt, raising my other leg, lifting me completely off the floor, and locking me in position at his waist. I love this show of pure masculine strength. It's such a freaking turn-on.

He takes the few steps required to get to my bed and sits on the edge with me wrapped around him. He slows the kiss, moving to lick and kiss along my jawline, up to my ear. "You look so damn sexy in this getup, which means you can never wear it in public," he whispers.

I pull back, searching his face. I can't tell if he's joking or if he's serious. His expression is serious, which suggests he means what he's saying.

"Tell me you're joking." I pause, waiting for him to confirm that he is, indeed, joking, but he appears to be standing firm. "You can't be serious. You can't possibly think I'll be okay with you telling me what I can and cannot wear when I go out in public. I thought you were messing around with the bikini comments, but I'm starting to think you weren't joking at all."

He shrugs his shoulder, looking me dead in the eye. "I'm deadly serious. You're mine. That means nobody gets to see how sexy you are, except for me."

Uh, I don't think so, big guy.

I push away from him, or at least I try to push away from him, but he has a vise grip on me which isn't allowing any leeway.

"I'm not the kind of girl guys look at and think, *hey, she's sexy.* I'm also not the kind of girl who goes around flaunting my body. I never pair these items together, but I thought I would *attempt* to look sexy for you tonight. I wasn't sure I could pull it off until you looked at me and went all caveman." His clenched jaw is crazy tight as he huffs out a breath, but I place my fingers over his lips to stop him from speaking. "You have nothing to worry about. When I'm out in public, I generally dress conservatively."

He's still trying to interrupt me, so I press my fingers harder against his lips, shaking my head. "But it's *my* choice what I wear. I won't have you, or anyone else, tell me what I can and can't wear. I make my own choices. If I want to walk down the street in a negligee and hooker heels, then that's what I'll damn well do, and you won't be able to stop me. Understood?"

I remove my fingers, allowing him to speak.

He shakes his head. "You have no idea how striking you are."

Now it's my turn to shake my head. "You make me feel beautiful, but I was never beautiful enough to keep a boyfriend before. I'm still waiting for you to wake up and notice I'm not special."

Even though I feel more confident in myself and haven't felt the worry I originally did since dating Oliver, the thought of him leaving me for someone more attractive sneaks up on me now and then. Not that he gives me any reason to feel insecure. Quite the opposite. He makes me feel completely secure *and* adored. I look down at our laps because I can't bring myself to see the pity in his eyes.

Using his finger, he raises my chin. "That's on them. If they were too stupid to see what was in front of them, then they weren't the right person for you. And, quite frankly, I'm ecstatic they didn't, or I wouldn't be here with you now." He kisses the tip of my nose. "I'll attempt to tone down my caveman tendencies, but I can't make promises. I want to keep you all to myself. I'm not good at sharing."

I nod. "I guess that's as good as I'm going to get from you." I smile demurely. "It's not like you're ever going to have to share. I'm not *that* girl. I won't ever stray. Just keep it in check, okay?"

He nods and kisses my forehead.

"C'mon, let's eat dinner before it burns. I cooked Nan's chili."

Kissing the tip of my nose, he releases me to stand on my own feet. Grasping his hand, I drag him through to my kitchen, where I see the burner has already been turned off.

"I turned it off because I thought we'd be busy for a while." He shrugs, smiling boyishly. "I didn't want all of your hard work to go to waste."

Probably a good idea too, because we were seriously distracted there for a bit. I serve two bowls, and we move to my small dining table to eat and chat about our day. Oliver tells me he's getting on top of his work and that he's also happy with the preparations for an important meeting tomorrow morning.

After dinner, we clean up and move to the couch, each with a glass of wine to wind down from the day. We turn in for the night and pick up where we left off before dinner.

———

Even before I open my eyes, I immediately know I'm alone. I sense he's already left to start his day. I roll over to my bedside cabinet, grabbing my phone to check the time. I'm surprised to find it's after eight; I rarely sleep this late, but we were up half the night, loving each other's bodies.

I have a missed call from Roman. That must have been what woke me up. Maybe I can see the kids. I quickly press the icon to return his call.

"Hi. Thanks for returning my call," Roman answers, sounding frazzled.

"No problem. Have there been any fresh developments? Can I see the kids?"

"Sort of. Look, I was supposed to go into a meeting today to get an update on what's happening, but I can't go. Evelyn's sick and I don't feel right leaving her when she's feeling unwell." He huffs out a sigh, and I visualize him pushing his hand through his messy hair.

"I can come and look after her. That way you can go to the meeting. I don't mind." I climb out of bed so I can get ready.

"Nah, you're back at school on Monday. I don't want you to get ill. Can you go to the meeting on my behalf and then let me know what's happening?"

"Uh sure. Will it be okay for me to go, since I'm not an employee?"

"I'm pretty sure it'll be okay. It's a meeting for anyone interested. Not just employees of *The Parkerville Project*. Would you mind?"

"Not at all. I'll go, and then I'll call you with the rundown. What time does it start?"

"Thanks. It starts at ten. I'll text you the address. I can't tell you how much I appreciate this."

"No worries. I'd better get moving. Tell Evelyn to get better soon. Talk later."

"Bye."

I end the call and immediately step into the bathroom to get ready. After my shower, I dress and check my phone for a text from Roman.

ROMAN

Thanks again

The meeting is on the 38th floor of Stone Tower, 1151 Mayfield Ave in the city center

ME

No worries. Chat later

I'd better get moving, or I'll never make it in time. I grab my purse and keys and make my way into the city. While I'm on the bus, I figure I could meet Oliver for lunch, so I send him a message.

ME

Hey boyfriend, I'm coming into the city at the last minute. Want to meet for lunch?

He said he was going to be busy this morning. Hopefully, he'll see my message before lunchtime and respond. I step off the bus and make my way toward Mayfield Avenue. I don't come into the city often, so I use the map app on my phone, which I'm surprised works on my older phone.

The building it directs me toward is completely different from all the other tall buildings around it. Slim gray bricks of different sizes and shades are stacked for the first three floors, and as I raise my head to look up at the structure, the bricks change to stone, cut in slim lengths to form a chevron pattern for the rest of the tower. Above the archway for the main doors are large stainless steel letters spelling out **STONE TOWER**. The building is like nothing I've seen before, and as much as I try, I can't see all the way to the top.

I must remember to tell Oliver there's a building in the city with his name on it. That should give him quite the ego boost, though he probably already knows about it since he works in the city.

I step into the lobby, which continues with the gray stone theme on the floors, enhanced by stainless steel counters, behind which sits a very attractive woman.

The woman's smile is friendly as I step up to the counter. "Welcome to Stone Tower. Can I help you?"

"Hopefully. I'm here for a meeting regarding *The Parkerville Project*. I believe it's on the 38th floor, but I wanted to check where to go." I shuffle on my feet.

"Oh, lucky you checked, it's actually on the 48th floor. Conference room five. You can take the elevator up."

"Thanks. Have a great day." I smile, waving as I walk away. Luckily, I checked. Maybe it was moved, or maybe Roman accidentally pressed the wrong number when he messaged me.

"You, too."

I press the up button, then step into the elevator when it arrives, and press the button for the 48th floor. The elevator is decadent, all mirrors and stainless steel, with a gray stone floor that matches the façade of the building. I arrive at the correct floor quickly and exit to find another desk.

The older lady behind the desk raises her head and smiles at me. "Can I help you?"

"I'm here for *The Parkerville Project* meeting in conference room five. I think I'm slightly early, but I didn't want to be late."

"Oh, of course. I always think it's better to be early than late. Please complete this sign-in sheet, and I'll show you through."

I write my details on the sheet, providing my name, contact email, and phone number. I see I'm the fifth person on the list. The woman then comes out from behind her desk to show me to the correct room.

"There's tea and coffee over on the side table. Help yourself to any of the pastries."

I walk over to a chair at the back of the room to drop off my purse. Then I make myself a cup of coffee and select a pastry, since I didn't eat breakfast in my rush to get here. The other attendees are milling about and chatting, but I don't know anyone, so I keep to myself. I get comfortable in my chair tucked in the back corner and watch as more and more people arrive. The room becomes crowded, making it so I can no longer see the front of the room, but it doesn't matter as long as I can hear what's being said.

Right at ten o'clock, a man clears his throat to gain everyone's attention. When I set my phone to record the meeting, in case I miss anything important and Roman wants to hear what they said, I notice a message on my phone screen.

BIG O

Hey Sunshine, I'd love to catch up for lunch

Where do you want to meet?

I'm unable to respond as the man introduces himself. "Good morning everyone. My name is Marcus Trainor, and I'm the CEO of *The Parkerville Project*. As you are aware, we are currently having some financial difficulties and have called this meeting to inform all interested parties of what's happening. First, I would like to extend my appreciation to Mr. Stone for allowing us the use of his building for this meeting. I would also like to take this opportunity to thank him for the major contribution his charitable foundation, *The CornerStone Foundation*,"—I've heard that name before—"has made to our project over the past many years. Without its ongoing support, *The Parkerville Project* would have closed its doors long ago. It was also Mr. Stone, who stepped in when the trouble first hit. He worked tirelessly to identify what happened to the money, which was supposed to be paying our mortgages and wages for our paid staff." He pauses as a chair scrapes. "Without further ado, I would like to introduce Mr. Stone."

Everyone claps politely, then Mr. Stone clears his throat and speaks. "Thanks, Marcus, for your kind introduction." I know *that* voice; the deep, rich timbre, but in a different context. He continues. "It has been my pleasure and honor to support *The Parkerville Project*." I suck in a breath because Mr. Stone is *MY* Oliver.

I can't hear anything else over the rush of blood in my ears. My breath stalls in my chest and I'm growing dizzy. All the noise and air have been sucked out of my space as if I'm in a vacuum. Closing my eyes, my body shakes as a tremor moves through it. I can't believe I didn't put two and two together:

Stone Tower,

The CornerStone Foundation,

Mr. *Stone*,

Oliver *Stone*—*my boyfriend*.

I need to get out of here, but I don't want to make a scene, and I certainly don't want Oliver to know I'm here. I'm so embarrassed. I wait for a semblance of calm—taking deep, measured breaths—then I rise slowly from my seat and walk quietly toward the door on shaky legs. Luckily, I'm on the shorter side and the room is packed—he probably won't see me leave.

As I pass through the door, I glance up to find Jase gaping at me. He attempts to reach for me, but I move quickly past him, shaking my head. I can't deal with him right now. Making a beeline for the elevator, I struggle to keep my tears at bay. Thankfully, the car arrives quickly, and I step inside, pressing the button to close the heavy doors. As the doors close, Jase watches me with concern.

Maybe I should have taken Emma up on her offer to check his social media. I'm such a fool.

What in the hell is he doing with someone like me?

He could have any woman on the planet.

I catch the bus home, put myself to bed, and sob my heart out until I fall into an exhausted sleep.

FORTY-TWO

-oliver-

THE MEETING COMES TO A CLOSE, AND AFTER A LONG DISCUSSION WITH Marcus, I finally make my way to my office. I'm about to sit down to check my phone to see if Kate's suggested a place to meet for lunch when Jase interrupts me by throwing a sheet of paper on my desk. He looks thunderous—anger rolls off him in waves—I don't think I've ever seen him like this before.

"What's this? And what's up your ass?" I pick up the sheet of paper, noting it's the sign-in sheet for the meeting.

"Look at the names on the attendee list for the meeting. Then *you* tell me what's up my ass."

I scan the document and all the blood leaves my face. I look up to Jase, then back down at the page, hoping against all hope that I read the name in the fifth space incorrectly.

"Tell me it's not true. Kate was in that meeting?" I point back in the general direction of the conference room.

"Yep. But she left early, close to tears. I tried to stop her, but she brushed me off." He shakes his head, pacing in front of my desk with his hands on his hips. "You hadn't told her, had you? I told you to tell her, man. You fucked up. You fucked up big time."

I get up, tipping my chair over in the process, collect my phone and keys, then stalk out of my office without a word.

I need to get to Kate.

I need to explain.

I need to *fix* this.

I can't lose her.

247

She's the best thing that's ever happened to me.

With city traffic, it seems to take forever before I bang on Kate's front door. I figure she wouldn't appreciate me letting myself in at this point.

There's no response, so I bang harder, calling her name. Still no response, so I take the risk and let myself in. Moving through her silent home, I search from room to room, hoping she's here. I finally get to her bedroom and my heart shatters.

Pieces falling at my feet.

Leaving a bloody mess on her floor.

I did this to her.

Curled up in the smallest ball in the middle of her bed, she's hiding under her blankets, hugging the pillow I use. I take my shoes, jacket, and tie off, then climb in behind her slight form. Wrapping my arms around her, I endeavor to work out a way to make this better, but my mind isn't cooperating.

After several minutes, she begins to stir, and I *feel* the moment she realizes she's not alone. I swallow hard and kiss the back of her head.

"Please let me explain," I whisper.

She shakes her head, attempting to extricate herself from my hold. "Please leave. I don't want you here. I don't even know you," she grits.

I tighten my hold. "You *do* know me. You know me better than anyone. I'm not leaving until you let me explain."

She starts to struggle against my hold, so I loosen my grip because I don't want her to hurt herself. She stands from the bed, brushing her tangled hair from her face. Her eyes, red and puffy, create a fracture in my heart—*I* did this to her. I'm such an asshole. I watch her steel herself, standing ramrod straight; she looks me straight in the eye as I sit up.

"I said I want you to leave. I don't want you in my home. Please give back my key and leave now, or I *will* call the police."

I can't believe she won't hear me out. "Please, Kate. It'll be okay. Let me explain."

"No!" she shouts, her face red with anger. Her small hands fisted at her sides. "Get out! I don't want you here. I don't know who you are. I can't believe I let you into my life, my home, my family, and my bed when I barely know you at all." Her breasts rise and fall as she takes a deep breath. "Get out!" she screams, her body shaking in rage when I don't move. I stand because I don't want to make things worse. Grabbing my jacket, tie, and shoes, I remove her key from my chain, place it on her table, then step toward the front door.

"I'm leaving. *For now.* I'll give you space, but I'm not letting you go. I told you, you won't be able to get rid of me even if *you* want to end this relationship, and I meant it."

I leave and close the door quietly behind me, ensuring it's locked.

Knocking on Margie's door, I ask her to watch over Kate for me and hand her my business card in case she needs anything. Climbing into my car, I drive back to my empty penthouse, feeling like the biggest piece of shit on the face of the earth.

I'm empty.

My heart left in pieces on Kate's bedroom floor.

Pulling out a bottle of scotch and a glass, I pour myself a drink. After swallowing it down and feeling it burn, I forfeit the glass, making myself comfortable on my couch with my new friend.

FORTY-THREE

-kate-

As I work to calm my breathing, there's a knock at my front door. My temper rises again. Why can't he just leave? Leave me alone! "Go away!" I shout through the door.

"I'm not going anywhere, young lady. Now open this door, or I'll get my key and let myself in."

I quickly move to open the door to let Margie in, and tell myself that I'm relieved it's not Oliver, but there's also a minuscule amount of disappointment that he gave up so easily. I shake off the thoughts and remind myself he was doing what I asked him to do.

Margie studies me closely. "You look awful, Katie-girl. What happened?" She leans into me, wrapping me in a fierce hug, hitting the back of my legs with her walking stick. The small amount of composure I had gathered breaks apart, and my tears start all over again. I'd have thought I would be too dehydrated to cry anymore, but apparently, I have an endless supply of tears.

"Oh, Margie, I'm such an idiot. If there was a prize for the biggest idiot, I would win, hands down."

Margie guides me to my couch, then heads to my kitchen to make me a cup of tea. Tea fixes everything, according to Margie. She's able to walk short distances without her walking stick already. She's truly astounding.

"You're not an idiot. Not at all. Now tell me, what has you in such a state, and poor Oliver looking like his puppy just died?" She pats my thigh and hands me my cup of tea.

"You saw him?"

"He knocked on my door, asking me to keep an eye on you. He looked ... broken. Much the same as you do." She sighs. "You young people don't know a good thing when you find it." Her gaze is wistful, as though she's remembering her own good thing. "Tell me what happened, Katie-girl." Her voice is soft and coaxing.

Closing my eyes, I draw in a deep breath. "He's Oliver Stone. *The* Oliver Stone. He owns a freaking building in the city and has his own charitable foundation." I look at her puzzled face. "I had no idea who he was. I'm such an idiot."

Margie still looks puzzled. "So? Who cares if he has a building and a charitable foundation? Why does it matter?"

"He lied to me. He told me he worked in corporate investments." I huff. *How can she not understand what this means?*

"He *does* work in corporate investments. It says so right here on his business card."

She pulls a card out of her bra and hands it to me. Clear, bold text slaps me in the face:

I flip the card over to find his contact number and email. "Why do you have his business card?"

"He gave it to me in case I needed anything. Such a sweet boy." She takes the card from me, slipping it back into her bra as though it's a prized possession. "Now tell me why it's such a problem that he owns a building and has a charitable foundation?"

I turn to face Margie, thinking about how to explain it to her. "Maybe he didn't lie, as such, but he also wasn't completely honest with me. I already felt at a disadvantage in our relationship because of the way he looks as compared to the way I look." Margie tries to butt in, but I hold up my hand to stop her. "I had become comfortable with the idea that he was in this relationship for the long haul. That he wouldn't dump me in favor of someone prettier or more interesting.

He … he made me feel beautiful. I was starting to relax in our relationship. But now this." I slap my thighs. "He's obviously incredibly wealthy, and that takes him way out of my league. I'm a kindergarten teacher struggling to pay off my mortgage and driving Nan's car. I buy the cheapest clothes I can find and get my hair cut once every six months to save money." My breath shudders. "I wouldn't have any clue how to live in his world. Let alone keep a man like him interested in me long term." I wipe frantically at the tears streaming down my cheeks as Margie moves in to offer me a comforting hug.

This discovery has cut to the core of my past hurts. One of my previous boyfriends at college thought it was okay to date multiple women because he had money. He couldn't understand why I was upset about his philandering ways when I discovered his infidelity. He informed me that all wealthy men have a wife at home and lovers on the side—it was almost expected of a man with a solid bank balance.

"My dear, dear girl. I have a feeling that might be exactly the reason that boy withheld the information from you." She pulls back, tracing her eyes over my face, and wiping my tears away. "I also think that maybe, just maybe, he wanted to live in *your* world, not the other way around."

"He must have been having a good laugh at my expense. I was always telling him he's too frivolous with his spending, buying me coffee and pastry every day, as well as lunch. That weekend away seemed extravagant. While I was blown away by it all, he appeared to be comfortable with the luxury and decadence of having a butler and a yacht with a full staff." I sniff, getting up to find my tissues to blow my nose and clean up my face.

"I doubt he was laughing. He probably thought it was refreshing. Can you imagine his life? I bet everyone around him wants something from him. But you only wanted *him*. Maybe that was what he was looking for. Don't be so hard on the boy. At least allow him the opportunity to explain."

I nod, but I need a little time to organize my thoughts and emotions. "I think I need time to digest this new information."

"Fair enough. But don't take too long." She stands, balancing against her walking stick. "I need to get back home. My show's about to start." I stand too and hug Margie, then walk her to the door. I watch her until she goes inside and I hear the locks engage, then I step inside to lock myself in for the night.

I check my phone, noticing I have a couple of missed calls from Roman. Shit, I completely forgot the reason I was in that meeting in the first place. I'll call him tomorrow. There are also several texts from Oliver.

BIG O

I'm sorry

I can explain everything

Please don't shut me out

I notice he didn't call me *Sunshine*.

I can't blame him, since I was screaming at him to leave me alone the last time I saw him. Certainly not my finest moment. Turning off my phone, I have a steaming hot shower, followed by a cup of hot chocolate. Then I put myself to bed for the night.

Sleep is difficult to find in my blistering cold and lonely bed without Oliver. I guess I'll have to get used to it.

———

I must have fallen into a fitful sleep because I wake to banging on my door.

Looking out of my window, I see Oliver's car parked in my drive-way. I'm not ready to see him. I need some time, some space. I stomp to my front door and without opening it:

I tell him to go away.

To leave me alone.

To give me some space.

I hear a muffled, "I'm sorry, Kate." And a thud vibrates through the door, which triggers another stream of tears. He sounds achingly sad and defeated—the same as me. I turn my back to the door and slide down the wood until my butt hits the floor, waiting to hear his footsteps take him away. It takes what seems a million minutes until I hear him walk away and his car engine roar to life. I cover my face with my hands, letting the tears flow, pouring out my heartbreak in the only way I can.

Eventually, I pull myself together and try to go about my day as usual.

It's better this way.

Better that I leave him *before* he leaves me.

Not that it hurts any less.

As I go through the motions of my regular Saturday chores, my laptop taunts me. It would be easy to type his name into the search bar, and I do well to resist the temptation through most of the day.

I return Roman's call from yesterday, apologizing profusely for letting him down. I told him I became unwell in the meeting and had to leave. He was completely understanding, telling me there are a lot of illnesses circulating at the moment. He got the information from one of his colleagues who attended the meeting. Apparently, it was Oliver who worked out what happened to the money. He's the one ensuring a conviction is brought down on the perpetrator.

I'm really proud of him. He's been working hard to sort out the problem.

The *Parkerville* situation must have been the work issue that caused him to disappear right before Christmas. *Why didn't he tell me then?* He could have easily explained he was working to sort out the problem of the closures of *The Parkerville* properties.

———

After a dinner comprising toast, because my stomach is so unsettled, I sit on my couch, attempting to read my latest book. I can't concentrate on the words on the page with all the confusion in my head. Looking across at my laptop, which has been taunting me all day, I chew on my thumbnail, debating whether to take a quick peek.

The laptop wins.

I put my book down and pick it up, turn it on, and open my favored search engine. I type **Oliver Stone** into the search bar and hit the return button. Instantly, the results load and at the top, it says: About 142,000,000 results (0.45 seconds).

Crap!

The initial results are for Oliver Stone, the American film director, but as I scroll further down the page, there are some pages for *my* Oliver. I click on images and the screen fills with hundreds of images of him. Mostly in suits entering or exiting special events. He appears different, more stoic, less free.

Scrolling through, there are several of him with extremely attractive women, lots and lots of different women. Each one is extremely pretty—model-worthy. There are quite a few of him with a petite blonde woman. I wonder if that's Sonia—if it is, she looks eerily similar to Crystal. The two of them look spectacular together.

My stomach rolls and folds on itself—my meager dinner fighting its way to the surface. Taking deep breaths, I manage to keep it at bay.

Shifting back to the *all* tab, I notice the first link is his company website. I click through to find information about Oliver Stone, the CEO of one of the most successful corporate investment companies in the US. The information is very bland and generic, telling prospective clients about his educational background, achievements, career highlights, and goals. Nothing personal to find here. I click out and check a few gossip sites, each one speculating about his relationship status with the latest woman on his arm. I come across an article from forbes.com, listing the richest men in America—Oliver is second on the list, and first for men under thirty-five. He's touted as a genius in his field, the likes America has never seen.

My head spins with the information, and I close out of the search, shutting down the machine as if it's burned me. I don't know what to think.

Yes, I knew he had more money than me. It was obvious in the car he drives, the suits he wears, and even his casual jeans are an expensive brand. But never in my wildest dreams did I think he was a billionaire! He certainly never gave off that vibe with me.

A freaking billionaire, for goodness' sake!

What in the hell is he doing with me? I don't understand. I look around my humble house and try to see it through his eyes. I wonder what he thought of it.

I repeat my routine from last night—hot shower, hot chocolate, and then bed. Once again, sleep is an evasive creature, and it's like I've been put through the wringer when I once again wake up to banging on my front door. Looking out of my window, I see his car in my driveway *again*—I don't have the energy to respond today. I sit in silence, hoping he'll go away.

I feel even worse.

Today is his birthday, and I know he has nobody to make a fuss over him. But my heart is cracked like glass—it won't take much to shatter it completely.

I can't do it.

I can't let him in

My phone alerts me to a new text.

BIG O

Please let me explain

Let me in. We need to talk

It was never my intention to hurt you

I think I need to stay with my parents for a few days, just in case this becomes a daily occurrence I'm not prepared to deal with. I start back at work tomorrow, and I need to be at my best for my students. I pack what I need, letting Margie know I'll be gone for a few days and she can call me if she needs anything.

———

When I arrive at my childhood home, a sense of calm and ease that comes with familiarity washes over me. My brother's car is parked in the driveway, which also lifts my spirits. We share a special bond—not sure if it's because we're twins or because we've always been close. He's not only my brother, but he's also my best friend.

I move to grab my duffel out of my trunk, preparing myself for the bombardment of questions I'm bound to encounter when I announce I'm staying for a few days.

Toby must have been at the front window because he comes out to help me with my duffel before I even close the trunk.

"Hey. You moving in?"

"Uh, yeah, just for a few days." I hug him from the side, hoping he won't notice my still puffy eyes.

He studies me closely. "What's up? You've been crying and now you're moving in with Mom and Dad. Something's wrong."

I wave him off. I should have known he'd notice. "It's nothing. Don't worry about me. How come you're here?"

He lets it go, knowing that I'll talk to him when I'm ready. "I'm going to be busy in the recording studio starting next week, so I wanted to spend as much time with Mom and Dad as I could. You know what my life gets like when I get in the zone." He laughs lightly. "The entire world ceases to exist, except for my music." I nod because I'm well aware he gets one hundred percent absorbed into his creative process when he's working on an album.

We step inside and Mom and Dad are waiting at the entrance with concerned expressions. Mom leans in for a hug. "Wow, aren't we extra lucky today? Both of our children decided to spend the day with us."

Dad pipes in, "It looks like she plans to spend more than just a day with us, Love."

"Hey, guys. Do you mind if I stay for a few days? I need a break from my place for a bit. Is that okay?"

Mom waves me off. "Of course, Katie-girl. This will always be your home. You know we love having you with us. I'll put some fresh bedding on for you."

She wanders off to change the bedding, while Toby takes my duffel through to my childhood bedroom. I'm not sure where Shane is. He's usually Toby's shadow, not that he needs his bodyguard when he's home with us.

Dad wraps his arm around my shoulder, and guides me into the kitchen. "C'mon, I was making a cup of coffee. You want one?"

"Thanks, Dad. I'd love one."

He winks at me, then gets to work, making my coffee the way I like it. When he's done, he nods his head toward the closed-in back porch and we make our way outside. We're settling in our chairs when Mom and Toby make their way out to join us.

"What's up? Maybe we can help?"

"Toby, Love, leave her be. She'll talk when she's ready." Mom smiles gently at me, setting off the waterworks all over again. I can't believe I have any water left in my body at the rate I've been crying.

"I'm such an idiot. A complete and utter idiot," I mutter.

Mom moves closer, stroking her hand gently up and down my back in comfort. "Now I doubt that's true. Why don't you tell us what happened? Then we can decide for ourselves."

I look up into the faces of the people I trust most in this world. They've always been upfront and honest with me. Like the time I wanted to sing as part of a duet with Toby, but I sounded like a dying cat. Mom gently told me I couldn't hold a tune, but maybe I could be his manager since my strength was being organized. I know they'll be honest with me.

"I found out that Oliver isn't who I thought he was. I'm such a fool. I can't believe I didn't see the clues."

Toby sits forward in his chair, clearly on the defense. "What do you mean *he isn't who you thought he was*? Did he cheat on you? Is he married or something? I'm pretty sure he was single. I'll kill him."

"Calm down, Son. There'll be no talk of killing anyone," Dad says firmly.

"No, nothing like that. He's *Oliver Stone*." I look at them with wide eyes, like *duh*. "*The* Oliver Stone. *The billionaire*, Oliver Stone," I say with an exasperated huff.

Mom, Dad, and Toby all look at each other in confusion. Don't they get what this means? What is *wrong* with these people?

"Uh, I hate to break it to you, Sis. But I already knew who he was. I assumed you knew." He shrugs, appearing amused at my lack of knowledge.

"How did *you* know? And how would *I* know? I don't keep up with the business world and I'm not on social media. I had no idea. I felt blindsided. I mean, I figured he earned a lot of money judging by his car and clothes and stuff, but I had no freaking clue he was a billionaire!" I throw my hands up in frustration. I look at Mom and Dad. "Did you guys know?"

They both shake their heads in the negative. "We're still getting over the surprise that he's the boy we cared for when you two were babies. What does it matter?" Mom asks gently.

While Dad says, "He seemed pretty normal to me." He shrugs. "How does his being a billionaire change anything?"

All three of them look at me, waiting for my answer. I can't believe I have to spell this out to them. "It changes every freaking thing."

Dad rubs his chin in contemplation. "Am I missing something here? I don't understand why the size of his bank account changes anything. That boy is so far gone for you, it's not funny." He watches me, waiting for my answer. "Toby's loaded, but you still love him."

How is that even the same thing? Toby's my brother. Of course, I'm going to love him.

"Well, for starters, he wasn't honest with me. What else don't I know about him?" I count off on my fingers. "Second, I don't know how to be the girlfriend of a billionaire, and third, and probably most importantly, what's he doing with a girl like me? When he can have anyone he freaking wants. He'll probably have a bevy of women at his beck and call, just like Keith did. Remember Keith? The one who thought because he had tons of money it was okay to date several women at once." I suck in a necessary breath because all of that came out in such a rush.

Mom tsks me, while Toby responds, "It seems to me you were doing an okay job at being the girlfriend of a billionaire because he was hoping to keep coming to our family dinners for as long as you'd let him." He glares at me pointedly.

Damn him for making sense like that.

Then Mom butts in. "In any new relationship, there are going to be things about the other person that you don't know. You learn about them along the way. That's a natural development. You can't expect to know everything about a person in such a short time. I can guarantee you haven't told him everything about you."

True, but hiding that you're a billionaire is pretty major. It's not like learning he doesn't hang his towel up after his shower—*right?*

"I didn't think we brought you up to be judgmental of other people. He shouldn't be punished for mistakes made by other men you've previously dated." She looks at me with disappointment, making me feel small.

Dad huffs, looking at me sharply. "I need you to explain the *third* comment. Something about *a girl like me?*"

What is it with these people? They don't see the disparities between the two of us. I *know* they're my parents and all, and they're supposed to only see the good parts, but let's be realistic here.

I straighten up. I need them to hear what I say. Understand what I say. "I already felt like I wasn't pretty enough to be with him."

Dad attempts to interrupt, but I hold up my hand in the universal sign of stop. Mom's looking at me with sympathy because we've already had this discussion.

"Please, let me get it all out before you tell me you think I'm wrong." I fiddle with the bottom of my T-shirt. "He is *incredibly* good looking and I've had an awful time keeping the interest of past boyfriends."

"That's because they were crap boyfriends. That had nothing to do with you. Just, maybe, poor choices on your part," Toby interrupts with a growl.

I smile timidly. "Either way, they've all strayed for someone prettier or more interesting. Or because they felt they were entitled to date more than one woman at a time. It took Oliver a while to convince me to give him a chance because I don't trust he'll stick around. He's breathtakingly handsome, kind, and generous to a fault—he certainly *could* have the cream of the crop. The images I've seen of him online with a bevy of attractive women support this." I take in a shuddering breath. "As you know, he persisted, and I gave in. He was very convincing and, to be honest, I was beginning to feel beautiful. I was growing more confident and less worried he would cheat on me. That took a lot of faith on my part." I stand up and move to the railing, leaning my back against the post. "But this adds an extra layer for me. Not only is he *that* good-looking, but he's also loaded as well. How appealing is that to most women out there? I can't compete and I can't risk my heart. I'm already in deep with him. I don't think I would survive."

Toby stands, wrapping his arms around me in a tight hold, allowing me to cry into his shirt. "Hey. You know, I saw him out to dinner with another woman. I could plainly see she was flirting with him—like a full-on assault. I heard him shut her down. Point blank. I honestly don't think you need to worry about him cheating on you, or being interested in anyone else." He squeezes me tighter, kissing the top of my head. "When I confronted him about it, he was genuinely upset that I would think him capable of cheating on you. My gut tells me he's a good guy."

Mom passes me the tissues to blow my runny nose. I must look like a complete wreck. "Maybe the attraction to you is that you're *not* after him for anything other than the man he is? Perhaps he could see your genuine interest in him as a person, rather than what you could take from him. Maybe, just maybe, you give him something else he's been searching for—something all the money in the world can't buy," she says, smiling softly.

Dad pats the chair next to him, encouraging me to sit down. "I recognized in him the same determination I had to win your mother over. He made his interest in you, and a future with you, very clear to all of us. He's an intelligent man. You have to give him credit that he knows what he wants out of life. I think you need to let him explain."

Everyone seems to be on Oliver's side. "But he kept something huge from me. Don't you understand? I-I don't know him."

"Just give him a chance. Okay?" Mom nods at me. "He must have had his reasons. Now I need to get lunch started. You three relax."

"I need time to get my head around it."

She squeezes my shoulder as she passes, reassuring me she understands. Gradually, Dad moves inside to watch TV, and Toby goes to work on some song that won't leave him alone. Thank goodness I'm back at work tomorrow. The kids will keep my mind busy and away from all things Oliver. I head upstairs to my bedroom to unpack for the few days I'll be here, choosing an outfit to wear tomorrow. My phone alerts me to a text.

BIG O

I miss you x

The tears roll from my eyes, and slowly down my cheeks, dripping onto my phone screen. I miss him too, but I'm not sure I can trust him, trust his intentions. I'm exhausted and completely wrung out.

FORTY-FOUR

-oliver-

I GET INTO THE OFFICE AT THE ASS CRACK OF DAWN. NOT EVEN A workout can extinguish the anger I have trapped inside of me. I *know* I only have myself to fucking blame, but the need to fucking punch something is strong. I spent most of the weekend working; attempting to take my mind off Kate, but it's not fucking possible. She takes up all the real estate.

Hours pass as I work on our major accounts. Employees begin to trickle into the office; lights turn on, computers boot up, and a steady stream of idle chatter breaks my silence.

The fucking noise is annoying as fuck.

I glance up from what I'm doing to find Jase leaning against my doorframe. "I don't pay you to stand in my fucking doorway, staring at me. Get to fucking work," I grumble at him.

He steps inside, closing the door behind him. "You look like you've gone ten rounds with Tyson. Are you okay?" He makes himself fucking comfortable in the chair opposite my desk, resting his foot on his opposite knee, slouching back like he has all fucking day to fucking sit and fucking chat.

"No. I'm not fucking okay and I don't want to fucking talk about it. I just want to get on with my fucking work. Can you get me the files for the Rhinecourt account? I've had an idea I want to follow up on."

He rises from his chair, nodding sharply. "Sure. I'm here if you want to talk, though. I know I'm *only* your assistant, but I also consider us friends."

Well, he knows how to make me feel like a fucking piece of shit.

He taps my desk and steps out to get the file I requested. He quickly returns, places it on my desk without speaking, and closes my office door with a snick behind him. I get to work on the account, discovering my idea will work; making Ms. Rhinecourt an additional thirty million dollars within two years.

My phone buzzes from Jase's line. "Yeah?"

"I have Gloria from *Coffee and Cookies* on line one for you."

"Can't you fucking deal with her?"

"I tried. She specifically wants to speak with you. Sorry, boss." He sounds somewhat apologetic.

"Fine, put her through."

I press the correct button to accept the call. "Hello, Oliver Stone speaking."

"Oh, hi, Mr. Stone. My name is Gloria—"

"I know who this is, my assistant informed me. How can I help you?" I know I'm being a fucking dick, but I'm not in the fucking mood.

"Oh, of course. Um, I've been delivering coffee and pastries to Kate, as per your request."

That perks me up.

"I wanted to let you know she canceled the ongoing order today. She also said that no matter what you said, she would no longer accept the gift of coffee and pastries daily."

Fuuuck! I'm losing her.

"Thank you for taking the time to let me know personally, Gloria. Please send through the final invoice and we'll be sure to get that squared away for you."

"Sure. No problem. If it's any consolation, she looked devastated."

"Thanks. But it's no consolation to me to know she's upset. Good-bye, Gloria."

I disconnect the call and throw my pen across the room. I wish it was something more satisfying, to be honest. I don't get any satisfaction knowing she's devastated.

I'm the fucking asshole who's made her feel that way.

I only ever wanted to make her happy.

Protected.

Loved.

Secure.

I've failed on every level.

Honestly, if I think about it, what do I know about relationships? The last healthy relationship I witnessed was my parents' relationship when I was seven. I only ever viewed that relationship through the eyes of a child. Clearly, I don't know what I'm doing. She's probably better off without me in her life. She deserves to have the best—the best husband and an incredible family of her own. I don't know the first thing about any of that.

The thought of ending things with Kate leaves me feeling cold. I can't fucking do it. I'm going to fucking fight for her if it's the last thing I fucking do. Selfish, I know. But too fucking bad. I pace my office, stopping to look out over the city when there's a knock on my door.

What the fuck now?

"Come in," I call out.

Jase opens the door and steps inside, closing the door behind him for the second time this morning. "What was that about? Gloria was pretty cagey and wouldn't tell me anything. Demanded to speak only to you."

I tuck my hands into my pockets as my shoulders slump. "Kate canceled the ongoing coffee and pastry order. She said she would no longer accept the gift from me. She asked her to stop bringing the delivery, no matter what I said." I huff out a breath, running my hands through my hair. Jase's expression is full of concern and sympathy. "I know you're dying to tell me *I told you so*, but I don't fucking need it right now."

"I wasn't going to say that. I would never kick you while you're down. There's no fun in that." He shrugs. "What are you gonna do?"

"I don't fucking know. She won't talk to me. Won't even answer her front door. Hasn't returned any of my messages. I think I've lost her. The one woman I want, and she doesn't want me." I slump down in my chair, releasing a deep sigh. The fucking irony.

"Well, you're not going to give up, are you? That's not the Oliver Stone I know."

I rub my hands down my face, noticing that my normally short beard is getting out of control. "Of course not. I'm trying to fucking give her some space and time to come to terms with what she's learned about me." I glance at Jase. "It might kill me to give it to her, but I fucking will. I owe her that fucking much. Then I have to come up with a plan to win her back."

"Well, if there's anyone with enough determination to break through the fortress she's building against you, it would be you." He leaves my office, closing my door with a sharp click.

I'm close to calling it a day. I can't concentrate for shit and my new friend, *Lagavulin*, is calling my name when a new email catches my eye.

Re: Update on Banking Situation
From: Marcus Trainor
To: Oliver Stone

Hello, Oliver

I've just received word from Mutual Banking Trust that our ninety-day deadline to pay the remainder of the mortgage started when the first payment was missed, which was two months ago. This means we have thirty days to raise the funds to save the properties.

I've been looking at the number of kids we have on the books and I think we can realistically reduce the number of properties by two. This solution will mean we have no room to take on any additional kids, or we will have to house them in our central location for longer periods, which isn't ideal. As you know, the beauty of the homes is that it gives the kids a sense of belonging somewhere. It's like a home with a parent and siblings.

We have seventy-six kids on the books at the moment. We can move a couple of kids around to fill thirteen properties to capacity, offloading two homes.
These changes will reduce the mortgage slightly.

Please let me know if you have any further suggestions or any other way you think we can solve our problem.

Kindest regards
Marcus
CEO
The Parkerville Project

I read the email twice, my jaw clenching. This is a fucking disaster. *What kind of sick fuck steals from homeless kids?* I can't wrap my mind around it. My head thumps a steady beat as a result of the email on top of everything I'm already dealing with in my personal life.

My line buzzes again. "Hey, I'm sorry, but I have Glen from *Lenny's Luscious Lunches* on line one. He will only speak with you."

Fuck, here goes. I bet she's canceled the lunch orders now.

"Put him through." I pick up the correct line. "Hello, this is Oliver Stone."

"Hi, Mr. Stone. My name's Glen from *Lenny's Luscious Lunches*. We had a standing order to deliver a range of lunches to Kate Summer over at Northwood Elementary at your request."

"Yes, I'm aware. How can I help you?" I don't know why I ask when my gut is telling me exactly why he's calling.

"Well, when our delivery guy took lunch to her today, she canceled the ongoing order. She said we were to stop delivering lunch to her, no matter what you said." He sounds unsure of himself. "Uh, I wanted to check with you that she had the authority to cancel the order?"

I clear my throat. "Of course she does. If she no longer wants lunch, then that's most definitely her prerogative. Please send the invoice to finalize the account. Thank you."

"No worries. Bye."

I disconnect the call before I crush the phone in my hand. She's certainly sending me a clear fucking message—she no longer wants to have anything to do with me. I want to talk with her, but there's no point while she's in class. She never accepts any calls. I'll stop by her place later this evening when I know she'll be home.

Stepping out of my office, I catch Jase returning to his desk with a coffee. He spots me. "Did you want one?" He gestures to his cup. "I can make it."

"Nah. I'm okay. You have a minute?" I nod my head toward my office. "Bring your tablet and coffee."

He collects what he needs, following me into my office. We both sit, and I turn my screen around to show him the email from Marcus.

"Fuck, thirty days?" He looks at me in disbelief. "What can we do to get that kind of money together in thirty days?"

"That's what I hope we can brainstorm. I don't want them to lose a single fucking property. This is too damn important. Even if I have to put work on hold *again*, I'm going to sort this shit out." I run my hands through my hair, looking at Jase. "Any ideas? We need to raise $10,000,000 to buy the mortgages outright, staff wages, running costs, and everyday costs associated with raising kids quickly." I click my fingers with a snap.

Even though I have an abundance of money on paper, most of it's tied up in assets and portfolios. The money I have on hand won't cover the mortgage. I can donate some to the cause, but not enough. "I can personally put in two million, leaving us eight to find."

He shakes his head. "You've already lost enough money because of this disaster. How can you be happy to contribute even more?"

"This is important to those kids. They need a stable environment. It means a lot to me too because of my history, but mostly, it means the world to Kate. She's devastated about what's happened to the kids. I need to sort this out as quickly as fucking possible for the kids, for me, and especially for Kate."

Jase sits, rubbing his stubbled chin, thinking but remaining quiet.

"Remember that gala dinner I went to last year? It was organized to raise awareness and money for the city's homeless women's shelter."

Jase nods. "Yeah, vaguely. Tickets cost a bomb if I remember correctly."

"Exactly. It was $5,000 per ticket. They also held an auction and raised close to $6,000,000. Maybe we could do something like that?"

Hope blooms that perhaps we can pull this off. The tickets will have to be more expensive and we would have to sell a lot of them, but I think it might be possible.

"It'll be difficult to pull off in the time frame we have to work with." He doesn't appear convinced.

"Well, we have no choice. We fucking have to. I'm going to take the lead on this project. Let's work out which accounts I can pass off to the team. I'll keep the most important ones, allowing me to focus on organizing this event."

Jase stares at me as if I've lost my mind.

Maybe I fucking have.

I usually begrudge taking time away from my *real* work, and yet here I am doing it for the second time in less than a month. We spend the next few hours going over our accounts, and I offload most of my accounts to my team, leaving me with half a dozen to manage. Once the gala's over, I'll pick them back up. Jase and I also make a basic list of where to begin and what we'll need to do.

To get the ball rolling, I spend the afternoon contacting the necessary people and organizations I need to contact. I shoot an email to Marcus, informing him I'm working on something which may help. I send emails to a couple of large, reputable hotels, explaining my purpose and asking if they'd be prepared to host such an event at a heavily discounted cost, allowing us to give as much money to the cause. I write emails to galleries, travel agents, designers, and importers to request donations that can be used in the auction. I've requested items with a minimum value of $10,000. This way, bidding can start at a reasonable figure—giving us the best return. I've also asked them to put me in touch with anyone else they think might be in a position to help. I can't do any more than that for today, so I call it a night and drive to Kate's.

———

Her car isn't in the driveway when I arrive, but I get out to knock on her front door, anyway.

No answer.

I try calling her, but my call is sent straight to voicemail, which is no surprise. I try knocking again, louder, knowing she won't answer. I don't want to give up, so I sit on her front step to wait for her to come home. After what seems like hours, but is probably less than fifteen minutes, I hear Margie's locks disengage and her door open.

She steps out with her walking stick. "What are you doing sitting on Kate's step?"

Taking a deep breath, I stand. "Hi, Margie. I'm waiting for her to come home. Any idea when that'll be?"

Margie studies me closely. "You look like shit, young man. Come in. I'll make you a cup of tea."

I follow her inside a space that's a mirror image of Kate's. Margie sets about making tea in her small kitchen, while I sit at her two-person dining table. She places a pot of tea on the table, along with two china teacups and matching saucers. We've done this several times before when she first came home from the hospital.

"Kate's gone to stay with her parents for a few days. She seemed rather upset, saying she needed some family time." She studies me closely as if she'll find answers to why Kate was upset. "Want to tell me what happened?"

Maybe Margie can help me out if I tell her what I did. "She found out something about me she wasn't expecting, and I guess she didn't like it."

Margie pats my hand. "What did she find out? What were you hiding from her?"

"I was eventually going to tell her, but I knew she would balk at being with me if she knew. I needed her to be fully invested in our relationship. Before I told her, I needed her to be in love with me. It was the only way I could think to keep her." I sigh, gazing into my tea. I realize I can't keep someone who was never mine to begin with.

"You're talking in circles, young man. Why would you think she wouldn't want to be with you?" She looks at me sternly, as if I'm not giving Kate full credit for the type of person she is.

"I'm a billionaire, Margie. There's no other way to say it. She was already gun-shy to date me because she had some ridiculous notion that she's not beautiful or interesting enough." I snort in disgust. "Which is utter bullshit!"

"Mhm. I agree with you there." She nods sagely.

"When we first met, she looked at me with interest. Like a woman does when she likes what she sees. It was purely based on physical attraction. Do you know how many times a woman looks at me in that way?" I look at Margie and she shakes her head in the negative. "Never. Exactly never." I breathe. "It was refreshing to be ogled for my body, and not my bank balance." Margie snorts a laugh. "At university, women could see my earning potential based on my academic program. Once I started my company and made money, I still attracted women who were after my bank balance, not me."

Margie nods along. "I don't think many men would consider that to be a burden."

She's probably right, and for me, it wasn't a burden until Kate came along and showed a different kind of interest—one I liked.

"You're probably right. But it was something new for me. I'll never forget how she made me feel like a man, instead of a meal ticket. There was something truly special about her, and I immediately felt drawn to her. I couldn't fight it. I tried to find her because I couldn't stop thinking about her. As I told you, I even hired a private investigator, and then I bumped into her. To me, it was a sign we were meant to be something to each other." I shrug. "I sound like a fucking pussy."

Margie pats my arm. "I get it. I really do. Kate's a very special young woman. She has the power to draw people into her orbit, and she doesn't realize her potency because she's especially sweet." She sips her tea, then glances up at me. "But you've hurt her. She feels betrayed ... lied to." Margie squeezes my arm to stop me as I try to interrupt. "I know you didn't tell her any untruths, young man, but you also weren't completely honest with her. I can understand why, because I know you had a difficult time convincing her to spend time with you. But when you had the chance, you should have told her. I think it made things much worse with the way she discovered your secret."

I nod because I fully agree; it would have been much better if she'd learned who I was directly from me, instead of the way she did.

"What can I do? She's completely shut me out. She kicked me out, won't speak with me, and won't even return my texts. My calls go directly to voicemail, and now I find she's left her own home to avoid me."

I can't believe the lengths she's fucking gone to.

"You have to give the girl time. She needs to come to terms with the reality of who you are and what that means. Give her some space. It's what she needs right now. Maybe if she misses you a little, you'll have a better chance of winning her back." She squeezes my arm, looking at me with compassion.

"Thanks. I guess I'll go home and let you get on with your evening." She stands with me, hugging me in a way I desperately needed. It's ironic. I'd gone years without that type of affection, never giving it a second thought. Until now. Now, I miss that simple gesture of intimacy so very much, and I'm terrified I'll never have it again.

Once again, I head home to my empty penthouse—*alone*.

———

A knock on my office door interrupts me as I respond to an email from the *Four Seasons*. Annoyed at the interruption, I snap, "Come in."

I remain focused on the email offering me a great deal for the privilege of hosting the gala. They've even offered us the use of their PR people as well as their event manager.

A throat clears.

Looking up from my computer, I find Jase standing next to a very pissed-off Toby, with Shane hovering near the door. I sit back in my chair, gesturing for both of them to take a seat.

Toby doesn't waste any time. "You've hurt my sister, and I told you to watch your fucking back if you stepped out of line with her. You wanna explain what happened before I pummel you into the ground?"

I explain everything to him, in detail. How much his sister means to me, what I hoped for in the future, how she found out about who I am, and why I kept my secret. As I work through my explanation, his anger dissipates as his shoulders relax and the tension leaves his face.

"If she would let me explain, we could put this behind us and move forward together. I don't want anyone else but her. She's it for me." I shrug. "I want her in my life, but I'm prepared to give her time. Then I'm going after her, and nothing is going to stand in my way," I tell him, raising my eyebrows to punctuate my plan.

Toby nods approvingly. "Sounds fair to me. If I can help, let me know. I want my sister to be happy. She was happy with you, and I could see her confidence steadily growing."

Jase pipes in. "Did you get the email you were expecting from the *Four Seasons* about the gala?"

"Yeah, I was just reading it. Their offer is incredibly generous."

"What's going on?" Toby asks.

Jase explains what I'm attempting to achieve for *The Parkerville Project*. "Oliver's putting his business on hold to work on this gala because it's immensely important to the kids and Kate."

Toby looks thoughtful as he rubs the stubble on his chin. "Do you have the entertainment organized yet?"

Jase and I look at each other. "Shit, didn't think of that."

"I could do it. Not to be boastful or anything, but I *am* a four-time Grammy winner. I can pull a pretty decent crowd. I would also be happy to auction off some of my time, or something along those lines." He shrugs carelessly, as though he hasn't just made my day.

Shane steps further into my office, away from the door. "You'll need to check your calendar, Toby. Things are getting busy for you."

Toby waves him off. "We'll work around it. No problem."

Not only is he prepared to help me win Kate back, but he's also prepared to help with the gala.

I get up from behind my desk, stepping around to shake his hand. "Thanks, man. That would help us out, and it means the world to me you've even offered."

"No problem. What date is the event? I'll let my manager know so she can get in touch with you. We can even use my PR people to help spread the word."

I share the necessary details, and he leaves my office, looking much calmer than when he arrived. I also feel a marked improvement in my mood, knowing I have his approval and support when it comes to Kate.

FORTY-FIVE

-kate-

THE PAST WEEK AT WORK FELT LIKE A CHORE, WHICH MAKES ME EVEN more miserable because I've always loved my job—it's something in which I've always found solace and joy. But right now, it's taking all of my energy to put one foot in front of the other as if I'm walking through molasses. I don't even want to get out of bed in the morning —ugh. One day seems to run into the next, and I'm not sure what day it is, or how much time has passed.

My world is drab and gray without Oliver.

I'm lifeless and disinterested in life, work, eating, reading, the kids —*everything*. But this was my choice; something I need to keep reminding myself. I could have let him explain, but it was more important to me to protect myself.

It's better this way.

I fake it for my students, but Emma sees right through my façade. She keeps begging me to open up to her, but I'm worried she'll say *I told you so*. After all, she suggested I search him online. None of this would have been a surprise if I'd done what she suggested.

I trudge through the week, with a promise to Emma that we'll meet for our regular coffee and cake catch-up next weekend. She even invited Margie along because she knows I won't deny Margie an outing to her favorite coffee shop.

———

Oliver hasn't contacted me for a few days—I guess he's given up.

I figure it's safe to move back to my place and get back to my routine. Mom and Dad are worried I'll have too much time alone and spend my time wallowing, but I felt awful leaving Margie on her own and need to be near her.

Seeing the evidence of Oliver in my space hits me hard when I open my door and wander around my little home. Socks he left behind. His toothbrush and shaver on the bathroom counter, and a couple of T-shirts and workout shorts in my bedroom. The hardest of all is his scent on my bedding and the towel he used that still holds the intoxicating scent that encompasses him. The scent I associated with warmth, caring, home … *love*. I strip my bed, remaking it with fresh linens, blankets, and a quilt. I change the towels and put everything into the washing machine.

On a mission, I find a box and move from room to room to collect and pack his things. I'll let him know he can come and collect them from my front porch. I save one shirt, tucking it under my pillow. Losing him completely is something I can't bear.

Maybe I'm a masochist?

Sleep is hard to come by, and I end up burying my nose in his shirt, using his scent to help me fall into a fitful sleep.

———

Saturday afternoon comes around, and I collect Margie so we can meet Emma for coffee. I'm not looking forward to this because I know they're going to meddle. Margie and I arrive at the coffee shop to find Emma already seated at our favorite table by the window. We all greet each other with hugs and move on to the important business of ordering our coffees, along with a selection of delicious cakes and slices we can all share. The conversation starts out light as Margie and Emma catch up, allowing me to zone out. My friends eat; however, I can't bring myself to take even a small bite. I usually love my coffee, but even that's lost its appeal.

Margie clears her throat and places her fork on her plate. "How are you doing, sweet girl?"

"I'm okay." I look anywhere but at Margie because she'll see right through my lie.

"No, you're not. You've been struggling all week, and I want to know why?" Emma huffs, watching me with a look that's somewhere between sympathy and a motherly scowl. *Geez.*

"Did she tell you what happened, Emma?" Margie asks.

Here we go.

"No, she won't share. Which means I can't help her." Emma seems hurt, making me feel like the lowest of the low.

Margie goes ahead, sharing my heartbreak with Emma.

In detail.

As though I'm not even sitting at the same table as the two of them.

Nothing's left out.

Emma looks at me with a *what-the-fuck?* look, and I shrink into my seat.

"What the hell is wrong with you? Anyone would kill to be in your shoes," Emma whisper-yells at me in exasperation.

"Exactly! He could have anyone. It's just a matter of time before he cheats or leaves me for someone much more suited to his billionaire lifestyle." I huff. "I'm already in too deep. When that happens, I won't survive. I need to get out before I'm in any deeper."

Emma calms slightly, her expression full of compassion. "I hate to break it to you, girl, but you're already in as deep as you can possibly be."

Something over my shoulder catches Margie and Emma's attention. Margie smiles and Emma sits up straighter, smoothing out her hair. I turn around and am shocked stupid to see Oliver striding toward our table with purpose—his intent written all over his handsome face. He looks stunning; as usual.

How on earth did he know I was here? I don't remember ever telling him about this place. It's not as though the café is in a prominent position, and he saw me in the window as he walked by. I turn back toward Margie and Emma, noticing Margie wink not-so-subtly at him.

She wouldn't have. Would she?

"Hello, ladies." He nods with a half-smile toward Margie and Emma, and then his mesmerizing green eyes zero in on me. "Kate."

Margie stands, hugs him, then introduces him to Emma. "Emma, this is Oliver, Kate's beau."

Oh my gosh, he's not my beau anymore. Did she listen to a word I said?

He holds out his hand to greet Emma. "It's great to meet you, Emma. Kate's told me a lot about you."

Emma blushes, placing her hand over her heart. "Nice to meet you as well. I hope she's only told you the good things about me. I wouldn't want you to get the wrong impression." She giggles like a schoolgirl, and I roll my eyes. *Oh, Emma.*

"Most definitely only good things. She holds you in high esteem." He turns to me. "Kate, do you have a few minutes to talk?"

I can't talk to him here in front of my friends. I know I'll become a mess and break down, and I certainly don't want to do that in a public place.

"I can't right now. I'm catching up with my friends." I turn my back on him.

Margie and Emma both do a double-take, their eyes growing wide. I know I'm being a total bitch, which is out of character for me.

He steps to the side, moving into my periphery. "I've given you time. I've been extremely patient. It's time you allow me to explain." His voice is deceptively calm, but his body is as tense as a rubber band ready to snap.

I stand, turning to face him. "I need more time. I can't put a time frame on coming to terms with the reality of not knowing the man I was sleeping with." I whisper-yell at him.

Several people in the coffee shop are now watching our exchange, making my annoying blush rise.

Shoving his hand through his hair in frustration, he mutters something unintelligible under his breath. Then he bends forward, situates me over his shoulder fireman style, wraps his arm around my legs, and stands up to exit the coffee shop. At first, I'm downright shocked I don't react, then I animate and begin to struggle in his hold. When I glance up through my unruly hair, Margie's smiling and Emma's clapping her hands and bouncing on her toes like the kindergarten children I work with every day. He keeps moving, ignoring my attempts to wiggle free. Nobody seems to think anything of a man walking down the street with a struggling woman slung over his shoulder.

What is wrong with people? He could be a serial killer for all they know!

He stops at his car, releasing the locks, then climbs into the passenger seat, positioning me so I'm straddling his lap.

I've missed this. This intimate contact with him.

One strong arm bands around my lower back, holding me tight to his hard body, while his other hand cups the back of my head. I've nowhere to go, and it's impossible to avoid his eyes in this position. He's studying my face intently, and I wonder if he can see my pain and hurt from his betrayal.

The lack of sleep, the lack of life.

He still looks as handsome as ever, even with dark circles under his eyes, an untrimmed beard, and messy hair.

I shouldn't, but I can't help but notice the firmness of his chest beneath my hands and his muscular thighs beneath my butt. It's not fair. Being this close to him devolves my ability to think rationally. This is a dangerous situation for me to be in with him.

"I need to explain. You're being unfair, and I won't let you throw away what we have. It's too special to let go without a fight." He reverently tucks a lock of hair behind my ear, glancing between my eyes and my mouth. "Give me ten minutes. If you don't like what I have to say, I'll walk away. It'll kill me to do it, but I'll honor your wishes."

I nod. "Okay." I'm surprised at the steadiness in my voice.

His chest rises and falls under my hands as he takes a deep breath, closing his eyes for a moment. "Remember when we met?"

I nod.

"I thought you were gorgeous from the instant I laid eyes on you. You were all sweetness, sunshine, enthusiasm, and bright smiles. You hugged Jase and me like we were old friends." He huffs a laugh. "When I noticed you checking me out as though I was a piece of meat, it made my day."

My body heats as my blush rises from my chest. I was hoping he hadn't noticed that.

He gently strokes my cheek with his thumb, looking at me with devotion. "I love your blush," he whispers.

He holds firm as I attempt to break eye contact by tilting my head down. "You're the only woman I've ever met who looked at me like a man, rather than a walking line of credit."

The sincerity in his gaze shocks me. I assumed he had women all over him all the time, solely based on *how* he looks. I berate myself because I never took the time to think about our relationship from his side, and some of the fight leaves me.

"When I came home, I couldn't spend time with another woman without comparing her to you, and how you made me feel in the short time I spent in your company. The connection I felt with you was nothing I'd ever experienced before—it was immediate. To be honest, the unfamiliar feeling knocked me on my ass. I think our childhood connection explains that somewhat."

Well, that's a bit of a surprise.

"I tried to get you out of my head, tried to convince myself I had built you up in my mind to be better than you were, but I couldn't shake thoughts and images of you out of my head. I even hired a private investigator to track you down."

He's told me this before, and it's no less creepy this time around. "You realize how creepy that sounds? Right?"

He nods sheepishly. "I know. Jase told me I was acting like a crazy stalker."

I can't help the chuckle that escapes.

"When I laid eyes on you at the renovation project, I couldn't believe my luck. I thought the universe was finally working in my favor. I knew I had to have you in my life, but you were so very wary of me. You were caught up in the idea that you weren't beautiful or that you wouldn't be able to hold my attention. Which is utter bullshit!" He sighs. "I knew I had to tread carefully with you." He glances out of the windshield, then back to me. "I felt as though you were never as invested in our relationship as I was. It felt as though you had one foot out, ready to run in the opposite direction," he whispers, his expression pained.

I attempt to interrupt, but he continues. I've clearly hurt him. The fortress I've kept around me, the one he's been working to break through, has ultimately damaged the man I know I've fallen in love with.

"I was prepared to move this relationship along at your pace, as long as you would let me be a part of your life. I thought once I felt you were fully invested like I was, I would tell you about my money."

At this moment, I feel small and mean. I made him feel as though I was never fully invested in us, which couldn't be further from the truth. I've unintentionally hurt him, and that hurts me.

"I never intended to keep it from you, but I didn't want you to have another reason to keep me at arm's length. I sensed my money would be an issue for you." He breathes deeply. "I am truly sorry you found out the way you did—it was never my intention. I never wanted to hurt you. I've only ever wanted to make you happy." He looks deeply into my eyes, his voice gravelly. "Please accept my apology."

Looking into his eyes, all I see is sincerity, heartbreak, and truth. I nod as tears fill my eyes, spilling over to track down my cheeks. "I accept your apology, as long as you'll accept mine. I didn't realize how much I was hurting you by holding back to protect myself."

His shoulders visibly relax as the tension leaves his body.

"I'm scared." He keeps my head steady as I try to look down at my lap. "I *am* more invested in this relationship than you realize. I'm in deep, and I know I won't survive *when* you tire of me." I swallow hard. Now's the time to explain my fears. "I, uh, dated a guy in college who had money. Old family money, but lots of it. I found out he was dating several women at the same time. When I confronted him about it, he blew me off and said it was expected for guys with money to have a wife as well as lovers on the side. He didn't understand what the big deal was."

He brushes his warm lips over my mouth with a gentle touch. "That guy was obviously a dick. It's not an expectation for wealthy men to be with several women at the same time." He kisses the tip of my nose. "I want you, Kate, *only* you. You're everything I didn't know existed in this world." He kisses me gently again, keeping it chaste. "I don't think you realize what *you* give to me. When I'm with you, I feel a sense of peace I haven't felt since I was a boy and Mom was still alive. I feel at home with you, as though I can finally take a breath. That feeling is beyond anything my wealth can buy me. You give me *so* much." He kisses the tip of my nose as punctuation.

I breathe deeply and look at him, studying him carefully, in awe of how vulnerable he's being. "I'm sorry my past relationships have had such a negative impact on us. I feel awful because I promised I would work on my issues, but I can see I never did. I only pushed them aside." I slide my hands through his hair, massaging his scalp, bringing them to rest at the base of his neck, allowing me to play with the strands resting on his collar. "I don't know how to be the girlfriend of a hot billionaire." My voice is small and unsure.

He laughs, and the final tension he was holding leaves his body.

"That's the whole point. I didn't want you to be the girlfriend of a *hot* billionaire. Underneath all of that, I'm just a man who wanted you to be *my* girlfriend." He rubs my cheek with his thumb, smiling at me. "Think you can do that?"

I'm still unsure. "I promise to try. But I don't know the first thing about your world; living in your world. Is that why I've never been to your apartment? Because you already know I won't know what to do? Or how to act?"

He shakes his head from side to side. "No. Not at all. I don't care about all of that. It's not important to me. I want to be in *your* world, where the sun shines and there's joy and love; *that's* why I never took you into mine." He looks out the window again, as though he can't look at me. "It also would have been obvious how much money I had. I live in the penthouse of Stone Tower." He huffs, pushing his fingers through his hair; I can see that's why his hair is such a mess. "Before you came into my life, I only left my building for business meetings or socially expected appearances at fundraising events. I was pretty reclusive. The life I led was sad and hollow. I didn't realize it before I met you. The business of making money was my sole focus. I'd been hurt as a child and as an adult, so I locked myself away. I don't have friends, and you know I only have my father."

My heart breaks for this wonderfully complicated man. He's had such a sad and lonely life, surrounded by people who don't see him as a person—only as a means to an end.

"What about Jase? I thought he was your colleague and friend. Who is he to you?"

He looks sheepish. "He's my assistant. I employed him over six years ago now. Over the years, we've grown close. He's almost like a brother to me." He shrugs. "If it's any consolation, he's pissed at me for not telling you sooner." He kisses the tip of my nose. "We were working on the school, and then again on the renovation where we met for the second time because he was trying to improve people's perception of me."

"Well, I'm happy to know you've had at least one person in your corner." I huff. "All those times I told you that your boss expects too much of you. You *are* the freaking boss!" I sigh. "You must have been having a good laugh at me."

"Never, Kate. Never. It made me feel like absolute shit that I was keeping something monumental from you."

I lean in to kiss him, gently pressing my lips against his mouth. At the feel of his lips against mine, I release a heavy sigh of relief. I thought for sure I would never touch him in this way again. His lips move against my mouth, licking his tongue over my bottom lip, encouraging me to open. We get swept up in long, drugging kisses, and our breaths become choppy.

He pulls away and his eyes flit between mine. He still seems worried. "I need to confess a couple more things to you before we move forward." He glances down and then back up at my face. "Full disclosure. No more secrets."

Oh, gawd. This doesn't sound good. I brace myself for whatever he's about to tell me and nod, encouraging him to go on.

"There's no easy way to confess. It's probably best if I just say it. When your car broke down, I asked Max to replace everything mechanical. Your car is pretty much brand new, apart from the body and interior." My mouth drops open in shock, and I'm lost for words. "I wanted to buy you a new car, but I realized you were attached to it because it was your nan's car, so I worked around it." He brushes his nose along mine. "Please don't be mad. It kept letting you down and I was worried you'd be left in a dangerous situation."

I'm stunned. "Oh my gosh! You sweet, generous man. Thank you for taking such good care of me, even when I didn't know you were doing it." I smile gently. "Nan's car does mean a lot to me. I can't explain how much it means to me that you were respectful of my sentimental attachment to it."

"There's one more thing."

Ugh. This is crazy.

"I paid for Margie's hospital stay, operations, physical therapy, and in-home nurse recovery program. She didn't have private insurance to cover the additional costs associated with her surgery. She would have ended up with an enormous bill which she shouldn't have had to deal with."

Oh. My. Gawd!

This man.

How can I be upset with his kind generosity toward someone he's only recently met? I think he takes my shocked silence as displeasure.

"Please don't be mad, or use this as an excuse to walk away. I only meant to help—"

I cut him off, pressing my lips to his in a kiss full of gratitude and appreciation for his kindness. I lick my tongue across the seam of his lips, encouraging him to open to me. He presses in closer, sealing our mouths, and uniting us as deeply as possible with our clothes on. His hand tightens in my hair, tilting my head to take the kiss deeper when there's a knock on the window.

I startle away from Oliver, and we both look out of the tinted glass; finding Margie's face pressed up against it, attempting to peer inside. We burst into laughter at the sight as he unlocks the door, alerting Margie to move away. Once she's out of the way, Oliver opens the door, helping me out, then following close behind. He tucks me into his body, allowing me to wrap my arms around his torso.

Margie looks between the two of us, and her expression tells me she's happy with what she sees. "Oh, thank goodness. You've made up."

She steps into us, wrapping her arms around us both in a tight hug. She's strong for a woman her age. I glance across, finding Emma holding my purse with a genuine smile as she holds up two thumbs and winks at me.

I look toward Margie but ask Oliver. "How did you know where to find me, anyway?"

Margie smiles brighter, while he clears his throat, putting his hands in his pockets. "I texted him." She responds proudly. "You were being a stubborn brat, and I wasn't having it anymore."

Oliver attempts to hold back a laugh while Emma lets loose a loud chuckle. I can always rely on Margie to be straight with me.

I step forward, embracing her in another hug, full of gratitude. "Thank you, Margie. I love you big time, lady."

"I love you too, Katie-girl. Now go and have some hot make-up sex."

She winks at Oliver while patting me on the arm. Emma chokes on nothing, and Oliver bursts out laughing. My annoying blush takes over my whole body as if I'm on fire. I should be used to her lack of filter, but she still catches me off-guard sometimes.

"Emma's going to drop me home." She reaches back to Emma, who's still holding my purse. "Here's your purse. Off you go."

FORTY-SIX

-oliver-

OXYGEN FINALLY FILLS MY LUNGS. I FEEL AS THOUGH I HAVEN'T TAKEN a proper breath in the last two weeks. There's sunshine in my world again, color and purpose. The relief of having her with me again is monumental, and something I certainly don't intend to take for granted. I can't believe the assholes she dated in the past. They have a lot to answer for, and I wish I could go back and punch Brandon in the face again.

"How about I take you to my place? I can show you where I live and work."

She looks up at me with a tremulous but grateful smile. "I would really love that."

I take her hand and open the passenger door, allowing her to situate herself inside. "We'll come back to get your car later. Okay?"

"Of course." She nods, putting on her seatbelt, beating me to it.

Closing the door, I make my way around the front to the driver's side. Getting in, I admire Kate sitting in the passenger seat. "You look perfect sitting there." I didn't think I'd ever have her in my car again.

"I think I would look even better if I were sitting there." She winks, gesturing to my seat.

Laughing, I let her know that's not happening anytime soon. I'm very protective of my baby. We make our way toward my building in relative silence, our hands entwined on the console between the two seats, enjoying having each other close.

"About Margie." Kate faces me. "I don't want her to know I paid her medical bills."

"Why not?"

"She received the best possible care. That was my goal, and it's enough for me. I don't need her gratitude or feeling as though she's indebted to me for any reason."

She contemplates what I'm saying and nods in acknowledgment. "She won't find out from me. Your secret's safe." She squeezes my thigh. "Just so you know, I think what you did for her is highly admirable and extremely generous."

As we get close to Stone Tower, she leans forward, studying the building through the windshield.

"You know, I was quite taken with this building when I first saw it. I thought about how it was coincidental that there was a building with your name on it." She shakes her head. "I can't believe I didn't put the pieces together then."

Squeezing her hand, we make our way into the parking garage to park in my allocated bay. Exiting the car, I take her hand, guiding her to the elevator. I place my hand on the security panel to call the elevator.

Her eyes widen as she laughs. "This is very James Bond. Very schmancy!" She nudges my arm with her shoulder.

Smiling, I wink at her. Once the doors open, I drag her inside, pinning her to the wall with my body. "My handprint is my security. This elevator only stops at my penthouse when I press my hand to the panel. Otherwise, it's a regular elevator, requiring the user to select a floor." I gesture to the panel. "You'll notice my floor isn't available for selection."

She looks across. "The top floor is forty-nine. How many floors does your building have?"

"Fifty. I have the top floor, and the roof is also only accessible from the penthouse. There's an indoor pool and entertaining area up there. I'll show you later. The view across the city is spectacular. I'll get your handprint added by security."

Being back in her orbit settles me. Feeling her body against mine, having her smiles, her laughter, her eyes on me—soothes my soul. Leaning closer, I run my nose from her ear down her neck, gently biting her collarbone.

She shivers from my attention, fisting my shirt in her hands, drawing me closer. The elevator comes to a stop and the doors open to my foyer, interrupting us.

I normally appreciate the speed of the elevator, but I'm cursing it this time.

FORTY-SEVEN

-kate-

OLIVER STEPS BACK FROM ME AND HIS HOME COMES INTO VIEW.

A gasp bursts over my lips.

I don't know what to take in first. The first thing I notice is all the glass and the cold, sterile atmosphere of his place. It's akin to being in a fishbowl—a very decadent fishbowl. I make a beeline for the windows and am immediately overwhelmed by the view. It's magnificent.

"I bet this looks sensational at night."

Moving from window to window, I take it all in. Turning back around to face the room, my heart sinks for Oliver. It's devastatingly cold and sterile. Don't get me wrong, it's elegantly furnished and decorated, but there are no signs a person lives here—no photographs, no tossed shoes, no personality, no warmth. It drives home what he was telling me in his car.

My heartbreak must be written all over my face because his expression is one of concern. Stepping toward me, he takes me in his arms.

"What's wrong?" He leans back, looking between my eyes, studying my face, while skimming his hands soothingly up and down my spine.

"Nothing's wrong. I'm sad looking at your space—it seems cold and lonely. I guess I didn't fully comprehend how lonely your life was for you until I saw your home."

He kisses my nose. "*I* didn't realize it until you came along. This has only ever been a place to eat, sleep, work out, and shower. Your place feels like home to me." Taking my hand, he kisses it reverently, then steps back. "Let me show you around. Then I'm going to pack a few days' worth of clothes and we're going back to your place."

He shows me from room to room, which all look pretty much the same. The whole place is decorated in various shades of gray, from the dark-stained, almost black, timber floors to the light-gray, almost white, painted walls. The rooftop is the most divine feature, besides the view from every room in his penthouse. The Olympic-sized pool with a built-in spa at one end is to die for. Talk about how the other half lives. I don't think my eyes could grow any wider if I tried.

Oliver takes me downstairs to his offices, which occupy the next two floors below his penthouse, some of which I've already seen. The gray stone floors, steel, and glass provide a modern feel to the space. His office comprises a suite of rooms—one being his actual office, a large meeting room, a fully contained kitchenette, and a well-appointed private bathroom. Windows line all the external walls, affording an outstanding view, which I bet he rarely takes time to enjoy.

"Do you use all this space?" I find it unbelievable that one person needs this much space at work. It's like a mini apartment.

"Well, yeah. Mostly." He looks around as if he's seeing it for the first time. "I guess it must seem decadent, but I put in long hours and a lot of it is about convenience. This way, I don't have to waste time running upstairs."

We head back up to his penthouse after he uses his handprint at the elevator, which blows my middle-class mind. He seems in a hurry to pack up and get out of here.

"What's the rush?" I ask. *Maybe he doesn't like having me in his space?*

"Hmm?" he responds almost absentmindedly, without looking up from what he's doing.

"You seem as though you're in a rush to get me out of your apartment."

He puts down the T-shirt he was holding and steps into me. Cupping my face in his large hands, he tilts my head back gently to peer directly into my eyes. "Since I started spending time at your place, I don't enjoy being here. It feels cold and lonely. These past two weeks have been hell," he breathes. "I spent as much time as possible in my office to avoid the loneliness. I only came up here to shower and change. I got little sleep because I couldn't settle without you near." He kisses my forehead and the tip of my nose as my heart smashes into tiny pieces all over the floor.

I swallow down my guilt. "I'm sorry."

I've been such a bratty bitch. If only I'd given him the chance to explain the day I found out. I was distraught and went straight into self-preservation mode, and I wasn't thinking rationally.

I hurt him ... *deeply*.

I don't deserve this man. But I'm not letting him go again.

"I'm honestly sorry I acted so horribly toward you. I'll never forgive myself." I feel sick to stomach.

He shakes his head in the negative and smiles gently. "You have nothing to be sorry for." *Well, that's an absolute lie.* He kisses my forehead and the tip of my nose as if to reassure himself I'm here. Since the café, he's had his hands or some other part of his body in constant contact with mine. "Promise me you won't ever leave me again," he whispers, his vulnerability palpable.

Pressing up onto my toes, I kiss his bristly chin, ensuring I have his eyes when I throw his words back at him. Unequivocally telling him, "I promise you won't be able to get rid of me, even if you try." I only hope I can keep my fears at bay to keep my promise.

He takes my mouth in a possessive kiss, which heats my body and curls my toes instantly. I lose all sense of time as the kiss progresses to something deeper, something that expresses the loss we both felt over the past two weeks. It's full of relief for our reunion and the promises we've made to stay together.

Oliver finishes packing, and we make our way down to his car. I can't wait to get him back to my place. I'm going to show him some tender loving care. I need to make up for my unforgivable brattiness these last weeks.

FORTY-EIGHT

-oliver-

THE TENSION I'VE BEEN CARRYING ACROSS MY SHOULDERS SINCE KATE kicked me out dissolves as soon as I step foot back inside her home. My breathing deepens, and that sense of peace and calm only she provides washes over me. I spot a box packed with my clothes near the front door, and I look at Kate, setting off her gorgeous blush.

"I collected all of your things with a plan to return them to you." Her gaze drops to her feet.

Stepping closer, I use the tips of my fingers to tilt her face up to mine. "I guess that's to be expected. Let's unpack all this later. I have some reacquainting to do."

I take her mouth in a rough kiss, expressing all of my frustration over our separation. I work hard to restrain myself, gentling the kiss and slowing down to savor our reunion. My body's alight with anticipation of having her tight pussy wrapped around my cock. Without breaking our kiss, I lift Kate beneath her ass, encouraging her to wrap her legs around me; noticing she's lost weight. Her arms automatically wrap around my neck as I kiss her all the way to her bedroom—I need a bed for this. I want to take my time with her. I need to show her how much I missed her and how much she means to me. Later, I can take her hard and fast against the wall. One of my favorite things to do.

As eager as I am to get to the main event, I need to slow down and take my time—I have two weeks to make up for. I lay her gently on the bed, still tasting her mouth, absorbing her breaths, stroking her tongue. Our hands roam, reacquainting ourselves with each other's bodies. I remove the fabric between us—desperately needing to feel her skin against mine. As more of her silky skin is exposed, I trail my hands and lips over her body—tasting, touching, licking, and nipping, paying special attention to her luscious tits.

Her breaths quicken as her body trembles in response to me. "You have too many clothes on." She eagerly pushes and pulls at my clothes. "Get them off. Please. I need to have your skin against mine."

I kiss the tip of her nose and push myself up from her bed to remove the offending items as quickly as possible. "Anything for you, Sunshine."

I can't tear my eyes away from her. She's fucking stunning. The puffiness of her lips from my kisses fills me with male satisfaction, and I mentally congratulate myself for marking her spectacular tits with a beard rash caused by my eager attention.

Removing my shirt, I discard it quickly while she watches with half-lidded eyes. Sitting up, she shuffles to the edge of the bed, coming close enough to reach me. She immediately releases my belt buckle, quickly followed by the button and zipper in one swift motion, and then she wiggles my jeans from my hips so they fall to the floor. I toe off my shoes, then slip my jeans and socks off. As I stand upright, I remove my boxer briefs and kick them away. My heart is beating desperately fast, and I'm worried it's going to explode out of my chest.

She leans forward quickly, licking straight up my cock, from my balls to my tip, then she takes the length in her mouth and moans. The vibrations shoot through my cock to my balls, and I can't stop the groan that escapes in pleasure—my head dropping back on my shoulders in ecstasy. Her hot, wet mouth surrounding my shaft is unreal. It takes all of my willpower to fight the urge to grab her head and fuck her mouth into oblivion. It's such a turn-on to know she's as desperate for me as I am for her.

I attempt to pull away, but she grabs my ass, holding me close. *Who am I to argue with the lady?* She sucks and licks my cock like it's her favorite treat and she's been deprived for too long. The vibrations caused by her little moans send my cock into hyper-drive. It feels so fucking good to have her mouth on me, taking me into her warmth, but I need to be inside her tight pussy when I come—which will happen too soon if I don't stop her.

"Your mouth's sensational, but I need to be inside your hot pussy when I come," I groan as she pulls away.

I push her onto her back, drop to my knees and spread her legs further apart with my shoulders. Studying her glistening pussy, I use my fingers to spread her lips. "You're already so fucking wet." I slide a finger inside slowly, and we both groan at the sensation. "Your pussy's gripping my finger extra tight to welcome me home." I slide out and back in slowly, then lean forward to swipe my tongue up her slit to her clit, nipping gently with my teeth.

Her hips jolt off the bed, and I place my hand on her trembling stomach to keep her still until I've tasted my fill. She moans long and low and attempts to thrust her hips in time with the pumping of my finger. As I slide out, I replace one finger with two, causing her to whimper. I scan her curvy body, finding her massaging those firm tits, her head thrown back in ecstasy. Her pussy convulses around my fingers as she falls apart, and her body trembles while her legs tighten around my head. I gentle my fingers and my kisses, then slowly move up her body, lavishing her trembling flesh with kisses until I get to her breasts, which I suck into my mouth.

"Oh my god," she whispers reverently. "I can't believe how good you are at that." She giggles, and it's one of the very best sounds.

I want to hear it every single day.

"What's so funny?" Smiling, I look up at her flushed face. Feeling fucking fantastic that I can make her happy.

"Nothing. I'm just happy." She sighs. "I missed you more than I ever thought would be possible."

"You missed my tongue and fingers," I state as a joke. I know exactly what she means—I missed her desperately.

"Well, I missed those too, but I missed *you* beyond belief. The time apart made me realize how important you are to me, and how much I love spending time with you."

She moves in to kiss me, but it's impossible to be passive. I swipe my tongue over the seam of her lips, encouraging her to open to me, and our tongues move in a familiar dance. *I love that she can taste herself on me.* I bite her bottom lip, then lick away the sting. Shuffling her up the bed, I position myself between her thighs, swiping the crown of my throbbing cock through her slick, swollen folds.

Locking eyes, I slowly slide my cock into her tight heat. I hold in place, maintaining eye contact to check she's still with me. Her pussy feels heavenly, strangling my thick shaft. Right here is where I belong, and I vow right now we'll never spend time apart again.

She attempts to tilt her hips, encouraging me to move. "Please move. I need you to move," she pants.

I teasingly slide almost all the way out and then back in, slowly.

"Anything for you. Watch my cock sliding in and out of your tight pussy. Watch us joining, the way we're meant to."

She looks down between our bodies, groaning. "Feels so good." She brings her feet up to press into my ass as she tilts her hips upward. "Harder. Please!"

I slide out, careful not to leave her body, and then slam back in. I repeat the process over and over—a gentle slide out, a hard slam in. A sheen of perspiration forms over both of our bodies, making our hot skin slick. The scent of sex fills the air, a heady scent that turns me on further, making my cock lethally hard. Her pants and my grunts add to the sound of skin slapping against skin.

Her internal walls begin to contract, strangling my cock. I hold on to my rhythm as long as I can until I feel her quake and break apart beneath me, permitting me to let go. My thrusts become frantic, leading to my own explosive release. Tingles shoot down my spine as my balls tighten up; blackness forms around the edge of my vision as I come, and come, and come some more. I throw my head back with a long groan and my entire body shudders with my orgasm that doesn't seem to have an end.

I collapse to the side of Kate, rolling her with me, while keeping my cock inside the haven of her body. I gently swipe away the hair stuck to her face, checking she's okay as we both catch our breath. She graces me with a shy smile and nuzzles into my neck like a kitten.

I kiss the top of her head. "I'm gonna want to repeat that. Several times."

She giggles and I groan as her walls squeeze my half-spent cock. This is the only place I want to be for the rest of my days.

I tenderly carry her into the shower and can't resist the pull to take her again. Holding her against the tiled wall, I pound relentlessly into her body until she cries out her release and I swiftly follow with my own. I'm never going to get enough of this kind-hearted, sexy woman.

After we've dried off, Kate prepares a plate of cheese, crackers, and fruit for a picnic on her bed. As I move the pillows to make us more comfortable, I discover one of my T-shirts hidden under her pillow. Holding it up, I raise an eyebrow at her in question, eliciting a shy smile and her breathtaking blush.

She casually shrugs her bare shoulder. "I couldn't bear to let everything go. I was going to keep that one, hoping you wouldn't notice." She turns away from me, embarrassed.

I carefully draw her face back to mine, kissing the tip of her delicate nose. "You can keep them all."

As we eat, I mention the gala I'm organizing and how Toby offered to be the entertainment. When I explain we only have two weeks to gather the funds to save the kids' homes, she immediately offers to help in any way she can. We make a plan for her to stop by my office to look through what we've done so far on Monday after she finishes work. Tickets went on sale last Monday, making fine-tuning the event a priority.

I also tell her about my visit with my father and his counselor. I think we cleared the air during our two-hour meeting. He carries a great deal of guilt for the accident which killed Mom, but his biggest burden is not being the father I needed growing up—that he checked out, leaving me to grow up on my own. It was probably the most honest and open discussion we've had, and I'm hopeful we'll be able to forge some kind of relationship moving forward. Kate's ecstatic for me, which I knew she would be. I now have a standing appointment every second week with him and Dr. Wyatt at *Square One*.

We spend the rest of the weekend in bed, reacquainting ourselves with each other's bodies and showing the love and affection we have for each other, without saying *the* words. I have this desperate need to have some part of me touching her constantly—as if the constant touch reassures me she's still with me. Kate's easy with her affections, and I feel the fractured part of my soul settle for the first time in a very long while.

FORTY-NINE

-kate-

OVER THE LAST TWO WEEKS, OLIVER AND I HAVE WORKED SEAMLESSLY together, preparing for the best gala event possible. He and Jase had already done the bulk of the work before I stepped in to help. Mom, Dad, Toby, and even Margie have helped wherever possible, and I *know* we've given the event the very best chance of success. The response from the rich and famous has been mind-blowing. Tickets sold out within forty-eight hours, and offers came in from far and wide for the use of vacation homes, personal jets, and dates to be auctioned for the cause.

Tonight's the big night, and it seems I have a flock of humming-birds taking flight in my stomach. Oliver insisted on taking Mom, Margie, and me shopping for our dresses and shoes for this event; which I reluctantly agreed to after we had a massive argument. I laid down some serious boundaries regarding his use of money where I'm concerned.

I don't want it.

I'm not interested in it.

I don't want his money to change who I am as a person; who we are as a couple. I *know* he has money, lots of it. I know there will be certain aspects of life with Oliver I will have to accept, but I don't want him ever to think I'm with him because of his money or for what he can give me.

He wasn't happy, but he eventually acquiesced to my *unreasonable* request—his words. If it were up to him, I would have had a full day of pampering with someone doing my hair and makeup. I wouldn't have felt like me.

I shower, wash my hair, shave, and scrub my body with extra care, ensuring my skin is smooth and silky. I've never been to an event like this and as excited as I am, I'm also nervous I'll struggle to meet society's expectations of what a billionaire's girlfriend should look and dress like. I only hope I don't embarrass him.

Maybe I should have taken up his offer of a stylist.

I blow my hair, styling it into smooth waves down my back, and apply my makeup, with a focus on my sapphire eyes, balancing it out with a pale matte lip color. I blew my budget to purchase some sexy red lingerie to wear beneath my dress to help me feel empowered.

I slip my feet into my red satin sandals, which have a single strap across my toes, painted in the same color, then get to work wrapping and tying the lustrous laces around my ankles and lower calves. Standing, I'm a little wobbly because I'm not used to wearing such high heels. I've been practicing for the last few days, but the wobble is real. Ballet flats are my go-to for work and my Converse for the weekend, so I feel a little odd; it's strange being this tall.

I carefully slide into the elegant, full-length black V-neck, off-the-shoulder satin dress. The fitted bodice shows off the top of my boobs sensationally—*Oliver may well swallow his tongue.* Hidden within the gathers of the full skirt is a long split, which goes all the way to the top of my thigh. The dress is very demure until I step forward, exposing the full-length split—making me feel sexy. The best thing about this dress is the hidden pockets, meaning I won't need a purse—*yay for me.*

I spritz some of my favorite perfume on my pulse points, finishing with the diamond stud earrings my parents gave me for my twenty-first birthday. There's a knock on my front door as I shove my essentials into my pockets.

I hurry to the door as quickly as I can in my heels, opening it swiftly to find Oliver, looking absolutely edible in a dark green tux that appears almost black. Fitted to perfection across his broad shoulders and tapering in at his slim waist, showing off his masculine physique. My eyes rake down his body and up again in heated appraisal. When I finally make my way up to his face, I see the same appreciation in his eyes, making my heart skip a beat and my skin warm. I can't believe this incredible man looks at me the way he does.

He steps into me, one hand wraps around my waist, the other slides to the back of my head under the fall of my hair. He pauses and then kisses my forehead. "You look otherworldly." He sucks in a sharp breath. "You've stolen all the air from my lungs." His warm hands come up to cup either side of my face as he whispers, "Can I kiss you?"

I can only nod. The reverence in his voice has stolen my voice and my heart. I can't help but wonder how many times I can fall in love with him. He moves in slowly, and my eyes close of their own volition to prepare for the potency that is Oliver. At first, his kiss is gentle, almost sweet, before deepening, becoming more demanding. I'm unsure how long we kiss, but we're interrupted by a throat clearing. He presses his forehead to mine, winking at me with a soft smile and a warm chuckle.

"C'mon, you two, we don't have all night." Margie huffs. "I imagine it would be poor form for the hosts to arrive late to their own event." We all snicker at that comment, making our way toward the waiting limo after locking up.

Once we're settled and on our way, Margie studies the two of us for several beats. "I must say, you two make a handsome couple. You'll make beautiful babies."

I almost choke at her blasé statement, but Oliver takes it in stride. "If our daughters are as kind-hearted and as beautiful inside and out as Kate, I'll be the luckiest man in the world."

My heart melts and I feel completely secure with Oliver right now. I lean across to whisper in his ear, "I'm hoping we have little boys who have a generous spirit and look just like their daddy." Then I kiss his neck, just below his ear. "I didn't get a chance to tell you how edible you look in your tux, Mr. Stone."

He kisses my exposed shoulder, making my body heat. I have to keep reminding myself we have Margie in the car, and our PDA needs to be kept suitable for public observation.

Margie turns to us with a small smile. "I'm extremely proud of you two. I know tonight's going to be a tremendous success and I want to thank you for including an old lady." Margie's eyes have a glassy sheen to them as she nods sharply, then turns away to stare out of the window. The outfit Oliver bought Margie for this evening is lovely: a muted mossy green, with lace sleeves and overlay. Its fitted bodice with a scoop neck gives way to a straight skirt, stopping at her ankles. She looks great all dolled up. I feel my own eyes burn with tears, which I barely keep at bay.

We arrive at the *Four Seasons*, which has been awesome throughout the entire process of putting together such a large-scale event with very short notice. They only requested a heavily discounted payment for the food and beverages for the evening. The hotel kindly donated everything else, including the room hire, table settings, staffing, the emcee, PR, valet parking, the auctioneer, and the event organizer.

The driver opens our door, allowing Oliver to exit the car first. He assists Margie out of the car and then helps me manage my exit, holding out both arms to escort us down the red carpet, past the paparazzi. Flashes explode as journalists thrust microphones into our faces, posing questions about who Margie and I are, as well as the designer of my dress and shoes. I can't believe anyone would be interested in who made my dress and shoes. I'm extremely nervous, and can't even remember off the top of my head. My choice of outfit had nothing to do with the cost *or* the designer, only that I liked it and hoped my boyfriend would think I was beautiful wearing it.

Margie goes ahead, leaving the photographers to get shots of Oliver and me together. All the while he whispers, "how sexy I am" and, "how he can't wait to take my dress off later tonight", helping to calm my nerves in this unfamiliar situation.

He has a confident air, which reminds me of all the photographs I've seen of him walking red carpets into events like this one with different women. It's a bitter pill to swallow, but I manage. He has a history that happened before me that can't be erased because it makes me jealous or uncomfortable. He does nothing but dote on me, build me up, and show me how much I mean to him. We haven't said those three words yet, but we *show* each other all the time.

Oliver slows to a stop in front of one particular journalist who garners his attention. "Mr. Stone, who is your date this evening?"

He steps closer to me, pulling me in with an arm banded tightly around my waist, looking down at me with smoldering eyes. "This stunning woman is Ms. Kate Summer."

I smile and nod my acknowledgment to the journalist.

"You're not usually the type of woman we see accompanying Mr. Stone to these events. How do you know each other?"

Did he really say that to me? What a jerk!

Pressing my shoulders back, I raise my chin. "You mean a *real* person—right? Instead of the fake women who only want to be seen with him to raise their profile? Is that what you meant?" I'm proud of the strength in my voice because his comment was way out of line and dug at the very core of my past hurts. I showed some spine and stood up for myself without being rude.

Go me!

Oliver steps in, whispering in a deadly tone, "You can fuck off. How fucking dare you be disrespectful to my date! I will fucking dismantle your pitiful excuse for a life, piece by fucking piece."

If you were looking on, you would have no clue as to the anger emanating from Oliver. Externally, he looks as calm as a lake, but I can feel the tension rippling off of him.

The reporter looks panic-stricken by Oliver's response to his inappropriate question.

I tug his arm, encouraging him to move along, allowing us to get on with our night; I'm not about to let some jerk ruin our evening.

"Are you okay?" he whispers close to my ear, his warm breath on my neck.

I smile at him. "Yeah, I am. Thank you for standing up for me."

"You stood up for yourself, but I couldn't let it go. I wanted to show that asshole we're a team." And that's exactly what we are.

I kiss the underside of his jaw with appreciation.

As we step inside the ballroom, my jaw drops at the spectacular sight. Everything is beyond stunning. From the table settings to the balloons and flowers, kindly donated by *Blooms and Balloons*, to the decorations donated by *Event Hire*.

And the large photographs showcasing the kids experiencing the day-to-day life in the homes provided by *The Parkerville Project* are a masterful addition. Each photograph is accompanied by the story of how the child came to live in one of the homes. We thought the photographs and stories would help loosen people's purse strings when it came time for the auction planned later this evening. People are already studying them, so I think they'll work a treat. Some of the older kids will be in attendance for part of the evening, sitting at the tables with the attendees. It will be such a unique experience for them.

We also have an electronic tally showing the amount of money already raised and the amount we still need. Currently, the tally sits at $5,000,000, which includes Oliver's donation of $2,000,000 and the sale of tonight's tickets, minus the food and beverage expenses. We need to double the amount with the auction. After perusing the donated items, I feel our goal is easily achievable. The money we need will cover purchasing the mortgages outright, utilities, staff wages, health care and psych services for the kids, school supplies and after-school tutoring and activities to keep them on track, as well as food and clothing for the next several months; until the missing money is recovered—*hopefully*.

Marcus approaches us with an enormous smile and a striking woman on his arm. He takes Oliver's hand between both of his, shaking vigorously with appreciation. He then takes my hands, repeating the process, almost jarring my arm out of its socket.

"I can't thank the two of you enough for all you've done to help us help the kids." His happiness is infectious, and we smile broadly in return.

"It's been our pleasure to put this event together. Let's hope we reach our target of $10,000,000 tonight."

Marcus nods and then draws our attention to the woman beside him. "Please allow me to introduce my lovely wife, Celia."

She smiles, nods her acknowledgment, and shakes each of our hands with a gentle calmness; quite the juxtaposition from her husband. We make small talk for a while until the manager of the hotel approaches us to confirm some minor details for the evening; ensuring we're happy with everything thus far.

The room is filling quickly and I'm embarrassingly star-struck by the number of celebrities in attendance. Even though Toby's famous, I'm very much removed from that part of his life. I've been to his concerts, but I've never met any of his famous friends. He likes to keep our family separate from his stardom and the things that go along with it.

Oliver retrieves a couple of drinks for us when we spy Mom and Dad. He purchased a table so Jase, Margie, Mom, and Dad could attend the event. At $8,000 a ticket, it wasn't in the budget for them. We cross the room to welcome them, hugging in our usual exuberant greeting. Mom gushes over how I look in my dress, while Dad and Oliver catch up. Right on seven o'clock, the emcee announces the entrée will be served, inviting everyone to take their seats.

A hush settles over the room as guests are served and begin eating —a tasting plate of seared scallops in a herb butter sauce, small medallions of steak, dauphin potatoes, and seasonal greens. The food is beyond divine.

Marcus approaches the podium to thank everyone for attending, encouraging them to open their hearts and wallets later in the evening during the auction. He introduces Oliver, inviting him up onto the stage.

Oliver strides to the podium with sure steps and a confidence that can't be faked. Everyone in the room applauds, and he waits patiently for them to settle.

"Thank you, Marcus, for your kind introduction. Thank you, everyone, for paying the ridiculous amount of money to attend this evening." Everyone snickers, and I notice they're nodding in agreement with one another. "*The Parkerville Project* means the world to me because I was once a kid who lived in one of the homes they provide." Audible gasps sound throughout the room, and I'm shocked he's shared such a personal part of his history with the people here. It's not something he likes to speak about, and it took him a long time to share it with me. "I ended up with nobody to care for me when I was seven. The why and how aren't important for this story, but where I ended up is. The people at *The Parkerville Project* took me in and cared for me. They kept me safe and nourished, and gave me a home." He looks at me. "More recently, they unknowingly facilitated a serendipitous second-chance meeting with my beautiful girlfriend, Kate." Everyone turns in my direction, attempting to work out who he's talking about. "Normally, I would throw wads of money at a problem rather than giving my time. I always considered my time better spent making *more* money." People around the room nod in agreement. "But Kate and Jase, my longtime assistant, have shown me the importance of also volunteering my time. The value of rolling up my sleeves and using my skills to help others is something they've taught me, and I can't thank you both enough for the valuable lessons." He nods in our direction, and I can't help the thrill that runs through me at his words. "Of course, money is always a big help, and that's exactly why you're all here tonight. Please donate generously for the kids so they can return to their homes as soon as possible. Thank you, and please enjoy your evening."

Oliver returns to our table amid pats on the back and plenty of handshaking. Everyone stops him for one reason or another. Men and women alike attempt to get a piece of him. The women are blatant and outright slimy in their intentions, reinforcing what he's told me and why he values our relationship so much. He and Jase share a manly handshake slash back slap, slash hug thing men do.

As he sits next to me, he takes my hand, kisses it tenderly, then kisses my exposed shoulder. "Thank you, Kate." His quiet words hold a deeper meaning, filling my heart with gratitude for him.

I turn, overwhelmed with emotion, and kiss the top of his head.

Dinner arrives, and we all settle down to eat our meal, chatting excitedly about the various celebrities in our midst. Margie, Mom, and I excuse ourselves from the table to visit the ladies' room and freshen up. As we exit the ladies, I can hear Toby on stage, playing to the audience. Some people have moved to the dance floor, while others stand in small groups talking, and others make their way along the auction table, looking at what will be offered for auction within the hour.

I find Oliver in the crowd and come to a screeching halt. A stunning woman with a petite frame and white-blonde hair is practically glued to Oliver's side. Her large breasts press against his body, while her hand glides down his jacket, feeling his pecs. I can't believe what I'm seeing, and I lose the ability to breathe for a moment. The surprising thing for me is that I realize I trust my boyfriend completely and my lungs fill with air. I have no thoughts in my head that he may be more interested in her than in me. He's given me zero reasons to feel insecure in this situation, and I'm not going to let my experiences with men rule my behavior.

Mom and Margie notice my inaction and step closer to me, following my line of sight. We all stop to watch them for a minute. The tension radiating off Oliver is obvious; his shoulders drawn as tight as a bow, his head pulled back as far away from the woman as possible. He's politely working to extricate himself from her hold without causing a scene. I step forward without thought, my need to step between them and get that woman away from my boyfriend at the core of my actions. I come around behind them, approaching from the other side, and Oliver's relief when he spots me is obvious.

I thrust my hand out toward the woman. "Hi, I'm Kate, Oliver's girlfriend." She studies my hand as if it's covered in crap. "And you are?" I prod.

She makes no move to separate from *my* boyfriend. However, he ups his game, stepping away from her and closer to me. He wraps his arm around my waist and pulls me into his body, finishing with a kiss on the top of my head, and I feel the tension in his body subside.

She looks at Oliver in disbelief. "I'm Sonia. We were engaged not all that long ago. I can't believe he hasn't told you about me." She brushes her long locks over her shoulder. "I'm his great love. Some would say, I'm the one who got away." She smiles a fake, saccharine smile at him. "I was telling him I would love to catch up with him sometime soon." She smirks at me, attempting a coy shrug. "For old times' sake. You know how it is?"

I thought so. This *is* the ex who's been stalking him to get him back.

"And I was just telling Sonia, I wouldn't catch up with her if she was the last woman on earth." He kisses the top of my head again and looks at Sonia. "Thank you for supporting *The Parkerville Project*. Enjoy your evening." He sounds as if he's speaking to a stranger, and I can't stop the million and one questions that fly through my mind.

Oliver guides me to the dance floor, taking me in his arms and holding me tight against his body. Tipping my chin up, his eyes capture and hold mine. "You're the only woman in this room I see ... I want. Don't let that vapid woman cause you to question how important you are to me." He takes my mouth in a possessive kiss that isn't suitable for public viewing, but I relish in the feel of his mouth on mine.

"You want to hear something great?" He nods for me to continue. "I trust you completely. You've given me no reason to question how you feel about me. I feel completely confident in our relationship." I kiss his chin. "I feel sad for her, though. Her desperation isn't attractive."

We dance for several songs until the emcee interrupts us, announcing its time for the auction to begin. Grabbing a couple of drinks, we return to our table as the proceedings begin.

As the auction gets underway, I excuse myself under the guise of checking in with Toby, but I want to find Sonia. Eventually, I see her coming out of the ladies' bathroom and make a beeline for her. We need to have a chat.

"Uh, Sonia." I'm proud of the strength in my voice, even though I'm extremely nervous about confronting this woman.

She turns around, looking me up and down with obvious distaste. "Yeah. What do *you* want?"

"I wanted to have a quick word with you. If you don't mind?" I'm not sure what I can say to her to get the message across that Oliver is with me. That she doesn't have any chance of reconciliation. I gesture to a couple of club chairs situated out of the way. "Mind if we sit for a moment? I'm not used to wearing heels and my feet are killing me."

We move forward, both sitting at the same time. "I guess you're wondering what I want to talk about."

"I assume you want to talk about Oliver."

I nod. "Yeah, I do. I wanted to explain some things to you. I want to make it clear you're wasting your time. When you dumped him for a richer man, you hurt him deeply. For a long time, he closed himself off and he no longer trusted women because of what you did."

She smiles a feline smile. She seems proud of her achievement. "Oh, I realized when I last saw him how much my actions had hurt him. He obviously still loves me if he's *still* feeling hurt after all these years."

This woman is delusional. I'm uncertain if anything I have to say will get through to her. But I try anyway. I explain how Oliver and I met. I tell her all about his efforts to find me again, and then to convince me to date him. I tell her about our recent breakup and the deep connection we share. I explain I want him for the man he is, not for the size of his bank account. I tell her the reasons he wants to have me by his side. The things I give to him that money can't buy. I can't tell her how much I love him, because I haven't told Oliver yet. The details I've shared are extremely personal, but I'm hoping she finally gets the idea; *there isn't any chance for her*. I didn't want to be unkind to her. For one, it's not in my nature, and second, she needs kindness, not hate or anger. I've probably shared too many intimate details, but I wanted to get through to her. I want her to leave my boyfriend alone.

FIFTY

-oliver-

I DIDN'T ANTICIPATE RUNNING INTO MY EX HERE, SO SHE CAUGHT ME BY surprise. Her calls, emails, and texts have ramped up over the past few weeks since her visit to my office, but it seems she's upping her game. I must remember to get Mike to investigate her. Something's changed and I want a heads-up before she becomes more of a problem.

I look over at Kate and spend a moment appreciating how stunning she looks tonight. She worries she doesn't fit into my world, but the manner in which she has presented herself tonight is proof she needn't worry about such things.

She's gorgeous in her cut-off shorts, when she first wakes up in the morning, covered in glue, paint, and glitter after a day at work, or anything else she wears. I've never seen her like this before. When she opened her door, I almost swallowed my tongue.

Seeing her standing next to Sonia reinforced for me that Kate is the person for me now and into my future. We've made a great team these past weeks, working together with Jase to organize this event. It's confirmed my original feeling that I want to marry her and make her round with my babies. She has such a genuine heart and soul, and I will be eternally grateful that she allows me in her orbit. I'll never take her precious gift for granted.

The auction is in full swing, the electronic tally showing $8,725,260. Kate's almost bouncing in her seat, excitedly watching the tally moving closer to our goal. A handful of attendees battle it out for an original artwork by a famous Japanese contemporary artist, who spends his time between Tokyo and New York. The piece eventually goes under the hammer for $1.8 million. Kate and her family are in utter shock, as the winning bid takes us over our goal for the evening. Amid cheers and whistles from everyone in the room, balloons release from the nets attached to the ceiling in celebration. Kate turns her excited face to me and grabs my face, slams her mouth onto mine, and kisses me through her smile and mine.

"We did it!"

I laugh. "We did."

The auction is momentarily paused for dessert to be served buffet style, and Toby returns to the stage, continuing his performance with Shane's ever-watchful eyes on the crowd forming on the dance floor. Tickets for his next album tour, including a backstage pass, are up for auction tonight. He's been more than generous with his time to help us —I can't believe I didn't know *who* he was when we met.

We gather the guys' favorite desserts for them to enjoy once this set is finished, then leave our desserts for later, joining the growing crowd on the dance floor. I feel a tap on my shoulder, and when I turn, I find Mr. Summer gesturing to swap dance partners. I reluctantly release my favorite dance partner to share a dance with Kate's mom.

"You are stunning tonight, Mrs. Summer."

She smiles shyly. "Why, thank you." She peers around my body, then looks back at me. "I wanted to have a quick word with you if that's okay?"

I nod. "Of course. Anytime." I brace myself. I'm unsure if this is going to bode well for me.

She releases a heavy breath, offering me a motherly smile. "I wanted to tell you how happy I am that you found your way back to our family. Despite the many difficulties you faced growing up, I'm extremely proud of the man you have become. I know I'm not your mother, but I wanted you to know I think your mom would have been very proud of the man you've become." Her words have unfamiliar emotions clogging my throat. "I also wanted to thank you. Kate's confidence has grown so very much since the two of you have been together." I'm shocked she's attributing Kate's increased confidence to me. "You're fabulous for her, and I'm truly happy you're in her life —*our lives*. I know it took a lot for you to convince our girl to give you a chance, and I'm very thankful you persisted."

Her approval means everything I didn't realize I needed. It's been twenty-five years since I've had a mother's approval and affection, which I'm only now realizing I've missed terribly. She must sense my turmoil because she rubs my arm tenderly and kisses my cheek.

We swap dance partners again, and I pull Kate in close, kissing her neck and exposed shoulder, then send her out in a spin and pull her back into my hard body—both of us laughing. My heart and soul feel lighter than I can ever remember, and I have Kate and her family to thank for that.

———

Toby performs his last song for the evening, and the emcee announces the auction will continue shortly, encouraging everyone to return to their tables. One hour later, and the last item is up for bid—tickets and backstage passes for a concert celebrating Toby's next album, which hasn't been laid down yet. It goes for $225,000, taking our final tally for the evening to $13,827,380.

Everyone in attendance cheers and celebrates the enormous success of the evening—popping champagne, making toasts, and reveling in our success. Kate's eyes are glossy with tears as Marcus approaches us. Throwing all formality out of the window, he pulls me up for an enormous bear hug and some healthy back-slapping. Then he draws Kate in for a tight hug of appreciation and repeats the process with Jase.

"I don't know how we can ever thank you enough for everything you've done. I am without words to express my gratitude to the three of you." He looks close to tears as Celia steps closer to offer her husband support.

The evening finally wraps up, and we say our goodbyes to everyone. Margie is spending the night at the Summer's home and since we're in the city, I'm taking Kate back to my place. I can't wait to get her out of that exquisite dress so I can worship her delectable body.

As soon as we enter my apartment, Kate's hands are on me, slipping my jacket off my shoulders and tossing it over the nearest chair. Next, she moves to my bow tie, and I gently grasp her wrists, stilling her. She looks up at me in confusion but stills when she sees the seriousness of my expression. I place her hands on my pecs, allowing me to cup her face gently in the palms of my hands, keeping it tilted up toward my own.

"I have something important I need to tell you before I spend the rest of the night worshipping your delicious body." I kiss the tip of her nose. "I love you, Kate," I murmur against her soft lips, causing her eyes to widen and shimmer. "The very first moment I laid eyes on you, I felt inexplicably drawn to you. I had never felt that magnetic pull toward another human being in my life, and it caught me by surprise. When we met the second time, I knew I couldn't let you slip away. Over these past months, getting to know you—your beautiful heart, your gentle nature, your genuine soul—only confirmed and solidified my initial feelings toward you." I kiss her cheeks. "I want to be clear. I have *never* felt this way about another woman. You're *everything* to me, and I don't foresee a time in my life when I won't want to have you in it; standing by my side, sharing my world." I take her lips in a gentle exploration, and she immediately opens for me, sinking into a kiss that expresses everything we both feel.

She reluctantly pulls back, smiling shyly. "I love you too. So much. I've been overwhelmed by how big my feelings are for you. It's wonderful to say the words finally."

She leans forward to continue our kiss, both of us smiling into it. We deepen it to a soul-searing level, and as usual, everything else falls away, and it's as if we're in a void where we're the only people in existence.

Without breaking the kiss, her hands move to undo and remove my bow tie, while my hands move toward her zipper. As I slide it down slowly, she unbuttons my dress shirt and pulls out my shirt tails. "You looked so freaking hot in your tux tonight. My panties have been drenched since the moment I opened my door."

I groan, leaning in to take her lips in a rough kiss, biting her bottom lip, then her top one. I swipe my tongue across and suck each soft pillow into my mouth, and my need grows exponentially with hers. I slide my hands over her smooth shoulders to shuck the straps at the top of her arms, making her dress slip down her body, gradually revealing a delicate red lace strapless bra, which displays her perfect tits like the delicacy they are. Sliding the dress lower, she has matching panties—a tiny triangle covering heaven, with ties at her hips for easy removal.

My cock jumps in excitement as a drop of precum moistens the tip. Holding out my hand for her, she steps out of the inky pool and I suck in a sharp breath as she stands before me in her sexy as fuck underwear and satin lace-up sandals. My eyes peruse her curves from the tips of her red-painted toes up her body to the top of her alluring head. She is a spectacular sight; creamy skin wrapped in red, with her crimson hair falling like silk down her back. My hands move without restraint, roughly grasping the back of her neck to draw her to my mouth. I kiss up her neck to her ear, tugging on her earlobe with my teeth.

"You are the most breathtakingly sexy woman I have ever laid eyes on."

She moans, pressing her body closer to mine, and slides my shirt from my arms with great difficulty, finally realizing the sleeves are trapped by my cufflinks.

We both chuckle, working to remove them, then tossing my shirt out of the way. Next, we both work to undo my belt, button, and zipper. While I toe off my shoes, she slides my underwear and trousers down my legs and discards them somewhere close by. I bend down to remove my socks and step her backward until I press her back against the cool glass of the window overlooking the city skyline.

She gasps at the chill as I press my warm body against her front, trapping her. I take advantage of her gasp, thrusting my tongue into her mouth as I slide my hands to her hips, releasing the ties on her panties.

It's like being together for the first time all over again. Her warm skin touching mine, her breaths fanning my face—*home*. One hand skims up to massage her breast through her bra, while my other hand slides from her hip to her pussy, which is drenched.

I groan.

She moans breathily.

My cock jolts.

Dropping to my knees, I position one silky leg over my shoulder and tease her clit with the tip of my nose, then I swipe her swollen lips with my tongue. Her hips snap forward as her hands fly to my hair, gripping it tightly as she moans her approval. I'll never get enough of hearing her sexy sounds and tasting her sweet pussy—it's like crack and I'm an addict.

I work her over with my mouth and when I know she's getting close; I slide two fingers inside her tight channel, causing her to break apart spectacularly. Her entire body shudders with her release, and her tits heave with her effort to take in a breath. As she comes down from her high, her head drops forward, a slow smile forming on her lips. She looks sated, but I'm not finished with her yet.

Releasing her leg, I move up her body, kissing, biting, and licking as I go. I slide one hand in between the glass and her back to release her bra and catch one of her magnificent tits in my hand—they've been teasing me all night. Using both hands, I squeeze them together, giving them the attention they deserve, and then I take each one into my mouth, sucking hard on the peaks.

"I love your tits. These pretty peach-colored nipples tighten up nicely, ready for my mouth to suck and bite."

She grips the back of my head, pressing me into the soft globes. "I love how you suck them. Please never stop," she mumbles, her voice desperate.

"I won't. I'll never stop sucking your gorgeous tits." Skimming my hands down her body to her ass, I pick her up, encouraging her to wrap her ivory legs around my hips. My cock's close to exploding as it gets closer to the haven that is Kate's pussy. I slide my shaft through her drenched folds, then line myself up and push in slowly.

Painfully slowly.

I feel every glorious inch of her tight walls welcoming my cock home. Bottoming out, balls deep in this sexy woman, I study her face carefully, ensuring she's with me every step of the way. What I see in her eyes fills me with a sense of contentment and satisfaction I've only ever experienced with her.

Kissing along her jaw, I take her mouth in a luxuriously slow dance of tongues, exchanging breaths. I begin a slow seduction of my hips, sliding my cock in and out her tight pussy with measured strokes that tease us both. The sensations make my cock weep in wonder at the bliss I've found.

She moves her hips in time with my thrusts, which gradually increase in tempo and power, driving us both higher into the stratosphere in our desire to come. Her walls spasm around my shaft as she comes on a long moan, and I can no longer hold back my release. My balls draw tight and I explode, whispering Kate's name reverently; my release leaves me breathless and my legs shaky. I carefully carry her to the dining table, laying her down gently, folding myself over her, because I'm not ready to leave her body.

She giggles, which feels awesome around my cock, and I lift my head to check what's so funny. She brushes her hair out of her face, looking up at me with sparkling eyes. "I hope no one saw my ass pressed up against your window." She bites her bottom lip. "That could be embarrassing."

I lean in, kissing her nose, then her forehead. "We're pretty high up and the lights are still off inside, which would make it difficult to see anything. I wouldn't put you at risk like that, because I don't want anyone else to see what's mine."

She looks satisfied with my answer, nodding her head. "That was the hottest sex I've ever had, and we've had some pretty hot sex."

I can only nod in agreement. The chemistry between us is off the charts, on fire, and knowing Kate inside and out makes our connection even stronger. I didn't know sex could be this spectacular.

"Every time we have sex, our connection grows stronger, and it feels more intense. I was close to blacking out then. You might kill me by orgasm." I kiss her nose as she giggles, pushing my still semi-hard cock out of her body. Lifting her in my arms, I carry her into my bathroom so we can clean up so I can defile her all over again.

———

My phone lights up with a call; Mike's name is on the display. "Hey Mike, what do you have for me on Sonia?"

"Hi, Mr. Stone. Well. Sonia's in a bit of a mess. She's been kicked out of her home, had her car repossessed, and all of her credit cards are maxed out."

"Huh. I knew something had happened for her to be coming after me. What about her husband?"

"He discovered she was cheating on him. That's why he kicked her out and cut her off. As you would know, she's never held down a job, so she has no income and no way to get one. I've been following her to upscale bars, where she's working hard to hook a new sugar daddy."

"How long ago did this happen?"

"From what I can gather, about four months ago now."

That lines up. "How did she manage to get a ticket to the gala?"

"As far as I can tell, the man she'd been seeing attended the event, and she was his date. They're no longer together. She's having a difficult time locking a man down."

"I see. Keep a general check on her and let me know if anything changes."

"Sure thing, Mr. Stone. Bye."

I disconnect the call, sitting back in my chair, looking out of my expansive wall of windows across the city skyline. It all makes sense now. That's about the time the messages, phone calls, and emails started. I'll keep ignoring her; she'll get the message eventually and hopefully move on.

I get back to work, familiarizing myself with the new data and analysis reports which have been put together by my finance department. We're looking good for this quarter, even though my focus has been elsewhere for the past month or so. The projections for the running expenses of the company over the next twelve months are also looking good. The coming year is looking to be our best year yet, which also bodes well for my charitable foundation.

————

It takes two weeks for *The Parkerville Project* finances to be sorted out with the bank and the foreclosure status to be dismissed. The money raised has paid off the mortgages and provided the organization with enough in reserve to cover the general expenses associated with the running of the properties, as well as staff wages, until we retrieve the stolen money. Everyone can finally take a breath.

Kate plans to spend her weekend helping the kids move back into their home and settle into their usual routine.

Checking my emails, I notice a new email from Marcus, so I click on the notification to see if there are any updates.

Re: Update on the embezzlement proceedings
From: Marcus Trainor
To: Oliver Stone

Hello, Oliver

We have a court date! Our lawyer will be in touch with you within the next few days to discuss the procedure from here and the probable dates you will be required to attend court.

She says things look promising for a conviction and the return of funds still sitting in offshore accounts. As you are aware, some of the money is gone, but most of it is still sitting there. The accounts were frozen immediately, preventing any further theft.

After the court convicts Errol, we're probably looking at six months before the stolen funds are returned to us. Thanks to you and your team, we have enough money to tide *The Parkerville Project* over until then.

Kindest regards

Marcus

CEO

The Parkerville Project

Well, that *is* good news! Things are looking up. I have the woman of my dreams, *The Parkerville Project* is in good shape, and my business is successful beyond my dreams. Life is good.

I make my regular call to check in on my father, and it seems he'll be ready to move into a halfway house within the next six weeks. It's the next logical step in preparing him for living in society as a functioning citizen. He'll still receive the support he needs while stepping out into the real world. They'll help him secure work and settle into a routine aimed at building his independence. Their success rates are high, so I'm feeling positive and hopeful for a more productive future for my father. I only hope this step allows us to build on what we've started over the last few weeks during the visits with his counselor. I miss the involved and loving father I had when I was a boy. Not that I would ever expect us to return to that.

My mobile buzzes with an unfamiliar local number, which I wouldn't normally answer, but it may be the lawyer Marcus spoke of.

"Hello. This is Oliver Stone."

Silence fills the phone for a few beats, so I check the display to ensure the call is still connected.

"Hello." I'm about to disconnect the call when I hear *her* voice.

"Oliver." It's a whisper. "I need your help."

"I'm not interested, Sonia. I've made my position crystal clear. Leave me the fuck alone."

I have my finger on the red button when she sobs, "I'm sorry. I don't have anyone else to call, and I'm scared. I don't know what to do or who I can turn to."

Fuck! I can't turn my back on her when she sounds desolate. Desperate. I know she must be in a bad place after the information Mike shared. "Where are you?"

She tells me her location, and I tell Jase where I'm going and why before leaving immediately. I plug the address into my GPS as I'm pulling out of the parking garage.

During the drive, I can't help but wonder what's happened to Sonia. *Why am I the only person she has left to call?* We've been over for a long time, and until recently I hadn't heard from or seen her.

Arriving at my destination, I find a parking space as close as possible to the address. It's a small café in a bohemian part of town. An eclectic array of people, bundled for warmth, are sitting outside enjoying the sunshine on mismatched wrought-iron chairs.

I exit my car, engaging the locks. A flash of white-blonde hair leaps at me, wrapping me in an embrace as I step around my car, catching me off-guard. It takes a moment for me to gather my wits and press against her shoulders, pushing her back. She doesn't appear distressed or even mildly upset, and I feel as though I've been duped.

"Sonia." I push her back further, stepping away from her body. "What the fuck are you playing at? You sounded distressed on the phone, so I came to help, but you seem more than fucking fine now."

She acts coy—which I know for a fact she's not—and places her hand on her chest in what I'm sure is an attempt to draw attention to her mostly exposed breasts. "It was the only way I knew to get you to come." She grasps my hand. "Come. Sit down, share a coffee with me."

I tug my hand free. "I don't have time to share a fucking coffee with you. You sounded distressed, and I came here to help. I thought you were in trouble. I have a busy schedule and I don't have time for this shit." I snap at her. She's delusional if she thinks I have any incli-nation to spend any time with her.

She pouts in a way that possibly works for a ten-year-old, not a fully grown woman. "Come on, Oliver. Surely you can spend an hour with me. I need to talk with you, and you've been ignoring all of my attempts to contact you. I had to do something drastic."

I drop my head, huffing out a breath in frustration. "Do you even have a problem?"

She shrugs one shoulder. "Other than wanting you back and you not giving me the time of day?" She steps forward again, attempting to touch my chest, but I step back quickly.

"Then I'm outta here. I've made it as plain as I fucking can. I'm not interested in anything to do with you. We ..."—I wave between the two of us—"are not getting back together. I have moved on so far from you and our pseudo-relationship, we may as well be in different galaxies." I glare at her pointedly. "Do not contact me via email, phone, or in person. I. Am. Not. Fucking interested. I don't want to revisit what we had, because I've learned that what we had was less than nothing."

I'm a few steps away from her when she calls out to me. "What we had was special! You may not remember, but I do."

I stop my retreat, spinning around to face her, frustration making my temper short. I take two steps forward until I'm in her space. My posture is intimidating and my tone says, don't fuck with me. "Oh, I remember everything, Sonia. What you meant to say was my credit card and my cock were special. There was nothing outside of that between us. I was a dumb fuck back then. I'm wiser now, and there's no way you can convince me to revisit what we had."

"You know I had a chat with your *girlfriend* the other night at the gala?"

She says *girlfriend* as though it's a dirty word, and my dumbfounded expression informs her of my ignorance.

"Yeah, she's all sweet and apple pie. Blah blah this and blah blah that. She thinks she has you locked down, but there's no locking down Oliver Stone, is there?" She rests her hand on my pec, looking up at me through obscenely long eyelashes. "You and I were great together in bed. You were always happy to have me on your arm for events. You loved having me spend your money to look my best, and we look so good together." This woman is delusional. "Not like that frumpy ginger you're wasting your time on. She's not right for you. She doesn't know how to be the wife of a billionaire CEO, and she doesn't know how to play the game. I can do all of that for you." She strokes her hand down my chest, making my skin crawl.

I grasp her hand, pushing it away. "Don't fucking speak about Kate. Don't even fucking think about her. She's a thousand times more woman than you'll ever be. The fact that she doesn't know how to *play the game* makes her perfect for me in every way. She's my future, and I won't let you, or anyone else, get in my way. Now leave me the fuck alone."

Her shoulders slump as her gaze drops to the ground, and she heaves out a long sigh. Tears fall from her eyes, making her appear defeated. Maybe she's finally got the message? "You love her," she whispers.

Tucking my hands into my pockets and rocking back on my heels, I look directly at her. "Yes. I do. She's the best thing that's *ever* happened to me, and I will not allow anything or anyone to take her away from me. Not now, not ever." I sound like a toddler who doesn't share his toys.

"I can tell by the way you defend her. She told me how hard you worked for her and how you wouldn't let her go when she was being difficult." She sighs, glancing away, then back to me. I'm surprised Kate shared so much with her. "You never fought for me when I walked away."

My eyebrows press down. I can't figure out if she's being genuine or if there's further subterfuge going on. "No, I didn't fight for you. You made your fucking choice, and it wasn't me. I was hurt and angry at the time, but I never considered fighting to get you back. Now, when I think about it, I'm relieved you walked away. Kate's shown me how powerful a loving relationship can be." She nods and I soften my tone. "Go find that, Sonia. Leave all the other bullshit behind and go find it. Don't worry about the money, find the real thing. It's worth more than any money you think you need."

I leave her on the sidewalk and drive away, feeling out of sorts. I go for a long drive, attempting to center myself, then make my way back to the office. I think I finally got through to her this time. When I arrive, I call Jase into my office and tell him everything that's been going on with Sonia over the past few months. His surprise and shock would be almost comical if I weren't feeling as off center as I am. His suggestion to inform the police mirrors Kate's, but I don't think it's necessary at this point.

I need to get through the day, then I can see my Sunshine. I'm taking her out for a casual dinner to celebrate Valentine's Day. Nothing fancy. We spend too much time hidden away from the world, and I want to show everyone she's mine. It's something Kate's avoided since the beginning when we ran into her ex at the pier. She also didn't feel comfortable with the attention she drew at the gala, and the speculation about who she was to me. She's gun-shy, which I can understand. But she needs to realize that all the other shit isn't important. What we have together is all that matters.

———

After spending the afternoon going over reports for our newest client and gathering the data to build a solid portfolio, I finally arrive at Kate's.

Her car isn't in the driveway, so I'm not sure if she's home, but I find her in the living room when I enter. I expected to find her dressed, ready for our dinner date, but she's sitting on her microscopic couch in leggings and a slouchy sweatshirt, looking at something. I step toward the couch and bend to kiss her.

I pull away to study her face; her blotchy skin and red eyes tell me she's been crying. "Hey. What's going on?"

She shows me what she's looking at, and my heart sinks to my feet —photographs. They appear very intimate *and* very damning and were obviously taken today.

Me looking down into Sonia's face; her looking up at me adoringly.

Sonia with her arms around me, her hand on my chest, looking up into my eyes.

Each one makes me sick to my stomach. Each one explains the tears—*once again* caused by me. The images captured don't show the true events of the brief encounter I had with Sonia today. But to someone who wasn't there, they look intimate—as if we're lovers.

"Where did you get these?"

I'm fucking fuming. I move around the couch, ready to explain the images aren't what they seem, but she stands quickly, wrapping her arms around her body as if she needs to protect herself from a physical blow. We'd made fantastic progress and I'll be damned if I lose her over this bullshit.

"How long have you been seeing your ex?" she whispers, unable to make eye contact.

I reach for her, but she steps away, much like I did today when Sonia attempted to reach for me. My heartbeat explodes into a rapid staccato—panic overwhelming me. "I'm not with her. I haven't been with her for several years. You know this. These pictures don't show what truly happened today." I step closer in a weak attempt to be back in her orbit. I'm cold and empty on the outer regions, and I don't fucking like it—not one single bit.

"Will you let me explain?" I ask. Not that I'll take *no* for a fucking answer this time.

She nods but doesn't look at me.

I need to stay calm. "Can we please sit while I tell you what *actually* happened?"

She nods again, stepping back toward the couch, sitting as close as possible to one end. I sit in the middle of the couch—because I'm an asshole like that. I don't want to leave an inch of space between us.

"She called me today from a number I didn't recognize. I've blocked her calls, texts, and emails. I already told you this. I answered the call because I thought it may have been the lawyer helping us with the embezzlement issue." I shove my hand through my hair, resting it on the back of my neck. "Anyway, it was Sonia. She was sobbing and sounded as though she was in trouble; she asked me to help her. She said she had nobody else to call. I should have fucking known better, but my conscience got the better of me and I offered to meet so I could help her." I drop my hand into my lap, huffing a breath. "When I arrived, I had barely made it onto the sidewalk when she pounced on me before I could register what the fuck was happening." I hold up the first photo. "I pushed her away immediately and was suspicious because she looked fine; absolutely zero signs of distress. She wants me back; correction, she wants my money back. She wasn't in trouble; she didn't need my help, and she wasn't upset." I get up to pace. I have too much adrenaline pumping through me to sit still. "Clearly, she wanted to cause trouble between us. I had no idea someone was taking photographs. I stupidly thought she genuinely needed help; that she was in trouble." I stop moving to look at Kate. "I'm sorry. There's less than nothing going on between me and her. I'm not interested in her in any way, shape, or form. *You* are my entire world. Why would I throw away what we have for something which was less than nothing?"

She stands and cups my face in her small hands. "I'm sorry. I should have known better, but those photographs hit every single one of my insecurities. Sometimes my demons overtake rational thought. I'm honestly sorry I doubted you, even for a second." She kisses my lips gently, then pulls back to study my face intently. "Can you ever forgive me?"

"There's nothing to forgive." I grasp her ponytail, tugging her head back and taking her mouth in a kiss full of apology and promise. Without this woman, I can't breathe. I'm not sure what it's going to take for her to finally realize the depth of my feelings for her, and that nothing, absolutely fucking nothing, will take me away from her.

"Maybe you should go to the police about her stalking you. She seems pretty determined and desperate. You don't know what she might be capable of." She wraps her arms around my waist, looking up at me. "I'm worried about you."

I pull her body as close as possible and kiss her forehead. "I'll be okay. I made it clear today I want nothing to do with her, and I think I finally got through to her. She should leave me alone now." *I hope.* "Where did you get those photos?"

"They were sitting on my porch in an envelope." She shows me the envelope with her name scrawled across the front in a feminine script.

Fuck! That means she came here *after* our meeting. Maybe I *should* get the police involved.

"Where's your car?"

"When I came out of work this afternoon, all of my tires were flat. I called Max, and he came to pick it up. It's a bit weird for all of my tires to be flat at the same time." She shrugs her delicate shoulder. "He's going to fix it overnight, so I'll have it back tomorrow morning." She steps into me, squeezing my torso. "How about I make you something for dinner? Then we can get some ice cream since I ruined our dinner plans. My treat." She steps toward the kitchen to put something together for me, when I grasp her wrist, stopping her.

"You didn't ruin our dinner plans. Sonia did. Put the blame where it belongs. You don't need to make me anything. I had a late lunch meeting. Just let me get changed and we can go."

"Okay. I should change as well. I don't want to embarrass you again." She walks past me into the bedroom.

"When did you ever embarrass me?"

She rolls her beguiling denim eyes as if I should know. "Both of the times we've been seen together in public."

I can almost hear the *duh* at the end of the sentence. I follow her into her bedroom, and as she opens her closet door, I slam it closed with the palm of my hand, startling her.

"You look perfect just the way you are, and before we go any further, I want to make something perfectly clear to you. So listen up and listen good. Not once have I ever been embarrassed to be seen with you. I'm always honored you give me the time of day." I lift her chin with my knuckle, ensuring she can't hide from me. "You are stunning to me—whether you're naked, dressed for work, lounging at home, or dressed for the gala." I cup her cheeks, perusing her face. "You are so fucking beautiful, Kate. I wish you could see what I see."

A tear slips down her cheek and my heart drops—I didn't intend to upset her. I would rather cut off my right arm than see her cry. "Don't cry, Sunshine. I never want to see your tears." I kiss the tear away.

"It's not a sad tear. It's a tear of acceptance. I think I finally get what you've been telling me from the start." She presses onto her toes, gently touching her lips to mine. "Thank you." Two simple words, but they're deeply heartfelt, easing my anxiety.

"Good. Now let's get moving. I want some ice cream." I slap her delicious ass as I pass her to change into sweats and a T-shirt.

She looks at what I'm wearing and smirks. "You realize wearing gray sweats will get you a whoooole lot of attention. Right?"

I look down at my pants and back up at her in confusion. "Why? What's wrong with them?"

"Uh, nothing's *wrong* with them. More like *everything's* right with them. If you know what I mean?" She winks at me. She's fucking talking in riddles now. "They say that a man wearing gray sweats is the equivalent of a woman wearing leggings."

I look at her in her leggings and while they shouldn't be sexy; they fucking are. They show off the curves of her luscious ass and hips, her shapely legs, and I get her meaning.

"Okay, I get it. Maybe we should *both* change?"

She laughs at me, stepping into her closet for a change of clothes, while I swap my sweats for jeans. The sound of her laugh is something I want to hear every fucking day I'm breathing. I stash the gift I had planned to give her over dinner into my pocket, and we head out for ice cream.

FIFTY-ONE

-kate-

Surprisingly, Oliver lets me pay for our ice cream, which I appreciate. He could have easily stepped in and paid what I'm sure is a negligible amount to him. I love that he gave me the space to feel as though we're equal partners—even though, financially, we're not.

After ice cream, we wander down the sidewalk, holding hands, stopping now and then to browse a window display. I treasure these simple moments with him. We're both very busy; Oliver with his business, and me with my job and volunteering, so the time we spend together always feels special.

I think his reassurances have knocked out the last of my demons. I don't think I need to second-guess our relationship or feel worried. He sees something in me that no other man has before. He values me as a person and what I bring into this relationship and cherishes me in every way, every single day. I mentally watch the last brick in my wall fall away, tumbling, breaking, disappearing. Gone forever.

"Come on. I feel like a cup of coffee." He tugs me into a cozy café and orders us each a decaffeinated coffee made to our preferred specifications. We wait for our order, then grab a booth by the window, allowing us to watch people walking by. He directs me to sit first, sliding in next to me, ensuring he's touching every part from my shoulder to my foot, sending electric currents through me. It's always like this with him. I've never felt anything like it before.

He digs into his pocket and passes me a pink calico pouch. "Happy Valentine's Day."

Embarrassment floods my chest with heat—I gave him a cheesy

heart-shaped helium balloon for Valentine's this morning. I had no idea what I could possibly get a billionaire that he doesn't already have or can't buy for himself.

"I've had this for a few weeks. I was waiting for the right time to give it to you." He looks down at it, then back up at me. "It's nothing expensive. I just thought you might like it." He must have noticed my worry over yet another gift. "Please. Open it."

I smile at him and open the pouch. Three small items slide out, each wrapped in pink tissue paper. I carefully open the first, sucking in a breath when I recognize the rose gold necklace with the rose quartz heart as the one I was admiring when we spent the weekend away. My eyes snap up to his. "How did you know?"

"I saw you discreetly admiring it at the artisan market. I approached the seller and asked her to contact me when it was finished." He nudges the other two small packages toward me. "She made it a complete set for me. Open the other two parts."

My hands are shaking as I attempt to open the small parcels carefully. As the pieces are revealed, I admire their beauty. Remarkably simple and delicate, yet stunning. He carefully places the necklace around my neck and closes the clasp, then places the bracelet on my wrist. I carefully remove the earrings I'm already wearing, placing them in the calico pouch for safekeeping, then attach the new earrings to complete the set.

Holding my hair away from my face, his eyes trace over the jewelry. "Stunning. Just like you. I knew they belonged on your body when I saw you admiring them."

I wrap my arms around his neck, pulling him toward me. "Thank you. They're gorgeous." I kiss him with gratitude and sit back to admire my bracelet. "I'm never taking these off. It means a lot to me that you went to so much trouble."

"It was no trouble at all. Anything that puts a smile on your face is worth the effort." He brushes a lock of hair behind my ear, kissing my lobe. "I always want to put a smile on your face. Every day, if I can," he murmurs.

I'm going to melt into a puddle of goo if he keeps this up. He thinks he's such an asshole, but he's never once shown that side of himself to me; however, I need him to know that I don't need gifts to make me happy. "You know I only need *you* every day and I'm a happy girl. As much as I love receiving gifts, I don't need them to make me happy."

I'm going to show him exactly how much I love his thoughtful gesture when we get home. Hmm, *home*. *When did I start thinking of my home as our home?* But it feels right—a natural progression of our relationship. *Maybe I should ask him to* actually *move in with me?* It's just that my place doesn't have a lot of space, and considering what his penthouse is like—enormous and spacious—I feel self-conscious about my home. I know he likes the homeyness of my place, but would he want to live there permanently?

———

As soon as the front door closes, I back Oliver up against it and drop to my knees, undoing his belt and jeans. He's already hard as granite, and his dick is fighting the constraints of the red boxer briefs I gave him for Christmas. I love that I have this effect on him. A man, powerful in his domain, is at my mercy—little ol' me. It's a heady sensation to feel this powerful, this desired.

"Whoa! Slow down. What's the rush?" He grips my hair, pulling my head back until our eyes connect and lock.

"I want to make you feel good. I want to show you how much I love your thoughtful and generous spirit."

I pull his dick out of his underwear, pushing them further down his muscular legs, allowing me to tease his balls without obstruction. He looks as though he's about to argue the point when I take the first swipe with my tongue from base to tip, followed by a gentle swirl around the crown. His salty precum touches my tongue as I take as much of his shaft into my mouth as I can. I tighten my grip around the base, coordinating my strokes to drive him wild.

He tries to be polite, keeping his strokes shallow—that won't do. I want him to lose control, the way I do when he's working me over with his talented mouth. I double my efforts, increasing the pressure of my hand, while I bring my other hand up to tease his balls again. I moan around his dick and his answering groan spurs me on.

His hips thrust and the hand holding my hair pulls tight in a bid to control my movements. Slowly but surely, he's letting go. I've lost control of my saliva and it drips out of my mouth, and my eyes water from the fullness and the pressure of my hair being pulled—exactly what I want from him. I'm getting wetter by the second and my breasts are full and heavy. It won't take much to push me over the edge to ecstasy. My moans and his grunts, together with our heavy breathing, fill the silence of my home as he gets closer to coming undone. He attempts to pull my head away, but I hold on tight to his firm ass, showing I want the complete experience—I want him to come in my mouth. He gives me so much; rarely does he not meet my needs before his own.

I gently tug at his balls, using my finger to massage his taint, breaking his control. His hot cum squirts down my throat in ribbons, coating the back of my tongue, and I work hard to swallow it all down so I can lick his dick clean. His legs weaken, and he slides down the front door to the floor, pulling me into his body and sealing his mouth over mine in a deep kiss full of satisfaction and gratitude.

Nuzzling into the side of my neck, he whispers words of praise and gratitude while gathering his composure. Awkwardly, he carries me through to the bedroom, almost tripping over his jeans trapped around his ankles, making us both laugh.

———

Saturday morning seems to come around fast. I wake in a tangled mess of limbs and blankets, snuggled up to my favorite person. Today's the day the kids get to move home. All the work Oliver and Jase did to find the missing money and organize a successful gala while putting his work on hold was astounding. He was determined to make things right for the kids, and I couldn't help but fall in love with him a little more—make that a *lot* more.

Attempting to extricate myself from the tangle, I wiggle toward the edge of the bed, but I don't get far when Oliver pulls me back against his firm chest.

"Mmmm. Where do you think you're going, Sunshine?"

I love the deep raspiness in his voice first thing in the morning. I can't believe this is my life. Every day for the rest of my life, I'll get to wake up with this man—*hopefully*.

"I was going to the bathroom. It's almost time for me to get ready. It's the big day today."

He tugs me around, positioning me exactly where he wants me. "Not before I get my good morning kiss." I know he won't let me go until I capitulate, so I press forward to peck his lips.

"Uh, uh. Not good enough." I knew it wouldn't be enough, but I have this thing: I prefer to brush my teeth first, even if he doesn't mind morning breath.

He tightens his hand at the back of my head, preventing me from pulling away as he leans forward, and then he takes my mouth in a good morning kiss to end all good morning kisses. His kisses leave me disoriented, and it takes several beats to recover my senses.

"Now you can go to the bathroom." He kindly releases me with a satisfied grin, allowing me to make my escape before I pee myself.

When I return, he's dressing. I know he's still behind with his work and will probably spend his time catching up while I help the kids settle back at home. I step behind him, wrapping my arms around his sculpted torso and lay my head between his shoulder blades. "Make sure you don't work too hard today. Okay? Remember to stop for lunch, at least."

He looks over his shoulder at me, then grasps my hands and twists around until we're face to face. Tucking a lock of hair behind my ear, his eyes soften. "I love how you worry about me." He reverently cups my face in his large hands. "I didn't know what I was missing until I met you." Leaning forward, he kisses my forehead, then steps back to continue dressing. "I'm coming with you today. I want to help the kids settle back in. I'll catch up on my work next week."

"You don't have to do that. You've already given up so much of your valuable time to help them. Truly. Concentrate on your work. I'll help them over the weekend while you catch up on your folios, or whatever you call them."

"No, I'm helping. I don't want to miss out on seeing you over the weekend. Work can wait. Now get dressed while I make us breakfast." He smacks my butt as he walks out, making me jump.

I quickly dress in layers because I know that even though it's cold outside, I'll get hot from the physical activity. Roman dropped off a key yesterday, so I'm going to the house first to clean it thoroughly, as well as stock the kitchen with essentials. I hope to get it all done before the kids arrive this afternoon. I bet they're so excited to get back into their own place and have their own space again. I can't imagine what it was like living in the central facility with everyone else.

There's a knock at my door as we're finishing our breakfast. When I open the door, it's Max. I'd forgotten that he had my car.

"Hey, Max. Thanks for fixing the tires quickly for me." I feel the warmth of Oliver at my back.

"No worries." He seems a little unsure. "Look, I don't know how to tell you this, but your tires were slashed. They didn't go flat by themselves."

What? Who would do something like that?

Oliver steps around me. "How could you tell they were slashed?"

"Well, there was a two-inch incision in each tire that could have only been made by a knife."

"You're sure?" Oliver's tension ratchets up.

"Yeah, man. You might want to let the cops know." He hands me my car keys and the invoice, but Oliver grabs the invoice before I can.

"Thanks, Max. We'll get on to it. Do you still have my credit card details on file?" Max nods. "Good. Use that to pay for the new tires and tow."

I try to butt in and argue, but he looks at me sternly, shaking his head. "No arguments."

I reluctantly agree, the tension in my muscles releasing over the worry about how I was going to pay for the repairs. "Okay. Thank you for your help." I turn to Max. "Thanks, Max."

"No problem. See you guys later." He leaves, and Oliver closes the front door, engaging the lock.

"Thanks for paying for my tires, but you don't have to do that." I'm not sure how to feel about my tires being slashed on purpose. "I wonder who would slash my tires? In the school parking lot, of all places. Thank goodness whoever did it didn't hurt any of our students."

Oliver's deadly quiet, staring at the closed front door. Then he looks down at me. "I have a suspicion who damaged your tires, and I'm not fucking happy about it." He steps away from me. "Let me make a quick call, okay?"

"Sure." He looks beyond pissed.

———

The first thing we do when we arrive at the Lloyd Street home is open all the windows and doors to let fresh air into the house. Oliver's mood has improved since we left my place and he gets to work outside, cutting the grass and tidying up, while I strip all the beds and replace them with fresh linens. While they're washing, I clean the bathrooms and kitchen, then Oliver comes inside to help vacuum while I dust. The place looks pretty great.

It's almost lunchtime, so we lock the house and drive to the market for what we need, stopping on the way for something to eat. We make quite a team, me and Oliver. It's fantastic to have him with me, and he doesn't seem to mind doing such mundane chores. It makes me think about what it would be like to work together to raise a family.

We're unpacking the last of the groceries when the kids come barreling through the door with Roman.

"Hey, wipe your feet! Kate's been working hard to clean up for you guys." As he comes around the doorway, he notices Oliver. "Oh, hey, Oliver. I didn't expect to see you here." He reaches out to shake Oliver's hand in that manly kind of way.

The kids crowd around, absorbing me into a group hug of epic proportions, amid a flurry of "Missed you, Kate", "Thanks, Kate", and "You're awesome".

I've missed these guys a heap, and it's fantastic to see them again. To be here to welcome them back to their happy space makes me feel all warm inside.

Returning their hugs, I let them know how much I missed them. "Now put your stuff away. We have a lot of catching up to do."

They take off to their respective rooms to unpack, or maybe a better description is to dump their stuff.

"Thanks for getting everything ready for the kids. I couldn't manage to do all of this"—he waves his arms around the kitchen—"*and* keep them out of trouble."

"We were happy to help. I'm relieved they're finally home."

While there's a sunny break in the weather, Oliver takes the boys out for a game of basketball, while the girls and I catch up on all our girlie stuff.

Ivy leans close to me. "So, I guess you know who Oliver is now?" she whispers.

I'm taken aback by her question. "What do you mean?"

"Well, last time he was here, I felt like you didn't know who he was, so I didn't say anything." Her eyes twinkle as her smile grows. "He's *Oliver Stone*. Only the richest man in America under the age of thirty-five." She lets out a girlish squeal.

Ah, I see. She knew who he was because ... of course, she did. She's always reading business journals and magazines. "So you knew who he was, but didn't tell me. Why not?"

Suddenly, her fingernails are super interesting and she can't look at me. "Um, I didn't want to ruin anything. You seemed happy, and I figured it wasn't my info to share."

I embrace her tightly. "You're very sweet, Ivy. You're right, I didn't know, but I do now." I pull back, studying her. "It was a shock at first, and I didn't like that he'd kept the information from me. But we've worked it all out now."

"He was really kind to me when I asked if I could shadow him at work. I'm not sure if he realized I knew who he was, but he was way cool. He told me I'm welcome to come in any time over school vacation so it doesn't interfere with my schoolwork."

"He thinks with your enthusiasm and drive, you'll be very successful in the corporate world." I have to cover my ears to protect them from the high-pitched squeal she releases.

We hear the boys come inside, and that's our cue to move into the living area.

"Who wants to make cookies?" I call out as we walk into the kitchen. The response is a unanimous "yes," so we work together to make a couple of different batches, using the same base recipe.

The time spent with the kids always seems to fly, but today seems to have passed at lightning speed. Before I know it, it's time to leave, allowing the kids to get to bed. Hugs are given freely, filling my heart to the brim with love and joy, because the kids, including Blake, also included Oliver.

———

Today's the day I get to catch up with Ella and Bob. I'm looking forward to seeing them. It'll be two years at the end of June since I last saw them. I can't believe that much time has passed. Oliver's come along too because he's interested in helping with the construction. He told me his *CornerStone Foundation* is a major contributor to the work Bob and Ella do with their *Schools for Everyone* Project. *Why does that not surprise me?* He told me that school was his one constant during his childhood and adolescence, and that's why helping Bob and Ella's project is important to him, though he usually only donates money.

Oliver's been in and out of court as a witness for the embezzlement case over the past few weeks, so he's been working late at the office most nights to keep up with his clients. I don't mind; I just miss him when he's not with me, so I'm grateful he came along.

Last Monday, we went to the police about my tires. Oliver told them everything that's been going on with Sonia and I told them about the photographs being left on my doorstep. They're following up to see what they can find, but I'm worried she's become unhinged. Oliver also has his PI, Mike, looking for her, but he hasn't been able to locate her yet.

Walking into the café holding hands with my guy, I see Ella and Bob have already secured a table by the window. Ella notices us first, her face lighting up with a genuine smile. She's out of her chair and walking toward us with her arms open wide, ready to embrace us. Our reunion is full of big smiles and warm embraces, as if we're old friends.

Ella holds my hand and then grasps one of Oliver's, swinging them between our bodies. "Oh my, look at you two." She looks at Oliver. "So I guess you found her, huh?"

I look between Ella and Oliver. "Yeah, I did; purely by chance."

"I'm very pleased. I felt terrible that I couldn't share her information when you requested it; confidentiality and all that."

"I understood, even though I was frustrated." He looks at me with adoration. "It all worked out how it was supposed to."

"Seeing you two together makes my heart happy." She tugs on our hands. "Come. Sit. Let's chat."

We order coffee and cake, then Bob and Ella update us on the progress of the last school they worked on, which was the one where I met Oliver for the first time.

"Your program was easy to implement. The teachers have moved forward in leaps and bounds. They use what you left for them as a base, and now they build their ideas from that," Bob tells me with pride clear in his voice.

The teachers I met with had little confidence in themselves, so I spent a lot of time building their self-belief while I was working with them. "They were wonderful when I worked with them. I'm not surprised they've taken what I left and built on it themselves. I'm so happy to know they found their confidence."

"So, how is the next project coming along?" Oliver asks.

"Good, good. As you know, it's another island community in the Molucca Sea this time. The region suffered a tsunami, and the local government is stretched thin with funding. They have an entire community to rebuild, so they contacted us to ask if we would be willing to help rebuild their school."

Oliver nods and my heart breaks for the community. The loss, tragedy, and utter devastation they've experienced is unbelievable.

Bob continues, "At the moment, the teachers are working under a hastily constructed hut with no resources. We're hoping to start work at the beginning of July. We're in the process of getting the school design finalized and recruiting volunteers to assist with the construction and setup." He looks at Oliver. "Thanks to your foundation, our funding support is strong. We're able to purchase the materials we need to construct the school, as well as the required resources to help the teachers with their program."

Ella takes over from Bob. "The devastation is heartbreaking. The sooner we can get the school up and running, the sooner the community will feel as though it's getting back to normal. As you know, school is more often than not the heart of any small community. Kate, if you could work your magic with the elementary teachers, we'll have another fabulous school supporting the children and the community."

"Of course. I'm excited to work with you again. I had fun last time. You can also count on me to help with the construction." I squeeze Oliver's thigh under the table. "We'll come together, and both help with the construction, and then, while I work with the teachers, Oliver will work remotely so he can also help set up the classrooms."

We continue to chat about the plans for the new school over coffee and cake for the next hour or so. It gives me such a burst of energy. I'm excited to start on this new adventure. The best part is being able to work on this next project alongside Oliver.

FIFTY-TWO

-oliver-

Arriving at work on Monday morning, I find Jase already has my coffee on my desk and my computer on, ready to go.

"Morning, boss man." He's always upbeat, but he's more upbeat than usual this morning.

"Morning," I say suspiciously, while he makes himself comfortable in the chair opposite my desk.

"So, I caught up with an old college friend on Friday night. He's a real estate agent, working predominantly in the high-end property market. You know, for rich guys like yourself." He smirks and I nod, indicating for him to get to the point. I need to get in touch with Mike to find out what he has on Sonia. "He has an incredible property on the books down where the old power station used to be. Remember, it was all redeveloped a few years ago?"

"Yeah, I remember. Properties situated on the riverfront."

"That's the one. Well, this property was built across four standard blocks, so it's enormous. House, pool and hot tub, spectacular gardens, a dock with a fire pit, a four-car garage, and a smaller home at the back of the property for live-in staff. It was built when the development was first undertaken, but it's been sitting empty for the past two years. Never been lived in."

This is interesting. It wouldn't be too far from the office, not too ostentatious for Kate, and space for Margie to come with us. Yeah, whenever I think about asking Kate to move in with me, I know I have to make plans for Margie as well. There's no way she'd be happy to leave Margie behind. "Sounds promising. Is there anything online I can look at?"

"Uh, yeah. That's why I've already turned on your computer. I already have the page loaded."

Now his organization this morning makes more sense. I wake up the computer to browse the photographs. It's a stunning property. Red brick, timber floors, lots of light, white trim, granite countertops, stainless steel appliances, a stunning double-sided stone fireplace, a mudroom, a master suite, and six bedrooms, each with its own attached bathroom. I don't think we would have to do much to it—just add furnishings. It screams settled-down family life, which is exactly what I want. I can't believe how quickly my thoughts on settling down have changed since being with Kate, but it's all I can think about.

I glance across at Jase, who's sitting with a smug smile. "Perfect, isn't it?"

I nod, returning his smile as my excitement builds. "It looks pretty damn good. I don't want to live with Kate in the penthouse. It's too cold, and she'd balk at anything too ostentatious. This is perfect. Not too over the top, but enough room for us to make a family together. Can you set up a time for me to view it in person?"

He rises from his chair. "Sure thing. I'll call Simon now."

As he reaches the door, I stop him. "Jase." He turns around with his hand gripping the door handle. "Thanks, man. Be sure you're available for the viewing appointment. I want you with me when I take the first look."

He seems surprised, but nods as he steps out to do my bidding. I'm unsure how he fucking knew I was ready to find a place for Kate and me but sometimes he knows what I'm ready for before I do.

I grab my phone and call Mike. "Hey Mike, what do you have for me on Sonia? I want this sorted out as soon as fucking possible."

"I can't locate her; she's disappeared. However, I found CCTV footage that shows the school parking lot from across the street. It clearly shows a blonde-haired woman hanging around Kate's car on the morning of February 14. I believe that's *before* you met with her?"

"Yeah, it was after lunch that I made the mistake of meeting with her."

"Right. Maybe your chat with her wasn't wasted. She hasn't bothered you since then. Am I right?"

"You're right. I haven't heard from her, but she *did* deliver the photographs to Kate's place after our chat."

"That could have been the photographer following through with his instructions. It could all be over for all we know."

"Maybe. I would still feel better if I knew where she is and what she's up to."

"No problem. I'll keep looking."

"Thanks, Mike. Bye."

I disconnect the call, feeling antsy and unsatisfied with the conversation. I need a conclusion. I need to know she won't bother us again. I need to know Kate's safe.

FIFTY-THREE

-kate-

EMMA, HER BOYS, AND I STEP OUT OF THE SCHOOL BUILDING AT THE end of another day. We stop to chat next to her car for a few minutes while she straps her boys into their seats.

"Did I tell you the house next door is up for sale?" Emma asks over her shoulder.

"No. How do you feel about that? You like your neighbors."

"Yeah, I do. I'm going to be sad when they move, but they need something smaller to maintain at their age, and I can understand where they're coming from. Ever since we moved in, they've always been good to the boys and me, so I'll miss them."

"You'll be able to visit them and have them over to your place." I nudge her shoulder with a wink. "You never know, maybe a hottie will buy their place and you'll have some nice eye candy."

Her face lights up. "Ohhh, I like the way you think."

She finishes strapping the boys into their seats. "Bye, boys. Be good for your mom."

"We will." Emma rolls her eyes at me. "Bye, Ms. Summer."

———

Arriving home, I'm surprised to find Oliver's car already parked in my driveway. It's only four, way too early for him to have finished work for the day. I quickly collect my things to rush inside; hoping everything's okay.

"Oliver!" I call as I open the front door.

He walks out of the bedroom, wearing jeans and a T-shirt, looking casual and relaxed, an enormous smile on his handsome face as he leans into me, kissing me chastely. He takes my bags from me and places them in their designated spaces. Since he's home early and we have time, maybe now would be a good time to ask him to officially move in with me.

"Is everything okay? You're home early."

Placing his hands on my hips, he pulls me into his body. "Everything's perfect. I have something I want to show you, but I have a question to ask you first." He takes my hand, leading me to my couch. He sits, positioning me on his lap, then cups my face gently in his warm hands. I'm not sure what's going on, but he seems serious.

"Okay, you have my undivided attention. What's going on?"

"It's something I've been thinking about for a while now, but I wanted to wait until I was confident we were both on the same page." He draws a deep breath. "We fit together seamlessly, and I know I never want to let you go. I feel we're completely in sync and I'm pretty confident you feel the same way."

I can only nod as my heart speeds up to the point I'm worried it's going to explode out of my chest. My palms are clammy, and my breaths scarce.

"Hey. Take a breath. It's okay, I'm not proposing." He grins at me, and I release the breath I was holding. "Yet! But I was wondering if you would do me the honor of moving in with me?"

Ahhhh, he must be a mind reader. I can't help the bubble of laughter that bursts out of me. "Oh my gosh. I was going to ask you the very same thing. I wasn't sure how you'd feel about moving in here with me, or if we should move into your place. But then I'd have to leave Margie and I'm not comfortable doing that." I ramble like an idiot as he attempts to hide his smile.

"Is that a yes, Kate?"

"Yes! That's a huge yes from me." I press forward, planting the biggest kiss on him I can.

"You've made me the happiest man. Now for the second part. I want to take you somewhere. Do you want to get changed before we go?" Judging by his attire, it's going to be casual, so I change into jeans.

As we get closer to the city, he turns toward the river. "I love the river. I don't spend much time here. Occasionally, I'll stroll on the walkways along the banks for an afternoon." I can't remember the last time I spent the afternoon doing that.

He smiles at me. "We should definitely do that sometime."

I nod, then turn my attention back to the window to admire the fancy houses overlooking the river. It would be amazing to wake up to a view like that every day. Oliver pulls into the driveway of a breathtaking home—which is enormous—featuring red bricks and large windows surrounded by white trim, as well as steps that lead up to a large porch, which would be perfect for a swing seat, but currently sits bare. The extensive garden and surrounds are something from a Pinterest board, but it feels as though nobody lives here.

"Whose place is this?" I ask as Oliver opens my door.

He takes my hand, dragging me out of the car. "I don't know, but's for sale and I wanted to bring you through to look. Jase's friend from college is the agent selling the property. He brought Jase and me through for a viewing this morning, and I think this would be the perfect place for us." He studies my face closely, observing my reaction. My eyes must be as big as they've ever been, and I think I can feel the paving from the driveway scraping my chin.

"You can't be serious. This place is enormous. We don't need anything this big. It's only the two of us." I flick my eyes between the house and Oliver.

At that moment, a man steps out of the house; he must be the agent. Oliver takes my hand, almost dragging me toward the house as the agent steps down from the front porch.

"Hey, Simon. Thanks for letting me view the home again today. This is my girlfriend, Kate."

We all shake hands.

"No problem. Welcome, Kate. I hope you like the home. Everything's open for you, so I'll wait out here. Take as long as you need and don't hesitate to ask questions about the property."

I manage to find my voice so I don't seem rude. "Hi, Simon. Nice to meet you."

Oliver's clearly excited as he impatiently drags me forward, up the timber steps, and onto the wide timber porch. The porch wraps around the house, with several sets of white French doors opening onto it. The riverfront is in plain view from the side porch, and I bet it's even better from the back.

"Oh, Oliver." I breathe. "Before even going inside, I can tell this home is something special." I've never seen a home like this in real life —it's unbelievable.

"Wait until you see inside and the rest of the property. You're going to fall in love with it."

He takes me in through the double front doors, which are more glass than timber, and I can imagine walking through these doors after taking our boys to football practice. The light-colored timber floors are finished with white baseboards, which continue to the trim around the doors and windows. The foyer is roomy and airy with a cupboard for coats, shoes, and umbrellas. I'm giddy thinking of having a life here with Oliver and a family we make together.

There's no furniture in the house, making it appear larger than it probably would if it were furnished. The entire home is on one level, with an attic for additional storage, making it feel homey. The enormous double-sided stone fireplace with a gas fire is charming, reminding me of the fireplace at the beach house we stayed in. I can imagine curling up in front of it, wrapped in Oliver's strong arms with a glass of wine and a good book on a cold winter's day. The image is powerful and vivid—stealing my breath.

The walls are all painted the same pale mossy green, which will go with anything and complements the riverfront location perfectly. The to-die-for kitchen faces along the back of the property, complete with a dining area, which has French doors lining the entire wall, opening onto a wooden deck. I don't know where to look; there are too many standout features. I picture nights when Oliver makes us breakfast for dinner; me cooking his favorite risotto and building a life together. My heart feels full to bursting.

As we walk through the home, I can't help but get caught up in Oliver's excitement as he shows me the large walk-in closet, sitting area, and private ensuite in the master suite. It has its own set of doors, exiting onto a private deck with a hot tub, separated from the main deck with privacy screens. He wiggles his eyebrows at me, pulling me into his body. "Imagine what we could get up to in that hot tub." I can't help but giggle and moan at the same time, feeling his hard length pressing into my belly. "We could even skip suits."

"Oh, that sounds perfect." I press up to kiss his soft lips, then step back to look around. The view across the river from the bedroom matches that of the view from the kitchen, dining, and informal living areas.

For as large as the house is, I can imagine life here with Oliver and our future family—earnest, loving little boys with Oliver's dark hair and green eyes.

As I explore all the rooms, including his and hers offices and an enormous room for a gym, which looks suspiciously like a dance studio; I'm amazed at the amount of thought and planning. As I open and close cupboards, taking in every nook and cranny, Oliver quietly observes me. Once I've checked everything over inside, he guides me outside, through the French doors onto the back deck.

"Wow!" It's all I can say as I look out across the property. Apart from the view, the spectacular gardens from the front of the house continue here. An impressive pool takes up space beside a gorgeous limestone patio with jasmine growing over the rafters, covering a stunning outdoor grilling area. I point to what seems to be a small house. "What's that place?"

Wrapping his arm around my shoulder, we stroll along the red brick-paved path toward it. "It's a smaller home. I thought Margie might like to move with us; it's the perfect size for her."

Oh, my heart! This man.

I throw myself at him, leaping into his arms and wrapping my legs around his hips. "You are the sweetest man, Oliver Stone. Don't let anyone tell you otherwise!" I kiss his lips through my smile and his. This can't be my life. For real, this only happens in fiction novels.

He carries me the rest of the way, putting me down on a cute front portico. We wander through what could be Margie's home, designed in a similar style to the main house. He then shows me our personal dock and boat shed. Near the dock is a stone fire pit, set in the middle of a red brick-paved circle.

I turn to Oliver. "This place is spectacular. I think the original owner thought of absolutely everything when he had this home built." I grasp his face in my hands. "Is this where you would like us to live?"

"Only if *you're* here with me."

"I would be honored to live here with you. But——" He cuts me off with a finger on my lips.

"No buts. If you think you'll be happy living here with me, that's all I want to hear." He shakes his head in the negative when I try to interrupt. "I *know* you're going to give me some spiel about not being able to contribute financially to something like this. I don't care. I *can* and I will. Please let me do this for us." He removes his finger, kissing my lips.

"I can sell my place. What's left from repaying the mortgage I'll put toward this house. Please, at least, let me do that. It'll probably only cover the cost of the fire pit, but I would feel better if you let me contribute my meager amount."

He looks at me in that full-on Oliver way and nods sharply. "Okay. I'll let you do that. But then that's the end of talk about money, and who pays for what. Understand?"

His tone is firm, and all I can do is nod. I'll just have to contribute in other ways. As we walk back up to the main house, a laugh bubbles out of me.

"What's so funny?" he asks.

"I was thinking I'll probably have to stop working so I have the time to clean this house. It's so freaking big!"

"I'll have my cleaner come through here once a week, instead of the penthouse. You won't have to worry about any of that."

I don't respond to his flippant comment about a cleaner, especially since it's my least favorite thing to do. I have to accept there are things he can afford to do and will choose to do. I can't fight him on every-thing to do with money, or we'll argue all the time, but I *will* maintain the importance of him not spending obscene amounts of money on me. I won't be like his ex, who spent his money on treatments and spa days, unnecessary clothes, and expenses. I need to be certain he knows I'm with him for *him*, and *not* for his money. That *HE* is what's most important to me.

We wander around to the front of the home, and I spot Simon on his phone. When he sees us, he ends the call and walks toward us.

"Hey, guys. What did you think of the property?"

He looks down at me, then looks at Simon with a smile. "Put in the offer. You know my maximum bid, but let's see if we can get it for the best price possible."

"Sure, sure. I'll get in contact with the seller's agent today. Any questions about the property?" He looks at me, but I shake my head in the negative.

After Simon confirms all of Oliver's details, he walks inside to lock up, and we drive to a riverside café for dinner. I can't believe we're going to be moving in together, and into such a spectacular home.

Oliver wants us to work with an interior designer to furnish the home to our liking. He feels at home at my place because of the cozi-ness and wants to bring that feeling into our new home. He doesn't want to say anything to Margie about the new house yet, just in case the seller doesn't accept his offer on the property.

Over the last week, Oliver's been busy with work, and we've spent our evenings planning for our move into our new home. His offer was accepted, and he's contacted an interior designer to work with us. Tonight, he wants to have Margie over for dinner so we can share our good news and invite her to move into the smaller home on the property.

I've already changed and am cooking dinner when there's a quick rap on my door before it opens. "Hey, Margie. How was your day?" She barely uses her cane these days.

"Hi, Katie-girl. It was okay. I baked a lemon-curd pie for dessert. I haven't baked one of these in years, so I was a little rusty, but I think it turned out okay."

"It smells delicious. Pop it on the counter and take a seat. Do you want anything to drink?"

"Nah. I'm okay. You keep cooking. I'm a little early, but I thought we could catch up before Oliver arrives. I feel as though I barely see you these days."

Guilt rises. Oliver and I get caught up in our bubble, forgetting about everything else. "I'm sorry, Margie. I've neglected—"

She cuts me off with a "tut" and a hard look. "Don't apologize to me for falling in love and spending time with your fella. That's how it's supposed to be."

We chat, catching up on the happenings in the street and how Margie's doing with her physical therapy, while I continue preparing dinner. She looks strong and confident in her movements, which is an enormous relief that she's okay.

Dinner's almost ready when Oliver arrives home. *Home.* I adore the sound of it.

"How are my girls?" He steps into the kitchen, kissing me semi-chastely. He then moves to Margie to hug her and kiss her on the cheek, which makes her day, judging by the flush of her cheeks.

"We're great. Margie was telling me about the happenings in the street. How was your day, *Dear*?" The term of endearment is kind of a joke between us now that we're *officially* going to live together. As silly as it sounds, it makes me feel even more secure and settled in our relationship.

"It's much better now I'm home with my girls, *Dear*." He winks at us, causing Margie to giggle like a teenager.

Margie and I set the table while Oliver changes, and we sit down together for dinner. Oliver waits until there's a natural lull in the conversation, then clears his throat. We're both a little nervous about Margie's reaction to our news.

He takes my hand while he looks at Margie. "Margie, we have some news."

Margie's face lights up, and she places her silverware down, gesturing for him to keep going.

"I've asked Kate to move in with me, and she said *yes*."

Margie squeals in delight. "Oh, I'm so happy for both of you. Although I thought you were already living together."

"I guess we were, but we've made it official." He looks at me, and I nod for him to share the next part of our news. "There's more news we would like to share with you, Margie."

"Oh, do tell. Don't keep an old girl in suspense."

"We've bought a house together on the riverfront. Our offer was accepted, and once it's settled and furnished, we'll be moving there."

Margie's joy slips slightly. "That sounds like a lovely spot to settle into your life together. I'll be sad to lose such a wonderful neighbor and friend because you've brightened up my days, Kate. You too, Oliver."

He nudges me to share the next part of our news. "Well, you can't get rid of us that easily, Margie. The property has a place for you and we would be thrilled if you would consider moving with us." Margie shakes her head, her eyes suspiciously glassy. "Before you say *no*, let us show you the property on the weekend—then you can decide. We truly hope you choose to come with us."

"Oh, you two gorgeous kids. You know how to make an old woman feel wanted, but I don't want to cramp your style."

"You wouldn't be cramping anything. You would have a home of your own; completely separate from us. Wait until you see it. It's spectacular. The original owner thought of everything."

"I … I don't know what to say."

"Please say you'll at least consider it," Oliver implores. "We would love to have you with us."

She's clearly lost for words, and her only reply is a gentle nod. She has no family, so we're all she has. As we finish dinner and move on to Margie's delicious dessert, Oliver pulls out his laptop to show her the house via the online listing. I can't wait for the weekend when we show Margie around the real thing. We're also going to meet with the interior designer to walk through how we want the interior decorated.

The rest of the week goes by in a blur of work, spending time with Oliver, and poring over images online to create Pinterest boards for our new home. I don't know if we have too many ideas or not enough. We've pinned pictures of the stuff we like that seem to follow a similar theme. We want our new home to be warm and inviting, homely and comfortable. I've never had to think about furnishing and decorating every room in such a large home. I don't want to mess it up, and I don't want it to look like a hodgepodge either. I guess the designer can look at what we have and get a feel for the house to help us work it out so it flows as it should.

Margie comes with us to the house on Saturday morning, falling in love with the place instantly.

"Are you certain you want an old bird living here with you?"

"Of course we do, Margie. We love you. We would be crazy to leave you behind." I wrap my arm around her shoulder, squeezing her.

"I'll give you the money from the sale of my house to put toward this place."

"You will do no such thing. Use the money to go on a vacation or something," Oliver suggests firmly. There's no way he would accept Margie's money.

"You could go on a cruise with Nan. She'll be due to go away again soon," I offer.

Margie smiles cheekily. "That sounds wonderful. But only if you're positive."

"We're one hundred percent positive."

"Okay. I'll move in. I don't know how I can ever thank you enough for this."

"Agreeing to move in is thank you enough." He pulls her in for a hug, and my heart doubles in size.

We walk through the property with Gina, showing her the ideas we pinned for each room. I'm not sure if she's being polite, but she seems impressed with our collection of boards for the house.

"You've done all the work for me. These ideas are fantastic and work well with the style of the property and its location. What exactly do you want me to do?"

Oliver responds, "We want you to pull it all together. I'm busy with work, and Kate already has a lot on her plate. Neither of us has the time to source everything we need to make this empty house become the home we want it to be. If you can source everything we need and put it together, so all we have to do is move our personal belongings in. We would be most appreciative."

"No problem. I can do that for you. I can probably access pieces you wouldn't normally be able to find in a furniture store, anyway. With my resources and contacts, this should be a piece of cake. What's your deadline?"

Oliver looks at me, and I shrug my shoulders. I hadn't thought about it. It's not like we don't have somewhere to live while Gina does the work.

"How about three-to-four weeks' time? Does that work with your schedule?"

"Absolutely. As I source the larger pieces and soft furnishings, I'll have them stored in the garage. Then, once I have everything here, I'll get my team to move everything into place."

"Sounds good." My head ping-pongs between Oliver and Gina, attempting to keep up with their conversation.

"I'll email through a contract on Monday, which will need to be approved, signed, and returned at your earliest convenience. Once I have that, I'll move forward. This is going to be a lot of fun."

"Feel free to contact either of us with any questions as they arise. I look forward to seeing the end result. Thanks, Gina."

And just like that, Oliver's bought a home and organized to have it completely furnished, ready for us to move in. My head is spinning. I'm not sure I know how to feel about someone else doing all the work of making our house a home. I guess that's how wealthy people do things. It will certainly make my life easier.

After Gina leaves, we wander out to the back deck, looking across the river. The view is stunning, and I can imagine weekend get-togethers with family and friends. Quiet evenings, drinking a glass of wine, just the two of us. Oliver and I playing with our children on the expansive grassed area, or in the swimming pool. I see it all clearly—as if I'm watching a movie. The future I'd almost given up hoping for. I look up at Oliver and push onto my toes to kiss his cheek. "Thank you."

Wrapping his arm around my shoulder, he pulls me in tight to his body as our eyes connect. "You don't have to thank me, Sunshine."

"Yeah, I do. You're making sure we have a welcoming and beautiful home. I don't want you to think I take *anything* for granted."

"It's only going to be a beautiful home because I'll be sharing it with you. Without you, it's just a big house on the riverfront."

This man slays me with his words. He lost an unthinkable amount as a boy, went through more than he should have growing up, was used and rejected as an adult, and yet he still shows me every day the wonderful and caring man he grew to be. I have to be the luckiest woman on this earth.

"Thank you for not giving up on me. I love you, Oliver Stone. Today and for all the days yet to come." I kiss his chest where his heart steadily beats—sure and strong. "Thank you for being mine."

epilogue

FIFTY-FOUR

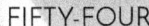

-kate-

WALKING ONTO THE BACK DECK, MY HANDS FULL OF DISHES TO ADD TO the buffet table, I'm especially light, happy, and grateful.

Moving into our new home five weeks ago was a dream come true. Oliver made it easy by hiring Gina to do all the legwork and organization. Then he hired people to pack up and move everything we wanted to keep from my place, Margie's, and his penthouse. All I had to do was wake up in the morning at my place and then fall asleep that night in our new home. Not that we got a lot of sleep that night—if you know what I mean.

Margie loves her new home. She wakes every morning and walks down to the dock to enjoy a cup of tea while watching the city come to life across the river. She misses the antics of Pete and Joe from down the street, but I have a surprise for her today. I invited them to our housewarming party—she's going to be ecstatic.

"Hey. I've loaded all the coolers with drinks and put out all the plates, silverware, glasses, and napkins. Anything else you need me to do before I have a quick shower?"

His demeanor is much lighter now. Especially since we received an email from his ex, apologizing for slashing my tires and sending the photographs she had taken. She'd already attacked my tires *before* meeting Oliver, and the photographer was following through on their prearranged plans. She was remorseful for her actions and made it clear she's come to terms with the way things are now. It was such a relief to learn she's moved across the country to live in New York and try her luck at finding love there. Her email seemed genuine, and I think it gave Oliver the closure he needed to completely let go of his anger toward her.

"Nope. I think we're all good out here. I have a couple more dishes to bring out. Our guests will start arriving soon, so you'd better scoot."

I press onto my toes, kissing him chastely. As usual, he takes over and I'm left dizzy and disoriented. His kisses always have that effect on me—I think it will always be that way. He smirks as he wanders off toward the bathroom to shower and change; knowing exactly what he does to me.

Once everything is on the table and I do a last check, I take five minutes to sit on the back deck, enjoying a cold Sprite before our guests arrive on this perfect spring afternoon.

Oliver steps out onto the back deck, wearing jeans and his red Converse, which he bought to match mine. His hair's still wet from his shower and his black T-shirt molds to his muscular torso perfectly. My eyes devour him, the same as they do every time I see him. Now that I know him on such a deep level, I think he's even more attractive than when I first laid eyes on him.

"Stop looking at me like that. We don't have time." He chuckles as he grabs a beer out of one of the coolers.

"I don't know about that. You can be pretty creative when you want to be." I wink at him.

We've christened every room in this house—it was a mammoth task, but it had to be done. I think we only have half a dozen more walls to wear in, and then we can start all over again.

I'm torn from my musing when the doorbell sounds, and together, we greet our first guests.

———

The man at the door takes me by surprise. I've never met him before, but I would recognize his features anywhere. He's an older version of Oliver, not as tall or fit, but definitely Oliver's dad. Oliver invited him to join us this afternoon but wasn't sure if he would make the effort to show. I'm glad he did. For Oliver's sake.

Oliver stops short of the door—"Dad."—taking a moment to recover his equilibrium. "Hey. I'm happy you could make it. Come in, come in."

My family and our friends are pulling up in the driveway, so we step out of the doorway and into the foyer. Oliver quickly introduces me to his dad. "Kate, this is my dad, James Stone. Dad, this is my girlfriend, Kate."

He reaches out his hand to shake mine, but I step straight into him, wrapping my arms around him in a hug. He's going to have to get used to the fact I'm a hugger. The sooner he learns, the better. He's stiff at first, taking a moment to relax; reminding me of the first time I hugged his son. "It's nice to meet you, Mr. Stone," I whisper in his ear and as we pull apart, he echoes my words.

My family arrives next with Shane, and I'm excited to show them our new home. I wouldn't let Mom visit until today because I wanted everyone to see it at the same time. Oliver introduces his dad to my family, and they head through the house toward the back deck to make themselves comfortable.

Margie wanders through in the nick of time to see Pete and Joe arrive. "Oh my goodness, Katie-girl. Why on earth would you invite these two old pains in the ass to your housewarming? They'll probably destroy the joint." She winks at me as she moves forward to greet the two old guys.

I get distracted when I see Emma arrive with her two boys in tow. She's laying down the law because I can see Austin rolling his eyes from here. I made sure to let her know I would have a quiet space, close to the action, so Lachlan can escape if the noise and activity level become too much for him. I hug Emma and ruffle Austin's hair. Lachlan rarely makes eye contact, so I quietly say "hi" to which he waves. Emma and Margie hug and move through the house to the back deck together with Pete and Joe; stopping on the way to show Emma and Lachlan the quiet room.

Jase arrives next. I wink at Oliver because he plans to offer Jase the key to his penthouse today. He doesn't want the place to go to waste, and he figured it would be a good bonus for him. Jase will be surprised, but I bet he'll be happy to get out of the shared situation he's been living in for the past four years.

He leans in close, greeting me with a kiss on the cheek, to which Oliver growls. I'm sure Jase does that on purpose to wind him up.

"Hey guys, nice digs. I'm happy this all worked out for you." He leans in, greeting Oliver with the half-hug, back-slap thing they do.

"We have you to thank for the house. We probably wouldn't have even known about it without you and your friend, Simon." Stepping closer, I hug him to show my gratitude.

Celia and Marcus, and Ella and Bob are hot on his heels, taking the few steps onto the front porch. It won't be long before we begin work on the new school with Ella and Bob. They already know Celia and Marcus through various charity functions. "It's so great you guys could come this afternoon." Leaning in, I hug each person in turn.

"Thanks for inviting us."

"Go through to the back deck. Help yourselves to the food and drinks. We'll be through in a minute."

Marcus holds back for a moment. "I wanted to thank you and Margie for donating your homes to our New Adult program. It's a great initiative. Just because a child turns eighteen doesn't mean they are automatically self-sufficient. Giving them a place to live while they get on their feet will set them up for life."

Oh, that makes me truly happy. It's fantastic that Margie and I could do something to help the young adults leaving *The Parkerville Project.*

"Margie and I were happy to gift you our homes. We didn't need them anymore." My mortgage is the only expense I have these days. Once it's paid for completely, I'll gift the deed to the *Project.*

Roman and the kids are piling out of their people mover. They're our last guests to arrive. The kids are excited to spend the afternoon with us. They have their swimsuits on, ready to jump into the pool. It's not quite warm enough for me yet, so I won't be going in today, but kids don't seem to notice the cold as much as we do. They high-five and fist-bump Oliver as they pass, making their way through the house like they own the place.

Oliver steps forward to shake Roman's hand. "Hey, Roman. Thanks for bringing the kids this afternoon. It means a lot to us that they could come."

"Wild horses couldn't keep us away. They certainly have plans to make good use of your swimming pool." He laughs as we walk to the back of the house, joining all our guests on the deck.

Oliver wraps his arm around my shoulder, tugging me into him, and kisses the top of my head. I look up at him, and my heart stops at his smile. He looks relaxed, happy, and content to have everyone here celebrating our new start. This must be unreal for a man who grew up without consistent people in his life. After another squeeze and a quick kiss, we separate to chat with our guests.

The afternoon is great fun. Between showing our family and friends through our new home and around the property, and laughing at the antics of the kids in the pool, the afternoon is passing quickly. Lachlan even seems to be coping with all the ruckus with Evelyn's help. She's such a sweetheart; she's been stuck to his side like glue.

FIFTY-FIVE

-oliver-

I'M FUCKING NERVOUS. I DON'T EVEN GET THIS NERVOUS WHEN I MEET A new client or take a risk on the market. The kids are having fun in the pool and I don't want to disrupt them, but if I don't get this done soon, I'll go insane.

I'm so lost in my thoughts that I don't notice Dad come up behind me until he pats me on the back. "You've done well, Son. Your mom would have been very proud of you after everything you've endured." He says, choked up, with guilt written all over his face.

"Thanks, Dad. Finally, I'm where I belong. It's taken a long fucking time, but I'm there."

"It's a bit of a twist of fate, hey? Kate's family taking you in when you were a boy?"

"Yeah. When I made the connection, it blew me away." I look across at Kate, finding her laughing with Emma. I can't believe how lucky I am. "I'm the luckiest man on the face of the earth to have found her and her family."

"She's a special lady. Beautiful, as well. She reminds me a lot of your mother. You're a very lucky man; make sure you hold on tight to that one, and never let her go."

"Oh, don't worry about that. I plan to keep her."

"Good, good."

Jase sidles up alongside Dad and me. "Kate certainly knows how to put on a good spread of food. I don't think I'll have to eat for at least a couple of days." He rubs his flat stomach in appreciation.

"She was worried there wouldn't be enough food." I rub the back

357

of my neck, dragging the key for Jase out of my pocket. Not that he needs a key once security scans his handprint; it's more symbolic than anything else. "Uh, I have something for you." I hold the key up to him, motioning for him to take it.

"What's this?"

"The key to my penthouse. It's about time you moved out of that shared house and my penthouse is sitting empty now." His eyes grow wide. "Security is set to scan your handprint on Monday morning. This key is a backup, in case something goes wrong with the scanner."

"I don't know what to say. You pay me well and all, but I'm not sure I can afford that kind of rent."

"Consider it a bonus. I don't want any payment. I want the space to be used."

I'm unprepared as he embraces me in a solid hug, almost knocking me off balance.

"Thanks, man. I was getting pretty tired of living with a bunch of dudes. It'll be nice to have my own space."

"I only brought my personal belongings with me. The place is still fully furnished, so you can move in whenever you're ready."

Jase grabs us a couple of beers, and we toast his new living arrangement. I probably could have let him move in months ago, because I haven't slept in my penthouse for quite some time. Kate was thrilled when I told her I was going to let Jase move into the penthouse. She even put together a welcome gift for him as a surprise when he moves in. I thought letting him live there was enough of a gift, but she wanted to make it special.

I catch Roman gathering the kids out of the pool, so I wander over to check they have everything they need to follow through with my plan. Blake still gives me the evil eye from time to time, so I guess he's still pissed I'm with Kate and he's not. When I spoke to Roman and the kids about my plan, he gave me the *'you better not hurt her, or I'll come after you'* spiel. I'm man enough to admit he made me feel a little nervous, increasing my respect for the eleven-year-old. The kids are ready to roll, which means I need to get Kate into position.

I find her giggling with Margie and her nan under the limestone patio. The jasmine growing over the beams smells divine, but not as good as Kate's natural scent.

"Ladies. Would you like to join us on the back deck? I would like to thank everyone for coming this afternoon." Margie already knows my plan; I think almost everyone here knows what I'm about to do.

Everyone except Kate.

We stroll toward the deck, and it takes everything I have to keep myself steady and my nerves at bay. Our family and friends mill around, waiting for us.

I take her hand to guide her up the steps to the large wooden deck. Wrapping my arm around her shoulder, I tug her into me and lay a gentle kiss on the top of her head. I'm beyond grateful for this woman.

Clearing my throat, I begin. "I would like to thank all of you for sharing in the excitement of our new home. Kate and I want you to know we have an open-door policy, and you're all welcome. Any time." Kate smiles up at me, squeezing me around my middle. "I never thought I'd have this. A home, with family and friends to share it with." I kiss the top of Kate's head again, holding her impossibly closer. "But now I do. It's all thanks to this woman by my side. Who, I hope, will choose to stay by my side until my last breath."

Everyone steps aside to allow the kids to walk forward with their poster board signs. Six of her favorite kids in the world, each one holding a sign with a single word:

KATE, WILL YOU PLEASE MARRY ME?

It probably only takes her a few seconds to read the signs and realize what the message says, but it feels like a lifetime.

When she turns back to me, I'm on one knee holding the ring I chose for her. A 1.5-carat pink Argyle heart-shaped diamond from Western Australia, surrounded by a halo of smaller colorless diamonds, in a rose gold setting. The band is also micro-pavéd with smaller color-less diamonds. The entire ring sparkles like the sun, which was my goal, because she's my personal sunshine. I chose the pink heart-shaped diamond to match the set I gave her on Valentine's Day.

The blush I love and adore rises up her neck and her eyes glisten, while her hands cover her chest—as if to prevent her heart from escaping.

"Kate, please do me the honor of becoming my wife. Be my part-ner, my lover, my best friend, the mother of my children, my now *and* my future. Let me love you, cherish you, and build my life with you." She's already nodding yes. "Let me be the last man to kiss you, share your bed, your body, your heart, your soul, and your mind. Kate, will you marry me?"

She's still nodding as tears stream down her cheeks.

"I need the words, Sunshine." I smile up at her.

She drops onto her knees in front of me, wrapping her arms around my neck and pulling me into her. "Yes. A thousand times yes. I'll marry you."

We meet in the middle to seal our promise of forever with a tender kiss. I'm more than aware we have an audience, one that includes my in-laws, but I can't stop myself from taking the kiss I want. Cupping the back of her head, I tilt her face the way I need, allowing me to deepen our kiss. Opening her mouth with a sigh, I slide my tongue in to dance with hers—swallowing her sighs and taking her breath. Gentling the kiss, I pull back a fraction, feeling Kate's breath on my lips as she slowly opens her eyes.

We both grin.

Remembering I still have the ring, I manage to pull back enough to slide it onto her left hand, where it will remain for the rest of our days.

We both climb to our feet amid cheers from family and friends, and everyone surrounds us in congratulatory hugs.

This is exactly where I want to be for the remainder of my days—building my life with Kate, our families, and the friends we gather along the way.

THE
SUMMER
TWINS
book one

*bonus
epilogue*

loving
SUMMER

DEBRA ST JAMES

ONE

-kate-

I can't believe I'm here. Here in this room, in this house, in this dress. It's completely surreal and so far away from where my life was nine months ago. Oliver gave me exactly four weeks from the day he proposed to organize our wedding. He wanted me to be Mrs. Stone before we traveled overseas to work on the next *Schools for Everyone* project, which begins in ten days. We'll be enjoying our honeymoon between now and then in charming Broome, Western Australia. Oliver wanted to show me the place where he got my pink diamond. I'm so freaking excited to have ten uninterrupted days and nights with him—as my husband, no less.

Sleep was almost impossible to come by last night. Sleeping here, alone in our bed, in our home was ... odd. Even though Mom and Emma were down the hall, it felt strange to be here without Oliver—I missed him. His presence, his touch, his smell, his warmth, his affection. We both felt it was important to follow the tradition of sleeping and keeping the bride and groom apart until the ceremony. Oliver opted to stay in the city with Jase in the penthouse while I remained in our home. I've decided, though, that I never want to be separated from him ever again in my life.

We decided on a morning wedding, followed by lunch. Thank goodness, too, because I couldn't have possibly waited all day to see my guy. Everything happened in a bit of a whirlwind this morning. Waking at five after such a restless sleep meant I wasn't looking my best. Mom came to the rescue with cold cucumber slices for my eyes, which worked a treat, and a perfectly made coffee to wake me up.

Mom, Margie, Nan, Emma, and I then enjoyed a breakfast of various fresh fruits, delicious yogurt, and muesli on the back deck, as several contractors arrived to add the finishing touches to our back garden, ready for our wedding. I didn't want anything too heavy to eat because I knew I'd be nervous today. After that, it's been a continuous stream of people in and out of my space. Mom directed me to the shower, where I scrubbed, shaved, and washed every single part of my body. The hairdresser and makeup artist arrived soon after seven to transform our hair and faces. They're a twin-sister duo that made the whole experience loads of fun. We connected instantly with our shared twin status. After they finished, we all went our separate ways to dress; though Mom stayed to help me into my wedding dress before leaving, so she could get dressed quickly.

Looking at myself in the full-length mirror, I turn this way and that to admire my simple, yet elegant, dress. I chose a dress similar in style to the one I wore to the gala. Oliver absolutely loved me in that dress, so I found the closest I could find for our wedding day. The shiny satin material hugs my torso with a draped bodice and a surplus off-the-shoulder portrait neckline, which makes my boobs look amazing. It has a light, floaty box-pleated full skirt, with a chapel-length train, and pockets—*yay for me!* At the back, the neckline forms a deep v-shape, meeting a line of tiny buttons that follow my spine down to my butt. I contacted Maria, the elderly lady from the artisan markets who was making intricate lace overlays for dresses the day we were there. I explained I had admired her work five months ago down at the pier. When I asked her if it was possible to make me a veil in the timeframe I had to work with, she insisted she could do it for me and deliver it to my door personally when she came up to the city to visit her grandchildren. She did spectacular work. The delicate nature of the lace complements the solid structure of the fabric of the dress perfectly. On my feet, I'm wearing the same red satin lace-up sandals I wore to the gala and I've got the sexiest set of red lingerie I could find hidden beneath the ivory fabric. Oliver knows I adore my red shoes and underwear; I think he'd be disappointed if I didn't wear them in some misplaced attempt to follow expected protocols. I made sure to wear the jewelry Oliver gifted to me on Valentine's Day and kept my makeup simple and fresh. Oliver's one stipulation was to ensure he could still see the dusting of freckles across my nose, which I usually attempt to hide with makeup. I'm wearing my hair in a similar style to how it was when we first met.

Emma walks in wearing her bridesmaid dress. I wanted her to have something she could wear anywhere. She chose a light blue strapless full-length tulle dress with an A-line skirt and sweetheart neckline. It has a long tulle ribbon that allows her to change up the design. For today, she has it coming up over one shoulder, between her breasts, and wrapping around her waist to define her sexy hourglass figure. Her dark hair is in a similar braid to mine and her makeup is light and fresh. She always looks pretty, but today, her level of pretty is on a whole other level. When she spots me across the room in front of the mirror, her smile grows. She's genuinely happy for me, even though her marriage didn't work out well.

"Oh my gosh, Kate. You look ... I can't even think of a word to describe you." She comes closer, circling me, studying every part of my dress. "You're beyond breathtaking." Her eyes are glassy, and I can feel my own emotions welling up inside. "Oliver's going to swallow his tongue."

I let out a small chuckle because I was hoping that would be Oliver's reaction when he sees me walking toward him down the makeshift aisle in our backyard.

"Don't you dare make me cry. I don't want to mess up my makeup and be all red and blotchy." We hug carefully, trying not to ruin our hair or makeup. "You look gorgeous, Emma. If only your sexy new neighbor could see you now." We both laugh because her new neighbor only ever seems to catch her when she's looking her worst.

"I feel fabulous in this dress. It's unbelievably comfortable and very flattering. Who knew a bridesmaid dress could be tasteful?" We giggle again, because we spent quite some time searching the internet for the perfect dress, and while Emma's dress is classy, some were questionable.

Mom steps back into the room after getting changed with Margie and Nan. They all freeze in place, eyes wide. Moving forward, they surround Emma and me, admiring our dresses, hair, and makeup.

Nan is the first to speak, grasping my hand in a tight grip, "You look just beautiful, Katie-girl. Stunning. Your pop would have been proud of the woman you've become." She hands me a dainty pale blue handkerchief. "Your pop gave this to me on our wedding day, sixty-five years ago. I want you to carry it with you today. Keep it close to your heart." Her eyes are shiny, and I'm fighting to keep my eyes dry. My nan and pop had such a deep love and respect for one another. She was profoundly lost when he passed eight years ago.

"Oh, Nan. Thank you ever so much. I'll cherish having this piece of you and Pop with me today. I only hope my marriage lasts as long as yours and is full of as much love and respect as yours was." I lean forward to embrace her in a tight hug; working hard to keep my emotions under control.

As I pull away, Margie steps forward with a gift for me. A dainty lace horseshoe attached to a delicate ribbon, which I assume ties around my wrist. "My mother gave this to me on my wedding day. It was given to her by her mother on her wedding day. I don't have a daughter of my own to pass this on to, so I would be honored if you were to wear this today, and eventually pass it to your daughter on her wedding day." Oh my gosh! I'm gonna cry, there's no doubt about it. I press forward, embracing my dearest friend.

"Margie." I breathe. "I would be honored to carry this tradition. Are you sure you want to pass it to me?" I feel her nodding against my shoulder. "Then I will cherish it with all my heart." Squeezing her tight and my eyes tighter to combat the tears threatening to fall, I pull back. "Thank you."

Mom's next, handing me a small pouch. My hands are shaking as I open it. Carefully dipping my fingers inside, I grasp the item and lift it out of the pouch. A delicate antique rose gold locket slides out—it's stunning. I look up to Mom for guidance.

"It opens. Take a look."

Using the edge of my nail, careful not to chip the pale pink polish, I open the locket. It has three parts, each holding a photograph. One of Nan and Pop, one of Mom and Dad, and one of Oliver and me from the day he proposed. The tears I've been fighting to contain fall over my bottom lashes, trailing down my cheeks.

"Oh my. I didn't mean to upset you. I wanted you to have a little of each of our happiest days with you today. I thought you could attach it to your bouquet." She pulls me forward, embracing me tightly against her breasts. Carefully, stroking my hair, avoiding the Jasmine flowers threaded through my intricate braid.

I pull back slightly, allowing me to see her face. "I'm not sad, just overwhelmed by all these extremely thoughtful gifts." I kiss her cheek. "It's perfect, Mom. I'm going to treasure it forever."

I gather all the ladies together in a group hug, showing them how grateful I am for their love and support on this special day. Having them all here, supporting me, and loving me has meant the world and made the day beyond wonderful. We separate and Mom works to attach the locket to my bouquet of Jasmine flowers. It was the one thing Oliver insisted on. He loves the scent of my jasmine body wash, shampoo, and conditioner. I ensured to have the jasmine scent everywhere possible because I wanted to make him happy.

I step into the bathroom to make sure my makeup is still intact, freshening up my lipstick. I'm ready to get to my groom. Even though I saw Oliver yesterday, I've missed him.

A knock sounds on the bedroom door, and Emma moves to open it to find my dad. That must mean it's time. Hummingbirds are flapping around inside my stomach—a mixture of excitement, nervousness, and eagerness taking over. Dad looks around the room before his gaze settles on me, his only daughter. He told me how Oliver nervously asked permission for my hand in marriage before he proposed to me. It was endearing to hear how Oliver bumbled his way through the tradition the week before our engagement. Apparently, Dad told him it wasn't his place to give permission, only I could give that. But he gave his blessing for a long and happy marriage—welcoming him to the family in a more formal sense. Oliver gave none of his nervousness away because I was blindsided at our housewarming party when he proposed in front of our family and friends. Dad steps through the room, kissing Emma, Mom, Nan, and Margie on the cheek before stopping in front of me. The look on his face is one of fatherly love and pride.

Taking each of my hands in his, he leans forward, kissing my forehead. "Kate." He whispers. "My beautiful daughter. You're the most stunning bride the world has ever seen, behind your mother." He winks at Mom and they share a special moment. "Today, I may be walking you toward your future, but always remember, your mother and I are always here for you. Through good times and bad, we're in your corner and want you to succeed in life as well as in love." Oh no. Here I go again. The tears I managed to control seep forward, threatening to spill over my lashes. I release his hands and surge forward to hug him. Holding him close, I whisper my thanks in his ear before stepping back to regain control of my emotions.

He turns to the other women in the room. "You all look beautiful, ladies. But it's time for Kate to take the last remaining steps toward her future."

They each come past and kiss my cheek, wishing me luck, before leaving the room. Emma will wait at the back door for us before making her way down to the limestone patio, where I'll take Oliver as my husband. Dad squeezes my hand as we walk toward the back door. I hear the music change to an acoustic version of *A Thousand Years* by The Piano Guys and that's our cue to begin walking. Emma steps out first, across the deck, and down the stairs to the pathway leading to the patio. Once she's halfway along the path, Dad and I step out of the house onto the back deck. My heart's beating a million miles a minute. This moment feels surreal as I take my last steps as a single woman.

TWO

-oliver-

THE MUSIC DISAPPEARS AS EMMA APPROACHES THE PATIO. I KNOW THAT any moment now, I'm going to lay my eyes on my Sunshine. I hear Jase suck in a breath and look across to see what he sees. Kate and her dad are stepping onto the path which will finally lead her to me. From here, she looks as though she's gliding toward me, an ethereal beauty, stealing all the breath from my lungs.

As she moves closer, everything around me falls away.

All I see is her.

All I hear is my heart beating a million miles a minute for her—only her.

All I feel is anticipation for the moment she reaches me.

The smile that spreads across her face as she reaches the patio lights up my cold world in a way I never knew was possible. Breathing is almost impossible as her dad passes her delicate hand into mine with a nod of affirmation that I will always put Kate first.

Kate steps up onto the low podium to stand in front of me. Her smile is contagious, and as I suck in a breath, my smile matches hers. One of joy and relief that we're finally here, in this place—together. About to become husband and wife. I bend forward, gliding my lips gently across Kate's, taking both her hands in mine.

"Hey," I whisper.

"Hey," she responds in like.

The celebrant clears her throat to gain our attention. Without breaking eye contact with Kate, I nod for her to begin. She gains everybody's attention and shares why we are gathered here today—as though it's not obvious. She reminds us that the hands we are each holding will be the hands to hold us in our times of need and despair, times of utter joy and happiness. These hands will be the ones to work together to grow and care for our family. They are the hands of our best friend, our lover, our life partner. She shares that the hands we are each holding will touch us in comfort, passion, and tenderness.

"I now invite Oliver to share his vows with Kate." We each wrote our own vows. We felt it was important to make promises that were important to us, as individuals and as a couple.

Clearing my throat and taking a breath, I begin. "Kate. When you came into my world, you brought the sunshine with you. I didn't realize how gray and colorless my life was until I met you on that veranda, half a world away. After finding you a second time, I knew I couldn't let you go. You made me work hard to be in your life, to prove that I meant what I said—that I was a man of my word. I promise you today, and all the days we're together, that I will always be a man of my word. You can rely on me and my promises until I draw my final breath. I promise to be trustworthy, open, and honest. I promise to always put you and our family first. To show you every day in every way, how important you are to me—that you are my world. I promise to never take for granted the peace you give to me. I promise to always show you the respect you deserve, and appreciation for the person you are. To always be true to you and the family we create together, to support you, and encourage you; to lift you up when you're down and be by your side when times get tough. I will forever cherish you—mind, body, and soul. I promise to laugh with you and have adventures with you. I promise to love you, your mind, your heart, your soul, your body—every moment of every day for as long as I draw breath. I promise you won't be able to get rid of me, even if you want to." I smirk at her. "I love you Kate, my Sunshine, my heart." I step forward, pressing tender kisses to her forehead, the tip of her nose, and her lips.

As I pull back, Kate's plush bottom lip trembles as she blinks rapidly, attempting to keep her tears at bay.

The celebrant breaks our moment. "Such meaningful promises, Oliver. Kate, would you like to share your vows with Oliver now?"

Speaking without words, I check she's able to say her vows. A gentle nod is the only confirmation I need, so I step back slightly to give her space. She takes a deep breath and begins.

"Meeting you was the biggest surprise and my greatest fear. Your devotion to me challenged my self-belief, shattering my carefully constructed walls as you patiently worked to chip away at my defenses. You persisted, and now here we are. I feel blessed beyond belief to have you in my life, making promises to me for our forever. You have shown me time and again that you are a man of your word, a man of honor, a man I can trust. You are everything to me, Oliver. My best friend, the holder of my heart, the keeper of my soul, my partner in all things, my lover, my confidant. I cherish every moment we've shared and all the moments still to come. I promise to always put you and our family first, to share adventures with you, and to walk through this life by your side. I promise to be your biggest supporter, your loudest cheerleader through your successes, and your soft place to land when times are tough. I promise to honor you, believe in you, trust in you, have faith in you. I promise to lay with you every night— sharing my life, my dreams, my hopes, my heart, my soul, and my body with you. From this day forth, I promise, you won't be able to get rid of me, even if you want to." She finishes with a smile and I release a chuckle at her final vow. "I will love you forever, Oliver Stone."

Pressing up onto her toes, she kisses my forehead, the tip of my nose, and my lips. We stand, forehead to forehead, blue eyes to green for untold moments. This woman is my forever. It's all I see when I look at her. We share a secret smile before the celebrant takes over again.

"Those promises were very meaningful, Kate." She looks out toward our family and friends. "I am duly authorized by law to solemnize marriages according to law." She looks back at Kate and me. "Before you are joined in marriage in my presence and the presence of these witnesses, I am to remind you of the solemn and binding nature of the relationship into which you are now about to enter. Marriage, according to law, is the union of two people to the exclusion of all others, voluntarily entered into for life." She looks at me. "Oliver. Do you agree to voluntarily become bound to Kate to the exclusion of all others, for as long as you both shall live?"

"Yes, I do." I have no doubts at all that I want to spend my remaining days on this earth with Kate.

She smiles at me, then looks at Kate. "Kate. Do you agree to voluntarily become bound to Oliver to the exclusion of all others, for as long as you both shall live?"

"Yes, I do." Her voice is sure and strong. The look in her eyes tells me of her determination and conviction.

"Kate and Oliver. Do you have rings you would like to exchange as a symbol of your never-ending love for each other?"

Jase steps forward, digging into his pocket for the rings. Kate's ring is rose gold, with pavé set colorless diamonds along one half of the band length, and a hand-engraved design on the other half. It looks like two bands placed together and it matches her engagement ring perfectly. My ring is platinum with a diagonal brushed rose gold rope inlay. As we place them on each other's fingers, I feel light-headed, knowing Kate is finally mine, in every sense of the word. I grasp Kate's hands in mine. Pulling her into my body, I press my mouth against hers in a kiss to seal our future. I had every intention of keeping the kiss suitable for public viewing, but just like every other time with Kate, I lose myself. Her hands wrap around my body, grasping onto my back, as though she never wants to let me go.

"I pronounce you husband and wife. You may now kiss the bride. Not that you needed permission from me or anyone else." Everyone laughs while I continue to devour my wife.

My wife.

My fucking wife!

I manage, barely, to pull myself away. Touching her forehead with mine, we share another smile before turning to our family and friends. Everyone cheers for us as I hold our hands above our heads in celebration of this moment. The beginning of our forever. We sign the necessary documentation before walking hand in hand toward our guests to receive their congratulations.

THREE

-kate-

HE'S MY HUSBAND.

My freaking husband!

I can't believe it. Inside, I'm squealing like a ten-year-old girl over her favorite boy band.

As we step down from the low podium to receive congratulations from our guests, the music begins to play—*Here Comes the Sun* by the Beatles. Oliver wanted to choose the song and kept it a secret from me. A smile graces my face as soon as I hear his selection for me. He always says that I bring the sunshine with me, but *he* makes *my* world brighter by being in it.

Our family and friends surround us with excessive amounts of love and joy. Hugs are given freely and smiles are wider than I've ever seen. Everyone is happy for us, happy to share this special day with us. I feel especially blessed at this moment.

We spend time having photos with friends, family, and our bridal party before Oliver and I break off to have some intimate photos, just the two of us. We're having a particularly special moment with Oliver pressing me up against the side of the boat shed when he lifts me, encouraging me to wrap my legs around his slim hips. I know these photos are going to be my favorite because they're indicative of our sexy times. He's looking into my soul, checking I'm okay, just as he always does when we're in this position. Leaning closer, he takes my lips in a gentle kiss, making my heart rate pick up and my body heat with need.

"I can't wait to get you out of this spectacular dress, *Wife*."

Moaning, I nip his bottom lip. "I can't wait to get you out of this tux, *Husband*."

He takes my mouth in a scorching kiss, forgetting the photographer until he clears his throat to gain our attention. Laughing, we separate and he carefully places my feet back on the ground.

With the standard photos completed, we join our family and friends in the large, see-through tent which was erected in our garden yesterday. Hanging on thin strands of thread across the entrance to the tent are hundreds of origami hummingbirds in various shades of blue. I chose the hummingbird because Oliver's shown great resilience throughout his life, and throughout our relationship, he's become lighter, more joyful. I thought they were also appropriate because whenever I look at Oliver; I feel like I have a dozen hummingbirds taking flight in my stomach. Hanging from the rafters of the tent are dozens and dozens of glass jars of different sizes filled with baby's breath flowers; for our everlasting love. Long strands of Jasmine flowers adorn each table, atop blue chiffon material running the full length and draping onto the floor at either end. The whole place looks stunning. As we were selecting the decor for our special day, I had no idea if everything would look okay together, let alone how stunning it all looks.

Overlooking the river, we eat delicious food, drink scrumptious wine, dance, laugh, and devour our velvet chocolate wedding cake. Before I know it, it's time to leave our guests to make our way to the hotel Oliver organized. We fly out for our honeymoon tomorrow evening. After our honeymoon, we're flying directly to meet Bob and Ella.

———

The hotel is out of this world. Overlooking the ocean, rocky formations rise out of the shimmering waters of the Pacific Ocean. The warm breeze causes the sheer curtains to billow into the room. I have my husband at my back, holding me close. I press back into his body, luxuriating in the rasp of his stubble against my neck as he kisses his way down from my ear to my exposed shoulder.

"As gorgeous as you look in this dress, I need you out of it. I need my skin to be pressed against yours."

Turning in his hold, I wrap my arms around his neck, playing with the hair at his nape. Pressing up onto my toes, I press gentle kisses to each corner of his lips, before sliding my tongue across the seam, encouraging him to open for me.

He doesn't hesitate.

He never does.

He welcomes me home every time, then promptly takes over, devouring me, stealing my thoughts and my breath. This kiss is everything—every word, every promise we made today, everything we've felt during our time together. It's lush and breath-stealing. I never want it to end, but at the same time, I want a whole lot more than this kiss. Slipping my hands around to the front of his collar, I deftly undo his tie, throwing it over the back of the luxurious chair to our left. Next to go is his jacket as I slide my hands underneath the lapels, loving the way the diamonds in my new wedding ring catch the light streaming in through the billowing sheer curtains. I throw it over the tie and begin undoing his shirt buttons, but he reaches up to grip my wrists, stopping me. Looking up into his face, his lips form an affectionate smile.

"My turn, Sunshine."

Kissing his way from below my ear, down along the crook of my neck, to my shoulder, he incites a moan of appreciation for the softness of his lips and the raspiness of his short beard. He slowly spins me around until he can reach the line of tiny buttons holding my dress to my body. Pressing gentle kisses to my exposed flesh, he patiently releases each button from its loop. My dress loosens and begins to slip down my body, exposing the red lingerie hidden beneath. I hear Oliver suck in a breath as his fingers falter for a moment.

"I didn't think I could get any harder, but seeing this red lace on your body, hidden by the purity of white satin ... damn, Sunshine. You're every wet dream come to life."

"Well, that makes us even then, because *you're* my wet dream come to life. Your body is a work of art, your mind is wicked sharp, your soul is genuine and noble ... but your heart. Your heart, Oliver, is kind, compassionate, steadfast, and true. I'm honestly grateful to have you in my life."

Looking over my shoulder, I seek out his lips to seal my words with a kiss. His tongue slides inside my mouth and my whole body sighs in welcome. I need him inside me now. I don't think I can wait another moment to feel his body connected to mine in the most primal way.

"Oliver, please."

"In good time, *Wife*. I've got you."

He continues undoing the final buttons, and for the first time since trying on this dress, I curse how many of the damn things there are. Finally, he releases the last button from its delicate loop and the bodice of my dress droops down, completely exposing my red bra. His warm hands slide around from the buttons to my bare midriff, up to cup my breasts encased in lace. Squeezing them together, he groans at the sight of them basically served up on a platter. I was hoping this would be his reaction. Releasing my breasts, his hands slide down, pushing my dress over my hips and allowing it to fall to the floor. I'm standing in a pool of white satin, wearing red lace, and my red satin sandals. He steps around, careful not to step on the white puddle until he's in front of me. The carnal look on his face makes me wet and throb. The ache becomes unbearable. I need him to touch me.

"I'm not sure what I ever did to deserve you, but I'm never letting you go."

He takes my hand so I can step out of the satin puddle. Leaning down, he collects the mass of smooth fabric, draping it carefully over the second chair by the window. Then he steps into my body, pressing his hard dick against my belly, taking my lips in a hard kiss, full of clashing teeth and dueling tongues. It's easy to get lost in him. His hand cups the back of my head, directing my mouth exactly where he wants it. I manage to regain some of my faculties and begin to blindly undo the buttons of his shirt; my fingers brushing his firm abdominal muscles. I need to get it off him. I want my skin against his more than I want my next breath. Finally, he's exposed to me and I press against him, soaking in his masculine warmth. My body warms at his bare touch. My nipples, hard as diamonds, try to burst through the flimsy fabric, keeping them contained.

Oliver reluctantly pulls away from me to remove his cufflinks, my gift to him on our wedding day—square stainless steel, engraved with our first initials and today's date. I asked Jase to give them to Oliver when they were getting ready this morning. As he carefully removes each one, he reverently rubs his thumb over the flat surface.

Looking up at me, he smiles gently. "Thank you for my gift. It was unexpected. I love them." He gently places them on the small table next to the chair before removing his shirt and carefully draping it over his jacket. Releasing his belt, he slowly removes his trousers, shoes, and red socks, revealing the red boxer briefs I bought him for Christmas. A giggle escapes me at the sight of 'Property of Kate' printed across his tight ass. As he turns toward me, my giggle freezes at the sight of the head of his dick poking out the top of his briefs.

Oh my!

Pressing my thighs together, I lick my lips. As my eyes slowly make their way up his torso to his face, the throbbing in my pussy grows more acute. I think I'll come the second he touches me—I'm thoroughly turned on.

His eyes are nearly black and his voice gravelly as he draws me forward. "Come here, *Wife*."

Pulling me tight against his body, his rock-hard dick pressing into my stomach, he takes my mouth in a deep kiss. Our tongues tangle and slide, while our hands roam across each other's bodies. Deftly, he releases my bra, freeing my swollen breasts. We both groan at the sensation of my hard nipples pressing into him. The sensation making me even wetter. My hands roam down to his ass, pressing him tighter against me as I attempt to increase the friction against my clit. He's remarkably switched on to my needs; he knows exactly what I'm trying to do as he positions his thigh between mine to help with my situation. The kiss is utterly decadent. I don't want it to end, but I need more. Oliver grabs my butt and glides my pussy back and forth, increasing the friction and leading my body into an orgasm which takes the edge off my need but leaves me wanting more.

So much more. I need my husband's dick inside my body.

Stepping forward, I guide Oliver's back toward the floor-to-ceiling glass doors. I press him against the cool surface before sliding down, taking his underwear with me as I sink to my knees in front of him. As he steps out of the briefs, his dick bobs forth, almost striking my cheek. Taking him in hand, I lick from the base to the tip, eliciting a deep groan from him, turning me on even more.

This man is incredibly sexy.

This man is my husband.

My Husband.

Freaking heck!

I want to drive him to the brink, then I want to climb him like a tree and impale myself on his length. Grasping the base of his dick in my hand, I take him in my mouth as far as I can without gagging. He grasps my hair and thrusts forward, hitting the back of my throat, stealing my breath.

"Yeah, Sunshine, take my cock. Take it all the way."

I swallow hard, causing him to groan and thrust again. He's trying to let me have control, but it's not in his nature to relinquish it easily. His hands tugging my hair, guiding my mouth back and forward over his length, makes me feel positively powerful to know that I can cause him to come undone. Holding onto his hard thighs, feeling his muscles tense and contract with his thrusts into my mouth, adds a whole new level to the sensations he's building within me. To an outsider, it may seem I'm at a disadvantage in this situation, but I get as much from doing this for Oliver as he does. It's taking everything inside me to resist touching myself at this point. I want the build-up to be protracted so that when he slides inside me, the feeling is as powerful as it can possibly be. To distract myself, I slide one hand up his thigh to cup his balls. Massaging them gently, while my other hand grips his shaft and my mouth slides rhythmically up and down, I feel him coming close to breaking point. His moans and grunts have escalated, and I know he's close.

He uses my braid to pull my head away from his dick, which is glistening with my saliva. Looking up at his arresting face—he's clearly holding on by a thread. I take the hint, standing up, I remove my panties and climb him like a tree. He turns, pressing my body to the glass as he impales me on his slick dick. Nuzzling into the side of my neck, he kisses from my shoulder up to my ear before drawing back to study my face. He must see what he needs because he begins to move. Slow, even glides in and out of my hot pussy.

It feels decadent and oh-so-good.

My body sighs in delight.

I tighten my legs around his hips, locking my feet behind his ass, drawing us as close as possible. I'm totally at his mercy—relying on him to take me where I need to be. He's never left me unsatisfied before, and I'm positive he won't today. The best I can do is hold on for the ride.

Our connection feels deeper somehow, dare I say, spiritual.

FOUR

-oliver-

COMING HOME. THAT'S WHAT THIS FEELS LIKE FOR ME. HAVING MY cock deep inside, Kate, my wife.

My Wife!

Knowing she's legally bound to me; that I have her forever gives me a sense of peace deeper than anything I've experienced with her thus far. Freedom I've not experienced before. A level of acceptance I've not felt since I was a young boy with an intact family. I feel like a pussy, but the strongest feeling I have is that of security. I'm finally secure knowing that she's mine. My future, my family, my everything.

My dream come true.

I'm working hard to keep my control intact, but her pussy makes it fucking hard—pun intended. My steady rhythm is about to be shot to hell as her walls flutter around my cock. She's close to her second orgasm of the afternoon, which will only be the beginning if I have my way. I don't plan on leaving this room until we have to leave for our flight tomorrow. Every time I slide my cock in, I make sure to rub her clit, sending her skyward. Her pussy constricts around my shaft, strangling it in the best possible way. Maintaining my steady rhythm through her release is impossible, and I pick up speed and power. As she breaks, I breach her ass with one finger, prolonging her release and increasing the pressure around my cock. As she cries out, I groan. I'm determined to take her straight into another orgasm. I pick up the tempo again, thrusting my finger in her ass, and rubbing her clit on the upstroke. She shudders again and before her climax ends completely, her internal muscles begin rippling again, sending me into overload and I can't hold on any longer. She bites me where my neck meets my shoulder, as my cum splashes her internal walls. Locking my knees to stop myself from collapsing, I press my cock in as deep as possible and ride out my orgasm. Moving my hips back and forth slowly, easing us both down from our mutual high, I struggle to take in a breath. My chest heaves and my vision becomes fuzzy around the edges. I take Kate's mouth in a soft, gentle kiss. A kiss of appreciation for allowing me into her body, sharing herself with me in the most intimate of ways.

Keeping my softening cock inside Kate's pussy, I slowly move us away from the window to sit on the edge of the bed. Our kiss continues—our connection soul-deep. We both slowly pull away, eyes half-mast, a small smile growing across Kate's lips.

"That felt more profound. Do you think it's because we're married now?"

"This whole day's been profound, Kate. I'm not surprised by the intensity of what we just did." I nuzzle her neck. "How about a bath?"

"That sounds divine."

I wrap my arms around Kate's body, encouraging her to wrap her legs around me, before rising to head into the bathroom to draw a bath in the large tub. When I made the booking for today, I requested all of Kate's bathroom products be waiting for us. Sitting Kate on the marble vanity, I fill the tub, adding generous amounts of jasmine bubble bath. Once it's full, I collect Kate from the vanity and step into the tub with her before sinking us both down into the warm, sudsy water. Positioning her back to my front, I glide my hands over her slick body, paying special attention to her firm breasts—I love her tits. As Kate leans back into my body, she releases a deep sigh.

"Today's been the absolute best."

"Yes, it has. You're tied to me forever. No escape for you." I kiss the side of her neck, which she tilts further, allowing me better access.

"That goes both ways, Mister. You can't get away from me either, you know."

"That suits me just fine. I don't want to get away from you. Ever." I kiss her neck again. "What was your favorite part?"

"Am I allowed to include what we just did? Against the window, no less." She giggles and the vibrations wake up my cock.

"You can include anything you want, Sunshine."

"Saying our vows and affirming our promises to each other in front of our family and friends. Knowing we're legally tied together was one highlight. Our first dance as husband and wife will be something I'll always cherish. The way you held me close—cherishing me with your words." She releases a deep sigh of pleasure. "The way we just made love for the first time as a married couple is definitely on my highlight reel. That was something else, Husband of mine."

My male pride is certainly feeling a boost. I nuzzle into her neck, drawing her body closer to mine.

"How about you? What was your favorite part?"

"That's easy. Making you mine, both legally and physically. I love knowing that you're mine in every sense of the word. Call me a Neanderthal, but I want to beat on my chest and tell the world that you belong to me. Today, placing that wedding band on your finger, tying you to me in the legal sense, feels like the equivalent of dragging you to my cave."

She giggles at my description. She thinks I'm messing around, but I'm deadly serious. I love having those rings on her finger, telling every other asshole around that she's taken—that she belongs to me.

She twists around until we're front to front and slips onto my erection, distracting me from my thoughts. We take it slow this time. Gliding together, building up slowly to our release, lips locked, bodies as close as they can be. Linked. Intimately joined in the best possible way.

We spend the rest of the afternoon, night, and the next morning locked together. Enjoying each other's bodies, feeling immeasurable pleasure before checking out to catch our flight to Broome for our honeymoon. I want to show her where her pink diamond came from and the northern area of Western Australia looks like the perfect spot for our first vacation together. It's also only a short flight away from where we'll be working with Bob and Ella in ten days.

We've flown to Vancouver, Brisbane, Perth, and finally, we've landed in Broome. I plied Kate with alcohol before each takeoff, so she didn't stress out—it seems to have worked. We're finally in paradise after twenty-four hours. It's winter here, though you wouldn't know it, with the temperature sitting at a warm eighty-six degrees. It's early afternoon as we leave the airport and make our way to the hotel I have booked overlooking the Indian Ocean. We're both travel-weary. After checking in, we follow our dedicated host to our villa. Despite her tiredness, Kate's eyes are wide with wonder.

"Wow, Oliver. This is magnificent. I didn't know places like this existed."

Looking around at our villa, inspired by the Asian and Colonial cultures which settled this area hoping to make a fortune gathering pearls, I'm impressed by the attention to detail. I crack open the bottle of sparkling wine that's been left on ice for us, pouring two glasses. Passing a glass to Kate, I kiss the tip of her nose, nudging her to look around with me.

"It looked spectacular online, but it looks even better in real life." I'm impressed. This is a tiny town, pretty much in the middle of nowhere; famous for its pearling history and exceptional beaches. To have a hotel of this caliber is unbelievable. We wander from room to room before stepping outside to check out our private courtyard, complete with a plunge pool and gazebo. We finish our drinks, placing the glasses on the outdoor table between two comfortable-looking loungers. I can't wait to get Kate naked in that pool. She sees the intent written all over my face.

"You have a one-track mind, *Husband*." She laughs, playfully shaking her ass as she moves to step back inside.

"With you as my wife, it's impossible to think of anything else." I catch up to her, banding my arms around her waist. Picking her up off her feet, I carry her inside and unceremoniously throw her onto the king-size bed. Her giggling stops as she studies my face—close enough that our breaths fan each other. Seriousness falls around us as she leans up, pressing a kiss to my lips. I push forward, my tongue licking the seam of her lips in invitation. She opens readily, taking me in, teasing my tongue with hers. Her head falls back onto the bed with a moan and I follow, using the hand at the back of her head to direct her mouth where I want it. We get lost in each other as is usual for us. Both of us enjoying the peaceful tranquility of the setting after spending hours upon hours sharing such confined spaces with others on several planes. I don't know how I kept my hands off of her for such a long time.

She pulls away. "I desperately need a shower. Let's unpack and freshen up."

I roll off of her and stand, pulling her up with me. We quickly get ourselves situated and into the shower, where I proceed to defile her against the tiled wall, as I plan to do every day while we're in paradise. We have a brief nap before our booked activity of a sunset camel ride along the pristine beach, right outside our hotel.

FIVE

-kate-

I CAN'T BELIEVE I'M ON THE BACK OF A FREAKING CAMEL, TRAIPSING across the whitest sand I've ever seen, with the love of my life at my back and the sun sinking further into the horizon by the second. The sky's painted in the most glorious shades of oranges and pinks. The scent of the sea and the warm ocean breeze on my face are pure magic.

This is now my life.

My life with Oliver, *my Husband.*

He's organized everything for this vacation of ours. All I need to do is enjoy the experiences with him by my side. This place is like something out of a postcard, the colors unlike anything I've seen before. The camels are calm and friendly, if not a little smelly, as they steadily stroll across the firm sand along the edge of the shore. It's a little nerve-racking being up so high, but I've got Oliver at my back, making me feel safe.

Oliver presses forward, kissing between my shoulder blades. "Is this okay? I wasn't sure if you would balk at sitting atop a camel. But the photos of this excursion were unbelievable, and I wanted to share this experience with you."

"Oh, Oliver. This is beyond amazing. I'll remember this for the rest of my life. Thank you." I reach behind my body for his hand, bringing it up to my mouth, and pressing my lips to the center of his palm. We enjoy the one-hour trek along the beach and back again before having photographs with our traveling companions and wandering back to our villa, where we're greeted by our host and a scrumptious seafood meal.

We fall into bed, exhausted from our travel and the time difference. After making slow, tender love, we curl our bodies around each other and fall into a restful sleep.

———

Today sees us wandering around the quirky township after a delectable breakfast of fresh tropical fruits delivered to our room. The red soil is a stark contrast to the pristine white sand and aquamarine waters of the beach we traversed last night. Holding hands, we partake in a tour that shares the long and colorful, sometimes deadly history of the area. Oliver insists on purchasing a set of delicate drop pearl earrings as a souvenir of our time here. He still doesn't get that I don't need all these gifts—I just need him. He's always so surprised when I remind him of that.

The combination of Asian and Indigenous cultures is something neither Oliver nor I have ever before experienced, making this an exceptional memory for our long life together.

———

Each day we experience new and breathtaking sights. We've flown over the Bungle Bungles, an awe-inspiring geographical feature, the likes I've never seen. The red rocks, change color right before our eyes as the sun sets. We've seen humpback whales frolicking in the warm waters as they make their way south along the Western Australian coast. For such enormous creatures, they move through the water gracefully. Watching them made us both feel small and insignificant. The pure delight on Oliver's face as he watched the enormous creatures is something I'll remember forever. He's like a little boy who's been given free rein in a candy store. I couldn't help but attack him with kisses.

We've flown to and hiked through the Mitchell Falls, before riding in a helicopter to experience the waterfalls and gorges from above, giving a whole new perspective to the location. The whole time, Oliver ensures our bodies are in close physical contact. Either holding hands or touching in some capacity. Kissing, snuggling, and nuzzling constantly. It's totally out of this world to be sharing these experiences with him. My heart's full to bursting to have this man as my husband sharing this vacation with me.

We kayak the pristine Indian Ocean waters, coming across a pod of friendly dolphins, catching the waves playfully alongside us. When we get back to our villa, Oliver tenderly massages the soreness from my arms and shoulders as a result of three hours of paddling. Then he massages other parts of my body, setting my body on fire until we both come and almost black out.

———

On the final day here, we fly to Horizontal Falls, where we'll cruise before swimming near their base. Oliver's bought out the entire tour for the day, meaning we're on our own with the tour crew. Oliver and I change into our swimwear so we can relax on the deck and enjoy the view of the cliffs and falls.

"That bikini's not going to work here."

I look down at my bikini in confusion. "What? Why not? It's the only one I have with me."

"Because it's too revealing, and the crew will see more of you than I'm prepared to share."

What the ...?

"Pardon? What do you mean 'share'? It's a bikini. It covers all the necessary bits, and it's not even as revealing as some other bikinis I've seen. It's not like anyone's going to be touching me, or even looking at me. They know I'm with you." I flash him my wedding and engagement rings in exasperation. "You're being ridiculous!"

"No, I'm not. They were already checking you out when you were fully dressed. They won't be able to keep their eyes off of your sexy curves when they see you in those scraps of green material."

"I'm not sure what you expect me to do. This is the only bikini I have, and I'm not missing out on catching some sun."

He passes me my white beach coat cover-up that falls to my ankles, with lace around my waist and ties in the front. It's pretty see-through. I'm not sure it's going to hide anything, but I guess if it makes him feel more comfortable, then out of respect, I can do that for him. I put the garment on and turn around. "Is this better? Do you feel better now?"

He nods slightly, even though his eyebrows are still drawn down low over his mossy eyes. "Thank you," he whispers, kissing my forehead. Then he leads me up onto the deck.

We get situated, and the view is magnificent, including the man laying on the deck chair next to mine. The crew meets our every need, barely allowing our glasses to empty or our ice to melt.

———

On the eighth day of our honeymoon, we take the one-and-a-half-hour flight to a place called Kununurra. A strange-sounding name, for a place that looks as though it's been forgotten by time. Home to the largest man-made lake in the southern hemisphere. The decommissioned mine near here is where Oliver sourced my pink heart-shaped diamond. He learned of it from Lena Rhinecourt, an investor he's been working with.

We travel by helicopter to *The Homestead*, which Oliver has booked out for our two-night stay. The view from the helicopter is breathtaking—the rugged, untouched earth is utterly mesmerizing. It feels completely decadent to have the entire homestead to ourselves. We're greeted by a divine lunch that could be served in any Michelin-star restaurant overlooking the magnificent river. It's like heaven in the middle of nowhere. After lunch, we wander hand in hand along the pathways through the bushland and finish the day in the enormous bathtub situated on the terrace overlooking the river with a glass of wine each.

"What's been your favorite part of our honeymoon?"

I have to think for a few moments. There have been heaps of awesome sights and experiences. But I do have a favorite, which may surprise my husband. "Of all the interesting things we've seen and experienced, my most favorite part of our honeymoon is …" I poke his rock-hard abs with my toe. "Having you all to myself for such an extended time. Sharing all of this with you is more than I ever could have asked for."

His eyebrows rise in surprise as he grasps my foot and drags me across the bath before taking my mouth in a full-on assault. He manipulates my body easily, sliding smoothly inside my wet heat. It always feels out of this world when we're connected like this. We're eye to eye in this position, his breaths mixing with mine. "I love that out of everything we've done and seen, you still think I'm the best. I've got to be the luckiest man on the planet." He kisses me again before beginning a steady glide in and out of my body. "My favorite experience is always being inside you. I love you, Kate." He picks up speed and power, driving us both to the edge before tipping us over into oblivion. With the sun setting over the river, Oliver inside me, and new adventures ahead of us, I'm the happiest I've ever been.

———

We spend the morning on a guided hike through gorges, making Oliver and I feel like the only people left on earth, and the afternoon enjoying thermal pools which feel awesome for our tired legs. It's certainly been an energetic vacation. The amount of hiking, climbing, swimming, paddling, and sexing we've done has certainly burned the calories. I'm definitely not complaining, since I get to burn all those calories with my hunky husband.

The last day of the honeymoon comes way too fast and I don't want to leave our personal bubble to join the real world again. Once again flying by helicopter, we make our way to the newly decommissioned Argyle diamond mine. It was one of the largest mines for diamonds in the world and one of the very few which sourced rare pink diamonds—like the one in my engagement ring.

The tour is very impressive and informative; and when the operator tells us that pink diamonds sell for one million dollars per carat, I nearly faint. I have to take slow, deliberate breaths to steady myself. He notices me looking down at my engagement ring and smiles.

"Ah, I see you have one of our exquisite diamonds. Looks like one-and-a-half carats to me." He nods toward Oliver. "You've got good taste, mate."

Oliver pulls me tight into his side. "I don't think I have good taste. I think I have exquisite taste." The operator catches Oliver's meaning, nodding and laughing in acknowledgment. I feel like I should lock my engagement ring away for safekeeping. I had no idea it was worth that much money. I'm going to be scared to lose it now that I know it's worth beyond the sentimental value that it holds for me. Oliver, as usual, picks up on my internal conflict.

"Don't even think about locking the ring away for safekeeping. The point of it is to show the world you're mine. The price doesn't factor into it." He raises my left hand to his mouth, kissing my ring reverently before kissing my lips chastely.

After the tour, we fly by helicopter back to Kununurra, to catch a flight to Darwin, and then onto our destination to meet Bob and Ella.

SIX

-oliver-

"FUCK, THIS HUMIDITY MIGHT JUST KILL ME!" WE'VE BEEN HERE forty-eight hours and I'm already suffering from the excessive humidity. I've got another fourteen days to deal with these energy-sapping conditions. It's the wet monsoon season, meaning the morning air is heavy with moisture waiting to burst from the clouds. In the afternoon, when it finally rains, it's a fucking relief, but we can't work because of the torrential downpour.

The work site is a muddy mess, making it difficult to traverse without slipping on your ass. Which has already happened to me. Kate thought it was fucking hilarious until she attempted to help me up and I pulled her down into the mud with me. She didn't think it was so funny then. Ha!

The only upside is watching the joy on my wife's face as she works alongside me and the other volunteers to build this new school. She's in her element; helping people.

I love her.

I never thought I'd find what we share. That I'd find the woman of my dreams; let alone marry her.

Someone I can trust completely.

Someone who loves me for the man I am.

Someone who loves me down to my very soul.

Even though we're halfway around the world, when we're together, I'm *home*.

pinterest

I went crazy putting together a Pinterest board for Kate and Oliver's story. If you're interested, you can check it out here:

https://tinyurl.com/lovingsummer-pinterest

THE
SUMMER
TWINS
book two

second
chance
SUMMER

DEBRA ST JAMES

inspiration

This story was inspired by the lyrics ...
—> *No Such Thing by John Mayer* <—

reader discretion required

This book contains incidences of domestic violence, which may be upsetting to some readers.
Check here for a more comprehensive explanation on Debra's website.
https://debrastjamesbooks.com/second-chance-summer-content-warning/
The above explanation <u>does contain spoilers</u>.

characters in this story

Some characters in this story are Deaf or Hard of Hearing. They are depicted using American Sign Language (ASL). ASL is a common form of sign language used in the United States and many parts of Canada. It incorporates these five parameters: hand shape, palm orientation, location, movement, and facial expression/non-manual markers.

It has its own grammatical rules and syntax. Therefore, some of the dialogue, shown within quotes, throughout this work is a translation of ASL to English for this novel. Please be aware that when it states someone is signing and speaking simultaneously, they are communicating through Simultaneous Communication (SimCom), which is different from ASL. This is a common form of communication between hearing individuals and those who are Deaf or Hard of Hearing.

The use of capitalization for the terms Deaf and Hard of Hearing demonstrates that the person identifies as a member of the Deaf Community.

I would like to take this opportunity to thank Kimberly and Fiona for their insights into the Deaf Community and their invaluable suggestions, which helped to make these characters as authentic as possible.

playlist

No Such Thing … *John Mayer*
Crush … *Jennifer Paige*
Love Song for No One … *John Mayer*
Vultures … *John Mayer*
I Just Wanna Live … *Good Charlotte*
Style … *Taylor Swift*
Love Me Do … *The Beatles*
Sweet Home Alabama … *Lynyrd Skynyrd*
Three Little Birds … *Bob Marley and the Wailers*
Isn't She Lovely … *Stevie Wonder*

You can check it out here:

https://tinyurl.com/secondchancesummer-spotify

ONE

-toby-

[senior year]

SITTING AT THE TABLE IN THE FAR CORNER OF THE CAFETERIA, TO AVOID notice, I watch Cassia walk in with her group of friends. They're all laughing and having a great time, something I generally find difficult to do in mixed company. I'm not sure why I'm the way I am. I generally only feel comfortable around my family and some close friends (which are limited). Music takes a lot of space in my head—I tend to get lost in there quite a bit—which doesn't make for a good friend, in most people's opinion.

As usual, Cassia looks beautiful with her chestnut hair falling below her shoulders in soft waves. As she looks up, our eyes lock across the crowded room. Sounds cheesy, right? But it's the norm for us. I'm connected to her on some fundamental level I don't understand. I also find her incredibly hot. She just has to walk into the room and my dick misbehaves, embarrassing me to the point where I have to escape being in her presence as soon as possible. The way I always leave whenever she's around, I'm sure she thinks I hate her.

Cassia excuses herself from her friends, then walks toward me with a shy smile. Luckily, I'm sitting down, so she won't see my hard-on. Stopping in front of me, she tucks her silky hair behind her ear. "Hey, Toby."

"Uh, hi, Cassia. How are things?" I manage to sound somewhat put together, which is a bonus.

"Great. The girls and I were just talking about prom. You going?"

I wouldn't be caught dead going to prom. I don't want to see her dancing with that douche she dates on and off, Jake Simmons. Kate's going with Michael Fitzpatrick, who hangs out in the same group as Jake. I don't think Michael and Jake are best buds, but they *are* friends. I told Kate that I think she'd be better off going to prom with her girl-friends than with Michael. He seems like a dick to me.

"Nah, not my scene." I look down at the table because I don't want to see the pity in her graphite-colored eyes.

"Oh, that's disappointing. I was hoping we could share a dance."

My head snaps up to hers. "I thought you'd be going with Jake."

She shakes her head in the negative, swishing the long, silky waves around her shoulders. Her lips spread in a half-smile. "Nope. We broke up." She rolls her eyes. "Again."

She doesn't seem too upset about another breakup. I don't know what that guy's problem is. He's constantly breaking up with her, then chases her down after realizing his mistake, begging for forgiveness. If she were my girl, I'd never let her go.

Shane wanders toward us, coming in behind Cassia. He wiggles his eyebrows when he sees we're talking. He knows I have a crush on her, so he likes to take every opportunity to tease me about it. "Hey, guys. What's up?"

Cassia turns toward Shane with a genuine smile, one that lights up her entire face. "Oh, hi, Shane. We were just talking about prom. Toby's being a boohoo and not going. What about you? Are you going?" She looks hopeful.

He tucks his hands into his pockets, looking between the two of us. "Maybe. Not sure yet."

"It should be a fun night. You two should definitely come." She looks over her shoulder to acknowledge her friends, who are calling her back to their table. "Anyway, I need to go. See ya in last period, Toby."

"Yeah, see ya around."

I watch her long legs carry her away from us, wishing I wasn't such a loser. Shane looks at me with raised eyebrows as he sits down. "You should definitely go to the prom. I hear Jake broke up with her again. This could be your chance, bro."

A large body moves in front of me. When I tilt my head up to see who's blocking my stellar view, I find Jake.

"Whatcha lookin' at, Emo Boy?" His beefy arms are crossed over his bulky chest. Just because he's the captain of our school football team, he thinks he rules the school. Actually, he *does* rule the school, and I hate him. I hate him because he has Cassia and doesn't treat her with the respect she deserves.

I don't even bother making eye contact with the jerk. "Nothin'."

"Good, keep it that way, Emo Boy. She's no one to you. Got it?" He snarls down his nose at me. Since I'm sitting while he's standing, he's pretty much towering over me like a giant brick wall.

"No problem." I'll say anything to get the guy out of my face. He seems satisfied with my answer, raps his knuckles on the table, and walks away to join his so-called friends. I'm pretty sure half the guys he hangs out with are only friends with him because it's safer for them. If you're not his friend, it leaves you open to being bullied by him.

"You should tell him to fuck off," Shane suggests, knowing I'll do nothing of the sort. "So, are you gonna go to prom?"

I doodle in my notebook that I always carry with me. "Nah. They'll probably get back together by then. It's not worth the hassle."

———

The last period is music appreciation, my favorite class. Music centers me, quiets all the noise in my head, and allows me to be who I really am. My teacher, Mr. Hastings, pretty much lets me do my own thing, guiding me when I need it and leaving me alone when I don't. I also like the class because Cassia Phillips is in it—the only class we share. She is in no way musically inclined, only taking the class because her mom wanted her to take it. She wants her to be 'well rounded'. She plays the flute, which causes all sorts of issues with my dick, as she purses her pouty lips to blow across the embouchure hole. She struggles to maintain the appropriate pressure, causing a lot of frustration on her part, while all I can think about is kissing her soft lips.

Since I'm not a chatty person, everyone pretty much leaves me alone, but Cassia always sits next to me during our music history session. "Hey again." She smiles at me, making my insides flip upside down.

Struggling to make eye contact with her, I flick my eyes over her shoulder. "Yeah, hey." I sound like a douche. I get so damn nervous when she's around. For once, I wish I could be the cool kid.

"You ready to learn all about Dylan's crash and burn when he decided to use an electric guitar instead of his trusty acoustic at the Newport Folk Festival in 1965?"

I'm impressed she's interested in Dylan. He's definitely one of my idols, and I aspire to be as famous as he is one day. I raise my eyes to hers. She's fidgeting ... biting her lip ... looking unsure. Raising an eyebrow, I nod slightly as one side of my mouth lifts to give her the approval I think she's looking for. She stops fidgeting, then smiles back. "It should be an interesting discussion."

"Yeah, it'll be interesting to find out what everyone's views are. I, for one, think Dylan's music was great, whether he played acoustic or electric guitar. It was all about the lyrics, the storytelling." I think it's the most number of words I've said to her, ever. The surprised expression on her face supports this idea.

Mr. Hastings walks in, interrupting our bonding moment over Dylan.

TWO

-cassia-

I'M CERTAIN TOBY HATES ME. TODAY WAS THE MOST HE'S EVER SAID TO me, and it was only because we were talking about something close to his heart. Maybe that's the key? He usually only says a few words to me because I approach him to strike up a conversation. Otherwise, he would never speak to me. I love hearing the timbre of his voice when he talks—and when he sings, oh my gosh, *so good*—so I purposely go out of my way to chat with him. My friends always tease me because they know I have a huge crush on him. He makes my heart beat faster and my belly flip. Watching him work his guitar, I imagine the way his hands would feel on my body. Today, when he looked at me with his denim-colored eyes, I'm sure the breath in my lungs seized.

Perhaps if I stopped going back to Jake, I'd have a chance with Toby. Probably not—he always seems to be in a hurry to get away from me, and I'm not sure why. I've repeatedly gone back over the years in my memory, trying to pinpoint if I ever did anything to him to make him dislike me, but I can't think of anything. Two thick arms wrap around my torso from behind, scaring the crap outta me. Glancing over my shoulder, I put a face to the arms. Ugh, Jake. "Let me go, asshole."

"Now, that's no way to talk to your boyfriend." He squeezes me tighter with one arm, while the other comes up to grab my boob, hard. "Ouch. Let me go."

"I'm never lettin' you go, Sia." Stupid idiot. This is what happens. He breaks up with me and then he acts like nothing happened.

"You already did remember?" Wiggling free, I turn to face him.

"You broke up with me because I didn't want to have sex with you on Friday night. Or did you forget?" He had a game on Saturday, so I'm sure he hooked up with someone else. Jake can't go without sex for more than two days at a time. He figures that if he breaks up with me before he hooks up with someone else, it doesn't count as cheating.

"Awww, you're upset. I didn't mean it. You know I never mean it." He pulls me into his huge body, snuggling down into my neck the way I love. He may be an idiot, but he can be so sweet to me. I like having a boyfriend; it makes me feel special and important to someone outside of my family. He pulls back, taking my school bag to carry, then grasps my hand to lead me out to his car. Throwing my bag on the back seat, he pins me against the side of his car, kissing me with apology and sweetness. Pulling back, he looks into my eyes. "I'm sorry, Babe. I was stupid. Please forgive me."

As I'm about to forgive him, *again*, Toby passes by with Shane and Kate. Toby looks my way and our eyes connect on a deeper level, as they always seem to. I'm sure I'm the only one who feels it, though, because he never seems affected. He doesn't stop, just keeps on walking, shaking his head … *in disappointment*, maybe? I'm pretty sure him being disappointed that I'm with Jake is wishful thinking on my part. Then he turns away down the sidewalk, exiting the school grounds without giving me another look. Looking back at Jake, I see the sincerity in his eyes, and I know he'll spend the rest of this week making it up to me.

I put on my sternest voice. "I forgive you. But this is the last time, Jake. I mean it."

He leans forward again, taking my mouth in a hard kiss filled with relief. He doesn't mean what he says and does half the time. He doesn't think things through, and he can be a spoiled brat when he doesn't get his way. Friday night was like witnessing a toddler's tantrum. He wasn't getting his way, so he wanted to hurt me by breaking up with me. I'm certain he's learned his lesson this time.

THREE

-toby-

[present]

"Hey, Xanthe," I sign, "I'm early."

Shane makes himself comfortable on a seat in the front lobby area.

Her face lights up as she leans in for a hug, then pulls back to greet me. "Hey, Toby." Signing as though she's playing guitar for my sign name. I'm proud to have recently been given a sign name by the people I interact with within the Deaf Community—it took almost four years to earn it after I became somewhat capable in ASL—which I still struggle with at times. Xanthe is Hard of Hearing, so she always signs with me to help me practice my newly acquired skills. I have a lot of time for Xanthe and her husband, Louis, who have worked tirelessly to set up and establish this brand-new facility for Deaf and Hard of Hearing kids. "I'm happy you could make it today."

I use my hands, facial expressions, and body language, combined with clear speech, to allow for lip-reading, as my signing is still a little clunky to communicate in ASL with Xanthe. "I can't wait to get started. Show me where I need to set up."

She indicates for me to follow her, taking me on a tour of the impressive facility and explaining the purpose of each area. She then shows me to a large room with wooden floors and large windows. There's a heap of colorful balloons spread around the room, making it look like a party is about to take place.

"The kids will be surprised to have a real-life musician play for them today." She shows me where everything is so I can set up and

409

then leaves me to my own devices. I take a moment to tune my guitar, strumming a new melody I've been experimenting with.

I'm so lost in my head that I fail to notice the little girl who's now resting her hands on my guitar. Her eyes are closed, her lashes resting on the apples of her cheeks as she's absorbing the vibrations of the strings through the body of the guitar via her hands. She's wearing a serene smile as she enjoys the melody I'm playing on repeat until I get it perfect. I don't want to stop because she's obviously enjoying the experience. After a few more minutes, she opens her eyes, revealing gorgeous pewter-colored irises, and smiles up at me. She's a cute little girl.

She signs to me, "I liked that."

"Thanks. I'm still working on it," I sign back to her.

"I love the guitar."

"Yeah?" I smile. I love it when I find a fellow guitar enthusiast. "I hug the guitar, too."

She giggles. "I think you mean you *love* the guitar, too."

"That's what I said."

"No, you didn't, silly. You said, 'I *hug* the guitar, too'." She shows me the difference between the two signs. They're so similar. I still get some signs muddled. "I've always wanted to learn how to play."

"Really? Why?"

"Why not?" she immediately responds.

"Because it would be hard," I sign. Her face drops a little. I'm still a newbie within the Community, and occasionally I make a faux pas, and I fear I've just made one. My ignorance surrounding the capabilities of Deaf and Hard of Hearing people still colors my thinking sometimes, but I'm working to shut those old thoughts down.

"That's okay. I like learning things that can be hard." She smiles at me. "Would you teach me?"

Uh, this was meant to be a one-off session to entertain the kids as part of their school vacation program. She's making a puppy dog face while holding her hands together in the begging position. I must be a complete sucker because this is going to require a regular commitment from me. "Okay. Okay." I laugh at myself and the situation I now find myself in.

She jumps up and down, spinning around with the biggest grin on her little face, and now I'm glad I've agreed to teach her. Not that I know where to even begin to teach a kid how to play the guitar. I've never done it before. I'll have to ask Mom for help since she's the music teacher of the family.

"Thank you. Thank you. Thank you," she excitedly signs.

I can't stop the spread of my lips in response to her sheer happiness at my agreement to teach her how to play the guitar. But then her face suddenly drops, as if she's remembered something terrible. "What's wrong?"

She shrugs. "I don't have a guitar to learn with."

"Oh, no problem." I wave away her concern. "I possible bring one of my old ones that you possible use while you're learning until you possible get one of your own." Her face lights up yet again, and she giggles. It doesn't take much to make this kid happy. I have several old guitars sitting at Mom and Dad's from when I was younger. I'm sure one of them will be the perfect size for her.

"Oh, you're silly. You kept saying *possible* instead of *can*." She shows me the difference between the two signs. "See the difference?"

That's twice I've stuffed up my signs. "Uh, yeah, thanks. I'll try to remember." I practice the two signs, trying to commit them to memory.

"That's okay. I sometimes make mistakes, too."

"You'll need to get permission from your parents." Her smile widens as she nods energetically. We're interrupted as a handful of kids of various ages make their way into the room. My new friend stays close to me but welcomes her friends with a wave. They've all spent quite a bit of time together over the past few weeks, and probably most of them attend the same school. Xanthe's close behind. She notices my new friend standing next to me, away from her friends.

She signs to me, "I see you've met Poppy." Looking at the little girl with affection.

So, her name is Poppy; it suits her. She's vibrant, like the color of the flower I assume she's named after. I nod, then let Xanthe know she conned me into giving her guitar lessons. She bursts into laughter before letting me know that Poppy's very good at getting people to do her bidding. *Oh, great*, I've been had by a kid. Kate's going to get a real kick out of this.

Xanthe introduces me to the kids by fingerspelling my name, then using my sign name from there on out. She explains how we met, and the kids' faces light up as they all wave to me. I'm not convinced Poppy got all the information because she was fascinated with stroking the timber of my guitar. I plug my guitar into the amplifier, put in my earplugs, and cover them with headphones for double protection. The amplifiers are loud to increase the vibrations through the wooden floor, so I make sure to protect my hearing. The kids lay on the floor, close their eyes, and lose themselves in the vibrations as I strum my way through a couple of my slower songs. Normally, I have my band playing with me during a concert or recording an album. Today, it's just me and my trusty guitar. After a couple of songs, Xanthe gets the kids to stand up. They grab a balloon each, and she does what she does best.

Sign my music to the kids.

Which is how we met four and a half years ago. I saw her signing at a concert, and I was hooked. I knew I had to get her to work with me, signing my concerts, and making them accessible to the Deaf Community. She's already familiar with my music, so it's smooth and fluent for her and the kids. The kids' faces light up with lips stretched wide as they experience my more upbeat songs for the first time.

I'm on top of the world.

Poppy's front and center, moving to the music with evident enjoyment written all over her body. Being part of this experience with these kids, who seem to have a natural rhythm, could easily become addictive. They're so appreciative and open with their joy. Maybe it won't be so bad to spend time with Poppy and teach her how to play the guitar.

After the class is over, Poppy comes over to me. "That was so good."

I bow, flattening my right hand, then placing the tips of my fingers to my lips before moving it out and down toward Poppy with a smile. "Thank you." We stand, smiling at each other until she realizes it's time to go. "I'll come back next Friday at the same time. See you then, Poppy."

"Okay," she nods. "See you then." She uses my sign name the way Xanthe showed the kids.

I touch her shoulder gently to gain her attention because she's already turned to leave. I wait until she's looking at me. "Make sure you get permission. Okay?"

She nods emphatically, waving over her shoulder as she runs out of the room.

I pack up my guitar to head out to find Xanthe and Louis before I leave, so I can let them know I'll be back at the same time next week for my first lesson with Poppy. I didn't think to check with them if it would be okay before agreeing to teach Poppy. Thankfully, they give me the all-clear. Me teaching Poppy how to play the guitar is exactly the sort of thing they want to happen in this space. Their mission is to bring the joy of music and dance to kids in a deaf-friendly way. They got into it because they have a passion for music and dance and wanted to share that with others. As their own hearing deteriorated, their love for and appreciation of the arts never waned.

"Why the balloons?" I sign to Xanthe. I was puzzled why the kids were holding onto the colorful spheres during the session.

Her eyebrows rise along with a knowing smile. "They're great at amplifying the vibrations of the sound waves in the air. It adds to the entire experience for them."

"That's so freaking clever. I would never have thought of that." I shake my head in amazement at the different approaches that can be used to share the music experience. I never used to even consider that a Deaf person would be interested in music since they can't hear. After spending time with Xanthe and Louis, I've learned it isn't true. They've dispelled a lot of myths.

As I'm leaving the building with Shane, I spy Poppy climbing into a car with an older lady. She looks like she could be Poppy's nan. They're signing animatedly when the lady glances up, making eye contact with me. I nod in acknowledgment, and she smiles in return as Shane and I keep walking toward my car.

"What was that all about?" Shane observes.

"That's Poppy. The little girl who conned me into giving her guitar lessons, starting next Friday." I huff out a laugh, brushing loose strands of hair behind my ear.

Shane does a double-take between Poppy and me in disbelief. "*She* conned you. You're a grown-ass man, for god's sake. You need to learn to say no occasionally, bro." He shakes his head. "You have enough going on at the moment writing your next album. You shouldn't be adding more shit to your schedule." He shakes his head at me.

I know he has my best interest at heart, but I want to do this for Poppy, and well, for me, too. I think it'll be fun. I've just gotta work out where to start. "It's cool, Shane. I'm pretty sure this won't be a problem. It might even give me some inspiration. Win-win."

He shakes his head at me with a half-smile. We've known each other long enough that he knows I won't change my mind. He won't get in my way or try to stop me. "Where to next, Boss Man?"

I look at the time. Mom should be home. I might visit her so I can find out how to teach guitar to a kid. She'll be able to give me some idea about how to get started, at least. "Let's head to my folks. I need to ask Mom how to teach guitar."

That's enough to cause Shane to burst into laughter. Deep, happy laughter sounds fantastic coming from my long-time best friend and bodyguard. He's seen so much shit during his time in Syria as part of the Special Forces Operational Unit. To hear him laugh eases a deep worry inside me. He's not been the same since he came home, and I worry he'll never be the Shane I knew before he signed up.

FOUR

-toby-

ARRIVING AT MY CHILDHOOD HOME, MY SHOULDERS RELAX SLIGHTLY AS I step up to the front door. I'm a pretty laid-back guy, but I'm wound up because I don't want to let Poppy down. I'm hoping Mom can give me some guidance on where to start, as well as what techniques I should use, since she's been a music teacher for over thirty years. It's not like I can use a standard teaching approach.

Maybe I bit off more than I can chew?

I knock on the door out of politeness, then walk straight in with Shane on my heels, calling out to Mom as I go. She steps out of the kitchen, wiping her hands on a dishtowel. Her face lights up when she sees the two of us coming toward her. "Hey, Mom." I wrap my arms around her in a tight hug, then step back to let Shane hug her, too.

"Hey, Mrs. S."

"Hello, boys, this is a lovely surprise. I didn't think I'd see you until your birthday on Sunday. Come through. I've made a brownie slice."

Shane and I smile at each other because we both love Mom's brownies, and if my nose doesn't deceive me, I have a feeling these are still gonna be warm. It takes me back to my school days, coming home from school with Kate and Shane to the smell of fresh baked goods. Following her into the kitchen, we find the brownie slice on the cooling rack in the middle of the counter.

Oh, yeah, they're still warm.

Mom potters around, making us each a cup of coffee, and then cuts the brownie into equal portions. She knows Shane and I love this treat, so she cuts and plates a generous serving for each of us. We sit around the table so we can catch up.

"Have you heard anything from Kate and Oliver?"

"Oh, yes. They checked in on Wednesday to let us know they arrived safely on the island. Kate was stressing out about her engagement ring because she found out how much it was worth on the honeymoon." Mom laughs.

"Well, it wasn't going to be cheap if Oliver had anything to do with it. What did she expect?"

Shane shakes his head. "Kate's gonna have to get used to how much money that guy spends on things. He can afford it."

Mom and I nod in agreement.

"So, what have you boys been up to today?"

"We just finished at *Music for my Heart*. Remember, I said I was volunteering there for an afternoon?"

"Oh, that's right. How was it?"

"It was great. Interesting and loads of fun."

"Your son got conned by a little girl," Shane adds with a smirk. He thinks it's hilarious that Poppy conned guitar lessons out of me. Mom's eyes flit between the two of us, waiting for an explanation. I explain how I met Poppy, our conversation, and that I've agreed to give her guitar lessons starting next Friday. I even tell Mom that I've offered the use of one of my old guitars. I must remember to get it out of the attic for her. Before she can play it, I need to fit new strings.

Mom's entire face softens as a smile curves her lips. Eyes, exactly like mine, look at me with pride and affection. "I'm so happy you're using your talent to teach others. What sort of hearing loss does this little girl have?"

"She's profoundly deaf, according to Xanthe. She was feeling the vibrations through the body of my guitar. The kids also used balloons. I've never seen anything like it before."

"Oh, my. That's amazing. I would have never thought to use balloons. I might try that with some of my younger students. It'll be fun." She pauses. "You'll need to employ some different techniques than what you normally would for a hearing child."

"I know. That's why we came over. I wanted to ask for your advice. First, I've never taught anyone how to play the guitar. Even though I'm competent, I'm not sure I know where to start with lessons, let alone for a Deaf person." I'm realizing that I *am* in over my head.

"She's going to rely on touch and vibrations more than a hearing person. *Feeling* the vibrations of the lower notes will send the signals to the brain, the same as ours receives the signals through *hearing* the sounds."

"Yeah. That's what we did today. The kids laid on the floor. We turned the speakers up loud, and they experienced the music through the vibrations. Then Xanthe joined in, signing the lyrics and music to the kids to give them a more robust experience as they held the balloons. They loved it."

"There's a music teacher I've heard about in London who teaches guitar to Deaf and Hard of Hearing children. Maybe look him up. I'll try to find his name for you."

"Thanks, Mom. That'd be great."

"No problem. Just remember to have fun with it. Remember, you want to build a love for the instrument, not just learn how it works or how to play it." She pats my hand to reinforce her point.

"I will, Mom. Promise. I'll do some research to see what I can find. I need to get one of my old guitars out of the attic, so she has one to use." I stand to take my dishes to the sink. "Be back in a minute."

I turn on the light in the attic and make my way to the area where I've stored my guitars since childhood. I have several sizes that Mom and Dad bought me as I grew. I find my half-size guitar, which I had when I was about six or seven. I'm not sure how old Poppy is. She looks quite small, so this should be a good size for her. I suppose I could buy a new one, but I like the idea of her using one of my old guitars. I grab the guitar, dusting it off as I leave the attic in the dark once again.

I step into the kitchen to find Mom washing the dishes and Shane wiping them. "I found my first guitar." Holding it up, I show her the small instrument. It brings back a lot of memories for me. Wonderful memories of Mom and me sitting together practicing *Love Me Do* by the Beatles. Two simple chords for most of the song, introducing a third in the bridge. "I think our first song will be the same one you taught me. Do you remember what it was?"

"Of course I do. *Love Me Do* by The Beatles. Such a fun little song and a brilliant choice for a first song to learn. I'm sure she'll love it."

FIVE

-cassia-

I DRAG MYSELF IN THE FRONT DOOR AFTER NINE, WHICH IS USUAL FOR A Friday night—especially lately. A lot of my work is for weddings, which predominantly happen on the weekend. Therefore, the latter part of my week is always busy, requiring me to work late most Friday nights.

Ever since I donated the floral arrangements for a big fundraiser for *The Parkerville Project*, I've been run off my feet. Most of the attendees—make that all the attendees—were very wealthy, and they seemed to like the quirky arrangements I put together for the table centerpieces. When Mr. Stone contacted me to ask if I would be interested in helping, I jumped at the opportunity. I was flattered that he had been impressed with my work whenever he purchased flowers from me, that I offered to provide all the floral arrangements for free. Even though I did it to help the kids, I've benefited tenfold from the event with the uptake in sales; it's put my little business on the map. Where I used to have at least two weekends a month off, I'm working events every weekend now, and it's all thanks to those centerpieces. I'm going to need to employ another staff member to help, so I don't spend every weekend away from my daughter.

The front of the house is dark, so I make my way toward the back of Mom's home. I moved back after I found out I was pregnant and would be going it alone. I needed Mom's help and support. I find Mom on the couch with my little girl curled up next to her, wearing her favorite purple pajamas, sound asleep.

"Hey, Mom. Sorry, I'm so late. The order for the wedding tomorrow was huge, and I needed to make sure the arrangements made it to the venue intact. I'll have to head over tomorrow morning to place everything and deliver the bouquets to the bride and boutonnieres to the groom. It should only take about four hours. Thank goodness." I sigh. "I need a break and I miss hanging out with my girl."

"It's no problem, Cassia. It's why you moved back home, remember? So I could help you. I love looking after my granddaughter." Mom looks lovingly at my little girl as she strokes a lock of hair that's fallen over her cherubic face behind her ear.

"She tried hard to stay awake to see you when you got home. She has some exciting news to share with you, but it's gonna have to wait 'til tomorrow." Mom stands up, ready to carry my baby upstairs to bed. Not that she's a baby anymore. She just turned seven.

"I can carry her, Mom. You sit down."

"Okay. I'll go up to get her bed ready so that you can lay her down."

I drop my purse on the table as Mom quickly walks ahead of us to prepare her bed. Carrying her behind Mom, I place her carefully on her pale purple sheets, kissing her forehead before Mom bends down to do the same. Mom leaves the room, allowing me time with my girl.

I use the light spilling in from the hall to take a few minutes to watch her sleep, then lean down to tuck her in and kiss her goodnight one last time. I wasn't quite as stealthy as I should have been, causing her to stir. When she sees it's me, her entire face lights up in happiness, which makes every single part of my heart feel close to exploding. She's the best thing I've ever done in my life. My greatest joy. I turn on the lamp next to her bed to make it easier for us to communicate.

She sleepily signs, "Hello, Mommy."

I sign, "Hey, Baby Girl." I brush the hair away from her face.

"Guess what happened today?"

"You won a vacation to the moon?"

She laughs. "No, Mommy. Don't be silly."

Sitting on the side of her bed, I settle in for a chat. "Well, tell me then. What happened today to make you so happy?"

"I'm going to learn how to play guitar from a real-life guitarist."

I'm not sure what qualifies someone as a 'real-life guitarist'. "Oh, yeah, anyone I know?"

She signs his name as the universal sign for 'guitar'. Well, that's an apt name for a guitarist, I suppose.

"How did you manage to get someone to agree to give you guitar lessons?" She's skilled at convincing anybody to do anything she wants. I'm not sure how she does it, but her success rate is extraordinary.

She shrugs her shoulders, giving me her most innocent face. "I just asked, Mommy, and he said 'okay'. He's even going to bring a guitar for me to use." Her little hands are flying fast and furious, conveying her excitement.

She's been asking to learn the guitar for the past two years. I'm not sure why she has such a fascination with the instrument, but it's something she really wants to do.

"You'll need to make sure you practice at home in between lessons."

She nods vigorously.

"When will you have these lessons?"

"On Friday afternoon. I already asked Gramma, and she doesn't mind taking me after school." She holds her hands in the begging position. "Please say it's okay, Mommy."

I bet that's how she got the guitarist to agree to give her lessons. "Of course it's okay, Baby. If Gramma is happy to take you and you promise to practice between lessons, I think it will be great for you."

She springs forward, wrapping her little arms around my neck, kissing me all over my face in absolute joy. We chat about her afternoon at *Music for my Heart* and how she spent the rest of her day. I let her know that I have work in the morning, but then I'll be free for the rest of the weekend. She snuggles back into her comfy bed, and I tuck her in again, kissing her goodnight. "I love you more than all the stars in the sky and grains of sand on the earth." She smiles at me, and I turn off her lamp to head downstairs to catch up with Mom.

"You were up there a while. I assume Poppy told you her news. She was so excited, bouncing in the back seat all the way home." Mom laughs.

"Yeah, she did. She's so freaking excited. I'm thrilled for her. Thanks for agreeing to take her to her lessons."

"No problem. I think it'll be fantastic for her. A challenge."

I nod in agreement. "She loves to be challenged. This will be just the thing." I lean forward to hug Mom. "I'm gonna have a shower, then head to bed. I'm exhausted."

"Sure thing, Honey. Sweet dreams."

"You, too. See you in the morning."

"I want Lisianthus flowers in their double form in purple, pink, and white in my bouquet and for our table centerpieces, at the church, and anywhere else we need flowers. I want them everywhere. I want to be swimming in them. They're just so beautiful." The bride-to-be is fierce in her love for the floral bloom. They are beautiful flowers, and I can envision the displays clearly.

"For your bouquets, I can do a tight round design using a minimum of fifty blooms wrapped in satin ribbon to match the dresses. For the table centerpieces, I would suggest a more whimsical display, softer with more movement. I can incorporate the same blooms, tying them in with some Lavender and Baby's Breath." I pull out my extensive collection of photo albums, which I keep on hand for clients. Flipping through, I find the collection I'm looking for, placing the open album on the table between us. Her eyes light up as she nods in agreement. "Something like this?"

"That's perfect. Exactly what I had in mind," she gushes.

We spend the next forty-five minutes finalizing the number of tables, bouquets, boutonnieres, and pedestal displays at the entrance of the church and reception. The wedding is three months away, so I make sure to put all of my notes into the system. I activate my calendar alerts to order the flowers and for the event itself. I set the order up in the system, which takes a significant amount of time because I have to calculate the number of flowers I'll require. When I place the order, I add an extra five percent to the quantity to allow for damaged blooms.

The bell over the door tinkles, letting me know someone's entered my store. I love my little shop, which belonged to my gramma, who is also a florist. I spent many afternoons and school vacation days here helping her with designs and arrangements. She still comes in every Friday morning to help me out with my weekend event orders. Stepping out of my office, I'm almost bowled over by my rambunctious daughter, followed closely by my mom. She hugs me tight around my waist, and I lean down to kiss the top of her head.

"Hi, Mom. It's so great to see you guys. You just missed Gramma Iris." I sign as I speak, so Poppy knows what I'm saying. I generally sign for Poppy, so she's not left out of conversation wherever it's appropriate. Some conversations aren't for little people, so I don't sign those if she's in the room. She gets mad at me sometimes, but I've explained to her that some conversations aren't meant for children.

"Poppy wanted to show you her guitar and tell you all about her lesson this afternoon."

I look down at Poppy and sign, "Was it as good as you hoped it would be?"

"It was better, Mommy." She shows me her guitar. "The best. Look at my guitar."

"It's not yours. Just on loan."

"No, he said I could keep it. It used to be his when he first learned to play. He was even younger than me." She's moving her hands so fast that I'm having trouble keeping up with her. "He even put different-colored strings on it for me to help me learn the different chords. Isn't it cool?"

"So cool." I smile at her. "You are one lucky girl."

"Let me show you what I learned today."

She sits on the chair opposite my desk, straps on the guitar, positions it tightly against her stomach, and places her fingers on the strings. She's focusing hard on getting them in just the right place. Then she strums the first chord. My heart's in my throat as moisture fills my eyes. I'm so happy she's doing something she's been wanting to do for ages. I'm so proud of her for making her dream a reality. I never want her to miss out on any of the things she wants to do.

"That sounds awesome, Poppy. I'm so proud of you." I glance over at Mom. She has the same look of pride as I do. "Did you have fun?"

"Oh, yeah. So much fun, Mommy. He's really funny, and he said that I might be able to go on tour with him when I'm older."

Geez, he needs to slow down a bit. Talk about getting her hopes up. "Uh, we'll see, Baby Girl. You need to get through school before you start thinking about touring the world with a band." Plus, I don't want to think about her growing up and moving away from home—not just yet, anyway.

SIX

-cassia-

MY PHONE LIGHTS UP WITH AN INCOMING CALL FROM MY SISTER. I quickly answer it because she rarely phones me, especially on a Sunday.

"Hey, Vi."

I hear sniffling on the other end before she answers. "Hey, Cass. I'm sorry to bug you on a Sunday, but I didn't know who else I could talk to."

"It's okay, Vi. You know you can call me anytime. What's happened?"

"It's Allen." She sniffles.

"Is he okay?"

"Well, if you call him getting shit-faced every weekend and hooking up with anyone with a vagina, okay. Then yeah, he's okay," she spits at me.

"Oh my gosh! I had no idea, Vi. How long's this been going on?" Far out. I had no idea they were having trouble in their marriage. I mean, Allen's always been a bit of a dick. He's often flirted with me behind Vi's back, but I shut him down, never giving it a second thought.

"Since I got pregnant with Jasmine, if I'm honest. But it's escalated over the last twelve months or so. I don't know what I should do." Her voice is shaky as she shares her secret.

"Have you spoken to him about his behavior? Told him it's unacceptable?"

"Yeah," she sighs. "When I call him out about it, we always end up

425

in a huge argument. I'm tired of going over the same shit with him. Either he wants to be in this marriage, or he doesn't. If Jasmine and I aren't what he wants anymore, then I would prefer him to leave rather than act like a nineteen-year-old frat boy."

"I hear ya, Sis. It's not good enough. Do you think he's waiting for you to end the relationship rather than manning up to do it himself?"

"Possibly. But I need *him* to leave. I don't want to have to move and uproot Jas if I can help it."

"You can always move in with us. There's plenty of room here. I don't know what I would've done without Mom's support. She's been a godsend."

"Yeah, I know. Thanks for reminding me, Cass." She pauses. "I guess now that I've admitted my marriage is in trouble, it makes it easier to ask for help. I haven't wanted to say anything to anyone before this, but last night was the last straw."

"What happened last night?"

"Nothing worse than usual, but he stumbled into the house after three this morning, his shirt all undone, stinking of another woman, and I don't just mean her perfume. It was disgusting." That would be awful. I remember Jake coming to me after we'd broken up, wanting to get back together, smelling of someone else. It was foul.

"Oh, Vi. I sort of know how you feel. Jake used to do that all the time, but we weren't married. I'm sure it's a thousand times worse for you."

"Don't devalue your experience because you and Jake weren't married. It's still just as bad. Men think they can do whatever they want and it'll be okay."

"Why don't the two of you come over for the afternoon? Leave the asshole to stew. Mom and Poppy made shortbread."

"Yeah, I think I might do that. I'll see ya soon."

"Great. I'll let Mom and Poppy know you're coming over. They'll be so happy."

"Okay." She pauses. "And, Cass. Thanks."

The call disconnects, and I'm heartbroken for my big sister. After what Dad did to Mom, and what Jake did to me, I always looked at Violet's marriage, hoping that not all men were immature assholes. But I guess they are.

I walk downstairs to let Mom know Vi and Jas are coming over to visit. Poppy's ecstatic because she adores her little cousin and dotes over her whenever they spend time together.

"You'd better put away anything unsafe for Jas. Okay?" I sign.

"Okay, Mommy." She darts upstairs to tidy her bedroom, making sure it's safe for her three-year-old cousin. Not that her cousin will play in her bedroom because it's upstairs, which isn't safe, but it's a great way to get Poppy to tidy her bedroom. Yep, I'm totally winning at this mom gig.

Mom smiles, winking at me because she's the one who taught me the strategy. I update Mom on what's been going on with Vi.

She hangs her head, then looks back up at me. She looks livid. "What is it with men? What's so hard about being a decent human being toward the people you supposedly love?" She slaps her thighs, shaking her head in disbelief. She just verbalized precisely what I was thinking.

"I don't know, Mom. What's so hard about owning up to your responsibilities and acting like an adult?"

"Exactly, Cass." She starts cleaning up the kitchen like a madwoman. Wiping over the counters as if they've wronged her.

I check the playroom to make sure Poppy's put away her Lego blocks, which would be dangerous for Jas. I'm finishing up when there's a knock at the front door and Jas runs in, looking for Mom.

"Gamma. Gamma. Gamma." Her little squeals precede her through the house.

I step out of the playroom to greet my sister with the hug she needs. Without words, I wrap my arms around her, pulling her in tight to me. Her body sinks into mine as she absorbs my support. "Things'll work out, Vi. I promise."

She nods, pulling away from me to wipe the tears from her face. Vi's coloring differs from mine. She takes after our father more than I do. I look more like Mom. Mom steps out of the kitchen carrying Jas on her hip, immediately pulling Violet into her for a fierce embrace. I wrap my arms around both of them, making a huddle of support for my heartbroken sister. She must have been through hell these past years, and not once has she let on to us that there was a problem. It must be a relief for her to have it all out in the open now and be able to lean on us for support. We separate to make our way into the kitchen, where Mom sets about making us each a cup of coffee to have with our shortbread. I flick the light switch, which flashes the lights throughout the house, to let Poppy know to come downstairs.

It doesn't take long before we hear Poppy's feet on the stairs and Vi braces herself for Poppy's onslaught. Sure enough, Poppy throws herself at her aunt's body. *That's my baby girl all over.* Luckily, she's gentler when she greets her younger cousin. She gets down on her knees to greet Jas. They hug so tightly that they fall over in fits of giggles; watching the girls instantly improves the mood in the room. We all sit to enjoy the yummy shortbread and hot coffee for the grown-ups, while the kids have a cup of milk. Poppy updates Violet on her guitar lessons, offering to play for her later; I have to translate a little because it takes Vi a little while to get back into the swing of ASL whenever she visits. After they've caught up, Poppy takes Jasmine into the playroom.

Mom reaches across the table, taking one of our hands in each of hers, squeezing in silent support. "I'm sorry, girls."

Vi and I glance at each other in confusion. "What are you sorry about, Mom?"

"I ... I think I've done a disservice to you both." I attempt to inter-rupt her, but she stops me with her hand held up in the universal sign for stop. "Your father leaving left its mark on all of us. I never bothered to put myself out there again to meet a decent man, and I think I may have done more damage than I thought. You girls have never had a positive male role model in your lives. Your father left when I was preg-nant with Cassia. Then my father died when you girls were so little, and then, well, then I put all my focus on raising you girls while working to put a roof over our heads. I never bothered to build another relationship, to model a positive relationship for you girls." Her head drops between her shoulders in defeat. She looks back up at us. "I'm so sorry."

Vi and I climb to our feet, embracing Mom on either side. "No, Mom. It's not your fault. Our relationships, or lack thereof, have nothing to do with you. You've always taught us to be strong and inde-pendent. To get on with what needs to be done and move forward. That's a great lesson. The best." I tell her.

"Yeah, Mom. The only people at fault here are the guys who seem to have difficulty acting like decent human beings."

"That's the thing. You girls never had that male role model."

"Once again, not your fault, Mom. Honestly. Don't carry that on your shoulders." I hug her extra tight to make sure she gets the message.

Violet looks at me, then at Mom. "You never told us why Dad left. I think we're old enough to know now."

Mom looks between the two of us, and I can see the war inside her

—whether to keep us in the dark or to share her experience with us. I quickly check on the girls in the playroom to find them playing together happily. As I sit down, Mom begins to share her story.

"Your father and I were happily married, and we'd always talked about having a family, but he only wanted one child." She looks at me sympathetically. "I wanted more, but I accepted that he only wanted the one. We were ... well, I *thought* we were happy. Things were going along smoothly enough, I suppose, with a baby in the house. Then I got sick with the stomach flu. Didn't really think anything of it," she shrugs, "but not long after that, I started feeling ill and my boobs were sore. When I sat down and thought about things, I realized I'd missed my period. So I took a pregnancy test without telling your father and found out I was pregnant." She gets up to make us all another cup of coffee. I sense this is difficult for her to share with us, even after all these years. "I was terrified to tell your father I was pregnant again. Obviously, the stomach flu caused the pill I was taking to be ineffective, so I felt completely responsible for the situation. I kept putting it off and putting it off until I couldn't hide the swell of my stomach any longer. He noticed my boobs had become bigger and my stomach wasn't as flat as it usually was. He confronted me about it." She sighs, carrying the coffee back to the table. "I don't know what I was think-ing; not telling him straight away. What did I possibly think could be the result? Anyway, he was furious with me. Accused me of trapping him with another child." She braces herself, looking directly at me. "A child *he* never wanted." She squeezes my hand. "I'm sorry, Cass. This is painful, and I want you to know it wasn't your fault that he left. It was his own. There was never a time I didn't want you."

I can only nod. Some part of me always felt it must have been my fault he left, and Mom just confirmed it for me.

"So, he packed his things and left. I've never heard from him since that day. Technically, we're still married because we've never divorced."

Now that *is* a shock. "You need to track him down and divorce his ass, Mom," Violet rightly suggests. "If Al walks away from me, I'm gonna divorce his ass as soon as I can."

I see red. "Why are you waiting for Allen to walk away from you? You can walk away from him, you know? Take the power away from him."

"You are more than welcome to move in here. The three of us could make a formidable team, working together to raise the girls. Supporting each other." Mom reminds Violet.

"I know I could and should walk away from him. But I want him to do it. It'll make it easier for me when it comes time to divorce his ass. I don't want him to have access to Jas. I'm hoping a judge will be less likely to award Al time with his daughter if he's the one to walk away."

"Maybe, maybe not." I wrap my arm around her shoulder. "Whatever happens, know that we're here for you. Okay?"

"Yeah, I know."

Violet decides to stay for dinner, so we head into the playroom to play with the girls. Then we take them to the park to get some fresh air for a while.

Saying goodbye to them both after dinner hurts my heart. Knowing what they're going home to makes it hard to let them go.

SEVEN

-toby-

"Hey, bro. You ready to head over for your lesson with Poppy?"

Shane's voice startles me. I was caught up in this new song I'm writing and I didn't hear him come up to my studio. If it weren't for him, I'd miss heaps of appointments when I'm in the zone.

"Uh, yeah. Sure thing." Before I lose the notes I was working on, I place my Fender on its stand and write them down. I grab what I need for today's lesson, then follow Shane downstairs to the garage. I'm really excited to show Poppy the new app I downloaded onto my laptop. It uses the computer microphone to convert the sounds from the guitar into interesting visual interpretations. I found out about it from the guitar teacher in the UK that Mom was telling me about. He uses it with his Deaf and Hard of Hearing students. I think she'll like it and I'm pretty sure it'll make our lessons fun.

"Have you decided whether you're going to the reunion tomorrow night?"

"Yeah, when I FaceTimed Kate on our birthday, she convinced me to go. She gave a compelling argument about taking the opportunity to apologize to Cassia for always blowing her off in high school. She thinks it'll be good for me."

"I think she's right. It's something that's weighed on your mind. It would be good for you to close that door."

"Yeah, I guess." I brush my hands through my hair, looking out of the car window as we drive. "I just don't want to spend time with

431

anyone else. None of those assholes gave me the time of day back then."

"You don't have to talk to anyone else. I'll make sure to keep everyone else away from you. After all, that's my job. Right?"

"Right."

Arriving at *Music for my Heart*, we exit the car and make our way inside. Xanthe is the first person we see. Her whole body expresses her happiness when she sees us. Her joy is unmistakable.

"Hey, guys. So, you're definitely making this a weekly thing with Poppy?" she speaks as she signs.

"Hi, Xanthe. Yeah, I committed to her and I intend to keep it. I found this awesome software which I think will make our lessons so much better for her. I even purchased an extra copy for her parents to load onto their computer at home." Shit, I hope they have a computer at home. Most people have computers, right? I guess I'll find out today. If she doesn't have one, I'll get her one.

"I've heard about that program. We're still setting everything up, but we should definitely get it for the center. You're taking this seriously."

"Absolutely. You know I don't do anything by half," I sign as I speak.

Xanthe laughs, nodding in agreement. "Oh, I know. You're a workhorse."

She walks me to the room where Poppy and I had our first two lessons. She's picking it up surprisingly fast for someone so young— much the way I did. As I set up my computer, Poppy runs into the room with the guitar I gave her, throwing herself at me in greeting. The guitar she's holding whacks me on the back of my legs. She's an incredibly vivacious little girl. I can't help but fall for her, which sounds weird. We step apart, and her little hands move wildly, telling me all about her at-home practice this past week. I'm equally excited to share my discovery with her, so I show her the program on my laptop.

I play our song to show her how it *should* look on the computer using the program I downloaded. While her eyes are on the laptop screen, her hands are on the body of my guitar. She looks mesmerized by the patterns being created on the screen in time with my playing.

Poppy signs to me. "Wow. That's amazing."

"I know. I think it's going to help you learn how to play the guitar."

"Me, too."

"Do you want to show me how you're doing? Then we'll look at how it comes out on the screen."

"Okay."

She puts on her guitar with the different-colored strings, pressing the body close against her stomach to maximize the vibrations, and begins to play as she watches the laptop screen. The smile forming on her cute little face is magical to watch. As she plays, she makes minor errors here and there, and I make a note of them on the music tabs so I can show her when she finishes. I can't correct her as she goes because she's focused on her fingers and the screen; I also don't want to distract her. I've caught on quickly that I need to give all of my instructions before she begins playing. I also ensure I have direct eye contact with her during any breaks. That's why I wait until she looks up after the last note to sign, "That sounds great, Poppy. I can tell you've been practicing."

"Oh, yeah. I practice all the time."

"I can tell. Do you like the program?" I point to the laptop.

"Yeah, it's really good. I can *see* my playing." She smiles proudly. "I'm making those sounds." She points to herself, then to the screen.

"Yes, you are. I bought a second copy of the app." I give Poppy the thumb drive. "You can load it onto your computer at home."

She nods as she takes the thumb drive from me. "Thank you."

"No problem. Do you have a computer at home you can use?"

"Yeah, we do. Gramma needs it for drawing the gardens she builds, but she lets me use it sometimes."

She never seems to mention her dad. It's always Mommy or Gramma. "What about your mom or dad? Do either of them have a computer they're not using, so you don't take time away from your gramma's work?"

"Oh, I don't have a daddy. Me and Mommy live with Gramma. I guess I can use Mommy's when she's home. She doesn't use it much because she works so much that when she's home, she likes to spend time with me." I had a feeling that was the situation, but it's none of my business. Heaps of parents don't live together anymore.

"I'm sure you have a daddy. You wouldn't be here without one." I nudge her shoulder.

"Oh, yeah, I guess so. I've just never met him." She shrugs as if it's not a big deal. I'm at a loss as to what kind of asshole abandons his daughter—especially a daughter as cool as Poppy.

"Let me know if it's not working out. I can get you a laptop."

Poppy jumps up, giving me an awkward hug, trapping her guitar between us. "Thank you. Thank you. Thank you. You're always so kind to me."

"I'm happy to help. I'm playing teaching you how to ..." I shake my head and wave my hand as though I'm erasing my words. "I mean, I'm *enjoying* teaching you how to play the guitar. It brings back memories from when my mom taught me how to play." I explain that Mom's a music teacher. It's because of her that I started playing guitar.

We get back to our practice for the rest of the hour. I'm in awe of her determination to master the chords, to master this instrument. She has a quiet determination about her, and I know she's going to succeed in her quest to master the guitar. Her mom must be so proud of her desire to succeed. I know I am, and I've only known her for a few weeks.

I get the feeling that Poppy makes everyone she meets fall in love with her.

EIGHT

-cassia-

Our prom theme was Vegas Nights, so the organizing committee used the same theme for our ten-year reunion. I don't know how to feel about tonight. I'm excited to see old classmates, but I'm dreading running into Jake. I have nothing to say to him. I don't want to have a confrontation in front of other people. My stomach turns at the thought of facing him tonight after what happened the last time I saw him.

Searching through my closet for something to wear that suits the theme and makes me look somewhat sexy and sophisticated. I push hanger after hanger aside until I come across my dressy black jumpsuit that I'd forgotten I had. If I pair it with my patent leather stiletto sandals, I think I can look somewhat sexy. It comes down low in the front as well as the back, which means I'm gonna need my boob tape and adhesive bra to keep the girls relatively contained. As I'm searching through my dresser for the tape, my thoughts switch to Toby. I wonder if he'll show up tonight? Ever since I received the invitation to this reunion, he's the one person who has been foremost in my thoughts; he's the one person I truly want to see. He didn't bother attending prom. I don't want to get my hopes up, especially now that he's famous.

I would love to see him again so I can congratulate him on his success. *Oh, who am I kidding?* I want to see his hotness up close and personal. I've followed his career via social media, and I'm really proud of his success—and from what I've seen, he's one hot dude. Women throw their panties at him when he's on stage; he's *that* hot.

Poppy's at a friend's house until tomorrow, allowing me to take my time to pamper myself so I treat myself to a bath with my favorite cinnamon bun bubble bath. Soaking quietly in the tub, my thoughts wander back to Toby in high school. He was always so withdrawn. He never socialized with too many people. He barely tolerated me chatting with him, finding any excuse to escape my presence. I know the jocks used to give him a hard time, but he wasn't the only person in high school to be subjected to their immature, self-inflated egos.

I'm lost in my thoughts, not noticing how cool the water's become until I shiver. I release the plug and step into the shower to finish my routine. I wash my hair, shave everywhere that needs shaving, then use my cinnamon scrub to make sure my skin glows. It's time to work out what to do with my hair that can't seem to decide if it's wavy or straight. Before I had Poppy, I had nice, even waves in my hair. After pregnancy, my hair doesn't know what it wants to do. It drives me crazy, and most days, I end up tying it up in a messy ponytail to keep it out of the way. I straighten it, then put in some loose waves. My hair is longer now than it was in high school, reaching halfway down my back.

I wonder how different everyone looks?

I don't get the opportunity to dress up or go out very often, so I'm taking my time to put some effort in for tonight. Plus, I'm hoping to catch a certain someone's eye, *if* he shows up. Putting on my makeup, I go for dramatic eyes with subtle lips and then choose my jewelry. Mmm, what to choose? Looking at my selections, I gravitate toward the butterfly pendant Poppy gave me last Mother's Day. I remember how excited she was to give it to me. When I asked her why she chose it, she said it was because butterflies are deaf, just like her. She thought it was awesome, while my heart cracked a little for my baby girl. Wearing the pendant she gifted me will help me feel confident and strong because she's the strongest person I know—the way she goes after what she wants with such determination is inspiring. Taking one last look in the mirror, I'm reasonably happy with what I see. I look pretty good for a mom—not that everyone there will know I'm a mom.

As I make my way downstairs, I realize it's nice to be dressed up as a woman, not just a 'mom'—I feel sexy instead of practical for a change. Mom steps in, taking my hands to hold them out from my sides. "You look gorgeous, Cassia."

"Thanks, Mom. I'm a little nervous, to be honest. I'm hoping Jake won't make a scene."

"Surely he won't do that sort of thing in front of everyone." Mom grumbles. "If he starts anything, just hold your head up high and walk away from him. He doesn't deserve a second of your time or your breath."

"Thanks, Mom. I'll do my best to avoid him. I'd better get going—my Uber's waiting. Don't wait up. I'll see you in the morning."

"Have fun, Love."

"I will. Night."

———

Stepping into the function room, I'm surprised at the amount of effort that went into the decorations. It looks amazing; the organizing committee did a fantastic job. I take a minute to get my bearings before stepping all the way inside the room. Peering around the ample space, it takes me a little while to recognize the faces from my senior year. Locating my high school girlfriends grouped over near the drinks—*of course, where else would they be?*—I make my way toward them, but I don't get far before a beefy body steps in my way. I haven't even been here for five freaking minutes, and he's already all up in my grill.

"Hello, Sia. You're looking mighty fine tonight."

I look at him closely. He looks okay. Still bulky, but not so much in a muscular way like he was in high school through to college. "Hi, Jake. I don't want any trouble tonight. I just want to spend time with old friends and have a good time." My heart's racing in my chest as though I've run all the way here. Why did he have to be the first person to speak to me? I haven't even had the chance to have a drink to settle my nerves.

"I'm not looking for any trouble, Babe. You're lookin' hot, but I wanna have a good time with old friends, too. Maybe we can catch up for old times' sake?" He finishes with a sleazy wink as he trails his finger up and down my arm. I shift slightly, so he's no longer touching me. *Uh, whatever.* I feel like I need to go home to bathe again now.

"Not interested, Jake. Not even in the slightest. Now, if you'll excuse me, I see some old friends I want to say hi to."

He blocks my escape. "Who's looking after the kid tonight?"

Who does he think he is? Like he cares. "That's none of your concern, Jake. Remember, you didn't want to complicate your life with a kid. Certainly not a deaf one," I spit out the last sentence.

Stepping around him, I plaster a smile on my face, then make my way toward my group of friends from high school. We lost touch when I found out I was pregnant. Our lives were moving in totally different directions; while they were out partying, I was throwing up and growing round with a baby. I don't begrudge them for losing contact. I was concentrating on growing up, getting ready to be responsible for another human being, while they were focusing on how many shots they could down and remain standing. The girls spot me, squealing in delight. I walk faster to make it to them, and we share an excited group hug. It's great to be surrounded by my old friends. It almost feels as though no time has passed. As our excitement calms, I take in each of my friends, noting changes in their appearance. Of course, we all look older, that's to be expected, but the girls all look fantastic. My eyes stop on Sam's belly; it seems to me as though she has a slight baby bump. My head snaps up, and she signals for me to keep my discovery to myself. I nod discreetly to confirm that I'll keep my lips sealed.

"How are my girls?" I look around the group. "You all look so incredibly gorgeous."

"Not as gorgeous as you do, girl. You're one hot momma." Jessica touches her finger to her hip like its sizzling. All I can do is shake my head, smiling at her antics. She hasn't changed one bit.

We spend the next hour drinking while catching up on the last ten years. Everyone seems oblivious to the fact that Sam's not drinking any alcoholic drinks. I'm surprised to find that none of the girls have settled down. They're all still single, footloose, and fancy-free—even Sam. I internally consider this prospect. Would I want to be like them? No, I don't think I would. I love my daughter, the life I've built, and my little shop. I don't think I would change a thing at this point in time. Suddenly, the entire room quiets. I look around, attempting to work out why. When I look toward the entrance, I find my answer.

Toby Summer has arrived.

This'll be interesting to watch. No one gave him the time of day in high school, but now that he's famous, I'll bet everyone wants a piece of him. He's with his twin sister, Kate, and his best friend, Shane. There's also another man I recognize as a regular client of mine—the one and only Mr. Stone. I recently worked on his wedding, not that I interacted in person with him or his wife, who I figure must be Kate by the way he's holding her close to his side. The foursome make quite an impact standing at the entrance. Kate's the first to break away, making her way toward her group of friends from school; her husband hot on her heels.

As I look back toward the entrance, my eyes connect with Toby's. With our gazes locked, it's like no time has passed at all. Those same tingles I used to experience every time he was near take hold.

He's totally smoking hot. Hotter than any image I've seen of him online. In person, there's a presence about him that wasn't there ten years ago.

He says something to Shane, then makes a beeline straight for me. Stalking forward like a panther. *Oh, wow!*

He's different; there's a confidence about him he never used to have. The lanky kid who would sit out of the way to avoid people now draws the eye of everyone in the room as his sure strides bring him to me. People attempt to get his attention, but he ignores them without breaking stride, as though I'm the only person he sees. He stops directly in front of me, making me tilt my head back to take him in. Those tingles I mentioned before, they've become a full-on assault on my senses now he's this close to me. He smells so freaking good, matching how good he looks in his casual suit. His hair's longer now, tied up in a bun, and that beard. *So freaking sexy.* What I wouldn't give to feel the rasp of it between my thighs.

"Hey, Cassia." His voice is so much deeper, richer than it was when we were seventeen.

"Uh, hey, Toby." My shaky voice exposes my nervousness. "I'm surprised you came tonight." Maybe I shouldn't have said that. It sounded pretty rude, so I quickly add, "I'm glad you could make it."

"It was touch and go there for a while, but Kate and Shane convinced me to come along."

"Well, I'm happy to see you. You look … uh … good." *Geez, girl, get it together.* You're being ridiculous. You used to talk with him all the time, whether he wanted to or not.

"I'm happy to see you, too, Cassia. You look as stunning as ever." The girls behind me let out a collective sigh. I can *feel* their eyes ping-ponging between the two of us. "I was hoping we could chat for a couple of minutes." *Oh, wow.* This is new. He never once sought me out in high school. "Would you mind joining me at the bar for a drink?"

I'm a little shocked, but manage to respond with a nod of my head. I turn to the girls, waving awkwardly, letting them know where I'm going. Not that I needed to tell them. They had a front-row seat to our conversation. They're all either fanning their faces, widening their eyes comically, or signaling for me to hurry and follow after Toby. Stepping away from the group, I hurry to catch up with him as he heads directly to the bar. He situates himself at the far end, away from everyone else —I see some things haven't changed. I sit beside him after he pulls out the stool for me, which is welcome since I've been standing in these heels for over an hour now. They may look sexy, but they are so freaking uncomfortable.

He studies me intently for a few seconds, as though he's cataloging the changes he sees in me. "What would you like to drink?"

"I'll have a lemon drop martini, thanks." I love my Vodka-based drinks.

He orders himself a beer along with my drink. We don't speak while we wait for our drinks to be served, but it doesn't feel awkward. It gives me the time I need to recalibrate. Once the bartender places the glasses in front of us, Toby slides my drink closer to me, then picks up his beer, indicating he wants to make a toast.

"To second chances." His toast is a bit cryptic. He taps his beer against my glass before taking a swallow of his drink. I watch, mesmerized by the dance of his Adam's apple, before realizing I should take a drink of my own. Sipping my drink, I sigh in appreciation of the sweet but tart taste of the cool liquid. When I open my eyes and look across at Toby, I find him staring at me.

Wiping gingerly at my mouth, I ask, "Do I have something on my face?"

NINE

-toby-

GOD, SHE'S STILL SO FUCKING BEAUTIFUL—NO, THAT'S NOT TRUE, SHE'S even more beautiful now—I can't take my eyes off her. When I stepped through the doorway to the function room, my eyes automatically started seeking her out. When I finally decided to come to this reunion, I decided my first action would be to apologize to Cassia for the way I treated her in high school. How I always made excuses to escape being in her presence. Now that I'm here, standing next to her, I'm too over-whelmed to say what I need to say. My wayward dick, as usual, is misbehaving in her presence.

I snap out of it to respond to her. "Uh, no. Nothing on your face, Cass."

"Oh, okay then. That's good." She takes another delicate sip of her cocktail. I watch her throat work to swallow the concoction and all I can imagine is her throat working over my cock. *Shit, that's not helping my situation.* "I believe congratulations are in order." I'm not sure why she's congratulating me. My confusion must show because she clarifies, "For all of your success. I knew you were a talented singer and guitarist in high school, but I never imagined the success you would go on to have. It must feel amazing to have followed your passion and have it all work out so well for you."

Ah, okay, that's what she's talking about. I shrug my shoulder, tucking a wayward lock of hair behind my ear. "I guess so. I just did what I love; what I'm good at. The rest sort of followed on from that." I sip my beer because what I'm about to say next is going to sound ungrateful, even though I *am* incredibly grateful for all of my successes and achievements. "I don't enjoy being in the limelight, though. I would rather be left alone." I glance over my shoulder, noticing several people who wouldn't give me the time of day in high school waiting for a chance to talk to me. Shane's doing his job and keeping them away from me—as he promised he would.

"Yeah, you always preferred your own company back then. I figured with your fame, you'd be used to all the people by now."

"Nah. I don't think I'll ever get used to that side of things." We're quiet for a few minutes; she drinking her martini, me drinking my beer. I'm generally not great with conversation or making small talk, so I don't know how to broach the subject of high school, but I'm determined to apologize to her. I guess now's as good a time as any. "Uh, Cass, I've thought about you a lot over the years." Her eyes widen in surprise as she chokes on her drink. *Oh, shit,* that didn't sound good. I pat her on the back to help her out. "Uh, I mean. Fuck, I don't know what I mean. What I wanted to say was I've often thought about how I treated you in high school." I take in her puzzled face. Clearly, she's forgotten all the times I would make a hasty exit. "You know, always making excuses to leave. Not participating in the conversations you made an effort to strike up with me." She nods as if she now remembers. "I owe you an apology for all of that."

"Don't worry about it, Toby." She waves off my apology. "Sometimes I was too much for people. I've toned down a lot over the years. I'm possibly more tolerable now." She laughs. I can't believe she thinks she was too much for anyone.

"It wasn't that. It was ..." Fuck, this is going to be embarrassing. "Me. All me. I was the one with the problem because I had a crush on you." There, I said it. I don't think her eyes could get any bigger as her lips part in surprise. With my stomach rolling from nerves, I huff out a laugh. "Every time you came near me, my teenage dick would stand to attention. I had to get away from you because I was terrified I'd embarrass myself." Well, there—I've laid it out as plain as day. She can laugh at me and tell me what an idiot I was.

She lays her hand on my arm. The heat from her touch burns through my skin. "Oh, Toby." She's smiling. I guess that's a positive sign. Maybe she doesn't feel creeped out by my confession. I never meant to tell her *why* I acted the way I did. I only wanted to apologize for my behavior. "You weren't alone. I studied up on Dylan like I was going to be graded on it so that I could hold a two-minute conversation with you." My head snaps up to study her face, seeking any dishonesty —all I see is sincerity. "I had the biggest crush on you, too." She gestures to her friends. "They all used to tease me relentlessly about it. They gave me a hard time for dating Jake when I should have been with you. If you had asked me to go to prom with you in the cafeteria that day, I would have said 'yes' in a heartbeat."

I can't believe what I'm hearing.

She felt the same way I did.

Everything I thought I knew about high school has been tilted off its axis. What I thought was a fantasy could have been a reality. One I could have acted on had I been courageous. But who's courageous at seventeen or eighteen, really? I mean, I was fearless with my music, not so much with people.

How would things have been different if I'd manned up and asked her to the prom, as Shane suggested? I'm trying to collect my equilibrium when she returns her hand to my arm.

"Toby, are you okay?"

I turn to face her directly. "I wish I'd been brave. I can't believe I missed my chance with you." My disappointment floods through me like a giant wave.

She smiles slowly, biting her full bottom lip as she does. The same one I used to imagine kissing. "Who says you missed your chance?" She clinks her glass against my beer. "To second chances, you said."

My lips spread wide as I return the gesture. "To second chances." We each drink, smiling at each other as if we've shared a secret.

Kate and Oliver break our moment. Kate and Cassia do the usual girly hug in greeting. They weren't close in school, but they were friendly. Kate's come into her own since dating Oliver. He's been great for her confidence.

She turns to me excitedly. "Guess what just happened. No, you'll never guess. I'll just tell you." She looks up at her husband, and he winks at her. "Michael Fitzpatrick just apologized to me for setting me up to go to prom alone. Can you believe it?"

Oliver looks like he wants to smash something when Kate mentions Michael's name. I guess she filled him in on what went down.

Cassia smiles. "It seems it's the night for apologies." She winks at me, but Kate and Oliver are completely caught up in each other, so they miss it.

Kate turns her attention to Cassia. "What have you been up to the last ten years, Cass?"

Shit, I'm such a douche. I didn't even ask her what she's been doing. What is her life like? Is she with anyone? Maybe not, because she sort of insinuated that we might have a second chance. Well, I hope that's what she was saying. She tucks a silky chestnut lock of hair behind her ear. "Well, I went to college, like most other people. Then I took over my gramma's florist shop."

"Oh, wow. That's so cool. Would I know of it? What's it called?"

"I'm pretty sure you do." She smiles, looking between Kate and Oliver. "I did the floral arrangements for your gala *and* your wedding."

"No way!" Kate and Oliver appear stunned. "You own *Blooms and Balloons*? That's your shop?" Cass nods. "Your flower arrangements are freaking awesome." Kate's almost squealing.

Oliver holds out his hand for Cass. "I thought you looked familiar." Kate looks between Cass and Oliver, trying to work out what's going on. "When I ordered the flowers I had delivered for you, I stopped in at *Blooms and Balloons*," he tells his wife. "That's how I became familiar with her work. When I was organizing the gala, she seemed like the perfect person to put our table centerpieces together." He looks back at Cass. "You did outstanding work. I had no qualms in recommending you to our wedding coordinator when it came time to organize the flowers."

"I loved, loved, loved what you did for our wedding. Oh, and the balloon drop for the gala. That was ah-mazing."

"Why, thank you." She does a little curtsy. "I was proud of that balloon drop. I was trying to think of something that would be memorable when you guys reached your goal."

Jake comes in behind her, wrapping his beefy arm around her waist and snuggling into her neck. My entire body goes into alert mode, my pulse increasing as my muscles tense. I had the impression that Cassia was unattached when she suggested we might get a second chance, but here's Mr. Beefcake wrapping himself around her like the snake he is. *What the fuck?*

I relax slightly when Cass tries to extricate herself from his hold, but he won't release his grip; if anything, he holds on tighter, sending a smarmy look my way. She continues to push against him, whispering something in his ear. I move forward, ready to step in if necessary; Oliver must read the cues too, because he seems to stand taller, looking more formidable than usual. Finally, Jake releases Cassia. The relief emanating from her body is palpable. It's obvious she doesn't like the man anymore, which is somewhat of a relief. He tries to move back into her space, but she pushes him away.

"Leave me alone, Jake. I told you, I'm not interested."

Oliver steps forward. "The lady asked you to leave her alone. I suggest you do so." His tone would typically be enough to get anyone to do his bidding, but Jake's not just anyone.

"Who the fuck are you?" he slurs. It's obvious he's had too much to drink. "Think you can tell me what the fuck to do." Kate puts her hand on Oliver's arm to calm him.

Shane quietly joins the group, sensing there's going to be trouble. He's no longer the skinny kid from high school; he's a trained killer now. Jake senses he's outnumbered *and* out-muscled. Looking around at our group, he raises his hands in surrender, sways, and steps away from Cass.

To us, he says, "Later." To Cass, he points and says, "I ain't done with you." Stepping backward from us, he turns, leaving the function room. We all turn to Cass to ask if she's okay, but she's folded in on herself, her arms wrapped around her waist.

She looks scared.

I step closer, checking with her if it's okay to hold her. She nods a little, so I wrap her in my arms, pulling her close. She fits against me like a missing puzzle piece and smells fucking sensational; spicy and sweet. I whisper in her ear, "You okay?"

She nods slowly in response.

"You want another lemon drop martini?"

"Yes, please."

Oliver steps up to the bar to order drinks for everyone in our group. The mood has dropped from the happy, upbeat vibe of before as we sip our drinks. We make light conversation about what we've each been up to over the past ten years. I do my best to ignore old classmates who think it's okay to interrupt us to get a piece of me. They didn't want a bar of me back in high school—they can fuck right off now. I only came hoping to catch up with the woman still in my arms.

Cass's friends join our group, expanding the circle and lightening the mood considerably. After several hours of reminiscing about various high school events, stupid shit different kids got up to, and bitching about some of the teachers; people start calling it a night and the crowd dwindles. Her high school girlfriends all want to head out to a club, but Cass declines. I need to think of something so that I can spend more time with her—I'm not ready to let her go yet. I want to know what that was about with Jake.

"You wanna get a drink somewhere?"

She smiles broadly, seemingly happy that I want to spend more time with her. "Yeah, that'd be great."

TEN

-toby-

I'M CURRENTLY THANKFUL SHANE DROVE SEPARATELY TO THE REUNION tonight because it means I'll have Cassia all to myself in my car. Walking to the parking lot, I guide Cass with my hand firmly pressed against the curve of her exposed lower back, right above her sexy ass. The feel of her warm, silky skin against my palm is testing my resolve to be a gentleman. It's taking all of my strength to stop my hand from sliding down to cup her firm behind.

"Is this your car?"

"Yeah, this is it." I'm proud of this baby. When I found it for sale, I knew I had to have her. I'm a fan of Sam and Dean, and well … I just had to have her. She's not exactly the same as their beast, since mine's a convertible.

She glides her hand along the front panel. I can't believe I'm jealous of my car. "Is this like the car from *Supernatural?*"

I think I'm in love.

"Same make and year. However, theirs is a hardtop."

I open the door for her, and she gracefully lowers herself into the passenger seat. She looks mighty fine sitting in my car. Stepping around the front of the car, I join her inside. After starting the car, I turn to Cass. "Where would you like to go?"

"Uh, do you have issues with being out in public? Like, do people bother you a lot?"

"Yeah, it bothers me. It's something I've had to get used to."

"How about we just go back to your place then?"

My eyebrows almost hit my hairline with surprise at her suggestion. If I have her alone at my place, there's no telling what we might get up to. I'm not sure I have the self-control to keep my hands off her, especially if this is my only chance to have her. "Yeah, I'm not sure that's such a good idea."

"Why not? Then we don't have to worry about you being spotted by your fans, and we can talk in a quiet space." She tucks her hair behind her ear. "Or maybe you don't want me in your private space?"

"I would love to have you in my private space, Cass. Maybe a little too much." I clear my throat. "I'm not sure I could keep my intentions pure or my hands to myself."

She smiles across at me. "That's okay with me."

Okay then. I put my foot down, making my way home in record time. She seems restless in her seat, adjusting her position every few minutes. Not another word is spoken, but I sense the tension building between us. That spark that was there in high school ... yeah, it's intensified into a low-burning ember.

Pulling into the garage, Cass speaks for the first time. "I like your place. It's very rock star." She clasps her hands tightly together; her lips press closed suddenly.

I laugh. "You think? I bought it for the view from every room across to the bridge, which looks spectacular at sunset."

We step out of the elevator that brought us up from the garage, entering the foyer on the lower level of my three-story home. It's all timber, steel, and glass.

Cass has her mouth on mine before we make it five steps inside, surprising the hell outta me. I've been waiting for this kiss for longer than a decade. I want to take my time; savor it, slow it down, and enjoy it. Pressing my lips against hers, I cradle the back of her head while tugging her hips forward, ensuring there's zero space between us—the press of her full tits against my hard planes—the silkiness of her hair in my hand, and the softness of her plump lips against mine are more than I ever imagined. Her arms wrap around me, her hands coming up to press my shoulder blades, pushing me into her ever closer. Our mouths open, and our tongues meet for the first time. I know, in this moment, there will never be another woman for me.

She's it.

Cass moans into the kiss, stealing my breath, while all the blood in my body redirects to my cock. It's throbbing in the confines of my pants, trying to find its target. I walk her backward, trapping her against the glass of my living room window. The only light is provided by the moon. I press my hard cock into her soft body so she can feel what she's done to me.

"Are you as wet as I'm hard, Cass?"

"Why don't you find out for yourself?" she responds without missing a beat.

Oh, yeah, don't mind if I do, but I have no fucking idea how to get her out of these clothes. I step away, manhandling her until her back faces me to check for a zipper or something. The thin straps tie in the middle of her spine. I kiss my way along the graceful curve until I reach the ties, biting and tugging them undone with my teeth. Releasing the ties, I loosen the front, hoping it's enough to expose her breasts. Preparing myself to see what I've only imagined since I was sixteen, I turn her back toward me. Slowly, my eyes wander down from her captivating face, her slender neck, to her delicate collarbones, and finally to those mounds I've imagined holding. Her top is somehow still stuck to her chest. I don't understand why it hasn't fallen to her waist as I expected. I gently pry the material away from her supple skin, but it doesn't release as I would expect. She looks down, peeling the fabric away from her skin gently.

"I had to use boob tape. I didn't want to expose myself inadvertently at the reunion. Give me a sec." She gives a breathless laugh as she peels the fabric away, giving me a perfect view …

Wait!

How come I can't see any nipples? I look up at her face, and I'm sure my confusion is apparent. Her boobs are pert, but there are no nipples as far as I can see in the little light available.

She blushes. "Sorry. I couldn't wear a regular bra with the design of the top. Give me a minute, and I'll have these off." She turns her back to me—I'm not having it. I want to watch her reveal herself to me.

"Uh, uh, uh. Let me watch."

She's looking down, not making eye contact with me. "I'm a little embarrassed. I hadn't planned to get naked in front of anyone tonight, and … well … this isn't very sexy."

"Maybe it's not the sexiest, but it's you. You went to a lot of trouble to get dressed—to look good. No, more than good—you look fucking sexy tonight, and I want to see how you made that happen. Let me see you."

She bites her bottom lip, so I press in to take over, biting the plumpness gently before sucking out the sting. Pressing my lips harder against hers, I swipe with my tongue, requesting permission to enter. She opens and our tongues reacquaint, sliding against each other, learning each other's taste. I pull back to allow her to remove whatever it is she's wearing in place of a regular bra. As she works on one side, I gently peel the second side. She's careful not to pull too hard or fast, holding her skin taut to reduce the sting as the adhesive pulls away, so I mimic her technique.

Finally, *fucking finally*, her tits are fully exposed for my perusal. I soak them in, admiring their fullness, and the slight teardrop droop to them. Taking one in hand, I test the weight before closing my hand over the globe and squeezing gently, realizing the bra has left behind a significant amount of sticky residue.

"How do you get this stuff off your boobs?" I marvel at what women go through to look good in their clothes. Men just have to put on pants and a shirt, and we're done. I wouldn't have the patience to be a woman.

"Oh, uh. I don't use these very often because I rarely go out. When I do, I usually rub it with some olive oil. It seems to do the trick. Maybe we shouldn't bother. I can just head home." She tries to cover her embarrassment with a deprecating laugh. "Can we forget this happened?"

"That'd be a no." I walk into the kitchen, dragging her behind me. "I have olive oil in the kitchen. Let's get this shit off your magnificent breasts so I can get down to business."

She giggles at my determination to get her into the kitchen. I know I'm acting like a madman, but I'm not willing to wait any longer to get my hands and mouth on her. It's been more than ten years, and from what I can see, it's definitely been worth the wait. Wrapping my hands around her trim waist, I lift her easily to sit her ass on my counter, so I can source the materials I need to get this show on the road. I find what I need, then carry everything over to Cass. I tip some olive oil onto my palm before rubbing my hands together to get it warm. Gently, reverently, I massage her soft breasts, paying particular attention to the areas with the most adhesive. I rub, caressing her until her nipples form peaks and goosebumps cover her skin. Teasing her nipples with gentle touches, squeezing the globes with firm pressure, makes her breaths come faster, the pulse at the base of her neck fluttering rapidly. Her hands come up to the back of my head, sliding into my hair as she pulls at the elastic I used to keep it in place. Trying to maintain my focus while her fingers comb through my hair, I work her breasts over until I feel the sticky residue dissolve. I desperately need to get my mouth on her. Reluctantly pulling away, I find a soft, clean cloth in the drawer. As I wipe the excess oil off her body, I manage to tear my eyes away from her breasts to peer at her face. Her eyes are molten, searing into me.

"Toby, please kiss me."

I don't have to be asked twice. I throw the cloth into the sink, moving forward at the same time as Cass to meet in the middle.

This kiss is slower—seeking, tempting, teasing.

Using only our lips, we slide back and forth gently, building up to something more, something intense and life-changing. I can't resist slipping my tongue out to glide along her plump bottom lip. Cass sighs softly, her warm breath moving across my mouth, and I use the opportunity to slide inside, deepening our connection. Her hand tightens in my hair, as though she doesn't want this kiss to end.

Me neither, Gorgeous. Me neither.

I need to get my mouth on her tits. I used to fantasize about her breasts in high school, and now that I have the opportunity before me on a silver platter, I'm not willing to miss out on getting my fill. I trail my kisses down to Cass's jawline, then further down her neck until I reach her collarbone. Nibbling, licking, and kissing my way further down, I finally reach my target. Leaning forward, I suck a nipple into my mouth. I taste it with my tongue before pulling back slightly to nip and bite around the areola; she tastes like olive oil with a hint of cinnamon. I swap over, paying the same attention to the other globe. She moans in pleasure, grasping the back of my head to hold me in place.

"You like my mouth on you, Cass?"

"Yeah, yeah, I do. Don't stop. Please don't stop."

Not planning on it anytime soon.

I glide my hands slowly down each side of her body, grazing her rib cage with the aim of removing her pantsuit, but it's stuck on her hips. It must have a zipper somewhere. Cass reads my intention, releasing the zipper on my behalf, allowing the fabric to slip down to pool on the counter. Encouraging her to raise her hips, I slide the material down her body until it's free of her sexy shoes. Starting at her ankles, I glide my hands slowly up the inside of her silky legs, pushing them wider apart as I go. In this position, I can smell her arousal even before I nudge my nose into the apex of her thighs. Dragging upwards, seeking her clit, I rub gently with the tip of my nose, garnering a sigh from my girl as she pulses her hips forward, seeking more friction. I search out the top of her underwear so I can remove the lacy fabric from her body. She lifts her ass again, and as I slide the lace down her legs and over her strappy shoes—they're staying on—they're sexy as fuck.

Standing to my full height, I pull her ass forward so she's balancing on the edge of my kitchen counter and slam my mouth down onto hers. I need this woman to come so that I can get inside her pussy. I press in as close as possible to grind my hard length against her exposed pussy, which I noticed is groomed to perfection. Her heat sears me through my trousers and boxers. I can't wait to feel her internal muscles squeezing the cum out of my cock.

Trying to slow myself down, I tenderly press her back so she's lying on the counter. Slowly, I glide my hands down the length of her body before squatting down to position her feet over my shoulders, opening her as wide as possible to my mouth and fingers. I can't resist watching her opening tremble as I delicately run my fingertips along her outer lips from the base to the top, pinching her clit gently. Her body shoots up from the bench with a jolt as she releases a long moan. I'm finally living out my fantasy, but I'm worried any moment now, teenage me is going to wake up, and this is all going to be a dream.

I press her body back down. "Don't move. Take what I'm gonna give you."

Her clit pulses. Oh, yeah, she likes my command. I can't believe how fucking lucky I am to be touching her like this. I'm determined to make this an experience she'll remember forever. I double down on my efforts, kissing her pussy like I would kiss her mouth. Biting and nipping her lips as I insert first one finger, then another into her tight channel. My dick leaps in eagerness to be where my fingers are, feeling her muscles pulsing and tightening around it in readiness for release. I work at a slow, steady pace to tease her along. I don't want to rush this. I intend to take my time, cherishing every moment, and tucking it away in my memory banks for inspiration. Cass begins the slow climb, and I feel her walls tightening, strangling my fingers.

"You're so fucking wet. Listen to my fingers sliding in and out of your hot pussy."

The slick noises seem loud in the quiet darkness. Cass moans as her pussy walls tighten and begin to flutter. I carefully bite her clit, pressing down with my tongue while pressing more firmly against her g-spot. She shatters, her walls pulsing relentlessly against the invasion of my fingers as I slow my movements, gentling as she convulses. Her legs tighten around my head, her heels digging into my back, holding me in position. This experience with her is better than anything I've had up to this point, which shouldn't be a surprise.

After all, it *is* Cassia.

ELEVEN

-cassia-

Woah. I know it's been a long time for me, but I don't ever remember having an orgasm that powerful before. He's as masterful with his fingers as I imagined he would be. The sounds my pussy made while they were inside me were almost obscene. If I hadn't been completely caught up in the moment, I would have been embarrassed. My muscles are relaxed, but I'm still turned on.

I don't allow myself to date, and I definitely don't do one-night stands, because Poppy is my priority. I highly doubt someone as famous as Toby does repeat performances, so this will be the only night I'll have with him, and I'm certain it's going to be one I remember for the rest of my life. I'm going to take full advantage of my one night out.

"Did you like my mouth on your clit and my fingers in your tight pussy?" God, he has a dirty mouth. I never knew that could be such a turn-on.

"Yeah, but I want your dick."

"You'll get it when I'm good and ready to give it to you."

He's put me in my place, and embarrassment floods me. I close my legs to regain my modesty, but Toby blocks my attempt with his body —which, I might add, is still fully clothed, putting me at a further disadvantage. Turning my head to the side, I try to block him out, but he's not having that either.

"Uh, uh, uh. What's up, Cass?" He gently directs my eyes back to his, holding my chin between his fingers. "Talk to me, Bun." I search his face. I'm not sure what he means. Was he calling *me* Bun? Why? He must read my confusion. "You smell like a cinnamon bun. All sweet, with a hint of spice." He nuzzles his nose up the side of my neck to that sensitive spot behind my lobe, where he licks me, then places the softest kiss.

"Nothing," I whisper. I'm embarrassed that I got so carried away that I basically demanded he fuck me. Maybe he doesn't want to go that far with me. I mean, I did pounce on him the minute we entered his home. I'm not sure what came over me. He doesn't know me, and I don't really know him. I'm mortified as I mentally run through my behavior since we arrived.

"I felt you fold in on yourself. So don't tell me 'nothing' when I know there's something."

"Really, it's nothing. I should probably get dressed and get out of your hair. I've already taken up too much of your time." I'm struggling to avoid his eyes in my embarrassment.

"If you want to leave, that's your choice. I won't hold you here against your will, but I don't understand the sudden change. Did I do something wrong? Have I upset you?" His eyes implore me for an answer, but I'm not sure what I can say as his voice drops to a whisper. "Talk to me, Cass."

"Uh, I'm a bit embarrassed. I ..." I try to look away—once again, he's not having it. "I, uh, got caught up in the moment and ... uh, well ... I'm not that girl."

"What girl?" He's completely confused.

"The girl that pounces on a guy I barely know. The one that gets so caught up in what's happening that I say things I wouldn't normally say; act in a way I wouldn't normally act. To be honest, I'm mortified with myself."

"I'm confused. So, are you saying you weren't into what was going down?"

Geez, this is unbelievably awkward. "Of course I was into it. But I got all demanding, and then you basically told me to slow down. You don't want to go that far." *Ugh. I just want to be invisible.*

His head tilts to the side. I can see him thinking. "When did I say I didn't want to 'go that far'? Because let me make something absolutely clear. I've wanted to get in your pants since I was sixteen years old."

Oh, uh. Wow. I'm shocked speechless. It takes me a minute to process his words, then formulate my response. "I guess I assumed when you said you'd give me your dick when you were 'good and ready' that you didn't want to go that far tonight." I try to sit up, but he folds his body over mine, pressing his clothed chest to my bare breasts.

His breath tickles my face as he closely studies my eyes. He presses in closer, taking my mouth savagely. His kiss alone brings me back to life, sending all of my pulse points pounding out a rhythm I can't ignore. I try to rub my pussy against his hard shaft, but the way he has me pinned makes it impossible.

"What I said is 'You'll get it when I'm good and ready to give it to you'. Which means you need to trust me to take you where you need to go. Don't try to take over. I'm in charge here, and I make the decisions. Outside of the bedroom, I'm more than happy to be on equal terms, but here, I won't tolerate you attempting to take over. Understood?"

I swallow hard, and his eyes snap to my throat as he releases a groan. I can only nod in response to him laying down the law.

"I need your words, Cass." He nuzzles the side of my face before whispering, "I need to know you understand what I'm saying, Gorgeous."

I nod again. "Yeah, I understand what you're saying."

"Good girl." He tucks his arms underneath me. "Now wrap your legs around my hips. I'm taking you to bed."

My clit throbs, and my pussy pulses in response as I wrap myself around his body. He lifts me easily, carrying me upstairs to his spacious bedroom. We land on his massive bed as one unit, his body weight forcing all the air from my lungs. Toby studies me closely, then pushes himself up to stand at the edge of the bed.

"Move up the bed, rest your head on the pillow. Spread your legs. I want to see your wet pussy." I quickly situate myself as directed, pushing down my internal discomfort at being on display to follow his instructions. His eyes travel languidly down my body like a caress as he removes his jacket. Leisurely, piece by piece, he methodically removes every stitch of clothing, revealing a muscular swimmer's body. His muscles flex and contract as he moves about, making my mouth water for a taste.

"Run your fingers along your slit. Show them to me. I want to see how wet you are."

He stands completely naked, waiting for me to comply. I slide my eyes over his body, stopping at his cock, standing gloriously hard and proud. While keeping my eyes on his cock, I slowly run my hands down my body, passing over my breasts, across my soft abdomen (thank god only the moonlight lights us), to my pussy which is so ready for him, it's pulsing. I gently caress the outer lips from the bottom to the top before moving inward, collecting my natural lubricant on my fingers. His cock bobs forth as if it's trying to get to me. I hold my fingers up for him, and he lunges forward in one fell swoop, taking them in his mouth and licking them clean.

Holy shit. That's so hot!

He guides my fingers back to my pussy, sliding them the same way he used his fingers, collecting more of my juices. He makes a show of licking my fingers clean. "Mmm, my new favorite flavor." Pressing down, he takes my mouth in a hot kiss. I can taste myself on his tongue, and even though I wouldn't have thought it could be sexy, it is. Everything he does turns me on more than I thought possible. I get lost in the kiss, my heartbeat increasing against his, my mind focusing solely on the moment we're sharing. I need to remember every detail so that I can draw on this experience on lonely nights.

"Turn over. I want to see your sexy ass while I fuck you." He pulls away, leaning over to the bedside drawer, retrieving a condom. I take the opportunity to turn over, scrambling to my hands and knees. I realize I haven't touched his cock. I haven't done anything except kiss him and hold on to him. I feel slightly cheated. Looking over my shoulder, I watch him roll the latex down his long, thick shaft. He's beautifully well-proportioned, and I can't wait to have him fill me up; just the thought has me almost dripping. I drop my head between my shoulders in anticipation of the first push of his cock into me; instead, he smooths my hair back from my face, clasping it firmly in his hand. His other hand comes around from behind, cupping my chin, directing my head where he wants it to go. He kisses me again, roughly this time, dominating my mouth, holding me hostage in our lust. Using his grip on my hair, he tugs my head back further, exposing my neck to his mouth. His soft beard grazes the sensitive skin, feeling fantastic and adding to the sensations overwhelming me.

His warm breath touches my ear just before his whispered words. "Are you ready for my cock, Cass?"

He thrusts fully into my core, forcing me forward, not allowing me to respond. I'm only stabilized by his hand holding onto my hair. I gasp for air, trying to regain my balance, but it's difficult. He leans back down over my body. "Your pussy's like heaven. So fucking tight around my cock." He kisses my neck again. "You feel how good my cock fits in your tight hole?" I can only whimper in response. Keeping his dick situated deep, he rotates his hips, hitting my g-spot, sending shudders throughout my body. My toes curl in preparation for his onslaught.

"You ready, Bun?" His chest leaves my back. I immediately feel the loss of his heat. "Answer me."

I suck in a breath. "Yeah, I'm ready." I try to brace myself, but the way he's holding me makes it difficult. He secures my hair tightly, then grasps my hip with his other hand before withdrawing his cock until only the tip is inside me. Biting my bottom lip, I prepare for what I anticipate will be a rough fuck. He slams back in, fast and hard. Pause. Swivel. Slow withdrawal. Pause. Slam. He sets up a fierce rhythm, and I match him. Pushing back into his firm body as he thrusts into me. He feels divine—I can't hold back my moans or my whimpers. His pace increases as he releases my hair and grasps both hips firmly. Taking over completely, he pulls me onto his cock—over and over and over again. His fingers feel like a branding iron on me, searing my skin, and even if he doesn't leave a visible mark, an indelible one will remain there forever in my mind. My breaths come in short pants. My skin's slick.

"I can feel your hot pussy tightening around my cock. Worshipping it. Trying to squeeze the cum out."

His words are so hot. I moan, "Oooooh, god!"

"You want my cum?"

"Mmmm. Yeah."

My body tightens from the tips of my toes to the tips of my fingers. My heart's pounding so hard, I'm not sure if it's trying to escape my chest. Like a supernova, I explode. Shattering into a thousand pieces, the brightest light scorches me to my very core.

Oh my god!

I try to collapse forward, but his grip on my hips prevents it. My ass is still high in the air while my head and shoulders rest on his soft bedding. He hasn't slowed down through my orgasm, still chasing his own. In this position, his dick is rubbing my g-spot without needing to twist his hips. His thrusts increase in speed and power as his hand comes around to massage my clit.

"Oh, god." I moan out. Low and deep, all the way from my belly. I think I'm gonna come again. I never believed having multiple orgasms was real.

"Come for me, now, Gorgeous."

After a few more thrusts, he pinches my clit, setting me off again. I'm going to pass out from orgasm overload.

His dick pulses as he lets out a long, low, sexy groan. Holding me in place, he presses tightly against my ass as he fills the condom with his release. His rough fingers tighten their grip on my hips to the point of pain—interestingly, I like it. I need to know he has hold of me, as I float out of my body during my moments of bliss.

Maintaining our physical connection, he lies to the side, pulling me with him, spooning me from behind, our sweaty bodies connected at every available point. Toby wraps his arms around me, each hand grasping one of my boobs. We lay in silence as we each catch our breath. That was possibly the most amazing sex I've ever had. Mind you, I've only had sex with one other person, while Toby's probably had heaps of sex with loads of different women.

As sated and as comfortable as I am lying here in Toby's arms, I need to pee. There's no way I want to end up with an infection.

"Uh, Toby. I need to go to the bathroom." I try to wriggle my way out of his arms, but he squeezes me tighter.

"Just give me a few more minutes," Toby whispers in my ear.

A few more minutes before he kicks me out? Or will he want me to stay the night? Which I can't do, anyway. I need to get home before Mom wakes up and notices I haven't come home. *God, I feel like a high schooler staying out beyond curfew.*

I guess I should luxuriate in his solid arms for as much time as he'll allow. It's not likely I'll get this chance again. I snuggle back into his embrace, the cooling sweat of our bodies causing our skin to stick together. He kisses the back of my head, making my whole body sigh at the sweetness of the gesture, which is such a juxtaposition to how he showed affection during sex. It's like he's reverted to the sweet Toby I remember.

I must doze for a moment because I wake to Toby quietly extricating himself from the bed and me. I'm assuming to deal with the condom. I take the opportunity to get up so I can deal with my own business in the bathroom.

"Sorry, I didn't mean to wake you. I needed to deal with the condom. You can stay there. I'll be right back."

"Oh, that's okay. I need to go to the bathroom myself."

We both deal with our business. I'm unsure whether he wants me to leave or stay. I wouldn't mind snuggling a little more with him. Stepping out of the bathroom, I find Toby lying in bed, with the opposite side of the bedcovers pulled down, inviting me to join him. I would definitely love to join him; however, I should head home.

"Come on. Get in."

"I should probably head home. It's late." His eyebrows slash down over his gorgeous blue eyes, and his jaw tenses beneath that short beard of his.

"What's the rush? Got someone waiting for you?" *Shit.* I don't want to tell him I live with my mom and daughter. I don't want to tell him I have a daughter. She's already been rejected by the one man who should never have done so. What would Toby, a musician, think of Poppy? This isn't anything serious. I'm not about to share *everything* about me and my life with him.

"Uh, no. I just figured you'd want me out of your hair."

"Nope. Not ready to let you go yet, Bun. Come on." I step closer to the bed, and he reaches out, grabbing my hand to pull me down on top of him. A surprised laugh escapes, leading to a round of giggles from both of us. It feels good to laugh, to relax.

Toby raises his head off the pillow, brushing his lips gently across mine. "I want you again."

I pull back to study his face. He's deadly serious. There's no way I could take his dick again after the rough sex we just shared. It's been a while for me, so I'm raw and sore. If we go again, I'm worried I'll do some serious damage.

This is embarrassing, but I need to let him know it won't be happening anytime soon. "Uh, I don't think so. My hoo-ha couldn't take another round like that tonight."

Doesn't mean I can't get him off, though. I didn't get a chance to touch or explore his body before, and I don't want to explain that I'm tender because it's been so long since I've had sex. I kiss my way down his body, starting at his beard-covered chin. I tickle my fingers through the soft bristles before moving down, kissing down his throat, torso, and abdomen—which is cut like granite. I follow the sexy trail of hair that leads to his hard dick, which is bobbing on his stomach. His hands slide to the back of my head, clutching my hair. His hips lift, seeking my mouth. Tentatively, I touch my tongue to the tip of his cock, running it over the head like a lollipop. He groans at the contact, then pushes my head down further. Shifting to make myself comfortable, I take his penis as far as I can without choking and swallow around the shaft. His hips shoot up in response as he releases another groan.

"Your mouth feels so good around my cock. I used to picture this exact scenario when you were playing the flute in high school. Your pouty lips blowing across the embouchure hole used to get me so hard."

I can't believe what I'm hearing. He gave me the impression he didn't like me—*at all.*

I swallow against his cock in response, garnering another low, sexy groan. Working my hand and mouth in tandem, I slide up and down his shaft in precise glides, squeezing the base each time I slide down. The lubrication from my mouth makes the movement easy. He guides my head in the way he wants, thrusting his hips up and hitting the back of my throat. I have to work hard to breathe through my nose because he's restricting my airway.

As sore as I am, my pussy feels empty as my clit throbs in time with my strokes.

"Swallow on my cock again," he moans.

So I do. His cock pulses, so I gently grasp the heavy sac below, massaging it with my other hand. That seems to push him over the edge because he tries to pull my head back to release himself from my mouth, but I stay firm.

I want his cum in my mouth.

I want the opportunity to taste him, just as he tasted me.

One last squeeze and swallow and he releases his orgasm on a long groan, his hand squeezing my hair so tight it's making my eyes water. I must look a sight at the moment, with my eyes watering as saliva runs down my chin. Slowing my hands and mouth, I coax him through his release, swallowing his salty cum before licking his shaft clean.

His hands loosen around my hair, then he reverently smooths it away from my face. "You didn't need to do that, but I'm glad you did."

I position my hands on his firm abdomen, resting my chin on them to look up at him. "I wanted to. I felt duped that I didn't get to touch you before."

"I'll remember that for next time." My eyes widen involuntarily at his statement. I'm surprised he's talking about a 'next time'. I figured this would be a one-and-done scenario for someone as famous as he is. "Now that I've had you, I'm gonna need to do that again, and if you won't let me have you again tonight, then it'll have to be another night. Soon." He gently brushes a lock of hair behind my ear, then places his hands underneath his head, looking down the length of his body at me. "I don't wanna wait another ten years to see you again."

"Oh." Is all I can say. This development is completely unexpected; one I'm uncertain about.

"Are you interested in catching up again?"

Does he mean like a booty call? Part of me would definitely be up for more of what we did, but the other part of me needs to shut this down.

"It might be difficult with my schedule at the shop. I get very little downtime, and I'm pretty busy when I'm not working." *Looking after my daughter.*

"Pretty sure we can work around your schedule. Mine's pretty hectic, too. I'm in and out of the studio, writing and laying down my new album, which will be followed by a tour when it launches."

For a moment, I forgot he's a famous musician, so he probably *is* only looking for a booty call. I was getting ahead of myself. He pulls me until I'm lying flat on top of him, one leg sliding between both of his. He groans at the contact. I try to pull away because I'm worried I've hurt him.

"Uh, uh, uh. You're not going anywhere." He directs my head to lie on his chest. His heartbeat is strong and steady. It's profound to listen so closely to the part of him that's keeping him alive and vital. Time passes without words; it feels comfortable to spend this quiet time with him—as though this is common practice for us.

We must have fallen asleep because I wake to the very early rays of the new day. I quietly and carefully remove myself from Toby, collect my shoes, and head downstairs to get the rest of my clothes. Dressing quickly, I step out of his spectacular home to call myself an Uber.

TWELVE

-toby-

I CAN'T REMEMBER THE LAST TIME I SLEPT SO SOUNDLY. I ALWAYS HAVE some melody or lyrics making themselves known at the oddest times. If I don't get them down, I've often lost them by morning, never to be retrieved again. I roll over, seeking Cass's warm body, only to turn up empty-handed. I sit up, looking around my bedroom.

Shit, I hope I didn't dream last night.

Getting up, I notice her shoes are missing, so I jog downstairs only to be filled with disappointment to find her gone. Slapping the granite counter with my palm, I run my hands through my hair, searching for something to tell me it was real.

That it wasn't a dream.

A fantasy.

The cloth I used to wipe the oil away from her tits is still in the sink, and the olive oil bottle still sits on the counter, making me feel marginally better, but pissed that she snuck out while I was sleeping. We didn't even exchange fucking phone numbers.

God, I'm stupid.

She never did answer me properly about catching up again. Maybe it was a one-and-done thing for her, something she can check off —*fucked a famous musician*.

I stomp back upstairs to have a shower and get dressed, remembering how she felt against me. How my cock felt inside her pussy. How we *fit* together like the perfect rhythm and melody.

Feeling motivated, I spend most of the day in my studio writing a melody that's stuck with me for the last couple of days. It's come through strong this morning, so I need to get it out. The words to complement it come quickly after waking up alone this morning.

Why can't you see me for me
Instead of the man you think me to be
I'm standing here in front of you
A simple man asking you to see
The man I am; the man you need

Shane steps into the studio, making me realize I must have lost track of time because he was set to pick me up for our regular Sunday dinner at my parents'. He doesn't come to dinner as my bodyguard but as my long-time friend. He's spent many Sundays at my parents' home, so he's casual and relaxed since he's not on the clock.

He smirks at me. "So, last night, huh?"

I glare at him, telegraphing that I don't want to talk about Cass.

"Jake's still a dick. Nothing much has changed there. He just looked softer around the middle." He smirks, patting his taut midsection.

I nod in agreement. "Yep. I agree with you there, brother. Nothing much has changed with him."

"I wonder what's going on between him and Cass? Do you think they're still together? Did you get a chance to talk to her after we all left?"

I got to do a whole lot more than talk to her last night, but I want to keep that to myself. It feels wrong to talk about what we did with anyone outside the two of us.

"I don't think they're still together; the way she pushed him away last night." Fuck, I hope they're not still doing that on-again, off-again shit like they did in high school. Maybe that's why she didn't give me an answer about seeing each other again. If she thinks she can leave me hanging, she has another thing coming. "He seemed pretty pissed last night."

"Yeah, maybe." He brushes his hand over his short hair. "You gonna catch up with her again?"

I stand up, placing my Gibson on the stand in the corner. "I dunno, man. I'd like to, but I'm busy, and she's probably busy with her business. Our lives are pretty different." I'm definitely hoping for a repeat of last night, but I want more than just great sex with her.

———

It's Friday, and I'm waiting for Poppy for our fourth lesson. She's picking it up quickly. She says she practices every spare minute and performs for her mom and gramma. I hope I can focus on her because I've done a shit job at it all week. My mind has constantly drifted back to Cass and the night we spent together before she snuck out on me. I'm kicking myself because I didn't even see her face as she came, and now I may never get the opportunity.

Poppy runs in with her usual excitement, throwing herself at me and hugging me in greeting. She's such a loving little girl. I'm not sure why her dad's not around, but he's missing out big time. We catch up for a few minutes as she updates me on her vacation adventures.

"Gramma took me to the movies and the park. But I've still been practicing every single day. I love playing the guitar," she rapidly signs. "That app is awesome. Mommy and Gramma love watching the patterns it makes when I play."

"That's great. It's fun watching the music come to life on the screen. Show me how far you've come this week." With the amount of work she puts in, she'll have our first song mastered in no time. "How are your fingers holding up?"

She shows me her little fingers; they're pretty red. The blisters, which are common for new players, seem to be starting to heal over. "They're okay. They've been a bit sore, but Gramma soaks my hands in warm salty water. It seems to help." Smart lady.

She situates herself on the chair before putting on her guitar. It's the perfect size for her, and it makes me happy to see my first guitar being used once again, rather than gathering dust in Mom and Dad's attic. The colored strings have helped Poppy pick up the different chords easily. While she's getting organized, I set up my laptop, loading the *Whitecap* program ready for Poppy to play. The program, together with the colored strings, helps her to *see* the music as she plays. She has a natural talent for the guitar, which contributes to the speed with which she's picked it up.

She starts the intro perfectly, G, C, G, C, and strums through to the bridge, introducing D, C, G, D, C, G. She plays through the song, hitting most of the chord changes correctly, making a few small errors here and there. As she finishes, her face lights up as her cheeks lift; her gray eyes sparkle with joy. She's so damn proud of herself, and I'm equally proud of her. For only her fourth lesson, she's done a remarkable job. We high-five, and then we laugh with joy over her success. My heart feels full to overflowing knowing I was the one to teach her, bringing this joy into her world.

"You are an awesome guitarist, Poppy. I'm proud of you."

"Me too. Mommy and Gramma have been listening to me every day. They're proud of me, too."

"I bet they are. Are they sick of listening to that song yet?" I laugh, remembering the countless number of times I played this song until I had it perfected. Kate and Dad grew sick of it, but Mom understood how important it was to me to get it just right. "Hey, how about you take a break and I'll play this new song I'm working on."

Poppy nods, removing her guitar so she can sit close to me. She places her hands on my guitar, watching the laptop as I play. It starts as a simple melody, which builds in difficulty and intensity as the song progresses. Once I've finished playing, Poppy looks up at me as a broad smile takes over her lips.

"I really liked that. Have you finished it with the words yet?"

"Not ..." Uh, what's the word I need here? Oh, that's right. "Completely. I'm still tweaking it. I wrote some lyrics this morning. They haven't been easy to come by."

Poppy frowns. "Why?"

"I've been distracted this week. I'm sure they'll come soon."

"I bet they will." It's a little weird getting support from a seven-year-old. The thing is, I know it's genuine from her.

"I thought you could start learning a new song. It uses the same chords, C, G, D, and introduces F on the solo. What do you think? Are you ready?"

She jumps up and down with her usual excitement. "Oh, yes! I'll still keep practicing the first one, but it would be great to learn a new one, too."

I find Poppy quite an interesting child. She has that childlike wonder and exuberance, yet at times, she shows a level of maturity beyond her years.

"Come on then. I'll play it for you." She places her hands back on my guitar, and I play *Sweet Home Alabama* by Lynyrd Skynyrd. We spend the rest of the lesson going through the intro for the song. Poppy's eagerness is contagious. I feel motivated to head back to my studio so I can work on my new song after the lesson's finished.

Poppy's gramma arrives to pick her up at the end of the lesson, and for the first time, she comes inside. She's standing in the doorway with a ghost of a smile, watching Poppy and me play together, as Poppy watches the colorful patterns move and change on my laptop screen. Poppy hasn't noticed her yet, but I heard the door open, so I looked up to see who was there. I motion with my head for her to come further into the room. Poppy notices my movement and turns to see what's going on.

She stops playing and removes her guitar quickly, then she runs to meet her gramma with the same enthusiasm she greeted me at the beginning of the lesson. I watch their exchange, full of happiness and love. I guess they would be closer than many grandparents to their grandchildren because they live together. I step forward to introduce myself, but Poppy beats me to it, signing my name sign—guitar—to her gramma. I don't bother correcting her, stepping closer to shake her hand.

"Hi, I'm Rose, Poppy's gramma. It's nice to meet you. Poppy talks non-stop about you and practices the guitar religiously," she signs as she speaks to me.

"Hi, Mrs.—" I realize I don't know her last name.

"Oh, please call me Rose." She waves me off.

"Well, Rose, it's nice to meet you, too. I can tell how hard Poppy's working on perfecting her technique and the song by how quickly she's mastered it. You must be sick of listening to *Love Me Do* by now," I sign as I speak.

She laughs as she nods. "Only a little." She says it with a grin, so I know she's not too bothered.

"Well, we started learning a new song today. She can switch between the two, giving you guys some variety."

"Oh, that's great." She stops signing. "Look, I stopped in today because Poppy's mother wanted me to thank you for teaching Poppy and to ask if we needed to be paying you for your time."

Poppy stomps her foot, looking frustrated. "Gramma, sign, please!"

"It's my pleasure. I've never actually *taught* anyone how to play guitar before. My mom had to tell me where to start." I laugh lightly. "She's the music teacher in the family." I shove my hand through my hair. "You don't need to pay me anything. I'm really enjoying spending time with Poppy."

Poppy interrupts. "Your mom's a music teacher? That's so cool."

I nod to Poppy. "Yeah, she taught me."

"Oh, okay. So you're not a music teacher then?" She seems confused.

"Uh, no." She doesn't seem to know who I am, which is fine by me. "I play and sing. I've been playing since I was younger than Poppy. I'm competent, but I'm not a teacher, as such."

"Sorry, I … we assumed you were a music teacher. Are you certain you want to keep teaching Poppy? We could probably get her a proper teacher."

"No, Gramma. I want to keep learning with Guitar." Her little eyebrows are drawn down low over her silver eyes.

Oh, shit. I don't want to stop working with Poppy. I've grown fond of the little girl. I love her spark, her energy, and her determination to learn and master something that would be quite difficult for her. There I go again with my assumptions about the capabilities of someone who is Deaf or Hard of Hearing—I mentally kick my ass.

"If you feel she would do better with a proper music teacher, you're more than welcome to seek one out for her, but I would love to keep working with Poppy. If that's okay?" I pause, hoping she sees as well as hears my sincerity. "Teaching her has helped me just as much as it's helping her. However, I understand if you would prefer she is taught by a professional."

"Oh, no. Poppy loves working with you. I didn't mean to imply you weren't professional. I didn't want to impose on your time if this isn't what you do. Are you sure we can't pay you for your time, at least? What about compensation for the program you sent home?"

"I'm certain. I don't need or want any payment. Not even for the program. It's fine, I promise."

"Okay then. Thank you so much. She's thoroughly enjoying these lessons. Poppy's wanted to learn to play the guitar for some time, and it's great to see her being challenged," she signs to Poppy, "Are you ready to go?"

Poppy nods and then collects her guitar. She hugs me goodbye and confirms that we'll meet again next week for her lesson.

THIRTEEN

-toby-

I can't keep going like I am. It's been just over two weeks, and thoughts of Cassia have invaded every minute of my day since the reunion. The only time I've had a break has been when I've worked with Poppy. I may not have her phone number, but I *know her flower shop's name*, so I plan to pay her a surprise visit today after my morning swim.

From the outside, *Blooms and Balloons* is a cute little shop. Cassia has flowers in various-sized pots outside the windows, made of smaller panes that curve in toward the door. I stop, watching her through the window. She's busy putting flowers together in some type of complicated arrangement. She has a serene smile, one that shows she genuinely enjoys what she does.

I feel like a bit of a creeper, so I step inside and, instantly, am overwhelmed by the scent of flowers. Hundreds of flowers in various colors, sizes, and shapes. The bell over the door tinkles, alerting Cassia to my arrival. When she looks up, she freezes—I've caught her by surprise.

I tuck my hands in my pockets to keep myself in check. "Hey, Cassia."

Her back straightens as she stiffens. "Uh, hey, Toby." She finishes tying off the ribbon on the arrangement she's working on, then places it gently on the counter. She makes no move to come to me, so I step forward.

"You left before I woke up the other morning." I push my hair back from my face. "Why?" I sound pissed. Which I am, but I don't want

471

her to think ... actually, I don't know what I want her to think or not think. I'm just pissed, and to be honest, hurt that she left the way she did.

Her eyes are darting everywhere but at me. That just won't do. I step around the counter, which looks to be made from wooden pallets, to get into her space. She can't avoid me when I'm this close to her. The pulse point at the base of her neck is fluttering like crazy, and she's biting that delectable bottom lip. That was her tell in high school. I see it hasn't changed. She feels uncomfortable and nervous about my question. *Good.*

She looks gorgeous, her hair tied back in a simple ponytail, minimal makeup, and her pale pink *Blooms and Balloons* apron. I reach forward to tenderly tuck a loose lock of hair behind her ear, my fingers following the line of her jaw to her chin, directing her to look up at me.

I whisper, "Tell me why you left, Cass."

She doesn't retreat from me or pull away from my light touch, which is a good sign, but I can see her thinking. As though she's formulating a response for me. "I needed to get home. That's all."

"That's all, huh?" My eyes inspect her face for deceit. In my line of business, people lie to me all the time. While I can tell she's not lying, she's also not being completely honest with me. "You couldn't wake me up to say goodbye?"

"Well, there was no need for both of us to be awake so early. You were sleeping peacefully. I told myself that if you didn't wake on your own when I got up, I'd leave you to enjoy your sleep."

"So, you were being ... thoughtful?" I tense my jaw. "Considerate?"

She latches onto those words, nodding eagerly. "That's right. I was being considerate."

"Sure you were. I was hoping to cook you breakfast and spend at least part of the day with you. I was ..." I look away, searching for the correct word. "disappointed. Disappointed to wake up and find you gone; no note, no goodbye."

Cassia's lip-biting has taken on a life of its own. I want to take that bottom lip between my teeth and bite it, suck it, lick it. *Fuck!* That doesn't help the constant issue I have with my dick whenever I'm around this woman.

"Sor-ry?" She seems uncertain in her apology.

"You need to make it up to me. Have lunch with me this week. A friend of mine owns a Greek restaurant close to here; good food, and the atmosphere is private. A quiet place where we can talk."

She's fidgeting, her eyes darting around her shop while I'm waiting for her to refuse. The expressions that cross her beautiful face suggest she's working through various responses and weighing up her options.

FOURTEEN

-cassia-

I CAN'T BELIEVE I AGREED TO HAVE LUNCH WITH TOBY. THIS WEEK IS crazy busy, and I don't have time, but more importantly, I'm surprised he wanted to see me again. I felt terrible to refuse his request, so I agreed to meet him for lunch today at his friend's restaurant. He offered to pick me up, but I told him I'd rather make my way to the restaurant than have him pick me up.

I've never been here before, and as soon as I step inside, it's like I've been transported back in time to a traditional Greek taverna. Not that I've ever been to a traditional Greek taverna—I'm basing my impression on what I'd imagine it to be like. It's darker inside than it is outside, and it takes my eyes a moment to adjust. If the delicious aromas are anything to go by, the food is going to be amazing. It's more upmarket than I was expecting, and I feel underdressed in my skinny jeans and work shirt—but I *am* on my lunch break. It's not as busy as I would have expected, but I guess it *is* a weekday.

The host greets me with a smile. "Welcome to *Cristo's Taverna*. How may I help you?"

"I'm meeting a friend. I assume he has a reservation. Toby Summer?" I finish as though I'm asking a question. I'm not sure if he would have made the reservation under his name or not. I'm not sure how secretive he has to be when he goes out.

"Your lunch companion has already arrived. Allow me to show you to your table." She guides me through the taverna to a table hidden away in the back corner. I guess Toby has to take some measures to maintain his privacy when he's out in public. We reach the table to find

Toby on his phone. He looks up, noticing my arrival as the host steps away to get back to the greeting podium. He quickly finishes the call, then stands up to pull out my chair, encouraging me to sit down.

"Hey, Cassia. I'm so happy you could make it." He sits down, his knee touching mine beneath the table, sending electricity shooting through my body. He picks up the water bottle, motioning toward my glass, waiting for my approval before filling it.

I quickly sip my drink before responding. "Hi. Of course, I made it. I said I would join you for lunch." I glance around the taverna. "I've never been here before. It feels as though I'm in Greece. Not that I've ever been to Greece. I mean, it feels like I could be in Greece. I mean, it feels authentic." *Geez, Cass, shut the hell up already!* Toby presses his lips together; I think he's trying to contain his laughter.

"It's pretty authentic. My friend Cristo is of Greek descent. His family has owned and operated this taverna for three generations. Before that, they owned and ran a taverna back in Greece. So it's in their DNA. The food is amazing. You're in for a real treat."

"What do you recommend?" Hopefully, he knows what's best, which will save us some time with the ordering process. I only have an hour.

"I thought we could start with their Thursday special: a tasting plate which includes Epiros Feta, Dolmathes, Octapodaki tou Yiorgou, Garides Skordates, and Soutzoukakia. Then I thought we could have Moussaka for our main meal, and we'll see how we go for dessert." He puts down his menu to check with me. "How does that sound?"

"That sounds delicious, but it seems like an awful lot of food for the two of us."

"I'm hungry. I'll eat whatever you don't." He pats his trim stomach for good measure. I remember exactly how amazing those abs of his felt beneath my hands.

The waiter stops at our table with a bottle of wine Toby must have ordered before I arrived. I really shouldn't have a drink because I have to go back to work, but I think I'll need a glass to get through this lunch. My nerves are running rampant. I got the distinct impression the other day that he was upset with me for leaving before he woke up. I'm worried about how he's going to deal with the *'issue'* today. The waiter pours us each a glass of wine before placing the bottle on the table, then takes our order.

Toby picks up his glass, then indicates for me to pick up mine. "To second chances, Cassia."

I tip my head in acknowledgment. "To second chances." We clink our glasses together, then drink.

"How's your week been so far?" he asks.

"Busy. I have two weddings this weekend, so it's rather hectic. I can only spare an hour for lunch today." He nods. "It's great to be so busy. I have Sally, a trainee, who puts together basic arrangements. She does the more straightforward stuff, but I prefer to handle the more complicated orders myself. I'm a bit fussy, wanting every single order that leaves my store to be truly unique. I really need to employ someone else, though, even if it's just doing office management and ordering, freeing me up to make the arrangements." I tuck a lock of hair behind my ear. "How about you? What have you been up to?"

"I'm currently writing songs for a new album, which I'll record before the end of the year."

"How do you come up with new ideas for your music?" I'm genuinely curious about where his inspiration comes from.

"From experiences, people, how I'm feeling, things happening around me. Anywhere, really. I have a great song that I'm thrilled with, but I can't seem to get the lyrics straight for it."

I take another drink of wine. "Is that how you work? The music comes first, and then the lyrics come second?"

"Sometimes. Other times, it's the other way around. It depends. Sometimes a bridge will come to me, and I work around that to write the rest of the song. I don't think I've written two songs the same way. It's weird like that."

The server delivers our tasting plate, interrupting our conversation briefly. The food looks divine and smells fantastic—I can't wait to taste it.

"This looks amazing." I place the napkin on my lap as Toby begins scooping a portion of each item onto my plate, then repeats the process with his own. We both take a bite of food, and I can't help the appreciative noise that escapes me. Embarrassed, I look up from my plate to see if Toby noticed. He's looking at me with his food paused midway to his mouth. "Uh, sorry. Couldn't help myself. This octopus tastes delicious. So fresh and tasty with the zesty lemon and subtle oregano."

"Never apologize for enjoying your food. The food here is always fresh and tastes delicious."

Discussion ceases momentarily while we enjoy the various foods and flavors. Everything is so scrumptious.

Toby wipes his mouth with his napkin. "Did you enjoy the reunion?"

"Yeah, it was great to catch up with old friends. Most people looked pretty much the same, just older. Though I don't think I would have recognized Shane if I fell over him in the street. He looks so different from what he did in high school."

Toby nods in agreement. "Time serving overseas in the Special Forces will change a guy."

"Oh, I didn't know. Where did he serve?"

"He spent some time in Syria. Saw some horrendous shit over there. Since he's been home, he hasn't been the same. He doesn't talk about it. He, uh, actually works for me as my bodyguard." He looks sheepish sharing that information with me, as though he's embarrassed he's so famous he needs a bodyguard.

"It must be hard to go through war over there, then have to come home and function as if you haven't seen and done terrible things. I didn't know he worked as your bodyguard."

"Yeah, I don't need one, but I wanted to keep an eye on him, so I created the position. He doesn't know that, though, so please keep that information to yourself." What a kind, generous thing to do for a friend. It makes Toby that much more attractive in my eyes—a man who takes responsibility with his actions rather than his words.

"Sure. No problem." Does that mean he thinks I'll be seeing Shane again? The server comes to clear our dishes, topping up each of our glasses with wine at the same time.

"So, do you keep in touch with anyone from high school?"

"No. The other night was the first time I'd seen the girls since we were nineteen. I got busy, and we lost touch." That's an understatement. I wonder what he'd think if he knew the reason why I became so busy.

"What about Jake? You still see him?"

"Uh nope. The last time I saw him was just over five years ago now." I don't want to talk about Jake or why our relationship ended for good. It'll expose Poppy, and I don't want to do that. She's had enough rejection. I refuse to open her up to more. "I don't want to talk about him. He's of no importance to me."

He nods thoughtfully as the server returns with our main meal, which smells out of this world. The béchamel sauce looks as though it's been baked to perfection. The next few moments are silent as we dig into our Moussaka; enjoying the combination of flavors on my tongue.

I'm about halfway through when Toby puts me on the spot. "At the reunion, Jake still seemed ... interested in a relationship with you. What was that about then?"

"Toby, I don't want to be rude, but I don't want to talk about Jake. We're done. Over. Have been for a long time. I'm happier for it. That's all there is to it, as far as I'm concerned." He doesn't look like he wants to drop the discussion about Jake; however, he must conclude there's nothing left to discuss.

We continue eating in silence. The atmosphere between us is awkward; however, I'm not sure how to break the sour mood. "So, do you have any humorous stories from your tours?"

He places his knife and fork down, taking a moment to think. "Actually, I do. My nan thought she'd surprise me by turning up to one of my concerts. I had no idea she was there, and I don't know if you're aware, but women often throw their panties on stage when I'm playing." He blushes, which is adorable. "Well, she noticed the women were taking their underwear off to throw them onto the stage. She was mortified and worried that I would be touching 'dirty' panties." He huffs out a laugh. "I don't know how she did it, but she managed to get on stage and used my bass player's mic to tell off all the 'filthy young ladies' in the audience. She said, and I quote, 'If you want to give my grandson your panties, bring a clean pair. Don't be throwing your dirty, smelly underwear at my Toby.' Security managed to guide her gently backstage, where she waited for me to finish my set before proceeding to lecture me about touching other people's dirty underwear."

I can't believe what I'm hearing and burst into uncontrollable snort-laughter; Toby joins me. Once we settle down, I ask, "Are you serious?"

He deadpans, "Completely."

"Oh my gosh, your nan sounds hysterical. How embarrassed were you?" I'm still giggling.

"Utterly embarrassed. It was a few years ago now, yet I *still* get asked about it in interviews sometimes." He shakes his head. "I wonder if it will ever go away?"

When I asked him if he had any humorous stories, I never imagined a story involving his nan. It makes him even more appealing in my eyes. He could have easily shared something that would portray him as the star he is; instead, he chose a funny anecdote involving his family. It suggests how close they are. I touch his hand. "I think it's sweet she was worried about you."

He uses the opportunity to turn over his palm so he can hold my hand. "We're a pretty close family. We catch up every Sunday when we're all in town; we enjoy spending time together. Most of the time, it's me who can't make it because I'm on tour, and I miss them when that happens."

"I think it's pretty rare these days to find families who *like* to spend time together. I'm close to my mom and sister, too."

"I didn't know you had a sister."

"Yeah, Violet's two years older than I am. She didn't like to be seen with her little sister at high school, so it wasn't common knowledge we were related then. She's married and has a three-year-old daughter with her husband."

"Cool. Do you like being an aunt? I can't wait for Kate and Oliver to start a family. I'm gonna be the coolest uncle." He puffs out his chest as though it will be his most outstanding lifetime achievement.

"I'm sure you'll be the coolest." I giggle. "I do love being an aunt. It's truly special to be part of their lives."

His mood suddenly changes from light and happy to serious as he squeezes my hand. "Are you ready to tell me the real reason you snuck out of my place early on Sunday morning?"

I knew this was coming, so I've been thinking about what to tell him. I figure I can go with part of the truth. People always say to stick with the truth as much as possible. "Look, it's a bit embarrassing, but I moved back in with my mom about eight years ago. I didn't want to arrive home after she had woken up and make her aware that I had spent the night somewhere; it feels disrespectful to her, and she would have asked me loads of questions." I bite my bottom lip. "As it was, I felt like I was back in high school breaking curfew." I give a light laugh, hoping to lighten my statement.

The surprised expression on his face shows he wasn't expecting that as my answer. "I didn't know that. Fair enough. I understand not wanting to be disrespectful to your mom. I would have probably done the same thing." He squeezes my hand, bumping my leg with his own to regain my focus. "I still would have preferred you to have woken me before you left."

"I'm sorry about that. I didn't know the protocol in that situation. I never do one-night stands. I figured you'd want me out of the way."

"Never. I don't want you out of the way. *Ever.*" The sincerity in his voice suggests he means this. But what does that really mean? Does he want us to hook up again? I'm not sure I could do it. My heart's already begun to get involved, and that's definitely not something I want to happen.

"When can we catch up again? I know you have two weddings this weekend, but are you free next weekend?"

Oh, shit! What can I say? I don't want to ask Mom to look after Poppy so I can go on a date if that's even what he's asking for. She already helps me out so much with her. "Um, what did you have in mind? I'll have to check my schedule."

"I enjoy going to *Brady's Pub* now and then on a Saturday night to watch live bands. I was planning to go next Saturday night with this guy I met a while ago through Oliver to watch an up-and-coming band. It would be great if you could come along, too." Oh, so it's not a *date*. I'm unsure if I'm disappointed or not. It sounds as though he's inviting me out as a friend.

"That sounds like fun. I'll have to let you know after I check my schedule for that weekend."

"Fair enough." His lips lift in a half-smile. "That means you'll need my number."

"Yeah, I guess I do." He gestures for me to get my phone out, so I reach down to pick up my purse. The strap catches under the leg of my chair, and everything spills out onto the floor—how freaking embarrassing. I mean everything. Tissues; wet wipes; band-aids; tampons; the arm from Poppy's Barbie doll. It's a genuine mom purse, you know—all the things I need to carry at all times. I try to scoop everything up quickly before Toby notices, except he's already bent down to help me.

"Wow, you sure carry a lot of stuff in your purse. It must weigh a ton." He laughs as he picks up the doll's arm, raising an eyebrow at me.

"Uh." I laugh awkwardly, thinking quickly. "That belongs to my niece, Jasmine." He hands it to me, and I add it to the collection in my purse. I glance at the time and am shocked to see that lunch has taken well over an hour. "I really need to get back to work. I have a lot to do."

He stands, then pulls out my chair for me. "I'll walk you back. I still need to give you my number." He pays for our meal, and I thank him for buying me lunch today. Shane steps in behind us, taking me by surprise. I didn't realize he was in the restaurant.

"Hey, Shane."

He tilts his head. "Hey, Cassia. How're things?"

"Great, thanks."

Toby holds my hand as we walk back toward my shop, and I marvel at how nice it feels to hold a man's hand in this way. Every time we've touched, whether it be our hands or our legs, I've felt that spark with him. Hell, I don't even need to be touching him to feel the spark between us. As we arrive, he pulls me around in front of him, wrapping his arms around my waist. Pulling me in tight to his body, he kisses my lips gently, as though he's unsure of my reception, but I press in tighter, returning the kiss. Toby pulls back to whisper in my ear. "It's hard to do, but I'm keeping it PG in front of your shop to be respectful of your business. Now give me your phone so that I can give you my number."

I pull out of his embrace and tackle the mess that is my purse to find my phone, unlocking it before handing it to him for his number. He inputs his information, then sends a message to his phone to get my number. He kisses me once again before we part ways with my promise to let him know about next Saturday night.

FIFTEEN

-cassia-

I NEVER GO OUT THIS OFTEN, BUT I'M STANDING IN FRONT OF MY mirror checking out my reflection once again. When I told Mom I'd been invited out by a high school friend I reconnected with at the reunion, she all but pushed me out the door. She was unbelievably happy to see me going out to spend time with friends. I didn't tell her the person was of the male persuasion; that would have led to too many questions and too much excitement. I've lost count of the number of times Mom's lectured me about 'putting myself out there' and 'you'll never meet anyone if all you do is work and hang out at home with me'.

I've chosen to keep my outfit simple. Pairing my black ripped skinny jeans with my white boyfriend shirt and the stiletto sandals I wore to the reunion. No boob tape or adhesive bras in sight—*just in case*. I've straightened my hair and put on minimal makeup. I've always been a bit of a no-fuss kinda girl, which suits my busy lifestyle since becoming a mom and business owner. I also don't want to look like I'm trying too hard to impress anyone, or Mom will get suspicious.

Saying my goodbyes to Poppy and Mom, I tell them not to wait up for me. Poppy's not used to seeing me dressed to go out socially, so she makes a big deal about how pretty I look, hugging me extra tight. I remind her to behave for Gramma, not that I need to. She's always such a good kid. I'm incredibly fortunate to have her in my life. I know Mom will spoil her tonight, giving her extra dessert.

Arriving at the pub on time, it's unsurprisingly busy for a Saturday night. I can't hear a live band playing, but there is definitely music pumping over the din of conversation. Unfortunately, the place is bigger than I expected, and as I make my way slowly through the crowded space, I'm not sure I'll be able to locate Toby and his friend here. The next thing I know, I'm wrapped in two arms and lifted off of my feet, causing me to squeal in surprise as I attempt to escape the stranger's grip.

"Fancy seeing you here, Sia."

Ugh, I know that voice. I heard it three weeks ago for the first time after a five-year absence. "Put me down, Jake." My tone brooks no argument. I'm livid that he thinks he still has the right to put his hands on me after all this time and everything that's gone down between us. "Now, Jake. I mean it." He squeezes me tighter, pushing all the air out of my lungs, so I increase my attempt to break free. I remember the shoes I'm wearing, so I thrust my foot back into his leg, causing him to release me, finally.

"You fucking bitch!" He raises his hand, ready to strike me when a couple of good Samaritans standing close by step in to help me. They step in between the two of us, using their bodies as a shield.

"You need to leave the lady alone, man. She doesn't seem interested." Samaritan number one says.

"Don't you fucking tell me what to do. She's my woman. I'll do whatever the fuck I want!" He sneers at the guy.

Samaritan number two looks over his shoulder to check the accuracy of the statement. "I'm not his woman. He's crazy." When I look around, I notice we've attracted quite a bit of attention from the surrounding people, one of which is Toby. He's moving toward me with malice in his eyes. Shane's close behind with a third guy bringing up the rear.

"What the hell is going on?" He looks at me. "Are you okay?"

Good Samaritan number two speaks up, "This guy's been giving her a hard time. He says she's his girl. She's saying she's not." He shrugs as if he doesn't know who to believe. Toby looks across, noticing Jake for the first time. If he was concerned that Jake and I were still together before, he's really going to think we're still on and off now.

I feel like I need to clarify the situation. "I'm NOT with him. We haven't been together for years." Of all the places we could bump into each other, it had to be in a place where Toby would be, too. It's unbelievable in a city this size that we happened to be in the same place at the same time—I guess it happens. Toby pulls me to his side, offering his support.

"What the fuck? Are you with Emo Boy now?" Jake sneers at me. The good Samaritans have stepped away, and I don't blame them. Jake looks about ready to explode. I can only hope he doesn't mention Poppy. He looks at Toby. "You always did have a hard-on for her in high school." He spits on the floor at my feet. "Enjoy her while you can, Emo Boy. She *always* comes back to me." Jake turns on his heel and storms away, pushing his way forcefully through the crowd. I finally release the breath I was holding in anticipation of the possible bombshell he could've dropped—fortunately, he didn't.

Toby pulls me into him, holding me tight as he strokes my hair. "You okay?" he whispers in my ear. I'm shaking now. I guess the release of adrenalin has kicked in, and I can only nod. "Come on. Let's go sit in our booth." He guides me across the tiled floor to the other side of the bar. Toby helps me sit, and I slide across the seat, allowing him to join me. Shane and the other guy slide into the other side. Toby pulls me back into his body, helping me to feel secure after what's transpired. He pulls his head away to study my face. "You sure you're okay? You're trembling."

I finally find my voice. "Yeah, I'm okay. It was just unexpected. I haven't seen him for years, then suddenly I see him twice in one month. Each time, he seems like he's been drinking too much and has acted like he still has the right to touch me. Which he doesn't." I look pointedly at Toby to make it clear that I'm not comfortable with Jake touching me. Toby tips his chin in deference. I hope it's the end of the conversation. He looks at Shane and the other guy. "This is my friend, Jase Parker. He works with Oliver, Kate's husband. And you already know Shane."

I smile at the guys. "Hey, Shane, good to see you again. Nice to meet you, Jase."

"You, too." He smiles. I feel like I'm sitting with the hot guy club among these three men. Looking around at my surroundings, I notice several women eyeing the men at my table. Yet I'm the lucky one sitting here with them. A couple of women step closer to our table as though they're going to approach the guys.

Shane stands. "What would you like to drink? We have a tab running." He situates himself between the women and our table, effectively blocking their approach.

"I'll have a Vodka tonic. Thanks." He acknowledges my request, then heads off toward the bar. The drink will help calm me down.

Toby places his hand on my thigh under the table, and the heat that travels up my thigh to my core is instantaneous.

"So, you've known Toby since high school, huh? Any embarrassing stories you're willing to share about our boy here?" Jase smiles as he winks at me.

"Uh, not really. We didn't hang out in the same circles, and whenever I tried to strike up a conversation with him, he'd find some excuse to leave."

"Hey, I've explained and apologized for that." Toby laughs, his breath rushing across my cheek. I look at him, appreciating the beauty of his face relaxed with joy.

"I feel there's a story here. C'mon, don't leave me in the dark, man." He looks at Toby.

Shane returns partway through the conversation. "It's because Toby had a crush on Cassia in high school. He couldn't be in the same room with her without getting a ..." His words fade away as he gestures to his crotch. The guys laugh at Toby's expense and, the good sport that he is, he joins in with them. The conversation lightens the mood and has everyone laughing. He doesn't seem to mind being the butt of the joke.

Conversation flows freely after that, then at ten, we make our way downstairs to the basement where the pub showcases live bands on a Saturday night. I didn't know this part was down here. The wooden floors look well worn, with years of patrons enjoying music in the space. Wooden paneling on the walls makes the space feel intimate. Green Tiffany pendants dangle from the high ceiling, providing dim light for the ample space.

We listen to the first set. The guys seem to enjoy the music, although it's not my style. I prefer Toby's style more than anything. That pop, rock, sometimes acoustic sound he seems to pull together. These guys are playing really heavy rock, and to me, it just sounds like a whole lotta noise. Jase has gone off to catch up with some other friends, while Toby wants to talk with the band during the break, so I stay with Shane.

Shane steps closer to me. "Hey, Cassia, I wanted to check something with you."

"Yeah. What is it?"

"Are things really over between you and Jake?" I'm uncertain what my relationship with Jake has to do with Shane. "I don't want Toby to get his hopes up, that's all. If you're still on and off with Jake, you need to make that clear to Toby. Don't let him think there's hope where there's none."

I think it's sweet that he's looking out for Toby, just as Toby's looking out for him by giving him a job. "Shane. I'm not involved with Jake in any way, shape, or form. You needn't worry about that. I promise. But what makes you think there's anything between Toby and me?" I'm interested to know if Toby told Shane about our night together.

"You know his high school crush?" I nod. "It never went away. You were the primary reason he attended the reunion. He was hoping to reconnect with you, maybe see where things could go between the two of you if you were single."

Wow. Toby hasn't said it in so many words, but he sort of implied he wanted me in his life. I wonder how Toby would feel if he knew what Shane's just told me? I'm starting to think I need to cut this, whatever this is, with Toby off. As much as I like him and thoroughly enjoyed spending time in his bed, a relationship between us would never work in a million years. There's no way he'd be interested in me if he knew I had a daughter. With Jake, no less. His world revolves around sound, while the most precious person in my life lives in a world of silence—even though she's learning the guitar. He travels all over, performing to thousands upon thousands of screaming fans, meaning he's away for probably most of the year. He probably sleeps with women worldwide; that's why he's so talented in bed. I doubt he's looking to settle down and be a committed partner. I'm not prepared to expose Poppy to his lifestyle or his possible rejection of her.

What in the hell am I doing here?

Toby's nowhere in sight, but I feel the urgent need to leave. "I've gotta get going. Can you please tell Toby I needed to leave?"

Shane seems surprised by my sudden need to leave. "Uh, sure. Of course. Do you need a ride? We can take you home."

"No. No, that's okay. I'll get an Uber. Bye, Shane." I step away from him. "Enjoy the rest of your night." Turning to leave, I make my way as quickly as possible through the crowded room, up the stairs, through the packed pub, and out the front door. By the time I reach fresh air, I'm almost gasping with an impending panic attack. I calm myself down with solid deep breaths, then use my app to request an Uber. Walking down the street to an open café, I wait inside for it to arrive.

My phone rings in my back pocket, so I pull it out to read the display. Toby. *Shit!* I contemplate sending it to voicemail, but that feels wrong since I just abandoned him in the pub.

Before I can get a word out of my mouth, he frantically speaks. "Where are you, Cassia?"

"Didn't Shane tell you? I had to leave. I wasn't sure how long you'd be, and I couldn't wait around." Sort of true.

"Is there some kind of emergency or something?" Or something, I guess.

"It was just time to leave. My Uber's arrived. Gotta go. Bye." I disconnect the call as I confirm my ride is actually my ride. As I'm settling into the back seat, my phone rings again. It's Toby.

Should I send him to voicemail?

I need to cut ties with him.

It would be best this way.

I've been contemplating what to do for too long, and my voicemail picks up the call, deciding for me. I breathe a sigh of relief that I don't have to talk to him now as the alert on my phone tells me he's left a message. I'll listen to it later. My phone rings again. Shit, he's not giving up. I probably should answer the damn thing.

"Hey—"

Toby cuts me off. "Don't hang up on me again. Do you understand?" he snaps before pausing. I open my mouth to answer, but he keeps on talking. "You have a habit of leaving me without the opportunity to say goodbye or to set up another time to catch up. Do you have some kind of issue with me?"

The only issue I have with him is the perceived future I imagine playing out. I can't express that to him, though.

"Am I a checklist item on your bucket list or something? Fucked a famous musician. Tick," he grumbles.

"What in the hell did you just say to me?" I can't believe he said that to me. How dare he speak to me like that. I'm the total opposite of some groupie who just wants to sleep with him. "Don't you dare presume something so crass about me. You don't know me. Who I am. The things that are important to me." I huff out a breath. I don't think I've been this mad for a long time.

"I'm sorry, Cassia. I don't know what else to think. You keep blowing me off." He releases a huge sigh. "I like you, okay. I fucking loved being inside you. I would like to explore a relationship with you, but I'm getting the distinct impression I'm on my own on that front."

He's sincere in his words; I can tell. "Look, Toby. You're not on your own. I like you, too. And I loved what we did at your place. It was by far the best sexual experience of my life." The Uber driver looks up at me through the rear-view mirror, reminding me I have someone who can listen to my conversation. I drop my voice to a whisper. "I'm not sure a relationship with you is possible with your career. That lifestyle is not something I'm interested in. I have other commitments and priorities that must come first for me at the moment. I'm sorry, but I think it's for the best if we leave things be." I'm greeted with silence on the other end of the phone. I look at the display to check he's still there. "Toby. You there?"

"Yeah. Just taking a minute to digest what you said and come to terms with the disappointment. But you're probably right. I don't want to force you into something that doesn't *appeal* to you—I respect you too much for that. Unfortunately, my lifestyle isn't conducive to a steady relationship, no matter how much I want one. See ya, Cass." He sounds resigned. As though he's acknowledging the prospect he'll have to face his entire future alone. I'm sure that's my imagination, though. I bet he has women lining up for him after his performances. I doubt he spends too many nights alone.

He disconnects the call before I can say goodbye, giving me a taste of my own medicine. Well, he gave up quickly. I guess he's not genuinely interested in a relationship with me, and he was looking more for a hook-up—which isn't me.

He's like all the other men—out for a good time.

Slumping back into the seat, I feel hollow inside. I never imagined tonight would go the way it did. First with Jake, and now with Toby. If only I felt like I'd made the right decision.

SIXTEEN

-toby-

WELL, I GUESS THAT'S THAT THEN. OVER BEFORE IT EVER REALLY started. I'm confused as to how our night turned out so ... *shitty!* I was confident she felt the same sparks, the same connection I did whenever we touched. Hell, we didn't even need to touch for me to *feel* it—but I guess I was on my own. It reinforces the notion I'm not going to find someone to accept me as long-term partner material with my career. Ever since Kate settled with Oliver, I've been thinking about my life and how I want it to look; and I know, without a doubt, that I don't want to be alone.

I'm still staring at my blank phone when Shane pats me on the back. "What's up, bro?"

"Uh, nothing. I think I'll call it a night. You guys enjoy the band. I'll catch up with ya tomorrow. Let me know when the next decent band's playing, Jase."

I don't give either of them a chance to ask any further questions, waving over my shoulder as I make my way through the crowd to head home—*alone*.

———

Poppy comes running to me as soon as she enters the room, launching herself at me. I've learned to brace myself for the onslaught of her exuberant greetings. She's always so happy to see me and show me how much she's improved since our last lesson. She pulls back, studying my face.

At least someone's happy to spend time with me. I sound like a crybaby, but Cass's rejection still fucking stings.

Her head tilts to the side. "Are you okay? You look sad."

"Yeah, Poppy. I've been sad, but seeing you makes me feel happier." If she's astute enough to pick up on my mood, I'm not going to lie to her. People experience all types of emotions in life. There's no need to pretend you always feel fantastic when you don't. I don't need to give her any details—just acknowledge that her assessment was accurate. "Come on, show me how you're going with your new song."

"Okay." She steps back into me, throwing her little arms around my hips, squeezing me tight. She steps back and signs. "When I'm feeling sad, Mommy gives me the biggest hugs, and that always makes me feel better. So I'll give you this hug now, and then I'll give you another one before I leave. Hopefully, they'll make you feel better."

My throat feels tight, making it hard to swallow. This kid slays me. She's so open and honest with her affection and friendship. She is a true credit to her mom and gramma. "Thank you. Your mom is right about hugs. Just seeing your smiling face made me feel better, but that hug. It was the best hug I've ever had. Thank you." I muss her hair before indicating for her to get her guitar to show me how she's going with her practice.

We settle into our lesson. I'm more than impressed with Poppy's progress on the new song. I only introduced it to her three weeks ago, and she started back at school this week, so I assume she's had less time to practice.

"You pretty much have it nailed. Anyone would think you've been playing guitar a lot longer than you have." I sign to her when she finishes. The smile that lights up her face is magnificent. She's proud of herself and with good reason. I don't understand why her father's not in her life, because she's a daughter I'd be proud to have. "Okay, now show me *Love Me Do*. Have you been practicing that one, too?"

She nods. "Yes, I have. I don't have as much time now I'm back at school, but I still make sure I practice every day."

"How has your first week back at paper been? Do you like your teacher?"

She giggles at me. "You're funny, Guitar. It's school, not paper." She shows me the difference between the two signs. They're very similar. Instead of brushing the base of my palms together, I need to clap them without making a sound.

"Thanks, Poppy. So, do you like your teacher?"

"Oh, yeah, she's nice, and all my friends are still in my class."

"That's good. It makes a difference when you have a teacher you like. My sister's a kindergarten teacher."

"I want to be a kindergarten teacher when I grow up. Can I meet her?"

"I'll ask her. Maybe she could come to one of our lessons."

"Cool." She spins around in her excitement.

Once she calms down, she settles in, and she's pretty much spot on with every note. I wave my arms in the air for her as she finishes, then she curtsies to me. We're having a good laugh when Xanthe steps further into the room. I was so focused on Poppy that I didn't notice her enter.

"Poppy, you sound fantastic. How many lessons have you had now?" Xanthe signs, speaking at the same time.

Poppy looks at me tentatively, showing the number eight.

Shaking my head with a smile, I correct her. "Seven. You've only had seven lessons."

Xanthe makes a big show of looking surprised. "You play like you've been playing for a lot longer than that. You were born to play guitar, girl."

You can almost see Poppy glowing with pride right before our very eyes. She should feel damn proud of herself—her consistent hard work and determination have brought her to this point quickly.

"I stopped in to ask a favor," she signs to both of us. "You know the Labor Day concert we have coming up?" Poppy and I both nod. "One of our performers has had to pull out because they've had a change in circumstances. I was wondering if you guys would be interested in doing a duet?" She holds her hands up in the begging position.

I look at Poppy and sign, "It's up to you, Poppy. I'm happy to do whatever you decide." I really am. If she feels up to the challenge of performing in front of others, I'll support her, standing by her side all the way.

She barely takes a moment to think it over, agreeing readily to the duet for the concert. She is one brave young lady since we only have two lessons to get prepared for it.

"Great. If you could let me know what song you guys want to perform so I can add it to the running sheet, that'd be fantastic. Oh, I'm a happy girl. I can't wait to see you guys play together on stage." She hugs each of us before bustling out of the room.

I look at Poppy. "Which song would you like to do? *Love Me Do* or *Sweet Home Alabama*?"

"Can we do *Love Me Do*?"

"Of course. Let's get started on working out an arrangement."

We work solidly for the rest of the lesson, working out the parts we'll play together. The parts I'll sing, and some parts Poppy can sign while I play. I feel energized and possibly more excited than when I play to a packed stadium. When we part ways at the end of the lesson, I stop in to let Xanthe know which song we'll be performing.

SEVENTEEN

-cassia-

I drag my exhausted ass in the front door with thoughts of a warm shower to ease my tired legs, then flopping face-first onto my bed. As much as I love my daughter and can't imagine my life without her in it, I'm hoping she's already in bed so I can just sneak in to kiss her goodnight. I've worked my schedule so I only have to work tomorrow morning this weekend. Walking through the house, I find Mom and Poppy in the kitchen making hot chocolate; it *is* only seven-thirty, after all. Poppy has her back to me, so she doesn't know I'm watching her.

She's growing up so fast. I miss the baby years: holding her while she slept; that yummy baby smell; her coos, giggling, and babbling. She was always such a happy baby; she's still a happy child. I thank my lucky stars every single day that I have her in my life. She turns around, noticing me, and immediately stops what she's doing to run to me. Throwing herself at me, I pick her up to hold her close. She grasps my cheeks, drawing her face back to look at me closely, then kisses the tip of my nose—she's such a sweetheart.

"Hello, Mommy."

I put her down so I can sign. "Hello, Baby Girl. What are you guys doing?"

"We're making hot chocolate with marshmallows." She shows me the bag of marshmallows as I notice the remnants of icing sugar on her cheek.

"Oooo, marshmallows. The best."

We work together to get the hot chocolate prepared, then carry it into the living room.

"You're home earlier tonight," Mom observes.

"Yep. I only need to work tomorrow morning, then I have the rest of the weekend off," I speak and sign at the same time so Poppy knows we have lots of time together this weekend. She jumps up and down with excitement. I spend a lot of time feeling guilty for the limited time I spend with my daughter. I've put an ad in the local community paper looking for an office manager in the hopes it will free up some of my time, allowing me to leave work earlier during the week.

"That's so good, Mommy. I have some news, too."

Mom winks at me with the biggest grin, making her look younger.

"I'm going to do a duet with my guitar teacher in a concert at *Music for my Heart* over the Labor Day weekend. You'll come to watch, won't you, Mommy?"

"I wouldn't miss it for the world, Pop. That's amazing. Does your teacher think you're ready?"

"He let me decide. We're going to do *Love Me Do*. We were working out the best way to play it today. Wait 'til you see what we're going to do. I'm so excited." I can tell she's excited. She has so much energy that I don't think she'll sleep tonight. She's almost jumping out of her skin. "I'm going to practice extra hard. We only have two lessons until the concert."

"You'll be great, Poppy. You're already doing so well with that song. You're going to smash it for the concert." I hug her close.

We all catch up on our days over hot chocolate. I feel revitalized after spending this time with the people I love most in the world.

"Come on, Pop. Time for bed."

She says her goodnights with hugs and kisses before trudging upstairs to get ready for bed. She works through her nightly routine independently while I get her bed ready for her to hop right on in. Tucking her down, ready to read a story together, she stops me.

"Mommy."

"Yeah, Baby Girl. What's up?"

"Why don't I have a daddy like everyone else?"

I knew one day I would need to answer this question. So I've been preparing my answer for her depending on how old she was when she asked. She's astute enough to pick up when I'm not completely honest with her, but I don't want to go into too much detail. "You *do* have a daddy, Pop. Or else you wouldn't be here. It takes a mommy and a daddy to make a baby."

"Where is he? How come I've never met him?"

"He was my boyfriend for a long time during high school and through college. When I told him I was pregnant, he wasn't ready to be a daddy, and that's okay. Not everybody is ready to be a mommy and a daddy at the same time. I moved back here with Gramma so we could all be a big family." I smooth her hair down her back. "Why are you asking about your daddy, Baby Girl?"

She shrugs. "I was just wondering."

"That's okay. You can talk to me or ask me about anything. Okay?"

"Okay, Mommy. Can we read the story now?"

"Sure."

We snuggle down together while I read the next chapter of *Charlie and the Chocolate Factory*. One of my favorites from my childhood. It's a little slower than usual to read and interpret it in ASL, but I'm so happy to share one of my favorites with her and have her enjoy it as much as I did.

I pop the book on her side table before hopping out of bed to tuck her in for the night, but she stops me.

"Mommy, do you think I could ask my guitar teacher to be my daddy?"

I startle at her question. I have to temper my response because I'm so surprised. "Why would you want to ask him?"

"He's really nice. He's kind to me, and he's been very patient. He's been sad, and he said I make him happy." She smiles at me. "I like it when I can make people happy. I really like him, Mommy. He's the best."

"That's great, Poppy. I'm glad you like him, and he's good to you. But you can't ask somebody to be your daddy." Her little face drops, so I rush to add. "There's no reason he can't be your friend, though." I brush a lock of silky hair behind her ear.

"You wait until you meet him after the concert, Mommy. You'll want him to be my daddy, too." Only if her guitar teacher was someone like Toby, I think to myself.

"Maybe, Baby Girl. We'll see, okay?"

"Okay, Mommy. I love you."

"I love you more than all the stars in the sky and grains of sand on the earth."

I kiss her goodnight, turn off the light, and step out of her room.

Then close myself in my room, down the hall. Leaning against the door, I look up at the ceiling to prevent the tears from falling; I had no idea she had been thinking about not having a father. I didn't know it bothered her to the degree that she wanted to find herself a dad. Once I get myself somewhat together, I make my way downstairs to speak with Mom.

Mom knows me too well. She reads the defeat in my posture and the look of failure on my face. She knows something's up. "What's up, Cass?"

"Poppy just asked about her dad or lack thereof." I brush my hand through my loose hair, reminding myself I really should get it cut.

Mom places her hand on her heart. "Oh, I guess we knew the questions had to come one day."

"Yeah, I know. It's just that … she wants to ask her guitar teacher to be her daddy."

A smile breaks out across Mom's face as her eyebrows almost hit her hairline. "Well, she has good taste. He *is* rather handsome, *and* he's been very good to her."

I chuckle mildly. "Oh my god, Mom. She can't go around asking just any man to be her daddy. I didn't realize she was missing having a father. That we're not enough for her."

Mom wraps her arm around my shoulders to comfort me. "Of course, we're enough for her. She's just at that age when she's noticing what her friends have and wondering why she doesn't have the same things. It doesn't mean we're not enough or that she's missing out on anything. She's just making sense of the world around her." She nudges my shoulder. "You were about her age when you asked me the very same question. Mind you, you didn't have someone lined up to be your daddy."

I'm shocked I would do such a thing. "No way. I would never have done that."

"Well, you did. It's only natural, Honey. Wait 'til you meet him at their concert. You may just want him to be her daddy, too." She snickers. *Oh, she's so damn funny.*

"I doubt it very much, Mom." I kiss her forehead. "I'm going to bed. I need to start early tomorrow."

"Night, Love."

"Night, Mom." I turn to head back upstairs. Halfway up the stairs, I turn around. "Thanks, Mom."

She nods, then heads back into the kitchen to shut off the lights.

EIGHTEEN

-cassia-

POPPY AND I STEP OUT OF THE FRONT DOOR TO VISIT THE PARK, followed by ice cream from her favorite ice cream shop, *Brain Freeze*. She loves the quirky characters the ice cream artists make out of ice cream and candy. As we're closing the front screen door, my sister's car pulls into the driveway. We haven't heard from her much since last month's visit, so I wasn't expecting her today. Poppy runs toward her car once it's parked. I follow along behind with a sinking feeling in my gut. As I get closer and see her face—her red, swollen eyes and messy hair—I know my gut was right. I step around to open her door, crouching down until I'm at eye level. Her tears burst forth, and I lean forward to engulf her in my arms. It's awkward, but I do my best to offer comfort. Her body shudders as her tears wet my shoulder.

Poppy's climbed into the back of the car entertaining Jasmine, while Vi and I cry together. I feel the pain of losing her marriage, as my hope fades for my own happily ever after with the demise of my sister's. Finally, I pull away, gently wiping my sister's tears with my thumbs.

"C'mon. Let's go inside." Undoing her seatbelt, I help her out of the car, then lean into the back to retrieve Jasmine. She's smiling and chatting happily as she squishes my cheeks between her chubby hands.

"Herro, Aunt Cass!"

"Hello, Jolly Jas!" I nuzzle her nose with my own, squishing her impossibly closer. This poor baby doesn't understand the turmoil her mom is going through at the moment. As we turn toward the house, Mom comes down the front porch steps, walking quickly toward Vi with her arms open wide. Violet runs into her arms, sobbing as Mom embraces her eldest daughter tightly.

"Come on, Love. Come inside." She guides Vi inside, as I follow behind with Jas and Poppy. I can't explain to Poppy that we won't be going to the park or for ice cream today because I have my hands full, but as soon as we get inside, I'll explain it to her; though she probably already has an idea that things aren't all that great with her aunt.

I explain the situation to Poppy without going into too much detail. She's such a gorgeous girl that she automatically responds it's okay, we can go to the park and get ice cream another day. She then gently guides her cousin into the playroom after I've done a quick check that there's nothing dangerous for a toddler in the room. Unfortunately, I may have to move anything hazardous upstairs to Poppy's room because I think Violet and Jasmine will be here for a while.

We get the kids settled in the playroom, then settle ourselves at the kitchen table, which always seems to be the location of choice for our discussions. Finally, Mom gets us all a drink—alcoholic, of course—it's the obvious choice for an occasion like this.

"He kicked us out!" Vi blurts. More tears are pouring down her face.

"He did what?" Mom and I respond at the same time.

"He said we're dominating his life. He feels like he can't breathe because we're always there."

I'm at a loss. Isn't that what a marriage and family are? Am I missing something here? "What does he mean, 'you're always there'? Isn't that where you're meant to be?"

"How am I supposed to know? He says Jasmine's too needy, that I'm so focused on her I don't pay him any attention other than to tell him what needs to be done around the house. He said, and I quote, 'you don't treat me like a man'."

How dare he act like an immature asshole, kicking my sister and his child out of their home. I feel like the top of my head's going to explode like the emoji.

Mom scoffs, "That would be because he's not acting like a friggin' man." She takes another drink. "If he wants to be treated like a man, he needs to behave like one. Kicking his wife and child out of the family home is certainly not acting like a man in my book."

"Why didn't he just leave? Why did he kick you guys out? What an asshole!" I feel positively violent on her behalf.

"He said his wage paid the mortgage, so it's his home, not mine. It doesn't matter that my wage paid the other bills and put food on the table." All I can do is blink in disbelief. I can't imagine how my sister feels.

"Are you serious?" Mom's voice is growing louder the angrier she gets. "I feel like I never even knew him." She's hurt. And to be honest, she should be. She welcomed Allen into our family as if he were her own son. This isn't just a breakup for Violet. It's a breakup for the whole family.

"Deadly. He thinks because he contributed more financially, I have fewer rights." She looks between both of us, her bottom lip quivering. "He said he doesn't love us anymore. There's nothing about the two of us that interests him. He's outgrown us." Her sobs break free.

We both lean in to hold Vi tight, offering her support in the only way we can right now, as all of our hearts break for her and for Jasmine. I'm not sure how long we stay like that, but the girls find us embracing in the kitchen and join in the hug fest. Eventually, we pull ourselves together and get busy organizing sleeping arrangements, pulling together essential items to get Vi and Jas through a couple of days. She left with nothing. The asshole didn't even give her a chance to pack a bag. Luckily, my sister and I are similar sizes, and I still have Poppy's old clothes that don't fit her anymore, ready to give to my sister. She's going to have to go back at some point to pick up their things, but she needs a few days' grace period to pull herself together.

NINETEEN

-cassia-

TODAY'S BEEN PRETTY QUIET FOR ORDERS, SO I USE THE OPPORTUNITY to catch up on paperwork in my office. Checking my emails for responses to my office manager ad, I find I have one reply, so I click on the attachment to read through the application. Disappointment fills me as I read, finding they have zero experience in office management. I'm all for giving people an opportunity to expand their skills, but I need someone who can walk straight into the position and get started without training them *how* to be an office manager. I shoot back a response, thanking the applicant for her interest and letting her know she was unsuccessful in her application.

My phone rings. The screen displays Sam's name.

"Hey, Sam."

"Hey, Cass. How are things?"

"Oh, Sam, where do I even begin? I'm so busy, I don't know where to start. Today's been my quietest day, so I'm catching up on paperwork." I respond with a chuckle.

"Oh, no. I was hoping we could catch up for lunch sometime."

"I could catch up today since I'm doing office work. I've already put together my orders for the day, plus a few extras, so I have enough arrangements on display for any last-minute call-ins."

"Sounds good. How about I pick up something, then come to you? That'll save you some time."

"You're an angel."

"I know," she says with a laugh. "I'll see you soon."

We disconnect the call, leaving me feeling lighter, knowing I'm going to have some girl chat time. I haven't had the opportunity to catch up with girlfriends since falling pregnant with Poppy. There was a playgroup when she was little, but the other moms seemed to pity me —which I didn't need or want. I found it difficult to bond with them, so I kept my distance. Once she started school for Deaf and Hard of Hearing children, I took over the shop from Gramma, which didn't afford me the opportunity or time to catch up with other school moms. I get stuck into my work, so I don't feel I have to watch the clock while Sam's here.

The bell over the front door tinkles, alerting me to someone entering my shop and forcing me out of my small office. I put on my best welcoming expression for the potential customer only to find Sam holding a large paper bag filled with what I hope is our lunch. We squeal in happiness, moving forward simultaneously to hug. We pull apart to spend a moment taking each other in. It's been just over four weeks since the reunion and Sam's bump has become more prominent.

"Are you going to tell me about this and why I couldn't say anything at the reunion?" I gesture toward her baby bump with my chin.

"I've been dying to talk to you about it. You're probably the only one who'll understand." I nod because I get it. I was in her shoes when I found out I was pregnant. None of my friends could relate to my situation and weren't interested.

"Come through. We can eat in my office. The space is small, but we can make it work."

We get ourselves settled. Then Sam pulls out the delicious-smelling food from the paper bag she was carrying. The first few moments are silent as we dig into the chicken and avocado paninis Sam chose for our lunch today.

"Come on, girl, spill. How many weeks along are you?"

"I've just hit sixteen weeks, so I'm feeling quite good. Unfortunately, I had terrible morning sickness which seemed to last all freaking day."

"I hear ya! I was the same during my pregnancy. Felt great during the second trimester, then started getting tired easily during my third trimester." It feels like such a long time ago, yet it seems like it was only yesterday. It felt amazing to be growing a human inside my body. "Do you want to talk about the father?"

Sam sucks in a deep breath before shrugging. "Not much to tell." She wiggles in her seat, looking away from me. "We'd been on and off for a while. Then, when I got pregnant, he wanted me to get rid of it. I couldn't do it, Cass." I can only nod because her story sounds so similar to mine. "He wasn't interested in continuing the relationship if I didn't have an abortion—he's not interested in being a father. I guess I'm on my own." She shrugs.

"He sounds like a real douche. He's certainly not someone you would want in your baby's life." He sounds exactly like Jake. "You've made the right choice for you, Sam. If he's not prepared to join you in this experience, then it's his loss."

She nods. However, I sense she's not convinced. "I know. It would just be nice to have a partner who's as invested in this baby as much as I am." She looks up at me with glassy eyes.

"I understand. I was in the exact situation you are in now. That's why I moved home. I needed help physically, emotionally, and financially. I couldn't have done it without Mom."

"My sister wants me to move in with her so that she can help. I'm seriously considering the offer. But I also need to get out of corporate. I can't put in the long hours expected with a baby on the way. Then, after the bean is born, I want to spend some time at home with him or her."

"What type of work do you do in corporate?" I take another bite of my delicious lunch.

"A bit of this, a bit of that. Anything from office organization to financial stuff." She shrugs.

Oh my gosh, could Sam be the answer to my prayers? I wonder if she'd be interested? I have nothing to lose by asking.

"I'm looking for someone at the moment who can take over running the office side of things. It's taking too much time. I need to focus on designing and constructing the arrangements and meeting with clients." I'm excited about the prospect of offloading the office stuff I hate so much. My passion is working with flora and balloons. "I'm not sure I can pay what you're earning in corporate, but it would be fewer hours, with only four days a week."

Sam's face lights up. "Are you offering me a job?"

"Uh, yeah. I'm offering you a freaking job." I can't keep the excitement from my voice. "Do you think you'd be interested?" I have every finger and toe crossed, hoping she says yes.

"Hell yeah. I'm interested. I'd have to give notice where I work, but I could start immediately after that." She pauses, looking around my office. "What about the time I'd need off when the baby's born? I

wanted to have some time off before putting him or her into daycare."
She caresses her small bump.

"I could pay for some time off, but probably not as much as you
would get with your current job because you'll have been with me for
less than six months. After the baby's born, we can look at reduced
hours for a while, and you could even bring the baby into the office if
you like." I'm thinking on my feet here. "We can work it out as we go
along. You could even do some of the office stuff from home, to be
honest. Anything to make life easier for you." Which will also make life
easier for me, too.

Sam jumps up out of her chair, pulling me up before engulfing me
in a hug, her hard stomach pressing against my softer one. We jump
around like a couple of loons, me excited to have solved my time
issues, her for simplifying her life. Finally, we settle down to work out
some of the initial details, completing the employment forms, benefits,
and banking info. We finish lunch, then Sam heads back to her office
while I get stuck into my paperwork. Ugh!

––––––

"Thanks for making that adjustment. You saved my ass." It's a relief to
have the issue sorted out.

"No problem, I'll update the order and then send through a confirmation email."

"Excellent. Talk to you next week."

"Bye."

I end the call with one of my suppliers just as the bell over the door
alerts me to a new customer. It's been hectic today for some reason. I
step out of my office with a smile on my face, ready to greet whoever is
visiting my little shop. When I look toward the door, my heart drops to
my feet. *What in the hell?*

"Hey, Sia." Jake's eyes wander down my body, making me thankful
for my work apron.

"What are you doing here, Jake?" I can't keep the disdain out of
my voice.

"Aren't I allowed to buy flowers?"

"Of course you are. But this seems a little too contrived for my
liking. I haven't seen you for five years, and suddenly, since the
reunion, you seem to be making regular appearances. What's
going on?"

"Nothin', Babe." He steps closer to me. "I told you, I ain't done with you."

"Well, I'm done with you. Please leave my shop and don't come back." I cross my arms in front of me, adding an extra barrier.

"And I told you, I'm here to buy flowers." His voice has a hard edge to it.

I narrow my eyes, sensing a lie. "Who are the flowers for?"

"Mom. She's been sick, so I thought I'd get her some flowers."

My shoulders release as I drop my hands to my sides. "Oh." I feel terrible now. "What's wrong with her?"

"She has bronchitis. Had it for over a week now." I'm relieved it isn't too serious. I always liked Jake's mom. Though I was hurt she never reached out to me when I got pregnant with her grandchild.

"Well, I hope she recovers soon. Do you have an idea of what type of flowers you'd like to give her?" I remember she loved peonies.

"I dunno. What do you think I should get for her?"

"Well, if I remember correctly, her favorite flower is the peony. So I could put together a simple arrangement for her."

"Sounds good."

"It'll take me about thirty minutes. You wanna come back?"

"Nope, I think I'll wait." Ugh, I was hoping he'd leave and come back. I don't want to make small talk with him.

"Okay. I'll just collect everything I need."

I can't leave the front of my shop unattended for long periods. It's okay to step into my office to answer a quick call, but to work out the back on an arrangement will take too long. Normally, in this situation, I make the client's arrangement and chat with them about the recipient and the reason behind the gift. I enjoy hearing the different stories behind someone's choice to purchase the gift of flowers or balloons.

I step out back and take a deep breath. I don't want to have to spend any time with Jake, but I have to maintain a degree of professionalism, no matter who he is. I wish Sally were here. I hate being in the shop with him by myself.

I collect a rope-style pot, gorgeous pale pink peonies, a hydrangea bloom, a couple of flowering cabbage, and some biodegradable oasis foam. I carry the items out to the front of my store, placing them carefully on the counter. Jake's made himself at home on the stool on the opposite side. I don't bother making conversation. I always pre-soak my oasis so it's ready for use, but I have to shape it before placing it in the pot. Once that's done, I anchor one side of the pot with the flowering cabbage, then the opposite side with the white hydrangea bloom, leaving room down the center for the peonies. Cutting and trimming to get the right height, I carefully place them to fill the space between the flowering cabbage and the hydrangea. I wander out back to collect a couple of peony buds to add interest to the arrangement. I finish off the display by adding them in, then adjusting the other stems slightly, looking at it from different angles to make sure it's balanced and interesting from all perspectives.

"How's this?" I present the pot to Jake.

He looks between the arrangement and me several times before speaking. I'm worried he doesn't like it. "It looks beautiful, Sia. You're great at this." Well, I hope so. It *is* my business, my livelihood.

"Thanks. I would hope so since I rely on this for my income."

We sort out the payment; I add on an extra twenty percent as a douche tax. *Ha!*

"Can I take you out on a date tonight, Sia?" I hate that he calls me Sia. It's not my name, and it isn't cute.

"No. I'm busy."

"Busy with what?" He straightens up. "You seeing that loser, Emo Boy?"

"It's none of your business, Jake. I'm not interested in spending any time with you now or in the future. Say 'hi' to your mom, and I hope she feels better soon."

"No, I want to know. What are you so busy doing tonight?"

"I said." I pause, looking him directly in the eye. "I'm busy. It's none of your damn business."

He steps around the counter so quickly. I have no time to react. He grasps my throat, lifting me slightly, so I'm balancing on my toes. My heartbeat picks up speed. I'm honestly scared. I don't know *this* Jake. The old Jake used to have a temper, but he would never put his hands on me like this. I bring my hands up to claw at him, trying to get him to release me, but I'm not making any headway.

"Tell me, what the fuck you're busy doing tonight?" He shakes me. "And don't give me none of that attitude." He loosens his grip slightly, allowing me to speak.

"I … I'm looking after our daughter, Jake. I can't go out at the drop of a hat. I have to make plans." He releases me, and I take in gasping breaths. Reaching up, I rub my throat, which is tender from his hard grip. He leans into my space again, and I'm too paralyzed to move. I don't know what to expect when he nuzzles down into my neck, kissing the red marks I'm certain he's left behind.

"Sorry, Babe. I didn't think about that. How about tomorrow night?"

Is this guy for real?

I'm not sure what he expects from me. I've told him repeatedly that I'm not interested in a relationship with him. His recent behavior is scary, which makes me even more determined to stay away from him.

"I … I can't. I can't get a babysitter at short notice like that. Plus, I don't like leaving her with a babysitter on a weeknight. She has routines and school and stuff." Hopefully, reminding him I'm a mom puts him off.

"Saturday night then?"

"I can't Saturday night. Poppy has a concert that I can't miss."

"What the fuck does a deaf kid do in a fucking concert?" I don't want to give him any information about Poppy. He doesn't deserve to know anything about her.

"It doesn't matter, Jake. It's important to me to be there for her. I won't miss it." Especially to spend time with him.

He steps back from me, huffing out a breath, mumbling something to himself. Then, grabbing the arrangement I made for his mom, he walks toward the door. "As I said, Sia. I'm not done with you. I'll be back next week. You *will* go on a date with me. I guarantee it." He opens the door, leaving my shop before I can respond.

Tears stream down my cheeks as I begin to shake. I have to sit down so I can control my breathing before I fall. I get the sense that he's not going to leave me alone until he gets his way.

Somehow, I have to remind him I'm a package deal.

It's not just me.

I have a daughter.

His daughter.

The one *he* never wanted.

It takes me some time to collect my thoughts and feel stable enough to stand up without feeling like my jelly legs will fail me. I'm beginning to wish I'd never gone to that damn reunion and put myself in Jake's sights again.

TWENTY

-toby-

"No way, Peta. I'm not gonna exploit the Labor Day Concert to promote my upcoming album." I slash my arm through the air, gesturing my displeasure at the idea. Peta's been dying to use my guitar lessons with Poppy to our advantage. In her eyes, this is the perfect opportunity. Poppy's family has put their trust in me—a complete stranger—allowing me to work with her at *Music for my Heart*, assuming she's in safe hands. Using her in this way feels underhanded and filthy. I won't allow it. "That's the end of it. Find another way to start promoting my new album. That's what I pay you for."

"Come on, Toby. You said yourself she's a cute kid with a ton of potential. It's not gonna hurt anybody if we record your duet at the concert and leak it to social media."

I adore Peta. She works hard for me and always has my best interest at heart, but I can't agree to this, especially since she doesn't want to get permission from Poppy or her family. She doesn't even want Poppy to know anything about it, to ensure she comes across naturally on camera. I'm not up for exploiting a kid, especially one who has burrowed her way into my life as deeply as Poppy has. She brings out the protective side of me, and I'll do anything to prevent exposing her to the public and their oftentimes vicious scrutiny.

"Poppy and her family don't even know who I am. They thought I was a music teacher. There's no way they would agree to your proposal, and I refuse to do it without their permission. Forget it. Think of something else." I brush the loose hair back from my face. "What's wrong with the usual press tour? It's always been effective in the past. I don't see why we can't do the same. I don't even mind doing some behind-the-scenes footage in my studio showing me working through the songs."

Peta holds her hands up in surrender. "Okay, okay. Alright, I won't use this golden opportunity to promote your new album. I want to show your compassionate side; remind everyone that you're a great guy." Shane snickers from behind me, so I throw him the bird over my shoulder in thanks. "Would you agree to visit the children's ward at the hospital again?"

"Sure thing. I don't have a problem with that scenario because it's set up for that purpose. I'm not blindsiding anyone." Peta should know me well enough by now. I'm pretty easygoing when it comes to my promo, so long as it's all above board. "Set it up, then let me know when and where. I'll be there." I stand up, ready to leave. "Remember, I have a standing commitment every Friday afternoon. So that won't work."

"Okay. See you next week for our regular meeting."

I wave over my shoulder as I clear the doorway. "Let's head over to *Brady's* for a couple of drinks."

It's one of the few places I can hang out on a weekday where people generally leave me alone. Maybe it's because I've been a regular there for a little while now—ever since Jase introduced me to Finn, the owner. I enjoy watching the new bands on Saturday nights, and their Wicked Wings Wednesday special is a favorite of ours.

"Sounds good to me," Shane responds. We head across town toward the pub. I can already taste the wings.

Stepping inside, I can't help but think about the last time we were here with Jase and Cassia. That night certainly didn't end the way I was hoping it would. I had plans to take Cass back to my place. I was hoping we could … I don't know what I was hoping for. Yes, I do. There's no point lying to myself. I wanted to repeat our night together after the reunion. I was caught entirely off-guard that she called an end to something that had only just begun.

We locate a booth toward the back and relax. A waitress, who's so busy eyeing up Shane I'm surprised she hears a word we say, takes our order. After she steps away, Shane locks his gaze on me. "What's going on with you, bro?"

I give him a 'what are you talking about' look, which is completely disrespectful because Shane probably knows me better than almost anybody. He returns the look with interest that says, 'what the fuck, man'.

"C'mon, what's up? You haven't been yourself since the pub the other Saturday."

We're interrupted as the waitress delivers our drinks, lingering longer than necessary, hoping to gain Shane's attention. Good luck, lady. He ain't interested. She eventually gets the hint and leaves, allowing us the privacy to return to our conversation.

"I dunno. You know I had a crush on Cassia in high school." He nods. "When we reconnected at the reunion, she admitted she had a crush on me, too. I thought maybe something could grow between us, but then she suddenly went cold and shut me out. I guess I wasn't enough in high school, and I'm still not enough now." I shrug, attempting to play down how hurt I feel because I don't want to come across as a pussy. "I think she's still on and off with Jake, even though she won't admit it. He seems to be all up in her space every which way she turns."

"When I spoke to her, she said she wasn't involved with him in any way. She seemed pretty adamant." He looks away, pulling at the collar of his shirt, then looks back at me, but not directly at me. "Uh, I may have put my foot in it and said something I shouldn't have."

He immediately has my attention. "What did you say?"

He pulls a grimace. "Uh, I may have told her your crush from high school never went away, and if she's still on and off with Jake, she should be upfront with you and not mess you around."

What the actual fuck! That explains the sudden turnaround. I glare at him.

"Sorry, bro. I thought I was helping you. I didn't think I would scare her off. You want me to clear things up with her?"

I know his heart was in the right place; my brother had my back. "Nah, man. If she scares off that easily, she wasn't interested. It's probably for the best. My career isn't conducive to a steady relationship, anyway. I'm not sure what I was thinking."

Our wings arrive, halting our conversation as we pretty much inhale the food. The wings taste so fucking good, and it allows me to reassess things internally. Cass *is* the type of girl I would change my lifestyle for: slow down and stop touring so I could spend more time with her. It isn't like I need any more money. I could record an album every couple of years, then be selective about where I perform and how long I tour. Other artists do that and manage to stay relevant.

They've even found that by making themselves less available, they have greater success. But I'm getting ahead of myself. I would actually need to meet someone who wants to be with me—the person—not the me that's famous for my music. I hoped that could be Cassia.

We go over our schedule, then Shane drives me home before heading to his place. I lay in bed, reminiscing about fucking Cass here; how her body felt against mine. It was as though we were meant to fit together like lyrics and melody.

TWENTY-ONE

-toby-

PETA MEETS US OUTSIDE THE FRONT ENTRANCE OF *MERCY VALE General Hospital* with a grin that takes up almost half of her face. She's practically bouncing on her toes with delight. She lives for these PR opportunities. Because I've been locked away in my cave and not in the public eye so much these past few months, this is the first public appearance I've had in a while. Saturday will be the concert, but I refuse to let her use Poppy and *Music for my Heart* for my gain. She leans in, wrapping her slim arms around me. She's so tiny that the top of her head only comes up to the middle of my chest. "Hey, Toby. Today's gonna be great."

We've worked together for a long time, and she's like another sister to me. We often rib each other. She can be pretty sassy at times, but she's a genuine person who wants me to be as successful as possible. Our relationship has quietly built over the years; the level of trust and respect we have for each other is based on a solid foundation. Not that we don't have our moments. "I'm looking forward to it."

She steps back, gushing, "The hospital was incredibly happy to have you back again. You know how much they love you."

"You know I always enjoy coming here to play for the kids and their families. It reminds me how lucky I am." I've never had serious health issues, nor has anyone in my family. My heart breaks for the kids and families I visit here now and then.

"You and me both. You ready to make our way upstairs to the ward?" She seems to be ignoring Shane, making me wonder if they've had words. Occasionally, they clash over Peta's expectations and

Shane's need to control a situation; I often end up in the middle, being the peacemaker.

"Absolutely. Let's get this show on the road."

Shane nods, following quietly behind Peta and me as she gives me a rundown of the program for this morning, speaking quickly.

Glancing over my shoulder to check on Shane, I catch him shaking his head. "What's up?"

He looks at me. "Nothin'." He opens and closes his hand like a talking mouth behind Peta's back, as he rolls his eyes with a half-smile.

I remind Peta that Poppy and I have our last practice session this afternoon, ensuring she remembers I need to finish up here by two-thirty to make it across town for our lesson. As we step out of the elevator, we're met by the hospital's PR people who run through their expectations for our visit, reminding us of their rules, who we can record, and who we can't film or photograph. We're then led through to the ward, where we're greeted by the Registrar, who will stay with us throughout our visit, ensuring we follow protocols.

Shane tries to be as unobtrusive as possible, and to be honest, he didn't need to be here today; it's not like I'm in a high-security risk situation here.

We step onto the ward, and the smell of disinfectant and bleach immediately assaults my nose. At least the children's ward walls are a cheery yellow color as opposed to the usual beige you see in the rest of the hospital. They've also gone the extra mile, painting murals of superheroes and princesses along the solid lengths of wall. It certainly brightens the space, making it feel more welcoming. We walk past a playroom designed for younger kids and step into a room designed for older kids, complete with TVs and gaming stations. The atmosphere is one of anticipation, with half a dozen kids waiting with their parents for our arrival. A hush moves through the room as the kids realize we've arrived; smiles fill their sweet little faces as their eyes light up. I can't imagine what these kids and their families are going through, spending more of their life in the hospital than out of it. The stress on these parents as they watch their sick kids, unable to fix whatever the problem must be ... is unfathomable. Some of these kids are very sick. Like so ill, they may not make it.

"Hello, everyone! How are we all today?"

I only hear positive replies: "We're great!"; "Never been better."; "I'm fantastic."

It blows me away that they can be so unwell, yet still be so positive.

Every time I visit and spend time here, it's always been the same. They're beyond grateful for every day they have; for every minute they feel well enough to leave their bed and experience some normality in their day. It makes me feel on top of the world that I can add something positive to their day. That I can give them something else to focus on, even if it's only for a couple of hours. Scanning the room, my eyes land on a familiar face. I nod in acknowledgment as my heart cracks for him and his family. They were hoping he was in remission the last time I saw them two years ago, but here they are again. I make my way toward them, greeting them like the old friends they are to me.

"It's great to see you again, Toby." Fiona leans in to hug me, and her husband, Daniel, shakes my hand. To be honest, I'd rather not be seeing them here again. It means Mathew is unwell again, but I return her hug and his handshake before crouching down to chat with Mathew.

"Hey, Mat. How's my man?" We fist bump, and Shane steps closer to say 'hi', sharing a fist bump, too. We've gotten to know this family quite well over the last three years; we even had them come to my final concert on my last tour, complete with backstage passes. He got a real kick out of it.

"Good, man. How's your new album coming?"

"Not too bad. I should be further along than I am, but I've been distracted. I have some excellent stuff, though. You want me to play something new today?"

His entire face lights up. "Yeah, would ya? That'd be so freaking cool."

"No problem. How've you been feeling?"

He shrugs, glancing over to his parents; they're busy talking with Shane and Peta, so they're not paying any attention to us. "I put on a good face for Mom and Dad, but I'm tired, Toby. Tired of fighting this disease. Tired of seeing Mom and Dad so worried about me, spending all of their time coming back and forth to the hospital when they should be spending time with Flo and Georgie."

I reach out, grasping his shoulder, and give it a gentle squeeze. "I can only imagine how tough it is for you and them. But you know they would never not want to be here with you." I make sure I have his eyes locked with mine. "They love you, man. They want to spend as much time with you as they possibly can. When you're feeling tired, lean on them; take your strength from their love for you." I muss the little hair he has left. "I'd better say hi to the other kids and families. Okay?"

"Thanks, Toby. I needed that pep talk. I'm sorry I was a downer."

"You're never a downer, Mat. Let me know what you think about my new stuff, okay?"

"You know it. I'm your biggest fan. I'll always tell you how I see it." We fist bump.

"I know, Mat." I wink at him. "Talk later?" He smiles, lifting his chin to me.

I make my way around the room, probably spending about an hour chatting with the kids and their families. Shane and Peta also spend time engaging with them, and when the kids learn Shane was a real-life soldier in a real-life war, the questions come flying thick and fast.

Attention then focuses on me, and why we're here today, so I grab my guitar and situate myself on a stool in the center of the room. I start out playing my more familiar songs, strumming and singing the popular tunes, gradually moving toward less familiar songs, and finish with some of my new stuff that nobody's heard yet. I'm always nervous about sharing my recent work. I never know how it's going to be received, whether my fans are excited by it or disappointed.

I'm relieved to receive a positive response to my new material from the small gathering, giving me hope a wider audience will receive it well. I mean, I still have quite a bit of work to do to complete the album, and some of the songs I performed today may sound different by the time I've finished, the bones are there, and I'm happy with them so far. I'll be locking myself away with my band to begin recording them shortly, so I need to have them pretty close to being complete before then; I don't want to waste anybody's valuable time.

TWENTY-TWO

-toby-

TODAY'S OUR LAST PRACTICE BEFORE THE CONCERT TOMORROW NIGHT. First, I want to practice the song we're performing to ensure we have smooth transitions between our parts so it flows cohesively. I'm setting up my laptop when Poppy comes running in with her gramma hot on her heels. Poppy throws herself at me in her usual greeting, and I wave at her gramma as she smiles at us with affection.

"Hi, Rose." I hope I remembered her name correctly.

"Hi, uh, 'guitar'?" She says in a questioning tone, signing at the same time, using my sign name. I laugh in return.

"My name's Toby." I fingerspell my name.

"Well, Poppy only ever uses the sign for 'guitar' when she talks about you. I figured you had a regular name. We just didn't know what it was." She smiles warmly.

"That's okay. Are you coming to the concert tomorrow night?" I sign as I speak.

"Absolutely. I wouldn't miss it for the world. Poppy's mom will also be there. She's hoping to meet you after the concert, so she can personally thank you for the time you've spent teaching Poppy the guitar." She smiles at Poppy. "Do you know if I can purchase additional tickets? My other daughter and granddaughter will also be coming along."

"Uh, yeah. If you see Xanthe in the front office, I'm pretty sure she can sort that out for you." Well, I hope she can. I'm not sure about ticket sales. Poppy and I didn't have to pay because we're performing, though I've given a large donation to support the center.

"Okay, thanks." She signs to Poppy. "I'll be back in an hour to pick you up. Okay?"

"Yeah, Gramma. See you later." Poppy kisses her gramma, hugging her goodbye before she comes back to me. Rose leaves the room, closing the door with a click.

"Hey, Poppy. Are you concerned about the concert?"

"Why would I be concerned?" She fingerspells concerned, her eyebrows drawn low over her silver eyes.

Damn, I think I've mixed up my signs again. "Sorry. I meant ... are you *excited* about the concert?" I fingerspell excited.

The smile that graces her face is magnificent. Her eyes are alight with joy and excitement as she nods eagerly. Then she shows me she's a little nervous by rubbing her thumb and index finger together.

"It's okay to be nervous. Nerves help to keep you alert. They also help you play your best." She nods in understanding. "How's your week been?"

"It's been really great. I love having my aunt and cousin living with us now. It's so much fun playing with her every day, and she likes watching me play my guitar."

"How old is your cousin?"

"She's three, and she's so cute." She certainly loves her little cousin. "She's gonna come to watch the concert tomorrow night with my aunt."

"Well, we'd better get on with our last practice before the big event."

"Yay. Let's get started."

We play through the song once, the way we planned to play it tomorrow night. Poppy stops, looking thoughtful.

"What if we changed this part and did it like this?" She shows me what she means. I really like the thought she's put into it. Her change makes sense, making the transition smoother. She has a genuine talent for the guitar and a unique approach to arranging music.

I nod. "I really like that. Let's do that. C'mon, let's practice it."

We practice it a couple more times until we're both comfortable with the arrangement and the adjustments we made today. We have a little time to spare, so we do another run-through of *Sweet Home Alabama*, which is coming along nicely. Poppy is a quick study. Her dedication to the guitar shows in how fast she masters the chords and melodies of each song she's introduced to. I think her family will be proud to see her performing for others so quickly after first picking up the guitar. Even though they've been privy to her daily practice, it's going to be very different for them to watch her perform on stage as part of a duet. Even though I perform for a living, in front of thousands of people, this is the most excited I've been to perform in a long time, and it's because I'm going to be performing with such an amazing young girl.

"Well, I think we're ready."

"Definitely." She nods. "Are you still wearing blue jeans with a white T-shirt?"

"Yep. You?"

"Definitely. Although Mommy will probably want me to wear something girly." She rolls her eyes in disgust. "I'll tell her it's our costume. She won't be able to change it then."

I can't help the laugh that bubbles out of me. This girl cracks me up. She certainly knows how to get her way. "I'm sure you can be very convincing." Especially since I've experienced her skills firsthand.

TWENTY-THREE

-cassia-

DAMN IT! I LOOK AT MY PHONE. ON ONE OF THE MOST IMPORTANT DAYS of Poppy's life, I'm running late. I don't want to miss her very first performance. Finishing up quickly, I rush to my car, hoping to make it home with enough time to get ready quickly. Thankfully, traffic is on my side for once, allowing me to make the drive in record time. I barge through the door, run upstairs, and jump straight into the shower. Ten minutes later, I'm out, dried off, and dressed in black linen pants and a sleeveless blouse. I wrap my ponytail up into a bun, put on a coat of mascara, and run downstairs with my sandals in my hand to find the rest of my family.

Bursting into the kitchen, I find everyone ready to go. Poppy leaps forward, grasping me around my waist in greeting. She's wearing her jeans with a white T-shirt. I would have thought she'd wear a pretty dress for the performance. I look at Mom, hoping to telegraph, 'what were you thinking?' to which she shrugs. Then, gently pushing Poppy away from me so that I can sign to her, I ask, "Why are you wearing this? I thought you might wear a pretty dress."

She smiles up at me. "It's our costume. Guitar is wearing the same." Oh, how adorable is that.

I nod, smiling in return. "Okay. Are you ready?" I'm nervous for her, but I bet she's not nervous at all.

"Yeah, let's go." She pulls on my hand, leading me out of the house with Mom, Violet, and Jasmine hot on our heels. Poppy's practically bouncing out of her skin as she grabs her guitar as we step out of the front door. We lock up the house, piling into my car with Mom in the front while Poppy, Vi, and Jas get situated in the backseat. I had a car seat installed for Jas once my sister moved in with us. I figured it would make life easier than transferring one car seat between our cars.

Arriving at the venue, Poppy quickly jumps out of the car, ready to take off inside. I manage to grasp her shoulder, gaining her attention. "I wanted to tell you how proud I am of you, Poppy. I'm excited to be watching you on stage doing something you've wanted to do for such a long time. I love you so much, Baby Girl."

I hold her close, hugging her tight as I breathe in her little girl strawberry scent. I feel unexpectedly emotional about this milestone in her young life. When the specialists first told me she was profoundly deaf, never in my wildest dreams did I imagine a future for Poppy which included her playing guitar at a concert in front of a couple of hundred people. This is a dream come true for her. At only seven years of age, she's made it happen. I'm in awe of her. I marvel at what the future holds for my little girl with determination so strong and goals so solid she lets nothing stand in her way.

She pulls away from me, excitement all over her angelic face. "I gotta go, Mommy." She kisses me, then grabs her guitar to make her way to where she's supposed to be. I stand watching my baby go until she disappears through the doors. I'm not sure how long after that I stay lost in my thoughts of how grown up my baby has become. It's not until Mom and Violet embrace me on either side that I manage to tear my eyes away from the building.

"My baby's not a baby anymore," I whisper, more to myself than anyone else.

Mom squeezes my shoulder. "No, she isn't. She's growing up and taking life by the horns. Heaven help us when she becomes a teenager."

Her statement is enough to send the three of us into a fit of giggles, making the tears that had welled in my eyes fall onto my cheeks. Once we've settled ourselves down, we walk inside to find the auditorium. A young man greets us at the double doors, offering earplugs for the audience members to protect our ears because the music will be loud. We each accept a pair, then find our seats inside. Unfortunately, our seats are toward the back, as Mom swapped out our original seats to have four seats together. It's okay. I'll sneak down to sit on a lower step so I can record Poppy's performance on my phone. There will be fifteen acts tonight—Poppy is number eleven, so I have a while to wait until I see my little girl.

I take the opportunity to ask Violet how she went today. She had plans to return home to grab some more of their clothes and some toys for Jasmine.

"Ugh. Don't ask. I don't want to ruin our night out." Violet sighs heavily.

"What happened?" Vi and Mom share a look. Violet looks like she wants to punch something, or maybe someone.

"He wasn't going to be home, so I thought it'd be safe to collect some of our things." I nod because I already knew this part. "Well, the good news is he wasn't home. The bad news is there was another woman's clothes hanging in our closet and filling my drawers. All of my stuff had been dumped on the guest bed."

I'm pretty sure my jaw hits my knee. "What in the hell is that man thinking?" I reach over to grasp my sister's hand in a show of support as the lights in the room dim. Xanthe and her husband, Louis, take to the stage. A spotlight shines down on their proud, smiling faces as some people applaud, while others wave their hands in the air.

Louis speaks as Xanthe signs for the audience. "Welcome to our Labor Day concert, ladies and gentlemen." More applause and hand waving greet him. "When Xanthe and I first had the idea to create a space for Deaf and Hard of Hearing kids to learn how to dance and play music, we never imagined how successful it would become. It's been a dream of ours for a long time to bring the joy of music to everyone. Making music accessible no matter whether you are a hearing person, a hard of hearing person, or a profoundly deaf person is a goal that we can proudly say we have finally achieved." More well-deserved applause and waving fills the auditorium for the pair who have brought so much joy into the lives of all these kids and their families. "Ladies and gentlemen, we have quite the lineup for you tonight. A special guest is accompanying one of our students in her debut performance. So, keep an eye and an ear out for that special treat." A hum makes its way, like the build of a slow wave, through the audience. "Without further ado, please welcome our first performer, Adelaide Scott, dancing to Lady Gaga's *Poker Face*." Wild applause breaks out through the auditorium in welcome for the teenager, dressed in a teal outfit complete with black ankle boots, reminding me of the famous video.

As the evening progresses and performers come and go on the stage, my arms become sore from waving, my feet tingle from all the stomping, and my face aches from smiling so much. The happiness that shines out of each performer is contagious. I challenge anyone here tonight to walk out of here not feeling blessed to have witnessed such talent and utter delight. The tenth performance of the night is finishing up, so I gesture to Mom and Vi that I'm going to head down to sit on the steps to record Poppy's performance. As I'm getting situated, I glance across, spotting Kate and Oliver in the row adjacent to the step I'm sitting on. They're deep in conversation, so I'm unable to catch their eye. The lights change, indicating that the next performer will be coming on stage, so I get my phone ready to record, pressing the button to ensure I don't miss a single thing.

Poppy steps onto the stage holding her guitar. Her cheeks lifted high as a smile fills her beautiful face. She must feel the vibrations of everyone's feet stomping on the floor throughout the auditorium. My heart fills my throat. It's difficult to swallow down the emotion I'm feeling seeing my Poppy on the stage, standing proudly in front of a packed house for the very first time. Not one single ounce of nervousness. She takes her seat, then looks off to the side of the stage she just stepped out from. I guess her guitar teacher is about to join her. I zoom my camera out so I can capture Poppy *and* her guitar teacher as he enters. As a man steps out, it takes a moment for my mind to register who it is. My heart, which had taken up residence in my throat, has made its way down to my toes as the bottom falls out of my stomach while I fight for breath.

Toby Summer.

The Toby Summer.

My high school crush and famous musician, whom I hooked up with mere weeks ago, is *my* daughter's guitar teacher.

This has to be some weird cosmic joke.

How can this be?

Seeing him walk toward my daughter with a proud smile on his face to match hers is surreal—they obviously share a solid friendship. I think back over all the conversations I've had over the last two months with Poppy about her guitar teacher.

My stomach rolls as I remember ... oh my god! She wanted to ask *him* to be her daddy! She said that once I met him, I would want him to be her daddy, too. A nervous giggle escapes me as I think how right she was. I'd love for him to be her daddy—how crazy is that? He takes the seat next to Poppy. They both situate their guitars, with matching colored strings, against their bodies. Poppy looks so small next to him, and she hasn't stopped smiling at him, just as he hasn't stopped smiling at her. Then, with a wink, they begin to play together ... and it's magic.

Beautiful, soul-filling magic!

As I watch my daughter pause her playing to sign the chorus while Toby continues to sing and play, my face heats with the memory of his hands on my body. His fingers coaxing me toward completion, his whiskers close to my ear as his deep voice whispered words of encouragement. It takes a Herculean effort on my part to remain focused on Poppy's performance while keeping my phone steady for the recording. I sit, absorbing their rendition of *Love Me Do*, tears filling my eyes as I watch my daughter discover a love for performing that I hope will stay with her forever.

As the song comes to a close, the audience stands, stomping their feet with abandon for the two entertainers on the stage. I know a lot of it is for Toby. He's obviously the special guest Louis mentioned at the beginning of the evening. Still, I also know in my heart that Poppy shone in her debut and deserves the show of appreciation. She worked damn hard to get that song perfected for tonight's show—she did such a fantastic job. As the crowd applauds the two, they stand, hold hands, and bow—all the while smiling at each other. Their bond is plain for anyone to see, and I now understand why Poppy was keen to ask him to be her daddy. It's clear that Toby cares for and respects her—a connection beyond that of teacher and student.

They both seem to really admire one another.

They leave the stage while people return to their seated positions, so I turn to head back up to my family. As I do, I catch Kate's eye. She smiles as she waves at me. She looks back and forth from me to the stage and back again; I see the moment that understanding dawns on her. Her expression changes as she tips her head in acknowledgment.

I have to face Toby after the show.

He's going to find out I'm a single mom, and that Poppy is my daughter.

The daughter I never told him about.

I don't know how I'll make it through the last few performances without being sick. I'm light-headed at the thought of the conversation we're going to have. I only hope he doesn't make too much of a big deal out of it in front of Poppy.

Joining Mom, Vi, and Jas back in my original seat, they excitedly congratulate me on Poppy's performance—as if I had anything to do with it. I'm not even certain where she gets her talent from; it certainly isn't from me. Vi makes some off-hand comment about how hot Poppy's guitar teacher is while Mom looks on with a knowing smile. She knows Poppy wanted to ask Toby to be her daddy. She's met and spoken with him a couple of times; even hinted that Poppy had good taste in her choice of a daddy, but I don't think Mom truly knows who he is.

It's then I note the change in Vi's expression. She places her hand on my arm, leaning in close to me as we watch the video I recorded on my phone. "Um, isn't that Toby Summer? *The* Toby Summer. Didn't you go to school with him?" Her eyes widen as she remembers our teenage discussions late at night when we were supposed to be sleeping. "You had the biggest crush on him in high school, but you kept dating that douche, Jake," she whispers. A wide smile spreads across her face, and then she looks at me knowingly. "Wow. Just wow." Is all she says as she slumps back into her seat, still smiling at me. Wiggling her eyebrows up and down, she slaps her thighs. "Well, I think our night has just become a whole lot more interesting, Mom."

Mom looks completely confused. "Why? How do you know Poppy's guitar teacher?"

"Um, we went to high school together. We were in the same music class."

"Oh, well, isn't that nice. What a coincidence that he's the one teaching Poppy how to play the guitar."

"You said he wasn't a music teacher, that he said he was 'competent' and enjoyed working with Poppy." Mom nods while Violet laughs. "He's not just 'competent', Mom. He's a successful and very famous singer-songwriter."

All Mom can manage is a simple 'oh' as she nods her head. I don't think she fully comprehends the magnitude of Toby's fame or how amazing it is that he took time away from his work to teach our Poppy the guitar.

That guitar she has—*is his!*

He's the one who's gone over and above to provide Poppy with every opportunity to succeed in pursuing her dream of playing guitar. I have a whole new level of respect for him while simultaneously feeling terrible that I assumed he would reject Poppy because she's deaf.

Obviously, that wouldn't be the case at all.

I wonder how he's going to react when he finds out that Poppy's *my* daughter. I struggle to contain my nervousness for what's going to happen after the show's over—I have no hope of concentrating on the final performances of the night. As the concert finishes and all the performers return to the stage to take a final bow, my back aches from the tension gripping me from the inside out. Within the next few minutes, I'll come face to face with Toby, and my truth will be exposed.

We make our way out of the auditorium, walking toward the meeting place we prearranged with Poppy. My nerves are shot and my legs feel like jelly. I'm having trouble keeping my breaths even. Looking around, I spot Poppy at the same time she spots us. She runs toward us, leaping into my arms.

TWENTY-FOUR

-toby-

THAT PERFORMANCE WAS PROBABLY UP THERE WITH MY MOST memorable to date. Playing alongside Poppy was ... *amazing*. Amazing isn't enough to describe the feelings that performance with her evoked in me. I was unbelievably proud of her. It was an honor to be the one playing beside her for her debut.

Waiting in the meeting area with Shane and Poppy, Kate, Oliver, Mom, and Dad quickly come out of the auditorium. After I told Kate about Poppy wanting to become a kindergarten teacher, Kate's been itching to meet her. They walk toward us en masse, broad smiles on their faces. Hugs and pats on the back are gifted all-around in greeting before I get down to business introducing Poppy to my family. These are the most important people in my life, and I'm introducing them to someone for whom I have a lot of respect.

Kate's the first to step in to hug Poppy and tell her how much she loved her performance. The rest of my family steps in to greet Poppy and tell her how amazing she is. I interpret by signing on their behalf as people steadily file out of the auditorium.

Poppy looks up, taking off at the speed of light—she must have spied her family. I try to keep her in my sights, but there are too many people between us. The six of us stroll forward in the direction Poppy went. People stop me, congratulating me on my performance, but I'm short with them because I want to get to Poppy. I spot Rose smiling down at someone, so I follow her line of sight. She's fondly watching a woman crouched down, hugging Poppy tightly. She stands as Poppy wraps her legs around her, holding on tightly. Poppy waves at me over the woman's shoulder, who I assume is her mom.

Poppy directs her mom to turn around, and as she does, her face comes into view.

Everything around me stops.

All sound vanishes.

The breath in my lungs expels in a gush.

I shake my head, closing my eyes, hoping when I open them again, the person I see isn't the person I just saw. I open them slowly, hoping that my eyes deceived me. Looking directly at her, our eyes lock for a moment as she tucks her luscious bottom lip behind her teeth. She's struggling to make eye contact with me, her eyes darting between my family and me. Her delicate eyebrows slash down low over her steely eyes as she slightly shakes her head.

If she thinks I'm going to pretend that everything's fine between us, she has another thing coming. I'm furious with her, but more than that, I'm hurt. She never told me she had a daughter. As I run through our previous interactions, I *know* I didn't miss any clues. Even when I discovered the doll's arm in her purse, she brushed it off as belonging to her niece.

She obviously didn't trust me with her truth.

My family steps as one toward Poppy's family as my senses come back online. Kate's clearly excited that Cassia is Poppy's mom, as she hugs them both tightly, as though they're best friends. Which, to my knowledge, they're not.

I tilt my head. "Cassia."

She nods slightly. "Toby."

Rose steps into me, surprising me with an embrace. "Hello, Toby. Thank you so much. That was just wonderful. Wonderful to see Poppy so happy while in her element up there with you. It was amazing," she gushes as she signs.

"It was my privilege, Rose. It's been fantastic working with Poppy; to watch her grow. Her determination and grit are inspiring." I sign as I speak. I want Poppy to know that I admire her determination.

Rose steps back. "I believe you already know Poppy's mom, Cassia." I nod. She then directs my attention to another woman holding a toddler. "This is my eldest daughter, Violet, and her daughter, Jasmine."

I reach my hand out to shake Violet's hand. "Nice to meet you, Violet." Smiling at Jasmine, I speak directly to her, "Nice to meet you, too, Jasmine." She giggles, tucking her chin into her chest so she can burrow further into her mother's embrace.

I return Rose's gesture as I introduce my family. While they all engage in the initial getting-to-know-you conversation, my eyes never leave Cassia. She doesn't even look at me, and my temper boils. Past teenage hurts rising to the surface, reminding me I wasn't good enough back then, poking at the scabs, suggesting I'm still not good enough now.

Looking between Cassia and Poppy, I'm stumped as to how I missed the resemblance. Poppy's the spitting image of her mother, right down to the gray eyes. Mind you, Poppy's gray eyes are on the lighter side, more like silver, while Cass's eyes are darker, more like storm clouds. She looks my way, catching me watching her with her daughter. Cass smiles timidly as she places Poppy back on her feet before moving closer to me.

She lowers her voice to keep the conversation private. "Um ... I don't know what to say. I had planned to thank Poppy's guitar teacher for everything he's done for her, but never in my wildest dreams did I imagine that person to be you." Her eyes dart away, checking to see if anyone's paying any attention to us. "Toby ..."

I shake my head, stepping back, putting space between us.

There's nothing she can say to me to make this situation better at the moment. I'm too caught up in the fact that she kept such an important secret from me. Perhaps I had no right to know about Poppy for the short amount of time we spent together, but even before that, she kept her secret when catching up at the reunion.

Isn't that something you share when people ask what you've been up to for the last ten years?

She steps forward again, placing her hand on my arm. The sensation burns through my skin, shooting sparks up my arm before heading down to my dick. I'm frustrated that my body still reacts to hers in such an acute way. Obviously, my dick hasn't got the memo that we're pissed at this woman.

"Toby, let me explain. Please."

I'm at war with myself. Do I want to know what could possibly be her excuse for not sharing such important information with me? Or should I walk away, never to look back, protecting my heart? But, in all honesty, it's like shutting the gate after the horse has bolted. It's already too late; I'm already too invested—in her and her daughter.

I'm fucked.

Completely and utterly fucked because I know, without a doubt, that I'll allow her to explain. Just not here. Not in front of my family and hers. Not in front of Poppy, whom I adore; how could I not?

"Not now. Okay?" My voice is low and firm as I indicate with my eyes and head that there are too many people around us. This needs to happen in private. It's something that needs to be sorted out between the two of us.

"Okay." She swallows as she nods. All I can imagine is her swallowing around my cock and how it felt as her throat tightened and released around my shaft. "But Toby ..." She waits until she has my attention. "Thank you for everything you've done for Poppy. The guitar, the strings, the program, your time and patience with her. She adores you and looks forward to your Friday afternoon sessions."

I nod stiffly. "You're welcome. I adore her, too. Her dedication to the instrument has been inspiring."

Cass smiles then, and it's everything to me. Poppy has her smile. Her positive energy. Though Cass's has dimmed somewhat since high school, it's still there, lying in her depths. "I'll call you. If that's okay?"

"Sure." I feel the need to put her at ease, so I offer her a small smile, which does what I hoped. Her shoulders drop, and she appears to relax slightly.

Cass turns back toward our families. "Well, it's getting late. We'd better get our superstar home to bed," she signs, as she talks for Poppy's benefit. I love that she doesn't exclude Poppy from the conversation.

"Aaaaah, Mommy. Can we at least go for ice cream to celebrate my performance? Can we? Please." She has those same begging hands and puppy-dog eyes she used on me to get me to teach her the guitar. She's one gifted kid at manipulating people to get what she wants. I'll be shocked if Cass can resist.

She looks up and around at all of us, rolling her eyes with a beautiful smile on her face. "Oh, okay. Come on then. Let's go."

Poppy jumps up and down in delight, punching the air to celebrate her success. "You'll come, won't you, Toby?"

Ugh, what? How did I become part of the celebratory party? Poppy leans closer to me, putting me under the same pressure as she did her mom. I'm powerless to resist, even though I don't feel up to spending any more time in Cass's company tonight. Maybe if I invite everyone along, it'll make it easier.

"Okay, Poppy, I'll come, too." I look around at everyone. "Ice cream for everyone!" Cheers go up all around, and we make our way to the exit and our respective vehicles.

Cass asks, "Everyone familiar with *Brain Freeze*? It's Poppy's favorite ice cream shop." We all nod. You'd have to live under a rock not to be familiar with the place. It's only the best ice cream shop in the city. We all get into our vehicles, making our way to Poppy's favorite ice cream shop. This is the Saturday night of a rock star!

I get in the car with Shane, drop my head back against my seat, blowing out a long breath. I can sense Shane's eyes boring into the side of my head.

"Well, that was fucking awkward." He rubs his hand over his cropped hair. "Did you know Cass was Poppy's mom?"

Without lifting my head from the seat back, I turn to glance at Shane. "Nope."

He bursts into laughter. I'm not sure what's so damn funny.

"Only you, man. This shit could only happen to you. What are the fucking chances that the only time you decide to teach a kid you don't even know from a bar of soap how to play the guitar, she's the daughter of your high school crush?"

It's unbelievable, is what it is. What *are* the fucking chances?

Shane pulls himself together, starts the car, and we make our way to meet everyone for ice cream. "You realize I haven't had a chance to vet this place or book it out, so you're not bothered by fans?"

"Yeah, I know. Sometimes it's okay to be spontaneous. We'll manage."

We all arrive within moments of each other, moving into the shop together. The girls lead the way, with me, Shane, and Oliver following close behind. My eyes automatically lower to check out Cass's ass in those black pants that hug those sweet globes I had my hands all over mere weeks ago. Everyone orders their favorite selection and I pick up the tab—even for my billionaire brother-in-law, Oliver. Ha!

I make sure to keep at least one or two people between Cass and me at all times. I don't want to get into anything with her in front of our families. I don't want to spoil Poppy's big night or our celebration of her debut performance.

My phone lights up with a text from Peta.

PETA

I thought you said I couldn't use tonight as PR for your new album.

ME

What do you mean?

PETA

I mean, check out whose images are trending across
social media as we text

I switch out of my text messages to load my favored web browser.
Typing in my name before clicking across to images, my stomach falls
to the floor as I let out a curse—image after image of Poppy and me at
the concert tonight. Videos of our performance are trending. I feel sick
to my stomach, my hands shaking with pent-up rage. I switch back to
my messages.

ME

What the fuck, Peta?

PETA

I had nothing to do with it

Don't look at me

But I'm not gonna say sorry it happened

This is great for you

ME

Get them taken down

I don't care how much it costs

I'm fucking fuming. Shane notices the change in my mood and
quietly steps closer to me to check out the problem. I show him my
search results, and he sucks in a breath.

"I thought you told Peta to leave the concert out of any PR?"

"I did. She says she had nothing to do with it."

"And you believe her. She'd do anything to advance your career.
You know this." His expression is one of disbelief that I'm taking Peta's
word about this.

"I believe her. I trust her, man. She respects my decisions."

He raises his hands in surrender. "Okay, man. If you say so."

"I say so. There were a couple of hundred people in the audience.
Any one of them could have taken that video and those photos and
shared them on social media. What other people do is out of our
control. You know this."

He rubs his hand over his cropped hair. "Yeah, I know." I know it irks Shane when he doesn't have complete control over situations.

I should warn Cass and her family that Poppy's performance has gone viral. They need to prepare for the onslaught of attention that's about to come their way. Whoever uploaded the images and video named Poppy directly, meaning there'll be no escaping the spotlight for her. Moving closer to Cassia, I lightly touch her elbow to gain her attention. "Can I talk to you quickly about something that's just come up?"

She looks around. Her eyebrows slashed low as she tries to make sense of the fact I want to talk with her now, but agrees. I gently guide her away from the group.

"Look, I've just been made aware of a situation involving Poppy." Her body goes rigid as she pulls her elbow away from my touch. The best thing to do is to show her the images and video that's gone viral. I take out my phone to show Cass the search results. "I'm really sorry, Cass. I never intended to put Poppy in the spotlight like this. I've already asked my manager to get the images taken down. Unfortunately, they've already been shared hundreds of times, which will make it very difficult to remove all evidence of them."

Her hand covers her mouth, eyes wide, as she looks at my screen in what I can only imagine is horror. But when she drops her hand, her lips are spread wide. "Oh my gosh, Toby. Poppy will think this is totally awesome."

Um, what!?

TWENTY-FIVE

-toby-

I EXPECTED HER TO BE FURIOUS, DEMANDING I GET EVERY LAST IMAGE removed. "But the photographs and video name Poppy. Even though it doesn't say her last name, it says the concert's venue. It won't take much for someone to put two and two together to find her. This could be bad, Cass. I don't think you understand the gravity of this situation. Someone could take a liking to her and attempt to kidnap her. She could be in danger because of me." I brush my hands through my hair in agitation. I'm having trouble standing still. I need to pace, to smash something.

She places her hand on my arm again to draw my attention back to her. That sizzle gets me every time. "Toby, calm down. I think you're overreacting. Nobody's gonna try to kidnap Poppy. She'll get a real kick out of seeing her video going viral. Surely that's gotta be good PR for *Music for my Heart* and for you?"

I can't believe how flippant Cass is being. "Well, yeah, but PR, no matter how good, should never happen at the expense of a child without their permission. Poppy's a really cute kid. What if someone takes an unhealthy liking to her, Cass? I couldn't live with myself if something happened to that little girl. I fucking adore her." My heart's pounding wildly in my chest cavity. My adrenaline is coursing through my system, its fight or flight response kicking in. Anxiety fills every pore. I want to punch myself in the face for bringing danger directly to Poppy and Cass's door.

Before I can react, Cass has her arms around my torso, pressing her body against mine. "Toby, it'll be okay. I'm not sure why you're so worked up about this, but I don't think anything bad will happen. Take a breath."

Wrapping my arms around her, I tighten our embrace, kissing the top of her head. "Social media can be dangerous, Cass. You don't know what sickos are out there or what they'll do." I smooth my hand up her back, grasping her nape. "It's okay, though. I'll have Shane watch over her. At least until I feel comfortable that nothing's gonna happen to her."

She pulls back, studying my face closely. She must see my determination, my unshakeable resolve to keep Poppy safe because she nods once in acquiescence. Her agreement makes me feel marginally better, releasing some of the tension from my muscles. Only then do I notice the position I find myself in with Cass while both of our families look on. I quickly drop my hands and step away from Cass. It feels almost painful to disengage from her physically, but she doesn't want me in that way. I can't keep putting myself in a situation where I'm constantly rejected—it's too painful.

I need to speak with Shane about the changes to his schedule. I'm making my way over to him when I feel my phone buzz.

PETA

I have my guy working on removing as many of the images as possible

Don't expect miracles

ME

Thanks Peta

PETA

No problem

Still think it's great PR for you though

Of course, she thinks that. As my manager, it's her job to put me front and center of as many people as possible as often as possible. I know I make her life difficult by enforcing certain limitations on her. We've had many heated discussions because of those limitations. I remember the huge argument I had with her when I helped Kate work on the *Parkerville* house renovation. I thought she was going to quit on me; that was probably our biggest disagreement to date. She thought my fans had every right to see me sweaty, dirty, and shirtless. I disagreed.

I stand next to Shane. "I'm gonna need to change things around a bit with your schedule." He nods thoughtfully. "I want you to keep Poppy safe. These images could draw out any number of crazies. I don't want anything to happen to her because of me."

"If anything happens to Poppy, it won't be because of you. It'll be because of whoever took the fucking images and uploaded them to social media without thought or consideration for the little girl." He seems as pissed about the whole incident as I am, and that's saying something. "Of course, I'll keep an eye on her. No problem, but what about you?"

"I'll be fine. At the moment, I'm stuck in my studio most of the time. I only go to Poppy's Friday lesson, our regular meeting with Peta, and my parents' place on the weekend. No biggie." I shrug.

He nods thoughtfully. "Maybe we should get someone else on you while I'm on Poppy. I'd feel better."

"I don't need anyone, Shane. Honestly. If I have to go anywhere, we can work something out. Okay?"

He reluctantly agrees.

Cass gains everyone's attention. "As wonderful as this evening has been, it's time we get this superstar-in-the-making home to bed."

I'm the first to step forward to say goodbye to my amazing duet partner. "It was a privilege to perform alongside you tonight. It was an honor to be your partner for your first public performance. Thank you." I lean down to embrace her. When she wraps her little arms around my neck, pulling me in closer before placing a kiss on my cheek, my heart fucking melts like an icy pole. This kid is so easy with her affection, her joy, and her sheer happiness. I can't help but be affected by her.

She signs to me. "Thank you, Toby. For everything."

I can only nod in response because I'm too choked up. "See you next Friday, okay?"

Poppy nods to me before making the rounds, thanking everyone for coming and saying goodnight. I say my goodbyes to her mom and aunt, who's carrying a very sleepy Jasmine in her arms. After they've all left, I turn to my family, who are watching me like I've stolen the last cookie out of the cookie jar.

"What?"

Mom's the first to speak. "Oh, nothing! You and Cassia looked rather cozy there for a minute, and Poppy is the most adorable little girl I've ever met." Her voice gets higher in pitch as she finishes the sentence.

Kate comes up, linking her arm through mine. "You still have that crush, brother. Only now you can act on it. So why don't you ask her out on a date?"

I look at Shane. Only he knows what went down between Cass and me recently—not that he knows everything. I don't feel like spilling my guts to my sister in front of everyone, though, so I just shrug it off without saying anything one way or the other. Of course, Cass still owes me an explanation, which I'll be sure to collect.

TWENTY-SIX

-cassia-

The minute I saw Toby's face while I held my daughter after her performance, I knew ... *I knew* I'd made a huge mistake shutting him out. Now I need to make it right. I need to pull up my big girl panties and face the music. The way he worried about Poppy's safety filled my heart more than anything else he could have ever done or said. His care for her was obvious from the minute he joined her on the stage, which carried through to him agreeing to ice cream, as well as the concern he had for her safety. He's still the great guy he was in high school. He deserves an in-depth explanation of my behavior. I'm not looking forward to telling him who Poppy's father is, but he's possibly already guessed.

I was waiting to see if he would still follow through with Poppy's guitar lesson yesterday—I wanted to know if he was going to cut ties with her because of me, but he didn't.

I should have known he wouldn't do that to her.

He still showed up, working with my little girl as though nothing was amiss, showing me who he really is deep down. He also followed through with having Shane watch over Poppy. I think it's too much, but Shane's been taking Poppy to and from school, as well as to her lesson with Toby yesterday afternoon.

Knocking on his front door, my heart's beating a gazillion miles a minute—my legs are shaky. I didn't check if he'd be home, wanting to catch him unaware. I figured I'd have a better chance of explaining things if he didn't have time to work himself up about what I did, as well as how I've behaved toward him.

It's taking an age for anyone to answer the door. I'm beginning to think he's not home. I step back down the steps, looking up from the street, noticing the large glass doors to his bedroom are open to the balcony. I think I can hear him playing his guitar. Perhaps he can't hear me knocking on the door over his playing.

ME

Hi, I'm at your house

Can you please let me in

We need to talk

It seems to take ages for a response, but it's probably been less than a minute.

TOBY

On my way down

That sounded curt. I hope he's not still mad at me. Before I have the chance to contemplate his mood, the front door opens to reveal a shirtless, barefoot Toby wearing only ripped jeans sitting low on his hips, exposing that beautiful V I never got to lick. He seems annoyed I'm standing on his doorstep if his scowl is anything to go on. My idea to catch him by surprise may not work as well as I was hoping.

"What are you doing here?"

Not the greeting I would like, but I guess I have to expect it after the way I treated him.

"Uh, hi, Toby. I was hoping we could talk."

He pauses for a moment, then shakes his head. "Sure." He steps to the side, allowing me to pass. The scent of him instantly heats my blood from memories of our night together. "Is everything okay?" Even though he's pissed at me, he still takes the time to check in. I feel like such an asshole.

"Yeah, everything's okay. I owe you an explanation as well as an apology for … well, everything." I feel sheepish. Now I'm wondering if he was even bothered enough to want to know my reasons.

He gestures to the couch and as I sit; I look toward the window he had me pressed up against the night I was here. I look around the room, taking it in for the first time in the daylight. It's homely and comfortable. Not a place I would have imagined a famous entertainer, such as Toby, would live. "I'm just gonna go put on a shirt. Be back in a tick."

While he's gone, I get up to wander around the space. Looking out of the large windows, I admire the view across to the bridge. This must look spectacular at sunrise and sunset, with the colors and shadows playing across the structure. Stepping into the kitchen, memories of him carefully wiping oil over my breasts to remove the adhesive assault me. The memories make my nipples pucker and my breasts heavy. Everywhere I look in this room, there's a memory associated.

I don't know how Toby's lived here.

"You're everywhere in this room." His voice startles me. "Here as well as in my bedroom. One night and the memories won't fucking leave me alone." He runs his hands through his unruly hair, his jaw tense under his neat beard.

So he *does* feel it, the magnitude of that night. I'm glad to know I'm not alone. Maybe I should apologize first. "Toby ..." He looks at me with such interest, as though he can't wait to hear what's going to come tumbling out of my mouth. "I'm, uh ... I'm sorry."

He shoves his hands into the front pockets of his jeans. "What exactly are you sorry for, Cassia?" There's a bite to his tone, which I completely deserve.

"I'm sorry I didn't tell you about Poppy. I'm sorry I didn't give you a chance. I'm sorry I ended us before we started." I run my hands through my hair, as all of my apologies gush out in a rush. Trying to get my words straight, I pause, looking around the room. "I was protecting Poppy."

"Protecting her from what exactly?" he snaps back at me without pause.

This is the tough part to share because I've painted him with the same brush as Jake when I knew deep down he was nothing like him, but I did it just the same. I step back to the couch, taking the seat he offered me when I first arrived. He must sense the difficulty of what I'm about to share because his voice softens. "You wanna drink?"

"Yeah, thanks. Water would be great." He prepares two tall glasses of cold water, carries them over, and hands one to me. I eagerly sip the cool liquid, trying to soothe my dry throat.

Toby sits on the edge of the couch opposite me, elbows resting on his knees, hands draped between his legs. He studies me for a moment. "What were you protecting Poppy from, Cass? Because the longer you take to tell me, the longer I have to create all sorts of terrible scenarios in my mind."

"I was protecting her from rejection." I sigh. "Her father never wanted her. When he found out I was pregnant, he demanded I have an abortion." He sits up straight, sucking in a harsh breath. "When I refused, he left me. That's when I moved back home." I give him a meaningful look, hoping he remembers I *did* share some of my history with him.

He shakes his head. "I'm sorry, Cass. Obviously, the guy's a dick."

I nod in agreement. "I decided to raise Poppy on my own with my mom's help. I figured that was the end of it." I shake my head to myself as I remember Jake coming back around, claiming he wanted to be a family man, to bring our family together.

God, I was stupid. I brush my hand through my hair, then take another sip of my water, my hands shaking.

Toby moves to the cushion next to me, his knee pressing gently against mine, giving me the encouragement I need to keep going.

"I didn't hear from him for nearly two years. Then he started coming back around." I can't bring myself to make eye contact with Toby, looking at the glass in my hands instead. I wipe the condensation from the surface for something to do.

"He wanted to be a family—said he was sorry. He seemed genuine, so I gave him a chance. We started dating again, but I was reluctant to introduce him to Poppy until I was sure he was serious about hanging around." I sneak a look at Toby to find him listening intently. I wonder if he's worked out who I'm talking about. "Anyway, after a few weeks, he insisted on meeting Poppy. In hindsight, I probably should have warned him she was deaf, but I never did, for one reason or another. When he met her, he thought she was ignoring him. That's when I explained she wasn't ignoring him. She couldn't hear him." Toby leans in closer, the side of his body touching the entire side of mine. He wraps his arm around my shoulder, pulling me in tight, kissing my temple.

"He lost the plot completely. He was furious I hadn't told him, furious that the child he fathered wasn't perfect in every way. He tried to punch her in the head, but I stepped in between, taking the strike. I pushed and screamed at him until he left. He thought the punch would 'sort her out'."

Toby pulls back suddenly. "What the fuck! Who in the hell thinks it's okay to strike a child? What in the actual fuck?" His voice is getting louder, angrier. "How could anyone think Poppy was less than perfect? In every single way?" He's completely pissed on Poppy's behalf, so I place my hand on his hard thigh in an attempt to calm him down.

"He said some truly horrible things. He accused me of trying to trap him with a freak for a child. I gave him back as much as he gave me. I was furious that he couldn't see the treasure that Poppy is, while feeling devastated on her behalf that her father rejected her in such a horrible way. Her parents are supposed to love her unconditionally." Toby presses in, kissing my forehead, before tilting my face toward his. With his hands cupping my face, his thumbs wipe away the tears tracking down my cheeks. "He said he didn't want her, and since I was her mother, he didn't want me either. Which I was fine with, but I was heartbroken for Poppy. I was hopeful for her to have a father figure in her life; I wanted more for her than I ever had."

"It's his fucking loss. Poppy *is* amazing. I would be proud to have a daughter like her. Any man would. He sounds like a fucking bastard."

"Anyway, once I came to terms with everything, I sought a lawyer and requested, no demanded, he sign away his rights as her father. He happily signed the paperwork, which made me feel better knowing he had absolutely zero rights when it comes to her. I didn't want him to be able to come back into her life in the future or to have any say." I sigh. "I'm so thankful Poppy's too young to remember his visit or the subsequent argument." I gather my courage to look at Toby. "I guess you're wondering who Poppy's father is."

He huffs out a breath. "I have a feeling I already know who the bastard is, but maybe you should tell me." He brushes his hand through his hair as he looks out of the window. The tic in his jaw tells me he's bracing himself.

I whisper, "Jake. Jake's her father. We were still on and off—"

I don't get the opportunity to finish my sentence when Toby suddenly bolts up from the couch, storming over to the windows. He rests his arm on the frame, his shoulders tense, his face like thunder. "He was always a fucking asshole. Even in high school. I could never understand why you kept going back to him."

I stand up, angry at him. "Don't you dare throw my mistakes back in my face. You don't know me, my background, what I was feeling, what I was searching for."

He storms back to me, stopping mere inches from me, and getting right in my face. His anger rolls off him in waves, smashing into me. "Only because you didn't deem me worthy enough to date back then." His voice is harsh as he brushes the hair out of his face. "I wanted to be with you, Cass; I would have treated you so much better."

"You! You never gave me the time of day. You treated me like I was somehow less than. I thought you hated me!" I snap.

He huffs out a breath, gentling his voice. "I've apologized for that and explained my behavior." He looks away, glaring at the window before softening his features to look back at me. "I would have treated you with the care and respect you deserved. I may have been a teenager, but I would have been better to you than he was." He gently, carefully cups my face in his hands, using his thumbs to wipe my tears. "Let me show you now."

I freeze in place. My body locked from head to toe. I can't possibly put Poppy at risk like that. She already loves Toby so much that she wants him to be her daddy.

If we don't work out … we couldn't possibly work out … with his career, his lifestyle.

He leans forward, gently pressing his lips against mine in a tender touch. His breath caressing my mouth, his eyes locked on mine, twilight blue to stormy gray. "C'mon, Cass. Give me a chance. I'll be the man you and Poppy need."

My head shakes back and forth in the negative without my permission, my last form of defense against him. "I can't, Toby. I can't risk Poppy like that. It's not just about me and you—I'm a package deal. I have to put Poppy's needs above my own." I sob. "I'm sorry, Toby." Breaking away from him, I grab my purse and run out of his home. Making it to my car, I quickly start it and drive.

I drive aimlessly, ending up at the riverside.

I need to get myself under control before I go home, or Poppy'll know something's wrong, so I go for a walk to settle my thoughts.

The woman inside me was desperate to say yes to Toby—to beg him to be with me, and if it was just me, I would have jumped in with two feet and my eyes wide open. But … the mother in me, the protective momma-bear, can't put Poppy at risk of falling in love with a father figure, only to have him walk away when parenthood and family life are no longer what he wants—it's too scary. Her grandfather did it, her own father did it, and even her uncle's done it. Everywhere I turn, I see examples of men who don't live up to their promises, don't man up or stick it out when things aren't exciting or they're not the sole focus anymore—even the father of Sam's baby. Toby may think he wants this life, but it's not compatible with his career. Touring and performing across the country isn't conducive to a healthy family life—

I know that, and deep down, he knows it, too. His high school crush blinds him.

TWENTY-SEVEN

-cassia-

THE BELL OVER THE DOOR ALERTS ME TO SOMEONE ENTERING THE store but I have my hands full out the back with gorgeous sunflowers for a tall vase arrangement, so I call out to Sam to get the door. That woman's been heaven-sent—I don't know why I waited so long to employ someone to help with the business management side of things. I keep working on my arrangement, confident that Sam can handle basic customer inquiries after her two weeks of training until I hear a familiar male voice speaking loudly to her.

Of course, Sam knows Jake from high school, but she's probably never seen him like this. I quickly step out from the back to diffuse his temper before it gets out of hand like last time. Before I can make my presence known, I hear Jake cursing at Sam.

"What the fuck are you doing here?"

Sam's arms are crossed. Neither of them has seen me yet. "I work here, Jake. What are you doing here?"

"You fucking work here? Are you fucking with me? You've always been a trouble-making bitch!" He leans over the counter with menace in his eyes, dropping his voice. "You'd better not fucking tell Sia that I'm the father of that kid in your belly." He points at her stomach like he wants it gone.

"I haven't told her anything. I have no intention of ever telling anybody about the biggest mistake I've ever made. Don't worry. Your miserable secret is safe with me, asshole," she snaps back.

I suck in a breath as the shock of this revelation hits me.

That fucking asshole!

How many women has he knocked up and repeatedly refused to take any responsibility for? I steady myself, preparing to face this jerk head-on. I'm almost certain he won't put his hands on me in front of Sam, so I'm going to lay everything out on the table. Stepping out of the doorway, I catch them both by surprise. Sam's obviously uncomfortable with the thought of me knowing that Jake is her baby daddy as she fidgets with her shirt buttons, looking everywhere but at me. Jake continues to shoot daggers from his eyes at Sam. He finally turns toward me with a smile as if he wasn't just cursing out my friend, and employee, and the mother of his child.

"Jake."

"Hey, Sia. You're looking hot as usual." I can't believe he's speaking like that to me, in front of his baby momma, no less.

Crossing my arms in front of my body, forming a barrier, I step in front of Sam. "What are you doing here, Jake?"

"I came to follow up. I told you I'm not done with you—I meant it, Sia." Out of my periphery, I see Sam leave the front room to head back into the small office. I can't believe he's doing this in front of her.

"And I told *you*, Jake, I'm not interested. I can't believe you think it's okay to come into my shop and curse out my staff. A woman who is carrying *your* baby, then thinks it's okay to pursue me in front of your baby momma. You're a disgusting pig."

He steps threateningly around the counter, getting into my space, the same way he did last time. I suck in a breath because I thought I would be safer having someone else in the shop while he was here. Obviously, he doesn't give a shit. Stroking the side of my face, he whispers, "You jealous, Babe?"

Ugh! As if.

Pulling my face away from his hand as though it's burned me, I step back quickly, breaking physical contact with him. "Why would I be jealous? I don't care what you do anymore, Jake. I haven't cared for a long time because there is nothing between us—not for the last five years since you attempted to punch Poppy in the head and treated her as though she was less than because she's deaf!" My anger is ratcheting up. I'm finding it difficult to keep control of my emotions or the tone of my voice level. "Nothing's changed on my end, so I'm not sure what you think is going to happen here?" I wave my hand between us.

He softens his tone. "I miss you, Babe. I want you back." He grabs hold of my hips, rubbing his pelvis against my belly. "We were good together. Remember?"

Ugh. Actually, I've had much better in recent times. I try to pull away, but his grip tightens on my hips. "I'm a package deal. Remember?" I hold his eyes with my own. "The package you never wanted. Remember?"

He releases me, stepping back as though I've scolded him. "Let's just spend some time together, you and me."

"No, Jake. It'll never be just you and me because Poppy and I are a package deal. Stop wasting your time." I turn to walk away from him, hoping he gets the message to leave, but he stops me with a tight grip around my wrist, dragging me into his body.

"I fucking told you, I ain't finished with you yet. Get that through your pretty little head." He drops my wrist forcefully and pivots around, walking out of my shop. My whole body sags in relief, shaking from the exchange as Sam pokes her head out of our little office.

"Is he gone?"

I give her the side-eye because she damn well abandoned me out here with him. Where's the loyalty? "Yeah, he's gone." I spin around on her, pointing to her bump. "You wanna explain what's going on?"

She looks sheepish but is saved by the bell over the door and a new customer. I spend the next twenty minutes with my customer, who wanted to buy an arrangement for her grandparents, who are celebrating their sixty-fifth wedding anniversary. I know there are plenty of couples who have long, happy marriages in my line of work. I just don't have any positive examples in the people close to me. It always seems like it happens for everyone else, but never for me.

As soon as she leaves, I step toward the office and lean on the doorframe, arms folded, waiting for Sam to notice I'm there. After a few seconds, I know she's seen me but is pretending she hasn't. I huff out a breath, drop my hands to my sides, and take one step into the room. "Sam?"

She ducks her head. "I feel ashamed of myself. I never wanted you to know Jake was the father of this baby. He certainly didn't want to be the father." When she first told me the father of her baby wasn't interested, I remember thinking her story was so similar to mine—I never contemplated that it was *exactly* like mine.

"Oh, Sam." I lean in, awkwardly wrapping my arms around her. "You have nothing to feel ashamed about. He's the asshole who gets women pregnant, then doesn't face his responsibilities. That's on him, not you."

"But, you see, this time, it's on me." Tears track down her face. She looks utterly miserable. "I got pregnant on purpose."

I feel as though she's slapped me, and the words tumble out before I can stop them. "What were you thinking, Sam?" I realize after they're out of my mouth that I sound like a judgmental bitch. "I don't mean it like that. It's your choice to start a family, but why Jake?"

"I've loved him since high school." Shit, I feel like she just knocked me on my ass. My eyebrows shoot to my hairline, and I'm surprised they didn't fly off my face completely. "I'm so sorry."

"I had no idea, Sam." She nods, looking away from me, obviously finding it difficult to face me with her truth. "Why didn't you ever say anything when we were in school?"

"You loved him, and I know he loved you. I was an easy lay whenever the two of you had a break." She shrugs her shoulders, looking down.

"There was a reason we kept having 'breaks,' Sam. We didn't work. We were all wrong for each other, but I was desperate to keep him because it made me feel special; like I was important to someone outside of my family." Laying my teenage thoughts out like that to Sam makes me feel exposed. "You already know I didn't have a dad in my life, and looking back now, I was desperate for male attention. *Any* male attention was better than nothing in my mind back then." I look away because I feel ashamed of myself now. "I was young, insecure, and stupid back then."

Sam stands to hug me tight as we sob into each other, coming to terms with our self-imposed shame. I'm ashamed of my back and forth with Jake in my late teens, while she's ashamed for loving someone she thought I loved. Back then, in my teenage heart, I thought it was love, but looking back with an adult mind, I know it wasn't. I gesture for her to sit, then I sit opposite her, the desk between us.

"So, what happened?"

"I hadn't seen Jake since high school. Then I bumped into him in a bar about six months ago. We hooked up, and he started coming around regularly. He made it pretty clear it was only for sex, but I wanted more. I still loved him." She fiddles with a piece of paper on her desk. "I thought … no, I hoped if I were pregnant with his baby, he would stick around. It was my pathetic attempt at trying to keep him. I'm so stupid." She sobs. "He's never wanted me. It's always been you. Even now, I'm pregnant with his baby, and he still wants you."

She doesn't say it with jealousy, more in resignation that things haven't changed in all these years.

"He doesn't want me. Not really. I'm not sure what game he's playing, but I'm not interested. He didn't want me when I got pregnant. When he found out Poppy was deaf, he certainly didn't want her because, in *his* eyes, she's defective." My anger rises back to the surface just thinking about how he exploded that day five years ago. I look back at my friend. "What are you going to do?"

"Stick with my plan, I guess. I'm having this baby. I already love the bean to pieces. If Jake doesn't want to be involved, that's his right, I guess. Especially since *I* did it on purpose."

"I'll help you wherever I can, okay? You realize Poppy's your baby's big sister?" As the tears in her eyes build again, she nods, accepting our ties through family as well as my help. "You're not alone." We hug again, sealing my promise.

TWENTY-EIGHT

-cassia-

THE BELL OVER THE DOOR TINKLES, SO I LOOK UP TO FIND GRAMMA Iris in my doorway. Happiness fills me as my eyes land on her. "Gramma." I step out from behind the counter to embrace her.

"Cassia, lovely girl. How are you doing today?" She squeezes me extra tight before we release each other.

"I'm great. I thought you weren't coming in today."

"Well ... I wanted to surprise you. I thought you could take the afternoon off. Sally, Sam, and I will look after the shop for you. I know you only have one event over the weekend, and I'm sure you're already organized for it." She looks me up and down. "I've booked you a hair appointment and a pedicure—" I try to cut in, but she keeps speaking over the top of me. "No arguments. You never do anything for yourself. My treat."

I lean back in, squeezing her extra tight in appreciation for her thoughtful gesture. She's right, I never take time to do anything for myself. If I'm lucky, I'll be able to make it to Poppy's guitar lesson this afternoon. She'll be so surprised. "Thank you, Gramma. I'm not gonna say no. I can't remember the last time I had my hair done or my feet treated. What time is my appointment?"

She looks at her watch. "You need to get a move on. You have twenty minutes." I kiss her cheek, then step into my office to grab my purse and coat, saying goodbye to the girls.

"Thanks, Gramma. See you on the weekend for lunch on Sunday." I kiss her cheek again, waving over my shoulder as I step out of the shop before she answers. I'm so freaking excited for a couple of hours of pampering. I know the shop's in expert hands, meaning I can relax and enjoy the afternoon.

———

I step out of the salon, feeling like a million bucks. Gramma had organized a shampoo, highlights, cut, and blowout. While the highlights were working their magic, I had my pedicure. It felt completely decadent to be pampered for a couple of hours—I feel like a new me!

I manage to get to *Music for my Heart* halfway through Poppy's lesson with Toby. Shane's sitting just inside the doorway as I enter. "Hey, Shane, how are things?" I don't see him all that much because I'm gone by the time he arrives to take Poppy to school and I generally don't get home until closer to dinnertime.

"Hey. Good, thanks, Cass. How 'bout you?"

"Good thanks. Um, so I was wondering how much longer you're going to be watching over Poppy?" I can't believe he's still driving her everywhere, as well as watching over her whenever she's out of the house. It seems like overkill to me.

"Until Toby decides things are safe for her, I guess." He shrugs as if it's no big deal.

"And when might that be?"

"Dunno. You need to ask him. But I don't think he'll be in a hurry. He had an unpleasant experience with a stalker a few years back. He doesn't want anything to happen to Poppy."

I didn't know; now his response to the video going viral makes sense. "Oh, okay. I guess I'll talk to him about it then." I gesture toward the room Mom told me they use for the lesson. He nods and goes back to looking at whatever's on his phone. He's never been much of a talker.

I make it down to the music room and peek in through the glass window in the door. My breath gushes out of my lungs at what greets me. Toby's sitting behind Poppy, his hands over hers, showing her the correct position for her fingers on the neck of the guitar. Her head's resting against his chest as he adjusts her fingers accordingly. The smile on my daughter's face is breathtaking. The level of comfort they have together is clear for anyone to see.

I'm not sure how many minutes pass before Toby looks up, noticing me in the window. He nudges Poppy, pointing toward the door. Once she sees I'm here, she scoots away from Toby, takes off her guitar, and runs toward the door. I open it, stepping inside to catch her little body as she slams into me, both of us laughing. I set her on her feet as Toby slowly makes his way over to where we are.

"Hey, Cass, this is a surprise." He seems reserved, greeting me as he would any acquaintance. I guess I can't blame him for being guarded.

I sign as I speak, so Poppy knows how I came to be here. "My gramma surprised me with an afternoon of pampering. I finished in time to surprise my girl." I slide my hand down Poppy's hair. "I wanted to watch you practice." I look at Toby. "I hope you don't mind?"

His eyes are locked on me. "Of course not. You're welcome here anytime." He looks down at Poppy. "Wanna show your mom what we've been working on?" She nods eagerly, then heads back to where they were when I arrived. They settle in and, with the biggest smile on her face, Poppy begins to strum a song I recognize instantly. It's upbeat and modern compared to the two songs she's already mastered. It was played to death on the radio when Poppy was a year old. I remember dancing around the house to this song, shaking my ass all over the place, and making Poppy giggle like crazy. I'll have to tell her when she finishes.

After she finishes, she asks me, "Do you know that song, Mommy?"

"Of course I know *Shake It Off.* When you were a baby, I used to dance with you around the house to this song. You used to giggle like crazy. You loved it so much." She's so excited that I know the song, while Toby smiles.

"I'd pay to see that." He signs as he speaks. "You shaking that sexy ass of yours." He tucks his hands into his pockets for the last part, smirking at me. I'm thankful he didn't sign that in front of my daughter.

I glance across at her to see if she has any idea what he just said, but I think the angle Toby's standing probably blocked the movement of his lips from her view. Sometimes, she can pick up the odd word here or there by watching a person's mouth while they speak, but it's a lot for her to take in.

He smiles, rubbing his thumb across his bottom lip—he's so freaking sexy, and he doesn't even need to try. I tuck my newly styled hair behind my ear, darting my eyes anywhere but at Toby. Maybe it was a mistake to turn up here. I should be doing my best to avoid him at all costs.

Poppy signs to Toby, "Let's play all the songs I've learned for

Mommy, like a concert." Toby nods in agreement, so Poppy situates a chair for me. She regularly checks between the computer monitor and Toby as they play. Her love for him is evident every time she looks at him. It's heartwarming while being scary at the same time. I'm worried she's getting too attached to him since I'm sure he'll have to abandon these lessons at some point. When his album's finished, he'll have to tour, meaning he'll be away for months. I make a mental note to speak to Poppy about it so I can prepare her for when the lessons stop. I tear my eyes away from my daughter to watch Toby. My heart stutters to see my daughter's affection returned—he truly cares for her.

As they finish, Toby encourages Poppy to bow. I wave my hands in the air and stomp my feet as heavily as I can on the wooden floor. I walk over, picking up my baby to give her the biggest hug. My heart feels so full with her in my life; I'm incredibly proud to call her my daughter. It's the end of the lesson, so they pack everything up. I notice Poppy put her guitar in a case. "Where did you get the case?"

"Guitar gave it to me today." Now I know that Guitar is Toby's sign name, it makes more sense.

My eyes shoot up to him. "Thank you, Toby. You didn't have to do that. You've already done so much for her." I sign directly to Poppy. "Did you say thank you?"

Toby answers instead of Poppy. "Of course she did. It was my pleasure to give her a case for the guitar. After all, she *is* a professional." He signs that last part, especially to her, as he winks.

"Mommy, can we go for ice cream, please?"

Well, if I can't take my girl for ice cream on the one day I get off from work early, there's gotta be something wrong with me. "Of course, Baby Girl. Get your stuff, then say bye to Toby."

"No, Mommy. Toby can come, too. Please." Oh, boy, she's put on the puppy-dog begging eyes, which will make me look like an asshole if I say no.

"Toby's probably busy—" I don't get to finish before he butts in.

"I'm not busy at all. My afternoon's wide open, so I'd love to come for ice cream with two beautiful ladies." Poppy jumps up and down in excitement, while I brace myself to spend the next hour or so with the man who sets my body on fire and my heart into a crazy rhythm.

"Okay then. Let's head out. We'll meet you at the ice cream shop. You remember Poppy's favorite place, right?"

"Of course. But I'll come with you guys. Shane can follow in my car." *Oh, shit!* I don't know if I can be stuck in such close proximity to him, but Poppy's celebrating like crazy.

"Okay, let's go." We all make our way out of the building, collecting Shane on the way. Toby gives Shane an update on our afternoon plans. I can tell he's surprised by the turn of events, by the way his head snaps up and his eyes capture mine.

I hear ya—*I've been railroaded, too.*

Before I get the chance, Toby helps Poppy into her booster seat, ensuring she's strapped in safely with such care and attention. He then opens my door because I'm frozen in place, watching his interaction with the most precious person in my world. Eventually, we get on our way, so I use the opportunity to speak to Toby about Shane.

"I wanted to ask you how much longer you think Poppy needs to have Shane driving her around?"

"Until I feel there's no threat." Oh-kay then, his tone brooks no argument. He doesn't elaborate either, but she *is* my daughter, and I need to know what's going on.

"Shane mentioned you had a stalker a few years ago. Are you worried that person might come after Poppy?" His body tenses, including that jaw of his I love, as his eyebrows slash down, causing creases in his forehead. I don't think he's happy I know about his stalker.

He looks out of the window before looking forward again. "He shouldn't have told you about that. It's not relevant. I'm just more aware than the average person of how social media can impact your private life." He briefly glances across at me. "I feel better knowing Poppy's safe. It helps me to sleep better at night." His voice is soft, vulnerable.

Without taking my eyes off the road, I nod in acceptance, whispering, "Okay." Tightening my hands on the steering wheel, I tell him, "If you ever want to talk about it, I'm a good listener." He nods, his jaw tense. "Thank you for keeping Poppy safe."

His body relaxes into the seat as he looks out of the window. "I would do anything for that little girl." After watching them together, I believe him.

TWENTY-NINE

-toby-

WELL, HOW PERFECT IS MY AFTERNOON TURNING OUT TO BE. ICE cream with the two girls I want in my life.

I was pissed at Cassia for running out on me before I could have my say. I've gone back and forth between feeling pissed, hurt, and hopeful that she cared enough to talk to me in the first place. She's scared, and I get that. I get she feels the need to protect her daughter, but she needs to realize she doesn't need to protect Poppy from me— I'm not the enemy here. I could have bought Poppy all the ice cream in the world when she wanted me to come with them, unknowingly giving me the opportunity I needed to spend more time with her gorgeous mom.

Poppy and Cassia make their ice cream selections: peanut butter crunch in the form of a penguin for Poppy, while Cassia goes with the chocolate chip. I place their order along with mine (macadamia crunch) and Shane's (raspberry swirl). A couple of teenage girls think they're being covert as they snap photos of me on their phones while I order. Shane approaches them with our usual request—I'm happy to have a selfie with them if they delay posting the photos to social media for a couple of hours. Most people readily agree, allowing me the opportunity to enjoy whatever I'm doing without hoards of people descending on us. This time, though, I'll also ask the girls to delete any photographs they have of Poppy and Cassia. Once they agree, I pose for a couple of selfies with each girl with the promise they'll delay posting them, allowing us to enjoy our ice cream in peace.

We opt to sit outside to enjoy the pleasant fall weather we're blessed with today. With Poppy completely focused on her ice cream, I take the opportunity to study Cass with her daughter. They're very similar in appearance, but also in their mannerisms. They both light up when they're in each other's company. Their love and bond with each other is so strong; it's beautiful to watch.

"—huh?" I glance at Shane. He said something that I missed because I was too busy watching my girls.

He lifts his chin, gesturing across the road. "Jake was watching the girls from over there. You want me to follow him?"

I search around but can't see any sign of him. "He's gone now, but make sure you keep an eye out for him. I don't want him causing trouble." I'm not sure if Cass wants it to be general knowledge that Jake is Poppy's father, but it's fucking creepy that he was watching them from the opposite side of the street.

Poppy breaks me out of my head when she thrusts her ice cream in my face, gesturing for me to have a taste. I check in with Cass that it's okay with her since I'll be licking her daughter's ice cream, but she just shrugs as though it's not up to her to decide. I take a lick, making a big show of liking the flavor. She screws up her face when I allow her to taste mine.

"I don't like vanilla ice cream. It's too boring," Poppy signs one-handed. Cassia bursts out laughing as my eyebrows hit my hairline. I pass my ice cream to Shane so I can defend my ice cream choice to a freaking seven-year-old.

"It's not *just* vanilla. It's macadamia crunch. It's delicious." I make a big show of taking another taste, followed by a lick of my lips.

Glancing up at Cass, she's squirming in her seat, looking everywhere but at Poppy and me—it's good to know I have *some* effect on her. Poppy laughs, screwing up her face yet again, shaking her head in the negative. I guess she's entitled to her opinion on ice cream flavors, even if she *is* wrong. Handing my ice cream back to Shane, I tell her exactly that, eliciting more giggles from her as well as her gorgeous mom.

Once we've finished our ice cream, Poppy insists we should visit the park. She's obviously enjoying having her mom home early from work and is planning to take advantage of every minute. She looks across at me with her sweet face. "Can you come, too?"

I don't even bother to check in with Cass. I'm enjoying my time with them way too much to have her deny me. "Of course. Let's go."

The four of us walk to the park, Poppy holding Shane's hand, while Cass and I walk behind them. "You don't have to come to the park. You're allowed to say no to her."

"I know I can say no to her, but I don't want to." I nudge her shoulder with my arm. "Unless we're encroaching on your mommy-daughter time?"

"Oh, no, it's nothing like that. I do my best to make sure I get regular time with my girl, not as much as I'd like with running the shop, but whenever I'm not there, I'm with her." She tucks her hands into the pockets of her coat. "I just figured you probably have other stuff to do that's more important than hanging out with us."

I *do* have plenty to do. These songs won't write themselves. "There's nowhere on this earth I'd rather be than sharing ice cream, followed by a visit to the park with you and Poppy on this fine afternoon." I mean it, too—this is exactly where I want to be. I smile at her, then laugh at the way Poppy jerks Shane's arm back and forth as she skips her way to the park. Cass notices, too, letting out a giggle of her own. It's a rather comical sight—Shane's a big guy, yet he's willingly being yanked around by a small child.

As we arrive at the park, I step forward, picking Poppy up by the waist to run ahead with her until we reach the swings, causing her to giggle all the way. After situating her on the swing, I check with her if she likes to go high or stay low. She tells me she wants to go high, so I swing her high and higher still while she squeals with girlish delight, kicking her little legs back and forth the whole time.

Cass stands in front of her, signing like a crazy woman to hold on tight—maybe I got a bit carried away because she looks worried. I stop pushing for a bit, allowing the swing to slow, gradually reducing its height so Cass can relax. Finishing on the swing, Poppy takes off for the climbing frame.

She climbs up like a monkey, and my heart plummets to my feet as I realize I can't call out to her to keep her safe. I glance across to Cass to find she's watching Poppy like a hawk, clutching onto the lapels of her coat. I look back up, finding Poppy higher now, so I quickly climb up behind her, ready to break her fall if she loses her grip, but she makes it to the top with no mishaps. Then she proceeds to scare the absolute shit out of me by letting one hand go so she can celebrate getting to the top, throwing her little fist up in triumph. I quickly step up behind her, trapping her between the climbing frame and my body to keep her safe. We both climb down until we have two feet securely on the ground. I release the breath that had been trapped in my lungs in relief, knowing she's safe on the ground, where she belongs.

Cassia steps forward, hugging her close, before signing. "You always need to hold on tight with two hands when you climb up high."

Her little bottom lip trembles as her chin drops to her chest. "Sorry, Mommy."

She raises Poppy's chin with her finger. "That's okay, Baby Girl. Just remember next time. Promise Mommy."

Poppy nods. "Promise, Mommy." Cassia holds her close, brushing her hair back from her face affectionately, studying her. After a few moments, Cass ruffles her hair playfully, and we walk together toward the obstacle course. All four of us, including Shane, goof off through the obstacles, allowing Poppy to take the lead. She runs across the open grassed area to the next obstacle, which is quite a distance away. Other kids are playing baseball, while others are running laps around the edge of the grassy field. Chasing after Poppy, I see a kid hit a ball full-on with his baseball bat out of my periphery, then hear the distinct crack of maple against hide. As I look back toward Poppy, everything seems to happen in slow motion as the trajectory of the ball heads straight for the back of her head.

I can't call out to her to get out of the way, so I pick up speed, sprinting forward and dive, putting myself between the ball and Poppy. Twisting around, the ball collides against my shoulder, taking Poppy and me down to the ground—*motherfucker!*

It hurts like a bitch.

Shane and Cass come running up to us, dropping to their knees beside Poppy and me. Shit, I dropped Poppy when I got hit. Quickly sitting up, I check to find Poppy's okay. After Cassia's checked her over for herself, she turns her attention to me.

"Oh my god, are you okay? That ball hit you so freaking hard." The color drains from her face as the realization dawns on her that the ball should have hit Poppy. She looks back and forth between her daughter and me as tears fill her eyes. Her shaky hand comes up to cover her mouth, her wide eyes watching me as her other hand comes up to my arm where I'm holding it. Her shaky fingertips tenderly brush over my hand. Before I can brace myself, she throws herself at me, wrapping her arms around me, squeezing me impossibly tight. A grunt escapes unbidden, and she realizes she's unwittingly hurt my injured arm and quickly leans away.

Shane bends down to help me stand. I climb to my feet, feeling the effects of the impact on my arm. I bet I'm gonna have a fucking huge bruise. I try to lift my arm, but the pain is too much, so I drop it back down, holding it across my chest.

Poppy wraps her arms around my hips, burying her face in my stomach. I lightly smooth my hand down the back of her silky hair, holding her close. My heart's still beating like crazy at what just happened. In the blink of an eye, we could have lost this precious little angel.

The kid who hit the ball comes running over to us as Shane picks up the ball. "I'm sorry, Mister. I didn't mean to hit you." His wide eyes flit between all four of us, and his heavy breaths reveal his worry that we're gonna ream him out.

"That's okay, bud. It was an accident." Shane hands the kid his ball.

His body shifts, his expression changing from worry to recognition. He points at me. "Hey, you're Toby Summer. My sister has your poster on her wall."

I nod. "Yeah. I am. Would you mind keeping this between us?"

"Sure. Sure." He looks down at the ball in his hand. "Uh, would you be able to sign this for my sister?" He thrusts the ball forward.

"No problem. Are you sure?"

"Uh, yeah?" He doesn't seem sure. The ball is probably his, and if I sign it to his sister, he'll have to forfeit it. Shane keeps small photos of me on stage in his pocket for this very reason. He pulls one out, then hands me a pen.

"What's your sister's name, bud?"

"Ruth."

I sign the photo to Ruth, then hand it to the kid.

"Thanks, Mr. Summer." He walks backward, heading toward his friends. "Sorry again."

I wave him off. No point in getting mad over an accident. He's probably only about ten years old and he was thoughtful enough to ask for an autograph for his sister. Gotta give him kudos for that.

Cass still looks as white as a ghost, so I shuffle forward with Poppy still attached to me and wrap my good arm around her, pulling her into a group hug. I'm not sure how long it lasts, but I could get used to holding the girls this close. The upbeat mood has been broken, so I suggest we make our way back to the parking lot to head home. My arm's throbbing, and I desperately need to get some ice on it. Back at the parking lot, I manage to get Poppy strapped into her seat securely. "Be good for your mom. I'll see you next Friday."

"Thanks for looking after me, Toby." She wraps her little arms around my neck, kissing my cheek.

I tap the tip of her nose with my finger. "Anytime." I wink as I stand to my full height, wincing at the pain in my shoulder. Cass is standing close by and notices.

Drawing her eyebrows down low, she bites her bottom lip. "Our place is closer to here if you wanna come home with us. I can take care of your arm. Make sure you're okay."

If I were a better man, I'd say no and go home to take care of myself, but I'm not a good man because I'm going to use this opportunity to my advantage. I'm gonna take her up on her offer. I look across at Shane, catching the hint of a smirk because he already knows what my decision will be. He nods slightly, letting me know he'll take the car home, then come back to collect me when I'm ready. "You don't have to." I'm not sure how I manage to say the words with a straight face, but I'm proud of myself.

"It's the least I can do. Please. I'll feel better if I know you're okay."

"Okay. It beats going home to my empty place to take care of myself. But only if you're sure it's not too much trouble."

"Really, it's no trouble at all. I promise."

"Shane, would you be able to come and pick me up later?"

He plays along for Cass's benefit, looking at his watch, then back to Cass and me. "Sure. No problem. I'll see you guys later." He pops his head inside the car, waving to Poppy, then heads over to our car to leave.

THIRTY

-toby-

CASS HELPS ME SITUATE MYSELF IN HER PASSENGER SEAT, LEANING across me to buckle me in, putting her magnificent cleavage right in my line of sight. Her hair smells different from last time, more of a chemical smell, not the cinnamon scent I've come to expect. As she pulls back, our eyes connect and lock, charcoal to cobalt, our lips mere inches apart, breaths melding together. It takes everything inside of me to keep my good arm by my side, rather than grasping the back of her head to pull her to me so I can take her mouth the way I've been dreaming since we spent the night together. She breaks the moment when she pulls away to close the door. Walking briskly around the front of the car, she grants me the pleasure of watching her.

Clearing my throat, I thank her as we make our way to her home. I've never been there before; we didn't mix in the same circles, which was mostly my fault because I kept to myself, rebuffing her attempts at establishing a friendship. I was a stupid fool when I was a teenager.

We make our way inside the neat home, and Cass immediately switches into caretaker mode, signing to Poppy to get the medical kit. Looking around, it seems we're the only ones here. "Where's your mom?"

"Oh, well, when I found out I had the afternoon off, I let Mom know so that she could make plans. She and Violet decided to take Jasmine out to an indoor playground center, followed by pizza for dinner and maybe a movie." She gestures for me to follow her. "Come on; let's look at your arm."

I follow her into the kitchen, which includes a dining nook. "Can you lift your sleeve?"

The ball hit me at the top of my arm, so I don't think I'll be able to lift my sleeve that high, but I try.

"Just take your shirt off, Toby. I'll get some ice."

I struggle to get my shirt off in the usual way, so I have to take one arm out, then take it over my head to drag the material down my injured arm. I'm studying the bruise that's already forming when I hear Cass suck in a sharp breath. Looking up, she's right there with a bag of frozen peas, her eyes wide, but they're not on my bruised arm. Instead, she's looking at my bare upper torso. I unintentionally flex in response to her heated gaze on me, causing her eyes to snap up to mine, locking our gazes in an intimate moment. Poppy breaks it as she comes running into the kitchen with the medical kit, which I'm sure is unnecessary.

Cass immediately goes into action, assessing the bruise. "Shit, I can see the stitches from the ball imprinted on your arm." She gently presses the imprint, causing me to wince. I'm trying to be all manly, but it hurts something fierce.

Poppy drags a chair close to me on the other side and rests her head on my good arm, which I move out to wrap around her small shoulders. She's been very subdued since the incident in the park, which is unlike the Poppy I know and have grown to love. I squeeze her in close, kissing the top of her head. Cass pulls a chair closer on my injured side, carefully pressing the peas against the bruised area.

"I could have lost my baby today," she whispers. "You saved Poppy's life. I'll never be able to repay you." Her plush bottom lip trembles, and I want to take it between my teeth to bite, then kiss it better.

"I told you, I would do anything for her, and I meant it. In the short time I've known her, I've grown to care for her ... a lot—even before I knew she was your daughter." I love Poppy, but that might be too much, too soon, for Cass. I don't want to sound like a weirdo. Our eyes meet and lock again, and she nods slightly, smiling timidly. "She's been quiet since the incident." Cass nods. "Is she gonna be okay?"

"Yeah, I'll talk to her about it later. Make sure she's alright." She lifts the icy bag from my arm. "We should put some arnica on this; it'll help with the bruising." She picks through the items in the medical kit until she finds what she's looking for. Opening it, Cass gently applies a liberal amount to the bruised area, which seems to be spreading rapidly. At this rate, my entire upper arm is going to be black and blue. I'm not complaining, though, because I would rather have this outcome over the other possible one, which I never want to think about. "We'll give the ice a break for a bit, then put it on again." I nod. "Do you want some Tylenol?"

"Yes, please, if you don't mind. It's throbbing quite a bit." She rises to get a glass of water, then places two small pills in my hand along with the cool glass of water. I eagerly take the medicine, hoping to lessen the pain radiating from the site.

"Poppy, let's make some pancakes for dinner." That perks the little girl up. She jumps out of her seat to help her mom in the kitchen. I get up to help the girls, but Cass insists I stay where I am. I'm not complaining—I have the perfect view from where I'm sitting. The ladies get to work, and before I know it, they place a stack of pancakes on the table along with a variety of toppings and several flavors of ice cream. Poppy sets the table, and we all sit to eat. It's comforting to see her smiling again, the sparkle returning to her eyes.

Taking a pancake from the stack, I load it with strawberries, then drizzle chocolate sauce over the top before finishing it off with ice cream. Taking my first bite, my taste buds delight in the flavors and the light, fluffy texture of the pancake. "Mmm, these are delicious." I sign to Poppy, as I make a show of licking my lips. Cass's eyes are locked on my mouth, so I draw out the show, especially for her. We make short work of the stack in the middle of the table, after which Cass repeats the process with the frozen peas on my arm. Then we clean up the mess from our breakfast for dinner.

I don't want to overstay my welcome. I know Cass was reluctant to have me join them this afternoon, so I excuse myself to head home.

"Can't you stay to watch a movie with us?" I look up to Cass to check her reaction to Poppy's invitation. She smiles slightly, tilting her head to the side as though she's awaiting my answer.

"I can if you want me to." I look between the two as they both nod their heads. This is definitely my lucky day. Cass willingly spending time with me is something I thought I'd never have after the way we left things between us. "What movie are we gonna watch?"

Poppy jumps up and down. "*School of Rock*, of course."

"Of course." I laugh.

"Can we make popcorn, Mommy?"

"Sure. Go put your pajamas on. I'll get the popcorn." Poppy races upstairs without complaint, as Cass tells me to get comfortable in the living room after giving me the frozen peas for my arm. I situate myself on the side of the couch that will keep my bruised arm safe from any bumps or knocks, holding the peas gingerly against my bicep.

I'm lost in my head when Poppy runs into the living room, throwing herself onto the middle of the couch, before snuggling into my side. I soak up her warmth, her vitality. Breathing in her little girl scent as I thank my lucky stars, our afternoon didn't end up the way it could have. Cass steps into the room with an enormous bowl of popcorn, placing it on Poppy's lap as she sits on the other side of her daughter, kissing the top of her head and then turning on the TV to pull up the movie. As the film begins, captions display across the screen for Poppy's benefit.

We're about fifteen minutes into the movie when Poppy snuggles further into my side, so I drop the frozen peas to the floor to wrap my arm around her small body, tucking her in close. When I look up from her, Cass is watching us, her lips slightly tipped up at the corners; the love she has for her daughter written all over her beautiful face. My fingers itch to touch her, and I easily could, but I refrain. She's made her feelings toward me clear; she's not interested in a relationship with me and as much as I would love for this to be my life, to share times like these on the regular, I know it's not in the cards for me.

Rose and Violet pop their heads in to say hello briefly when they get home before taking Jasmine upstairs to bed. I wait for them to come back down to join us, but they never do.

About three-quarters of the way through the movie, I notice the little girl who's stolen my heart has slipped down to my lap; her breaths slow and steady. I pretend to be too caught up in the movie to notice because with her asleep, there's no longer a reason for me to stay. As the movie ends, I dread the conclusion of our evening. The credits roll, so I know my time is up when Cass presses pause; however, she surprises me when she turns in her seat. "Um, thank you again for today. I don't know what I would have done if you ..."

Her words trail off as she looks down at Poppy. My need to soothe her surpasses my need to protect myself from further rejection; lifting my hand from her daughter, I squeeze her shoulder, then gently caress her cheek with my hand. Her silky smooth skin presses deeper into my palm until I'm cupping the side of her face, her eyes fluttering closed as I caress the softness of her cheek. The moment between us feels deep. Deeper than any we've shared before, even the night we spent together, which was all about connecting on a physical level. Slipping my hand behind her neck, I pull her toward me and press my lips against her forehead in a barely there touch. She tilts her face upward, making it oh so easy to take her mouth, but that would be all kinds of wrong with her daughter asleep in my lap. "You don't have to keep thanking me. I would do it again in a heartbeat to keep her safe." I look down at Poppy. "You want me to carry her upstairs to her bed?"

"No, that's okay. I can manage."

"You don't have to manage while I'm here. Let me do it. Please." I implore her.

Nodding her head slowly, she relents. "Okay, thank you." I carefully adjust my position to allow me the space to scoop her up. Hiding my wince, I lift her without her waking, following Cass upstairs to Poppy's bedroom. I take in the explosion of purple as Cass pulls back the comforter and blankets, readying the bed for a sleeping Poppy. I place her as gently as possible onto her pale purple sheets, then step back slightly to allow Cass to do her motherly thing, tucking her daughter in. Once she's tucked in to Cass's satisfaction, we step out of the room to head downstairs.

I message Shane to pick me up. It would be easier to call a cab or an Uber, but the grief Shane would give me for doing that wouldn't be worth my while. Saying goodbye is the awkward part of the evening: do I kiss her like I desperately want to? Or do I keep it purely platonic, the way she wants to? Standing by the front door, waiting for my ride, I tuck my hands in my pockets to stop myself from reaching for her.

"Thanks for everything, Toby."

I wave off her thank you. "Please stop. Thanks for looking after me." I gesture to my arm, which is still throbbing like a bitch. "And for inviting me to spend the evening with you." I shuffle on my feet as I brush loose hair out of my face. "I, uh, had a really great time."

She looks surprised, huffing out a laugh. "Oh, yeah, this must have been a real highlight in your rock 'n' roll life." She tucks her hair behind her ear, her eyes skipping around everywhere but at me.

I pause, waiting for her to look at my face so I can respond. "Actually, yeah, it was. It's the best Friday night I've had in a really long time. I wouldn't mind all of my Friday nights being just like this one." Headlights shine through the window near the front door, highlighting that my time with Cass has come to an end. Her eyes widen in surprise at my confession, so I use the opportunity to lean in and cup the side of her face, pulling her forward to press my lips gently against hers. She doesn't pull away, so I press in firmer, using my tongue to lick at the seam of her lips. She opens for me, welcoming me inside her mouth. Moaning, I take the kiss I've wanted for weeks—my hand in her hair, my lips on hers, my tongue dueling with hers.

THIRTY-ONE

-cassia-

STANDING IN THE DOORWAY, WATCHING THE RED TAILLIGHTS DISAPPEAR while pressing my fingers against my puffy lips, I wonder if anyone else's kiss will ever sear my lips the way Toby's kisses do.

"What are you doing, Love?" Mom startles me out of my daze, so I quickly close the door, keeping the cold air out where it belongs.

"Uh ... I was ... uh ... just saying bye to Toby."

"Oh. I must say, it surprised me to find him here." There's no judgment in her voice, but there *is* a hint of curiosity.

Turning around, I face her, and the fear I felt from the afternoon washes over me. There's something about being in Mom's presence that permits me to let go. Tears well in my eyes from nowhere, tipping over the lower lids to stream down my cheeks.

"Oh, Mom. Where do I even start?" She recognizes how upset I am and guides me into the kitchen, sitting me at the kitchen table. Mom makes us both herbal tea before joining me.

"What's upsetting you so much?"

I tell Mom about the afternoon, from the time I left my shop until now. I'm sure to include every detail, not leaving out a single thing. All the color drains from her face as she learns how close we came to losing Poppy today. If it hadn't been for Toby's quick thinking and action ... I dread to think. Poppy was at a definite disadvantage. If Toby had been further away from her, or the timing had been different, then ...

"I need to be with my baby. I'll see you in the morning. Okay?"

575

She only nods at me. Still shell-shocked by the events of the afternoon. I ensure I lock the front door, then make my way upstairs.

I get changed into my pajamas, going through my nighttime routine, before climbing into Poppy's bed with her. She immediately rolls over, snuggling into me, as though she senses I need her close. I breathe in her little girl scent of strawberries, feeling the life inside of her wrapped in my arms and the tension finally releases from my body. Lying with Poppy safe in my embrace, I permit myself to think about tonight. Having dinner, then watching a movie with Toby felt almost … like being a family. It felt right having him here. Poppy's clearly in love with him, which Toby obviously reciprocates easily.

Maybe I could let him in.

Then, I remind myself of his career and his fame, and I can't see a way it could possibly work. I *know* he has women throwing themselves at him every which way he turns—I've seen it happen when I've watched him on television or followed him on social media.

Why on earth would he be interested in a single mother who could never really be part of all that?

But that kiss—it was incredibly intense—I could feel his blatant need for me. He asked me to give him a chance the day I apologized.

Should I?

Could I?

I look down at my sleeping daughter. She's already in love with him and I can see he feels the same way.

What if it doesn't work out?

She'd be devastated if she loses him from her life. If things don't work out between us, would he still be there for Poppy?

THIRTY-TWO

-toby-

IT'S TIME TO PUSH FORWARD WITH CASS. SHE'S NOT GOING TO COME TO me, and I know I want her and Poppy in my life from here on out. I know she's scared. From the little she's told me, I don't think she's had a man stick around in her life for one reason or another. I get the impression she's assuming things about me based on my career—that I'll be yet another man in her life who doesn't stick. She couldn't be more wrong, though. I just need the opportunity to show her.

Walking along the cracked sidewalk with the sun shining down, the closer I get to her shop, the more my heart rate increases. When I arrive out front, I breathe deeply several times to prepare myself to be rejected yet again, but I've decided I'm not giving up easily.

"Do you mind waiting out here?"

"Don't you want a witness to your crash and burn?" Shane laughs. It's great to hear him laugh, to see him lighten up, but I would prefer it wasn't at my expense. I already feel as though I'm stepping up to the gallows.

"Haha. Smart ass." I give him the bird over my shoulder.

Stepping inside Cass's small shop, the scent of hundreds of blooms infiltrates my nose. I stand in place, giving myself a moment for my eyes to adjust to the light inside.

What greets me makes my fists clench and my jaw tighten. Jake has Cass pinned against the wall with his body. I clear my throat loudly, attempting to garner their attention since the bell over the door failed to do so. Then, moving closer to them, I round the counter as Jake looks over his shoulder. When he spots me, he smirks slyly, then turns back to Cass, nuzzling her neck.

"What the fuck is going on?" I snap, sharp as the crack of a whip. I hear Cass suck in a sharp breath.

"What's it look like to you, Emo Boy?" Jake responds without turning around. His body jolts as though he's being jostled. I get the impression Cass is trying to push him away, but I can't be sure. Everything she's ever said about him leads me to believe she's not interested in a relationship with him, but then why is he here?

"Jake, move," Cass firmly states, though he ignores her, pushing his body further into hers. She clearly doesn't want him touching her. I step forward. Grabbing the back of his collar, I put all of my strength into pulling him away from her. He barely budges, but it's enough to give Cass room, allowing her to raise her arms to push at his chest as I pull at his shirt. He takes half a step away from her, glaring between the two of us.

"You two still fucking?" he spits out.

Before I can respond to defend Cass's honor, she snarls, "It's none of your goddamn business, Jake. I've repeatedly told you to leave me alone."

I step forward, getting in his face, my jaw tense, my fists ready to brawl. "You heard the lady, asshole. She's not fucking interested in you. Leave her the fuck alone."

"And I fucking told her I ain't finished with her yet," he grinds out to Cass before turning to me. "This is between her and me. Stay out of it, Emo. It's none of ya fucking business."

I step up to him. He has a couple of inches on me and probably close to eighty pounds, but I don't give a shit. "It's my fucking business because she's with me." Cass's eyes widen at my statement. I hope she catches on to what I'm putting down and plays along. "Get your filthy fucking hands off my girl." My tone brooks no argument. The bell over the door alerts me to another person entering. Glancing over my shoulder, I see it's Shane. He must have been watching through the window. He remains close by the door, holding it open for Jake and making it clear it's time for him to leave. These days, he's an intimidating motherfucker. He could easily kill Jake with his bare hands.

Jake turns toward Cass, pointing his finger sharply in her direction. "I ain't finished with you, bitch. Have your fun with Emo Boy, but you'll be coming back to me."

He turns to step past me, striking my shoulder with the side of his body, but I stand my ground. If it had been last week, I would have keeled over like a pussy after a nudge like that against my bruised arm.

"Have my sloppy seconds while you can. She'll tire of you, then come back to me. She always does." He heads for the door, closing in on Shane. He says something in a low tone that I can't hear. Shane follows him out, closing the door behind him, and returns to his position out front.

I remain standing where I am, looking out of the front of the shop for a few moments, gathering my calm. Dropping my head, I turn toward Cass when a woman steps out of the office, seemingly oblivious to my presence.

"Has he gone?"

My head snaps up at her question. I'm fucking pissed she left Cass out here to deal with that cocksucker on her own.

Cass shakes her head and huffs out, "Yeah, he's gone." She walks slowly toward me, as though she's unsure of my reaction to her. My eyes don't leave her as I hold out my hand. She doesn't hesitate to slide her smooth palm against mine, and I close my hand around hers, squeezing it in reassurance. She returns my gesture with a small smile, stepping closer to me. Then, using my hold on her, I pull her in, wrapping her in my arms.

"You okay?" I whisper.

Her eyes connect with mine, and I know what she's about to say is the truth. I see nothing but sincerity in her clear gray gaze. "Yeah, I'm okay. Thanks for stepping in." I nod, trying to rein in my anger and worry about what might have happened had I not been here. I came on the off-chance I could take her out to lunch, or at the very least set up a date for another time.

What would Jake have done if I hadn't stepped in?

Her employee obviously wasn't going to help her out. Glancing back at the woman who stepped out of Cass's office, I recognize Sam, one of her high school friends. My eyes drop and I notice a significant bump, which she instinctively covers with her hand when she sees me notice.

I lift my chin. "Hey, Sam. You okay?"

She seems surprised at my question but nods in answer. Cass goes to step away from me, so I drop my hands, feeling the loss immediately. Whenever I'm with her, I always want to touch her in some way. I look between the two women, wondering why Sam was in Cass's office.

"Sam works for me now," Cass answers my silent question. "She makes such a difference to my workday. I get home at a decent time now."

"I bet Poppy loves spending more time with you."

Cass's shoulders relax as she smiles. "She sure does."

"Does that mean you can spare an hour for lunch?"

Cass looks over her shoulder at Sam in question. "You don't need to check in with me, Boss Lady. Off ya go." She smiles at Cass, wiggling her fingers in a shooing motion.

"Okay, let me get my purse." She slips past Sam into the office, emerging quickly with her purse slung over her shoulder. Placing my hand on the small of her back, I guide her toward the door. We both wave to Sam over our shoulders as we leave. Stepping out into the pleasant fall day, she acknowledges Shane standing outside her shop. "Hey, Shane."

"Hey, Cass." He looks between us. "You need me to deal with Jake for you?"

Cass's step stalls for a moment, her eyebrows slashing down over her eyes. She looks at me as if to ask, 'Is he serious?' then turns back to Shane. "Uh, I don't think that would be a good idea. I wouldn't want you to get into any trouble. He'll get tired of coming around." She looks down at the ground. "Eventually."

Now that gets my attention. "How often does he come around hassling you?"

"I dunno. It's random." She glances between Shane and me before rushing to add. "I haven't led him on. In fact, I always tell him I'm not interested in anything with him. I don't understand why he's started coming around. My situation's the same as it was when he rejected Poppy five years ago."

"Have you called the police about his visits?" I'm agitated thinking about him touching her. He has no right to put his hands on her.

"What can they do? It's random. I can't predict when he'll show up or what he'll do."

I huff out a breath as I flick my eyes to Shane. He knows exactly what I want to do. Without me having to ask him, he lets me know with a nod of his head that he's onto it. I feel somewhat better knowing Cassia will be safer once Shane gets a guy over here to watch her. I grasp her hand as we make our way to the local diner a few blocks away from the shop. We order a couple of subs while Shane sits away from us to give us privacy. After a few moments of silence, as we take our first bites of food, Cass is the first to speak.

"So, I'm with you, huh?" Her metallic eyes are sparkling, and she has a cheeky grin on her beautiful face.

I swallow my food. "It was the first thing that came to mind when he wouldn't back away from you. Sorry about that." I'm not sure if she's pissed at me for putting it out there.

She reaches across the table, places her hand on top of mine, and squeezes it. I peer up into her eyes. "Thanks for your help. It seems you're always stepping in to help me."

I brush off her comment with a shrug of my shoulder. We both take another bite of our subs. "How long has Jake been hassling you?"

She seems uncomfortable, looking everywhere but at me. "The reunion was the first time I'd seen Jake since Poppy was two. Then he was at the pub that night, and he's come into the shop three times now. It's almost like he forgot I existed until he saw me at the reunion."

"Does he always put his hands on you?" My pulse picks up speed in anticipation of an answer I'm not gonna like. Her eyes dart away from me, then back again as she chews on her bottom lip, tempting me to do the same. Dropping her eyes to the table, she nods imperceptibly. If I wasn't watching closely, I might have missed it, but I was watching her like a hawk. I have to draw on every ounce of my self-control to stay seated and not get up to punch the shit out of something. He's always been a fucking asshole, but to put his goddamn hands where they're not wanted ... that's something completely different. "I don't want his filthy fucking hands on you ever again."

Our eyes lock across the table, stormy gray to blue, as I do my best to convey how serious I am about the situation with Jake. She nods slightly, then drops her eyes to the table. Using my fingertips, I gently raise her face to mine. "It's not your fault he's such a dick, Cass."

"I know." She releases a long breath. "I don't understand why he's back in my space being so freaking demanding suddenly. He didn't want Poppy or me before. It's not like anything's changed." She shakes her head.

"Has he said he wants Poppy?"

"No, it's always about me. It's as though he's ignoring the reality of what ended us in the first place—Poppy."

It's not my business, but I have to know. "Would you go back to him if he wanted to be a proper family?"

She looks over my shoulder, at something out the window, then down to her lunch, biting her lip. Shaking her head in the negative, she says, "Nope."

"Are you sure?" It seemed to take her a while to answer my question, as though she weighed up the options.

"Absolutely positive." She folds her arms on top of the table, leaning forward, giving me the perfect glimpse down her T-shirt.

Hey, I'm a guy. If I get the chance to look, I'm gonna look.

"I'll tell you why if you want to know." I'm not gonna say no, so I nod for her to continue. "I don't love him. I have zero respect for him, and I don't even like him. I haven't for a long time, not even when we were together all those years ago."

I wasn't expecting her answer. "So, why did you stay with him? I remember in high school, you were always on and off. Why not just dump him for good?" She looks over my shoulder again before looking back at me. She's finding it hard to meet my eyes. I get the impression she doesn't want to share any more with me. "It's okay if you don't want to talk about it anymore," I say, giving her an out.

She reaches across the table, and I meet her halfway, twining our fingers together. "No, it's okay. I stayed with him because having a boyfriend made me feel special." She looks up at me. "Stupid, hey?"

"Not stupid. It's how you felt."

She shrugs. "Yeah, but it was pretty pathetic to keep going back to him when I didn't even really like him. My, uh … my dad left my mom when he found out she was pregnant with me. Apparently, he never wanted two children."

What the fuck is wrong with the guys in Cass's life?

"The only male in my life was my grampa, and he wasn't one to make a fuss about his grandchildren. I guess, thinking back, I was looking for the love of a man, even if it was all wrong for me. I kept going back because some part of me always felt I was unlovable, and … well, Jake, I guess … showed me some form of love, even if it wasn't all that great." She shrugs her shoulder, letting out a self-deprecating laugh. "It's all I thought I was worth back then. I know better now, though."

I grasp her other hand, entwining our fingers. "It makes sense you were looking for male attention when you had none growing up. Jake was super popular. I can imagine for a girl, his attention would have felt pretty special."

Her shoulders drop as she nods in agreement, as though she's relieved I understand. And I do. I do understand, even though I hate it. I wish things had been different for her, but they weren't. She was doing the best thing for herself. It's all well and good to look back in hindsight and think about what you could have done differently, but it's unrealistic to judge your choices back then with the knowledge you have now. All it does is create a sense of failure, which doesn't help anyone.

We both eat a few more bites of our subs, enjoying our lunch when Cass surprises me. "So, are we together now?"

I study her closely, not sure where she's going with her question. I feel I need to weigh my answer carefully. I chew my food slowly, using it as my excuse to calibrate my thoughts into a sentence that won't scare her off. "I would like us to be, but I know you have concerns. I'm pretty sure I know what they are, but maybe you could lay it all out for me so we can talk about them. Clear the air, so to speak."

She nods thoughtfully. "Okay. First, I want to say that I *do* really like you, Toby. A lot." Well, that's a fantastic start. "I *know* my view of men is tainted by my experiences, and I apologize because I put you in the same category as the others. Which was wrong of me to do."

I nod, smiling. "Thank you for recognizing I'm not like the other men in your life. I've had a fantastic role model of what a husband and father should be. I know I won't be perfect, that I'll make mistakes, but I want to be in a relationship with you and with Poppy for as long as things work for everybody." Her posture changes. I can almost see her walls being constructed back into place—I've said something wrong. I run the last sentences back but can't work out my mistake. "Talk to me, Cass. I said something wrong, but I'm not sure what."

She shakes her head again, looking everywhere but at me. Her voice is low, almost a whisper, when she asks, "Does that mean, when things get a little rough or difficult, you'll leave?"

It's like I've been physically slapped, as my head snaps back in response. "No. I didn't mean that. I *know* relationships aren't all smooth sailing, that we have to be prepared to put in the work. Great relationships don't just happen. Both parties have to commit to it and work hard to make it a success. I *know* there will be not-so-fun times as well as great times, but I'm more than happy to be there for *all* of it. I meant that if we find we're not compatible, or you decide you don't want to be with me anymore."

"I'm sor—" I cut her off.

"Please don't keep apologizing. I get it. I do. You've only had guys who flake out on you when things aren't going the way they want. It was a fair question, but that's the last time you put me in the same box as them. I'm not them. I refuse to keep being punished for their mistakes. Okay?"

"Okay. I'm sor—" I shake my head with a smile, cutting off her apology.

"Now, tell me some of your other worries where we're concerned."

"Okay, so don't laugh at this, okay?" I nod. "Promise?" I signal, crossing my heart. She draws a deep breath, then, looking over my shoulder, she starts. "A while ago, Poppy asked me if she could ask you to be her daddy." My surprise must be written all over my face because she rushes on. "Of course, I told her she couldn't go around asking anyone to be her daddy. Plus, it was before I knew you were her guitar teacher. Although Mom said once I met you, I might want you to be Poppy's daddy, too." She's rambling now, which is fucking amusing as hell. "Anyway, I'm telling you this because I'm worried if we date, Poppy will get her hopes up, and if, for one reason or another, this doesn't work out, she'll be heartbroken. I also don't want her to lose having you in her life. She's grown to love you so much."

I reach across the table, grasping Cass's hand I squeeze it tight before entwining our fingers together again. "That won't happen, Cass. No matter what happens between us, I'll continue to teach Poppy guitar until she doesn't need me anymore. Okay?" She nods. "What if we dated for a while without telling her? Test the waters; see how we think things will go for us."

Her lips spread wide, filling my soul. "That sounds perfect. Only if it's okay with you?"

"I don't want to be your dirty secret, though, so keeping it on the down-low for Poppy's sake won't be long term ."

She nods in agreement. "I wouldn't want to keep it a secret for long. Just until we're sure."

"Okay. Anything else?" It surely can't be that easy.

She bites her bottom lip. "I *am* concerned about your career—the travel, the fans, touring, your celebrity lifestyle. I'm not sure where we can fit in with all of that. It makes me nervous, to be honest."

A valid concern.

"First, I keep mostly to myself when I'm home. I don't live a rock 'n' roll lifestyle—I'm pretty dull. I spend every Sunday afternoon and evening with my family at my parents' home, while my Friday afternoons are taken with a certain someone's guitar lesson. Other than that, I'm a homebody. It's too much hassle going out in public if I don't need to. Occasionally, I have to do publicity stuff, but that's always pre-planned. When I'm on tour, I'm there to work. It's my job as well as who I am as a person, which is my brand. I'm not prepared to damage either of those things by behaving in a less than appropriate way. I'm not sure what you think happens, but it's not a non-stop party. I don't hook up, get drunk, or do drugs." I brush my hand through my hair. "I hope that puts your mind at ease somewhat. I guess you'll have to trust me and see for yourself." I *have* been thinking about a future as a family man. I know things will have to change, but I don't want to go in too hard and fast with Cass today. I think I've been clear about who I am as a person.

"I actually do believe you."

"Good, now come here." I pull her forward by her hand so I can take the kiss I've been dying for. Licking my tongue across her lips, she opens willingly, inviting me into her mouth. Our tongues slide and tangle, reacquainting with each other.

Even though we were over before we started, I missed her taste, her touch, her scent … I missed … *her*.

We pull away from each other slowly, as if it's the most painful thing to do, then both of us break out in matching grins. I lean forward, stealing another chaste kiss. "Come on. You need to get back to work."

We walk out of the diner hand in hand, and I'm feeling on top of the world. Shane follows close behind. I know he'll give me shit about this later, but at the moment, I don't care. Once we arrive at her shop, I open the door for her to walk inside, knowing I have the goofiest smile on my face because she's agreed to be my girl.

Using my hold on her hand, I pull her back around to face me so I can give her a proper goodbye. With her hand still in mine, I wrap my arms around her, then lean down to take her lips until we're interrupted by someone clearing their throat. Pulling back, I press my forehead to hers as we share a smile. Moving to the side, we make room to allow the customer to enter the store. Cass breaks away, going into florist mode, so I watch her in her element until she's finished and the customer leaves.

"Are you gonna watch me like a creeper all day?" She laughs lightly.

"Maybe. I have nothing else to do." I smirk. "Seriously though, when can I see you again?"

THIRTY-THREE

-cassia-

I CAN'T BELIEVE WE'RE GOING TO SEE WHERE THIS THING BETWEEN US can go. When I woke up this morning, never in my wildest dreams did I think my day would turn out like this.

"Uh, let me check my bookings." I gesture for him to follow me into the office with a tilt of my head. "Hi, Sam, you can go to lunch now if you like. I have this covered."

"Thanks, Cass. I'm starving. It seems I'm always hungry, even though I snack in between meals." Sam laughs as she stands up, noticing Toby behind me. "Hey, Toby." She turns back to me and winks. I'm sure she'll ask for the lowdown later.

Looking at my calendar, I remember I only have one event this weekend, on Sunday. "Okay, I have a sixtieth birthday on Sunday, which leaves my Friday night free," I say with a hopeful lilt to my voice. "I'll have to check with Mom if she can look after Poppy for me, though. I'm sure it won't be a problem."

He jams his hands in the front pockets of his jeans, which hug his thighs like it's their job. "You wanna go out or come to my place?"

My preference will always be his place. I don't want to share him with anybody else. "Your place?" It comes out more like a question than an answer.

"Perfect. I'll cook dinner for us. Bring your suit; we can enjoy the hot tub after dinner." Toby pulls me in close to his body, nuzzling the side of my neck before whispering, "Or don't." He nips my earlobe, then pulls back with a cheeky grin on his gorgeous face. He kisses my lips briefly before pulling away and smacking my behind on his way out of the office. Winking over his shoulder, he asks, "Seven, okay?"

"Seven's great. See you then, handsome." He stops at that, turning to face me.

"You think I'm handsome?" Duh, every red-blooded woman in America thinks he's handsome.

"Of course I do. Along with every other woman on the planet." I roll my eyes.

"I don't care about every other woman, only you. Your opinion is the only one that counts." He turns, waving over his shoulder. I hear the door open and close. He's gone. I stand stunned for a moment, then a smile breaks over my face. I jump up and down on the spot like a child, squealing in delight. I'm so freaking happy. I'd better check with Mom that she can babysit Poppy for me before I get too excited.

ME

Hey, are you free Friday night?

I wait for her response with bated breath.

MOM

Hey Love, I don't have any plans. Why?

ME

I have a date

I'm squealing internally as I type. The decision was to keep it a secret from Poppy for now, but I figure it's okay to tell Mom.

MOM

May I ask who with?

ME

You may

MOM

Well ....

ME

Toby

MOM

Oh, I'm so happy you gave that boy a chance. He's such a sweetheart

588

ME

I know

But don't tell Poppy. We're gonna see how it goes for a while first

I don't want to get her hopes up

Okay?

MOM

Absolutely. I think that's a wise decision

Oh, I'm so excited for you

ME

Thanks Mom

Me too

I message Toby to let him know that Friday night is sorted from my end. I don't even try to play it cool in my texts, making sure he knows that I'm really looking forward to our date.

Friday can't come soon enough in my book.

THIRTY-FOUR

-cassia-

STANDING ON TOBY'S DOORSTEP, I'M EQUAL PARTS NERVOUS AND excited. I think the butterflies in my stomach have multiplied on the way over. As I raise my hand to knock on his door, I notice it shaking in anticipation of seeing him again. The door swings open before my knuckles make contact with the surface, revealing a relaxed-looking Toby wearing ripped jeans with a basic long-sleeve T-shirt with a heartbeat line running across his chest; part of the heartbeat makes a guitar. It's very fitting for him; even in high school, he was always caught up in his guitar or notebook during breaks. He has nothing on his feet and his hair's loose around his chiseled face, complete with a trimmed beard. I like this look on him—really like it. *A lot!*

A smile breaks out as he assesses me. I'm wearing something similar to him except I have a watercolor poppy on my T-shirt. I tug my tote higher on my shoulder. "Hey."

He turns to the side, gesturing for me to come in, stopping me as I step in line with him. "Hey." He nuzzles his nose into my neck before placing a gentle kiss there. "You always smell so damn delicious."

I giggle in response as his beard tickles me as much as his words do. Closing the door, he slides my tote off my arm, placing it on the side-board in the living room, where we pretty much mauled each other the night of the reunion. I flush with the memory of being pressed up against the window.

"I'm trying to be a gentleman and not maul you the instant you step inside my home, but you make it——" He looks down at his crotch, then back up to me. "—fucking hard." God, his words don't help to cool my overheated body.

The guy's incredibly sexy without any effort.

He smirks at me before taking my bottom lip between his teeth, nipping it gently before soothing it with his tongue. I open with a sigh, inviting his tongue inside as Toby cups my head with both hands, guiding my head where he wants it, deepening the kiss. He steals all the breath from my lungs, leaving me limp, relying on his strength to keep me upright.

"We should definitely stop before I get carried away."

My whole body pouts in disappointment as he pulls away from me.

I'm not ready to stop kissing him, so I grasp onto his T-shirt to pull him back into me to continue the kiss. He guides me until my back is against the window I was just reminiscing about, the coolness of the glass seeping through my clothes to my heated skin. I slip my hands underneath his T-shirt until I feel his warm, smooth skin beneath my touch. His muscles shift and tense beneath my hands as I glide them up to pull him tighter against me. It doesn't seem to matter how close our bodies are—it's still not close enough for me.

He pulls away, leaving us both panting hard, working to catch our breath. Toby rests his forehead against mine as a slow smile spreads across his chiseled face, producing one of my own. "I made dinner—"

"Will it keep for a while? I don't think I can wait any longer to have you inside me." I plead. Remembering the last time—the way he made me wait when I got carried away—I bite my bottom lip to shut myself up. He likes to be in charge of the sexy times, which means I need to be patient, trusting he'll look after me; but it's hard to hold back with him.

He must read the desperation in my eyes because he steps away. "Take off your jeans and panties." He points to the couch. "Bend over the couch. Wait for me. I'll be with you in a minute." His tone is sure, demanding—it says, 'do as I say'.

Why would I argue anyway?

I'm about to get exactly what I want. I do as I'm told and wait, feeling as awkward as hell. My ass is bigger than the average girl's , making me self-conscious about it. I use longer shirts to cover as much as possible. I'm caught up in my head, worrying about the size of my behind so I startle when Toby glides his hand up from the inside of my ankle toward where I want him most. Without missing a beat, his tongue follows the pathway, stopping at the top of my inner thigh, where I hear him take in a deep breath.

"You smell delicious, as usual. I can't wait until I finally get a taste." He reaches for my other ankle, and he repeats the process, following with his tongue. Goosebumps break out in his wake.

He spreads my legs further apart, wedging himself into position. It's then I feel the first swipe of his tongue. It's enough to have me tensing my thigh muscles in anticipation of the pleasure about to be bestowed on me. I know from experience Toby can make my body sing. His tongue swipes through my lips, lapping up the moisture I'm producing to prepare for his onslaught.

My body's on fire as he licks, nips, and plays me like he does the strings on his guitar. It doesn't take all that long, and I'm almost flying over the edge toward my first orgasm. He replaces his tongue with his fingers, causing me to lose all sense of cohesive thought. His fingers are then replaced with his dick as he impales me in one clean thrust. Pushing me down further into the cushions with one hand, he tightens his other on my hip and slams into me repeatedly.

"You're dripping all over my cock. I think you like it a little rough," he grunts between thrusts.

I nod my head, barely able to release the moan from inside me as he slams hard and fast into me over and over again. My hip bones repeatedly connect on the timber frame of his couch as he pushes me down as far as possible. I'm almost upside down, but I'm not about to complain when it feels so amazing.

"You make me lose fucking control. I just wanna keep slamming my cock into your body all night." My walls spasm around his shaft. I'm close to losing control. "Yeah, you like my dirty mouth *and* my hard cock."

"Mmmmmm—"

He wraps one hand around the front of my throat, tilting my head back and to the side. He slams his mouth onto mine as he continues to thrust in and out of me at a steady pace, keeping my orgasm balanced on the brink. I pull away from his mouth slightly so I can see him. The blackness of his pupils almost completely swallows the gorgeous cobalt color of his irises. He looks like a wild man, barely holding onto his humanity.

"Please, Toby." My whispered plea is enough to push him into action. He drags my T-shirt off me then scoops my breasts out of their fabric cage, pinching each nipple, causing me to cry out.

"I'll get you there in good time, Cass. Trust me." He bites my neck before soothing the tender skin with his tongue. He uses one hand on my boob to hold me in place as his other hand finds my clit, pinching it hard before rubbing it in smooth, firm circles. That's enough to send me flying over the edge into oblivion. My vision blurs around the edges, and I'm thankful for the couch holding me up at this point because I've lost all ability to hold myself. His thrusts continue through my orgasm, and it feels like my internal walls are never gonna stop spasming. My legs shake as Toby still thrusts in and out of my pussy. Both of his hands come up to play with my swollen, achy breasts. "Let's get another one. You ready, Gorgeous?"

"I ... I'm not sure I—"

He cuts me off. "Yes, you can. Hold on."

I thought he was pounding into me before, but he really lets loose now, skin slapping against skin, his balls slapping against the inside of my thighs, his fingers tight around my nipples ... and I'm falling again.

Into oblivion.

My body convulses from the tip of my head to the tips of my toes and everywhere in between. It's never been like this before for me, and I'm overwhelmed by how big my emotions are.

It's scary.

Toby follows me over the edge into oblivion, pushing his dick as deep as possible before pausing, his dick pulsing as he fills the condom. His hands smooth up and down my spine, followed by delicate kisses spanning from one shoulder to the other. I love the sensation of his raspy beard trailing over my skin, followed by the silkiness of his hair.

"Fuck, that was fantastic. I'm sorry. I don't seem to be able to control myself with you. I meant to at least feed you dinner first. I was gonna try to be a gentleman." He sounds annoyed with himself. I can't help but giggle at the hopelessness in his voice. "Stop fucking laughing. You're not helping my dick to calm down." He finishes with a groan, sliding slowly in and out of me. I can't believe he's still semi-hard after what we just did. As he slides in and out of my pussy, I can feel him getting harder with each stroke.

Twisting around so I can see him. "You can't be serious."

He leverages himself back up to a standing position, grasping my hips.

"Deadly."

Thrust.

"This is what you do to me."

Thrust.

"Every time you're near me."

Thrust.

"Ever since I was sixteen."

Thrust.

"Why do you think I always had to make a quick getaway?" He smirks, thrusting again, eliciting a moan from me. I'm going to be sore if we go again, but I don't have it in me to stop him. I want this; I want him again.

What the hell is wrong with me?

His hips are slower, more methodical this time around—almost leisurely. He slides almost all the way out before sliding back in slowly, playing my clit with his masterful fingers. He's not in a hurry and I'm enjoying the slow slide of his cock in and out of my pussy, relishing in the sensation of this slow build.

"Oh, yeah, fuck. Tighten those pussy walls around my cock." God, his words undo me, then I break. This time's different—slower, more languid as he breaks along with me—both of us falling over into the abyss together.

We stay connected, Toby lying over my back as I'm still draped over the couch. Sweating, heaving bodies feeling satiated from multiple orgasms within minutes of one another. I close my eyes, allowing myself this moment to just *feel*.

I come back to reality when Toby presses gentle kisses to the side of my neck before peeling himself from me and slowly, carefully sliding his softening dick out of me. We both moan at the feeling of disconnection from the other. I'm worried I won't be able to stand. My legs turned to jelly.

Toby carefully removes my bra before he turns me over to lift me bridal style, carrying me through his home. He disposes of the condom and then steps down into his hot tub. The warm water is heavenly against my jelly muscles and my well-used vagina. I sigh in delight at being wrapped in Toby's arms in the warm water as he places delicate kisses over my face—my heart pounding in happiness.

We sit, wrapped in each other's arms for silent minutes, enjoying the intimate connection. Toby breaks the silence first. "Cass?"

"Mmmm?" I don't want to break the spell surrounding us as the warm air collides with cool, forming a blanket of mist, blocking out the real world.

"I really want this to work between us." The vulnerability in his voice swiftly drags me out of my stupor, so I lean back to study his face. He reminds me of the boy from high school.

Where did my confident lover go?

Looking into his eyes, I need to put his mind at ease. "You remember what I told you at the reunion?" He looks puzzled. I can tell he's working through our many conversations from that night. "I told you I had a crush on you, too. It wasn't all one-sided then, and it's not all one-sided now. I really want this to work, too."

He leans forward swiftly, slamming his lips against mine, but as soon as they make contact, he gentles himself. His lips pressing against mine, exploring softly—quite the contrast to how he just took me bent over his couch. This man is a dichotomy of different facets, and I'm looking forward to learning about each and every part of him.

The kiss slowly deepens. It's a languid meeting of lips, tongues, teeth. He's kissing me as though he's learning every part of my mouth. I adjust myself so I'm straddling his legs, my most private place cradling his hard shaft. His hands cup my ass to slide me back and forth, ensuring he rubs my clit on the way forward.

Pulling away from my mouth, he grunts, "I love your ass. It's like a juicy peach I just wanna bite."

His words are enough to have my pussy convulsing and me coming on a loud, wanton moan. I've never been as vocal during sex—Toby brings out a different side to me, one I like. It turns me on that he loves my ass so much because I've always been self-conscious about it. I think it's out of proportion with the rest of my body. Jake added to my self-consciousness about it when he would often comment about its size and how much it would jiggle whenever I walked or ran.

"I love watching my dick disappear into your pussy between your delicious cheeks. So fucking hot, Cass. Everything about you is so fucking hot—you always make me so fucking hard."

I lean in, quickly pressing my lips to his in appreciation for his words. He makes me feel beautiful exactly as I am; no need to be fancy or try to be something I'm not. I want to show him how much I love his words, so I move off his lap. "Can you sit up on the side of the tub?" He looks confused. "Please."

That seems to do the trick, and he hoists himself up the side of the tub. His nipples peak instantly from the cold air, and I'm second-guessing whether this is such a good idea. It's a little chilly out of the water, but I go ahead. I swim forward, pressing myself between his thighs, using one hand to massage his balls, which have contracted up tight against his body to stay warm. I lean closer, licking his gorgeous shaft from the base to the tip, followed by a squeeze of my hand at the base.

Toby lets out a low groan, then focuses his cobalt stare on me. I make sure to maintain direct, solid eye contact with him as I take his dick to the back of my throat. My gag reflex kicks in for a moment, so I pull back slightly, but I make up for it with an intense suction action as I moan around him. He's no longer a passive participant as he grabs hold of my hair, dragging my mouth up and down his shaft. Even though he's taken over, he's careful with me, not pushing too much, just enough to make me even more desperate to feel his cock inside my mouth. He thrusts forward, so I moan as I swallow deeply around him.

"Fuck, Cass. Your mouth feels so fucking good. Swallow again."

I do as he demands, and he grants me another long groan as he attempts to pull my head away. I try to shake my head to maintain my position, showing I want to take him all the way. His jaw tenses as his brows furrow in intense concentration. I moan around his shaft again and swallow hard. I feel the pulsing of his cock, followed by warm ribbons of cum shooting down my throat. I can't keep up with swallowing it all down. I'm certain I must be a mess, with excess cum and saliva dripping down from my mouth.

He looks down at me with a crooked smile on his handsome face. The glazed look in his eyes almost undoes me. He's looking at me with immense gratitude, as well as care and affection, as he slides back into the tub, pulling me in for an open-mouthed kiss. It's so sexy that he can taste his cum on my tongue. He's kissing me right down to my soul, and I never want him to stop.

Pulling back slightly from each other, we rest our foreheads together as we share a secret smile. Unfortunately, my emotions are getting the better of me. I'm beginning to confuse the intense feelings of lust I have for Toby with love.

It can't possibly be love this early on.

Closing my eyes, I work to center myself by blocking out his potent stare. When I open them again, I'm calmer inside; more in control of my emotions. I remind myself it's all the hormones released by awesome sex, running rampant, which have me feeling so discombobulated.

THIRTY-FIVE

-cassia-

"C'MON. LET'S GET DRY. I NEED TO FEED YOU." TOBY HELPS ME OUT of the tub. Together, we race inside, leaving puddles of water all over his hardwood floors as we make our way upstairs to his bathroom. Goosebumps cover my skin and his as we make a run for it. I never got to appreciate his bathroom the last time I was here. I stop dead in my tracks in the doorway when I get a look inside. It reminds me of a fancy day spa with a giant shower head over the open shower area, but it's not the only shower head. There are ... hang on, let me count. Six. Six shower heads are coming out of the walls surrounding the space. It's going to feel amazing.

Toby steps in, turning on the faucet to get the water up to temperature, before inviting me to join him. Steam fills the area as I step into the decadent space. I close my eyes, raising my face to the water surrounding me, soaking up the luxury when Toby's slippery hands glide up my sides, from my hips up to cup my breasts. He's soaped up, ready to clean the hot tub chemicals from us.

Silently, reverently, he washes every single inch of my body, paying special attention to his favorite part—my ass. I return the favor, ensuring his gorgeous cock gets extra special attention. As we're drying off, I remember all of my clothes are downstairs and prepare to head down to grab them when Toby comes up behind me, slipping one of his sweaters over me. The arms are way too long while the body comes to mid-thigh, but it's cozy and warm. An additional bonus is the fabric smells just like him, which I inhale like a druggy trying to get my next fix. He passes me a pair of his woolen socks, and I put them on before we both head downstairs together, holding hands.

He sits me on the kitchen counter, exactly where I sat when he carefully removed the adhesive residue from my bra. I slide my fingers across the smooth surface with a smile as I remember that night as Toby finalizes our dinner. "Can I help with anything?"

He turns around, smiling. "Nope. You sit and keep looking gorgeous in my clothes."

It's rare I get spoiled like this, so I happily oblige. "Okay. Let me know if you change your mind. I'm happy to help."

He presses a kiss to my forehead, then keeps going about his business. "Whatever you've made for dinner smells amazing. I can't wait to taste it." My stomach grumbles—loudly. Toby laughs, and I love the deep, rich sound of it; the crinkles around his eyes, the lightness on his face.

The table's already set, and he places two bowls filled with the most delicious-smelling dish. I begin to wiggle my way off the counter when he comes over to carry me across to the table, sitting me in the chair. "I can walk, you know." I laugh.

"I know. But I want to spoil you. I want to ruin you for any other man. That way, you won't want to leave me." He's saying the words as a joke, but I sense it's a sensitive topic for him.

"Trust me, I love having you spoil me, and I'm not thinking of any other men while I'm here with you." I lean forward to kiss him gently on the lips. I take the first bite of my creamy pasta with shrimp, sighing in appreciation of the delicious flavors. "Oh my god, this is freaking delicious. Did you make this from scratch?"

"Yeah, I like to cook when I have the chance. Of course, I don't bother when it's only me, but this is one of my favorites."

"The avocado's so creamy ... and with the shrimp and feta—it's superb. Thank you so much."

"You're welcome." He smiles at me, and we eat in silence for a few moments, enjoying the delicious meal.

"Where's Poppy tonight?"

I swallow the food in my mouth. "Mom and Violet are treating Poppy and Jasmine to a fairytale princess movie night. A movie marathon at home with all the trimmings. The girls were incredibly excited."

Toby smiles, showing his affection for my daughter. "I'll bet they are." He takes another bite of food, chewing thoughtfully. "What was she like as a baby?"

Now, this is a topic I could talk about all night. "She was such a beautiful baby." He nods. "So happy and easy. She slept right through the night from about six weeks, which was wonderful for me once I got past my anxiousness that she was okay." He takes another bite of food, chewing and swallowing, as I do. "All of her milestones were met at all the right times, and she loved trying new foods as she grew. Her baby years were such a great time. I learned a lot about myself in those early years, too."

"Yeah, like what?"

"I thought I loved my mom, but my love for Poppy surpassed that by miles. I had no idea I could love another person as much as I love her. I learned I'm pretty resilient when I get shocking news. First, when I found out I was pregnant with Poppy. Then learning I would have to raise her on my own. And finally, when I learned my baby was deaf." I suck in a breath. The memory of that event seared into my very soul.

"When did you learn Poppy was deaf?"

"She was born profoundly deaf." Toby reaches across the table, taking my hand in his, giving it a gentle squeeze in silent support. "All babies are given a variety of tests when they're born. To test hearing, they use a probe in the outer ear to send a signal, then wait for an echo to bounce back."

"I never knew that."

I nod. "Yeah. When they tested Poppy, there was no echo. I noticed she didn't seem to respond to noises, loud or soft, at home, so I already suspected that her hearing wasn't the same as mine. When she was three months old, I took her in for more tests, which identified that she was profoundly deaf. She was born with no hearing nerves, so she's never heard a single sound." I take a fortifying breath. "I was hoping, you know—" Toby nods, showing his understanding. "I was hoping the first test was a mistake, but that second test left no doubt. She *was* born deaf."

"It must have been a tough time."

I nod, thinking back to that time, running through the emotions I felt. "It was the toughest. I drove home, handed Poppy to Mom, then went upstairs to my room and sobbed. I cried for her and I cried for me. I didn't want her to have to face the difficulties I imagined she would face throughout her life." Toby reaches across, using his thumb to catch a tear that's escaped. "That night, I watched my baby sleep, and I grieved for everything she would never experience. She would never hear my voice; hear me say the words 'I love you.' Hear the rain falling on the roof, laughter, music."

"I can't imagine being in your shoes, Cassia. You realize, though, you've done an amazing job with her. I don't get the impression she feels she's disadvantaged in any way."

"No. Once I got over my pity party because that's exactly what it was, I put on my mom hat and followed up with the various organizations that work with people like us. I didn't know that ninety percent of Deaf and Hard of Hearing babies are born to hearing parents. I ignorantly thought deaf babies were born to deaf parents. I'd never had anything to do with a Deaf or Hard of Hearing person. I decided I had to learn her world since she couldn't learn mine. I started learning to sign immediately, then began teaching Poppy along the way. She signed her first word when she was only nine months old." A smile spreads across my face. "I was so freaking proud of her. I was running around the house like a complete idiot. I was thrilled because it was the first time I really felt like we could do this. That we could communicate."

"I would've loved to have seen that. It would have been such an amazing feeling after the worry you must have had for her."

"It was such a relief. She blossomed from that point—nothing held her back. I engaged a tutor to come to our home to teach the three of us how to sign. I'm so proud every single day I get to call myself her mom. She's the greatest joy in my life."

"She's an amazing kid. You have every right to feel as proud as you do." He looks away from me, then back again. "She's incredibly easy to fall in love with, Cass."

I can only nod in agreement because Poppy brings out the best in the people around her.

"How about you? How did you learn how to sign?"

"Ah, well. I met Xanthe." He tells me how they met and the friendship that grew between them. "I decided I wanted to learn how to sign somewhat proficiently with my new friends. I also engaged a tutor to teach me. I'm still learning. Sometimes I mess up, but I love it."

It's almost like Toby was preparing himself to become part of our lives. It's mind-boggling.

THIRTY-SIX

-toby-

MY ADMIRATION FOR CASS SKYROCKETED THE NIGHT SHE OPENED UP over dinner at my place. It must be difficult for a parent to learn that your child isn't like you. To pick yourself up and work through what needs to be done, putting your child's needs and happiness first is admirable. She says that's the job of a parent, but not all parents put their kids first. Since being friends with Xanthe, I've witnessed first-hand how some parents won't accept their child communicates differently. They insist their child learns to speak and read lips, denying them the opportunity to learn sign language. It's heartbreaking for the child involved.

This last month, sneaking around with Cass any chance we can get has been amazing, but I'm tired of keeping it a secret. It's Cassia's birthday in two days, and I want to celebrate with her and her family. But I can't do that if Poppy doesn't know we're together. I'm not sure what's keeping Cass from telling her we're together because, in my opinion, we're perfect. I want a future with Cass and Poppy. When it's only the two of us, I feel like we're on the same page, but then she keeps putting off telling her daughter and I'm left wondering if I'm in this on my own.

I need to talk to someone who isn't Cass. Pulling out my phone, I press my sister's contact. She answers on the third ring.

"Hey, brother. How are things?"

"Hey, Squirt." I love teasing her about her size.

"Stop it! I owe you a pinch to the side for that." She's laughing, so I know she's not pissed at me.

"You got a minute to talk?"

She senses the seriousness in my tone, responding in kind. "Sure, Tobes. What's up?"

I tell her all about seeing Cass at the reunion and that we spent some time together that night—I don't tell her we hooked up. That part's too personal to share.

"Oooooo, I knew something was going on between you two after the concert. There was this hot, heavy vibe going on between the two of you."

"Uh, you're not listening, Sis. We weren't together then. I had no idea Poppy was her daughter. She didn't know I was Poppy's guitar teacher."

"Awwww, that's such a great story. It's like the universe was pushing you together."

Huh, I never thought about it like that. Maybe ...

"Anyway, I finally convinced her to give us a chance. She agreed on the proviso that we keep it a secret from Poppy until we're more certain about our relationship."

Kate whispers, "I think I know where this is going."

"Yeah, well, I have no doubts, Sis. We haven't said those three words yet, because I don't want to scare her off, but I can't imagine my future without her in it."

"Oh, Toby. That's incredibly sweet. I'm so happy for you."

I pace, the agitation in my body forcing me to move. "Yeah, well, she keeps putting off telling Poppy. It's Cass's birthday on Friday, so I want to be there to celebrate with her family, but I can't if Poppy doesn't know about us."

"I see."

"I don't know what to do, Kate. I'm tired of seeing her in secret. I would like to do some stuff together as a family, you know. Plus, it's getting harder to keep it under wraps when I see Poppy every week for her lesson."

"Have you talked to Cassia about how you're feeling? What you want? How you see your future together?"

"That's the thing. She's had such shitty luck with the men in her life. She's scared I'm going to be the same."

Kate huffs out a breath. "You remember the trouble I gave Oliver?"

"Yeah. How could I forget? You made him work incredibly hard to be in your life. He has the patience of a saint." I chuckle darkly.

"You, my brother, are going to need to have the patience of a saint. You need to earn her trust. A month isn't all that long in the scheme of things."

"But I want to be part of her birthday celebrations with her family." Again, I can hear myself pouting.

"What's missing out on this birthday, if it means having the rest of her birthday celebrations? Think of the big picture. You need to give her time, Toby. It sounds like she doesn't trust easily—it's something you're going to have to earn. It may take a long time."

She's not telling me what I want to hear, which is frustrating as hell. *Time.* It feels like my enemy at the moment, but I guess I don't have a choice.

"Thanks, Squirt." The misery in my voice is heavy.

"I'm sorry. It probably wasn't what you wanted to hear."

"Nah, that's okay. It's why I called you. I knew you'd give it to me straight."

"If she's anything like me, she's fighting hard against her demons to let you inside. But she won't be able to stop herself from falling in love with you, because you're the best person I know."

"Thanks, Kate. Love you."

"Love you, too, Toby." She pauses. "Talk later?"

"Of course. Say hi to Oliver for me. Later, Squirt." I quickly end the call, laughing to myself, so she can't retaliate. I'm a shit of a brother sometimes.

I guess she's right. Cass needs time; she needs to see I'm hanging around. She still doesn't trust me one hundred percent. I know this because even though she's on birth control, she won't let me stop using condoms. I almost forgot once, and she went ballistic.

THIRTY-SEVEN

-cassia-

I'M WOKEN BY POPPY JUMPING ON ME WITH THE BIGGEST GRIN. SHE'S already dressed for school, so she must have woken up really early, which is unusual for her. She usually tries to get up as late as she possibly can on a school day. My baby's not a morning person at all. Once my eyes are open, she signs the happy birthday song for me. She's done this since she first learned how to sign the song. I love waking up on my birthday to her wishing me happy birthday this way. We giggle as I pull her in close for a special snuggle, inhaling her strawberry scent.

After snuggles, I dress for work, then Poppy and I make our way downstairs, where I'm greeted with waffles for breakfast—my favorite. Mom makes the best waffles: crunchy on the outside, light and fluffy on the inside. She's been making it for my birthday ever since I was a little girl.

"Awww, thanks, Mom. I'm so lucky to be still getting my favorite breakfast for my birthday."

Mom turns around to face me. Stepping close, she places her hand gently on my cheek. "Happy birthday, Baby Girl."

"Thanks, Mom. You know this day is as much about you as it is about me."

"Oh, don't be silly. I just happened to be there." We both laugh because that's her usual response. Like she was visiting the hospital that day and found me in the parking lot or something.

Violet's busy getting all the toppings organized while Jasmine places the silverware on the table. They both grab me on either side, making a sandwich out of me, and wishing me a happy birthday. It's such a great start to the day, but it would have been nice to wake up in Toby's arms.

I know he's getting antsy with me, wanting me to tell Poppy we're together. I'm unsure what's holding me back. I know he's perfect for me and he adores Poppy so much. He still has Shane driving her everywhere she needs to go to keep her safe. I'm scared he's too good to be true; that as soon as things get a little tough, he'll pack up and leave me. It's what I've seen happen throughout my life. It's difficult to change such deeply ingrained beliefs overnight.

We all sit down to enjoy our special breakfast, which is very decadent for a weekday morning. As we're busy eating the delicious waffles, Mom looks at me knowingly over Poppy's head as she asks, "Will you be seeing Toby today?"

I shake my head in the negative. He wanted to take me to dinner, but I had to turn him down because I always spend it with my family. I couldn't invite him along because, well ... how do I explain his presence to my daughter? It makes no sense for him to attend my birthday dinner. If I were brave enough to take the chance to be open about our relationship, she would know all about him, and I could spend my birthday with the man I've fallen in love with.

If only I were brave.

———

"Good morning, *Blooms and Balloons*. This is Cassia. How can I help you?" I answer the phone professionally.

"Hey, Cassia. It's me, Kate."

"Oh, hi, Kate. How are you?" I wonder if she's calling about Toby?

"I'm great, thanks. Happy birthday."

"Thank you." I guess Toby must have mentioned my birthday to her.

"Look, I know it's really short notice, but a friend of mine is getting married next weekend, and I was wondering if you could do some flowers for the wedding?" She sounds panicked.

"Sure. What did they have in mind?" I grab my notebook and pencil to record the information.

"Roman and Alice want something simple. What would you suggest?"

I offer her my thoughts, and she chooses blush pink and cream roses. A classic choice for a wedding, and the blooms will be easy to source at short notice.

"Sorry, I can't stop to chat. I'm on a break. The bell's about to ring."

"No problem. I'll chat with you later about the details."

"Thanks for all your help, Cass. I appreciate it at such short notice." Her relief is clear to hear, making me smile. That's what I'm here for. I love to make the planning of an event easier for the organizer.

"You're welcome. Have a great day. Bye." I jot down the notes, then add the additional blooms to my order.

I busy myself putting together an order for a baby shower tomorrow afternoon, a mix of flowers and balloons. It's a lot of fun. The customer has asked me to put blue powder inside the balloons as a surprise for her guests. She plans to reveal the sex of her baby, which I guess is a boy. Sam's taking a long lunch break because she has an appointment with her obstetrician today and Sally's unwell, so I'm here on my own.

The bell over the door tinkles as I'm putting the finishing touches on the order.

I jump in fright.

I find I'm jumpy every time the bell over the door sounds, ever since Jake started showing up at random times, thinking he can put his hands on me. I don't feel safe in my own damn shop, and it pisses me off. As I look up to greet the customer, I automatically grab my secateurs. Doing my best to keep my fear hidden, I welcome whoever it is with a smile. When I see who it is, my shoulders relax, my guard drops, and I put the secateurs down. My smile becomes genuine and my heart rate picks up for a completely different reason. Rushing around my bench to get to him, I leap into his arms before he's ready, almost knocking him on his fine ass.

"Toby! I'm so happy to see you." My day's perfect now. He's the one person I wanted to see but thought I wouldn't.

He laughs. "Woah, Gorgeous. That's some greeting." He's holding me the best he can, my feet dangling off the ground. Finally, I lean in to press my lips against his, claiming the kiss I want for my birthday. When I pull back to look at him, his eyes are sparkling with laughter.

His face is perfect when he smiles …

Even when he doesn't smile.

He's just ... *sigh.*

"Happy birthday, Cassia," he whispers, leaning forward, taking my lips with his. This kiss is so much more than the kiss I took. He seems to reach down to my soul, owning every single piece of me on the way.

He pulls back way too soon for my liking, sliding me down his body so I can feel every inch—and I mean *every* inch—of him until my feet touch the floor. He doesn't let go until he's sure I'm steady. As I step back, I notice he's holding a gift in his hand. This explains why he couldn't hold me properly. He awkwardly thrusts it toward me.

"Uh, I bought you something for your birthday. I figured I couldn't get you flowers, since ..." He gestures around my shop. "I hope you like it."

To say I'm surprised he got me anything for my birthday is an understatement. The last time we spoke, he seemed pissed at me. I wasn't ready to tell Poppy about us, leaving him out of any birthday celebrations.

"Thank you so much. You didn't need to get me anything—" He steps forward to take the gift away from me with a smirk, but I tuck it in close to my body, protecting it from him. "But I'm glad you did. I love getting presents." I mean, what girl doesn't love to get presents on her birthday? Right?

He gestures with his chin. "Go on then. Open it."

I quickly place it on the bench, opening the card first. It has two mushrooms on the front with the words; *I have so mushroom in my heart for you.* I burst into laughter. I glance up to thank him, finding him standing with his hands in the pockets of his jeans, a gorgeous grin on his face. "It was too funny to pass up. I had to get it for you for your birthday."

"I love it. It's so damn cute." I prop it up on my bench and drag the gift closer. Carefully, I pull at the tape to open the paper so I can see what's inside. When I pull the paper away completely, I'm pretty sure my jaw drops to the ground. I glance up at Toby, then back at the box, then back to Toby again. "Oh, gosh, Toby. You shouldn't have. I can't accept such an expensive gift."

He steps around, lifting my chin with his fingers so I have to look at him. "You can and you will accept it. I wanted you to have it. You said yours was close to dying."

"Well, yeah, but I would have replaced it with a basic model, not a freaking *Kindle Oasis.*" Then I realize how rude I've been. "Thank you so much. This ... it's gorgeous. Totally over the top ... but the best present I could have ever asked for."

"You're welcome, Gorgeous. There's a waterproof cover in there, too. I also opened an account for you, so you can buy any books you like. On me."

"Oh, my gosh. Are you serious?" He nods in confirmation. "Thank you so much." He catches me under my ass as I leap into his arms, covering his face in kisses. Shane pops his head through the door, wishing me a happy birthday through his laughter at my juvenile display.

"Can I take you out to lunch for your birthday?"

I pull back, the disappointment in having to turn him down strong. "I can't today. I'm here on my own at the moment. Sam's at her obstetrician appointment, so she won't be back until nearly three. And Sally called in sick this morning." Watching disappointment coat Toby's face has me almost inviting him to join me for my family's birthday dinner tonight. Maybe I should bite the bullet and do it. My gut tells me he's not like every other man I know. He's loyal and committed. He'll always choose to be there for Poppy and for me, no matter what.

He covers his disappointment quickly with a smile. "That's okay. Have you eaten lunch yet?"

"No, I've been too busy. I'll grab something light later."

He nods thoughtfully, his brows drawn down low over his sapphire eyes. The bell over the door sounds, breaking our private moment. "I'd better let you get back to work then." He steps away from me. "Enjoy the rest of your day with your family. Bye."

Stunned at how quickly the mood between us changed, I only have time to wave goodbye before he's gone.

Turning my attention to my customer, I smile. "I'll only be a moment."

I quickly collect everything to carry into my office, buying myself some time to gather my thoughts. Stepping back into the front of my shop, I feel in a more professional headspace and deal quickly with my new customer, creating a unique arrangement for his mother-in-law's birthday. He wants it to be unique because she suddenly lost her husband two weeks ago. Apparently, his father-in-law always gave his wife flowers for her birthday. He didn't want her to miss out this year.

While working on the arrangement and listening to my customer's story, I realize time isn't always on our side. It's the final push I need to invite Toby to dinner tonight, so I text Mom to add two more people to our booking.

> **MOM**
> You're sure?

> **ME**
> Not really, but when will be the right time?

> **MOM**
> I think you're doing the right thing
> You can't keep him at arm's length forever

> **ME**
> I know

> **MOM**
> I'll change the booking

> **ME**
> Thanks Mom x

> **MOM**
> I'm proud of you for taking a big step forward
> I know how hard it is for you to do

The bell over the door tinkles again. Looking up from my phone, I nearly drop it in surprise. Toby's back, and he's carrying a takeout paper bag that smells like lemongrass and coconut. He smiles at me. "Since you couldn't come out to lunch, I thought I'd bring lunch to you."

My cheeks rise to match his and my heart grows exponentially. I'm now one hundred percent certain I've made the right choice to include him in my family dinner tonight.

I step from behind the counter to pull him in for a tight hug, whispering in his ear, "I love you." It sort of slipped out, but I don't want to take it back. His head snaps back, eyes wide in surprise, but I know he's happy I said those three words.

"You love me? It's not even *my* birthday." I nod as my lips spread.

It's true; I love him. It feels so freaking good to say it out loud. I've been feeling it for a while and I've had to work hard to keep it from slipping out over the last couple of weeks. I don't know how to explain how his body language changes; he almost melts in front of my eyes.

"Say it again."

"I love you, Toby Summer."

He pulls me back into his body, whispering in my ear, "I love you so much, Cass." He laughs. "It feels so fucking good to say those words out loud."

He spins me around in the air before planting a rough kiss on me, deleting all humor and raising the heat level to extreme in a matter of seconds. This is a kiss to seal those magic words, reinforcing their importance to each of us. Unfortunately, he pulls back from me sooner than I would like, making my whole body pout in disappointment.

"C'mon, eat while you have a chance." He drags me into my office, then proceeds to lay out a plethora of dishes on the office desk as I clear the paperwork Sam has sprawled all over the surface. He hands me the Pad Thai noodles, giving me the first taste. The flavors burst inside my mouth, eliciting an appreciative moan. Toby pauses eating his crispy chicken, eyes snapping up to mine. He quickly leans forward to steal a kiss, then goes back to eating his chicken as though nothing happened.

"This is delicious. Thank you for spoiling me with lunch on my birthday."

"You're more than welcome, Bun. Where are you going for dinner with your family tonight?"

Here's my chance to invite him along. "We're going to our favorite pizza place. It's the traditional meal for our birthdays." I swallow nervously. "Um, would you like to come along?"

His body stiffens as his knuckles blanch around his fork. I don't think he was expecting an invitation tonight. I mean, I wasn't expecting to invite him along until a little over an hour ago.

"Are you sure?"

"Positively certain. Never felt more sure about anything before. It's time to let Poppy know we're together." I feel almost giddy for tonight, especially at what this means for our relationship. I'm tired of sneaking around, keeping something significant from the most important person in my life. "Poppy will be overjoyed." I observe his face for what I'm about to tell him again. "After all, she asked if you could be her daddy."

Toby's cheeks lift immediately, as his whole face lights up in delight. "You know I would be honored to be Poppy's daddy." He reaches up, cupping the back of my head to pull me forward before capturing my mouth with his. I open immediately, letting him in. God, what I wouldn't give to be somewhere else, so I could have this man inside me. The food is forgotten as we become lost in each other. It's always like this between us. A small spark leads to an inferno in an instant.

"So, is that a yes to dinner tonight?" I whisper against his lips.

"Absolutely, it's a yes. Only because I love pizza." He laughs as he dashes out of the path of my hand, swiping at him in fun.

"Good. I had Mom add two more people to our booking. I figured Shane would also need to join us since we're out in public."

"Does that mean you're already taking me for granted? Assuming I'm available to have dinner with you on a whim?" He smirks at me.

"You don't have to come if you have plans." I sass back.

"Oh, don't worry, I'll be there for sure. Even if I had plans, I would cancel them in a heartbeat to spend your birthday with you." I think my heart just melted into a puddle; he always says exactly the right thing.

We continue eating our lunch, which surprisingly doesn't get interrupted by a customer. Once we're finished, Toby cleans up the mess, then kisses me goodbye with the promise to see me at dinner after his lesson with Poppy. He promised not to say anything to Poppy, preferring to tell her together at the restaurant tonight.

THIRTY-EIGHT

-toby-

"WE'RE GOING TO DINNER TONIGHT AT *OVER THE TOPPINGS PIZZERIA* for Cass's birthday. Can you check it out for us? See if it's not too late to book the place out?"

"Sure, I'll get onto it straight away." He pulls out his phone, searching for the number.

"Thanks, bro."

I feel like I've won another Grammy—actually, it feels better. Cass is showing me a level of trust she hasn't thus far. Introducing our relationship to Poppy is a big deal. One I won't take for granted. Even though Cass hasn't had any positive male role models in her life, I have. Dad was the best man, always patient and supportive. Firm but fair. He was always a solid, steady figure in my life. If I can be half the father he's been to me, I think I'll be doing okay.

A shriek breaks my musing, and Shane steps closer to me.

"Oh my god! It's Toby Summer. It's Toby Summer. I can't believe it. Oh, my god!"

Everyone who happened to be walking down the street, minding their own business, stops to see what the fuss is all about. This is how it starts. One person spots me, then suddenly, I'm surrounded by a mob —usually made up mostly of young women.

"Can you sign my shirt? Oh my god! Nobody's gonna believe me."

"Sure. Do you have a pen?" I often find it best to sign everything thrown my way. That way, I can go on with my day. If I resist, they generally keep following me around until I relent. But I have things to do, so it's best to agree to her request.

"Oh my god! You're gonna sign my shirt!" She turns around to the crowd forming. "Toby Summer's gonna sign my shirt!"

She digs through her purse, pulling out a Sharpie. Man, who happens to have a Sharpie on hand? Shane does, precisely for this purpose, but I usually ask the women if they have one on hand. That way, if they don't and I'm not in the mood, it's a good excuse to get out of the situation. Particularly when someone's as rude as this woman has been. She hands it to me, and I gesture for her to turn around to sign her back.

"No way. I want you to sign it right here." She points to her chest. Damn it. I hate signing women's breasts. I'm not sure what they think is gonna happen if I write across their boobs. Do they think I'll take one look at their rack and fall hopelessly in love?

"Okay, if you're sure." She nods vigorously, reminding me of a bobble doll. "Who shall I make it out to?"

"Deanna. My name's Deanna. D-E-A-N-N-A."

"Sure. Thanks, Deanna. It's always great to meet a genuine fan." As much as I don't enjoy being in the spotlight or having to deal with fans, I'd be a nobody if it weren't for them. I sign as carefully as I can, high up on her shirt, making minimal contact with her breast area. "There ya go. Have a great day."

"Can I have a selfie, too?" Some manners would be appreciated, but people often forget them in these situations.

"Sure." I step next to her, trying not to actually touch her, which is blown out of the water when she wraps her arms around me, squeezing me like a boa constrictor. Shane takes the obligatory photo and then hands the phone back to Deanna, signaling her to move along.

Shane and I spend the next forty minutes signing anything handed to me and taking selfies with strangers who feel they know me like an old friend. In between, he booked out the rest of the restaurant for the evening. The restaurant already had two other bookings besides Cass's, which we couldn't interfere with, but there won't be any others. I'm always aware of the lost revenue, so I pay for the privilege of booking out a restaurant.

To make up for lost time, we head over to Poppy's school together to pick her up for her guitar lesson. I'm not registered to pick her up from school, so Shane heads in to collect her while I wait in the car. I watch her holding Shane's hand, swinging it back and forth between them, as she skips while he walks toward the car. When she spots me sitting in the passenger seat, her whole body lights up with happiness. I step out to greet her properly, barely getting to my feet before she throws herself at me in her usual Poppy style.

Once I set her back on her feet, she signs, "Toby!"

"Hey, Poppy. How was your day?"

"It was the best. It's Mom's birthday today, so we had waffles for breakfast. I love waffles. Then, after my lesson, we're going to have pizza for dinner. You wanna come?" She looks between Shane and me hopefully.

Shit, I'm not sure if I'm allowed to tell her I'm coming to dinner tonight. I catch Shane's eye over the top of the car, indicating for him to situate Poppy in her booster seat. He comes around, guiding her into her seat, ensuring she's safely secured, and allowing me the opportunity to text Cass.

> **ME**
>
> Poppy just invited Shane and me to dinner tonight
>
> What do you want me to say?

It takes less than a minute for the three dots to bounce.

> **BUN**
>
> You can tell her I already invited you guys

> **ME**
>
> Are you sure?

> **BUN**
>
> Yep
>
> See you tonight lover boy

> **ME**
>
> Hey, I'm all man, or do I need to remind you?

> **BUN**
>
> Oh, I remember, but a refresher wouldn't go astray 😊

> **ME**
>
> It would be my pleasure
>
> See you tonight

I wait for a reply which doesn't come. A customer probably came in that she has to deal with. We drive across to *Music for my Heart.* Once we're all out of the car and ready to head inside, I tell Poppy that Shane and I will be joining her and her family for dinner tonight. She jumps up and down with the joy of a child who's been told she's going to Disneyland, not adding two adult males to the dinner reservation. But that's Poppy to her very core.

We spend the one-hour lesson playing the three songs she's mastered, then choose a new song for her to learn. We select a reggae number by Bob Marley, *Three Little Birds*. It's a great song, using three chords, reminding us not to worry about a thing. Poppy loved the video I showed her on YouTube. She eagerly decided it would be her next song and favorite. I sit behind her, demonstrating how to play, with my hand guiding hers, while she watches the colorful display on my laptop monitor. The lesson flies by and before we know it, we're heading back to the car to drop Poppy home.

Once it's only Shane and me in the car, Shane asks, "Do you think I still need to be watching over Poppy? It's been a couple of months since your concert duet went viral."

I think about it for a moment. "I know it's been a while, but what if someone's been waiting for the right time? I would never forgive myself if something happened to her because of me."

Shane nods thoughtfully. "I see where you're coming from, but remember, you have a press tour coming up after Thanksgiving. So who's gonna watch her then?"

I look out of the window, tension building across my shoulders at the thought of being away from Cass and Poppy for any length of time —even though it's only two weeks. "Let me think about it. Okay?"

"Sure. I'll do whatever you want. But I don't want to leave you unprotected while you're away. It leaves you vulnerable to crazies." He looks at me meaningfully. As if I could ever forget what happened a couple of years ago.

THIRTY-NINE

-toby-

ARRIVING AT *OVER THE TOPPINGS PIZZERIA*, CASS AND HER FAMILY ARE already inside. I spend a moment observing them interact through the glass window like a creeper, unable to stop the warmth building inside me.

I'm about to walk inside and join them.

Finally, our sneaking around is over. We can be together openly.

There are two other tables, one with an older couple sharing a pizza while looking lovingly into each other's eyes. The other table is a group of young women. They could be a problem, but I'm hoping not. Shane and I don't need to speak to know what the other's thinking about a table of four women drinking wine while laughing over pizza.

I'm not about to stay out here checking out the woman I love from afar when I have the opportunity to join her for her birthday, so I open the door to step inside with Shane close behind. Poppy's facing the door, which means she's the first to catch our arrival, and bolts straight for us, hugging my waist before giving Shane the same attention.

I know he's become quite fond of her over the weeks he's spent ensuring her safety. She takes each of our hands, pulling us toward the table. Cass offers a secret smile, and I wink back. This, here with Cass and Poppy and their family ... is where I want to be—*always*.

Rose steps in to greet me first. "I'm thrilled you could make it on such short notice." She pulls me in, embracing me as she whispers, "I'm pleased my daughter finally came to her senses."

I bow my head, closing my eyes—a shaky laugh bursts out of me. I didn't realize how nervous I was about having Cass's mom's approval.

It's always nerve-racking meeting the parents of the girl you're dating, and it's no less daunting doing it as an adult.

"Me too, Mrs. Phillips, me too."

"Rose. Remember?" She chastises me with her eyes.

Cassia steps closer, waiting to welcome me. I want so much to pull her into my arms and greet her the way I need to, but I want to be respectful of Poppy—who doesn't know we're together yet. I grin at her. "Hey, Cass. Happy birthday."

She blows all of my good intentions out of the water when she plants a kiss directly on my lips in front of everyone. I hear a series of gasps from the table of women. Cass flicks her tongue across the seam of my lips and I press in closer to hide my rising cock from the little girls who are standing too close for comfort. However, my hand has a mind of its own, holding the back of her head in place, stopping her from pulling away until I'm ready.

Poppy wraps her arms around both of us, squeezing our bodies together. It's then I remember where I am and the company I'm in. Reluctantly, I pull my lips away, touching my forehead to the woman who holds my heart—sharing a secret grin. Then, out of the corner of my eye, I catch a flash of a camera. Turning in their direction, Shane heads to the table of women. He normally offers them a portion of my time for my privacy in situations such as these. I trust him to do his job, so I bend down to pick up Poppy.

Poppy signs to me. "Mommy told me you're her boyfriend now." I look at Cass because I thought she was going to wait to tell Poppy until we were together.

"I couldn't hold it in any longer. I'm sorry I didn't wait for you." Cass signs to me as she speaks. I can't describe how happy it makes me that Cass was too excited about us to wait. I pull her into me with my free arm, kissing her temple. "I hope you don't mind."

It feels amazing to have both Poppy and Cassia—*my girls*—in my arms. "I don't mind at all, Bun."

We separate, and Violet says, "Hello," warily as we all take our seats around the table. Cass introduces me to her gramma Iris. I feel like I know her already after everything Cass has told me about her. She has a lot of respect for her gramma and they share a strong bond through their mutual love of floral design.

"Gramma, this is Toby. Toby, this is Gramma Iris," she signs as she speaks.

"Well, hello, handsome. It's nice to meet you finally." I go straight in for a hug with my free arm. I come from a family of huggers, so it's natural for me to greet Cass's family in this way.

"Nice to meet you, too." Shane and I pull out chairs at the table.

The red-checked tablecloths add to the traditional feel of the place as two guys work the large pizza oven in full view of the dining area. We chat around the table, comparing our favorite toppings and pretending to be grossed out by Poppy's preference for pineapple on her pizza. The point of difference between this pizzeria and others is that you build your own pizza. There are no boards on display for you to choose from a range of pre-designed pizzas. Instead, customers are encouraged to create their own one-of-a-kind taste sensation. The topping choices are extensive and include your regular options to create a savory pizza as well as sweet options to create a dessert pizza.

We each place our order with the waiter, a teenage boy with a wiry build, curly blond hair, and the unmistakable beginning of a fine mustache. His voice cracks as he introduces himself, preparing to take our orders on his tablet. We order wine for the adults and juice for the girls, which is brought out quickly along with a range of different warm breads. Poppy was quick to nab a seat between Cass and me, allowing me to rest my arm on the back of her chair, allowing me to play with her mom's silky hair.

Shane's sitting next to Violet, and they seem to be getting along. He's smiling freely while answering Jasmine's million and one questions. It's a change to see him relaxing and joining in rather than staying on the outer edges. Even when he spends time with my family, he's always slightly removed from the rest of us. Before joining the military, he was more relaxed around people, but he's different now—more withdrawn, quieter, slower to laugh and join in the conversation.

Pizzas of all varieties are brought out to the table, causing the conversation to die down momentarily as we all get stuck into our creations. Afterward, we all enjoy the birthday cake Rose organized for Cass. A red velvet creation with cream cheese filling and icing to match. Poppy and Jasmine end up with cream cheese all over their sweet little faces, giggling in delight at the reactions of the adults around the table. High on sugar, I pity Cass and Violet when it's time to get them to bed tonight.

As I regard everyone around the table, the night drawing to a close, I wonder what my chances are of getting Cass to come back to my place. I want to wish her a happy birthday properly. Leaning over Poppy, I tuck a lock of Cass's hair behind her ear, then lean closer to whisper, "What are my chances of wishing you happy birthday privately later?"

Her head turns quickly, our eyes connecting. The molten heat staring back at me makes my pulse race, directing the blood in my body toward my cock. *Fuck!* This is not the time nor the place to get a hard-on. "Let me get Poppy home to bed, then I'll come over. Okay?"

"Perfect." I lean in, pressing a gentle kiss to her lips. The same lips I used to dream of kissing in music class. I have to be the luckiest man alive. Our moment's broken by a throat clearing behind us, and I know it's time to pay up in exchange for being left alone during our meal. I excuse myself from the table as Shane does the same. We put some space between our group and the fans who've been reasonably patient this evening.

"Hello, ladies. Thanks for your patience and for being kind enough to wait until we'd finished our meal this evening."

My appreciation is met with various giggles, hair flips, hands pressed to breasts, as well as 'I'm sure you'll make it worth our while' responses.

Shane steps in. "If you would like to give me your phones, I'm happy to take a photo of each of you with Mr. Summer."

The ladies waste no time digging out their phones and opening the camera app before passing them over to Shane. Each one takes their turn, pressing their body as close as humanly possible to mine while posing for the photo. It astounds me to this day that people have no qualms about putting their hands and bodies all over a complete stranger. It's making me more uncomfortable than usual because I know my girls are mere yards away, witnessing these women fawn all over me. I hate it on a normal day, but tonight I feel downright dirty.

Attempting to extricate myself from their clutches, I work to put some space between myself and them, but it's an almost impossible task. They have me sign a menu, personalizing each one. I have to work hard to keep my smile in place as well as my friendly, professional manner intact, as they take every opportunity to put their hands on me. Shane picks up on my discomfort, informing the ladies it's time to move along.

Moving toward our table, I watch for any signs of annoyance from Cass, but I find none. Instead, Rose and Violet are scrutinizing me as I sit down.

"I'm sorry about the interruption to our evening. Unfortunately, stuff like that happens when I'm in public. I've found it best to spend time with my fans rather than ignoring them."

They nod in understanding while Cass turns to me.

"When it's only us, I always forget how famous you are. I think it's great you don't ignore your fans." I sigh in relief at her acceptance of this facet of my life. "But if I see another woman rub her breasts against you or put her hands on you as though she owns you, I'm not gonna be held responsible for my actions." She finishes her statement with a sweet smile, contradicting the tone of her words. Rose and Violet snicker as Shane's lips twitch, suggesting he's holding back his laughter. I notice she didn't sign any of that for Poppy's benefit.

"Are we all ready to head home?" I check with everyone.

A round of yeses sound out, and we all stand, gathering our things to leave the restaurant. Shane's already picked up the tab on my behalf, so I guide the ladies out the door quickly, hoping they're too preoccupied with putting on their coats to notice.

Rose stops near the cashier. "I have to pay for our meal. You all go ahead." She shoos the girls away, but I linger, letting her know the meal has already been covered.

She's not happy with me, making it known that as her guest, it was very rude of me to step in to pay for *her* daughter's birthday dinner. I apologize profusely as we make our way outside to join the others. The girls all pile into one car, Cass lingering beside the driver's door. I say my goodbyes to the girls and Violet in the back seat before stepping into Cass's body and pulling her tight against me.

"Will I see you tonight?" I'm unsure if she still wants to come over after witnessing the women from the other table fawning all over me.

Bringing her smooth hand up, she cups the side of my face. I automatically press further into her palm before grasping and kissing it. "As soon as I can get Poppy to bed, I'll head over. I'm not sure how long that'll take, though. Is that okay?"

"Of course. Don't rush. I'd wait all night for you, Cass." I kiss her palm again, then press my lips to her forehead. "Drive safely." I kiss her lips chastely before nudging her into the car to fasten her seatbelt.

FORTY

-toby-

I FEEL LIKE I'M GONNA COME OUT OF MY SKIN AS I WAIT FOR CASS TO show. It's only been an hour since we parted ways at the restaurant, but it feels like so much more time has passed. Then, finally, headlights shine through my front windows, letting me know she's here. I head out to meet her at her car, opening her door before she's aware that I'm there, causing her to almost hit her head on the roof.

Holding her hand to her chest, she chastises me. "Shit, Toby. You scared the crap outta me."

I pull her out of the car and press her up against the rear door. "I'm sorry. I couldn't wait the extra time it'd take you to come to me." Moving forward, stopping her words, I press my lips to hers in a desperate kiss. I'm hungry for her. I can't even wait until I get her inside. It's only when a car full of teenagers careens past, yelling profanities, that I remember where we are. Dragging my mouth from hers is a mammoth task. Breathing heavily, I press my forehead to hers. "Sorry. Couldn't help myself, as usual."

Her giggles lighten the mood. "I love how much you want me. You won't ever hear me complaining about your lack of control." She kisses me chastely. "Now, help me carry my overnight bag upstairs."

"Does that … does that mean you're … are you staying the night?" I finally get the words out past my surprise.

"Yep. Mom insisted I deserved a night away. She promised to take care of Poppy tomorrow. Gramma Iris will deliver and set up the flowers and balloons for the baby shower for me. So you have me all night as well as most of tomorrow."

"This is the best gift, and it's not even *my* birthday."

I can't contain my excitement at having her in my bed all night. To wake up wrapped around her in the morning for the first time. To not have her leave my bed in the middle of the night like a teenager sneaking around after curfew. She removes her car keys, then closes her door while I grab her bag. Locking her car, I guide her up the few steps into my home with my hand nestled into the small of her back. She stops dead in her tracks, sucking in a breath at what greets her.

"Is this all for me?" She glances at me over her shoulder, steely eyes wide. I nod, then press a gentle kiss to the side of her neck, below her ear.

"All for you, Gorgeous."

"It's beautiful." She turns to me, her eyes glittering with the reflection of the candlelight. Pressing upward, she captures my mouth with hers. I drop her overnight bag to the floor and cup her face in my hands, deepening the kiss. As is typical for us, an inferno builds quickly, and I have her pressed against the entry wall without realization. Lifting her underneath her ass, I encourage her to wrap her legs around me, allowing me the pleasure of grinding my rock-hard cock against her soft pussy.

Kissing her roughly, our breaths heavy and uneven, our tongues dueling, tasting, twisting, licking—I *know* I could kiss her for days and be a fortunate man. After a few moments, drawing on every single reserve of strength I have, I pull away, carefully sliding Cassia down my body until her feet make contact with the floor. Ensuring she's steady, I grasp her warm hand in mine and lead her toward the couch, where the wine is resting on the table, along with half a dozen candles. I have more spread throughout the space, giving a romantic glow to the room.

The lights of the bridge in the distance can be seen through the window, and I don't think I've ever felt this content in my private space. The only thing that could make this better would be having Poppy asleep upstairs and Cass's clothes in my closet.

We get comfortable. I pass a glass of wine to Cass, then collect my own. Carefully tapping my glass against hers, I make a toast. "Happy birthday, Bun. Here's to sharing the rest of our birthdays together."

We both sip the sweet wine and Cass leans in to snuggle my neck as she whispers, "Every." Kiss. "Single." Kiss. "One." Kiss. "Until my dying day." It's exactly what I want to hear from her. She pulls back.

"Thank you for all this." She gestures around the room at the candles. "You didn't need to go to this much trouble for me."

"You deserve to be treated like a princess. This was no trouble at all." I grasp the back of her head, pulling her lips to mine. Kissing her roughly, tasting the wine, feeling her breath.

Slowly pulling apart, I can see something's bothering her. "What's up?" I whisper, my forehead pressed against hers.

She bites her bottom lip, her eyes skating around the room before settling back on me. "Does it happen often?" My eyebrows pull down, trying to work out what she's talking about. "You know. The fans." Oh, right, *that*.

"It usually depends." How do I explain this without making my life sound unappealing to her? "I don't go out much. Whenever possible, Shane works to ensure I have minimal contact with the public. We didn't have time to plan for tonight, which means we didn't have our usual level of control. Today was unusual. I was stopped by fans twice. Once, after leaving you this afternoon, then tonight at dinner." I sip my wine as Cass does the same. "When I prepare for my tour, I'm out and about more, which means dealing with fans more often. Then, while I'm on tour, it can get pretty crazy. Otherwise, I work to keep myself as low-key as possible."

Cass nods thoughtfully. "It's to be expected, I guess." She pauses. "It's the first time I've witnessed it up close like that. Those women had seen you with me, yet they had no problem fawning all over you, touching you." She stands, stepping over to the windows, her back to me. "It was difficult to be a bystander. To watch them touch what I think of as mine." And isn't that music to my ears.

I stand quickly, pressing my body close to hers, touching her at every available point. I nuzzle my nose down into her neck, kissing her below her ear. "You're the only woman I *want* touching me, Cass. Remember that." I place several more kisses as she kindly tilts her head, allowing me access. Then, turning her around and pressing her up against the cold glass, I lock eyes with her—stormy gray to calm blue. "I have a two-week press tour after Thanksgiving." She tries to look down between us, but I tilt her chin so I don't lose her eyes. "I plan on telling the world I'm a taken man, Bun. It'll be crystal fucking clear to all women to keep their hands to themselves. I promise." She smiles then, her shoulders relaxing. I'd give anything to be the one to make her smile each and every day. "I can't wait to tell the world you're all mine." I swoop forward, sealing my words with a deep kiss that leaves no room for questions or doubts. "C'mon. I need to take you to bed."

Holding her hand in mine, we lock the front door before extinguishing all the candles. Carrying her overnight bag in my free hand, I guide her upstairs, mentally planning what I'm going to do to her first. Dropping her bag on the chair near the window, I draw Cass into me and wrap my arms around her, erasing any space between us. Her heart beats double time, mirroring my own—it seems we're both worked up. Her hands slide up my back, grasping onto my shoulders as her tits press against my chest. Having her in my arms like this is a dream come true for me; one I never want to wake up from. Tilting my head down, I press kisses to her forehead, and as she closes her eyes; I kiss each lid gently, reverently. I want to worship this woman until there's no doubt in her mind that she's the only one for me.

Stepping back slightly, I remove her clothing piece by piece, revealing her gorgeous body to me inch by glorious inch. Lovingly, I caress my hand from her hip to the indent of her waist, then up further to cup one teardrop-shaped breast. I brush my thumb over her nipple until it's pebbled to my liking; a perfect morsel for my teeth to nip and bite, my tongue to lick and taste, my mouth to swallow and devour.

Goosebumps break out across her body; her shallow breaths come faster. The pulse point at the base of her neck flutters a fast tattoo. My other hand follows the same path up the other side of her body, while I lean down to nip her perfectly pebbled peak, then soothe it with my tongue. I take as much of her breast as possible into my mouth, drawing on the globe with a deep suck. Releasing it from my mouth, I give her other breast the same treatment. It's surreal to touch her in such an intimate way.

Her hands slide up into my hair, releasing the tie holding it back. Tangling her fingers in the strands, she holds me tighter, moaning softly. "I love what you do to me with your mouth. Please, never stop."

I pull away, remaining in position, glancing at her face. "Never, Gorgeous. I plan to have my mouth on you as often as possible for the rest of my days." Crouching forward slightly, I lift her under her ass and as she wraps her legs around my waist, I carry her to my bed, settling her gently on the edge. Pushing her back, I kneel, spreading her legs wide with my shoulders. She gets the hint, placing her feet on the edge of the bed, dropping her knees, and opening herself up to me exactly the way I like. Resting back on my haunches, I use my fingers to slide open her pussy lips from the bottom up, pinching her clit as I reach the top before sliding back down to begin the process again.

I rub my trimmed beard along the inside of her thighs, making them shake as my fingers continue to caress her pussy. The essence coats my fingers, which I rub along her thigh, then follow close behind to taste with my tongue.

"You taste so fucking good. I want your cream all over my beard, so I can smell you every time I inhale." Finally, I can't hold back any longer. Diving in, I swipe my tongue from the base to the top, feeling her pussy throb as her moisture coats my tongue, covering my beard.

Cass releases a long moan. "Make me come. Please, Toby. Make me come." She whispers over and over, her hips moving to create the friction she needs to fall over the edge. I help her along, thrusting first one, then two fingers into her tight hole. The wet warmth has my dick trying to push its way out of my jeans to get to her. Sliding my fingers purposefully in and out of her body while I suck her clit into my mouth has the desired effect. Cass's hips shoot upward as she spasms around my fingers, spilling her delicious juices all over my face. Her breaths are harsh, her tits rising and falling in rapid succession. It's incredible that I'm the man who gets the privilege of sending her flying into oblivion.

She lays sprawled on her back, her lips widening sleepily across her beautiful face. She looks stunning in this moment, flushed from her orgasm, spread open, ready for me. I slowly crawl up her body, smoothing my hands worshipfully along her tanned skin, leaving goosebumps in my wake, kissing and licking until I reach her mouth. Meeting her lips with a smile of my own, our kiss is slow, languid— quite the opposite of the blood rushing through my body. Her hands reach up to pull me down onto her, pressing her heated body further into the mattress.

As if only just realizing I'm still fully clothed, she pushes at my shoulders. "You need to get naked. Now, Toby."

Her slim fingers tug and pull at my sweater in haste to remove it as if it offends her in some way. Pushing up from the bed, I grab the back of the collar to pull the offending sweater over my head before haphazardly throwing it to the floor. As I free my belt, button, and zipper, allowing me to slide my jeans and boxer briefs to the floor in one swift motion, Cass scoots up the bed, resting her head on the soft pillow. Dark, hooded eyes study me closely, her hands gliding slowly over her silky skin as I climb back on top of her.

My dick bobs forward, trying to get to her, but he'll have to wait a little longer as I reach across to the top drawer to retrieve a condom. Cass reaches out, stopping my hand as my fingers connect with the cool, wooden surface. Then, switching my focus from the drawer to Cass, she shakes her head in the negative. "We don't need it. I trust you, Toby."

My body sags at the level of trust she's chosen to give me tonight. I swallow hard, my dick seeking her entrance. "Are you one hundred percent certain?" I study her face closely for any sign she's unsure or second-guessing herself. "Because once I've been inside you bare, I'm not going back to using condoms ever again." She nods in affirmation. "I need your words, Gorgeous."

She swallows, maintaining eye contact as her response comes out sure and steady. "I'm certain, Toby. I promise. I don't want to use condoms with you anymore. I don't need the physical or emotional barrier."

I don't need any further assurances from her. I quickly get into position, sliding my fingers through her pussy to check she's still wet and ready for me, groaning when my fingers are met with her slickness. Prodding the eager tip of my cock at her entrance, I push her thighs open wider and drive my hard cock to the hilt, my balls nestled against her ass. Rising on my elbows, I kiss her slowly, passionately, tangling my tongue with hers, swallowing her sighs and her moans. Lost in the kiss, our connection, I move—the slow glide out followed by a slow glide in, ensuring I rub her g-spot and clit on the way. Cass's legs wrap around my lower back, moving her hips in time with mine as we make love.

We take our time, kissing, grinding, building toward euphoria.

I'm in no hurry knowing I have her for the entire night and into tomorrow. "I'll happily spend the entire night stroking my cock in and out of your tight pussy, Gorgeous." Her pussy tightens around my shaft at my words—we both groan.

Sweat coats our skin, our hearts speeding up with the exertion, as I lose myself in my woman's stormy eyes, her plush mouth, and her stunning body. This woman stole my heart when I was sixteen years old, and as we've grown closer over these past weeks, I've decided she can hold on to it, keep it, and never give it back.

Our momentum gradually increases, skin slapping against skin. Cass's hands feel sensational, grasping onto my back, digging her fingernails into my flesh. Holding her eyes, I increase my speed and power, building our orgasms toward their mutual peak. Cass's walls squeeze my dick in rhythmic flutters as I grit my teeth to hold on to my own. I want to get her there so I can build her straight into another one.

As she comes down, I gingerly slide out of her and roll to my back, pulling her on top of me where I want her, then slide back into heaven. We lay like that, connected in the most primitive way until Cass is ready for more.

"Mmmm. That was so good."

I pull her head down to me, eye to eye, licking at her lips until she opens for me. Mouths open to the other, sharing breaths as we slide our tongues together. Grabbing her peach of an ass in one hand, I guide her hips back and forth to meet my thrusts. I can't go as slowly this time; the need to release is overtaking rational thought. Increasing my thrusts, I power up into Cass's tight hole as she pushes down, meeting me thrust for thrust. Her silky walls tighten, making my shaft pulse. My balls tighten up, ready to shoot my cum into her.

"Get there, Cass. I can't hold on any longer."

"I'm almost there. Just need—" I circle her clit with my fingers, hoping to push her over the edge, and as I do, she erupts, permitting me to let go. I groan out as my cum fills her pussy. The satisfaction I feel at knowing that she trusts me enough to allow it fills my soul. She flops forward, her head resting in the crook of my neck. Wrapping my arm around her, I use my free hand to stroke her tangled hair away from her face so I can kiss her forehead. With a serene smile on her face, she mumbles, "Love you, Toby."

Placing another kiss on her forehead, I return her words, "Love you, Bun."

FORTY-ONE

-cassia-

T OBY WAS INSATIABLE LAST NIGHT, WAKING ME REGULARLY WITH HIS mouth on my pussy the first time and his fingers inside me the second. I was thankful I didn't wake up to his dick inside me because I'm not sure I could've handled it without having a flashback to the time Jake came home drunk, thinking it was his right to have unprotected sex with me while I slept.

At one point last night, I pushed Toby away before I realized who I was with. I'll have to explain why at some point—I don't want him to think I was reacting to him because I wasn't. But I'm unsure how to broach the subject with him in the light of day. I know he already dislikes Jake a lot; I don't think it would take much to tip the scales toward hate.

As I roll over, I realize the bed's empty. I'm bereft at the loss of a morning snuggle with my boyfriend.

Boyfriend!

It's rare I get to lie in bed in the morning. Usually, I have to get up straight away to get moving for the day, but having the day off from all responsibilities is affording me a unique opportunity to relax. Snuggling down into the blankets with a smile, I think over last night and the last few weeks.

I've never met a guy more solid than Toby.

Even when he was pissed at me for not telling him about Poppy and breaking things off, he still maintained his connection with my daughter without missing a beat. Because of that, I feel more confident than ever in my decision to open my heart to him fully. To let him into my life and Poppy's life, too.

"You're finally awake, sleepyhead." Toby breezes into the room, looking as happy as I feel, carrying two cups that smell a lot like coffee.

Scrambling to sit up, I hold out grabby hands. "Gimme, gimme, gimme."

Toby chuckles. "I guess you want one of these—" He gestures to the cups in his hands. "And not me." He playfully pouts, looking freaking adorable. Then, handing over a cup of coffee made just the way I like, he leans down, kissing my forehead. I melt into a puddle every time he places a kiss there; it's such a beautiful show of affection and care.

"Well, I want you, too. It's just coffee ..." I leave my statement hanging as Toby slides back into bed, carefully situating me exactly where he wants me without spilling a single drop of caffeinated goodness—quite a skill.

"How'd you sleep?"

Surely he's joking. It's not like we got a lot of sleep last night. "The sleep I *did* manage to get was great. It just wasn't a significant amount because my *boyfriend* kept waking me up," I huff out with a giggle. I give him wide eyes as though I'm annoyed, but I'm really not because those wake-up calls were something else.

Now I'm all hot and bothered again.

I'm not sure my hoo-ha could take him this morning after the night we shared. He wraps his arm around my shoulder, pulling me in tight before kissing the top of my—what I'm assuming—is a rat's nest of hair.

"I'm not gonna apologize for taking advantage of having my girlfriend in my bed all night. In fact, it would make me happy if that's where she slept every night." He throws it out casually, as though what he said isn't a big deal. I laugh in response because I'm not sure I have the words to respond. We both sip our coffee, enjoying a few silent moments. I guess now would be a good time to apologize for last night.

I look up at him. "Uh, I owe you an apology."

He looks down at me, eyebrows drawn low over his cobalt irises.

"For when I pushed you away. It wasn't anything you did. It just took me a minute to remember who I was with. I, uh ... had a terrible experience once, which led to all sorts of major life changes for me." I swallow hard, glancing away. I'm not sure I can tell him anything more; does he even want to know?

He squeezes me, regaining my attention. "You wanna talk about it?"

"You've gotta promise you won't get mad."

His body tenses against mine. I can sense him preparing for what I'm about to share. Finally, he nods in agreement, jaw tight, mouth tight.

"When I was dating Jake, I always insisted on using condoms. You remember how on and off we were? He would always sleep around when we were off. I couldn't trust him to keep me safe, so I kept myself safe." His jaw twitches, but he tilts his head for me to continue. "One night, he came home drunk. I was already in bed and asleep. I woke up to him having sex with me. When I realized what was happening, I tried to push him off me, but he's so much bigger and stronger than me. I couldn't get him to stop. Finally, he came inside me, which I'd never allowed throughout our entire relationship. I was so angry at him that I had to have an STD check because of his selfish ass. That's when I found out I was pregnant—which was a surprise since I was also on the pill. While I would never not want to have Poppy in my life, he took my choice away from me that night." The anger radiating off Toby's body is lethal, and his silence is unnerving. "Say something," I whisper. I desperately need to know he doesn't think any less of me. I know none of what happened was my fault, but other people can be judgmental.

"He fucking raped you is what he did. Not only did he take your choice away from you, he fucking raped you." He goes deathly still, and I'm worried about what he's about to say next as he pulls away from me, ensuring he's not touching me in any way.

Does he think I'm too damaged to touch now?

Am I about to be told to get out of his bed, out of his life?

"I hope you know I would never, *never* do anything like that to you. I will never have sex with you against your will." He swallows, taking his gaze away from me before we lock eyes again. "I'm sorry, Cass, so sorry, if anything I did last night made you feel unsafe or made you feel I was like that fucking asshole." He brushes his hand through his hair in despair as he whispers, "Please tell me you know I would never do that to you." He looks up at me, devastation in his eyes.

I place my coffee on the side table and raise myself to my knees, cupping his face in my hands, his beard tickling my palms. Ensuring I have my eyes locked on his before I begin. "You are nothing at all like him. Not in any way, shape, or form. Don't ever, *ever* think I put you in the same category because I don't." I lean forward, pressing a gentle kiss to his forehead, before pulling back again. "I trust you with the most precious part of my life, my daughter. Toby, I trust you with my heart and my body." His body almost deflates, and I'm unsure if he would still be sitting upright if I weren't cupping his face in my hands. "I know you would never take anything from me against my will. I also know you would never put your hands on me for any other reason than to show me love. I promise."

He leans forward swiftly. I don't have time to brace myself, as his hands cup my face and he takes my mouth in a gentle kiss. He pulls back, each of us holding the other, eye to eye. "I would rather break my own heart before I would break yours. Smash it to pieces all over the floor at your feet as a sacrifice to keep yours intact, Cassia. I love you and Poppy so much."

He leans forward, pressing his mouth to mine; I open willingly, welcoming him inside. Rising, I straddle his lap, feeling his hardness against my feminine folds. Wrapping his arms around me, he presses up, finding my entrance before sliding inside. Sharing breaths, eye to eye, we make love, wrapped in each other, sealing our bond.

———

"C'mon. I need to feed you. Then I wanna pick up Poppy so I can spend the day with both of my girls." *Could this guy be any more perfect?*

I laugh as he slaps my ass playfully. "Okay, okay. I'm getting up. Not sure my legs are gonna work, so you might have to help me out."

Bending forward, he picks me up as though I weigh next to nothing and carries me into his decadent shower. Washing me from head to toe; he keeps it chaste because I'm a little tender. We dry off and dress quickly, making our way downstairs for breakfast. Toby whips us up some scrambled eggs with toast along with another cup of steaming coffee. Then we're on our way to pick up my girl for a day of fun—just like a regular family.

FORTY-TWO

-cassia-

I FEEL SO FREAKING SICK. I CAN BARELY LIFT MY HEAD FROM MY PILLOW, but I need to go to work. Making my way downstairs, I find Mom and Violet look to be feeling the same as me.

"Morning," I mutter, only to be greeted by their murmured greetings, which is very unlike our regular mornings in this household. Then it hits: that spasming in my stomach—the need to hold on to its contents before they come exploding out of places they're really not meant to. I make a run for the downstairs bathroom and drop to my knees over the toilet. My misery seems to go on forever. Just when I think I'm done, more seems to come out of nowhere. *Ugh!*

I manage to pull myself up from the floor, flushing away the evidence of my misery until I catch my reflection in the mirror. Bloodshot eyes, clammy, pale skin, and vomit in my hair greet me—gross. I set about slowly cleaning myself up as best I can before heading back to the kitchen.

"I think I have the stomach flu." I manage to say before Mom rushes past me, straight for the room I've just vacated.

"I think we all have it. I need to go upstairs to check on Jasmine. She was burning up through the night." Violet gingerly steps out of the kitchen to check on her daughter, so I do the same. Slowly, following her upstairs, focusing on putting one foot in front of the other, we make it to the top of the stairs before Violet covers her mouth in fear, dashing for the bathroom. I can't believe we all have the same bug at the same time.

I open Poppy's door to find her still sleeping, which isn't unusual for her. I usually have to wake her on a school day. What *is* unusual—she's thrown all the covers off the bed and is lying exposed to the chill in her room. Stepping over to her, I gently place my hand against her forehead, which is burning to the touch. She's clammy and very pale.

That's five for five with the stomach flu on this lovely Friday morning. I wet a cloth, then place it gently over Poppy's forehead, trying not to disturb her too much. The best thing she can do is sleep. I get a bucket to place next to her bed, call Sam to let her know I won't be in today, then call Gramma to ask if she could work with Sally the whole day. Once everything's sorted, I make myself as comfortable as possible, complete with a sick bucket and blanket, on the chair in the corner of Poppy's room, so I can monitor my girl.

I'm unsure how much time's passed when the doorbell rings, causing the lights throughout the house to flash. I wait to see if anyone else will answer it, but it seems I'm out of luck as it rings again. I can't hear anyone making their way toward it. Barely dragging my ass up, I slowly make my way back downstairs to answer the front door. It takes a concerted effort, and by the time I get there, I'm covered in sweat as though I've run around the block a time or two. Looking through the stained-glass inlay of the front door, I see Shane. Shit! I completely forgot he comes through to pick up Poppy for school. I don't want him to get sick; I think it's best to communicate through the door.

"Uh, hi, Shane. I'm sorry. I forgot to call you this morning."

I hear a muffled, "Is everything okay?"

"Uh, no. We all have the stomach flu—all five of us. We won't be leaving the house anytime soon. I'm sorry you came all the way here for nothing."

"That's okay. I don't mind. Can I get you ladies anything to help?"

"No, I don't think so. Thanks anyway."

"Okay then. Bye. I guess I'll see you guys whenever you need me over the Thanksgiving break?"

"Thanks for everything. We'll be in touch. Bye, Shane." I'm about to step away from the door when I remember Poppy has her guitar lesson with Toby this afternoon. "Shane," I call out as loud as I can.

"Yeah?"

"Can you please let Toby know we're all sick and Poppy won't be at her lesson today?"

"Sure, Cass. Take care. Bye."

"Bye, Shane. Thanks."

I sag against the front door as though I've completed a mammoth task. I sigh to myself as I turn, looking at the stairs I have to climb. Then, just as I'm about to head for the kitchen to see what we have in the way of crackers, another wave hits me. I make a mad dash to the bathroom. I get myself cleaned up again, grab what I need from the kitchen, check in on Mom (who's doing about the same as me), then head back to Poppy's room in time to catch her as she sits up, covering her mouth, tears in her eyes. Leaning her over the side of her bed, I grab the bucket for her, holding her hair back so she can expel the contents of her stomach. Her whole body retches. It's painful to feel my baby girl in such a state.

Once she's finished, I slowly lead her to the bathroom, where I deal with the bucket and clean both of us up in the shower. Finally, we both climb into my bed. I replace the sick bucket on Poppy's side just in case. I so badly want to close my eyes to sleep, but I need to make sure Poppy's okay.

I'm not sure if I fell asleep, but my eyes slowly open to the god-awful sound of the doorbell again. *What now?* I lay still, hoping someone else will deal with whoever's there. I can hear muffled voices, so I'm assuming I can relax again, but my stomach's not having it. For the third time this morning, I jump up and dive for the bathroom. At this point, I have nothing left to expel, but that doesn't stop my stomach from trying.

I'm too exhausted to move, so I decide it's a good idea to rest my head on the lip of the bowl for a moment.

FORTY-THREE

-toby-
_____

WHEN SHANE ARRIVED ON MY DOORSTEP WITH THE NEWS THAT Cassia's entire family had the stomach flu, meaning Poppy wouldn't be at our lesson today, I quickly pulled myself together. First, I made a trip to the convenience store and the pharmacy. Stocking up on ginger ale, lemonade, crackers, Imodium, and Ibuprofen. I also bought fruit juice, peppermint and chamomile tea, as well as ingredients to make a chicken broth for them all. Then there was the matter of being granted entry into the house. Rose wasn't happy to see me on her doorstep, and it took quite a bit of convincing on my part to get her to open the front door to let me in. I think I only won the argument because I still had stamina while she's exhausted from the virus.

Now, standing in the bathroom's doorway, looking at my poor love wrapped around the porcelain bowl, I'm relieved I came. I stroke her hair away from her pale, clammy face then carefully pick her up to carry her to her bedroom, where Poppy's already asleep on one side of the bed. She's incredibly weak and out of it; I don't think she's even registered she's been moved. I head back to the bathroom to wet a couple of small towels to care for Poppy and Cass. Meticulously, I wipe each of their faces down with the cool cloth, then rest them on their foreheads. Leaving the room, I check on Violet, who's curled around Jasmine. They're both burning up, too, so I repeat the process with them. Rose is downstairs, asleep on the couch with the TV on low. She doesn't seem to be doing as badly as the others, but she's still mighty unwell. I set a ginger ale beside her with a couple of crackers, then head to the kitchen to make the chicken broth.

Mom used to always make this for Kate and me when we were sick. I swear it has some sort of magic in it because I always felt much better after slowly slurping down a bowl. While it's simmering on the stove, I do the rounds again. Everyone's still asleep. Thankfully, there has been no vomiting since I arrived, but I take the time to rinse each cloth, wipe their faces, and replace the cool fabric on each of their foreheads. As I'm tending to Poppy, her eyes open sleepily, presenting a dull, lifeless gray instead of the cool silver I'm used to seeing from her. She sits up suddenly, eyes wide, gesturing that she's going to be sick. I lean her over the sick bucket next to the bed as I hold her hair out of the way for her. Her little body retching with spasms is like a punch to my gut. Once she's finished, I carry her to the bathroom to clean her up as best I can, then sit her up in bed. Once she's situated, I run downstairs to get her some lemonade I've left sitting out. She sips it slowly before giving me a weak smile and laying back down, falling asleep instantly. Cass must be completely out of it because she hasn't moved a muscle the entire time.

I spend my day going from room to room, ensuring everyone's as comfortable as possible. I have to change Jas because she was sick in her sleep. Messing herself, her pajamas, and the bedding. I felt awful waking Violet to change the sheets. I worked as quickly as possible, then threw everything into the wash.

I'm shattered, and it's only been one day. These viruses can last for longer than a week. I may need to call in reinforcements if the girls keep being sick at the rate they are. During the brief bouts of incoherent wakeful moments, I manage to get a little of the broth into everyone, along with crackers and ginger ale for the ladies; flat lemonade for the girls.

Everyone seems pretty settled at this point, so I think I'll call it a night. I prop myself up in the chair in the corner of Cass's bedroom. This is my first opportunity to check out her space because I've been solely focused on looking after everyone. It's simple, not overcrowded with crap and, interestingly, not a floral pattern in sight.

Sitting quietly, observing my girls, I think about the future with them. Having them move in with me, living with me, spending every available moment together as a family. Planning vacations, as well as holidays together, has me thinking about Thanksgiving coming up in less than a week. I wonder if they'll be well enough to celebrate.

ME

Hey Mom

Would we have space to add six more people to our
Thanksgiving?

I don't have to wait too long for her reply.

MOM

Hi Love

Oh, I forgot to tell you, we're having it at Kate and
Oliver's this year. She wanted to have all the kids over
and they have more room

Who did you want to invite?

ME

I wanted to invite Cass, Poppy, and the rest of the
Phillips family

MOM

Oh, I'm so happy for you Toby. Poppy's just delightful
and her Mom's so pretty

I don't think it'll be a problem, maybe check with Kate

ME

Okay, thanks Mom

See you soon

MOM

Love you x

ME

Love you too x

I knew she'd be happy to have Poppy around. She's practically
been counting down the years until Kate or I made her a grandma.

ME

I heard you guys are hosting Thanksgiving this year

It takes a few minutes for her to reply. I almost jump out of my
chair when my phone eventually vibrates.

SQUIRT

Yeah, is that okay?

ME

Of course. I was wondering if it would be okay to invite Cass, Poppy, and the rest of their family? Six people in total

SQUIRT

Of course. The more the merrier

ME

They're all sick with the stomach flu at the moment

SQUIRT

Oh no!

ME

I'm not sure if they'll be up for the holiday, but I figured it wouldn't hurt to check in first

SQUIRT

Oh, absolutely. They're always welcome. Any time

ME

Thanks Sis

Talk soon

SQUIRT

Okay. Love you brother x

ME

Love you too x

Tucking my phone away, satisfied with my organizational skills, I do one last check on the women, then settle down in my chair for the night to sleep.

———

Coming into awareness slowly, I sense eyes on me. Pretending I'm still asleep, I feel little fingers poke at my beard, followed by little girl giggles. I can't keep my lips from widening as I slowly open one eye, followed by the other. I'm greeted by two little girls who look remarkably well, considering how sick they were yesterday. I've heard when kids get sick, they go down hard and fast, but they recover equally fast. I never gave it much thought, but looking at the two little sweethearts in front of me, I'm thankful for how fast the girls have bounced back.

Their color still isn't what it should be, but they're definitely well on their way to a full recovery.

I sign as I ask. "How are you girls feeling today?"

Jasmine and Poppy both reply eagerly with goofy smiles. Placing their right hand, flat palm, against their lips, then moving it forward to rest it in their left hand. Letting me know they feel 'good'.

I rise from the chair, stretching out the kinks in my neck and back. "Okay, let's get you girls some breakfast." I pick up Jasmine while I hold Poppy's hand as we tiptoe from Cass's bedroom.

I need to keep their food simple today, so I make them some plain toast and give them half a cup of juice each. They happily sit at the table, swinging their little legs back and forth, smiling the whole time. It's great to see them somewhat back to normal.

"How come you were seeping on the chair?" Jas asks me. Oh, no, once this kid starts with the questions, she doesn't know how to stop.

I sign for Poppy as I speak. "I wanted to make sure everyone was okay last night, and well, there wasn't another bed for me. So I slept in the chair."

The girls nod thoughtfully, and I'm hoping that's the end of question time. "But Poppy wasn't in her bed, and I wasn't in mine. You could haf sept there."

Smart kid. Violet's going to have her hands full with this one. "I didn't want to be too far from Poppy and your aunt."

"Do you love them?"

"Yes, I do."

"Are you gonna be Poppy's daddy now?"

"I would like to be."

"My daddy doesn't want me anymore." Her bottom lip quivers as her eyes get that sad look that little kids sometimes have when they're about to cry.

Oh, shit! What do I say to that?

"I'm sure that's not true. I bet your daddy loves you and wants you very much." I look around for something to distract the girls. "How about after we eat breakfast, you guys can have a bath, then we can watch a princess movie?"

"Otay," Jas responds with a serious expression that suggests she means business to get on with the job at hand so she can get to the fun stuff.

Poppy's lips are spread wide as she asks, "You want to be my daddy?"

"Yeah, Poppy, I do. One day."

She throws her arms around my neck, squeezing tightly. Her little heart beats strong and sure against mine.

The girls finish their breakfast. Then, I give them a quick shower because I'm not sure I have the skill set to bathe them. Once they're dressed for the day, I set them up in front of the TV with the movie of their choice, surrounded by their favorite cuddly toys. Watching the first few minutes to make sure the girls settle in, the wild red hair of the princess on the TV reminds me of my sister's.

I leave the girls downstairs to watch their movie and I make my rounds, checking on the adults. They're still pretty out of it, not fully aware of what's going on around them. I wipe the exposed skin of their faces and arms with a cool cloth and replace the drinks on their bedside tables. At least nobody's thrown up today. That's gotta be a good sign.

I think we're up to our third movie of the day. In between, Poppy and I have done some guitar practice, entertaining Jasmine with our tunes. The girls have managed to glitter-bomb my beard, and I think I've done a pretty good job of keeping everyone fed and hydrated. The final credits are rolling, and I'm about to make a fresh batch of broth for everyone when I spy Cass carefully making her way downstairs. I quickly clear the few steps between us to help her the rest of the way down.

"What are you doing up and about? I'll bring you whatever you need."

She looks wrecked, but still so fucking beautiful. She tries to smile, which looks like it took a lot of effort. "I wanted to check on Poppy. I feel terrible. I've been so out of it that I've totally lost track of time. I haven't looked after my baby girl." Her eyes glisten, filling up to the point a tear escapes down her still-clammy cheek.

"She's good. I promise. The girls have been watching princess movies. They also decorated my beard." I wave my hand around my face to draw her attention to it.

She looks up at said beard, and her eyes widen. She reaches up, pinching it between her fingers. "Is that … glitter?"

"Yep! I've also kept them fed and hydrated. I even showered them this morning. They're all good. Seriously, go back to bed, Cass. I have everything covered."

"But I'm her mom. I *should* be the one looking after her."

"You don't have to do everything now. I'm here." She sags into me, as though the weight of everything she's had to deal with on her own since she got pregnant has finally been lifted from her shoulders. Wrapping my arm around her shoulder, I guide her the rest of the way to the living room. "You can say hello to the girls; check for yourself they're okay. Then back to bed. Okay?"

"Okay," she sighs.

Stepping into the living room, the girls spot Cass straight away and head toward her. They can see she's still unwell, so they treat her gently with careful hugs around her legs and waist.

"How are you girls doing?"

"We're good. Toby's been watching movies and playing with us. He's funny, Mommy." Cass's relief is plain to see. She needs to get used to the idea that we're a team now. When one's down, the other picks up the slack. She doesn't have to do it all on her own anymore. I know she's had the support and help of Rose, but it's not the same as having it from a partner.

"That's great. Be good for Toby, okay?" The girls nod vigorously. "I'm going back to bed." She hugs Poppy close, then signs to her, "I love you more than all the stars in the sky and grains of sand on the earth."

I help her back upstairs. "Do you want to have a shower so you can put on some fresh pajamas?"

"I'd love that, but I feel pretty weak. I don't want to fall over in the shower."

"Okay. Give me a sec. I'll make sure everything's okay downstairs, then I'll be back."

I head downstairs to give the girls a snack, turn off the stove, and make sure everything in the kitchen is safe for the girls. I set them up with some coloring in, explaining that I'm helping Cass in the shower. They agree to stay put, so I head back upstairs.

I guide Cass into the bathroom, then turn on the faucets, getting the water up to temperature. I strip off, then remove all of Cass's clothes and help her step into the shower. I wash her body. Even though she's terribly sick, my cock hasn't got the memo. I can't help the erection coming to life as I wash my girl. She barely has the energy to stand, and my dick thinks it's time to come out to play. *Stupid fucker!*

Rinsing us both down, we step out carefully to dry off. I find a clean set of pajamas for Cass, then sit her in the chair while I change her sheets. Once she's settled in bed, I get dressed in the same clothes I was wearing before because I didn't think to bring anything else with me—my sole focus was on getting here as fast as I could yesterday. I dish up some of the broth I've made and carry it with some crackers back up to Cass after checking on the girls.

I do the rounds again, ensuring Violet and Rose are okay, giving them some of the broth, crackers, and ginger ale, too.

"Why are you helping us?" Violet studies me with suspicion.

"Anyone would help you guys out if they could."

"Nope. My husband never once looked after me or Jas when we were sick."

"Well, I don't know him, but I grew up in a house where my parents worked as a team. If one was down, the other stepped up. Simple."

"Sounds like a fairytale."

"It was my reality growing up. I don't know any other way to be."

"I guess you're serious about my sister, then."

"Like a heart attack. Her *and* Poppy."

She nods. "Good." She chews thoughtfully on a cracker, then adds, "Do you love them both?"

"With everything I am, Violet. I want to be the one to take care of both of them. I want to call them mine. Both of them. Not one more than the other."

She nods, giving me a timid smile. "They deserve that."

"Yes, they do. So do you. Don't settle for anything less." She nods. "I helped Cass have a shower before. I'm not comfortable offering you the same service, but I can sit at the door while you shower to make sure you're okay if you feel up to it."

She thinks about it. "Thanks for the offer, but maybe a little later. If that's okay?"

"Sure. I'll check in on you in a while to see if you're up to it then."

"Thanks."

I leave her to it and make my way downstairs to spend time with my girls.

FORTY-FOUR

-cassia-

I CAN'T BELIEVE TOBY HAS SPENT THE LAST THREE DAYS LOOKING AFTER all of us. Seeing me at my absolute worst and caring for two young girls while Mom, Vi, and I were pretty much out of it. He's surely going to be rethinking his stance on wanting to be with me now. No young, attractive, single guy wants to sign up for that.

"Toby's pretty great," Vi blurts out of nowhere as we're all sitting around the kitchen table nursing our tender stomachs with dry toast and ginger ale.

"He certainly is. Did you see the note he left on the kitchen counter about Thanksgiving?" Mom nods toward the sticky note I noticed earlier but haven't yet read.

"No. What about Thanksgiving?"

"We're all invited, Gramma too, to his sister's house for Thanksgiving dinner with his family. So sweet of him to think of us. I've been too sick to do any preparation for the holiday. His invitation is a blessing."

"Do you think Shane'll be there?" Vi asks, and I raise my eyebrows toward her in question. "He, um, he seems really nice. Jas likes him. A lot."

"I'm not sure. This is the first I've heard about Thanksgiving. Don't you think it's too soon to be sharing combined family holidays?" He may have changed his mind since he wrote the note. I don't want to get my hopes up. "His sister's married to Oliver Stone, the billionaire. Remember? I'm not sure they'll want all of us intruding on their holiday."

Vi's eyes widen. "That's right. That man is sex on a stick. So freaking hot. I couldn't keep my eyes off him after the concert when we went for ice cream."

"Violet!" Mom admonishes.

"What? He is. You've seen him!"

"You don't need to talk about him like he's a piece of meat. I brought you girls up better than that." Vi makes a show of rolling her eyes at me.

"Well, I'm sure he's a great guy, but I can only base my judgment on what I know, and since I only know what he looks like ..." She shrugs, leaving her statement hanging.

I agree with her. He is hot, but not as hot as Toby. Toby has a raw sex appeal you can't ignore.

"I've actually been to their house. Well, *not exactly* inside their house, but outside. I did the flowers for their wedding." I sigh. "It was such a gorgeous location and even though they could have had anything they wanted for the wedding, it was kept small and simple." I grab my phone. "I'm just gonna check if the invitation is still valid."

"Why wouldn't it be?" Mom's puzzled face is almost comical.

"He might have changed his mind after having to deal with all of us." I glance away. "He saw me at my absolute worst. He probably never wants to have anything to do with me now."

"Rubbish, Cassia. That boy is in it for the long haul. Mark my words."

> **ME**
>
> Thank you again for looking after us

He answers immediately, as though he was sitting on his phone, waiting for my message.

> **TOBY**
>
> You're more than welcome, Bun

> **ME**
>
> I really appreciated it
>
> Sorry you had to see me like that

> **TOBY**
>
> Like what? Sick? Everyone gets sick

ME

Yeah, but I was a mess

TOBY

No one looks great when they're sick

Even though you were sick, my cock still got hard in the shower

Oh, my gawd! Even though I'm not fully recovered, my body heats at his words.

TOBY

You're always gorgeous to me, Cass

ME

Thank you

I wanted to check about Thanksgiving

TOBY

Yeah, what about it?

ME

Are you sure Kate and Oliver want all of us over for Thanksgiving?

It seems like a lot

My phone rings. "Hey."

"Hey, Bun. How are you feeling today?"

"So much better. Still not one hundred percent, but better than I was. Thank you for looking after us."

"You're more than welcome. But you can stop thanking me. You've thanked me enough." He sighs.

"Okay. I wanted you to know how much I appreciated it."

"I know you did. It was my privilege to care for you when you needed it." He pauses. "I already checked with Kate the first night I came over. I want to spend all of my holidays with you and Poppy. If it means dragging your whole family with you to have that, then so be it."

I grow warm all over with his words. He doesn't mess around or play games. He knows what he wants, and then he works toward getting it. For some reason, he wants Poppy and me in his life. I'm incredibly blessed to have him in ours.

"Okay. Only if you're sure."

"We're sure. Kate's inviting the kids from the shelter where she volunteers, so it's gonna be fun. It should be a great day."

"I know Mom was thankful for the invitation. She feels underprepared for the holiday. Poppy'll love to see Kate again. She loved meeting your sister and thinks it's amazing that you're twins. That you were in your mom's stomach at the same time." I laugh lightly. Toby laughs, too.

"Do you need me to pick you guys up, or can you get there on your own? I know my preference would be to collect you and Poppy."

That's his gentle way of telling me what's going to happen, so I go along with it. I would prefer to go with him rather than show up. "Would you mind picking us up?"

"Of course not, Bun. I'll see you then unless you need anything."

"I think we're all good here. We're taking things slow and recovering. See you on Thursday."

"See you Thursday, Bun. Love you."

"Love you, Toby ... and thanks again."

We disconnect the call, and I let Mom and Violet know Thanksgiving is a go.

———

I'm so freaking nervous. This is only the second time I've met Toby's parents, and I want to make a good impression. The first time was ... awkward, to say the least. Toby was shocked to find out I was Poppy's mom, while I was stunned that he was Poppy's guitar teacher. I'm racing around my bedroom, trying to work out what to wear when Violet comes strolling in.

"What's up, Sis? You're all over the place." She plops down on my bed, looking around at the pile of discarded clothes.

Throwing my hands up in the air, I huff. "I dunno what to wear. I want to make a good impression. Plus, I want to erase the last images Toby has of me. I wanna look good, but I can't work out what to wear."

She stands and studies the clothes on the bed as well as the ones still in my closet. "What about these black, skinny jeans with this red sweater? You can wear your knee-high boots. They always look amazing on you."

"You think that'll be okay to wear to Thanksgiving with his whole family?"

"Of course. Why not?"

"I wanna look classy."

"You'll look classy and casual. Sexy even. C'mon, you're running out of time."

"Thanks, Vi. I'll be down in a minute."

She blows me a kiss as she leaves my room. The butterflies in my stomach are going crazy as I get dressed, finish off my hair, and apply a little more gloss to my lips. As I step into the kitchen, Mom's putting the finishing touches to one of the two casseroles she made as our contribution to dinner. Finally, Poppy and Jasmine are ready to go, looking as cute as anything dressed in matching outfits.

The doorbell rings—*he's here!*

I draw a deep breath, releasing it slowly, trying to calm myself as I walk as calmly as possible toward the front door.

Opening it, Toby's waiting on the porch, looking edible in worn jeans with a black sweater that hugs his torso. "Hey." He smiles, sapphire eyes twinkling at me.

"Hey." I step into him, wrapping my arms around his torso and kissing his lips softly. "How are you feeling? You didn't get the stomach flu?"

"I'm great. No sign of sickness. Are you guys ready to go?"

"Yeah, come in. I'll get our coats." He steps inside, closing the door before turning to face the room in time to catch Poppy as she throws herself at him. Gramma Iris steps out of the kitchen, laughing at Poppy's antics.

Toby's holding Poppy on his hip, her arms wrapped around his neck. "Thank you for looking after all my girls for me last week."

"No problem. I was happy to do it." He looks at Poppy, jiggling her on his hip, causing her to giggle.

We gather everything we need and step out the front door. Mom stops dead in her tracks, causing us to walk right into her, almost knocking the casserole out of her hands. I glance up to see what the issue is, noticing a stretched limo parked in front of our house. What the ...?

Toby notices us all gawking at the car. "I figured everyone would fit in this. Hope you don't mind."

Mom's the first to respond. "Not at all. I was surprised, that's all.

It's very thoughtful of you to organize a ride. I figured we'd be following behind you and Cass."

"This makes it easier. C'mon, let's go." He's nonchalant about organizing such a lavish ride.

We all walk forward to pile into the fancy car. I've never been in a limo before. It feels somewhat over-the-top to turn up to Thanksgiving dinner in one, but I guess it was a fair solution. As we get closer to Kate and Oliver's home, my butterflies become out of control.

I needn't have worried, though, because as we pull up, Toby's entire family steps out to greet us like we're old friends. His mom and dad warmly welcome my mom, while his nan and another elderly woman fuss over my gramma. It's like our families have always known each other—that's how comfortable it all feels. I watch Toby hug his dad in greeting and their easy interaction. I can see the bond they share; the love between them is obvious.

As we're about to step inside, a minibus arrives. Half a dozen kids pile out with a large man and a petite woman hot on their heels. His hair's a mess, as though he's been almost pulling it out. She looks put together with a wide, friendly smile. Kate runs forward, arms open wide, as Oliver follows behind, hands in pockets and a smile on his face. His adoration for his wife is blatantly obvious for everyone to see.

Once all the introductions are made and everyone's inside and settled, Kate and Oliver explain it's a buffet-style dinner today. A long buffet is already set up, waiting for the hot food, a non-alcoholic punch for the kids as well as a 'special' one for the grown-ups. *Lucky us!*

The Stone house is stunning. I remember admiring the home's exterior, but the outside doesn't hold a candle to how warm and inviting the inside is. For such a large house, it feels cozy and welcoming. In addition, Kate's gone all out with holiday decorations, adding to the atmosphere.

Toby hasn't left my side, always finding ways to be touching me, little touches here and there, ensuring we're always connected. It's definitely louder than I'm used to with so many people gathered together to celebrate the holiday. It makes me even more grateful for my family; that it's growing larger by joining Toby and his family.

Poppy's even made new friends, dragging Jas along for the ride. It hasn't taken long for the kids to work out a way to communicate; it always amazes me how kids seem to easily work their way around obstacles. Kate and Oliver hand out a journal to each of the kids they spend time with at the shelter.

"I love the tradition of giving the kids a journal each Thanksgiving. The first year, it surprised me they had anything at all to be thankful for, but they did. So we're keeping it going."

She hands Poppy a journal, too. In purple. "Here, Poppy. I heard purple was your favorite color." I translate for Poppy. Her delight at being included is clear as she quickly gives her thanks, then immediately takes it to Toby to show him her gift.

"Thank you for including Poppy in your journal giving. It was a sweet gesture." I nod toward my little girl and Toby. "She obviously loves it."

"No problem. Once I knew you guys were coming today, I *had* to include her. Unfortunately, Jas is a little young, so I didn't get her a journal. I bought her a coloring book instead." Kate's incredibly sweet, readily including the girls in her gift-giving tradition.

Mom is helping Toby's mom, Emily, in the kitchen along with Roman and Alice, who I learned only married recently. They were the friends in need of wedding flowers at short notice. Roman and Alice are the kids' caretakers at the shared home where they all live. James and David—Oliver and Toby and Kate's dads—are preparing the salad. I assume they were given the simple task, as they're possibly not competent in the kitchen. They all laugh at something Roman said. Mom looks comfortable. It's as though she's known them for years. She has a few friends she spends time with occasionally, but it would be great if she made friends with Toby's parents because I have a feeling he's gonna stick.

Poppy comes running over to me, waving her journal. "Look what I got, Mommy."

"I saw. You know what it's for, right?"

"Yeah. I have to write the things I'm grateful for."

"Exactly."

"It's gonna be a lot of things. I'm grateful for heaps of stuff." I laugh because that's typical Poppy. She finds only things to be happy about. She's rarely sad or down in the dumps. "Hey, did you know one of the other girls is called Ivy? That's another plant name. Just like us."

"Yeah, I heard that. She must be super cool, hey?"

"Super cool."

She runs off back to her new friends after ensuring I'll keep her journal safe. Gramma Iris steps back inside with Toby's nan, Kate, and their friend, Margie. They're all cackling at something and I feel the three of them together will be trouble.

FORTY-FIVE

-toby-

It feels right to have Cass and Poppy here with my family. They all meld together seamlessly, not that I thought they wouldn't. *Who wouldn't love Cass and Poppy?* The rest of Cass's family is just as cool and easygoing. Cass looks sexy as hell, making it murder to keep my touches chaste in front of everyone. It's been too long since I've had her. Which reminds me, I haven't told her how gorgeous she looks today.

Roman cuts through the noise with a loud whistle.

"Dinner's ready on the buffet, everyone. We'll serve the kids first. Then the adults can get their own."

Cass moves toward Poppy to dish up, but I stop her. "Can I do it?"

Her eyes widen at my question. "Sure. If you want to."

"I want to. Is that okay?" She smiles brightly, which reaches her eyes, giving me an emotional high. Who needs drugs when I have my girls?

"Definitely."

I collect Poppy as well as a plate, and we make our way along the buffet; her pointing out what she would like to eat. I note Shane's doing the same for Jasmine while Violet and Cassia refresh their drinks with the 'special' punch. Of course, Margie, Iris, and Nan have already had more than their fair share of that punch; Margie and Nan are already wild enough together, they don't need the help.

The kids are all settled at a smaller table with their food, and I collect Cass so we can make our way over to the buffet to fill our plates.

"I can't believe how much food there is. I should have worn my stretchy pants." She laughs.

I snuggle into Cass's neck to whisper, "I love you in these sexy jeans. I'm sorry I forgot to tell you how gorgeous you look today." I kiss her neck, right below her ear. "I'll be happy to help get you out of them later." Pulling away, I wink before moving further along the buffet to get some turkey. We settle in at the table, Cass sitting next to her sister, and me next to mine. Taking turns around the table, everyone shares something that they're grateful for.

Kate nudges me with her elbow. "I guess your patience paid off, Brother?"

"Yeah." I can't stop the goofy smile which fills my face. "You were right. In the end, I didn't need to push. She let me in all on her own."

"I'm so happy for you. She's a great lady and I adore Poppy." She takes a bite of her dinner, chewing thoughtfully, then swallowing. "I can't believe you're pretty much a daddy." Her eyes, which match my own, are looking suspiciously glassy. "You're gonna be such a great daddy, Toby. The best thing about this is I'm now an aunt and I've finally got a sister. Yay!"

"Thanks, Squirt." She shoves her pointy elbow into my side. "Oooomph. Geez, your elbows are deadly weapons." I rub my side in an exaggerated show, making her laugh.

The conversation is loud and is regularly broken up with boisterous laughter. Everyone's having a great time, enjoying fantastic food, surrounded by family and good friends. My heart feels full watching all the people I care about most in the world together in this one space, sharing a meal and enjoying the holiday together. I only hope I get the chance to show Cass exactly how grateful I am for her later on. I have a special surprise up my sleeve that I set up with Rose yesterday for later.

———

With stomachs full to bursting, we all load ourselves back into the limo, heading back to the girls' home. Hopefully, Rose has already packed an overnight bag for Cass and Poppy so we can head straight to my place.

We arrive at the Phillips' home and pile out of the car, carrying containers of leftovers, which will possibly feed everyone for the next couple of days. Kate always over-caters when she has an event. As we get inside out of the cool air, Rose rushes further inside their home and returns with a duffel, passing it to me. Cass looks between her mom and me quizzically. "What's going on?"

"You and Poppy are having a sleepover at Toby's house." She signs as she speaks. While Cass is shocked at the turn of events, Poppy excitedly jumps up and down in celebration.

Cass is shaking her head, eyes wide. "We can't sleep over at your place." She's making some weird gesture with her face like I should know better than to have a sleepover in front of her daughter. Cass doesn't know Poppy asked me when she could come for a sleepover. It happened at our lesson after Cass's birthday, when she spent the night. I set up a bedroom for her and I can't wait for her to see it. "I don't think that would be a good idea." She's glancing between her mom and me.

"Why wouldn't it be a good idea? Poppy's super excited about it," Rose answers.

"Yeah, but …" She stops signing. "Do you think that sets a good example for Poppy to see her mom sleeping in a man's bed when we haven't been together all that long? I mean, we've been together for a little while, but Poppy thinks we only got together on my birthday. I don't want to be a poor role model for her."

Poppy stomps her foot. "You stopped signing for me."

I sign, "This is adult conversation."

She crosses her arms with a pout—she doesn't like to be left out of the conversation.

Rose wraps Cass in her arms, beating me to it. "And don't you think it's good for Poppy to see you happy with a man who cares for you both so much? A man who puts you *and* your daughter first?"

I don't want to push her into anything she's not ready for; as disappointed as I'll be if they don't come, I have to let her make the choice. "It's okay if you're not ready, Bun. I understand what you're saying. I don't want you to do anything you're not comfortable with."

She bites her bottom lip, and I want to take over and bite it myself. It's been hell all afternoon, not being able to touch her in the way I really want to. Finally, she looks at Poppy's excited face and signs, "Do you want to have a sleepover at Toby's house?"

Poppy nods like a bobble doll, holding her hands in the begging position under her chin. I watch Cass carefully, observing the moment she gives in. "Okay then. Let's go have a sleepover." Poppy hugs her mom tightly around the waist while I release the breath I was holding, hoping to get the answer I wanted. We all say goodbye and I walk my future family to the waiting limo to take them *home*, which I desperately want to make into a family home with them.

The limo drops us off at my place, and once we're securely inside, Shane heads off, leaving me alone with my girls. The first night I brought Cass here, I never would have imagined I'd have her back in my space with a daughter in tow after the reunion. A daughter I'll proudly call my own one day.

"C'mon, I want to show you your bedroom." Cass sucks in a breath, graphite eyes wide. I take the duffel in one hand and Poppy's hand in the other, then climb the stairs. I show Poppy where her bathroom is on the way. I stocked it with the same strawberry bubble bath, soap, shampoo, and conditioner she uses at her house.

"Oh, Toby. You've gone to so much trouble for her," Cass whispers, her fingers held up to her mouth. "You didn't need to do all this." Wait until she sees Poppy's room.

"It was nothing, Bun. I want her to be comfortable here. I'm hoping you guys will stay over regularly." Maybe I'm pushing her too fast, but I can't help myself. She smiles at me, giving me a simple nod, her eyes suspiciously glassy.

We walk down the hallway. As we get closer to Poppy's bedroom, my stomach rolls in nervousness. I really hope I've done the right thing and they both love it. I suck in a deep breath, readying myself for the reveal to go either way as I open the door. Looking at both of the girl's faces the moment they see the room for the first time, I think I got it right if their smiles are any sign. Poppy doesn't hesitate, moving into the room. Spinning around to look at everything. I even bought her a new guitar and a laptop. That way she can practice while she's here.

"Oh my god, Toby. This is incredible." Cass glances at me before joining Poppy on her exploration. Then, as Poppy investigates everything more closely, Cass steps into me, wrapping me in her embrace. She presses a chaste kiss to my lips. "I don't know what to say. This room is everything Poppy loves. You're incredibly sweet to do this for her."

I wrap my arms around her, locking us together. "I want her to be happy here. I want to make this our home, Cass. I hope you know that." I finish with a kiss on her forehead as she melts into me.

"I never thought Poppy and I would have this." She looks up at me, stormy eyes glassy. "Thank you doesn't seem enough."

"You guys being here is all the thanks I need, Bun."

"I love you so much. I'm gonna show you exactly how much once she's in bed."

"I love you, too. Both of you." I press a kiss to her lips, grinding my hips into her stomach. "I can't wait until later."

Poppy wraps her little arms around both of us, pulling us as tight as she can with the cutest grin on her face. Then, she pulls back to sign, "Thank you, Toby. Thank you. Thank you. Thank you. I love it. I love everything. It's beautiful."

"You're most welcome, young lady." Then, laughing, I bend down to pick her up to include her in a family hug.

Perfect.

My life is perfect!

Cass changes Poppy into her pajamas in case she falls asleep during the movie, then we show her where we'll be sleeping in case she wakes during the night. I had nightlights installed down the passage to help her find her way easily if she wakes in the night and forgets where she is. We head downstairs, where I show Cass the switch I had installed to flash all the lights in the house for Poppy. That way, we can get her attention wherever she is. Cass's eyes look misty again—storm clouds brewing with rain—as she steps in to press a kiss against my lips.

"You are getting so lucky tonight, Mister," she whispers against my ear with a smile, waking up my dick. He's going to have to wait because I promised Poppy a movie tonight and I always keep my promises.

"I'm gonna hold you to that, Bun." I kiss her hard, then step away, making sure I don't get carried away. We head into the living room, where we load up the Disney Channel.

Did I ever think I'd be subscribing to the Disney Channel at this point in my life? *No.*

Am I happy that I am? *Hell yeah!*

I make popcorn before we settle in for a movie. Poppy takes up her usual position between her mom and me. I stretch my arm along the back of the couch to play with Cass's silky hair and I take a moment to admire my girls.

My house finally feels like a home.

About an hour into the movie, Poppy lays down with her head in my lap and her legs across her mother's. The trust she affords me whenever she does this fills me with gratitude and a sense of purpose I've not felt before. This little girl relies on the adults in her life to keep her safe, to love her unconditionally, and to allow her to be the person she's meant to be. That I'm now part of her circle fills me with a sense of pride that's unparalleled in my life. Even more so than the Grammy's I've been awarded and the albums I've released; or the success I've experienced in my career so far. This right here ... *this* is my purpose.

Cass switches off the TV and lights as the credits roll, checking that the front door is locked. I carry Poppy upstairs to her new bedroom as Cass follows behind. As soon as Poppy's tucked in for the night, gentle kisses pressed against her forehead and cheek, I eagerly lead Cass into my bedroom. Or should I call it *our* bedroom?

FORTY-SIX

-toby-

As soon as the door to our bedroom closes, my Bun has me pressed up against it, her lips smashed against mine, hands loosening my hair out of its elastic. I catch up quickly, my tongue swiping against her lips, demanding entry. We get lost in a kiss that's so fucking sexy. My cock's going to have zipper indentations on it at the rate it's expanding and trying to escape my jeans. I switch places, pressing Cass against the door, grinding my cock against her, eliciting a sexy moan which vibrates against my mouth. This woman turns me on like no other, lighting a fire inside me that can only be extinguished by her.

Kissing my way down her neck, I pull at her sweater. She gets the hint, lifting her arms so I can remove the offending item. Her tits greet me, cupped in black lace, presented to me like the gift they are. I'm thankful the lamp's on, so I can appreciate the gorgeous sight of Cass's body. Nuzzling them, licking the nipples through the fabric, I finish with a bite before releasing the front clasp. Kudos to whoever invented the front bra clasp, making life easier for men all around the world. Catching the gorgeous globes in my waiting hands, I knead them carefully, pressing them together and nuzzling them, just the way I dreamed of doing in my teenage bed. The reality of Cass, of being with her, far surpasses any teenage fantasy I could have ever dreamed up.

Cass tugs on my hair until I'm looking up at her; dark eyes, full of lust, look back at me. "I really need you inside me. It's been too long."

"In good time, Gorgeous." I slide down her body, releasing the button and zipper on her jeans. The boots make it difficult to peel the skin-tight denim away from her body, but I'm a man on a mission—nothing's gonna stop me from having my way with her. Matching black lace panties greets me and I take a moment to admire them up close as I inhale her arousal. It's like a fucking aphrodisiac, not that I need any help to get hard when I'm in her vicinity.

Sliding her underwear down her legs, I lift one shapely leg, balancing it over my shoulder, and take my first swipe of her pussy. I moan at her cinnamon taste. I don't know how she does it, but she always has that sweet, woody taste and scent that drives me wild. I get down to business, licking, stroking, nipping her lips, using my fingers to tease her clit.

Three knocks sound on the other side of the door, and I freeze, looking up at Cass. We both know we can't ignore Poppy. She's in a strange house and a strange bed for the very first time. I stand up, giving Cass my sweater to put on, covering her nakedness, and then open the door. Poppy's rubbing the sleep from her eyes as I bend down to pick her up.

Looking at Cass, she signs. "Mommy, I'm scared."

"Baby. You don't need to be scared. C'mon, let's go have a cuddle in your new bed." Cass looks apologetically at me as she reaches for her daughter. I give her a look I hope telegraphs it's okay and tell her I'll be waiting. I think it's best if they have some quiet time together in Poppy's new space to help her acclimate. Thinking I'm no longer needed, I step out of the way so the girls can get past, but Poppy reaches out to grab my hand, pulling me along with them. I guess she wants both of us.

All three of us lay in Poppy's bed, Cass and me on either side, sandwiching her in the middle. Poppy snuggles down under the covers. Feeling safe, she closes her eyes. We watch her as she falls asleep until I decide watching Cass watch her daughter is sexy as fuck. A ghost of a smile crosses her lips as she looks up at me.

"What are you doing, perv?"

"Watching my girlfriend love on her daughter. Did you know it's sexy as fuck watching you as a mom?"

Her eyes drop to Poppy again as her smile drops for a moment. "You have no idea how much of a turn-on it is that you love my daughter as much as you do."

We lay in quiet bliss, watching each other, watching Poppy, enjoying the moment together. Once Cass is certain Poppy's well and truly asleep, she gestures for us to leave the room. Once in our bedroom, I waste no time in picking up Cass to throw her onto the bed, so I can pick up where I left off.

"Get that sweater off. Show me your pussy."

I step back to remove my jeans. She wastes no time. Removing my sweater swiftly and opening her legs wide, she uses her fingers to caress her delicate pink folds for my benefit—eyes hooded and biting her bottom lip. She's a wet dream. I dive down, taking a swipe of her lips, licking her fingers as I do.

"Play with your tits. I've got this."

Her fingers quickly move out of my way, and I watch her glide them up her body until they reach their target. She presses them together, then teases her nipples. Once I'm satisfied she's on task, I leave her to it and focus on my own. Her warm channel greets my fingers with a tight squeeze as I pump them in and out with purpose. Seeking the swollen area that's not as smooth as the rest of her walls, I know I found the spot I'm looking for. Massaging the area in time with my tongue on her clit, her legs tense around my head as her silky pussy walls tighten around my fingers as she breaks apart beneath my mouth. Her moans and sighs make my dick harder than granite, if that's even possible.

"That's it, Gorgeous. You're a fucking sight to behold when you fall apart." My chest expands with pride that I'm the one to bring her pleasure. I'm the man who will give her the pleasure she deserves for the remainder of my days.

Removing my fingers gently as she finishes, I climb up her body, paying close attention to her breasts with my mouth as my cock seeks her entrance. She's so fucking wet from her orgasm. I have no problem sliding home. Braced above her, our eyes lock, and I pause. Taking a moment to study her face, I absorb her love for me.

"I love you, Bun," I whisper, my lips touching hers, my eyes locked on hers, my breaths exchanging with hers. I don't give her a chance to respond; I press forward to deliver a kiss that expresses the intensity of my emotions.

Joined, not moving, just kissing.

My hair curtaining us from the world.

Her warmth surrounding my cock.

Her breath filling my lungs.

Her love filling my soul.

Moving my cock incrementally in and out of her body, we build a rhythm. Our bodies move together as if we've done this a million times when, in reality, we've only been together like this on a few occasions. If she were living here, we could do this every single day. Slowly, steadily, we build and fall over the edge in mutual satisfaction, sighing and moaning against each other as we continue to kiss.

Cass peers up at me with a lazy smile touching her lips, her eyes serene. "I love you so much." She presses up off the bed to seal her words with a kiss.

Keeping our bodies intimately joined, I roll us to the side so I don't squash her with my weight. Then, using one hand, I brush her hair away from her face, laying a tender kiss on her forehead. "I want you to think about you and Poppy moving in here with me when I get back from my press tour."

Her eyes widen as her lips part, but I stay her words with my finger pressed against her lips. "Just think about it. It's a few weeks away yet. Okay?"

She nods. "Okay. I'll think about it."

We fall asleep, my dick still inside my gorgeous girlfriend.

FORTY-SEVEN

-toby-

I STEP INTO MY BEDROOM AFTER MY MORNING SWIM AND I IMMEDIATELY know something's wrong. I can detect the distinct sweet floral scent of a perfume that I hoped I would never smell again. Feminine underwear lies on my bed like an invitation, one I never want to receive again. Memories flood, knocking me on my ass as my breath leaves my lungs. This can't happen again. I refuse to let her rule my life a second time. My home is meant to be my sanctuary. It needs to be a safe place for Poppy, for Cass, and for me. If this psycho's back and thinks she can mess with my life, she has another thing coming.

I message Shane.

ME

Can you come up to my bedroom to look at something?

Within moments, I hear his heavy footsteps running up the stairs. I haven't taken my eyes off the garments on my bed as he comes up beside me. Looking at him, I see the instant he smells the perfume, and recognition sets in.

I tilt my head toward the bed and he follows, eyes widening as he spots what I found. "Fuck."

"Yeah, fuck."

"I'll call the psych ward to check she's still there."

"You do that, but I don't think she is."

I step out of my bedroom, slamming the door closed in frustration. I need to block it all out. Pretend it's not happening again. Stepping into my studio, I plan to lose myself in my music for a few hours while I wait for Cass to come over.

———

Making my way out of my studio, Shane catches me in the hallway.

His eyebrows are drawn down, his jaw's tight. "She's still in the facility."

I shake my head. "Are you sure?" *What in the hell is going on?*

Walking back to my bedroom, I open the door to check that what I saw this morning is still there. That it wasn't my imagination playing tricks on me. I wouldn't be surprised since I'm stressed about flying out —leaving Cass and Poppy behind. But then Shane saw it, too. So it can't be my mind playing tricks on me.

We both glance at the bed. The lingerie is still there with that awful odor still in the air, milder now, but still there. I'm fucking confused.

"Does this mean I have a copycat stalker?"

Shane shrugs. "I dunno, man. But she's still under psychiatric care. I made them check her room."

I stand, rubbing the back of my neck, trying to make sense of the situation. Shane's equally confused.

Light footsteps sound on the stairs, and we both step out of the room to see chestnut hair appear, followed by steel-colored eyes together with a smile I want to see every day. Cass comes straight to me, wrapping her arms around my waist. She smells different. I push her away.

"What's wrong?" She studies my face. "You look pale. Are you getting sick?" She holds the back of her hand to my forehead, checking my temperature.

I glance between Cass and Shane. "You smell different. What perfume is that?" Shane catches on, leaning forward, sniffing my girl-friend. I give him a warning look, so he backs away with a smirk on his face.

"You like it? I thought I'd try a new one. It's called Miss Dior."

"No, I don't fucking like it. I like the way you usually smell." Shane's eyes widen comically, and I realize how I spoke to the woman I love.

"No need to be so damn rude. What the hell is wrong with you?" she snaps.

We're both already on edge because I fly out tomorrow for my press tour and we're dreading the time apart. Add to that, finding my room smelling like a past nightmare means I need to temper myself. Shane looks as though he wants to step in to defend me, but I stop him with a shake of my head. Smart man that Shane is, he steps away from us. Leaving me to face the wrath of a pissed-off Cass.

Carefully placing my hands on Cass's shoulders, as though she's a grenade that may explode if mishandled, I pull her into me, snuggling her face into the crook of my neck. Kissing the top of her head. "I'm sorry. I shouldn't have spoken to you like that. Please forgive me." I kiss her again. "I don't want to fight when I won't see you for two whole fucking weeks."

She sags against me. "It's okay ... just ... don't do it again. Okay?"

"I promise, Bun."

I pull away, pointing over my shoulder. "Do those belong to you?" As her expression changes from forgiving to pissed again, I realize how my question sounded. I'm not doing very well this afternoon.

"Who the hell else is gonna be leaving lingerie on your bed?" She stomps over to the bed, snatching them up, waving them in my face. "I was planning to give you a sexy treat tonight before you have to leave tomorrow, but maybe I won't."

"Awww, don't be like that." I follow her, tugging her back into me. "Let me explain. Please?"

I sit on my bed, situating Cass on my lap.

FORTY-EIGHT

-cassia-

HE'S ACTING VERY UN-TOBY-LIKE. I'M NOT SURE WHAT TO MAKE OF him. The way he shoved me away from him when I hugged him, it ... well, it hurt. He's never spoken to me or treated me like that before—it was a shock. I know he's as anxious as I am about our impending separation, but he didn't need to take it out on me. Now, sitting on his lap, he's scanning the room, looking everywhere but at me. The tenseness in his jaw as well as the frown lines across his brows have me worried.

Finally, he looks at me. "A couple of years ago, I had a stalker." Shane mentioned something about that. "She, uh, she used to come in here and leave her ..." He rubs the back of his neck, tensing his jaw. "Her, uh ... dirty underwear under my pillow. Her perfume ..." He gestures toward me with his head. "Would be all over my bedding, as though she rubbed her body all over my sheets." I can't hold in the gasp as I glance at his bed. "It started with her sending me personal messages on Facebook and Insta. Several times a day, she'd let me know what she was up to, how much she loved me, and send me photos of her boobs and vagina. Never her face." He brushes his hair behind his ear. "Then she started sending me love letters and small gifts. It was constant. Every day, something else would turn up here at the house."

I open my mouth to speak, but I don't know what to say to him. I can tell he's caught up in the memories by the cloudiness in his normally bright blue eyes. I place my hands on his chest because I have to touch him. His heart's beating incredibly fast; I'm worried it's going to beat right out of his chest. "She made a photo album. Like a regular

671

family photo album of us together in different places, with kids, me coaching little league. It was fucking weird. The photos never showed her face and mine was always photoshopped onto different men." I suck in a breath because that's unbelievably twisted—what a sick thing to do. "I would sometimes come home to find my favorite meal set out on the dining table, with the table set for two, candles, the works. Then it escalated to the underwear and messing around in my bed." He releases a heavy sigh, so I wrap my arms around his shoulders to offer him support. "It took months to work out who it was and to actually catch her. The woman was very unwell. She ended up in the psych ward. She put me through hell, Cass ... and ... when I walked in here, smelled the perfume and saw the lingerie, it took me back there." He locks eyes with me. "I'm sorry I reacted the way I did."

I cup his face in my hands, pulling his face forward to place a gentle kiss against his smooth lips surrounded by soft bristles. "Thank you for sharing with me. I completely understand your reaction. It must have been an awful experience for you. I'm sorry I brought back those memories. I thought sneaking in to leave my lingerie displayed on your bed would be a sexy tease." I kiss him again. "I assume that's why you employed Shane."

He nods. "It definitely gave me the excuse I needed, but it's also why I've been protective of Poppy. People go to extreme lengths sometimes, and I didn't want her caught in the crossfire."

"I get it now. I do. But I also think it's time to call Shane off her watch. You need him while you're away. We'll keep Poppy close. I promise she'll be safe."

He shakes his head, his jaw tensing. "You don't understand how creepy these people are, Cass. They wait for any opportunity. That woman stalked me for months. The stuff she did ..." He glances away again before looking back at me.

I can see his fear and concern for Poppy, but I don't think she'll garner the same attention as Toby did with his stalker. "How about you take Shane with you?" He's already shaking his head. "Listen, please. I'll sleep better at night knowing you have him with you. If it makes you feel better, we'll keep your guy, Len." I only hope he sees reason. I soften him up some more, grinding down on his dick as I kiss him (maybe soften him up was the wrong phrase because he's as hard as a rock).

He kisses me back, grasping the back of my head to take control, pressing his dick harder into the softest part of me. Pulling away, pressing my forehead to his, I implore, "Please. For me?"

He huffs out a breath. "Okay. But I want you to know I'm not happy about the swap. Shane's been giving me a hard time about it, too. He thinks the risk to me is higher than to Poppy at this point."

I agree with Shane. "I think he's right." Toby nods lightly.

"Uh, do you mind if we have a shower?" he asks sheepishly. "I really need to get that smell off you."

I wriggle off Toby's lap, pulling him up with me to head to the shower. "Sure thing. I'll give this perfume away. You'll never smell it on me again."

He kisses my shoulder. "Thanks, Bun."

Toby treats me to some extra attentive loving in the shower, and even though it wasn't what I had planned for our last night together for a while, I'm certainly not complaining. What that man can do with his nimble fingers is nothing short of astounding. He certainly keeps my lady bits happy.

But more than that, he keeps *me* happy. I've never felt so safe, so cherished, so loved before. I know he would do anything in the world for Poppy and for me.

FORTY-NINE

-cassia-

WE STAND ON TOBY'S FRONT STEPS IN THE EARLY MORNING. THE CHILL surrounds us as we say our final goodbyes. "Why can't I come to the airport? Sam and Sally can hold the shop for a little while."

"I would love for you to come to the airport. Hell, I'd love it if you'd grab Poppy and jump on the plane with me, but there'll be too many people. I don't want to draw more attention to the fact that you guys are going to be here unprotected. Our photos are already all over social media. I'm terrified someone's gonna come after you guys. Humor me, please. Stay as close to Len as you can. Try not to go out more than necessary. I know I'm asking a lot, but it would make me feel better."

The tension radiating off his body is intense. I can feel it transferring across to me; making me feel unnecessarily worried. I push it down—I don't want him to sense that I'm worried. We don't need both of us getting worked up. "I can do that for you. Just work, school, and home for us for the next two weeks. But only because I love you." I agree with a smirk, punctuating it with a cheeky peck on his lips.

His body sags as he releases a long breath, kissing me on the nose. "Thanks, Bun. I appreciate it. And I only worry because I love you guys. You and Poppy are too important to me to put at risk."

I think the events of yesterday are still raw for him, making him more anxious than necessary. "I know. We'll be careful, I promise."

We share one more intense kiss, then I drag myself away from him to head to work for the day as he heads to the airport to begin his press tour. This time it's only two weeks.

How will I feel when he's away for months at a time for his actual tour?

Work is terrible. This place is usually my sanctuary, but today it's not offering the peace I typically feel when I'm here. Looking up into the corners of my little shop, I sigh at the sight of the hidden cameras Toby insisted on installing. I can't believe how quickly they worked to get them in. He said it would make him feel better to have the cameras recording inside since I didn't have Shane standing outside. He doesn't have as much faith in Len as he does in his best friend, so he wanted additional measures for my safety and Poppy's. I reluctantly agreed to give him peace of mind.

I can't concentrate no matter how hard I try. My mind is constantly wandering to Toby—wondering what he's doing, where he's at, who he's with. Not that I don't trust him. I do—one hundred percent. I just miss him and it hasn't even been a full day.

———

Toby and I have been messaging regularly back and forth for the last three days, but it's not enough. I miss him so much. I miss his smell, his touch, the rasp of his beard against my skin, the warmth of his body. He told me to be secure in my room, on my own, ready for his text tonight. So here I am. Poppy's in bed, and I'm in my warm fleece pajamas, reading the latest Bratva romance by Bree Porter on my Kindle. My phone vibrates with an incoming message.

TOBY

I miss your sexy ass

ME

I miss you too lover

TOBY

I want you in my bed

ME

I miss your bed so much

TOBY

I'm gonna fuck you for a whole day and night when I get home

ME

Promises, promises 😏 😉

TOBY

I always keep my promises

The things I'm gonna do to you

ME

What sorts of things?

TOBY

You're gonna sit on my face so I can eat your pussy for starters

I can't believe I'm sexting my boyfriend. I'm squealing inside like a teenager receiving her first love note.

ME

Yeah? That sounds so good

TOBY

Yeah, you're gonna cover my face and beard with your juices, so I can taste and smell you for hours

My dick will be so hard from licking your pussy

Then I'm gonna fill your pussy with my fingers, while you fuck my face

ME

Can I suck on your cock while you're eating my pussy?

TOBY

Fuck yeah

I'm so fucking hard for you

ME

I'm so wet, god I miss you

As I'm about to slide my hand into my pajama bottoms, my phone rings, scaring the shit out of me. I press to accept his call, holding the phone up to my ear.

"Is your door closed?" His voice is gritty—god, he's sexy. He's as turned on as I am.

"Yeah," I whisper.

"Good. Take your pajamas off." He's not messing around.

I put the phone on my nightstand, quickly stripping down until I'm completely bare. "I'm naked." I didn't realize how breathy my voice was until I heard him groan on his end of the phone.

"Good girl, now tell me … how wet are you?"

I dip my fingers down to my pussy. "I'm so wet, Toby. I wish you were here to lick up all of my cream."

"Slide your fingers down to your beautiful pussy and let me listen to them slide in and out of your tight hole."

Oh, god. His words.

I move the phone down to my pussy, then do as he told me. The noises I'm making are obscene.

I put the phone back up to my ear. "Did you hear how wet I am for you? Are you hard?"

"I'm so fucking hard for you. I'm stroking my cock so hard right now, imagining your tight pussy strangling it." His heavy breaths fill my ear.

"Mmmmmm. My fingers don't match up to your dick, but your words, they get me so hot."

"Rub your clit, Gorgeous. Just the way I would, small circles."

"Oh, god, Toby. It feels so good. I'm getting close. Are you close?"

"Yeah, Gorgeous, I'm close. Rub harder, then slide two fingers inside you. Imagine it's my fingers fucking you."

"Oh, oh, oh …" My pussy spasms around my fingers as my legs shake. I've never had an orgasm like this before while talking to my boyfriend over the phone.

"Yeah, fuck, I can feel your pussy squeezing my cock so hard. Mmmmmhm." He grunts as he comes undone. "Fuck, that's messy," he huffs out as he laughs mildly.

His statement's so unexpected that I laugh, too. "Oh, Toby. I miss you so much and I'm not talking about your dick. Though I miss that, too." I chuckle.

"I miss you too, Bun. I'm counting down the days."

"Me too. I saw you on The Tonight Show. Jimmy's such a funny guy." Watching Toby on television was surreal. I used to follow his career intermittently once he got big via social media and interviews on TV, but it's somehow different now I've spent time with him on a personal level.

"Yeah, he is. Not just in front of the camera, either. He had me in stitches beforehand, too."

I lower my voice. "I love how you're letting everyone know you're off the market. Thank you." I don't think he truly realizes how much it means to me that he's sharing his personal life with the world, so women back off.

"I needed to make it clear that my woman doesn't like sharing. Just as I don't like to share either." His voice is deeper, raspier as he tells me he doesn't like to share.

"You sounded so good last night." His voice is incredibly rich and warm. "I loved the new song. Is it going on the album?"

"Yeah, I wrote that one when you weren't giving me the time of day." He chuckles, but it's forced.

"I'm sorry about that. I was trying to protect myself when I really didn't need to." My stomach turns as I remember how I ended things abruptly with him. I'm thankful he didn't give up on me.

"No problem, Bun. It all worked out how it was supposed to."

———

I wake with a start, my phone stuck to my face. I must've fallen asleep while we were talking. I'm still naked as the day I was born from our sexting session. My body warms as I remember our text messages and conversation last night.

FIFTY

-toby-

I HATE BEING AWAY FROM HER. FROM BOTH OF THEM.

I've decided I'm definitely not doing my normal tour when the album releases. It's too hard being away from her and Poppy for any length of time. I know for a fact I won't make it if I'm away from them for six months touring the country. I *don't want* to make it without my girls for that long.

They're my priority now. The music's great and all, but they're my future, my world.

I answer the door to my suite, finding Peta standing with three cups of coffee. I take them from her so she can step inside. She's a petite firecracker who always has my best interest at heart, but I don't think she's going to like what I'm about to tell her this morning. "Morning, Peta."

"Morning." She breezes past me, making herself comfortable at the small dining setting where Shane's already set up. "Morning, Shane." I follow behind, placing the correct coffee in front of each person as Shane grunts his response. He barely tolerates Peta on a good day, and he's in a crap mood today for some reason. "Now, what was so important that you needed to see me desperately this morning?"

I don't quite know how to break it to her, so I think I'll just rip the band-aid off. "It's about the tour for this album."

"Yeah, I'm still finalizing the dates and venues. Then I'll work on seeking suitable support talent in each location. You wanna go with local talent, right?"

"Yeah, about that. I don't want to do an extensive tour this time."

Her eyes narrow as her back straightens; she looks like an angry pixie. "What the fuck, Toby? I've already invested months of time and effort into planning the damn thing. You can't just up and decide on a whim you're not doing your normal extensive tour." She's almost yelling at me as she finishes. I almost feel the need to protect myself against a physical attack.

"I have different priorities now."

"Oh, do tell. What are your priorities now?" she snarks at me.

"Cassia and Poppy. I don't want to be away from them for too long."

"You've been, what, fucking this chick for a month, maybe two at the most, and now you're going to throw everything away we've worked for? Are you for real?" She practically snarls.

"Watch your fucking mouth, Peta. I won't have you speaking about Cassia like that. She's the real deal for me and I have Poppy to think about, too. It's not only about me anymore." I stand abruptly, tipping my chair over in the process. "You fucking work for me. Remember that. Make it work."

"I know I work for you, asshole. You can't throw something like this at me, expecting me to be all, 'okay, Toby, sure thing, Toby.' We're talking about your career, *which*, until a few months ago, *was* your priority. So forgive me for not responding in the way you expected," she snarks at me, rolling her eyes. She looks across at Shane, who always keeps out of these conversations. "Did you know about this?"

He shakes his head in the negative. "Nope. And as far as I can tell, he's the boss, which means he gets to decide what he wants to do with his career. How he wants it to progress." I'm surprised he spoke up on my behalf, and I think Peta is too, because she slams her mouth shut, sagging back into her chair.

Shaking her head, she seems resigned. "Shit. Okay. What do you want to do then?"

"Well, I was thinking four cities, two nights in each. Allow three days in between for setup, pack down, and travel. We would need the largest capacity stadium in each city to make it work." She's nodding as she types like crazy to get everything down. At least she seems somewhat on board with my new plan. "If we make the final concerts at home, that makes the whole time away less than three weeks in total." Which makes it more tolerable.

"I think it's workable. Limiting your appearances makes you more appealing, anyway. The whole playing hard to get thing could definitely work in our favor." There she goes, putting on her marketing hat. "Okay, let me work with that. Are you still looking at early June?"

"Yeah, that still works." I can hopefully convince Cass to come along and bring Poppy, too. It wouldn't be too long for her to be away from her shop. Sally's reasonably competent, and I think she's looking for someone else to help.

"Okay, I'll get onto it and let you know. Luckily, we haven't set dates or have tickets on sale yet." She looks pointedly at me as she stands from the table, taking her now cold coffee with her as she hurries to the door. "You owe me big time for messing me around." She slams the door behind her, and Shane breaks out into laughter.

"She's an angry pixie today."

I nod. "That she is, but I *did* throw her a curveball. So it's understandable." I shrug, taking a drink of cold coffee.

———

I've been doing interviews all over the place for the last ten days. I've just about had enough. Can't these guys come up with some original questions? I've been answering the same questions repeatedly; I could almost answer them while I'm asleep.

The thing that pisses me off the most is when they play the video of Poppy and me at her debut performance. I get she has star appeal, but I refuse to use our performance together to further my career. Peta always thinks it's great when they pull the footage out, but I shut that shit down real quick. Social media's been blowing up about my over-protectiveness of the girls in my life—opinions are divided about whether I'm too controlling and protective while others think I'm 'so sweet'.

I don't care what anyone thinks. They're my girls, and I don't want anyone messing with them.

FIFTY-ONE

-cassia-

WORKING OUT BACK IN MY WORKSHOP, I'M COUNTING DOWN THE DAYS until Toby comes home. We've messaged, talked, and sexted every single day—but I miss him so much. I don't think it registered how much I've grown used to seeing him at some point every single day. If I'm not spending time at his place, he's visiting me at the shop or at home. Every single female in my family adores him, too.

"I'm going to lunch now. See you in half an hour."

"No problem, Sally. Can you pick me up a salad, and I'll pay you back?"

"Sure." She heads out to lunch. She's a great kid. I'm beyond thankful to have her here helping me in between her classes.

I have a huge wedding this weekend, so I'm putting together all the greenery today for the table arrangements. That way, I only have to add in the fresh flowers tomorrow. I hear the bell over the door tinkle, and I step out with a professional smile, ready to …

I freeze in my tracks when I see who it is.

"Wh— What are you doing here?" My heart beats a million miles a minute as I tremble.

"Can't I come to say 'hi' now? You think you're too fucking good for me now that you're fucking a star? He's telling everyone in America that he's fucking you and in love with *my* fucking daughter," he practically spits at me as he shouts. "You're my fucking family. Not his!"

Shit! I never considered how Toby's interviews would negatively impact us. He was worried it would bring out the crazies for him, jealous girls who feel he belongs to them, but neither of us banked on

Jake. "It's not like that, and you know it. You have no reason to be stopping by. We have nothing to talk about." My voice comes out steady, concealing my panic.

He moves lightning-fast around the counter to stand toe to toe with me. I tilt my head back to peer up at him. The veins in his neck and forehead are bulging, and self-preservation kicks in—the urge to step away from him is overpowering. As I make the first move to do so, he grabs my wrist.

"Ow, let go, Jake."

Out of my periphery, I see Sam step out of the office. "Leave her alone, or I'll call the police." Her voice is shaky, and she looks scared out of her mind as she holds her hand protectively over her protruding belly.

He snarls at her, releasing my wrist to step toward her. With only eight weeks to go, Sam's bump is significantly larger.

Jake gets right into her space, pushing at her shoulder. "Call the fucking cops," he snarls like an animal. "I ain't doin' nothin' wrong."

"You're intimidating us. That would be enough."

She steps back to head into the office, and his whole body seems to grow—the space he's taking up is overwhelming; his anger is like a living organism. Grabbing Sam by her forearm, he flings her full force across the small space. It's like the whole thing happens in slow motion as I let out a panicked scream. I can see what's going to happen, but I can't do a damn thing to stop it. She sickeningly smashes against the counter, baby first, then crumples to the floor, cradling her belly, sobbing. Jake bends down with his arm raised back, ready to inflict a blow. I quickly scramble onto his back, pulling on his arm with everything I have in me, screaming bloody murder.

He stands, attempting to dislodge me, but I hold on for dear life, scratching at his face like a madwoman. I sense we're moving, but I'm not wholly aware of it in my crazy attempt to get him away from Sam. Agony explodes down my back as he slams me into the solid wall—my head flies back, connecting with the brickwork. My vision goes blurry around the edges and it's tough to hang on, but I would rather take the brunt of his anger than he do any more damage to Sam and her baby.

"That's your baby in there, you fucking motherfucker!" I scream at him, trying to get my finger into his eye socket. I need to get him away from her.

Where the hell's Len?

I try to glance out the windows to see what's going on, but my vision's still fuzzy, and too much is happening at once.

"Stop fucking scratching me, you bitch!" He grabs my left forearm, twisting and pulling hard. Agony in my shoulder overwhelms me, forcing out a blood-curdling scream. I release him, having no other option as intense pain rushes through my system, almost causing me to black out—but I can't.

I have to fight.

He'll go after Sam. He never wanted the baby, and this is his chance to get rid of it. He's like a raging bull—his face red, saliva coating his mouth.

He slams me into the wall again. Without any purchase, I slide down it to the floor in a puddle of useless arms and legs. He takes the opportunity to kick my ribs, smashing them and forcing the air out of my lungs. Gasping frantically, I struggle to get any air and panic, which won't help me in trying to catch my breath.

I can't die.

I have Poppy to look after.

He can't do this to me, to Sam, to Poppy, to Toby, to my family.

Who in the hell does he think he is?

Does he think he can come into *my* shop and attack Sam and me?

My inner thoughts give me the strength to get up so I can keep fighting. I'm not going to let him do this to us.

He must've thought I was down for the count because he turned his back on me, moving his attention back to Sam. "I never wanted this fucking kid." He lands the punch to her stomach that I tried my best to prevent. We both scream at the same time.

He must spot my movement as I fight hard to sit up, working myself into a standing position to protect Sam, because he stomps over to me and, lifting his foot, he slams it down on the lower half of my right leg.

More excruciating pain floods me as I feel the snap of bones.

Falling to the ground, blackness fills my vision as I fall into oblivion

…

… *feeling like a failure.*

FIFTY-TWO

-toby-

O<small>UT OF THE CORNER OF MY EYE</small>, I <small>SEE</small> S<small>HANE STANDING OUT OF</small> camera shot, reading something on his phone—his face is like thunder. I can almost feel his anger radiating off him from here. He looks up at me, gesturing that he's stepping out. It's not like I can acknowledge him while I'm in the middle of my interview.

Once I'm done, the host thanks me for my time and I step away from the cameras and crew. Peta's standing to the side, eyes red and puffy, her bottom lip trembling with Shane beside her, looking as though he wants to kill someone. They glance at each other, then back to me. Dread settles in my belly, my gut telling me something's terribly wrong.

Looking between the two, I swallow the feeling of dread. "What's going on?"

Shane takes hold of my arm, guiding me away from the few people around us into a private alcove. He glances down at his feet, and when he looks back up at me, his eyes are glassy. "What the fuck's going on? Tell me."

"Uh, I don't know how to tell you this."

Peta starts crying. I'm assuming it's not the first time by her puffy red eyes.

My hands fist on my hips as adrenaline begins coursing through me to prepare for whatever they're about to tell me. "Just fucking tell me. What's wrong?" Their behavior shows only one thing—shoring up my feet, I brace for bad news.

689

"Cassia and Sam were attacked in the shop around lunchtime today."

"What!" I yell as I start moving. I need to get to Cass. "Where are they? Are they okay? What happened? Who the fuck attacked them?" Even as I ask, my gut tells me I already know who it was. I'll kill the motherfucker myself.

Shane and Peta fall into step with me. Peta's almost running to keep up. "They're in *Mercy Vale*. Sam's being prepped to deliver her baby via c-section, and Cass ... Cass is still unconscious."

I break into a run. "Get me on a plane, now!"

"You're already booked. A car's out back to take you guys to the airport. I'll sort everything out here, then I'll fly home. You guys can go. I'll find my way back to the hotel," she rushes out between sobs.

We get to the car in record time, thanks to the adrenaline powering me. Peta tries to hug me, but I'm in too much of a rush. It's going to take fucking hours to get to my girl.

"Toby. I'm so sorry this happened. I hope they're gonna be okay." I don't even acknowledge her in my rush—the anxiety of getting to my girl overwhelming all my senses. My heart is shattering beneath my ribs and will only be whole again if Cass is okay.

Sitting in the car on the way to the airport, I can't stop my leg from shaking or my foot from tapping impatiently on the floor of the car.

"What the fuck happened?" More importantly. "How did it happen? Where the fuck was Len?" He's next on my list of mother-fuckers I need to kill.

Shane takes a deep breath. "Apparently, Len was at lunch when the attacker came into the shop. When he came back, Cass was uncon-scious, and the guy had just kicked Sam in the stomach." *Fuck!* "He fought with the attacker, but he got away. He contacted local law enforcement. They're going to study the footage from the cameras inside the shop." He turns away, swallowing hard. "I'm sorry, Toby. I should have listened to you and stayed behind with the girls." Thank god we installed those cameras.

As furious as I am about what's happened, I can't let Shane carry that guilt. "You didn't know something like this would happen. None of us did. Don't go down that path, man." I grip his shoulder and squeeze, punctuating my point. "Can you tell me anything else? Do we know who did this to the girls?" My gut tells me I already know, but I need it to be said. I need to hear that motherfucker's name.

"Len thinks it may have been Jake. He's not sure. He didn't get a good look at the guy in the chaos before he escaped. Len says the guy was like a raging bull." Shane shares a look, suggesting he also thinks it was Jake. He hadn't been around for a while, but before that, he *was* getting handsy with Cass. Something's obviously tipped him over the edge, and he's snapped.

"What about Poppy? Is she okay? Is she safe?" I don't think I could handle having both Cass and Poppy victims of Jake's brutality.

"Fuck, I'll check in with the school. Give me a minute."

It's two-thirty in the afternoon. She *should* still be in school. Watching Shane's face carefully as he talks with the school officer, his face blanches and his jaw tightens. "Call the cops. Call them now and get them down to the school. He's already landed her mom in the hospital." He hangs up, immediately making another call.

"What the hell's happening? Is he at school? Is Poppy safe?" *Fuck!* I squeeze my knees tight to the point of pain in an attempt to keep myself still, but it's getting harder by the second.

Shane covers the mouthpiece. "He's causing all sorts of trouble in the office, yelling and cursing, throwing chairs around the room. But they won't release Poppy because he's not on the approved list." He holds his finger up, indicating he'll be a minute. While he's talking to the police, I stare out of the window, unable to contain my thoughts. My body thrumming with adrenaline.

When we arrive at the airport, I don't wait for Shane to jump out of the car. I know he'll follow. Instead, I sprint to the check-in desk to tell the woman who I am. Peta's worked her magic because Shane and I are immediately taken through the back passages to the correct gate and onto the plane without delay. As the plane fills, it's taking everything inside me to sit still. I need to get to my girls. I need to lay my eyes on them. The suffocating feeling is overwhelming and all-encompassing. The sheer terror Cass and Sam must have felt during the attack. Anger pulses through me at the weak excuse for a man who thinks it's okay to beat on women.

I'm going to go after him with everything I have. He's going to be sorry he was born. I'm not some weak sixteen-year-old kid he can bully around anymore. I'm going to make that son of a bitch pay for what he's done.

Shane gets off the phone after several calls. "Cass's family knows what's happened. They're on their way to the hospital. Do you wanna contact your family, or would you rather I do it?"

I shake my head in the negative. "I'll do it."

"Do it now, before we start moving, and you have to turn your phone off."

I nod.

With shaky hands, I pull up my contact list, pressing Dad's number. He answers on the fourth ring. "Hey, Son. How are all the interviews going? Your mom and I have watched every single one."

As soon as I hear his voice, I break down. I unashamedly let the tears stream down my face. Shakily, I whisper, "Dad."

His tone changes. He's immediately on alert. "What's wrong? What happened? Are you okay?"

I shake as my tears turn to sobs, and I struggle to take in a full breath. I feel more than see Shane slide my phone out of my hand. I drop my head into my hands, allowing the feelings of hopelessness and anguish to break free, barely aware that Shane's relaying the terrible events of today to my father. He disconnects the call and wraps an arm around my shoulders, letting me have my breakdown.

"Let it out, Toby. Once we're home, Cass is gonna need you to be strong. Let it out now." As the plane prepares for takeoff, I sit, sobbing in my best friend's embrace.

FIFTY-THREE

-toby-

WE BARGE THROUGH THE HOSPITAL EMERGENCY DOORS TO FIND MY whole family and Sally in the waiting room. Kate immediately engulfs me in one of her hugs, which I desperately needed.

"I'm so sorry this happened to Cassia. It's awful," she mumbles against my chest. When she looks up at me, blue eyes exactly like mine rimmed in red greet me; her nose red and her cheeks blotchy. We're particularly close, which means she'll be experiencing my pain as though it's her own, just as I did when she hit a rough patch with Oliver. I'm not sure if all siblings are as close as we are or if we're close because we're twins. I smooth my hand down her hair and raise my eyes above her head, making eye contact with Dad. He's scrutinizing my face carefully for signs of distress. I think I got all of my tears out on the plane. I tip my head to let him know I have myself together, and he returns the gesture.

Mom's holding onto Nan as they walk forward together. Oliver steps in to peel Kate away from me, giving me a very serious tilt of his head. His whole body's drawn tight. I can feel his anger over the attack from here. Mom and Nan step into me, giving me their love and support in the only way they know how—hugs and fussing.

"This is awful. Who would do such a terrible thing to such a lovely woman?" Mom's completely bewildered.

We've never had anything like this happen to anyone we've known. It's so far out of the realm of our experiences to date that it's difficult to understand why someone would do something so heinous. However, Shane and I know exactly who's responsible for this horrendous crime

693

against two women who did absolutely nothing to deserve his hate and anger.

"I have a pretty decent PI I use if you need him." Oliver offers.

"Thanks, but the guy's already been arrested. The police caught up with him at Poppy's school. He was trying to get to her and went berserk when they wouldn't let him have her." Thank god the school only allows the kids to leave the grounds with a registered person.

Mom gasps. "It wasn't random?"

I shake my head. "No. It was Cassia's ex, Poppy's father." Mom covers her mouth with a shaky hand, tears rolling down her cheeks. "But why?"

I shrug. I have no words for what he's done. I don't want to think about what his plans were for Poppy. But I'm beyond grateful he couldn't get his hands on her.

Shane messaged Rose to let her know what we found out and that we were on our way to the hospital. Cass's entire family is in shock, which is entirely understandable.

Dad wraps his arm around my shoulder, squeezing me close to his body. He heard my sobs over the phone, and I know he's worried about me. After all, he is a psychologist.

"You want me to stay with you or head back to the shop to get the footage for the police?" Shane asks.

"Go get the footage and take it to the police. That's the priority. We need all the evidence we have to make sure he gets put away."

Shane nods, looking uncomfortable. "Uh … did you want to … uh, watch the footage?"

"Why on earth would you want to watch what happened?" Mom butts in, her normally steady voice high-pitched.

Dad steps across to her, wrapping his arm around her. "It has to be his choice, Em."

She looks up at him. "I know. But it'll be horrible to see exactly what happened." Dad squeezes her shoulder, and she acquiesces.

"Yeah, I do. Make a copy to keep. I'll watch it when I'm ready." My gut's rolling. I don't know if I'll ever be able to watch the attack, but I want to have the option. Shane nods, saying his goodbyes to everyone else before pulling me aside.

"Give Cassia my love. Okay?" I nod and Shane turns around, walking purposefully out of the hospital to make sure Cassia's attacker gets the fullest punishment possible.

Rose walks toward us down the corridor, her face pale and blotchy, her eyes red and swollen. I meet her partway, not thinking twice about comforting her. Her body sags into mine as her hands clutch the sides of my shirt.

"Oh, Toby," she sobs into my chest.

Rubbing my hand up and down her back to soothe her, I whisper, "She's gonna be alright. She's gotta be."

"I don't understand for the life of me why Jake would do this to her."

"Did you know he's been hassling her since the reunion? He wants her back." I suck in a breath. I feel that all my talk about Cass and Poppy in my interviews may have been the catalyst that pushed him over the edge. "How is she? Can I see her?"

"Well, that's certainly no way to treat a woman you want to have in your life." She huffs, stepping away from me and acknowledging my family. "Thank you all so much for coming."

"We can't express how sorry we are this happened to your daughter. How is she?" Mom steps in to embrace Rose.

"Thank you. It's certainly been an afternoon." Her voice is shaky as her gaze skates around all of us. With a sad smile, she takes my hand in her own. "She's awake." She nods as if confirming to herself Cass is okay, swallowing harshly as though to gather her emotions. "She has a concussion, broken ribs, and a bruised spine. The lower half of one leg is broken, and they've put it in a cast. She also had a dislocated shoulder, which has been corrected, as well as bruising on her arm."

My stomach rolls and I'm worried I'm going to be sick. Hearing the results of the attack reignites my fury. "Can I see her, please?"

"Of course. Come on. I'll take you to her room."

I turn to my family. "Thanks for coming, but you may as well go home. I'll let you know how she's doing. Maybe you can come back to visit tomorrow." I don't want to share Cass with any more people than her mom and gramma at this point. "I'll tell her you all came and that you give her your love."

They all nod, hugging me as they leave. Rose and I make our way down the corridor toward my love. "I have to warn you. She's pretty bruised and sore."

Words escape me, so I only nod, swallowing down my bile. I'm doing my best to keep myself together because Cass doesn't need to see me broken; she needs my strength and my love more than anything.

Arriving at Cass's door, we both pause. Rose checking with me if I'm okay, and me taking a deep breath in preparation. Finally, she opens the door, and the world falls out from beneath my feet as I lay eyes on the woman I love.

Anger rises, but I push it down with equal force.

I don't know how anyone who calls himself a man can put his hands on a woman in anger and cause so much destruction.

I take four strides to reach Cass's bedside, and as soon as she sees me, tears immediately run down the side of her beautiful face, and her bottom lip quivers.

I want to take her in my arms, but she's so fucking broken.

Leaning down, I gently wipe her tears with my thumbs, laying a gentle kiss on her forehead, which appears to be free of bruising. Then, gently pressing my forehead to hers, I lock eyes with my love.

"I love you so fucking much. I'm so fucking sorry, Cass," I whisper against her lips.

She lets out a sob, and I softly cup her head, breathing in her pain. "You're safe now. He's been caught and they'll have to lock him up." I feel her nod gently, and I still her head. "Don't move, Bun. I don't want you in any more pain than you already are."

We stay like that, with me bent over her bed, dull gray eyes to blazing blue, sharing breaths until her eyes close and she dozes. When I look up, Rose and Iris are watching us closely.

"Would you mind staying with Cass?" She looks back at her mom. "We feel terrible, but we need to get home to check Poppy's really okay." Rose is worrying the end of her shirt with shaky fingers. "Mom also promised Cass she'd work with Sally to get everything ready for the wedding this weekend. We know she's in good hands with you."

"Of course. I'll be staying with her until she's discharged. Then I'll be taking care of her."

Rose nods as though she already assumed that's what I'd do. "Violet's home looking after Poppy and Jasmine. She'll probably want to come to see her sister's okay for herself."

"Sure. That's understandable. My family is worried about Cass, and they barely know her. I can't imagine what it's like for you guys." I swallow hard, dropping my eyes back to Cass. "If it were Kate, I'd want to be where she was."

"Thanks, Toby."

"Uh, hug Poppy from me, please. I felt homicidal at the thought of Jake getting to her and what he planned to do."

With glassy eyes, they nod, kiss Cass gently goodbye, then come around to me. Rose places both of her warm hands on my cheeks, peering up at me.

"She's incredibly lucky to have you. They both are." She pulls my head down to kiss my forehead, the same way my mom does. Iris hugs me, kissing my cheek. Then they both head out of the room with one last look at their daughter and granddaughter.

Alone with my girl, I pull up a chair. While holding her free hand, I study her. The bruising on her face and forearm. The tangles in her hair and dried tears on her face. Down her body to the cumbersome cast on her leg. I can't see her torso, but I imagine it's pretty bruised, considering she has bruising down her spine as well as broken ribs. My jaw tenses, and I know it's going to be that way for a while yet to come. My phone buzzes.

> **SHANE**
>
> I watched the footage of the attack
>
> You should be fucking proud of your girl. She fought him like a champion to protect her friend

I look back at Cass, sleeping soundly. Tears track down my face as pride fills me for the strong woman she is.

> **ME**
>
> Thanks bro

> **SHANE**
>
> I've taken it to the police and filled in the necessary paperwork

> **ME**
>
> I appreciate it, thanks

> **SHANE**
>
> No problem. Let me know if you need anything

> **ME**
>
> Will do

I sit watching my girl. Unsure of how much time has passed. A doctor walks in as Cass begins to wake, her eyelids slowly lifting, revealing her graphite gaze, locking me in place.

"Good evening, Cassia. How are you feeling?"

"She's been asleep—" I glance at my phone. "For about an hour. She's just waking up."

"Good, she needs to rest, but we don't want her sleeping too long with that concussion."

Trying to lift her head, Cassia whispers 'hello' to the doctor.

"Stop moving, Bun." Her eyes snap to mine, blinking back tears.

The doctor steps closer to Cassia. "Where are you feeling the most pain, Cassia?"

"Everywhere hurts," she whispers with a shudder.

"Okay, we'll get some pain medicine for you in a moment." The doctor flashes a light in Cass's eyes, records something on her tablet, then looks back up. "I need to talk with you about the results of our tests." Then she looks at me. "Would you mind stepping out of the room, please?"

The hackles on the back of my neck stand on end.

I'm not leaving her.

Now or ever.

Cass places her hand on my arm, squeezing it. "Toby's my boyfriend. I'm okay with him staying, Doctor."

She nods. "Okay." Dropping her eyes back to her tablet, she runs through Cass's injuries and what treatment they've done so far. "I also wanted to let you know the baby's fine. It's early enough that the injuries you sustained in the attack didn't impact the embryo." She smiles as though she's delivered news we were waiting to hear—I'm confused as fuck.

Why is she calling Sam's baby an embryo?

Cass looks relieved. "Thank you, Doctor. I'm so glad Sam's baby is going to be okay. I was so scared that … that he … he … what he did …" A loud sob escapes, preventing her from finishing. I brush her tangled hair away from her face, trying to calm her. The violent sobs can't be good for her broken ribs.

FIFTY-FOUR

-toby-

THE DOCTOR LOOKS CONFUSED. "WHO'S SAM? I WAS TALKING ABOUT you." Her eyes widen. "You didn't know you were pregnant?"

My eyes snap to the doctor as Cass blurts, "What?"

"I'm sorry, I thought ... I assumed you knew. Our tests show you're roughly six weeks pregnant." She looks at both of us with an expectant smile. When we don't respond in kind, her face drops. "Uh, I'll go sort out some pain medication for you and leave you two to talk."

Cass's brows wrinkle as she bites her lip. Her focus has turned inward, and I sense she's thinking about the news the doctor just delivered. I'm fucking ecstatic that we made a baby, but the longer she's turned inward, I worry she's not feeling the same. I squeeze her hand to draw her attention to me. She looks everywhere but at me, her eyes flitting around the room, trying to find somewhere to settle. She attempts to pull her hand away from mine, but I cover it with my free one to keep her in place. Finally, she looks at me, a steady stream of tears tracking down her bruised cheeks.

She doesn't want this.

She doesn't want a baby with me.

My heart cracks with the pain of knowing she doesn't want to have a baby with me.

"I ... I'm so sorry, Toby."

"Shhh, shhh. It's okay." No matter what she wants to do, I'll support her. It's what you do when you love someone unconditionally, even if they don't love you the same way.

"I religiously take my pill every day," she sobs. "I don't understand what happened. Oh, god! I should have insisted you keep using condoms." She looks devastated, and I feel gutted that I'm the cause. "I'm sor-ry, Toby. I didn't mean for this to happen."

I stroke her hair gently, calmly. "Shhh, shhh. It's okay. It's not your fault. It's mine. This isn't only on you. I was there as well, remember?" I smile sadly because my heart is breaking. "Neither of us meant for this to happen, but I can't say I'm unhappy about it."

She sucks in a sharp breath, then cries out in pain.

"Calm down. You can't afford to get yourself worked up. We'll work it out. Whatever you wanna do, Cass. I'm here, standing with you, supporting you. I promise."

More tears track down her face, and I fear I've said the wrong thing. "You mean, you're ... you're not upset? You're not angry with me?"

"Hell no. I'm fucking ecstatic that I knocked you up." My chest puffs up with pride.

She blinks rapidly. "Wha ... What did you say?"

I stand up, cupping her face carefully in my hands, locking my eyes on hers to make sure she hears me correctly this time. "Cass. I'm so blessed to have you and Poppy in my life, but this ... you being pregnant with my baby ... it's everything to me. *You're* everything to me. You *and* Poppy, this baby ... I couldn't be happier. You hear what I'm saying, Bun?"

She nods the best she can with me cupping her face. I lean down, pressing my lips gently against hers. A breath gushes out of Cass as she whispers against my mouth, "I thought you'd be mad."

"Never, Bun. Never."

Cass shakes her head, closing her eyes. "I was scared I was gonna lose you," she whispers on a shaky breath.

"I love you so much, Bun. I'm not going anywhere. We're doing this together. You're not alone this time." She opens her eyes, locking them onto me, and I smile, trying to reassure her.

A nurse enters the room, breaking our moment. "Sorry to interrupt, but I'm here to give you some pain relief."

Cass and I share a look. I know we're both thinking the same thing. I don't want her in pain, but is it safe for the baby?

"Will it be safe for our baby if I take that medicine?"

"Yes, it's totally fine at this stage of your pregnancy. Your baby is well and truly protected and safe."

Cass tries to adjust her position, sucking in a sharp breath and scrunching up her face. "Take the pain relief, Bun. You need it to heal properly."

She studies my face closely for long moments before turning toward the nurse. "Okay. I'll take it."

"Good choice. We don't want you in distress. It's better for you and the baby." The nurse goes about her business. She's an older woman who seems to be all about efficiency. Her movements are swift and precise before she leaves us alone again.

———

I haven't left Cass's side since I arrived last night. There's a sharp knock on the door, followed by two police officers stepping into Cass's room.

"Ms. Phillips, we would like to have a word if you're up to it."

"Surely, this can wait a few days. You have the footage from the shop. Isn't that enough?"

"I'm sorry, Sir, but we need to follow up with everyone involved." They turn back at Cassia, who nods.

"Can you remember what happened?" asks the second officer.

"Most of it, I think."

"Would you mind running through it for us?"

She nods again, glancing at me, then back to the officers. Slowly but surely, she walks us through the attack yesterday afternoon. My blood boils with violence for that cocksucker. I wanna get my hands on him and break his fucking neck. Vivid images play out in my mind of what I want to do with him.

Through tears, shaky breaths, and plenty of stops and starts, Cass shares the events of her attack. All the while, I hold her hand in support. Hearing her describe her attack in graphic detail, blow by blow, makes me feel so goddamn proud of her. The way she tried to protect Sam. Which reminds me, we need to find out if Sam and her baby are okay.

"Thank you, Ms. Phillips. We'll be in touch."

I want to hold my girl after listening to her recount the events of yesterday. I have no fucking words to express how brave I think she is. But I'm scared I'll hurt her if I hold her the way I want to.

Cass looks at me. "Would you mind doing me a favor?"

"Anything, Bun. What do you need?"

"I need to know how Sam and her baby are. Can you please try to find out?"

I gently squeeze her hand. "Of course. I'll find out for you. First, though, I need to tell you something." I brush her hair, which is still tangled from her ordeal, away from her face. "I am so fucking proud of you, Cassia. What you did yesterday ... you were so goddamn brave. I don't know too many people who would have stayed and fought rather than run to save themselves." I lean forward, kissing her lips, as more tears track down her face. "I love you so much, Bun. So much," I whisper.

"Thank you," she whispers back, her lips touching mine. "It was probably stupid, really. I'm a mom. I could have ended up much worse than this." She indicates down her body. "How would that have helped Poppy?" More tears track down her cheeks.

"Don't think about it now. You're okay. I'm sure Sam and her baby are okay. Jake's been locked away. He won't be able to hurt you again." I kiss her again. "I'll see what I can find out about Sam." I don't want to leave her alone, but I know she's worried about her friend and I don't want her to get upset. "Be back in a minute."

I step out of the room to find Shane and Violet standing outside the door. "Hey." I lean in to hug Violet. "I was about to see if I can find any information about Sam and her baby. You mind sitting with Cassia?" Violet looks as though she's been crying nonstop since she found out about the attack.

"Hey." Shane pats me on the back. "Sam's up in maternity. She had the baby last night."

"Oh, okay. Maybe I don't need to leave Cass to find out. Come in to say hello." We step back inside the room.

Cass's eyes widen as her lips spread in happiness at seeing Shane and her sister. He steps toward her, kissing her forehead. "Hey, Cass. How are you feeling?"

"A bit sore and sorry for myself, to be honest," she responds with a sad smile. "But thankful it's not worse than what it is."

"I watched the footage from the shop. You're a badass. I'm honored to call you my friend. What you did for Sam. The way you fought with everything you had. You were ... are amazing. Don't forget that."

Cass's eyes are glossy as she blinks rapidly at Shane's praise. It means a lot coming from someone like him. He steps back, allowing

Violet to step forward. She's frozen on the spot, her eyes tracking all over her sister's face and body.

Cass holds out her good hand to her sister, which seems to wake her up. She rushes forward, gently grasping her sister's hand as a loud sob breaks free and the girls cry together. We step back to give the sisters their privacy.

FIFTY-FIVE

-cassia-

MY WHOLE BODY ACHES AND THROBS. MY MIND'S SPINNING. I'VE BEEN attacked, hospitalized, and found out I'm six weeks pregnant. Sam had her baby boy, and I'm being discharged today.

It's been a lot.

Toby hasn't left my side. I'm missing my Poppy desperately, but I didn't want her to see me lying helpless in the hospital. I've decided, though, I'm not leaving here until I visit Sam. Toby rolls me toward my friend, and as Sam comes into view, tears fill my eyes.

She's okay.

Shane told me she was okay and the nurses also told me, but until this moment, until I saw her with my own eyes, I didn't fully believe them. The relief that fills me is overwhelming, and I'm grateful I'm sitting down, or else my legs may have let me down. Sam takes one look at me, covers her mouth, and begins to cry. Big, fat tears roll down her face. Toby rolls me forward quickly.

"Don't cry, Sam. We're okay. You're okay. Your baby's okay. I'm okay." I reach forward with my good arm to brush her hair away from her face, and she settles a little at my touch.

Toby quietly steps out of the room, giving us time together. I know it was difficult for him to do because he hasn't left my side since he arrived at the hospital.

"Thank you for everything you did, Cass. I … I don't know what would have happened if you hadn't been there. My baby—" She breaks into a loud sob, unable to finish the sentence.

"Shhhh. Shhhh. Everything worked out okay. We're all safe now. He can't hurt any of us anymore." Sam nods slowly. "Now, where's your beautiful baby boy?"

A smile forms as she sniffs and wipes away her tears. "He's in the NICU. I just came back from seeing him. He's so small, so helpless."

"You know he's in the best possible place. They'll care for him and give him everything he needs."

She nods. "His skin's so soft." She smiles, almost to herself. "His feet are tiny." She shows me with her thumb and forefinger. I remember when Poppy was that small. I lay my good hand on my stomach, thinking about the time I'll get to meet this little one.

"I can't wait to meet him. What's his name?"

She locks eyes with me. "Phillip." My eyes widen in surprise. Surely she didn't ... "I named him after you because you saved his life."

More tears trickle down my face as pride fills me down to my soul. "I'm honored, Sam, but I didn't do anything anyone else wouldn't have done."

"I don't care. If you hadn't been there to distract Jake, I don't know what he would have done." The thing is, I feel it's my fault to begin with. If Jake hadn't come after me, he wouldn't have hurt Sam. I feel the heavy burden of guilt for bringing that asshole to her doorstep.

We catch up for a while before Toby steps back into the room, suggesting we head home. We say our goodbyes, and Toby rolls me out of the hospital. Lifting my face to the sunshine, I soak in its warmth while I carefully suck in a lungful of fresh air. I have to be in a wheel-chair for a few weeks until my shoulder's healed because I can't manage crutches at this point. Communicating with Poppy is going to be a little slow for a while, too. I'm going to need to manage signing with one hand, something I haven't done a lot.

As we're driving home, Toby announces, "Once you're able, you and Poppy are moving into my place." I look across at him, eyebrows raised. "I'm not having you away from me any more than absolutely necessary."

"You don't think it's too soon to live together?" I sass at him. Secretly, I love that he wants us in his space as much as he does.

"Nope," he snaps out, sharp as a whip. "I've wanted you since I was sixteen. I've already waited too long."

I laugh at his grumpiness about the topic and point to my leg. "I won't be able to manage three flights of stairs in your house for a while."

"No problem. I've set us up in the guest room on the first floor. I figured we'd stay with your mom until you're out of the wheelchair and she feels happy enough to let you go." His tone is all business and I don't have any inclination to argue with him at this point. I *want* to be with him as much as he wants to be with me.

We pull into the driveway. My heart soars, finding Poppy standing on the front step waiting for us, with Mom, Violet, and Jasmine behind her. I want to jump out of the car and run to my little girl. Give her all the love I haven't been able to give her since Friday morning.

Toby quickly jumps out of the car, coming around to my side with the wheelchair as Poppy runs down the few steps to the grass, bringing her closer to me. Toby opens my door, and Poppy stops cold when she sees the sling holding my arm in place, the bruising on my face, and finally the cast on my leg. Mom prepared her; told her that someone had hurt me, but I think hearing about it and seeing it are two very different things for a seven-year-old. Her bottom lip trembles as her eyes fill with tears. I want to wrap her up and pull her in tight, which is impossible at the moment. Every time I move or forget about my ribs and breathe a little deeper, they send agonizing pain shooting through my body.

"Mommy. Are you okay?" I can only nod in answer.

Toby quickly helps me out of the car, and it takes me a moment to recover from the burst of pain caused by the movement. Then, we all head inside slowly and carefully, Toby carrying me up the steps before situating me on the couch.

Carefully Poppy—more carefully than I've ever seen her be—sits beside me on my right. Wrapping my arm around her carefully, I pull her in close, kissing the top of her head. We sit side-by-side for long minutes as Toby brings in my wheelchair while Mom makes us all a coffee.

Violet smiles at me. "It's good to have you home, Sis." She teases out the bottom of her hair with her fingers. A tell that she's bothered about something.

"It's good to be home. I missed you all so much." I sign one-handed.

"Aunt Cass. I missed you." Jas comes barreling toward me with the speed of a toddler, but her mom's quicker, scooping her up to hold her next to my face so I can kiss her chubby cheek. She giggles as I tickle her with my good hand.

"Come on, girls, I'll put a movie on and we can all chill out together," Vi signs as she speaks, pulling up the movie channel so the girls can choose an old favorite. And that's how we spend our afternoon, with me dozing while the girls giggle at the antics of the characters on the screen.

FIFTY-SIX

-cassia-

I'M FEELING ESPECIALLY GRATEFUL THIS CHRISTMAS. I HAVE TOBY IN my life, a baby on the way, and in a few weeks, we'll be living together like a proper family. It's something I've always dreamed of but figured would never happen.

Not for me, anyway.

But here I am, living the dream.

Toby's been living in a house full of women since I came home from the hospital. I have to admire his patience with the girls. He spends hours sitting and playing with them.

We plan to tell my family about our surprise baby this morning as part of their Christmas gift. I can't wait to see their faces. I'm so freaking excited. This time is completely different from the last time I got pregnant. I *know* he wants this baby as much as I do.

Before we tell the rest of my family, we want to share the news with Poppy first, just the three of us. Sitting on my bed, Poppy's almost bouncing out of her skin, waiting to find out the special present I told her she would get first thing this morning.

"Merry Christmas, Mommy!" She leans forward, gently pressing her body against mine. She learned very quickly that she had to be super gentle with me. "Merry Christmas, Toby!" She throws her body at him—gone is the gentle little girl. He kisses her forehead with a smile and a laugh.

"Merry Christmas, Baby Girl!"

"Can I have my special Christmas surprise now?" She's practically vibrating with excitement as she signs.

Toby and I look at each other. He tilts his head, letting me take the lead. "Well, we were wondering how you'd feel about being a big sister?"

"I would love that so much. When can I be a big sister?"

I look at Toby, and we share a proud smile. "How about in August? I already have your baby brother or sister growing in my stomach."

She looks between the two of us before jumping off the bed and running around the room like a headless chicken. I'm relieved she's happy about it. I was worried she'd be upset because she's been an only child for such a long time.

She stops dead in her tracks. "Really?" She looks at us expectantly, as though we're playing a prank on her. Toby and I both nod with wide smiles as she throws her little fists up in the air, jumping on the spot. "Can I see the baby?"

"Not yet, Baby Girl. Soon, though. We'll go to a special doctor where they'll take a photo of what's inside my stomach."

"Okay. But you're gonna have to stop calling me Baby Girl because I won't be the baby anymore." She doesn't seem sad about losing that title, which is a huge relief. "Can I tell Gramma?"

Toby nods, letting me know he's okay with her sharing our news. "Okay. But you have to wait until after all the other presents are opened first. Okay?"

She nods. "Okay."

"Alright, let's get ready for opening presents. Did Santa come last night?"

"He sure did. You should see all the presents. There's so many." Her eyes are wide as she runs from the room.

Toby helps me into my wheelchair, and we follow behind. Mom, Violet, and Jasmine are already in the living room waiting for us.

"Merry Christmas!" Mom calls out as she makes room for me next to the tree, bending forward to hug me.

"Mewwy Chwistmas, Aunt Cass." Jas sings out to us from her spot almost tucked underneath the tree. She can't possibly get any closer to the presents if she tried.

I giggle, then suck in a sharp breath, and then wince at the pain caused by the breath I just sucked in. My ribs still hurt if I forget and carry on as though they're not broken.

"Merry Christmas, guys," Vi calls out from the kitchen.

"Merry Christmas, everyone. Thanks for waiting for us. Is everyone ready to open some presents?" I sign as I speak.

Shouts of yeses fill the room along with arms raised high in cele-bration, and we get down to the important business of opening gifts.

––––––

An hour later, Poppy and Toby are making music videos on the creator cam he bought for her, complete with a green screen. Mom and Vi are picking up all the wrapping paper. Jas is playing with her new doll-house, courtesy of Shane and Toby, while I sip on a decaffeinated latte made for me in my brand-new coffee machine, courtesy of my very generous boyfriend. Once I'm recovered, he's gonna get very lucky.

He loved the personalized wooden guitar picks Poppy and I had made for him with various phrases, like 'You're my guitar hero' and 'You're my pick' engraved on them. I also got him a hemp bracelet to match the leather bands he likes to wear. This one has an outline of a guitar made from stainless steel as a feature to join the two ends. He put it on straight away. I keep catching him rubbing his thumb along the band.

Once everyone's back in the living room, I let Poppy know she can share our news. She makes sure everyone's sitting quietly, and she has their undivided attention. Then she signs, "I'm going to be a big sister!"

The silence seems to last forever; Mom and Violet look between Toby and me. Mom pointedly looks down at my stomach, then back up to my face, eyebrows raised in question. I nod like a bobble doll, tears filling my eyes. She jumps up, picking Poppy up off the floor, giving her the biggest snuggle, before sitting her on her hip and dancing around the room.

Violet steps over and cups my cheeks, looking into my eyes. "I'm so freaking happy for you." She looks across at Toby. "For both of you. This is such amazing news." She picks up Jas in happiness. "You're gonna have another cousin. Aunt Cass has a baby in her tummy."

Jas looks down at my stomach, as if she can see the baby, and then wiggles free of her mom's arms. Coming right up to me, she places her hands carefully on my stomach. She leans forward, speaking softly, "Hello, baby." My heart melts at Jasmine's cuteness.

Mom wraps her arms around Toby, holding him tight. "Thank you for making me a gramma again. This is the best news we've had in a while. Oh my gosh, Mom's gonna be so excited to be a great-gramma again. I can't wait until she gets here so we can tell her." She leans in, cupping my face, much like my sister did. "Thank you, Cassia. You two are going to make a great team." She kisses my cheeks and then steps away, looking as proud as can be, her eyes glassy, her smile wide.

———

We gather everything we need to take with us and pile into our cars to make our way to Kate and Oliver's home. Once again, they generously invited my entire family along for the fun. The afternoon is spent eating too much and opening more presents. I don't think I've ever experienced a Christmas quite like this before. We normally only have our little family together for the day, meaning it's pretty quiet. As I absorb the love, happiness, and friendships around the room, my smile grows as warmth fills my entire body. This is going to be my future. Holidays spent with family and friends—it's amazing to know there are so many more people to love Poppy.

Toby sits next to me. "Are you ready to tell everyone our news?" His sparkling eyes give away his excitement at sharing this news with his family.

"Yep. Go get Poppy, so we're all together. Then you can tell them." He kisses my lips too briefly for my liking and heads off to find our girl. It was easy to think of Poppy as *our* daughter. He loves her as much as I do. Poppy and I are his top priorities all day, every single day.

He brings Poppy in close to me before gaining everyone's attention. Everyone's watching him expectantly, eyes wide, waiting. I can't imagine what they think the news will be. My family all have knowing smirks on their faces, while Poppy's almost coming out of her skin with excitement.

He clears his throat and looks down at me with a wink, then back to his family and their friends. "Cass, Poppy, and I are expanding our family. Poppy's going to be a big sister!" he signs as he speaks.

At first, everyone's silent again. Then it's as though they all absorb the meaning of Toby's announcement at the same time as they all cheer, moving forward en masse toward us, engulfing us in warm hugs and loud congratulations. Even though they already treat Poppy, and Jasmine for that matter, as their grandchildren and nieces, I *know* this will be even more special because this baby will be part of Toby.

FIFTY-SEVEN

-toby-

I FEEL STUPIDLY NERVOUS AND OUT OF MY ELEMENT AS CASS, POPPY, and I wait in the obstetrician's waiting room. Women in various stages of pregnancy are seated around the room. Some on their own, some with small children, some with their partner. We thought Poppy should be here to see her brother or sister for the first time. She's practically bouncing in her seat with excitement.

A nurse steps into the room. "Ms. Phillips."

I can't wait to change her surname to Summer. Poppy's, too.

I indicate to Poppy that it's our turn. Standing, I push Cassia forward; with her arm still in a sling and her leg in a cast, it's been a necessary requirement. Cass is sick of it, and it's been hell watching her in pain, watching her frustration grow over the things she struggles to do at the moment.

Her gramma had to go back to working full time, pulling in a friend to help her and Sally out while Cass and Sam are out of action. It's been tough on Cass to let things go. She attempts to do as much of the paperwork for the shop as she can from home, but it's not enough for her.

The nightmares are the worst. More often than not, I'm woken up by her thrashing around in bed, crying out in pain because she's moved more than she should, fighting Jake in her sleep. I feel helpless as she lies sobbing, half in a dream, half awake. She's been casually talking with Dad about everything that had happened that day as well as the stuff that had happened years ago. He won't tell me anything they talk about and Cass just says she's 'getting there'.

"Hi, I'm Kelly. If you could, please follow me. I'll get you set up and ready for Dr. Hart." We step into a clinical room, which could do with being a little warmer. "I'll just check your weight and blood pressure. Are you able to stand on the scales?"

"Sure. But won't the cast on my leg make my weight incorrect?"

"That's okay. The doctor will consider all of that."

I help Cass onto the scales and the nurse records the measurement on her tablet. "Do you mind helping Ms. Phillips onto the table?"

"No problem." I pick Cass up to carry her over to the table, eliciting a giggle from her.

"I'm pretty sure she didn't mean you had to carry me here."

I kiss the tip of her nose. "I'd carry you everywhere if you'd let me."

Moving the wheelchair out of the way, I sit down next to the bed and situate Poppy on my lap, ensuring she has the perfect view of everything that's going on. First, the nurse takes Cass's blood pressure, recording the numbers on her tablet, and then takes Poppy's for fun.

"Okay, that's all for me. Dr. Hart will be in shortly."

"Thank you, Kelly." She smiles as she leaves us in the room alone.

We play eye spy with Poppy to keep her entertained until the doctor walks in a few minutes later. He's young and good-looking, and I'm not too fond of the idea that he'll have his hands on my girlfriend.

"Good afternoon, Ms. Phillips. Mr. Summer." A hint of recognition fills his eyes, but he remains professional. "And who is this young lady?"

Cass signs one-handed as she speaks, introducing Poppy to the doctor. He makes a big fuss of shaking her hand and congratulating Poppy on becoming a big sister. His award-winning smile stretches right across his face as he makes sure Poppy's included.

Maybe he's not so bad after all.

He washes his hands in the sink, then sits on the other side of Cass, pulling on a pair of gloves. "So, you think you're around ten weeks pregnant? Is that right?" Cass uses her free hand to translate for Poppy, as she normally does in public situations.

Cass nods. "It was picked up in a test when I was in the hospital for these." She gestures to her shoulder and leg. "They said the hCG levels suggested I was around six weeks pregnant. That was four weeks ago now."

He nods. "Well, let's take a look to see if they were right. First, please lift your shirt and lower your pants to your bikini line. Did you have a big drink of water before your appointment today?"

"Yes, I did. I have to warn you. I'm getting pretty close to needing to go to the bathroom."

"Excellent, we should be able to get a good, clear picture of the baby." He holds up a tube. "This may be a little cold, but we need to use it to help with the equipment."

Cass nods. "I remember from when I was pregnant with Poppy." Poppy's eyes are glued to her mom's stomach and everything the doctor's doing.

He squirts the gel on her stomach, then uses a flat probe to spread it out, pressing down firmly on Cass's midsection. He fiddles around with some buttons on his computer, and the screen comes to life. Poppy's eyes snap to the screen while I watch my girl's face light up at the sight of our baby in her belly. Finally, I look at the screen, and my breath catches at what I see.

Our baby.

The one Cass and I made together.

Seeing the little body complete with little stumps for arms and legs and a huge head on the screen makes it real. I mean, I knew it was real, but it was an abstract type of real. Now it's really real. It's fucking amazing to see the life we created in a grainy black-and-white image on the screen. The doctor freezes the image and uses the mouse to draw some lines.

"I'm taking some measurements to get an idea of your due date."

"Is everything looking okay, Dr. Hart?"

He looks at me. "Everything's looking perfect, Mr. Summer."

"Okay, judging by my measurements, your baby is about 3.3 cm from crown to rump." He inputs the figures, then looks at us. "I'd say you'll be due around August thirteenth."

We had done some calculations ourselves and had come to the same conclusion if the blood test had been accurate. Cass'll still be able to travel with me for my tour. She resisted at first, using the shop as her excuse, but her gramma said she didn't mind stepping in again to help, which took that excuse out of the equation. Every excuse she came up with, I found a solution.

"Are you ready to hear your baby's heartbeat?" He fiddles with something on the computer, and a rhythmic whooshing sound fills the room as the heartbeat line shows along the bottom of the monitor.

My own heartbeat ceases for a moment, then restarts as I listen to the fast beats of our baby's heart. I grasp Cassia's hand and soak in the moment, appreciating the wonder on her face as tears slowly escape, tracking down her cheeks. Poppy's mesmerized by the moving image, steeling her eyes away from the screen to look at Cass's stomach in awe.

Dr. Hart points to the screen. "Can you see the little flutter right there?" I release Cass's hand so she can translate. We both peer more closely at the monitor, then nod. "That's your baby's heart. The flutter you see are the chambers working to pump the blood around your baby's body."

"That's amazing." I'm in awe of the technology. I'm in awe of Cass. That she's able to grow a human inside her body. Her stomach's only got a slight bump at this stage, barely noticeable. It's hard to believe that what I see on the screen is inside her body.

Cass squeezes my hand as she whispers, "You know, Poppy will never *hear* her baby's heartbeat like this." More tears stream down her cheeks, and she releases my hand to wipe them away.

"She may not *hear* it the way we do, but she'll see it, and she'll be so in tune with everything, she'll probably *feel* it." I lean forward to kiss the back of her hand.

"Now, let me move around a bit here and we'll take some photos for you to take home for your album. We'll also send them to your phone if you like. Be sure to check we have your correct numbers."

He takes photos and prints them out, handing them straight to Poppy. "Here you go. Your little brother or sister," Cass signs for her.

Her little face lights up as she looks down at the images. She places them carefully on the bed to sign, "I'm gonna make a special photo frame when I get home." She holds the images up for us, then presses them against her little chest close to her heart. She's going to be a great big sister.

FIFTY-EIGHT

-cassia-

MOVING INTO TOBY'S HOME FEELS SURREAL. I'M WORRIED I'M GOING to wake up and it's all going to be a dream. Poppy was so freaking excited. She made sure to pack every single toy she had; she didn't want to leave anything behind—even though I told her she'd still have sleepovers with Gramma, Aunt Violet, and Jasmine. She's currently upstairs, situating all of her favorite things in their new homes while Toby and I share a glass of wine on the couch. Well, he has wine; I have sparkling water.

Thank goodness I no longer need the wheelchair as of yesterday, and I can use crutches now that my ribs and dislocated shoulder have healed. It makes it so much freaking easier to get around and communicate with my daughter. Toby wasted no time. He made it clear. As soon as the wheelchair was gone, Poppy and I were moving in with him—and here we are. I was given the okay to use crutches yesterday, and we moved in today.

"She's so excited to be living here. It's all she's talked about since I told her we were going to be living with you." I sip my water.

"I doubt she's even half as excited as I am seeing both of you here in our space."

He's had no trouble talking about his home as our home. He's made numerous adjustments to his home and life for Poppy and me. The flashing lights attached to the doorbell and the switches on each floor to flash the lights throughout the house to get Poppy's attention wherever she is. Her beautiful little girl's bedroom. All of our favorite bathroom products are in the bathrooms, and our favorite foods are in the cupboards. He's even made space for Poppy in his studio. He makes me feel like we're the most important people in his world.

He leans forward, kissing me until I'm dizzy—lucky for me, I'm sitting down and can enjoy it without losing my balance. He makes my body heat in anticipation for later, when Poppy's in bed and it's only the two of us. Pulling back, he's toying with the ends of my hair, eyes focused on the strands as he whispers, "How are *you* feeling about moving in?"

"Do you want my honest answer?" He nods slowly, swallowing hard. "I'm honestly happy to take this step with you, even though I'm a little scared. This is a big step for Poppy and me. I genuinely want this to work out more than anything." I kiss his lips gently then whisper against them, sapphire eyes to charcoal, "I feel deep down in my heart … this is where we're meant to be, here with you. Making a family. Together for always." I blink quickly, working to keep my tears at bay. The lump in my throat makes it hard to get the words out. "A *real* family full of love."

"That's exactly what we are, Bun. A *real* family." His mouth comes down onto mine and I open eagerly to greet his tongue. Grasping the back of my head, he directs the kiss, deepening it until we're sharing each other's breaths. He pulls away before I'm ready, our foreheads pressed together as we each catch our breath. "I'm gonna marry you, Cassia Phillips, and adopt Poppy as soon as I can."

Pulling back to see his face more clearly, I open and close my mouth several times before anything comes out. "What?"

"You heard me, Bun."

"Are you asking me or telling me?" I'm trying my best to be sassy; however, I'm not sure I'm pulling it off. I'd say yes right now to this man. I don't need a romantic, down-on-one-knee proposal from him.

"I'm warning you, so you can be prepared for when I ask you properly." He smirks and winks at me. "Now, where's my other girl? It's time for lunch."

Holy cow! This man's so sexy. I can't wait until tonight.

FIFTY-NINE

-cassia-

"I'M SO NERVOUS." I'M HAVING TROUBLE DOING UP THE BUTTONS ON MY blouse because my hands are so freaking shaky and I'm certain I'm going to throw up any minute.

"You have nothing to be nervous about. I'm not gonna leave your side." Toby takes over, doing up my buttons. "I much prefer undoing these, by the way." He winks as he secures each button in its corresponding hole, bringing a smile to my face and distracting me from my thoughts.

Once I'm dressed, I head out to the kitchen to grab a glass of water. Toby smacks my ass, almost causing me to spill it on the blouse he just secured for me. His hands shoot out to prevent it from falling, and we both laugh. I certainly don't have time to change. My nerves already have us running late.

On the way to the courthouse, I fidget with the fabric of my pants, picking at imaginary lint. Toby reaches his hand across to stop my fidgeting, glancing at me before returning his eyes to the road. "It's going to be okay. He can't hurt you anymore."

I swallow down my nervousness. "I know. It's just ... I never thought I'd be in this situation."

"I know. Nobody should have to go through this, Bun." I love it when he uses my nickname. "You know you weren't the only one. He's dangerous, Cass. The sooner he's put away, the better for everyone."

I nod. "I know." And I do. I'm not nervous about sending him behind bars. I'm worried they won't.

"You've told your story. Everyone else shared theirs. There'll be no reason for the jury to set him free."

I nod. "Thanks for the pep talk. I needed it."

"Any time, Bun."

Toby parks the car and then helps me out. Shane and Len arrive at the same time we do, and we all walk into the courthouse together. Sam's standing off to the side with an older woman who looks like an older version of her. We head in her direction.

"Hey, Sam." We hug in greeting. "How are you doing? How's Phillip?"

Her face lights up at the mention of her gorgeous little boy. "He's doing great. I love being able to snuggle him without all the wires. It's so exciting, but I'm also a little scared. I don't want to mess up being a mom."

"You won't mess it up, Sam. You'll be a great mom." I glance at her mom. "Plus, you have your mom to help you. My mom was invaluable to me when Poppy was a baby."

Toby notices the time and ushers us inside, ready for the final proceedings. Things happened incredibly fast after the attack. I'm not sure why, but I think our case has been pushed through quicker than what would usually happen. It may have had something to do with new policies being pushed through regarding domestic violence. I think the Governor wants to make a big show that he supports victims of domestic violence and he won't tolerate it in our State.

We sit together with Becky, the woman Jake beat up five months ago. When I met with the district attorney to give her my statement, she told me Jake was already considering a plea deal for an attack in which he killed an unborn baby. Apparently, he didn't want that baby either, so he beat Becky, kicking and punching her stomach repeatedly. She was taken to hospital and tragically lost her baby at twelve weeks. I share a deep connection with her; she's been through so much at the hands of Jake. It seems he started to become violent and unpredictable after our reunion.

On the other side, Jake sits with his attorney. Laying eyes on him turns my stomach, and I suck in breaths to keep from expelling the small amount of breakfast Toby insisted I eat. I fold my hands together tightly in my lap, attempting to steady the shakiness, but the one thing I can't stop is the way my heart beats. It feels like it's going to pound right out of my chest, and as I swallow down each breath; I feel like I'm struggling for air. Sensing my discomfort, Toby places his hand on my thigh. His touch and genuine concern help to settle me. I'm able to slow my breathing to get myself under control.

Jake's mom sits in the seat behind her son, fidgeting with her necklace, looking everywhere but at us—Jake's victims. My heart breaks for the kind woman I remember—her son has put her in a terrible position. She doesn't deserve what she must have been through since everything he's done came to light. But it goes to show the good person she is, that she's here to support her son even though he doesn't deserve it.

The bailiff breaks into my thoughts, calling the court to order. "All rise for Judge Albercombe." We all stand and the proceedings get underway.

I get distracted in my thoughts, remembering the days spent in this courtroom listening to Becky and Sam recount their stories. Becky's story was very much like mine.

She was woken in the middle of the night by a drunken Jake having sex with her. When she tried to get him to stop, he kept going. Then he wanted her to abort the baby when she told him she was pregnant as a result of the rape. The one thing I can say about Jake is that he's consistent—a consistent asshole of the highest order. I'm sure it makes me a terrible person, but I'm grateful Jake didn't do to me what he did to Becky and Sam. He never actually tried to kill my baby.

The days after the attack were horrendous for all of us. I remember the remorse written all over Len's face about stepping away to grab some lunch, leaving us exposed. Of course, he wasn't to know what was about to happen—the man's entitled to a break.

Sam was worried she would be judged because she got pregnant on purpose. Love can cause you to make questionable choices sometimes. It took a lot of support and encouragement on my part to get her to be completely honest on the stand about her pregnancy. She didn't want him to be seen as a victim. She didn't want the jury to sympathize with him and let him off the hook. I understood where she was coming from, but he nearly killed their baby that day. I got the distinct impression during the attack that it was one of his goals. He wanted that baby gone from this world, and it was only the quick actions of the paramedics and doctors which ensured Phillip came into the world as safely as he did.

I glance at Jake's mom. She looks pale as she closes her eyes, sucking in a breath. This must be incredibly difficult for her to hear. She has grandchildren I'm now certain she never knew existed.

I remember when it was my turn. As I made my way to the stand on my crutches, I made eye contact with the jurors, hoping they'd listen to everything Jake had done and bring down a conviction against him that will put him behind bars. Finally, I was sworn in, and my mouth went dry, my hands shook, and my vision went fuzzy around the edges.

I found my talisman and locked eyes with him, stormy gray to calm blue. I managed to take deep breaths as I started at the beginning of our story, all the way back to high school. As I walked the jury through all of my experiences with Jake, I felt the knots loosen, and it became easier to speak my truth.

Recounting the night Poppy was conceived was tough. In my mind, I was taken back to that place and time—my shakes intensified, and I had to grip my hands together to steady myself. I sought Toby again, and he centered me with his unwavering support from across the room. I was grateful I'd already shared my story with him; that he wasn't hearing it for the first time. I don't think I could have made eye contact with him if he was hearing it for the first time, along with the jurors and judge.

Moving forward in time, I recounted what happened when Poppy was two. I remember the audible gasp Jake's mom let out at her son's violence against me, as I protected Poppy against his fist. The fact he thought he could correct her hearing with a fist to the head showed how unstable he is. The only thought that kept me moving forward with my story was the hope we'd all be safer if he was locked away. I remember pushing through my discomfort to share the last few months.

The prosecutor warned Sam and me that he wanted to show the footage of our attack to the jury. We agreed with him, but when it came time for it to be shown, I wasn't certain I could watch it. Toby wrapped his arm around my shoulder, tugging me into his body as the footage began to play. The images were so clear. The sounds of violence and hate couldn't be ignored. I felt like I was living through it all over again: every punch, kick, and stomp. I remember the way the jurors responded to Jake punching Sam's pregnant belly. They didn't bother disguising their disgust and horror at the events they witnessed. It was difficult to watch myself lying unconscious on the floor as he kicked her belly right before Len entered the picture, pulling Jake away from us and fighting with him for several minutes before Jake escaped from the shop.

The trial has been a long process. I feel like I've been put through the wringer. I'm exhausted, mentally, emotionally, and physically wrung out. There's been so many horrible details shared and it's been a lot to absorb.

I don't know whether to feel better or worse that I wasn't the only woman he was mistreating and assaulting. Maybe if I'd said something to the police sooner, none of this would have happened. The shame and guilt I feel surrounding my younger self's choices are overwhelming, and it's difficult to reconcile that girl with the woman I am today. There's no way I would tolerate anything like that ever again. I only wish I'd come to this point sooner. Looking around at the other women sitting nearby, they both appear to feel the same way I do.

I'm so caught up in my head that I almost miss the judge's ruling.

"On one count of manslaughter in the first degree. Guilty. On one count of attempted murder. Guilty. On four counts of assault with intent to cause harm. Guilty. On one count of destruction of property. Guilty." He looks around the courtroom. "Jake Robert Simmons, you have a track record of abuse and violence against women, which this court will not tolerate. I hereby sentence you to serve twelve years in the state penitentiary with a minimum sentence of five years before consideration for parole." He bangs his gavel. "Court dismissed."

He stands to leave. Everyone seated on our side of the court seems to release a collective breath. My body sags into Toby's as the guards lead Jake away, but not before he says something to his mom, which has her shaking her head as tears trail down her cheeks.

Stepping out of the courthouse, the gray skies greet us, threatening rain—the weather matching our mood. This event has fundamentally changed me. The nightmares. My persistent wariness of being alone in my shop, which was once my sanctuary. The constant tangled thoughts over past actions and what I should have done differently.

I want to go back to a simpler time when monsters didn't attack women or murder unborn babies.

"Cassia. Cassia." A woman calls out as Toby and I carefully make our way down the courthouse steps. I know exactly who it is. I carefully turn around on the step, keeping myself as steady as possible on jelly legs. She takes a couple more steps down, coming closer to me. "Cassia," she whispers, her bottom lip trembling.

"Mrs. Simmons." Tears flood down her cheeks at her name on my lips. As much as I think her son is an appalling excuse for a human being, I don't feel any of that for her. She was always kind, warm, and welcoming to me. "Please don't cry." I want to reach out to her, but I'm unsure if my comfort would be welcomed.

"I ... I'm so, so sor— ... sorry. I h— ... had no idea ... about any of it." She blinks quickly, fiddling with her necklace. She takes a few moments to compose herself. "I feel as though I didn't know my son. I mean, I knew he had a temper, ... but ... this. I had no idea. I can't believe I have grandchildren that I never knew about. Never met." Searching her bag for something, she pulls out a handful of tissues. "I feel so ... responsible for everything that's happened." She sobs into the tissues, her whole body shaking. I look at Toby, silently asking him if I should comfort her. He gives a single nod, so I lean closer, placing my arm around her shoulders, rubbing my hand up and down her arm, attempting to calm her.

"Mrs. Simmons. Please don't take the blame for Jake's behavior. It's all on him." I try to keep my voice soft, soothing.

She nods, but I see the doubt in her eyes. "But *I'm* his mother. I *should* have known."

"How could you have? He was very good at showing people what he wanted them to see." I had no idea his temper could get this bad, and I dated him on and off for years.

"Thank you, Cassia. You're too kind. But this guilt ... it's something I'll carry with me until my dying day." She pulls away from me, having gathered her composure somewhat. "Please take care of yourself and your daughter." Her hand snakes up to her necklace again as more tears escape her eyes. She's genuinely upset at the thought of having grandchildren she didn't know about.

As she goes to step around me, down the steps with her head down low, I call out to her, "Would you like to meet your granddaughter?" I'm not sure what possessed me to invite her into our lives, but none of this is her fault. When I was younger, I remember feeling hurt she hadn't made an effort to meet Poppy or support me, but now I know she had no idea about any of it. I don't want to punish her for her son's behavior. Her steps come to a stop, and she turns to face me, an incredulous expression.

"Really? You would let me meet my granddaughter?" she almost whispers, her chin trembling.

I nod. "Yeah, I would. Poppy's amazing. You shouldn't miss out on getting to know her." The more I think about it, the more comfortable I feel with the idea. I know Jake's mom is a kind and loving person. I know she'll love Poppy with all of her heart, and why wouldn't I want to give that to my daughter? "Do you still live in the same house?"

"Yes, I do. But … are you sure?" Her eyes are open wide, shining bright with hope.

"Yep. How about we let the dust settle a little? Then I'll organize a time with you to bring Poppy over for a visit?"

She steps into me, embracing me tightly. "That would be wonderful, Cassia. I'll look forward to it." As she steps away, she looks a little taller; a little happier. After what she's been through recently with Jake, I'm glad I could give her something to look forward to.

After watching her walk away, Toby pulls me to his side. "You're such a good person, Cassia. I don't think too many women would do what you just did."

Pressing my head against his shoulder, I sigh. "It's not her fault Jake's such a monster. She shouldn't be punished for her son."

He nods, kissing the top of my head, making me feel cherished. "C'mon. Let's go home."

SIXTY

-cassia-

STEPPING THROUGH THE DOOR OF *OUR* HOME TOGETHER—IT STILL feels surreal to be living here with Toby—he slips my coat off my shoulders and down my arms, hanging it in the coat closet. He's always doting on Poppy and me, making every single day special. Today, after everything at the courthouse, I know, I *just* know, he's going to take good care of me. Poppy's staying over at Mom's tonight because I wasn't sure how I would feel after the judge delivered his verdict.

He steps into me from behind, wrapping his arm around me beneath my breasts. A sigh escapes me at the feel of his hard body pressed against mine. He uses his other hand to smooth my hair away, giving him clear access to my neck.

Nuzzling down into the space between my shoulder and neck, he whispers, "I plan to make long, slow, sweet love to you, Gorgeous. Starting now." He presses a gentle kiss with a glide of his lips across my heated skin.

This man turns me on just by being in the room. When he actually touches me, I have no hope of resisting him and why would I? Turning me around, he presses me up against the foyer wall, reminding me of the first night we reunited, when I did the very same thing to him. He swoops down, licking across the seam of my lips, and I open with a sigh as I sag against the wall. He wastes no time connecting our mouths completely. As Toby kisses me, I wrap my arms around his head, removing the elastic holding his hair so I can run my fingers through the silky strands.

I love his hair—the softness of it.

I love it when his weight's on top of me as his hair creates a private curtain around us, shielding us from the outside world.

Our tongues slide and taste each other, exchanging breaths, sighs, and moans. He presses his hard dick against me and my hips automatically seek the friction only he can give me.

I've learned to relax. To let Toby lead during our sexy times. He's always diligent in doling out my pleasure before his own; I don't need to worry. I *know* he'll get me where I need to go, which is so damn hot!

Pulling away, we both catch our breaths as our foreheads kiss. "I'm gonna need a bed for this. I wanna take my time." He bends forward, picking me up bridal-style, carrying me up three flights of stairs as though I weigh next to nothing. He stops next to our king-size bed, sliding me down his body slowly, my bump sliding against his taut stomach until he's sure my feet are firmly on the ground.

His hands instantly snap up to the fasteners of my blouse. "I've been dying to undo these little silver buttons since I did them up for you this morning."

The tension I was carrying in my shoulders begins to slip away as my body prepares to be taken care of in the best possible way. As each inch of skin is exposed, Toby leans forward, kissing down the front of my body. I sigh at the gentle press of his warm lips against my flesh, pausing on my bump and leaving a trail of goosebumps as his soft beard tickles me.

"I love how soft your skin is. I always want to have my hands, or better yet, my mouth, on you."

"I love having your hands and mouth on me. You always make me feel so good."

I jump slightly as he nips at my belly button before releasing the button and zipper on my pants. I won't be able to wear these pants much longer. He slips his hand inside my underwear, stroking my pussy lips, and my belly quivers.

"You're already so fucking wet and I've barely touched you," he whispers, as his fingers slip through my folds easily.

"I just have to look at you and I'm wet. My body knows what you can give me and instantly prepares for your touch," I whisper, as my hands reach forward to stroke the hard outline of his cock through his trousers. "Mmmmm." I look down at his crotch. "Can I have a taste?"

"Not yet. I need to take care of my pussy first." He grunts as I squeeze his shaft.

He pushes my pants and underwear down my legs, then takes my hand to help me step from the discarded items before helping me to remove my ankle boots. He flicks open the front clasp of my bra and slides his calloused fingers underneath the straps, sliding it and my blouse off to join the rest of my clothes on the floor.

Goosebumps erupt all over my body and my tender nipples do their best to gain Toby's attention. Leaning forward, he takes a bite of one, then soothes the sting with his tongue. I shudder as his mouth closes over the nipple and sucks—hard. Massaging the other breast with his hand, he pulls back. "I can't wait to watch you nourish our child with these pretty tits."

His mouth. How he uses it. The words he says. It's such a turn-on. Moisture slicks my pussy lips and I clench my thighs together in a lame attempt to lessen my reaction to him. *It doesn't work.*

He picks me up underneath my ass, laying me out on our bed like an offering. His fingers smooth down to caress my body, followed closely by his talented mouth, pausing over the bump of my stomach. If you didn't know me, you wouldn't know I was pregnant when I'm fully dressed. Naked, though, the curve is visible. Toby takes every opportunity to caress and kiss it. Each night, he talks and sings to our baby while he lovingly rubs body butter over my torso, making me fall more in love with him; if that's even possible. His kisses reach my pubic bone and, after giving me a sexy smirk, he literally dives in.

Tasting.

Licking.

Biting.

Sucking.

Fingering me until I'm a writhing mess of need, on the verge of exploding. Then, pushing my legs further apart with his shoulders, he sucks hard on my clit as his two fingers press up against the front wall of my pussy. Violent spasms erupt out of nowhere, and I fall into bliss —a trembling, quivering mess of liquid bones and muscle. I flop my hand up to my forehead as my lips spread wide. A sigh escapes as I lie in post-orgasmic bliss.

Toby climbs up my body like a panther, all slick and sure, pressing a gentle kiss to my lips. I can smell my arousal on him as I run my tongue along his lips, tasting myself as he groans.

"You know how fucking sexy it is when you want to taste your cum on my lips?"

"Mmmmm." I run my fingers through his hair. "Can I taste you now? You taste so much better than I do." His cock jolts between us, tapping my stomach. "I think your cock wants me to." I smirk sassily.

He sits up. Then he helps me upright as he gets into position at the edge of the bed. After tossing a cushion to the floor between his feet, he directs me exactly how he wants me—kneeling between his legs on the floor. Taking one of my hands, he wraps it around his cock, then grips the back of my neck, guiding my mouth toward his magnificent cock. As far as dicks go, I've only seen two in real life, so I'm no expert, but to me, his dick is perfect.

"Lick the tip, then suck it into your gorgeous mouth. I wanna see my cock resting on that delicious bottom lip of yours." He uses his hand at the back of my neck to gently guide me forward. "In high school, I used to imagine your plump lips surrounding my dick. It never took me long to come with that vision in my mind."

I groan. Knowing he masturbated to thoughts of me in high school should be creepy, but it's not. Instead, knowing he's wanted me for so long boosts my desire to please him. I take his cock in my mouth, pressing my tongue along the underside of his dick, as I moan long and low from my throat. His hand tightens on the back of my neck as he pushes me closer to his body, sending his cock further into my mouth to the back of my throat. Taking a deep breath through my nose, I manage to contain my gag reflex, swallowing around his shaft. He groans, thrusting his hips toward my face.

"Your mouth feels so fucking good, Gorgeous."

His praise turns me on, urging me forward. Increasing my strokes and sucks up and down his shaft, sliding it out of my mouth and back in with a suck. I cup his balls gently and use my finger to massage his taint. Even though I've just had an orgasm, doing this to him has me heating, preparing for another one. His grip tightens on my hair, and as he pulls on the strands, his hips thrust in time with my ministrations.

I moan, and he groans.

Before I can stop him, he has his dick out of my mouth, me on his lap, and his cock in my pussy in one swift action.

Straddling his thighs, we remain still, joined in the most intimate of ways. The connection we share reaches right down to my very soul. I thank the heavens above that Toby came back into my life. Then, with our eyes locked, we begin to move, slowly, surely, with purpose and promise. With one hand resting on his broad shoulder, I tangle my other hand in his hair, drawing him forward to my mouth. Lips open, our tongues caress each other as we build toward our peak.

My pussy walls flutter and begin tightening around his dick. In response, his dick jolts and grows impossibly thicker, putting more pressure against my g-spot. Finally, his hand snakes down, and his fingers press against my clit, sending me flying into the stratosphere. My whole body shudders as my pussy walls tighten around his shaft, gripping it with force.

"Fuck, yeah. I want your pussy strangling my cock every single day of my life. It feels like heaven." He slams his mouth over mine and thrusts deep, holding himself inside me as his pulsing dick releases his cum. I wrap my arms around his shoulders, pulling him in tight to me, every inch of my skin touching every inch of his.

Sweaty, slick skin against sweaty, slick skin.

Hearts pounding a matching rhythm.

Panting breaths gush in and out as we attempt to fill our lungs.

He brushes my sweaty hair out of my face and presses a delicate kiss to my forehead, the tip of my nose, then my lips. My sighs are met with a gorgeous smile.

"You're so fucking beautiful, Cass." He kisses me again. "When you come." He bites his bottom lip. "I'm the luckiest bastard in the world." He kisses me again. "Thank you."

His genuine gratitude for what some men take for granted increases my love for him and the man he is. I return his kiss, deepening the connection until I don't know where he begins and I end.

"I love you, Toby Summer." I kiss him again, stealing his breath in the same way he steals mine. "Thank you for being the man who showed me it's okay to open my heart." I press my forehead to his. "Thank you for loving my daughter and me as deeply as you do."

We stay locked together. Slick bodies pressed tightly, his dick nestled inside me for long moments. Connected physically, mentally, emotionally, and spiritually. This man is the one and only for me, just as I am the one and only for him.

———

After snuggling for a while, both of our tummies let out a hungry grumble, sending us into fits of laughter. I didn't eat much before court. It's now mid-afternoon after an intensive round of lovemaking, so I'm not surprised I'm starving. Finally, Toby rises out of bed, pulling me up with him.

"C'mon, Bun. Let's feed you and the bump." He steps over to the drawers and throws a T-shirt at me. "I got you a little something."

Aww, he's so sweet. He watches me closely as I smooth the T-shirt out on the bed, immediately bursting into laughter at the text on the front.

'Guitarists Finger Faster'

Toby smirks, then pretends to be offended that I'm laughing at the gift. He runs his hand through his messy hair to push it out of his face, contracting his bicep, drawing my eyes there. He notices, tensing the muscle even more.

I roll my eyes; he's such a guy.

"I thought it was appropriate." He smirks and shrugs as he pulls on a pair of jeans, doing up the zipper but leaving the button undone.

I put the soft T-shirt on, then step over to my boyfriend. Wrapping my arms around his naked torso, I peer up at his face. "I love it. Thank you."

He tilts his face forward, kissing the tip of my nose. "I love you, Cassia." His voice sounds raspy, and as I study his face closely, his eyes show me how deeply he means those words.

Pressing up on my toes, I press a tender kiss to his soft lips. "That works out perfectly because I love you, Toby Summer. I love you as my partner, my lover, my friend, and the father of both of my children."

epilogue

SIXTY-ONE

-toby-

I step inside *Cristo's Taverna* and give my eyes a moment to adjust to the dimness. Shane's close behind as usual; he knows why I'm meeting Rose for lunch. I'm sure Rose has her suspicions, but I didn't elaborate on why I wanted to meet here today. The host greets me by name, possibly because there's no mistaking who I am since I'm a regular here and I booked out most of the restaurant to ensure my privacy. I did a similar thing when I met Cass for lunch, back when I was trying to convince her to give us a shot. It's the only way to ensure a modicum of privacy.

Rose is already seated at the back table I prefer, perusing the menu. She glances up as I approach, giving me a smile that reminds me of her daughter. She stands, embracing me tightly. "My, aren't I lucky to be invited out on a weekday to share lunch with my favorite guy?"

"Hey, Rose. Thanks for agreeing to have lunch with me today." We both sit. "You're gonna love the food here. I brought Cass here a while ago. She enjoyed the authentic Greek cuisine."

"Anything I don't have to cook tastes pretty good to me." She laughs.

The waiter brings a bottle of water to the table, filling our glasses. "Would you like to share a bottle of wine today, Sir?"

I look to Rose for her input. "Sure. That'd be lovely."

"What do you like to drink?"

"Sweet white, if that's okay with you?"

"Definitely. That's Cassia's preference, too." I let the waiter know, and he steps away to get our drinks.

I gulp my water to soothe my dry throat. My hands are shaking so badly that Rose notices. Peering at me with a raised eyebrow and a small smile, she sits forward in her chair, resting her chin on her hand.

"It's lovely of you to invite me out to lunch, but I assume you have an ulterior motive for sharing a meal with an old lady."

"Wow, Rose. I'm hurt you think my intentions aren't what they seem." I hold my hand over my heart, giving her my best 'hurt feelings' face. "I was at least going to ply you with excellent wine and food before getting down to business." I smile at her and she laughs.

The waiter returns with our wine, pouring each of us a glass. "Are you ready to order?"

I look at Rose. I know she already perused the menu, and I know what I like here. "Do you know what you'd like?"

"Yes, I do. I'll have the kokinisto me manestra thank you."

"A great choice, Ma'am. And for you, Sir?"

"I'll have my usual, thank you."

"Certainly." He heads back into the kitchen with our order.

"And what is your 'usual'?" She takes a sip of her wine.

"I always enjoy the moussaka whenever I eat here. It's always a tasty choice, not that you can go wrong with anything on the menu." I rearrange my cutlery, centralize my glass, and unfold my napkin before folding it up again.

Rose places her hand over mine. "What is it, Toby?"

Tucking a lock of hair that's escaped my hair tie behind my ear, I sip my wine, hoping for liquid courage. "Uh, well, I have something I wanted to talk with you about."

She pulls her hand away to fiddle with her necklace, her eyes wide, as her shoulders rise around her ears. "Are Cassia and Poppy okay?"

"Oh, yeah, yeah. There's nothing wrong." I glance away, then back at Rose as her shoulders drop and she takes another sip of her wine. "I, uh, well … I … I wanted to … uh—"

Her eyes are twinkling as she fights a smile. "What are you trying to say?"

"I'm gonna ask Cass to marry me and ask Poppy if I can adopt her," I blurt out. "Geez, I had this entire speech worked out, and that was not how I was going to start the discussion." I huff out a breath. I'm so goddamn disappointed in myself.

"Oh, Toby. That's wonderful news. I'm beyond happy for the three of you." She stands, stepping around to me with her arms open wide, and I get up to meet her. She wraps her thin arms around me tightly, whispering, "I couldn't have asked for a better man for my girls."

My entire body, from the top of my head to the tip of my toes, relaxes. I knew I was tense because of my nervousness, but I didn't realize *how* tense I was. "Thanks, Rose. I appreciate you saying that." I squeeze her back, then we release our embrace.

Sitting back in our respective chairs, Rose is beaming, and I feel like I can breathe again. I don't think I've ever felt this nervous in my life, even when performing in front of thousands of people or sending a new song out into the world. The waiter brings our food, and we both dig in. It's probably good I got the difficult part out of the way because I can actually enjoy my meal.

Rose looks at me with excitement. "I hope you're going to do it soon. I'm not sure I'll be able to contain myself for long."

"I was planning on doing it this weekend." I tell Rose about my plan as we enjoy our delicious meal. She nods along excitedly, giving me praise for my choice of location as well as my craftiness.

We finish our meal, talking some more about Poppy and Cassia before Rose needs to leave for an appointment with a new client. Shane and I walk her out of the restaurant, parting ways with a tight squeeze and a kiss on the cheek. I feel lighter than I did when I walked into the restaurant.

I turn to Shane. "Did you enjoy your lunch?"

"Yeah, the food here is always great. I assume you got the all-clear from Rose for the weekend?" He smirks at me.

"Yep." I pop the 'p' like an adolescent. "She said, and I quote, 'she couldn't have asked for a better man for her girls'." I blow on my fingernails, pretending I'm buffing them on my shirt as my face cracks into a broad smile. I'm on top of the world. "Now I've just gotta put my plan into place."

"Well, I can't see a 'no' anywhere in your near future if that helps." He slaps me on the back. "Where to next?"

"I need to get to the jeweler to pick up Cass's ring. Then we can pick up Poppy from school and take her for ice cream. I have something I need to ask her."

———

Poppy orders her regular peanut butter crunch, while I order the macadamia crunch, and Shane has a raspberry swirl. The three of us find one of the back booths to enjoy our frozen treats in relative peace. Poppy's working like crazy to lick up the ice cream as quickly as possible. Cass and I always make sure there's ice cream in the house because it's one of the few things we can use to bribe her to do her chores. Shane sits on the same side of the booth as me, blocking me from public view, so we're left alone.

Once I finish my ice cream and my hands are free, I rub them down my jeans to wipe the nervous sweat away. I ask Poppy about her day, checking in with how her friends are going. I know I'm delaying what I really want to talk about. I can't believe how nervous I am to ask a seven-year-old if she thinks what I want to do is okay. Once I've calmed myself down and I'm satisfied Poppy's in a good place, I bring up the purpose of our outing.

"Hey, Poppy. You know how much I love you and your mommy, right?"

She nods and passes her ice cream to Shane. "I love you, too. And I know Mommy loves you lots. She's always kissing you." She screws up her cute little nose.

Good, I'm glad she thinks it's gross to kiss a boy. I hope she feels that way until she's at least thirty.

I ask her to come and sit next to me. Shane stands, allowing Poppy to sit in the booth while he blocks us from the rest of the customers with his body. Wrapping my arm around her shoulder, I kiss the top of her head and breathe in her little girl's strawberry scent. Pulling away, I put some space between us so we can talk.

"There's something I want to ask you, and I hope you think it's okay."

She nods, indicating I should get on with it.

I swallow down the buildup of saliva, taking a deep breath. "Do you think it would be okay if I asked your mommy to marry me?"

Instantly, her face lights up brighter than I've ever seen, and her hands move fast. "Will that mean you'll be my daddy?"

I smile. "Yeah. We'd be a family. The three of us, and when the baby comes, we'll be a family with the four of us."

"Yes! Yes! Yes! Please marry Mommy. I want us to be a family. I want you to be my daddy." She throws her little arms around my torso, squeezing me as tight as she can. I suck in a gulping breath and Shane gives me an 'I told you so' look.

I explain some aspects of my plan to Poppy, and she offers her input as well as a couple of suggestions for tweaks that could work in my favor. Gotta love a smart kid.

———

At six months pregnant, my Bun looks spectacular. She has that pregnancy glow about her, making her even more gorgeous than she usually is. The last three months, having Poppy and Cass living with me, have been more than I could ever have asked for. They've made my house feel like a home, full of the love and warmth I'm used to having. The three of us have started creating our own special traditions, like breakfast for dinner on Sunday nights after we've spent the afternoon with my family.

I can't wait for the weekend when I can put my plan into place to make them both mine permanently.

As Cass comes down the stairs after putting Poppy to bed, I carry hot cocoa for each of us over to the couch. She sits down with a heavy sigh. "Today was nuts. I'm not sure what's going on, but we were busier than usual. Sam was only in for a couple of hours, then she had to head home to feed Phillip. I'm exhausted."

"I know Sally's a big help, but have you given any thought to hiring another floral designer to help you out? What are you planning to do when the baby's born?" I lift her feet and she swivels her body so they're resting on my lap. I begin massaging them for her as she drinks her cocoa.

"Yeah, I definitely have. I have my eye on a new, upcoming floral designer. She's won a couple of local awards, so I've been putting together a proposal to woo her to my shop." She moans as my thumbs dig into the arch of her foot, waking up my dick. Settle down, buddy. I'm looking after our girl in a different way for now. I shift my legs, making room for the expansion.

"Oh, yeah? How are you gonna woo her?" I swap to her other foot.

"Well, I was hoping a couple of tickets to your final concert might do the trick. She's in your core demographic. Maybe even some back-stage passes?" She looks at me with hopeful eyes. As if I'd ever deny her anything.

"It's all yours, Bun. Anything you need to get her on board and into your store." She leans forward, offering me her luscious lips for a kiss, which I happily accept. Pressing my lips against hers, I cup the side of her head, directing and deepening the kiss the way I want it. Her breath mingles with mine. Our tongues tangle together. She tastes like cocoa and my Bun—my favorite flavor. "I actually, uh … have something I wanted to talk to you about."

She pulls back, studying my face carefully. "What's wrong?"

"Nothing's wrong, I just … uh … wanted to ask you something really important to do with Poppy." I struggle to get the words out. Reaching forward, I drink my cocoa to coat my dry throat, noticing my hand shaking as I grip the cup.

It's certainly been a day full of anxiety for me.

"Well, it's something. You seem a little … out of sorts." She nudges me with her toe, connecting with my dick. She looks up at me questioningly. "Are you excited to see me, or is that a banana in your pocket?" She giggles, breaking the tension I brought between us.

"I'll show you exactly how happy I am to see you later." I wink, twisting around to face her more directly. "You know how much I love you and Poppy?"

"Yeah, we both know how much you love us. We love you, too." She leans forward, kissing me again, settling my nerves slightly.

"Well … uh … I was wondering how you'd feel about me adopting Poppy. I want both of our kids to have my last name. It's important to me that our kids have the same surname." Cass's face goes soft as she offers me that ghost of a smile that she often does. "I mean, I know Poppy's not mine biologically speaking, but I think of her as mine. I love her as though she's my own and I would do anything, *anything* at all to keep her safe and happy—" Cass cuts me off with a press of her smiling lips against mine. I pull back slightly, whispering, "Is that a yes? Would you be okay if I asked her?"

She presses another light kiss against my lips. "Yes." *Kiss.* "Absolutely." *Kiss.* "One hundred percent." *Kiss.* "Yes." *Kiss.* She pulls back further, putting more space between us. "You're gonna make her so happy. I can't wait to see her little face when you ask her."

"You're sure?"

"Never been more certain about anything in my life. I know how much you love her, and I know how much she loves you. I love how you think of her as your own. How you support and care for her. She's one lucky little girl to have you *choose* to be her father."

"I would consider it an honor to be Poppy's daddy." I lean forward, kissing my girlfriend, hopefully soon-to-be fiancée. I spend the next few minutes running through my plan for the weekend with her. Only sharing the parts I need her to know. We clean up our dishes, lock the house, then head upstairs to bed, where I take my time to defile the woman I hope to make my wife.

SIXTY-TWO

-toby-

I'M AS NERVOUS AS ALL GET OUT THIS MORNING. THE BEAUTY OF MY plan is that Cass thinks I'm nervous about asking Poppy if I can adopt her, and Poppy thinks I'm nervous because I'm going to ask her mom to marry me. I barely tasted the chocolate chip pancakes I ordered for breakfast. Cass kept smirking at me over her decaffeinated coffee, while Poppy kept nudging me with her elbow when her mom wasn't looking.

Shane has the goods in his pocket, and he's set to take photos on his phone for me at the important moments.

"Are you girls ready to head out for my surprise?" I wink at Cass while I nudge Poppy.

Poppy's practically vibrating with excitement, as she pretty much climbs over me to get out of the booth we're sitting in. Cass and I laugh at her energy. Once I'm up, I help Cass slide out of her seat. She's finding moving around a little awkward. She says it gets even more difficult closer to the end. Watching her grow round with our baby has opened up a whole new level of overprotectiveness I have for her. She says I'm hovering and fussing too much, but I want to help her out as much as possible. I want to make her life as easy as possible while her body's working hard to create another human being. She needs to get used to it because I can't see myself stopping anytime soon.

We all climb into the car to make our way to the Japanese gardens. I came by earlier in the week to check it out, making sure the cherry blossoms were in bloom and to work out exactly where I want to propose to my girls. Large wooden doors greet us at the main entrance, and as we pass through, the tranquility of the gardens can be felt instantly. The weather is absolutely glorious for my plan.

Poppy stops inside the entrance for a moment to take in her surroundings with Cass in tow. A pond full of koi greets us, along with superb large pines towering over the pathway, creating a shady canopy for the lush greenery surrounding us. We wander over a low wooden bridge, past the open tea house on the right—we'll stop in there before we leave today.

The large Buddha statue greets patrons, and I snap a couple of photographs of my girls with him. I remember seeing a photo of *The Doors* posing with this very statue. We stroll further into the gardens on this perfect spring day, walking along the pathways which meander through carefully manicured plants and miniature trees. We're getting closer to the spot I've chosen. I asked Poppy to distract her mom when we reached the stone steppers.

Poppy looks at me and I give her the signal we agreed on over ice cream. She grips her mom's hand, pulling her to a stop between a pond full of koi fish on the left and a two-tier waterfall on the right. A realistic statue of a couple of herons rises out of the pond on the far side—it's the perfect location. Shane stayed back to take photographs. As Poppy signs to Cass about the fish in the pond, I get down on one knee, the ring safe in my pocket. With the sun at my back, I draw in a deep breath, waiting for Cass and Poppy to turn around.

She turns around, and it takes her a moment to register that I'm down on one knee in front of her—with my heart in my throat and hope in my eyes. Her eyes widen as she looks between Poppy and me. She was expecting me to ask Poppy about the adoption, and I will, but I wanted to have Cass as my fiancée first.

I make sure to sign as I speak, even though I'm shaking like a leaf, to make sure Poppy doesn't miss out. "Cassia." I half-smile. It's all I can manage while I'm this nervous. "I've had the biggest crush on you since I was sixteen. Never in my wildest dreams did I think I would actually be lucky enough to call you my girlfriend. But today, I'm a man kneeling in front of the woman I've fallen deeply in love with— the woman I want to share my life with, through good times and bad. When I think about the future, you're all I see. All I want." I smile up at her. "I promise to love you and our children with every beat of my heart. Will you do me the honor of marrying me? Becoming my wife?"

Now that I have all of that out, I look at Poppy and Cass properly. Poppy's holding her hands in the begging position, a cute smile on her face, wide-open eyes peering up at her mom. Cass's hands are clutched up against her chest, eyes glassy, a ghost of a smile on her lips as her chin trembles. She glances between Poppy and me, taking what seems like a hundred minutes to respond. I'm not sure she's going to respond, but she seems to become aware that I asked a question that requires an answer.

At first, she begins nodding slowly, teasing me. Then a smile slowly spreads across her gorgeous face. "Yes. Yes! *Yes!* I want to marry you and spend our days and nights together. Yes! I want to build a family with you. You're all I want, all I see."

I quickly get to my feet, scooping her body into mine for a luxurious kiss to seal our promise to one another, to our family, our future. Then, keeping in mind that we have young, impressionable eyes on us, I reluctantly pull away.

"We'll finish this kiss later, when we don't have little eyes on us," I whisper against her lips, forehead pressed to forehead. Cass nods in agreement. Both our faces split wide in a grin.

Poppy nudges me, pointing to my pocket, reminding me about the ring. *Shit!* I forgot to give Cass her ring. I pull it out of my pocket, and, holding her left hand steady, I slowly slide the platinum hand-engraved band on her slender finger. The three-carat solitaire diamond sits proudly on her finger, held in place with platinum petals, making it appear almost like a flower. I already have the matching platinum hand-engraved wedding band in the safe at home.

Cass studies the ring closely for several moments before looking up at me.

"It's gorgeous, Toby. So simple and pretty. I love it so much. Thank you." She leans forward, laying a hard kiss on my lips as Poppy wraps her arms around both of us. I hope Shane's getting all of this on his phone. Bending down, I lift Poppy up to join us. We stand, the three of us in a tight embrace for several moments. Soaking in the feel of my two girls in my arms, I absorb their goodness—the perfection of my family.

We wander deeper into the garden until we come across the Peace Lantern. This is where I want to ask Poppy an important question. I already asked Cass to distract Poppy at this point, allowing me the time to get down on one knee for her. When the girls turn around, I'm in position and the confused expression on Poppy's face is almost comical. She looks up at her mom before looking back at me. Cass nudges her slightly closer, and I suck in a deep breath to prepare for this next part.

"Poppy." I sign shakily. "I love you so much, even before I knew who you were. From the first moment I laid eyes on you, I knew you were going to become an important person in my life." She smiles shakily. "I was wondering if you would do me the honor of becoming my daughter? I would really like to adopt you so that you'll legally be mine."

She pounces on me, tears trickling down her cheeks, her little girl face split in a wide grin. She kisses my cheek and snuggles her face into the crook of my neck. I hold her close, rubbing my hand up and down her back. Cass squats down, pulling the three of us in tight, much the same way Poppy did a few minutes ago.

Poppy pulls her head away, putting some space between us. I look at her with hope and butterflies in my stomach. She brings her hands in front of my face and then, with a broad grin, she shows me two thumbs up. She jigs them up and down to make her point. I pull her forehead to my lips, pressing a relieved kiss there before tucking her in tight. After several moments, I let her down to stand on her own feet and dig into my pocket for the Return to Tiffany red double heart tag pendant. I got the one with the red heart because poppies are red. I thought it was fitting. I show her the necklace, then put it on her.

When I glance up at Cass, her face is glowing and her gray eyes are like storm clouds holding back the rain. Poppy shows Cass her necklace as she signs to Poppy how lucky she is to have me for her daddy. Poppy reminds Cass that they're both lucky. I have to interrupt them at that point because *I'm* the luckiest one of all.

I have one more surprise for my girls. I want to give it to them on the bridge that's shaped like half a drum, with the reflection in the water completing the other half. Together, with Poppy skipping between us, we head toward the bridge. Shane passes me the item I need for this part and then moves into position to capture the memories for me. Climbing the steep wooden structure, using the crossbeams for support, we reach the top, which matches exactly how I'm feeling— like I'm on top of the world.

"I have something I want to share with both of you." They both watch me in anticipation. I pull the CD out of my hiding spot. "I finished recording my latest album, as you both know. It's been mastered and pressed. I have the finished product here." I hold it up for them to see.

"The artwork's gorgeous, Toby. This looks amazing."

"Turn it over and look at the back." Cass turns it over, and I watch her studying it closely. I know immediately when she sees what it is I wanted to show them. With wide eyes, she looks up at me. I tip my chin, indicating she should let Poppy see. She passes it to Poppy so she can see. Her eyes snap up to mine as confusion fills her face.

"I hope you don't mind, but I put our song from the concert on my album. In addition, I've listed you as co-arranger, which means you'll earn royalties." I raise my eyebrows, waiting for her to notice what I've done.

Her face falls as tears fill her eyes so quickly they can't be contained, running down her precious cheeks. I look up at Cass in question, and her face mirrors her daughter's. My heart sinks to the bottom of my feet, through the bridge, and into the water below with a hefty splash.

"I'm sorry. I thought you'd like it." I shove my hand through my hair in exasperation. I can't believe I fucked up so epically. "I'll redo the CD and take it off. No problem. I'm sorry." My hands can't keep up with my verbal apology and I'm certain I've messed up some of my words. I drop to my knees in front of Poppy, raising her chin with my fingers as I wipe her tears away with my fingers. "I'm sorry, Poppy."

She shakes her head in the negative, then slowly signs, finger-spelling her new name. "You made my name Poppy Summer."

"Yeah. I'm sorry, I shouldn't have done that."

Her lips spread in a shaky smile, and she looks up at her mom as her smile grows wider. "He wrote my name, Poppy Summer."

Cass nods. "Yeah. I saw that." She has a watery smile as she looks down lovingly at her little girl, tucking a lock of hair behind Poppy's ear.

Poppy looks back at me. "You really *do* want me to be your daughter."

"Yeah, I do. You're the best daughter a man could ever wish to have. I love you, Poppy." She throws her body into mine, and with our arms wrapped tightly around each other. I stand on top of the bridge, on top of the world, with one of my girls in each of my arms.

Over Poppy's shoulder, I ask Cass. "Did I do the wrong thing? Was it too much?"

Cass shakes her head. "It was perfect, Toby." She comes in, closing her arms around us. "Thank you for loving us the way you do."

THE
SUMMER
TWINS
book two

bonus epilogue

second
chance
SUMMER

DEBRA ST JAMES

ONE

-toby-

As I do the final soundcheck of the tour, I reflect on the last three weeks and how different this one's been compared to previous tours. Having Cass and Poppy with me made the entire experience so much better—less lonely, more tolerable. I've never enjoyed touring. Being away from my family and home has always been difficult for me. However, sharing this tour with my two favorite girls has given me a new appreciation for the process. Some things I've taken for granted over the years, the girls have really enjoyed. We even managed to do some touristy-type things, which I don't normally do. We've certainly kept Shane and his security detail on their toes with our regular outings.

Poppy's soaked up the attention she's garnered along the way since our performance at *Music for the Heart* went viral all those months ago. As much as I tried to remove the video of our performance, it kept popping up. The two of us have a surprise planned for the audience tonight. Poppy and I have decided to finish the tour with our duet. It took a lot of persuasion on Poppy and Cass's part to convince me it would be okay since the plan has always been to live-stream the tour's final concert to millions of people.

They say I worry too much. I say they don't worry enough.

Poppy stands next to the stool alongside mine. "Are you ready, Daddy?" She must have signed 'daddy' hundreds of times since the first time I proposed to her and her mom, but it still makes my heart swell. I'm pretty sure it's always going to affect me deeply. The fact she's chosen to have me as her daddy makes me unbelievably humble.

She's not officially my daughter yet, but it won't be long now. As soon as the baby's born and Cass is ready to walk down the aisle, Poppy will become mine, too. I can't wait to have them both legally bonded to me.

"Yeah, I'm ready." I help her up onto her stool, then take my own, giving a signal to the sound and lighting technicians we're ready to start.

We run through our duet several times, and Poppy nails it every time. I'm the one that keeps messing up because I'm too busy watching my girl shine.

"You need to stay focused, Daddy." There goes my heart again. Her calling me that isn't going to help my focus.

"I'll do my best. Maybe if you weren't so amazing to watch, I'd have a better chance," I sign back to her. She giggles, but the ever-professional performer she is gets us back on track for a final run-through, which we nail.

Everything's set for tonight. After a final chat with the guys, Poppy and I head home to Cass. We've got a few hours to kill before tonight, and I think Cass wants Poppy to rest this afternoon. Good luck—this kid's wired!

TWO

-toby-

STEPPING ONTO THE DARK STAGE, THE AUDIENCE ISN'T AWARE OF MY arrival. Each of my bandmates takes their place and slowly the lights begin to illuminate the stage as Chris starts to play a slow beat on the drums; he's laying down a great groove. Whispers carry through the crowd as they notice we're here. Gradually their whispers turn into screams and cheers, which rise to a deafening level. My heart pounds in an excited rhythm.

There's nothing that can compare to the rush I get every time I step onto the stage. Knowing every single person out there is here to see me. To listen to my songs. To enjoy my music. The shy boy who would sit in the farthest corner of the cafeteria in the hopes he would blend into the wall now performs at sold-out venues in front of thousands of people.

I don't waste time. Just as we rehearsed, the band and I move straight into the first song of the evening. It's an older piece which is always a favorite. I like to warm up the crowd before dropping my new, less familiar songs. The lights overhead move over the audience and even though I can't see them properly, I can feel their energy coming off of them in waves.

Xanthe is off to the side, with a camera solely trained on her, which is projected on a forty-foot-high screen behind the band. She looks magnificent doing her thing for our audience. She really gets into the music, feeling it, expressing it from her very soul. Two large screens on either side of the stage show me and my bandmates alternating on each screen to keep it interesting. After three consecutive songs without a break, I take a moment to interact with the audience.

"Thanks for having us tonight! It's great to finish our tour on home ground." The audience goes wild. The noise is deafening and my cheeks split into a wide grin. The family I'm building with Cass and Poppy will always come first, but this, I love this. The feeling of being valued for my art ... or maybe not just for my art as underwear starts flying onto the stage.

I take a peek at Cass, who's sitting on a stool to the side of the stage, just out of view. She's laughing it up. Probably remembering the story I told her about my nan. Lucky for me, she, Margie, and Gramma Iris are touring wine country, making a general nuisance of themselves in Napa Valley.

We play another few songs, then I take a moment to introduce my touring band. These guys have been sensational to play with. I think it worked out well using them to record the album and then to tour with me over these past few weeks. We're tight and get along great. I'll chat with Peta about keeping them in mind for future contracts. As I intro-duce each member, the spotlight shines down, giving them center stage to do their thing for a couple of moments before I introduce the next member. It also gives me a few moments to catch my breath, wipe off some sweat, and grab a quick drink of room-temperature water.

We roll into the next song and I'm flying high on the adrenaline of the crowd. My new songs are being received with vigor and I know I've got another successful album on my hands. It's always nerve-racking the first few weeks after releasing recent work. Will my fans enjoy it? Will it attract new fans? Or will it be the album that kills my career?

Whenever I get the chance, I search out Cass and Poppy to the side of the stage, giving them a smile or a wink. An acknowledgment that I'm happy they're both here with me.

We're on the last song of the set. Of the night. Of this tour. It feels bittersweet for it to be over.

Normally, when I take a new album on tour to celebrate its release, it lasts months, not weeks. The shorter timeframe with fewer stops has been extraordinarily successful for me personally and professionally. As the song ends, we all say goodnight. The crowd cheers so loud I can't hear my own thoughts. I'm so pumped right now. The last three weeks have been some of the best of my life and it's because I got to do what I love with the two girls I love the most.

The lights go down and the roadies step on stage to remove everything except my guitar and two mics. They set up the two stools, center stage in the darkness. The crowd is chanting for more as Poppy and I carefully make our way toward the stools to take our positions, ready to perform the final number together.

It's quieter, more subdued. Nothing fancy, just a spotlight shining down on the two of us. Xanthe is still going to do her thing. One side screen is going to show the computer screen that Poppy and I use to learn new songs, while the other will show the two of us.

Slowly the spotlight becomes brighter, showing the audience the two of us situated in the center of the stage. Both with our guitars, ready to perform the song from the album. My heart is in my throat as I look across at the little girl who stole my heart within the first five minutes of meeting her. It's no wonder the rest of the world fell in love with her, too.

We begin, G, C, G, C, progressing through the song. Signing at different intervals and singing at others. The performance is the same as the one we did for the Labor Day concert, just tighter, more refined. This may be the last song of the night, but this will not be the last time we perform together. We finish with a flourish to a standing ovation from the crowd—just as many people calling out Poppy's name as they are mine. Her face lights up, her whole body vibrating with joy. I lift her, hugging her as we say our last goodbye of the evening.

The lights go dark and I carefully carry Poppy to her mom. The three of us embracing on a high—adrenaline rushing through my system and probably Poppy's, too. Peta and Shane give us our moment together, then guide us further backstage to meet Wendy. She was the generous, winning bid for backstage passes at *The Parkerville Project* fundraiser, which Oliver, Jase, and Kate put together to save the project from financial ruin.

I'm looking forward to meeting her and being able to thank her in person for her support of such an important project.

We arrive at the room. The guys are well and truly celebrating the end of the tour. I spared no expense for the after-party tonight. Celebrating with the band, crew, partners, and kids is a handful of people who have won various prizes, including backstage passes tonight. The vibe in the room is positively electric.

Xanthe almost knocks me on my ass with an enormous hug before pulling back. "Tonight was awesome. The energy of the crowd was incredibly intense. I think I'm gonna be pumped for days," she signs quickly.

Peta steps over with a woman and a teenage girl in tow, interrupting Xanthe and me. "Toby, I would like you to meet Wendy and Tatum. Wendy, Tatum, this is Toby Summer."

Wendy doesn't seem to know what to do with herself, while Tatum moves forward to engulf Poppy in a hug. "I can't believe I get to meet you. I'm such a huge fan." Her words come gushing out and Poppy looks to Cass for help. Cass signs on Tatum's behalf. "I wanted to tell you I think you're totally amazing, and I wish I could be your best friend."

Poppy smiles, signing while Cass speaks. "I'm always happy to make new friends."

Tatum must be at least fifteen, and the fact she's fangirling over a seven-year-old is quite remarkable. I would have thought kids that age were too cool to show their feelings outwardly. However, I'm not sure if I should feel left out. After all, I'm supposed to be the star of the show. I leave the three girls to their conversation, reaching forward to shake Wendy's hand. "Hello, Wendy. I'm so happy to meet you. I've been looking forward to personally thanking you for your generous bid."

She blushes, waving off my thanks with a flick of her wrist. "I bought it for my foster daughter." She gestures over her shoulder. "But I'm afraid since the fundraiser, her focus has moved from you to Poppy. She's in awe of the young girl's talent and tenacity. I must say, I'm in awe of the little girl, too. It's not easy learning an instrument, let alone when you can't *hear* that instrument in the usual way." She looks across at Tatum and Poppy. "She's quite an inspiring young lady. Such a positive role model for other young girls."

I nod in agreement. "She's shown nothing but determination in her desire to succeed at playing guitar. She's taught me a thing or two about tenacity." I look at my daughter and my chest fills with pride. The girl steals everybody's heart, and she doesn't even have to try. God help us when she's sixteen. I may have to look into putting her in a convent. "So Tatum's your foster daughter. Did she spend time in *The Parkerville Project* program?"

"Yeah. I met her through some volunteer work I do on occasion with the project. We hit it off, and I was in a position to take her in. I would like to adopt her one day, but her mom is still in and out of her life. Tatum's still hopeful she'll get her act together." She shrugs carelessly, but the tightness across her eyes tells me she's not so unaffected by the situation.

I reach across to squeeze the top of her arm to offer a modicum of support. "It's so easy to get attached. I fell in love with Poppy the minute I met her. There was no option for me."

Wendy nods slowly, a smile gracing her face. "She would be very easy to fall in love with."

"That she is."

THREE

-cassia-

LAYING ON MY SIDE WITH A PILLOW UNDER MY ENORMOUS STOMACH, watching Toby sleep, I count my lucky stars I'm able to celebrate his twenty-eighth birthday with him. That I'm the first person to wish him a happy birthday. Well, if he ever wakes up, I will be.

"You know it's creepy to watch me sleep." The rasp of his morning voice goes straight to my core and I press my thighs together. The sun's just beginning to peek above the horizon, sending a slight glow across our bedroom, enough to make out the smirk forming on Toby's lips. His hand snakes out, wrapping around my body as he shimmies closer until we're touching everywhere we can when I'm the size of a whale. He kisses the tip of my nose before placing a tender kiss on my lips. "How'd you sleep, Bun?"

I heave out a prolonged sigh. I don't want to talk about my lack of sleep. It's to be expected at this stage of the pregnancy. I move forward, placing kisses along his bristly jawline, whispering in between each one. "Happy birthday, Toby. I'm so thankful to be spending this day with you." Our eyes lock as I scratch my fingernails through his beard as his smile broadens.

"Waking up with you has got to be the best birthday present I've ever been given." He angles forward, his hard dick pressing into my hard stomach. The baby pushes out against the intrusion, causing Toby's eyes to widen comically. "Was that ..."

"Bub must have been feeling a bit squashed." I giggle. He pulls away from me, gliding his hand over my stomach. I take his hand and guide it toward Bub's foot just as it presses outward again. My stomach looks as though it's been invaded by an alien with the protrusion near my belly button.

Toby scoots down the bed, kissing my expanded stomach before saying good morning to our baby. He's going to be such a great daddy. He sings to the baby every night as he lovingly rubs cocoa butter on my belly, which often leads to other things. I was worried that once my stomach expanded, he wouldn't find me attractive anymore. I couldn't have been more wrong. He loved my body before pregnancy, but he's insatiable for it now. He's mesmerized by the way it's changed and how my body's nurturing and growing our child.

His hand lazily glides up over the bump and grips my swollen breast, plucking my sensitive nipple until it's peaked to his liking. His soft lips kiss their way down to the bottom of my baby bump. The feel of his bristles against my soft skin leaves goosebumps in his wake. He raises my leg, resting it over his shoulder, and I almost jump out of my skin as his tongue takes its first swipe of my swollen lips.

Oh my God!

"Ooooh." My hips jerk forward without my permission as he licks and nibbles at my pussy lips. This man knows what he's doing and I love being on the receiving end of whatever he gives me.

"Mmmmm. This is the best birthday gift ever!"

I huff out a laugh, which swiftly turns into a long moan as he slowly inserts a finger into my channel. As he slides his finger in and out of my pussy, adding another, my walls flutter around his digits. It doesn't take a lot to make me come in my current state. The pressure of the baby makes everything more intense. Finally, with his mouth sucking my clit and his fingers massaging my internal walls, I break apart with a cry on my lips. He keeps working me over until I come all the way back to earth, my body slick with perspiration. He kisses along the inside of my thighs before coming back up to me.

Leaning his head forward, he brushes the hair away from my face and takes my mouth in a wicked kiss. Rubbing my hand up and down his arm, his muscles twitch and move as he kisses me, massaging my tongue with his, feeding me my own taste.

"I love watching you fall apart. Knowing I'm the man who gives you bliss makes me feel like the king of the world."

Running my hands up his arm, across his shoulder, and into his silky hair, I lock eyes with the man I love beyond measure.

"You make me feel like a queen every single day, so it's only fitting you should feel like a king." I push him onto his back and awkwardly maneuver myself so my mouth is level with his hard dick. I planned to wake him up with my mouth on his dick, but he woke and beat me to it. Wrapping my hand firmly around the base, I swirl my tongue around the tip, tasting his pre-cum.

"Mmmmhm. I love having your mouth on me. This is certainly the best birthday I've ever had, and the sun hasn't even risen completely." His hand slides into my hair as he strokes it away from my face. Looking up the length of his trim body, his eyes are locked on me, watching everything I'm doing to him with an intensity I've grown used to seeing on him during our private moments.

His eyes are so full of lust; I can barely see any of the blue I love so much. I spend long moments loving on his dick as he massages the back of my head, running his hands through my hair like its precious silk. "Since it's my birthday, I wanna finish inside you. Climb on, Gorgeous."

I reluctantly release his shaft with a pop and a final lick to crawl up over the top of him. I try to look sexy, but I doubt I pull it off at this stage with my engorged boobs and huge belly. I do my best, though, and if the look on his face is any sign, he still likes what he sees.

"You are so fucking sexy, Cass. The way your body has grown and changed to care for our baby."

His words quiet the voice inside me that questions my appeal as a woman. His hands grip my hips as I straddle him. Holding his shaft upright, I slide the tip through my folds before placing the head at my opening. Toby thrusts his hips upward, sliding his cock inside as far as it can possibly go, and a long sigh escapes me.

"I love being connected to you in this way," I whisper with a breathy moan, as he glides out before thrusting his hips back up again.

His fingers dig into my hips and I know I'll have his finger marks bruised on my skin. I smile at the thought. His marks on me make me feel cherished and adored, sexy even. Leaning forward, I rest my hands on his pecs as he continues to thrust in and out of my body.

He takes my hands, locking our fingers together. "Let's turn you around, Gorgeous."

Nodding my assent, I lift my hips, allowing him to slide out. Toby helps me twist around and guides his dick back inside. Sitting up behind me, he wraps his hands across my breasts and stomach, running kisses along my shoulder up to my neck. I tilt my head to the side, giving him better access.

Sweat coats our bodies as we continue to build to our mutual release. We've had a lot of practice getting to the point where we can sync our releases. His fingers tweak each nipple in turn as his other hand slides down my body, locating my clit. His talented fingers play, press, and strum the sensitive bundle, pushing me ever closer to the explosion my body's seeking. I ride his dick, sliding up and down his shaft, my movements becoming irregular the closer I get to my climax.

"You're nearly there, Gorgeous. Give it to me."

One final pinch to my breast and clit sends me falling over the edge on a long, low moan that comes up from my gut. He presses up, freezing in place, his moan vibrating through my body as his release coats my internal walls. My muscles squeeze him tight, trapping him inside.

"Happy birthday, Toby," I sigh with a final shudder.

"Thanks, Bun." He returns between kisses along my shoulder.

We sit in silence, his arms wrapped around me, my arms covering his. These quiet moments after the rush are some of the best. Soaking each other in. The sun has risen higher in the time we've spent loving each other and Poppy will be awake soon; wanting to wish her favorite guy a happy birthday. Gingerly, we separate, and I immediately feel bereft at the loss.

FOUR

-cassia-

STEPPING OUT OF THE SHOWER, I HEAR THE TELLTALE SOUND OF LITTLE girl giggles coming from our bedroom. I quickly dry off to stand in the doorway, watching their interaction. They have such a strong bond. The way he dotes on her, supports and encourages her, fills my heart to overflowing. I can't believe I almost missed out on this because I thought it would be safer for Poppy to keep Toby out of our lives. My stomach twists and turns at the thought of Poppy missing out on Toby's love—of me missing out on Toby's love.

Bub kicks, breaking me out of my contemplation. Quickly dressing, I step out into the bedroom to find it empty. They must have gone downstairs for breakfast.

Stepping downstairs, I find them in the kitchen. Once again, Toby's spoiling my birthday plan. I wanted to make him pancakes for breakfast because they're his favorite. But he's already in the early stages of making French toast for the three of us with a side of maple bacon. Yum.

Stepping up behind Toby, I brush my hand down his back to gain his attention. The play of his muscles beneath his shirt as he turns to greet me sends shivers down my spine.

"I was going to make you pancakes for your birthday breakfast." I know my tone sounds like I'm pouting and I am a little. He spoils us so much, I wanted to do this for him.

Poppy notices me and moves in to wrap her hands around my waist in greeting—well, she tries to; they don't quite fit these days. Running my hand down her silky hair, I bend forward to kiss the top of her head.

"Did you sing happy birthday to Daddy?" I sign to my beautiful girl.

She nods eagerly and as I look across to Toby, his eyes soft as he looks at Poppy, I know her birthday wishes mean the world to him.

"Maybe next year you can make me pancakes for my birthday. You're already working hard to make me the best gift ever, so go and sit down. I'll bring over your tea." He leans over Poppy to land a gentle kiss on my forehead. My insides melt into a puddle of goo at his thoughtful gesture. He's been so caring and thoughtful throughout my pregnancy; waiting on me hand and foot.

FIVE

-toby-

"Tobes!" Kate cheers as she runs toward me. "Happy birthday!"

I laugh at her excitement. "Happy birthday, Squirt!" I wrap my arms around her, lifting her off her feet, and spinning her around a time or two. As I place her back on her feet, she takes a swipe at me.

"Stop calling me Squirt. I'm the big sister!" She's always so affronted at my nickname for her, but I know she secretly loves it.

Kate steps over to Cass. "Oh my gosh, you look so beautiful. You're positively glowing." She moves in for a hug and the smile that graces my future wife's face is spectacular. She's been feeling unattractive as her belly grows, which couldn't be further from the truth. "How's my niece?" She asks as she pulls away. She's not asking about Poppy. No. Kate's adamant that Cass and I are having a girl.

"Hey, we might be having a boy. So, don't be so sure of yourself." I like to mess with the girls. They all think I want a boy to even up the stakes in our house. Secretly, I want another daughter to take care of. But in all honesty, I'll be happy with whatever we have because it will be ours.

Oliver slaps me on the back as the girls give me the evil eye. "I'd better wish you happy birthday before you're drawn and quartered for that comment."

"Nah, they love me too much." I blow the girls a kiss.

"Yeah, I wouldn't push my luck if I were you." He laughs. The transformation from intensely serious to the guy who jokes around is impressive. Kate's done wonders to lighten Oliver up, while he's built up Kate's confidence and self-belief. I wasn't sure about the guy at first, but he's proven to be loyal and genuine. Of course, it doesn't hurt that he adores Kate beyond belief.

We make our way inside. I'm beginning to think that maybe Cass and I need to sell my place to buy a place more like this. Something with a backyard for the kids to play in and space to grow.

Mom and Dad are waiting in the kitchen; they wanted to wish Kate and me happy birthday before everyone else arrived. Kate and I pull Mom and Dad in for a special family hug. The four of us embracing tightly, rocking from side to side.

"Happy birthday, my babies." Mom whispers, squeezing us extra tight.

"Mooooooom!" Acting like a petulant teenager, Kate rolls her eyes. "We're a bit too old to be called babies. Don't you think?"

"You'll always be my babies. Even when you have babies of your own," she responds with a grin. Did I tell you how excited she is to be a grandma?

Dad laughs. "Happy birthday, you two. We love you both."

We sit around the table, Poppy on my lap. Mom and Dad give Kate and me our birthday gifts. I can't imagine how difficult it is for them to think of things to give us at our age. We can pretty much buy whatever we need or want. When we were kids, birthday gifts always included new swimsuits, summer clothes, a new backpack for school, or new shoes. Unwrapping the gift, I note Kate's is the same shape and size. Whatever we've got this year, it's the same thing.

Kate manages to get hers open first. It's some type of book. I quicken my pace so we can discover the surprise at the same time. While Kate's cover is red and mine is blue (cliché, I know); they are both photo memory books. We sit side-by-side, turning each page to find our life unfolding before our very eyes.

They've gone to so much trouble to give us a highlight reel of our youth, to our teens, and even into our adulthood. Kate and I went from looking quite similar when we were small, gradually becoming more different throughout our childhood. Then, finally, developing and changing in our teens to look quite different. I don't think people would realize we're twins when they look at us now. Poppy's getting a real kick out of seeing me as a baby, a child, and then a teenager.

I hear Cassia suck in a sharp breath as Poppy studies one of my high school band photos. Turning to check she's okay, Poppy jigs up and down on my lap, pointing to someone in the photo. Cass's eyes are wide as she looks at the same photo and a smile slowly graces her lips. I turn back around to study the image. Cass and I are standing next to each other. I remember when this was taken. I was willing my dick to behave for the photos until I could escape. Her cinnamon scent invaded my senses, and I was trying really hard not to take a breath or to even look at her. Because of that, I missed noticing her looking at me. In the photo, her face is turned toward me as I look directly at the camera. The look on my face says I want to be anywhere but there, while Cass looks like she wants to lean over to kiss me.

I can't believe I missed all the signs back then. *What an idiot!*

SIX

-cassia-

I WAKE UP IN A SWEAT AND THE SHEETS AROUND ME FEEL DRENCHED. I'M not sure what exactly woke me up, but I feel as though I've wet the bed in my sleep.

Shit!

I hope I haven't wet the bed—that would be highly embarrassing and utterly un-sexy. I've been up so many times through the night to pee and my back's killing me. Getting out of bed leaves me feeling short of breath and exhausted, but I manage—just. Toby stirs and I could kick myself for disturbing him, yet again.

I brush my hand over the sheet, then smell it. It doesn't smell like urine. It smells slightly sweet.

Shit!

That means my water's broken! That's probably what woke me up and why my back's killing me. A tight wave rolls across my belly, and I reach forward to brace myself using the mattress. More fluid escapes—and there's so much of it. I had forgotten about this from when I had Poppy. It's not just one release of fluid; it keeps on coming.

It's not time.

I still have another two weeks.

Using my breathing exercises, I inhale and exhale to get through the pain. It's not too bad at this point—comparable to my monthly cramps, but I know it's going to build into agonizing waves that continually crash over me until the baby comes out.

Oh, God! We're going to get to meet our baby soon.

Standing slowly, I steady myself to make my way into our bathroom. A warm shower is what I need. Then I'm going to have to wake Toby. I don't want him to roll over onto soaking wet sheets. Maybe I should wake him now?

Nah.

I'll let him get as much sleep as he can because it'll be hard to come by for a while. He doesn't know what he's in for with a new baby in the house.

Tears track down my face at the thought of Toby as the father of this baby. He treats Poppy as his own, but he didn't get the pleasure of holding her as a newborn or watching her grow. There's so much change in those first weeks, months, and years. He's going to be so great. My heart feels as though it's going to explode with the love I feel for him. I can't wait to watch him holding our baby.

My heart races as I think through everything that's got to happen between now and then. The work my body has to do.

Oh, God! I'm not ready.

A sob escapes. I'm so grateful I'm in the shower, hopeful the sound of the water is disguising the noise. Looking down at the floor, I notice the pink stain to the water and a glob of mucus. There goes the plug. This is happening really fast.

I'm unsure how long I've been bracing myself against the wall as the warm water runs over my back, but I sense a presence. I know, even before I turn around, that Toby's up. He steps in behind me, sliding one arm around my stomach while the other rubs my back as he places a soft kiss between my shoulder blades.

"Everything okay, Bun?" He kisses me again. "I noticed the sheets were cold and wet. Did you have an accident?"

My body sags into his hold as he kisses along my shoulder. Another wave abruptly washes over my stomach, tightening the muscles like a band being drawn around my middle.

"Woah, what was that?"

I can't answer as I try to breathe through the contraction. It takes all of my focus as my body tightens with the pain. Toby gently smoothes his hand down my back while still cradling my stomach, and my body relaxes as the contraction abates—for now.

I work to catch my breath. "That … was a contraction. The mess in our bed is from my water's breaking." I turn in his arms. "I'm pretty sure our baby's decided to come early."

His eyes widen comically, his mouth opening and closing. I don't think he's breathing.

"Toby. Are you okay?" I grab his arms, squeezing them, trying to break him out of his frozen state.

"Shit! Fuck! Okay." He runs his hands through his messy bed hair. "We need to get to the hospital. Now!" He looks around and steps out of the shower, grabbing our towels. "Why didn't you wake me up? We need to get moving." He's talking so fast as he hands me the towel while I'm still in the shower. The towel is soaked immediately.

"Fuck! I should have turned off the water first. Hang on, have mine. I'll get another one." He hands the towel to me once again while the water's still running, and I can't help but laugh at him in his panicked state. He's so adorable.

I turn off the water and step out of the shower. "There's no rush. I'll be having these contractions for hours yet. We'll need to time them, then make our way to the hospital as the time between each one gets shorter."

My breath is stolen as another tight wave strikes my midsection. Shit! That was close to the last one. Maybe Toby's right. I double over, trying to catch my breath. Toby's instantly there, holding onto me and counting me through my breathing. Once it passes, we share a look.

He dries me quickly, then helps me back into our bedroom, positioning me on the edge of the bed where it's still dry. Another contraction hits and I cry out. Toby drops to his knees in front of me. "What can I do?"

I grasp onto his hand, gripping tight as the pain takes hold. They're becoming intense very quickly. This is only the third … fourth contraction? I'm not sure, but it's happening really fast. My heart speeds up as I panic I won't get to the hospital in time and I'll have our baby here in our bedroom. No nurses or doctors to help us if anything should go wrong. The panic washes over me, and I'm struggling to catch my breath. I raise my head to Toby and he reads the panic on my face.

"It's okay, Bun. We'll get dressed and leave now." Our roles have reversed. He's instantly switched from the one panicking to the one who's calm and in control.

Once the contraction passes, he checks it's okay to step away from me. I nod sharply, closing my eyes to center myself. Toby helps me to dress, then dresses quickly as another wave hits me, almost taking my legs out from underneath my body as we make our way downstairs. I fear we're not going to make it to the hospital at this rate.

"Do you think I should call an ambulance? Or do you think it'll be quicker if I drive us?"

I don't know at this point. It's hard to think straight. It's taking all my focus to get through the contractions and recover my breath in between.

"Fuck. I'll drive us. By the time we wait for the ambulance, we could be halfway there. You okay with that, Bun?"

"Yeah. Let's go." I steady myself against the wall. "Promise me you'll keep driving when I have another contraction. I don't want to be stuck on the side of the road having this baby." I implore him with my eyes.

"I promise. Come on. I'll call your mom on the way to let her know what's happening. As much as I was missing Poppy, I'm glad she was sleeping at your mom's tonight."

Toby helps me into his car and as he's putting on the seatbelt, yet another contraction has me doubling over in pain, stealing my breath, and causing me to cry out.

"Fuck! I feel so helpless. Tell me what I can do."

Once the pain passes, I sag against the seat. "Just get me to the hospital before this baby comes out." I swivel my head toward him. "Please."

He kisses me briefly, then heads around to climb into the car. Within seconds, we're pulling out of his underground garage, on our way to the hospital. I only hope we make it in time. I spend the ride focused solely on getting through each contraction, trying my best not to distract Toby from driving. I feel like the baby's almost ready to slide right on out when I see the hospital's lights through the windscreen. The relief that travels through my body is instant. I know I'm in the right place to have our baby now. I can relax and let it all happen.

Toby parks haphazardly and yells something at me as he slams his door closed. I watch him take off at a sprint across the parking lot. I'm worried he's forgotten all about me here in the passenger seat, so I take a calming breath and make my way out of the car. As I'm about to stand upright, another wave takes over, so I hold on to the door for dear life so I don't collapse. The next thing I'm aware of is Toby helping me to sit in a chair. He crouches down in front of me.

"Nearly there, Bun. Hold on."

I nod, even though I'm not sure I can hold on for another second. My hair's sticking to my neck and face, annoying the shit out of me.

Everything's annoying the shit out of me. I don't want anything touching me—anywhere.

We make it inside and the bright lights hurt my eyes as another contraction takes hold, ripping a cry from my body.

"Somebody help her. I think our baby's almost here."

SEVEN

-toby-

THE NURSES ARE LOOKING AT ME AS IF I'M FUCKING CRAZY. MAYBE other men come running in here spouting off their baby's almost here, but our baby *is* almost here. Cass's contractions have been insane.

I can't believe what her body's going through and it's all my fault because I knocked her up. Not that I regret knocking her up, I'm just sorry she has to go through this. I feel fucking responsible for her current state.

An older nurse wanders over with a practiced smile like we've got all fucking day to stand around and chat. Another cry rips from the woman I love beyond measure so I crouch down in front of her, holding both her hands in mine. She squeezes the life out of them and I fear she's going to crush my bones. I should probably be worried she's going to cause permanent damage, but if she needs to crush my bones, then so be it. It's the least I can do for her.

The nurse moves forward more quickly and I notice a couple of others come around the desk to check on Cass.

"Let's get her into a room to check everything out."

The older nurse takes the wheelchair, waiting patiently for me to move out of the way before pushing Cass forward and ducking into a room. The three nurses work quickly to situate Cass on a bed, allowing me to keep physical contact with her the entire time. One of the nurses wraps a band around my girl's stomach before attaching it to a monitor. Instantly, I can see the baby's heartbeat on the monitor as well as her contractions. She fiddles with some switches and the sound of our

775

baby's heartbeat fills the room. The rapid thumping and swishing sound fills my ears and my heart.

The line showing her contractions rises quickly and Cass shoots forward, letting out the most incredible wail I think I've ever heard. The sweat coating her skin and the redness of her face have me worried that she's going to overheat.

"Can you do something for her? She looks like she's overheating. You've gotta help—."

"Oh my. The baby's crowning. It's not going to be long now." She looks up at me, excitement in her eyes. "Won't be long until you meet your baby." She taps Cass's leg as she smiles at us. The nurses move into action as I hold Cass's hand in mine.

My whole focus moves to Cass. She needs my support and I'm going to give her everything I have. "Hear that, Bun. Not long now. You're so strong and so brave." I kiss her sweaty forehead. "I love you so much. Thank you for making me a daddy again."

Another contraction hits. Cass's face screws up tightly, the pain evident in her features as her grip crushes the bones in my hand again. As it passes, I brush her damp hair away from her face, placing gentle kisses on her temple.

"Did you call Mom?"

I nod. "Yeah. The girls are on their way as we speak."

She nods, smiling at me, which quickly turns into another grimace.

"Don't push yet. Let's get you down the bed a little and we'll prop your feet up on these pads." She taps the pads on the side of the bed. The nurses are so calm, the lights in the room are dimmer than I would have expected and in between the contractions, Cass is as calm as anything—I'm so proud of my girl.

"Good morning, Cassia, Toby." Dr. Hart calls out as he enters the room, donning rubber gloves. "I heard Bub has decided to make an appearance a little earlier than we anticipated. I just finished delivering another baby when I heard."

"Hi, Doctor." I look up from my position. "Today's the day."

"Seems that way. Let's take a look." He studies the monitors, feels around Cass's stomach, and observes her opening. "Okay. Let's start pushing. We want gentle pushes at this point, Cass. Okay?"

"I feel like I'm gonna poop. I don't wanna poop on the table," Cass cries.

"You feel like that because the baby's engaged, ready to come out. It's okay."

One nurse wraps her arm around Cass's thigh, pulling it back and opening her wide. "C'mon, Daddy. Copy me with her other leg."

They count to ten, encouraging Cass to push. They repeat the process three times in succession, then allow her to rest. I'm in awe as I watch my girl work damn hard to deliver our baby into the world. The process is repeated over and over. Cass is looking tired as tears track down the side of her face, finding their way into her damp hair.

She looks so fucking beautiful in this moment.

One of the nurses gives Cass a towel and they pull on it like a tug o' war to help her through the next round of pushing. I look down between Cass's thighs to see our baby's head slowly revealing itself. With each push and cry of pain, more and more of the head becomes exposed, showing strawberry-colored hair. It's surreal to watch our baby coming out of my girl's body. She's the bravest person I know as she pushes, breathes, and pushes again.

Cass flops back against the pillow, looking utterly exhausted. "I'm so proud of you, Bun. You're doing so great."

"Okay, Mommy, the head is almost out. You ready to do three more gentle pushes?"

She nods as tears gently track down the side of her face. Taking a deep breath, she prepares for her task like the warrior she is. The nurse counts again and we both hold Cass's legs open for her, taking some of the strain. Cass cries out but pushes through like the queen she is.

"The head's out. Take a breather while I make sure Bub's safe."

My head snaps toward Dr. Hart. "Why? What's wrong?" My heart's thumping as though it wants to escape my body. I can only imagine my Bun's heart rate.

"Nothing's wrong, Dad. We like to check the cord isn't wrapped around the baby's neck before we do any more pushing at this stage. We also clear any mucous from your baby's mouth to ensure their breathing isn't compromised."

I relax a little at his explanation. Leaning forward, I kiss Cass's forehead, whispering against her skin, "You've done such a great job, Bun. I'm so fucking proud of you."

"Okay, everything's good down this end. You ready for the final stretch?"

Cass looks into my eyes, stormy gray to blue, and nods with determination.

We help her back into position, bracing her legs as she does the final work to deliver our baby into the world like the champ she is. I'm torn between watching Cass and watching our baby. A little scrunched-up face that's all red from exertion is resting in the doctor's hands and I'm in love.

My breath catches in my throat as the shoulders are pushed out and the rest of the body glides out of my love. The doctor expertly catches our baby, as it lets out an almighty wail. I tear my eyes away from the miracle in front of me to check that Cass heard our baby's first cry. Her trembling lips and glassy eyes tell me she did.

I move up to kiss those tears away. "Don't cry, Bun."

She clutches her hand to her chest.

"I'm so happy, Toby."

I can't resist, taking her lips in a kiss that's full of admiration and gratitude. Women are definitely the stronger sex. If a man had to go through what my girl just did, our population would die out for sure.

"Congratulations, Mom and Dad. You have a healthy little girl." Another wail follows as they lay our little girl just below Cass's breasts.

She's so small.

It's my job to keep her safe. To care for her. To show her she can do anything she sets her focus on. But above all, it's my job to love her.

Her little arms and legs flail about, her red face scrunched up tightly. She's not a happy camper at all. The nurses wipe off the excess mucous from her little body as Cass and I grasp hands, surrounding our baby with our love.

"Okay, let's deliver the placenta now." Our doctor tugs on the cord, pressing Cass's abdomen as we focus on our little girl. I'm not sure how much time passes before he clamps the umbilical cord and passes me a strange-looking pair of scissors. "Here you go, Dad. Ready to cut the cord?"

I nod, my hand shaking as I grip the scissors.

"Just between the two clamps." He points to the area I need to focus on.

I nod again, my voice escaping me. Placing the scissors in between the two clamps, I squeeze the handles. It's hard. I'm not sure what I expected, but it feels like I'm cutting through a cable.

"This isn't gonna hurt our baby or Cass, is it?"

"Not at all. I promise." He gives me an encouraging smile, nodding toward the scissors in my hand.

I squeeze hard and finally separate our baby girl from her mother. The nurses move our girl up higher onto Cass's chest, covering her with a blanket, which seems to calm her somewhat.

"You should talk to your little girl. It will help to soothe her in this strange new world."

I think we're both in such awe of our little girl that we lost our words for a moment.

A little girl.

We have another beautiful, perfect little girl.

We whisper to our baby, snuggling her close.

She blinks open her little eyes and we fall.

Hopelessly.

Endlessly.

In love with our baby.

"Do you have a name for your baby?"

We look at each other, a knowing grin broadening our lips. "Yeah, but we'll wait until her big sister's here before we share it."

"Fair enough. We'll just get everyone cleaned up." The nurses are moving around efficiently doing whatever needs to be done. "You two have some quiet time with your new addition. Then, whenever you're ready, you can tell your family to come back."

I look at the doctor in awe at what he's done today. "Thank you, Dr. Hart."

"My pleasure. Enjoy your little bundle. I'll see you in a few hours to check on you." He leaves us with the nurses and I offer them my gratitude for helping to deliver our beautiful girl into the world.

One nurse remains as we enjoy quiet moments with our baby. She's smacking her lips together and Cass lets out a small laugh. "I think she might be hungry."

As naturally as anything, Cass directs our baby's tiny mouth toward her breast. She latches on and begins sucking as though her life depends on it. With one hand stroking Cass's hair and my other stroking our baby's hair, I feel more love than I ever thought possible.

"I'm gonna go get Poppy. She should be here to meet her sister."

Without taking her eyes off of our girl, she nods to me. Reluctantly I leave my girls, but our family doesn't feel complete without Poppy and I don't want her to miss out.

Stepping into the waiting room, I find both of our families waiting on news. They spot me and stand quickly. My smile must be ridiculous at this point. I'm floating on air as I speak and sign for our families. "We had a little girl."

Poppy jumps up and down in happiness while quiet cheers fill the space as everyone moves forward to engulf me in congratulations.

"I've just come to get Poppy. Do you mind if we have a little while with the four of us, then I'll come and get you guys?"

"Of course. Go. Enjoy your new baby." Mom squeezes me extra tight.

"Won't be too long."

I grasp Poppy's hand as we walk down the hallway toward the other half of our family. Pride and pure joy make my steps light. As we breach the doorway, Poppy releases my hand and runs toward her mom and baby sister. She reaches forward, ever so gently to touch the baby's foot.

"What's her name?"

Cass nods to me to sign. I wait until Poppy's looking at me. "Her name's Daisy."

Poppy's eyes light up. "That's the name I picked."

Cass and I nod. "It was the best name."

I lift her onto the bed so that Cass can hug both of our girls. I scoot in, wrapping my arms around my three girls, thinking to myself how lucky I am.

Now my family feels complete.

I lean down, kissing the top of Poppy's head, followed by a kiss to Daisy's head, and finally, I kiss Cass's temple.

"Thank you," I whisper against her skin. "Thank you for giving me a family to love."

———

Not ready to say goodbye?
Sign up for my newsletter for a little more …
https://tinyurl.com/thesummertwins-bonus

Would you like to join Roman as he enjoys a long-overdue vacation in
Loving Roman?
An over-40s summer vacation romance novella
A steamy, low-angst, stand-alone over-40s contemporary romance
novella featuring a cinnamon roll foster carer and a single widow who's
forgotten what it's like to be a woman.
https://books2read.com/dsj-lovingroman

Find out what happens when Emma meets her new neighbor in
Stolen Kisses.
A neighbors to lovers romance
A steamy, emotional, stand-alone contemporary romance about a
single mom giving her all for her kids and a single uncle learning how
to be a dad while coming to terms with devastating losses.
https://books2read.com/dsj-stolenkisses

Shane's journey is an emotional one as he works to overcome his past. Read his healing story as he finds his HEA in

Everlasting Love.

A scarred cinnamon roll Hero/single mom romance

An emotional, steam-filled contemporary romance about a damaged cinnamon roll veteran who believes he's undeserving of the sexy single mom with a sweet daughter even though they may be exactly what he needs.

https://books2read.com/dsj-everlastinglove

pinterest

I put together a Pinterest board for Toby and Cassia's story. If you're interested, you can check it out here:

https://tinyurl.com/secondchancesummer-pinterest

debra's books

The Summer Twins

Loving Summer | *Kate Summer & Oliver Stone*

Second Chance Summer | *Toby Summer & Cassia Phillips*

The Summer Twins | Complete Series

Spin-off Novella

Loving Roman | *Roman Armstrong & Alice Reed*

Kisses

Stolen Kisses | *Emma Miller & Theo Drivas*

Moonlit Kisses | *Max Stanfield & Molly Lewis*

Unexpected Kisses | *Sarah Stanfield & AJ*

Kisses | Complete Series

Monday Knights | *novellas*

Enemy Kisses | *Finn Brady & Harriet Dubois*

Wicked Kisses | *Lincoln Kingsley & Sophie Chalmers*

Everlasting

Everlasting Love | *Shane Sutton & Violet Jamison*

Everlasting Promises | *Hope Sullivan & Benjamin Taylor*

Everlasting Vows | *Nixon Steele & Abigail Steele*

Debra has a list of her books available on her website.

You can find them here:

https://debrastjamesbooks.com

connect with debra

stalk me

You can stalk me pretty much everywhere!
https://debrastjamesbooks.com/connect/

How about joining my Facebook group?
https://www.facebook.com/groups/DebsBibliomaniacs

newsletter

Join Debra's newsletter to receive important updates before anyone else. Newsletters will be sent once a month unless something exciting is happening.
https://debrastjamesbooks.com/newsletter/

thank you

Thank you for taking the time to read my first two novels. I hope you've enjoyed spending time with the Summer Family as the twins each found their happily ever after. Writing a book is a funny thing, it's as much a journey for the author as it is for the reader and I've loved every minute of writing these stories.

Thank you for taking a chance on me; for reading my book. I truly do appreciate your time. If you've enjoyed reading about Kate, Oliver, Toby, Cassia, and Poppy, I'd love to hear from you.

I would like to thank Mr. St James and our two sons for their support and patience with me when dinner was late, or I didn't listen as attentively as I should have, or I didn't want to leave my cave because I was working on this baby.

I would also like to thank my beta readers, Stacy, Wendy, and Kelly (who stepped in at short notice). Your feedback and support meant the world to me. The fact that you were prepared to give up your valuable time to help me polish my story helped me immensely.

about the author

Debra St James is an author of spicy, slow-burn contemporary romance that features cinnamon roll heroes who listen to their women's hearts and their words. She takes her time to weave a detailed tapestry of genuine characters, real-life struggles, love, and romance to create engaging stories that will have you so immersed in the story that you'll never want to leave. Her stories are always guaranteed to take you on an emotional journey that ultimately ends with a HEA!

Debra loves to read romance. Her family often finds her with her nose stuck in her iPad, swooning over her latest book boyfriend. She writes part-time from her Perth home, which she shares with Mr St James and their two sons, whose antics often make her roll her eyes and laugh in equal measure.

Writing a novel had never been on her radar. One morning, she was enjoying a coffee by the river and a story sprouted, seemingly from nowhere. At 51, she pulled up the Pages app on her phone and began to type, giving life to her debut, *Loving Summer*.

The rest, as they say, is history!

Debra xo

www.ingramcontent.com/pod-product-compliance
Lightning Source LLC
Chambersburg PA
CBHW061936130726
47909CB00013B/1804